Yuin

GEOFFREY WALKER

 A catalogue record for this book is available from the National Library of Australia

ISBN: 9780648320708 (Paperback)
ISBN: 9780648320722 (Hardcover)
ISBN: 9780648320715 (Ebook)

Book Cover Design: Pickawoowoo, Laila Savolainen
Interior Formatting: Pickawoowoo Publishing Group

Printed & Channel Distribution
Lightning Source | Ingram (USA/UK/EUROPE/AUS)

Dedication

This book is dedicated to my daughters, Rikki-Lee Andrew (nee Walker),
Jessica Melanie Walker, Jodie Jeanne Wahby (nee Walker)
and my late parents, my Father, Harley Jersey Walker,
and my Mother, Jean Walker.

Table of Contents

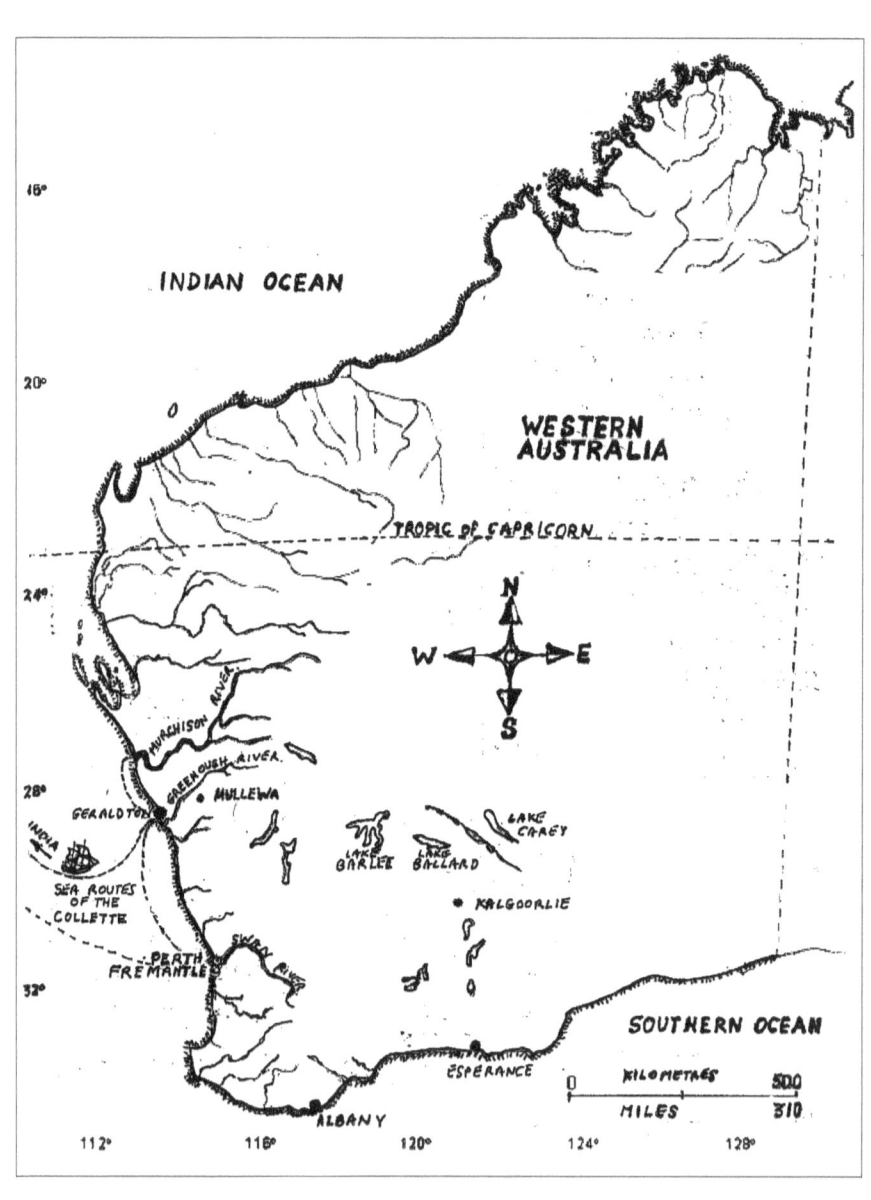

INDIAN OCEAN

18°

20°

WESTERN AUSTRALIA

TROPIC OF CAPRICORN

24°

N

W ◄─◆─► E

S

28°

MURCHISON RIVER

GREENOUGH RIVER

GERALDTON ● MULLEWA

LAKE CAREY

LAKE BARLEE

LAKE BALLARD

INDIA

SEA ROUTES OF THE COLLETTE

● KALGOORLIE

PERTH FREMANTLE

SWAN RIVER

32°

SOUTHERN OCEAN

ESPERANCE

0   KILOMETRES   500

MILES   310

ALBANY

112°   116°   120°   124°   128°

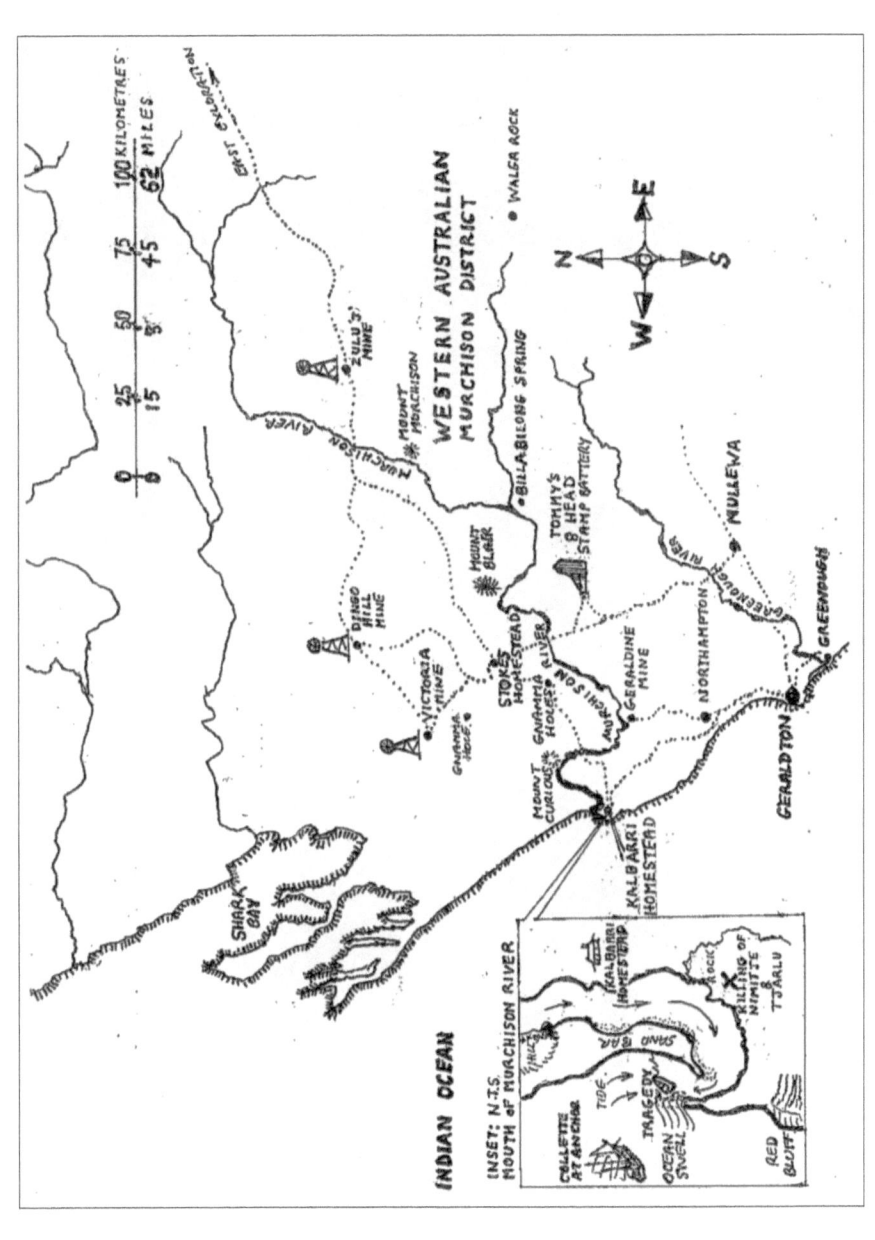

Preface

I am a Western Australian; bred and raised in the Eastern Goldfields town of Kalgoorlie and as you will read and have been fortunate enough to have spent many years in Africa as will be evident when you read this novel.

I began to write this novel some thirteen years ago when I became aware that the family history was silently slipping away. Having never written a book, it was indeed a daunting task, the main question being- where to begin. As with all tasks that I have undertaken in my lifetime, I like to have all of the material at hand before I start (tools if you like). The gathering of the actual recorded historical facts took some time as one can imagine, however as I will explain, I did have a lot of literary material already, and I made a point of engaging my mother in her later years, whenever she was able, to gather as much information as I could of our past history. With that knowledge and documents, she had saved, I considered it time, and so began. Because of the gaps in actual recorded family history, I decided to blend fact and fiction as my platform for this novel.

My Grandmother (Gertrude Banks nee Carlyon) on my mother's side, often reminisced to me as a child about her up bring in the Murchison River area and North to the interior and I would sit fascinated for hours as she told of those days of her upbringing and her interaction with the aboriginal people.

My mother as mentioned, kept or collected excellent hand-written records of that time, most of which I discovered after her passing, they being of family relations and other documents relating to her mother and father's history and also those my father's side of the family. I am fortunate, in that I have these documents in my possession. Sadly, my Father, Mother and Grandmother have all now passed to a place where beautiful people go. However, I am fortunate to possess an accurate and very long memory which has astounded many over my years, and as oft proven- even myself!

In the writing of this first novel of a trilogy, I have sort to lay the foundations for integration of the history in Mid-Western Australia, both factual and fictional and of course, in consideration of my own ancestry. I have included a lot of the characters who are part of Western Australia's actual history for this adventure, in particular with regards to the white man's claimed discovery of the Murchison River and the establishment of Geraldine (later to be officially named Geraldton).

Many of the happenings written here did in fact occur, according to recorded history.

I have made reference to a number of the settlement's government representatives and influential peoples, such as Lieutenant George Grey, Senior Police Constable John Drummond, Surveyor General Mr John Septimus Roe, William Burges (Magistrate), the Gregory brothers and Reverend Charles Clay, all of whom were influential in the development and establishment of the pastoral industry and mining in the area and therefore are part of that history. All of these people had significant influence in the area.

Kalbarri was the elder and leader of the Nhanda people at that time, and who are the original custodians of certain areas of the Murchison River and surrounding lands, all indigenous names given to characters in the book are also figments of my imagination or may have some vague reference to indigenous people of that time as told to me by my late grandmother.

As documented in the original story- the Nhanda legend of the "Give Away Girl", I have adhered to this as close as my research allowed, in that

I have woven that section of the story as I could imagine it would have transpired, placing myself as close as one could to that tragic situation.

Therefore, should any names or events differ from undocumented historical fact, it is unintentional and pure coincidence, bearing in mind that recorded history is indeed scant as I have discovered.

I make this point so as to avoid offence and out of respect for the indigenous owners of that part of history.

All other Caucasian, Chinese and African characters in this book and of the period are a figment of my imagination as are the establishment of certain buildings and mining operations by Nicholas Yuin.

This story will take you primarily with my creation of Nicholas Yuin on a journey beginning in the mid 1800s, from England to Cape Town in what is now South Africa. It will return you to Africa at Lake Nyanza (Bhantu); later to officially become Lake Victoria in 1852, and later Tanganyika.

The continuing journey will take you back to London and then by sea to the Murchison River in Western Australia's Midwest coast and inland, where the beginnings of a great adventure is to occur.

It is a novel of adventure, emotion and love, of high risk, danger on land and at sea, stepping into the unknown and multi-cultural integration, but above all it will lead to an insight of that exciting time of discovery in mid-Western Australia in the 1850's and beyond.

Geoff Walker

Introduction

Nicholas Yuin was born in March 1814 to wealthy parents in the mid-West of the English country side. This story tells of a young lad over whom tragedy cast its cloak at an early age.

Like all tragic events, there is a time when the events will either strengthen ones soul or destroy it. In Nicholas's case, the events that followed eventually turned him into a person of strong character and decency. His indomitable spirit serves him well in our journey as does his unshakable belief in his chosen paths, whatever fate may lay before him.

As his adventures begin, his persona evolves and his strong character develops, he finds deep seated and emotional love, an obsessive passion for geological mineralization and exploration and he forms a rare and balanced sense of fair play. He finds and implements the most valuable commodity of all decent men, an even-handed approach applicable to all situations. That is not to say he is perfect, no person can lay claim to that, but Nicholas Yuin applies and seeks honesty, trust, friendship respect and honour as a pre-requisite to his approach to life in general.

There are parts of this novel whilst on the African continent, that are tinctured with some personal experience and other sections have been through some in depth research, not the least being the phycological research. With this knowledge applied to this story and Nicholas and his adopted family, one must include those outside his family, their lives are intrinsically entwined in his adventure, as are that of his intended.

Africa is a continent that has a vast collection of countries and an equally diverse collection of unique and ancient peoples. The diversity and difference in tradition and heritage is on balance, as vast as the lands.

These countries are full of wonderful and unique wildlife, and while some of the animals are the most dangerous on Earth, Lion, Buffalo, Leopard, Hippopotamus and Elephant, to name a few and a litany of dangerous reptiles and insects, none is more dangerous than man himself, as will be demonstrated by peoples created in this novel.

In contrast, Australia too had, and still does have, a diverse collection of traditional peoples who are rightly protective of their heritage and ownership of lands. As we now know, that ownership spans over 60,000 years. As the traditional owners of the lands, its unique bounty and natural produce, these people have no peer.

Australia does not now have any real animal predators (mammal)– at least none that would naturally prey on human beings. It does however, have many large or poisonous reptiles and insects. But as in Africa or anywhere else in the natural world, it is important to re-iterate that we alone in our neglects are far more dangerous than any beast, reptile or insect. Nicholas Yuin will have first-hand experience of this during his excursions.

The dream of adventure, discovery and exploration are never far from the forefront of Nicholas Yuin's mind and so begins another stage of his adventures.

You will accompany him to the raw and largely unexplored region of the mid- west of West Australia and further into the harsh and extremely hot sun baked interior.

In the mid 1800's, Western Australia had only cursory exploration, especially with regard to the inland sections. The land generally was a hot inhospitable place and by the most, void of fresh water, at least for the uninitiated. Nicholas Yuin, in his exploration, will transport you to the harsh realities of this, the harshest of environments. Although, harsh and unfriendly as it maybe, some years produce good seasonal rains and it with it, brings periods when this land is transformed into the most beautiful landscape ever imagined with unique fields of colourful wildflowers and new growth, waving in the winds like the ripples of ocean, but like butterflies wings, fade within a short time.

Access was either by foot, or horseback, only the coast gave access to the peripheral of the land and most of that coast was of treacherous nature. Inland in particular, then and now is an inhospitable country. In the early days, only the very brave, determined or as it was oft deemed, the 'foolhardy', dared venture inland, but venture there, many did, including our intrepid explorer and his companions, as did my ancestors. However, their association and friendship with the people of the 'Nhanda' were to prove vital to their survival on many occasions, especially Nicholas himself.

It is here that Nicholas meets and bonds with several people, none more so however than his blood bond with a massive black man of Africa, an ex-Zulu slave. All of the other characters that Yuin meets and bonds with form essential parts and periods of this journey and by the most have significant roles to play in our story.

In this opening book and its lead to the future, the author has used his somewhat extensive knowledge of the 'Bush' and has introduced our Nicholas Yuin to entwine and begin the story with past family members. With this knowledge, the author has applied his family history as he knows it and as documented, and Nicholas Yuin begins his chance association with history. The author has created a blend of fictional and actual historical people, and for the most, the fictional characters walk the path, either in your imagination or as it would have been at that time.

Chapter 1

Yuin, 1849

*T*he dark cloaked figure stood at the starboard bow of the ship, gazing toward the line of a ferocious sea breaking at the supposed mouth of a river discovered and named but two and a half years earlier.

With one hand on the rigging, he rose and descended with the ship as it rode the heavy swell running relentlessly toward the distant shore. He stood almost ramrod straight, and for all intents and purposes looked to be affixed to the vessel such was his concentration. The only movement was the occasional flap of the hem of the dark green and black edged three-quarter cloak he wore and the occasional glint of the twin rows of brass buttons running down either side of the flaps of the coat.

Oblivious to the sounds of ship that one absorbs and accepts after such a journey as they had completed, his gaze never seemed to waiver. He eventually fished for his fob watch chain, hardly shifting as he glanced down, and saw it was just after 5.30am. He cast his eyes across the bowsprit and north along the beach, grey and shrouded in mist thrown up by the pounding of the breakers on reef and beach alike. The moderate breeze was now in his face and he could see a faint orange and pink tint colouring the rims of the cliffs and hills heralding the advance of sunrise.

Nicholas Ryan Yuin was a fine figure of a man by anyone's standard; he was tall, just over six foot three inches with long coal-black hair braided down his back to between his shoulder blades and tied with a fashionable black velvet bow at the end. An equally coal-black, close-cut beard covered an olive-skinned face beneath high cheekbones, and at his temples one could see just the merest hint of grey. The almond shaped eyes appeared to have an almost oriental tilt to them, however slight, although there was, as far as *he* knew, no Asian influence in his lineage. The colour of his eyes were unusual, with traces of hazel, but with a dominant amber tint.

Lines spread from each corner of his eyes, a legacy of many days spent outdoors squinting in harsh conditions.

He was a lean and fit man, confident and self-assured at thirty-four years of age. Proficient in any manner of self-reliance – as oft develops with such a man – who would by choice, prefer to do things alone. He was well-travelled, and in his years had learned and perfected a healthy respect for other cultures, people, their customs and crafts. His driving ethos was respect.

Yuin was tolerant of most things, to a degree, but had a penchant for immediate action. He had trouble controlling his reactions on occasion, oft to his regret, especially when anyone close to him or himself was threatened. One could sense he would brook no trouble from anyone. Those who knew him well enough would say that although he could be hard, sometimes stubborn, he was always fair and reasonable, an honorable man with high standards.

It was late August, and for three days now, the ship had been at anchor off the coast of this distant, sparse and unexplored land, waiting for the heavy Indian Ocean swell to abate, but it was as consistent as it was frustrating to this man who had gambled all to pick up the challenge to make this voyage.

There was never any doubt in Nicholas's mind as to whether he should have chosen this path, for just as he had undertaken all of the previous challenges in his thirty-four years – twenty-two of which he had spent away from England, his place of birth – he never looked back when he set his course. He strongly believed that to dwell on doubt was to admit defeat before you even started.

'Mr Yuin suh, begging your pardon suh, but the cap'n wishes a word, e's up on the poop.'

Nicholas at last tore his gaze from the mist-shrouded distant shore and turning to acknowledge the blocky figure of the bosun's mate standing beside him, nodded and said 'Thank you Alan.' He turned and strode toward the stern of the ship and poop deck.

Captain Strudwich was a sprightly looking man with piercing blue eyes, from each corner of which were deep rows of 'crow's feet' etched into his skin and which seemed permanently squinted from a lifetime at sea.

His eyebrows stuck out almost like verandas from his brow, such was their wild growth.

He lowered his well-worn telescope at Nicholas's approach and turned in greeting. Yuin noticed he too had been scrutinising the shoreline.

'Ah, Mr Yuin sir,' he said grinning and with a twinkle in his eye, 'I sense a change in the wind coming and I think by this evening we may, at last, have an easterly wind, which should help flatten out this damn swell.

'By tomorrow, at first light, if I am correct, we will send out the long-boat to see if we can sound for a passage into this river to transport your livestock and provisions.'

Nicholas, no novice to the way of the sea and weather himself, wondered how this wily old devil knew of the imminent change.

The captain saw the query in Nicholas's eyes, and tapped his nose. 'I can smell it man,' he said before Nicholas could say a word.

Not for the first time Nicholas was in awe of this man, with his uncanny seamanship and wisdom. It seemed he ran his ship as though he were part of it, and there was no man Nicholas would trust more than Captain Peter Strudwich in matters of seamanship.

'Below deck!' shouted the watch from up on the main. 'Cap'n, I see movement ashore in the lee of the red cliff, looks like folk sir!' he added with some degree of incredulity in his voice.

All eyes swung to the starboard side and the red bluff near the river mouth.

The captain swung up his telescope and glassed the shoreline. 'I see nothing! Where away?' he shouted. 'To the left sir, where the ridge runs down to the beach,' came the lofty reply.

Nicholas could see nothing but sea mist, but the captain muttered, 'Blacks!' and passed the telescope to him.

There appeared to be six that he could see, making their way down to the shoreline. It was too far away to make out any distinctive features, but of black skin they were.

Moving the glass up to the top of the bluff, he made out a solitary figure standing equally as straight as he himself had been some ten minutes ago. Although the distance belied any certainty, Nicholas had the distinct feeling that the figure was staring directly at him. An uneasy feeling settled over him – as comes over all men when facing the unknown.

The captain broke his reverie. 'I doubt there would be many of them around here,' he said. 'Too hard this country.'

But in his travels Nicholas had seen first-hand how native peoples could survive in the most inhospitable places you could imagine – and flourish. He immediately thought of the diminutive Bushmen of North Africa who could survive in one of harshest and inhospitable places on Earth – the Kalahari Desert.

The unease remained.

The next morning dawned as Captain Strudwich had predicted, a calmer sea with moderate swell, the dawn sky now painting pink and orange splashes on the curved backs of the ocean's dark sentinels as they silently rolled toward the shore. You could hear their dull roar as they broke over the reef and shoreline, over which hung a sliver of grey sea mist, although somewhat reduced in comparison to the previous day with the breaks further apart.

Nicholas clung halfway up the rigging, the rough prickle of ropes sticking into his bare arms. A warm breeze blew into his face from the shore, and he again stared at the land, an excitement now gripping him as he drew in the intoxicating smell and tasted the easterly wind.

He had expected a similar scent to that of Fremantle where the convicts were being driven to build a new harbour, but to him, this place had a raw untamed smell. It was a smell of imminent heat, danger and mystery.

The land breeze had now cleared the heavy mist revealing a red bluff and jagged cliffs coloured red, cream and chocolate with horizontal bands of mineralisation, an unusual sight and formation. From where the ship lay the cliffs looked for all the world like a giant book lying on its side.

So far, everything about this strange land seemed different in the extreme. Where Africa was raw, this land felt ancient and Nicholas instinctively knew that this expedition could prove to be his greatest challenge. His heart pounded with excitement and adrenaline coursed through his body.

As he swung down from the rigging the bosun greeted him. 'Morning Mr Yuin suh, looks like things be 'appening today and not before time if I may say so.' Nicholas grunted, and not wishing to break his feeling of anticipation, he strode off to inspect the longboat swinging on its snatches.

The boat was equipped with enough provisions for a possible delay in return, should it be necessary, there being no way to know what lay ahead of them.

No man to his knowledge had ever entered the river by the mouth, the only record registered attempt was by the survey ship HMS *Tenacious* in late November, 1839.

In Nicholas's research, he had read that, early in 1839, a Lieutenant George Grey had named the river "Murchison" after the then president of the Geographic Society of London, Roderick Impey Murchison.

Grey had sailed down the coast from the north in two whaling boats with twelve men. Unfortunately, the boats were wrecked in violent surf, many miles north of the river he was yet to discover.

Lt Grey and his men had set out south on foot and were destitute when they stumbled across the river about a mile north of the mouth.

Here they had found that upriver the water became fresher. They caught fish in crude traps they made and cut up some musket ball and shot wild duck with the only two muskets they had managed to salvage.

Grey and his men had stayed at the beautiful Murchison estuary area for a while recovering before heading further upstream then, beginning an epic journey on foot to the port of Fremantle.

Grey was the only one to complete the journey. Three days after the group began the trek from the river, the remainder of the men began to deteriorate, some still carrying injury from the beaching, and after discussion they decided to return to the Murchison, with Grey electing to carry on alone.

Months later Grey stumbled into the Perth area, emaciated, haggard and bedraggled.

His arduous journey was not in vain, a search party was organised and all but one of the men he had left behind survived. It was mentioned that the Blacks in the area had provided some help in the way of food for the men.

Grey was later promoted to the rank of captain for his courageous deed.

The river mouth had been noted in *Tenacious* log as being far too dangerous to attempt to enter. The ship's only attempt at a landing had ended in disaster with the loss of two seamen.

It was this very notation that had first piqued Yuin's interest and fired a burning desire to find out what lay beyond the 'impossible' landing.

It had been a chance meeting in a portside alehouse Nicholas was visiting in Cape Town, Africa, when he first heard of this river, along what was to become known as Australia's West Coast.

Quite by coincidence, the navigator of the *Tenacious* happened upon the dingy alehouse and had struck up a conversation with him. They talked of their travels and experiences, sometimes tragic, sometimes rewarding, and of wonders and fascination of all things discovered.

During the conversation the navigator told of the voyage to Australia. The attempt to enter the river and how the entire crew of the *Tenacious* longboat were almost lost attempting to enter the river mouth.

The boat was swamped. Two of the crew had leapt over the side to lighten the load, whilst the rest frantically bailed the boat. Minutes later the two crew men clinging to the side were lost, one being smashed into the side of the boat and the other snatched beneath the boat by something, presumably a shark.

Apparently, the frantic crew only had time to see a dark stain in the water before it too was ripped away by the vicious current.

Suddenly, a fierce undertow gripped the boat and dragged or pushed it through the waters – like some unseen hand – through the cross-chopped, foaming channel and back out to sea.

According to the navigator, it was as if the river had actually spat them back out to sea.

He went on, describing a narrow channel of boiling seas, where vicious rips met with heavy surf crashing over the reef running across the front and diverting the river's passage into the sea.

Beyond the turbulent mouth, it appeared, lay calm wide waters and a sandy beach, with low to medium timber beyond, almost beckoning in its serenity.

'Do'n matter, 'twas an evil river and the mouth was guarded by unseen demons!' the man had whispered in his drunken stupor.

The navigator's brief glimpse into the land beyond was enough to fire the hunger for adventure that had for years driven Nicholas halfway around the known world.

Nicholas had brought another round of rum and had proceeded to glean from the man any morsel of information he could about the place of mystery. He eventually compiled a list of names of some of the sailors involved and gained some information as to their possible whereabouts.

As Nicholas was to discover, this was to prove a very difficult task – the *Tenacious* was believed to have been refitted and her whereabouts were unknown, though some of the original crew were believed to be in London.

Nicholas had boarded the next available ship back to England and thus began to gather the scant information recorded about the HMS *Tenacious* voyage along the West Coast of Australia.

Chapter 2

London, 1847

On the fourth month since leaving Africa, he made land in England. There, in London, he sought out the crew of the longboat, or those he could find, to try to rekindle any memory or observation of this mysterious place.

Unfortunately, most information from the seamen was now laced with superstition, and as the rum took effect, so too were the facts affected and wild exaggeration abounded.

In the end Nicholas decided he would only find out the true facts if he went there himself. He needed financial backing and an expedition.

His drive and determination had him spend a full eighteen months seeking exploration rights and the right to lay claim to the land beyond the river mouth.

This was a frustrating and degrading time, for Nicholas found, not surprisingly, that the House of Lords and businessmen alike were all too reluctant to consider financing an ambitious adventure based on speculation and of what might be. They ridiculed the very idea.

It was during another fruitless attempt to persuade yet another reluctant ear to his plans and dreams, that Nicholas's patience finally ran out. His temper, held in check for months, erupted to the surface. Exploding like the proverbial volcano, Nicholas snapped his journal shut with a sound like a pistol shot and leapt to his feet.

His voice dripping with sarcasm and fury he snarled, 'Damnation! You narrow minded fools, the only risk you take is to walk from your desk to the privy!' and he stormed out of the stunned gentleman's office, hardly noticing the diminutive figure seated in the back of the room.

The wizened old gentleman rose up out of his chair and now struggled to his feet with the aid of a cane, and snapped, 'Close your mouth Jonathan, you look like a crocodile sunning itself on the banks of the Nile!'

'Well, what do you think!' he continued.

Before the man could answer Sir Gregory Scott enthused, 'I think our Mr Yuin has fire in his belly and a rare determination, just the sort of man we need!

'But Sir, if I may, there is no proof that this place can even support livestock, let alone human beings. Why, there may even be Blacks there, and God only knows how many at that…'

'Enough!' the old man's voice cracked like a whip, and he fixed the man in a fierce glare.

'Two things to remember! One, just because the inhabitants there are probably of black skin, doesn't mean they are not human, that the place is uninhabitable or that they are stupid, quite the contrary. And two! I am interested in Mr Yuin's prospecting prowess, not damn cattle!'

'But sir, Mr Yuin has not mentioned his ability as a prospector, in fact he has made no mention of mineralisation.'

'Exactly!'

Good God! Sometimes I think that I'm the only one who thinks around here, the old man thought.

Investigation revealed that Yuin's prospecting skills were of some note, Sir Gregory mused, and it was rumoured he had made a small fortune discovering deposits and selling leases in Africa and Canada, although the details were never clear.

'Jonathan, I want you to wait two days, then go and fetch our Mr Yuin, bring the man to my house. Make sure he brings all of his research about this dream of his.'

Jonathan Trewellan stuttered, 'With all due respect Sir Gregory, I do not think this is a very good idea, and what if he won't…'

'Make him come man! For God's sake! dangle the bait, he wants this expedition so badly he can taste it!'

The old man's fury at the negativity was getting the better of him, 'And if I hear the word "BUT", once more, you're fired!'

Trewellan winced and said, 'Very well Sir Gregory, as you wish.'

Trewellan at last found Yuin sitting on the sea wall opposite his lodgings, overlooking the River Thames. A half bottle of rum and an empty glass beside him.

He looked drawn and sullen, but his head was still up in that commanding manner that Trewellan found so unsettling.

'I beg your pardon Mr Yuin.'

Nicholas's head snapped around at the intrusion and fixed Trewellan with an unwavering gaze, one eyebrow raised, and with a look of complete scorn. He said nothing.

Trewellan felt his gut clench, the sheer force of character this man emitted was unnerving to say the least.

Trewellan, summoning his wavering courage, said to himself, I am the head accountant for G.A. Scott Investments & Co Ltd, a highly respected investment company, and right-hand man to the shrewdest businessman in all of England, get a hold of yourself man.

'Mmm...my employer, Sir Gregory Scott, would request your presence Mr Yuin at his place of residence,' Trewellan managed as he cursed himself for the use of the word request. He quickly added, 'That is if you please.'

Nicholas said nothing, his gaze never wavering, but his heart skipped a beat, when, after what seemed an eternity, he answered.

'And to what would I owe the honour of this command, should I even accept it? You have already made it very plain that you regard the very idea of this expedition as ludicrous.'

Oh! the arrogance of this man thought Trewellan, a retort at his lips. But Sir Gregory's threat rang in his ears, time to be a little humble he thought.

'Mr Yuin, my thoughts are not always those of Sir Gregory. I am sure if you were to accept his invitation it would be to your advantage.'

Could it be possible that at last someone was showing some interest in his proposal? Nicholas's thoughts were now racing, although his demeanor never altered.

He waited, weighing up the possibilities and trying to keep a lid on his mounting excitement.

'You may inform Sir Gregory,' he said frostily, letting the sentence hang in the air, toying with the man and causing Trewellan's heart to plummet to an all-time low 'that I accept the invitation.'

The man's bowels almost let go with relief. He looked up at Yuin's face, the almond eyes now dancing with mirth.

Trewellan nervously gave Nicholas Sir Gregory's instructions and address, and with some relief vanished into the mist.

The manor was set deep inside thick woods on the outskirts of London, the trees dripping with dew from the fog that swirled around like some ethereal gossamer cloak.

Nicholas was ushered into a study where a fire burned brightly in an ornate hearth. He looked around. The room was full of trophies, animal and artifact alike, a fascinating room.

As he looked, he recognised many of the mounted animal heads from Africa, Canada, Alaska, India and Asia.

There were artifacts from ancient civilizations – Mayan, Aztec, Canadian tribal, Asian and many more.

Dozens of books crammed a floor to ceiling bookshelf, some magnificently bound in tooled leather and gold inlay.

One wall was devoted to mineral specimens, literally hundreds, perhaps thousands, from base metal to precious. It was to this, that Nicholas was immediately drawn.

Each was scientifically named with small labels of gilded stiff paper. Some of the specimens he had never seen before.

The voice startled him. 'I have been collecting those for over fifty years, from all over the world, most of them personally, fascinating don't you think?'

Sir Gregory rose from the high-backed lounge chair before the fire, his face pinched with pain as he came to his feet and extended his hand.

The old man's grip was firm and dry and Nicholas could not help but smile at the stooped figure before him.

'Fascinating indeed sir, it is by far the best collection I have ever seen.'

Sir Gregory's pale blue eyes swept over the rest of the room as he said, 'I lost the urge to kill many years ago, I now think it barbaric to hunt for the sake of it. It is as selfish and pointless as suicide itself, but I think to get rid of these mounts would now be an insult to these once beautiful animals. Do you agree Mr Yuin?'

Nicholas slowly nodded his head. 'The Bushman of Africa could educate us all on how and when to hunt sir,' Nicholas replied. 'To them, all animals are here for a reason and all is to be shared, even their spirit.'

After some thought Nicholas added, 'If you destroy these trophies, you will not be able to educate others or share your knowledge of them.' He concluded, somewhat tongue in cheek and fixing Scott with an unwavering stare, with, 'You would be ridiculed for talking of the unknown.'

Sir Gregory chuckled. 'Touché Mr Yuin, touché.'

'Ah, I forget my manners, please sit down'. Ambling to the drinks cabinet he said, 'A whiskey perhaps?' He poured without waiting for an answer.

Once they were settled, Sir Gregory continued. 'Mr Yuin, I have asked you here to discuss your plans to explore the western coast of Australia, in particular one unexplored river of the mid coast.' He paused and studied Nicholas's face with intent.

'I have listened to your requests with some puzzlement. Can I be so bold as to ask to view your findings and documentation pertaining to your quest to travel to Australia?' The shrewd eyes pinched as his unblinking gaze remained locked on Nicholas's amber eyes, which were equally as steady.

A slight grin came to both faces as mutual respect flowed between them.

Nicholas handed over the papers, which were best described as scant indeed.

As the older man scanned the papers, Nicholas sipped the whiskey and tried to keep that rare feeling of euphoric wellbeing in check, which comes when you know you have met someone significant in your life.

'Poppycock!' the old man stated with some force.

'I beg your pardon sir?' an astonished Nicholas asked.

'I said, poppycock! You are no more interested in raising livestock in this place than I am in raising hell in a brothel on the docks of London. What you *are* interested in is exploring and prospecting north of this area because no other fool has been able to reach it!'

Nicholas felt his rage at this insult dissolve, and he burst out laughing. The old diamond was correct in every way. At last he had met someone with enough mettle and intelligence to understand what drove him.

They talked long into the night, of their experiences and of possibilities in the yet to be explored river region.

By the end of the evening, Nicholas had his backing and guarantees of ongoing support.

After what could be likened to a high-speed version of chess, he and Sir Gregory had struck a bargain and formed a business partnership. Nicholas had argued hard to hold 55 per cent of the deal – after all, it was he who would be risking his life.

The deal was struck, all binding and dependent on a solid viable mining prospect.

The establishment of the cattle station would go ahead as a cover to mask Nicholas's real intentions.

The last thing they would need was a mining rush and rival prospectors to contend with. Already they knew the Gregory Brothers had staked claims at the upper reaches of the Murchison area. Finance would be made available to fund the establishment and staffing. They decided on the simple title of Yuin Scott Pastoral Company as the name of their venture.

One of G.A Scott Investment Co.'s merchantmen, the *Collette*, would be commandeered for the voyage under Master Mariner, Captain Peter Strudwich.

Strudwich was an ex-British Navy privateer, regarded by many as one of the best seamen around.

Sir Gregory had produced a document detailing a Lieutenant Grey's voyage and epic journey for Nicholas's scrutiny. Nicholas was astounded, for he had tried for many months to obtain this information and had met rejection at every turn. 'How did you…?' he looked at Sir Gregory in query. The older gentleman's face was fixed with a sly twisted smile which said, ask no questions.

In the ensuing months whilst preparations continued, the bond between the two men grew and strengthened, the old man seeing Nicholas as the young man he once was, with the same drive and determination to discover, explore and conquer.

Sir Gregory had not felt so enthusiastic for life in years, and his arthritic pain seemed to markedly diminish as the preparations swept forward.

Nicholas on the other hand, felt an enormous respect for this highly intelligent old man, a man with vast experience and knowledge, and he drank from this pool of knowledge at every opportunity.

He was ever mindful of the extended hand of trust, and the opportunity, support and burgeoning friendship it represented.

What remained was to make the voyage and navigate the dangerous entrance to the river.

The day they were due to sail, Sir Gregory handed a large envelope in a leather satchel to Nicholas.

'You are to take this letter to the governor of the new colony at Fremantle en route to the Murchison. All has been arranged,' were Sir Gregory's parting words. They shook hands, the lines were cast and the sails cracked in a stiff breeze.

Chapter 3

The Murchison

Peter Strudwich and Nicholas both clung to the rigging some 25 feet above the deck, discussing how they would approach the river mouth.

'There must be a channel running parallel to both the reef and the sand bar beyond,' the captain observed. 'You can see the current flowing from starboard to port, and the actual river enters on the extreme starboard side by the rocks there.'

'Yes, and it must discharge on the port side, although I cannot see where,' Nicholas said uneasily.

The captain nodded his head in agreement. 'It is as well we have chosen a neap tide to attempt this Nicholas. Otherwise you could be fighting either the incoming or outgoing tide, the river's discharge and the swell breaking over the reef, all at once. I lay a pound to a shilling that is what happened to the crew of the *Tenacious*,' he mused.

'Nevertheless, this will be very dangerous. You still have the breaking swell over the reef and the river's discharge to contend with, though possibly to a lesser extent. Once you enter the channel you will have to row for your lives.

'Observe the hump of sea in the middle there,' Captain Strudwich continued as he handed over the glass. 'It's where the flow of the river meets the incoming tide. Watch it when you enter the channel, keep away from the middle and try to keep to the port side against the sandbank.'

Nicholas listened intently. The captain continued. 'Have a man stand in the bow with a long painter, if the bow even looks like swinging out to the centre, hard-a-port and row for the sandbank.' He turned to Nicholas, fixing him with his intense blue eyes. 'Listen up now! Your man in the bow must make the bank the moment it kisses the sand, too soon and he will be swept away. If that happens, you may all be lost.'

The long boat pulled away from the *Collette* with eight men aboard and there was not one of them whose gut wasn't clenched from nerves.

Fifty chains from the ship Nicholas glanced over the stern of the longboat to lift a hand to Peter Strudwich. As he waved a flash of something caught his eye. He saw a huge dark striped shark pass beneath the stern, its blunt nose telling him it was a tiger shark. Horrified, he said nothing.

As the oarsmen pulled the longboat towards the river mouth Nicholas stood in the stern, one foot on the tiller. 'Pull away lads, we will go about to port for a bit and see if we can see past the surf over there,' he instructed.

As they rowed along parallel to the reef, the sea seemed to smooth out somewhat, although Nicholas knew they had merely ridden the back of the swell before it slid over the reef.

Suddenly, Nicholas saw what he had been looking for. 'Boat oars lads, let's have a look at this.'

The opening was indeed to the port of the reef, and the incoming tide, although neap, was deceptive – it was running into the opening at some speed but slowed about halfway up the reef where it met the outflow of the river. The bow started to turn slowly to starboard.

'Row!' Nicholas shouted and threw the handle of the tiller hard to starboard, knowing that they must get out to sea and enter the opening on the far port side or be dragged onto the corner of the reef.

The sailors bent their backs to his command and slowly they began to make some headway out to sea.

They drew away from the mouth and out into calmer waters.

To the port and starboard, sea birds wheeled and dived into the sea, terns, booby's and gulls alike, feasting on shoals of baitfish. The hapless creatures herded into a mass and boiled to the surface as they tried desperately to escape the slashing jaws of the predators below. Occasionally, one could see fins of shark break the surface and large fish, their sides slashed in silver, jump clear of the sea to splash back into the turmoil.

The feeding fish and birds indicated the forthcoming change in tide. Even though the tide swing was minimal because of the neap tide, which was typical of a quarter moon, nonetheless he knew they must hurry or they would be fighting the odds even more.

He angled the boat across to the port side, parallel with the sand bar, which he observed ran for some distance north.

As they ran alongside the bank, Nicholas looked to the red cliffs and saw the solitary figure of a man standing like a sentinel, looking down on them, a long solitary spear held vertically by his side. But he had no time to speculate further.

'Put your backs into it lads! Here we go! Row for your lives!'

The incoming current picked up the longboat and now held in its grip, dragged it into the channel.

'Jesus Christ!' Nicholas said to himself in alarm as the boat shot into the churning water and began to buck like a wild horse, making it difficult for the oarsmen to maintain pull on their blades. The bow was plunging into the sea and the spray drenching all.

Nicholas had his full weight on the tiller to keep the boat from being sucked into the centre of the channel, but even so it was veering that way.

Ahead he could see the deceptively smooth looking hump stretching almost from side to side of the channel, a lazy fixed curl at its centre.

The boat slowly began to run toward the port bank. 'Get ready with that painter mister! Don't jump unless I say so, you got that!' he shouted.

'Yes sir!' Seaman Cox yelled back. Cox was down on one knee, hanging on for dear life, drenched and with a death grip on the bow.

The boat began to slow just as it approached the nexus of the incoming tide and the outgoing flow of the river.

Suddenly, the vicious undertow caught the boat and the vessel slewed.

Nicholas yelled, 'Pull! Pull!' as the bow began to swing to starboard. 'Come on! Come on!' Nicholas pleaded through clenched teeth for the boat to swing back to port. She steadied and moved toward the bank.

'Jump now!' he yelled. Cox leapt toward the bank, landing half in the sea and half on the bank.

He scrambled up onto the sand, and wrapping the painter around his shoulders, began to take the strain.

The painter was as taught as a bowstring as Cox dug in, but the bow of the longboat began to be dragged by the undertow.

'Sir, I can't hold her!' screamed Cox as he was steadily dragged to the water's edge.

'Lafferty! Take the tiller!' snapped Nicholas. The man scrambled to obey.

Nicholas leapt to the bow and dived straight in to the sea.

The current sucked at him like an invisible hand. He desperately struck out and threw one hand at the painter and hung on.

He struggled hand over hand toward the bank, Cox now almost up to his knees in sand, not a metre from the edge.

'Look out sir!' screamed Cox. 'Shark!'

Nicholas had no time to even look, one more pull and he hauled himself onto the sand. As he scrambled to his feet turning to throw his weight behind Cox, he saw the blunt snout of a large shark, not a foot from the edge of the bank swirl away, the dorsal fin about nine inches tall.

God almighty that was close, he thought.

They had no time to dwell on the incident as both men took the strain, the painter cutting into their shoulders and turning their knuckles white.

'We're holding her sir!' Cox gasped. 'Come on heave!' was all Nicholas could manage to grunt out.

They slowly made progress, the boat now almost halfway upstream from the hump in the middle.

The hull of the boat was just scraping along the sand at the edge of the bar, the sandy spit's end only about one hundred feet away. Two more men now leapt ashore to assist Cox and Nicholas while the rest poled the boat off the sandbank with the oars.

Ten minutes later, they lay scattered on the sand of the spit jutting toward the river's entry into the channel, utterly exhausted and dragging in ragged lungful's of sweet air.

'Bloody 'ell! Did ye' see the size o' that fookin' damn shark! I thought 'e 'ad you for sure sir,' one of the men said.

'I think maybe the damn thing was sent to help me out of the water,' gasped Nicholas.

The men snickered, relief palpable, the laughter dissolving some of the tension of the past hour.

They all passed around a pannikin of water then walked around the sand bar.

A beautiful estuary lay before them. The shallows were clear, shoals of small fish rippling the surface at their approach. Stingrays flapped out of harm's way, their wings beating as they shot to the depths and safety.

Flocks of graceful black swans glided through the calm waters, their bright red beaks in stark contrast to their ebony plumage, and many species of wild duck flew overhead and swam among the growth on the far side of the river.

Further along the port side of the sand bar were hundreds of banded stilt, their beautiful contrasting white plumage, chocolate coloured wings and long red legs vivid against the silver and white sands, streaked by the morning sun.

Scattered along the bank were piles of driftwood, their gnarled, sun-bleached trunks twisted and bent into all manner of shapes and sizes. Hermit crabs scuttled across the fine sand, seeking cover under the driftwood or rapidly digging themselves into the sand.

'Fookin' beautiful!' muttered one of the sailors as they all drank in the sight.

One of the men spotted a larger blue coloured crab, about a foot across, moving steadily toward deeper water, its long claws raised high in defence. The sailor dashed into the water to catch it and the blue crab immediately attached its nippers to the sailor's hand. Amid hoots of laughter and the man's howls of pain, it eventually let go and scuttled into deeper water.

The men's chuckling died away as a strange buzzing sound started to echo around the cliffs in front of them. The hair on their necks stood on end as the deep buzzing noise rose and fell in crescendo.

The din continued for ten minutes or so then suddenly died away, the echo drifting around them leaving only the sound of sea birds and the hiss of the surf, which now seemed to be abating.

'Be-Jaysus, what was that!' stammered one of them, his eyes flitting all over the cliff face.

They all seemed riveted to the spot, eyes now darting everywhere but there was nothing to be seen.

The only one not terrified was Nicholas, having heard it before, though not in Australia.

Another buzzing now started some distance away, although from where they stood it was difficult to detect from where.

'It's a message stick.' he said. 'In our language and in some parts of Africa, you would call it a bullroarer or buzz stick. It's a flat, thin, piece of wood about twelve to eighteen inches long and about two inches wide, it has a hole in one end and is tied to a length of twine about five or six feet long.'

The men stared at him. 'You whiz it around your head, like this,' he demonstrated, rotating his arm and fist around his head in a horizontal plane. 'The flat piece of wood spins on the twine as you whiz it around, giving off the strange noise. The harder you spin, the louder the noise and higher the pitch.

'The Bushmen in Africa also use it to signal each other, so I guess these people use it too, interesting.'

'What's it saying then sir?' asked Cox.

Nicholas pursed his lips, eyes cast upward and stoking his chin, replied, 'White man beat shark by nose, all bets off.' He shook his head, 'I don't know man!'

The men again lapsed into laughter and chuckles, the fear fading with it, which was exactly what Nicholas had intended with his flippancy.

He, of course, spoke the truth. He had not the slightest idea what message had been sent, but he did know that it meant there were likely to be quite a number of these people around them.

The unease returned as they made their way back to the boat and pushing off, rounded the elbow in the river.

The river was indeed serene and calm, shoals of small fish broke the surface as they quietly rowed into the wider section. The only other sound was the splash from the sounding weight as Cox threw it ahead and his soft call of the depth as they progressed upstream.

Nicholas again stood at the tiller silently scanning every foot of the banks, not that they could be in any danger out in the middle here, but because he was taken with the serenity of this place.

They were being paced by two dolphins, gently breaking the surface with a sigh of breath, their gleaming skin shining bronze in the morning sun.

The banks were lined with paperbark trees, and a kind of cypress he thought and what appeared to be some sort of acacia. Not very tall, Nicholas observed, but tall enough to build with perhaps when the time came.

Rocky outcrops of stone tumbled in layers down to the water's edge, in chocolate, grey and brown. Nicholas stared at them, then dismissed them as of no value other than perhaps as building material.

Wild duck careened past and flocks of pelican stood on the sandbank to port.

He steered to port as Cox began to call shallow depth and they were getting too close to the land side shore.

They rowed upstream for some five miles before Nicholas finally called a halt and said, 'Ship oars and we'll take arms lads, just as a precaution.

'No one is to fire a shot unless I say the word but be alert.'

They primed and checked their long rifles and pistols. Nicholas disliked pistols, apart from their inaccuracy, the muzzle flash and smoke from the discharge marred vision temporarily due to the close proximity of the weapon to one's face. At least with a rifle you were further away from the flash and most of the military versions were still able to be armed with a bayonet on the end of the barrel. Most of the men carried Royal Navy 1836 issue Baker rifles of .650 calibre, a flintlock with a two-grooved barrel, while the others had Brunswick's, not nearly as accurate but with a .704 calibre and a kick to match.

'We'll put to shore over there, on that small beach,' he said pointing to the starboard bank.

The longboat gently kissed the shore, Cox and two others leapt out, waist deep into the river to steady the boat. They stood still and listened.

No sound came to them other than the chirping and twittering of birds, of which there seemed to be many flitting amongst the trees and shrubs.

With a final look around Nicholas said, 'Alright men, let's go ashore, keep alert and those muskets primed, I don't think we will have trouble yet or they would have been on us by now.'

He leapt over the bow onto the dry sand.

At last! He was elated and charged with excitement. Striding to a rocky outcrop some thirty feet in height, he scrambled to the top. To his left, lay the river as it swept down toward the broader waters of the entrance. Turning to his right the river narrowed and curved away to vanish into the timber and scrub before reappearing briefly some miles further up.

Inland, he could see high cliffs jutting into the horizon, and like a hunter sniffing game Nicholas guessed this was where he would find his mineral traces, if they were here. He climbed back down, his eyes sparkling with anticipation.

'We'll scout around lads, look sharp. When we return, we will make camp here for tonight, by the rocks over there,' he instructed pointing to the hill he had climbed. 'Mr Lafferty, Mr Cox, stay and secure the boat.'

They walked some distance from the river, the Blacks and the bull-roarer's moan still vivid in their minds.

Small black flies swarmed about them, crawling all over their faces, attracted by their sweat and the moisture in their eyes.

They neither heard nor saw any sign of the Blacks, only thorny scrub and sand dunes, punctuated by rocky outcrops. These Nicholas examined briefly but found them to be only of limestone.

Returning to the boat, he said 'Lift the tiller Mr Lafferty, we'll run two ropes from the stern to timber and anchor the bow six feet offshore after we've unloaded.'

'Aye sir, will we…' his voice died away, and he stared past Nicholas. 'What is it man?' Nicholas turned to see what had stalled his conversation.

Two Blacks had appeared as if by magic and stood not twenty feet from the party.

They wore only a piece of paperbark hanging from their waist and a red ochre strip of some material around their heads, black curly hair tumbled about their headbands.

Both were heavily bearded, the older of the two having a long beard which was streaked with grey.

About five foot eleven in height, they were as wiry and lean as a drawn bow, and massive tribal scars crisscrossed their chests.

Each held a clutch of long spears tipped with vicious looking barbs.

'No sudden moves now lads,' said Nicholas before any of them could react. 'They could have taken us any time without getting this close.'

'I don't like it sir, they're armed!' someone said. 'So are you man, so are you,' said Nicholas quietly.

'Those spears look like they're for fishing to me, see the barbs?'

'No one shoots! Understood? And Robins put that damn musket up. Now!'

The older of the two, lifted his hand in some sort of indication. The other bent down, laying his spears on the ground beside him. He selected one with several long prongs, notched with the vicious looking barbs and what appeared to be a long piece of semi-curved wood, like a quarter section of tube. It was about two and a half feet long. On one end there was a sharp spike sticking up at an angle toward the other end which had a sort of handle, bound with a twine. He fitted the end of the spear to the spike and gripping the handle, lifted this to about shoulder height, left hand supporting the spear. He suddenly moved toward them. The sailors shifted nervously. 'Easy lads, easy now,' said Nicholas.

He was about six feet from the nervous white men when suddenly he raised his right arm with the sheath and spear and before anyone could react, threw the spear between Cox and the longboat.

'Hold your fire!' Nicholas called.

In an instant, the fellow was at the water's edge and retrieved a large flapping fish about two and a half feet long, its scales flashing silver in the sun. It was speared neatly through the gills.

The astonished white men stood open mouthed by the speed and gracefulness of the move as the Black walked up to Nicholas and laid the still flapping fish at his feet.

The older man said something that sounded like 'Gooda' and gestured with his hand to Nicholas.

Nicholas dipped his head in thanks, and astonished, asked, 'Did he just say "good"?' But the two had turned and vanished into the scrub.

This significant gesture elated Nicholas, allaying some of his previous unease. He turned to the open-mouthed men and grinning said, 'Gentleman, I believe dinner is served!' One of the men said, 'Sir, I reckon he *did* say sum'pin loik', gooda!'

Nicholas knew that this gesture of welcome was given in peace, but would things change when he attempted to set up a homestead he thought. Still he pondered: how did he know the word good?

It was one thing to welcome someone, but how would these people react when they realised he intended to stay.

Nicholas was not to know, but the older, white bearded Aboriginal elder was to play a significant role in his survival and future.

They spent two days at the river, exploring the area back toward the mouth and a few miles inland.

The most significant feature that caught their attention, were the red cliffs. On climbing up to the most prominent point, the cliffs provided a magnificent view up and down the coast and some distance up the river. They were made up, in part, of multiple bands of different coloured limestone, from cream, chocolate and red brown all sandwiched together. They lay in horizontal layers, and from a distance looked like the pages of a book.

Other parts of the cliffs were red and very hard abrasive limestone.

Nicholas examined these cliffs with some interest. Although they did not offer any trace of viable mineralisation, the shear magnificence of the colour and formation fascinated him.

There were many varieties of shrubs surrounding the river and beyond. Nicholas did not know what they were, or if they would affect his livestock – it was a risk he would have to accept.

He did notice some "blue bush" scattered further inland and recalled some of the would-be graziers in Fremantle talking of it. He wondered if it became more prevalent further inland, and if so, there might be good grazing for sheep in the future.

Kangaroos of several different types appeared to be in abundance. Some of the sailors had never seen the kangaroo before and were amazed at the agility of these marvelous creatures as they bounded effortlessly through the scrub, equally at home bounding up the cliffs and rocks scattered around the river. Here, the kangaroo was different to those around Fremantle, being predominantly of a rusty red colour.

The *Collette* rode at anchor some distance off the river mouth. She had moved to about one nautical mile distant, no doubt Captain Strudwich was cautious of the tidal fall.

From up here on the cliff face Nicholas could see just how dangerous the channel was, but he was also able to see the deeper parts of it and where to take advantage.

They would need the outgoing tide to return to the ship, using the flow of the river and the tide.

The passage through the channel would be a lot easier going out Nicholas observed – what worried him was returning, and the perilous attempt at passage with fully laden boats as the outflowing river and the sea pushing back against it, made forward motion very hard.

He decided that perhaps a better option might be to unload most of the stores and livestock onto the sand bar on the north side of the river's exit to the sea. This would enable a party of six men to walk up to the spit at the turn of the river, towing the boats and assisting the oarsmen to negotiate the channel until they entered the river.

They could then row upstream to the opposite side of the sand bar, reload the stores and livestock in calm water and transfer them to the far bank. He would discuss this with Peter Strudwich when they returned to the *Collette*.

They neither saw, nor heard from the Blacks again during their remaining time at the camp by the river. Nicholas again began to wonder what the reception would be when he started to establish his buildings, and these people realised he intended to stay.

He had heard rumours that there were already some white settlers inland, having trekked up from Geraldton and Greenough some years ago, but did not know where exactly or even if they had survived, let alone established any dwelling. Perhaps he wondered if the Blacks had had some interaction with these others, hence the English word.

With the knowledge gained from his observations and their hair-raising entry some days before, the exit from the river proved to be without incident. They did come perilously close to the reef as they turned out to sea, the neap tide obviously diminishing the undertow.

They rowed back across the mouth and Nicholas had Cox sound out the water off the sand bar north and for about four chains leading back to the west. The average depth came up at five fathoms.

This completed, they rowed back to the *Collette*.

They stepped back on board at eight bells and the men immediately set about lifting the longboat from alongside, the snatch blocks squealing as they hauled on the ropes.

Captain Strudwich gave quiet orders to his first mate, 'Haul anchor if you please Mr Birch, we'll make for the north side of the river mouth.' Birch was a heavyset man of taciturn demeaner to whom Nicholas had taken an immediate dislike to from first sight. Peter Strudwich had assured Nicholas that although a hard man, he was a good man at sea.

The first mate bawled orders and the sailors began to lift anchor and unfurl the topsails.

'We'll shift closer to shore, off the sand bar as close as we dare Nicholas, we should be able to transfer most of the heavy stock by tonight all being well,' Strudwich said. 'And we'll leave the livestock hobbled and tied for the night with shore guards.

In all, the livestock consisted of two good breeding cows, one huge bull, one bullock, three horses, ten sheep, and a crate of fowl consisting of about ten chickens and one rooster.

With the exception of two horses and the bull, all of the rest had been purchased and hoisted on board in the settlement of what was to be the new town of Geraldton at Champion Bay which they now knew to be roughly a day and half sailing to the south, weather permitting.

The only other exception being Nicholas's own horse, which had been picked up from Cape Town and endured the voyage to Fremantle, Geraldton and on to the river.

The dun was looking a little on the lean side by now and Nicholas thought the sooner he got him to the shore and some decent feed the better, and he could not wait to give him some long overdue runs.

The dun was a sturdy looking animal, not a magnificent horse by any standard but he stood sixteen and a half hands high and was tough and strong of heart. His distinguishing features were the long raking scars down both sides of his haunches and flanks.

Nicholas had come by the horse whilst on one of his many ventures into the African bushland hunting and looking for mineral deposits after his departure from the Lake Victoria region. He and his party had set camp within a thorn boma near the base of a low range of hills at the outskirts of the Transvaal.

They were aware of another hunting safari party camped some two miles to the south-west, one of Nicholas's scouts had seen them. On a more ominous note, the other residents of the area was a large pride of lions. 'I hope they have made a boma?' Nicholas said.

During the early evening they were reminded of the lions' presence by the occasional roaring.

Around midnight sounds of commotion erupted from the direction of the safari camp and several shots were heard accompanied by roaring and the terrified and hysterical whinnying of horses.

Nicholas and his party investigated at first light. On the way they came across the dun. Its flanks clawed by a lion. The terrified animal's eyes were huge and rolling in fear, he was bloody and trembling but his ears pricked toward them and the head was still up in defiance.

They scanned the area and surrounding thorn bushes for any sign of lions, but neither saw nor sensed anything. The horse had managed to seek refuge in a rocky cut, or gulch, in the side of the ridge that ran through the area, each side of which was heavily guarded by thorn bushes.

It was a miracle in itself that the hyena or lion had not brought the poor creature down during the night, let alone that the animal had ended up here in the cut.

Nicholas approached the horse talking softly and soothingly until the horse let him touch him. He inspected its haunches. Deep wounds lay open down the flanks and were already covered in flies.

He had lifted the rifle to put the animal out of its misery but was unable to pull the trigger.

The horse's eyes were like deep pools of regret. It was as though the animal was willing him to stay the shot.

They stared at each other, neither moving as the animal's life hung on the fraction of movement of Nicholas's trigger finger.

Nicholas suddenly lifted the rifle.

'Get the salve and antiseptic from the pack,' Nicholas had commanded, uncocking the hammers and lowering the rifle. 'We must stop the bleeding'.

A'buti, his Bushman guide and friend, had rolled his eyes, then he looked at the horse, staring into its eyes. 'He will be your brother or your death,' he stated with finality.

The little Bushman snorted in derision and waved his hand around. 'I look!' and trotted off.

He returned some 15 minutes later, chewing, his cheeks ballooning as he did so, and he carried some dark clay-like substance. He spat a green goo into the clay and mixed it well. They had quickly pressed the substance into the worst of the clawing. Leading the weakened animal, they then hurried on in the direction of the safari camp.

The camp was chaotic when they approached it, equipment was scattered and tents were down. One member was dead, mauled by one of the lionesses, which lay shot dead on the other side of the camp, and one of the porters had been clawed across his back. He sat against a tree shivering in fear and pain. Almost all of the horses had bolted and by now most likely would have been taken by lions or hyenas, or possibly still running.

Nicholas and his men had assisted as best they could, managing to round up three remaining horses which had survived by bolting out into the open plains to the east. By some miracle they had not been taken by the ever-present predators. They then helped with packing, the party now abandoning the hunt.

As they readied to break camp, one of the party, a ruddy faced individual with large ears and a handlebar moustache had approached the dun, inspecting the wounds. He then directed one of the bearers to fetch his rifle.

'One moment my friend,' called Nicholas. 'May I have the horse, since you are to destroy it anyway?'

'That horse used to be very good but now it will never be any good again man,' the fellow stated. 'Better to put it out of its misery but thank you for trying to save it.'

But Nicholas insisted, and the man finally gave way, and with a shrug gave it to him.

Back at his own camp, they hobbled the horse. The dun was skittish, tossing its head with his ears layed back flat, rolling its eyes and flaring its nostrils making it hard to handle. Mbutu sprinkled some sort of powder in his hand and placing it under the horse's muzzle. Amazingly, after a few minutes the grey seemed to settle somewhat.

'I shall call you Stitch if you survive this,' Nicholas stated, needle and cat gut in hand as he and the others once again tried to calm the animal so he could stitch the deepest wounds. However, wiping the wounds with clean lint had agitated the poor animal despite the 'magic' powder. A'buti had then sprinkled another of his herbal powders into the wounds, numbing the poor beast's pain. The stitching had continued, some one hundred and twenty of them. Good God! Nicholas thought as, wrists aching, he again strained to push the bloodied needle through the tough hide. 'Any man would die of the pain!' he muttered as he felt the tremors of the animal beneath his hands.

It took some time for the sturdy horse to recover and it spent the first four days plodding around the thorn bush kraal they had made with his head hanging down. Nicholas began to doubt if the animal would survive, but survive it did, and Nicholas had never regretted putting the effort into what most would have called a waste of time. He and the little Bushman spent many weeks healing the wounds. A'buti's skill with native herbs and remedies probably saved the horse more than anything.

One morning Nicholas woke to find the dun trotting around seemingly free of pain. He clucked his tongue and the horse immediately came trotting up to him and nuzzled his hand. Nicholas was elated.

In some sort of cliché Nicholas had reflected, the horse had the heart of a lion.

Chapter 4

Edward Raymond Birch

The unloading of the livestock and provisions went without incident. By dusk the animals were hobbled and tied on the sand bar. Four men stayed ashore to keep watch, a good fire burned brightly at their camp.

The rest of the provisions would be unloaded the following morning.

Peter Strudwich had the ship move back to its original anchorage, and as the sun vanished below the horizon, he and Nicholas stood on the poop deck in silence, absorbing the magnificent spectrum of colour as the final curtain on daylight fell to close the day.

Nicholas and Strudwich had talked at length over their evening meal and had argued over Nicholas's decision to begin this adventure alone. The captain said it was madness, he would be placing himself and the investment at great risk.

He was probably correct, thought Nicholas, however he deemed the risk was somewhat lessened by the gift of fish from the two Blacks. His thinking was that if he were alone he would pose less of a threat.

In any event, he had argued, the *Collette* was to return in about nine or so months' time with cattlemen and more stock or they would arrive overland from Geraldine.

The next morning found the ship bustling with sailors as they hove to, adjacent to the sand bar, then dropped anchor and commenced loading the boats with provisions, readying them for the short trip to the sand bar.

Nicholas walked among the men, chatting to a few, but his mind was already ashore and on the task ahead of him.

He was stepping over one of the long crates which lay upon the deck – his mind on the building task which awaited him once the ship left – when he collided with one of the crew, a huge black man, a heavy crate perched on the man's back. The two men and the crate crashed to the deck.

The first mate strode across the main deck and snarled, 'I'll teach you to watch where you're going you damned 'eathen!'

He kicked the man full in the face and snatching up a belaying pin from the fife rail, lifted his arm to swing it down on the unfortunate fellow's head, who was still on his knees from the collision and the kick, blood now trickling down his face and onto the deck.

His swing was stopped by a tremendous blow to the side of his head, felling him to the deck. Birch scrambled to his feet, a look of immeasurable fury contorting his face as he faced his attacker and wiped his face with his sleeve.

The man who had struck him was a Welshman; whose actual surname was Wilberforce but known only by the nickname of the 'The Whip' or simply Whip. He was purported to be a pugilist of some note.

The instant the first mate made a move, Whip landed two more lightning fast blows to his head, stopping Birch in his tracks. Poker faced, he said, 'Back off Birch, t'weren't the Negro's fault.'

Purple with rage, Birch snarled, 'By Christ! I'll have you both lashed!' his face now swelling and not just from the indignant rage. 'I told the cap'n that this bloody 'eathen would be nothin' but trouble,' snarled Birch, blood now trickling from his own nose such was the power of the blow. Whip said nothing, fists still up – he almost casually waited for the mate's next move, and Birch knew it.

Nicholas broke in, 'Hold! Mr Birch. As a matter of fact, it was I who collided with...' he turned to the Negro, still on his hands and knees. 'Stand up man, what is your name!' The man slowly got to his feet, eyes wide with astonishment at Nicholas's admission.

Then, eyes downcast, he said, 'They call me Jack, sah.' The voice was so deep it was like the sound of distant thunder.

The huge man towered over Nicholas, his massive chest heaving and blood trickling from his nose and into the black curls of hair on his chest. His face was round and his right cheek sported a scar about half an inch high in the shape of the letter 'J', whether deliberately done or by mishap it was hard to tell. His head was clean shaven and glowed like polished ebony.

He locked eyes for an instant and a glimmer of recognition between the two flared. Nicholas suddenly remembered the slave market in Cape town years ago. Good lord, he thought, could it be the same fellow?

Nicholas knew that to show recognition may complicate matters even more and so masked his reaction.

The giant of a man cast his eyes down and now was showing difficulty looking into Nicholas's eyes and Nicholas knew what was expected and why.

Even though officially abolished in England in 1833, slavery, forced upon these people, forbade them to look their "masters" in the face. Nicholas's anger flared within, but his eyes were kindly when he said gently, 'You can look at me when we talk man, no harm will come to you over this.' The deep voice rumbled 'Thank you sah,' and he lifted his head to look at Nicholas, the gratitude evident in his eyes. A slight frown suddenly creased the man's face and he now openly stared at Nicholas. They again stared at one another, Nicholas saw something deep behind the submissive look, long suppressed pride and dignity, but also something else.

Nicholas switched his gaze to the first mate, his amber eyes burning like coals.

'As I said, the fault was mine, there will be no lashing of either of these men, is that perfectly clear? Now, get back to work! All of you!

'A word, if you please Mr Birch.' Nicholas's gaze switched onto the man and frowning, he indicated the quarter deck with a jerk of his thumb, where the captain now stood having heard the commotion from the forward hold.

After trying to explain to the captain what had occurred, Nicholas had had enough of the belligerent first mate's interjection and ill manners.

'I'll have that black bastard's arse before this voyage is done and 'is cocky mates, you mark me words...' Birch fumed.

Nicholas stepped up to him, and towering over him, his eyes flat and devoid of anything as he barely gained control, said with a voice full of menace, 'You were fortunate that someone did stop you, you damn fool, you would have caved his head in, and if the Welshman hadn't stopped you, I certainly would have. Now, whilst I am financing this expedition, you will curb your unjustified ill treatment of the men working to assist me, are we clear about this Mr Birch?' The man held his gaze, Nicholas noting the hatred in his eyes. Birch glanced at the captain who nodded his head. 'As you wish,' he said, spinning on his heels and walking away.

However, Nicholas knew the man would make good his threat once the ship sailed and he was off the ship.

Peter Strudwich could not afford to let any one get away with making a fool of his first mate in front of the crew either, even if it was the right thing to do.

Strudwich had, on occasion, ordered the lash for very serious breaches of discipline by his men, and once to an enemy of the crown but other than that, hated the treatment, thinking it too harsh.

Nicholas, his hand stroking his chin, again thought of the building task ahead of him. Perhaps it would not be such a bad idea to relent and have someone stay to help. Indeed, the Negro's dark skin may be to some advantage.

He turned to find the captain's eyes upon him, and Strudwich said, 'You know I cannot let this incident go unpunished Nicholas, irrespective of what you believe. I cannot allow a seaman to trade blows with a first mate in front of the entire crew and get away with it.'

Nicholas nodded, then said, 'I understand Peter, but the Negro had done nothing, it was my fault entirely for not watching where I was going, yet you and I both know that Birch will find a way to have a go at him one way or another once I am ashore.' He went on, 'The other man, is another story, even though he was only stopping Birch from using the belaying pin on the Negro, I understand he must be punished.'

Peter Strudwich pursed his lips, a sly look came over his face. 'Of course, there is one way I could avoid trouble.' Nicholas stared at him and could sense what he was about to say. He could barely contain his amusement at the cunning old sea dog's attempt to manipulate him.

'I could punish them both, by sentencing them to go ashore for six months or so to assist you,' he mused.

Nicholas put a suitable amount of abject shock on his face as he looked at Strudwich.

Spinning to the stern to hide their faces from the crew, they looked sideways at each other and suddenly quickly grinned at each other, unable to keep up the game any longer.

Nicholas relented – it was a decision he was to often reflect upon.

As he turned away to continue with the work, Nicholas was thinking about the look on the huge Negro's face as he stared at him. Something was nagging at him in the recesses of his mind. Damn, could it really be the same young man he saw at the market in Cape Town? he thought, it was such a long time ago.

The longboats fully loaded, Strudwich assembled the crew who would carry out the short voyage and unloading. After the brief about the perils and pending danger, he called Wilberforce and the big Negro before him.

'Ye both are charged with insubordination, disrespect for a superior, that being the First Mate Mr Birch,' he called out loud and clear.

'The maximum punishment is twelve lashes of the cat!' There was a collective gasp from the men. It was a harsh punishment and a few in the crew had been lashed before but never twelve lashes. A fit man would be hard put to survive the punishment, for the cat o' nine tails' lash would cut deep.

Birch had the lid off the brine barrel smirking and was already drawing out the cat from its home when Strudwich called out, 'Hold Mr Birch if you please!

'After some consideration and even against Mr Yuin's protests, I have decided that it best to remove the two offenders from the situation.' He carried on. 'Forthwith, Wilberforce and Jack will be put ashore from the *Collette* until I decide otherwise, but in any case for a minimum of nine months at Mr Yuin's behest.'

Turning to the two, he said. 'You are to remain on land and assist Mr Yuin in his establishment of his venture, here at this river or wherever he directs, are you clear on this?' A quick glance between the two and they both nodded and said in unison, 'Yes sir, understood.'

There was stunned silence. Birch, furious, flung the cat back into the barrel and turned to face his captain. 'I pro...' Strudwich, expecting this, turned with fury on his first mate.

'The decision is made by your captain and is final!' he roared. 'You have anything further to add Mr Birch?' he added, one eyebrow arched.

Birch, seething with hate and anger, finally muttered, 'No sir.'

'Good, we are settled then!' he concluded, and walked up to stand at his usual station on the poop deck with Nicholas. He said to Nicholas out of the corner of his mouth, 'A satisfactory result I think.'

'Very good.' Nicholas responded.

The transfer of the rest of the provisions from the ship to the sand bar was carried out without any great trouble.

The men then concentrated on hauling the longboats up through the channel and then rowed them around to the calm waters of the river.

The loading and unloading would begin all over again once the site on the opposite bank had been chosen.

Jack and Whip had accepted their "sentence" without protest, although both had looked suitably downcast about being sent off the ship. Nicholas could sense the relief they must have felt at avoiding the first mate's wrath.

Whip's full name was William Wilberforce Whipple. He hated the name Whipple as he had been the brunt of ridicule with the name all through his early youth, and so had dropped it. Apart from the name Whipple, he was the descendant of a seafaring family from Wales and proud of it. He had been at sea since he was ten years of age, and Nicholas discovered to his delight, had been apprenticed as a ship's carpenter.

He was a wiry looking fellow, five feet eleven inches in height, and a gaunt, chiseled face with awry scarred eyebrows from under which peered steady brown eyes. The scars and puffed ears testimony to his love of competing in dockside boxing competitions, a rough school indeed.

He was thirty-eight years old and although a tough man, Nicholas was later to find him an amicable, compassionate man with an unbridled hatred of sadistic bullies of Birch's ilk, possibly a legacy of his youthful encounters.

Jack was yet to reveal his true African name or where he originated, although it was obvious that he had suffered greatly under the white masters he had previously been enslaved to.

Strudwich had told that he had been aboard one of the "Spanish prizes" that the captain had commandeered toward the end of his privateering years.

The unfortunate fellow had been found bound to the mizzenmast when the captured Spanish vessel was boarded, his back bearing several wounds from the lash and in addition he had been savagely beaten. Peter Strudwich had recounted to Nicholas how the big man had been hanging unconscious from the savage beating, a few strips of flesh hung from his back and he was covered in welts and bruises.

The ship secure, Strudwich had the man cut down and had his ship's surgeon attend the man's wounds, although the surgeon had doubts he would survive.

With a deadpan expression, beneath which rage boiled almost out of control, he had rapped out commands to find those responsible for the barbaric act.

Although the practice was a common punishment throughout the navies of most countries, including the Royal Navy, Strudwich had never seen such brutality as this – apart from the dried blood caked all over his body, this itself indicating he had been beaten earlier, there were even bruise marks upon the back of the man's head, buttocks and stomach, although these had not yet broken the skin.

Two men were brought before him, an aristocratic looking first officer, who was arrogantly demanding to be unhanded, and a heavyset man of ruddy complexion and bald pate, a great gut emblazoned with a crude tattoo of a naked woman, which hung over his belt. His arms and chest were still spattered with the Negro's blood.

Strudwich had begun to question the officer about the sadistic beating, and looking down at the man's boots, he saw a splattering of blood.

The Spaniard answered in arrogant silence, and looking down his nose, suddenly spat in Strudwich's face.

Without even the slightest hesitation, Peter Strudwich tore the pistol from his belt, cocking and aiming in one fluid motion, and shot the officer between the eyes. The officer collapsed to the deck, his body and boots beating the tattoo of death upon the deck.

Wrenching another pistol from his boson's waist he levelled it at the head of the man who had obviously carried out most of the punishment.

He was a hair's breadth away from discharging the weapon when he realised the man was actually smirking at him, his sadistic beady eyes squinting in amusement.

The pistol held steady between the man's eyes, then lifted. The grossly overweight sailor had suddenly grinned, his contempt obvious. Peter had grinned back, but *his* grin was as cold as a witch's kiss.

'Throw that piece of shit overboard,' he said to his first mate, flicking his head toward the Spanish officers body, 'and strip and lash this fat pig to the mizzen men, let's see if 'e finds a taste of his own treatment amusing.' Then, almost as an afterthought said, 'In stages, an hour break in between, and three at a time with lime on the tails if you please. Start on the bastard's fat legs first.'

The amusement and smirk had vanished from the Spaniard's face as it dawned on him what was to happen. Struggling and yelling, he strained back as they lashed him to the mizzen. He was thrown into the brig in irons six hours later when his screams from the lash had died to a blubbering whimper.

The sailors had rowed across from the sandbank to choose the best landing and site to establish the new dwelling and yards. Leaving the rest of the crew at the boat, Nicholas chose two men and the three men strode along the land side bank of the river, some half a mile from the base of the imposing red cliffs, they headed in that direction.

Nicholas was mindful that the Blacks had been heading down the ridge toward the area that they were now approaching and when first they had been spotted. He was mildly curious as to why they had taken the trouble to make the difficult climb down the ridge when they could easily have approached from the lower ridges. It could well be coincidence, or that they too had been atop the cliff observing the ship with the solitary figure, perhaps from another vantage point.

Knowing that he would have to choose the site for their establishment very carefully, not only against the elements and possible attack, but also so as to proffer as little offence to custom as he could, he thought some investigation was the wisest course.

As they reached the base of the rocks, Nicholas held up his hand to halt their advance.

A well-worn track could now be seen winding down the ridge and faded out onto a flat limestone ledge, which jutted out over the corner of the river. The deep blue-green colour of the water signifying some depth.

Here, the river's waters were clear, with moderate current. The faster moving waters were further along toward the point where the river turned to the right and raced out to sea.

To their left, the surface of the limestone was made up of many jagged peaks, far too sharp and uneven to walk on, and rose to a good ten feet in height, forming a natural barrier to the land beyond.

Climbing up onto the ledge and looking down to the clear water below, they could immediately see why these people took the trouble to climb down the ridge.

The water teemed with fish, of all sizes, some quite large. There were well-worn holes, ground into the flat surface of the limestone, possibly for grinding grain of some sort, and several places where fires had been lit. Scattered around the edges of the clearing, were many broken oyster shells and all type of small shell.

Toward the back of the ledge was an overhang of rock, about four feet higher than the ledge. About six feet in, the rear wall, eroded by the wind and elements, had been curved to a concave shape. Many strange markings in red, mustard yellow, white and browns were painted on the smooth surface.

Images of figures and handprints were most predominant, as were drawings of fish, complete with backbone. Sectioned paintings of kangaroo and snake adorned the wall in various places.

Although Nicholas had no idea what they represented, he realised that this place was significant to the Blacks and it looked as though they had been using this place for a great number of years, perhaps even centuries.

'We will leave this place alone, I think we may be causing some offense by being here, even now someone may be watching,' he said glancing around. 'We'll head back upriver and have a look further along…we need to find a place with some flat ground, somewhere where we have a clear view to where the *Collette* is anchored now, so when she returns we can see her.'

Nicholas was the last to climb down. As he dropped to his haunches to leave the ledge, a faint glint caught his eye. He was about to continue, when his curiosity got the better of him. He reached over and picked up the small piece of rock about half the size of his thumbnail. It was heavy despite the size.

The bright silvery mineral glittered in the sunlight and small amounts broke free at his touch. Unbuttoning the top clasp on his shirt and fishing around his neck he produced his father's gift, a small brass encased prospector's magnifying glass on a gold chain, or "specking glass" as some called it.

As the specimen came into focus, his heart raced – it was galena or lead ore. He quickly glanced around the area but immediately discarded any connection, quite obviously the specimen had been brought here from elsewhere.

To say Nicholas was elated was an understatement, the galena had to have come from somewhere around the area and his prospectors nose twitched like a bloodhound's.

He speculated that one of the Blacks must have picked up the galena and carried it here, possibly a child, for there seemed to be no obvious reason why it was brought here, and further, it was the only piece he could find.

To the uninitiated, this find might seem insignificant, but galena ore or lead sulphide often was mingled with, or signified, a variety of other important and valuable minerals such as copper, silver and sometimes gold. It did not necessarily mean that these other minerals were present with the galena, but the very fact that this type of ore was present could lead to many possibilities, the prospector's dream.

Galena itself was in great demand, for it is from this very mineralisation that lead is easily produced. Lead was used in water pipes, ships' ballast, military shot, bullets, roofing, printing and a variety of other uses. A significant find would be very prosperous.

Nicholas looked toward the distant range of hills and the smell of challenge swept over him.

Pocketing the specimen, he chose to say nothing of his find.

Reluctantly, he turned and climbed down to join the others, there was much to do and it was to be many long months before he could even begin to think of prospecting.

Chapter 5

The River Bares Its Fangs

The search for a good site for the base began and they split into two groups. After a time, they eventually all came together at a small clearing some 750 yards north of the ledge. On one side was an outcrop of the layered limestone twenty feet or so high and quite long, curving away from a small sandy beach of pebble and sand.

The clearing was reasonably flat and even ground, running back east for about 350 yards. On the south side it was bordered by a mixture of trees and dense shrub. Small eucalypts were in abundance along the side of the clearing as well as other tree types Nicholas did not recognise.

There was a small hillock roughly twenty-five feet high and made up of some harder type of limestone not far from the corner of the layered limestone, this was a good lookout point considered Nicholas.

Examination of the area found no trace or evidence of the Blacks having frequented the area.

'This will be where we will begin,' stated Nicholas. 'We have limestone, timber and a small landing, and the flat is quite raised from the river's edge should it ever flood, perfect!'

Whip walked among the stand of timber, and returning said, 'Not much body in the wood, but it will do, some is very hard timber which should cure very well. The others, well, we'll see.'

The transfer of the equipment began in earnest, the longboats making many trips to and fro, loaded to the gunwales with provisions.

The previous day they had decided to unload the livestock last, Strudwich predicting the wind would drop.

In all there were some twenty tons of material. There were five tons of cut and dressed timber for housing, another three tons of rough cut stockade posts, prospecting gear, water casks, coils of rope, calico, bags of lime, firearms and shot. Other items included pitch, black powder, tallow, dried and cured food and grain. Great sea chests hooped with brass and iron, full of linen, clothing, navigation and surveying implements and other general items. Most essentially, building equipment comprising of wood saws, chisels, mattocks and hammers etc.

There was even a small horse-drawn cart, broken down for the voyage, and a wooden wheelbarrow filled with snatch blocks and pulleys. A great load of bagged grain and feed for the stock making up the bulk.

Whilst all this was being brought ashore, Nicholas checked off each item as it was unloaded and directed where the gear was to be placed.

Whip and Jack were already making good use of the building and surveying equipment and were marking out an area for stockyards.

The last of their load to be transferred would be the livestock, and they wanted to have the holding yards ready for them if possible. The spread of the stockyards would make this a time-consuming task and therefore they would try to utilise the crew of the *Collette* whilst they could.

A makeshift camp was set up, consisting of a large sailcloth tent, and that evening they all sat around a fire for their meal and to discuss the next day's events.

Their meal consisted of salted pork and biscuit, a standard meal aboard ship for seafaring men, washed down with a pannekin of black sweetened tea.

Nicholas outlined their first task tomorrow – cut stockade posts from the stack of timber and some from the thicket of native timber whilst the rest of the crew dug the postholes for the fencing and grain store building.

With the sky rapidly darkening, they relaxed around the fire with a shot of rum and a squeeze of lime they had procured from Champion Bay as a deterrent to scurvy.

One of the crew was an Irishman with the inevitable name of Paddy O'Leary. He was a witty fellow, and true to his nature had everyone in fits of laughter with his raucous stories, punctuated by the most outrageous of lies.

Most of his crewmates knew that Paddy rarely ventured further inland than the dockside ale houses, for he had an inordinate fear of insects, snakes and spiders, particularly spiders. He was always on the lookout for them, even on board ship, but this didn't stop him from making up the most incredible stories and lies about his experiences with them.

The only reason he was ashore now was because he looked upon Nicholas with some awe and felt reasonably safe in his company.

During one of his tales of dubious origin, he was describing his terrifying experience with a giant spider in India, huge, with multiple shining eyes.

'Oi'm tellin' ya, d' bloody tings are two whole feet across! An' wi' great shinin' oiyes, dozens of 'em!' he began, rolling his eyes around for effect. 'Evil lookin' oiyes dat can swivel all around an' root ya to da' spot!

"Is bloody great fangs are as long as me finger, an' all drippin' wit poison!' he continued, dangling his fingers in front of his mouth for emphasis. The older men were rolling their eyes at him, although a few of the younger ones were teetering on belief, mouths open in rapt attention, such were his antics.

'Dey fix ya wit dem beady oiyes an' slowly creep toward ya,' he paused dramatically, arms akimbo and fingers rolling, bent down like claws. "Is great 'airy bloody legs movin' loik dis! Den! dey pounce on ya! Stick ya wit dem bloody great fangs, an' suck all o' ya blood *right out!*" The young fellows jumping as he near on shouted the last words.

Whilst he held his doubtful audience's attention, Nicholas spotted a centipede about six inches long, making its way up behind the ranting Irishman.

Nicholas broke in, 'You know Paddy, here in Australia there are some very strange creatures,' he paused and gave Jack a quick wink. 'Why only the other day Jack and I spotted the strangest and most ferocious looking spider we have ever seen, even in Africa!'

'Instead of eight legs, this one had at least a hundred of them!' He turned to Jack, who along with several others, had spotted the centipede. 'Isn't that true Jack?' Jack solemnly nodded his great shining head.

The Irishman gulped, seeing the serious look on Nicholas's face, and trying very hard to look unconcerned, said 'Never! B' Jaysus!' Looking around at the deadpan faces, he asked, 'Umm, ah, d' ye be tinkin' dat dare moit be any of the buggers around 'ere sir?

'An'…an' what be dis terrible critter be lookin' loik sir?' he asked, his eyes darting around the surrounding ground behind him and looking decidedly nervous.

The centipede was now beginning to climb onto the Irishman's sea boot.

Nicholas grinned, and pointing to Paddy's boots said, 'Like that one!'

Paddy quickly dropped his eyes to his feet, he went as white as a ghost and to his horror saw the olive green centipede with its bright red head and tail and yellowish legs, climbing across his boot.

The poor fellow's eyes bulged out of his head like two bloodshot onions, and with a gasp he shot to his feet, flicking his boots about like he was in some mad frenzied dance and screaming like a girl. He landed a full four feet behind where he had been sitting, and collapsed in a dead faint.

There was not a man who wasn't roaring with laughter, and it was a full minute before some of them scrambled to their feet, remembering that the multi-legged 'spider' was probably still crawling around, although they failed to find it.

It took two buckets of water from the river dashed into Paddy's face and many slaps about the chops before they could bring him around.

He was shaking like a leaf and not from the cold water either. He got up and without another word walked to one of the longboats and sat at the tiller refusing to come ashore, no amount of persuasion, even from Nicholas, would convince him to set foot back on land.

The crew reckoned he would get over it and were in no doubt that the 'spider' would grow to at least three feet long and have no less than five hundred legs inside six months.

The men took to their tasks the next morning with a will, except for Paddy, who still steadfastly refused to budge from the stern of the longboat, so Nicholas directed him to clean the boats and catch fish for lunch, which he accepted without so much as a word, but nonetheless it took a full fifteen minutes before he started.

Soon the fence posts started to be placed for the stockade, which would be some one hundred and twenty feet long and about sixty feet wide and split into four sections.

By late afternoon the next day, the perimeter of the stockade had been completed and a huge pile of the limestone had been either broken off or picked up and transferred to where the stock and dwelling would be built. They discussed the transferring of the stock over the next day, leaving the remainder of the work to Nicholas, Whip and Jack.

The men all retired early after the day's hard toil. As Nicholas prepared to bed down, he reflected that Peter Strudwich would come ashore tomorrow and say his farewell, I will miss him he mused.

Nicholas awoke about 1am – something was bothering him, but he couldn't put a finger on what, and try as he might, was unable to get back to sleep.

He got out of his blanket and walked to the burnt down fire. Stirring the ashes, he lifted the cast iron urn further into the coals. It wasn't long before the water was bubbling softly, he made two mugs of strong sweet tea and walked over to the man on guard.

The fellow was alert and had seen Nicholas arise. 'Mornin' sir,' he greeted softly, '...why thank you kindly sir,' he added when Nicholas handed him the mug of tea and squatted down beside him.

They said nothing for a while, both taken by the peace and tranquility that surrounded them, the only sounds coming from the muted snoring of the men back at camp and the occasional call of some type of owl, a soft 'Oo- Hoo'.

The night sky was as black as pitch, the brilliant stars giving the area a soft heavenly glow, as though some ghostly paintbrush had touched up the edges of the encampment and the river as it slid slowly by almost unseen in the dark. 'This be a very special place I be thinking sir,' the man said after a couple of sips of his tea.

'Do you think so? How so?' Nicholas asked even though he felt he knew the answer.

'Well, I ain't never seen such stars in all me life, an' look at that river, it's as though mother nature has put that sand bar just so, to keep it calm an' safe from all trouble an' strife.'

Rising to his feet Nicholas said, 'I hope you are right man, I'm going for a stroll over there,' he said pointing to the rocky hillock a short distance from the camp site. 'Right you are sir, be careful sir.'

Nicholas climbed the small outcrop and sat down facing the sea. Before him lay the river, silently sliding to his left, dappled with elongated silver strips of the reflected stars. The sand bar lay between it and the sea, the glow of the sentry's fire throwing an eerie orange hue onto the livestock hobbled nearby.

Further out to sea, a single pin prick of yellow light marked the position of the *Collette*, although you could not distinguish the ship at all from the sea at that distance.

Breathing in deeply through his nose, Nicholas drew in the smell of the dew on the land and scent of the river. It gave him a sense of elation that he could not explain, and he lay back on the rocks and gazed into the mystical kaleidoscope of the stars.

As he stared at the wonder of the heavens, wandering at will through the night skies and absorbing the beauty of the dark early morning, he drifted off to sleep.

He dreamed a tranquil dream, of the many things he enjoyed in life, the simple things that have no cost, but are priceless nonetheless – the sparkle of the Sun on a mountain lake in Canada; the soft mists of England, swirling around him and the kiss of moisture it offered upon his cheek; the smell of new rains upon dry land in Africa. No perfume exists like that of the first rains, especially on hot and dry lands, and no sound as welcome as the accompanying joyous patter of raindrops in newly formed puddles.

Later in the early hours, he had another dream so realistic he was a ball of tension even though in deep sleep, and his arms tightened around his chest. A woman's face appeared, fading in and out so frustratingly he could not distinguish or recognise her. The light glowed from behind her so that when she moved he could not even distinguish her hair colour. The glimpses he could gather of her were of such beauty he gasped in his sleep.

It seemed as if her face floated before him surrounded by the very mists that caressed his face earlier in his dream.

She had long tresses of hair, which fell about her face and eyes that glowed with warmth and love. In his mind he reached out to touch the beautiful face, and as he did so great tears silently slid down her cheeks. Her eyes were now tinged with great sorrow and she began to fade away. An enormous feeling of helpless anguish clutched at him. In silence he reached for her and tried to call her back, but she faded into the mists of his mind.

'Mr Yuin sir, wake up sir.' Nicholas jerked up to a sitting position, staring with bewildered eyes at the sentry. 'Sorry sir, I was worried sir, I thought I heard you callin' out.'

Nicholas wiped his hand over his face, and rubbing his eyes said, 'It's all right man, I had a dream is all.' 'You can go back now and thank you.' He looked around, the eastern skyline had a faint hint of light to its edge, signaling the coming dawn. 'Wait! I'll come with you, I think I could do with another brew, how about you?' They climbed down and walked back.

Try as he might, Nicholas was unable to keep his thoughts from his dream, such was its realism. The glimpses of the beautiful face kept wandering around his mind. He would gruffly push it out of his mind, berating himself, but back it came like pushing water uphill. Then, each time she appeared, the same wrenching feeling came over him.

He tried to find some connection in his past, but although Nicholas had bedded many a woman, he was very particular with whom he lay with. For Nicholas, there had to be some kind of challenge for even the most beautiful girl or woman to even pique his interest, and even then the slightest thing could douse any desire he may have had. She, therefore, would have had to have been someone very special, if indeed she really did exist.

His gut wrenched as the realisation of the fact that the only woman he had ever truly loved and still did, had been Victoria. Was it Victoria? Was this some kind of telepathic cry for him? Something was very wrong he sensed and he thought, Victoria, are you safe? Perhaps she was in danger or something had changed for the worst. Am I being paranoid perhaps? Why then, he wondered, was this feeling so intense, something he had never experienced before. He wondered why there were no other parts to his dream that would connect to the vision, or why, of all places, would he dream of her here, at the Murchison River. The more he thought about it, the more he became convinced the woman in his dream was Victoria and she had somehow managed to contact him through his dream. He tried to brush off the connection as fantasy but the feelings came rushing back as soon as he did. Good God, how I miss everything about her so much, he thought as her memory caressed his mind and his mind slipped back to when he had departed from the Amendson's homestead.

Nicholas had wasted no time when he left the shores of Lake Victoria, his heart heavy and his emotions in turmoil. Try as he might he could not drive Victoria out of his head and heart. On his return to his prospecting camp, he was taciturn to say the least and the two Zulu men, who he had hired in Cape Town to help him, looked at each other in confusion. Gone was the genial man who they had come to trust and care for. Nicholas was brusque and authoritative and everything had to be done quickly and he worked incessantly from dawn till dusk.

On return to their camp, they would prepare their meal and eat in near silence after which Nicholas would sit by the fire brooding over something until late at night.

Gradually, Nicholas began to return to the man he was. A full month and a half had now passed when Nicholas suddenly realised that he was wasting his time. His heart was just not in the prospect anymore and he knew he had probably missed the tell tail signs he normally would have noticed.

Time to move, he thought one day, and he ordered the camp to be struck. He knew the best antidote was a challenge and adventure, and so had headed back to Cape Town.

The call of an owl brought his thoughts back to the present.

He knew it would be fruitless to travel back to Africa as either way if she was in trouble right now, he would have to travel back to Fremantle or Geraldton first, then it would be a minimum of twelve weeks before he could make landfall in the nearest port in Africa, Mombasa, and another four to six weeks to travel to the Armendsons.

He decided he would write to Ludwig and Lillian voicing his concern and if they thought or wanted him to return. He would make sure he gave the letter to Peter before he left, knowing that the letter was certain to be passed onto the mail clerks in Fremantle. With luck the mail could be in Ludwig's hands in about three and a half months, maybe less. He went to his satchel and fetched paper, his quill and ink, and began to write.

In the letter he apologised again for his rude exit and how no matter what, declared that his love for Victoria would never die, despite the fact that she had rejected him and he had tried so hard to put his feelings for her aside. He talked about he now being in Australia, about the country and of his pending foray into the unknown. After some thought, he decided to tell of his intense premonition, but whilst doing so, was so gripped in uncertainty and fear for Victoria, he could find no other words and therefore he finished the letter feeling much worse than when he had started, apprehension and uncertainty gnawing at his stomach like an acid.

Eight o'clock that morning saw the *Collette* moored off the sand bar and the captain's gig pull away from her side. Nicholas could see Peter Strudwich standing in the boat's bow. As it neared the edge of the bar he glanced around. The morning sky was clear and promised a fine day. Strudwich leapt ashore and strode across the bar toward the inner river where the men were loading stock. Nicholas smiled as he watched – he was looking forward to seeing the captain.

The transfer of the livestock was well under way and there remained only the sheep and Nicholas's horse to be brought across. He had decided to bring the horse across last, partly because two of the longboats would have to come back through the channel, one skiff was to remain with Nicholas until the *Collette's* next visit. It made sense to have a lead on the longboats as a precaution, and all the better to have his horse on stand-by to take the strain if needed.

Nicholas would then take the opportunity to give Stitch a run up the beach of the sand bar, and then ford the river some miles upstream. This would give him the chance to have a look around before beginning the construction of the buildings.

Peter and Nicholas walked around the clearing inspecting the work already done and discussing what would be achieved by the time the *Collette* returned in about six to eight month's time, all things being normal.

'You have chosen this site well I think,' said Peter, looking around. 'You should find good water when your well is dug, where are you proposing to sink the shaft?' he asked. Nicholas led him to a small shrub covered rise in the ground which appeared to be of broken and weathered limestone, some two hundred feet south east of the stockade. 'This should give good support to the shaft walls and reasonable digging,' Nicholas said. 'I expect to find water at about fifteen feet, it's far enough from the river, so I am hoping with the lime stone filtering the water it will be clean and drinkable.'

They continued walking around the area chatting amicably and talking of what the future may hold until it was time to make the last crossing to the sand bar.

Reaching into his waste coat Nicholas passed a flat brown paper parcel tied with twine to Peter and said, 'Could I impose upon you to see that this letter gets to the mail in Fremantle? It is of great importance to me.' Peter eyed the script on the front, which simply said; *L & L Amendson, Mombasa, onto Herrgarden Grande: Lake Victoria.* Peter said, 'Mombasa? I will be calling into there on my voyage back to pick up dispatches and stores for the company, I will hand deliver it to the Dutch embassy, but first I will check in Fremantle to see if any ship is sailing direct to Mombasa. The embassy in Mombasa have a mail chain in place, and they share this with the German embassy, it may well get there quicker yes?' Nicholas agreed and expressed his gratitude. He knew the Amendsons received mail from the mail chain and so would be sure to get it.

All of the boats were now ready to row across to the bar, Nicholas and Peter being the last to board.

'Right lads, let's push...' the words stalled in Peter Strudwich's mouth as the sound of the bullroarer started and built up to a crescendo, then died away. Some of the crew, who were just ashore for the first time, looked at each other with fear in their eyes until the others explained what the noise was.

Nicholas had left Whip and Jack behind to keep an eye on the stock whilst he went over to the bar. He was now a little worried that if there was trouble, they would be exposed, with no cover or place to shelter.

Strudwich looked at Nicholas and said, 'Are you sure you need only two men with you lad, I mean there may be any amount of Blacks out there and they just might see weakness in leaving just two men here.'

Nicholas thought for a minute. 'Yes, I acknowledge what you are saying, but by the same token, if there were a large force out there and they wanted to make a point, or were aggressive, then I feel that they would have attacked long before now.'

Another bullroarer, further away, could now be heard – it was difficult to pinpoint where exactly but it was further inland and upstream.

'Look sir, up on the cliff, ye can see some o' the buggers!' one of the crew said pointing. All looked to the cliffs.

There appeared to be four in the group. Nicholas thought he could recognise the older of the two who had offered the fish on their first encounter but the others were indistinguishable.

'Glass if you please Mr Cox,' Nicholas said holding out his hand to the seaman. He swung up the telescope and brought the group into focus.

It was indeed the grey bearded elder accompanied by a youth and two young women, one of whom looked about twenty years of age, bare breasted and covered only by a small loin cloth. The other was much younger, perhaps twelve or thirteen years old.

The youth was a striking looking fellow, and although thin, he was lean and muscled. He stood perhaps an inch in height above the old man and held his head high. None appeared to be armed, except for the elder who had a strange curved piece of wood in his hand, or perhaps there were two, it being difficult to tell at this distance.

Nicholas handed the telescope to Peter Strudwich, who stared at them for some time.

'It doesn't appear as if they are threatening in any way Nicholas, and they are not armed as you observe.

'We'll carry on, push off lads.'

They rowed across without further incident and teamed up with the rest of the crew on the sand bar.

The crews readied their longboats for the risky exit from the river, six men on ores, one in the bow, and one on the tiller bar. They rowed around to the spit, beaching on the east side in the slower water.

Nicholas saddled Stitch and the colt trembled with anticipation, his eyes rolling, and was as skittish as a cat on ice.

It had been many months since anybody had sat on him and Nicholas was anticipating an interesting few minutes until Stitch got used to the idea again.

He swung up into the saddle. Nothing happened – Stitch just stood there. But the instant Nicholas took one hand off the reins to pat the horse's neck, he exploded into action, rearing, then bolting north along the sand bar at full gallop.

Nicholas, caught almost completely unawares, hung on for dear life and it was some two hundred yards before he managed to regain his posture on the horse, and he burst out laughing and whooped with joy at the exhilarating feeling. He let the grey have its head and they galloped out of sight up the beach, disappearing into the sea mist from the surf only to reappear some miles further along as the beach swung out to the nor 'west.

Gradually, Stitch began to slow down, the pent-up energy almost expended, and Nicholas turned the grey around and began a slow trot back to the spit.

The beach was magnificent, he now was able to observe. Fine white sand and turquoise water fading into a deep royal blue on the other side of a long reef. The surf hissed in, long lines of white foaming wavelets ran across the reef some two hundred feet out and slipped into the turquoise lagoon behind the reef before finally curling, to their mild annoyance, onto the sandy beach.

On his left, low hillocks covered with scrub and grasses hid the inland and river from view.

As Nicholas rode back he came across a strip of rust-coloured sand running down from the sandy hills. 'Whoa boy!' he said pulling up his horse. Stitch lifted his head and whickered softly, ears pricked and nostrils flared, he pawed at the sand.

Nicholas could see that the growth at the base of the hills where the stained sand came from appeared to be more prolific and was a lot brighter in colour than the surrounding bush.

Small olive-green parakeets flitted among the shrubs and little black and yellow birds with long curved beaks sang a melodious tune as they jumped from branch to branch.

There had to be water here, Nicholas thought, though it seemed a most unlikely place.

He dismounted and led his horse over to the base of the hill, tying off Stitch to a hardy shrub, he walked through the bushes until he was about eighteen or twenty feet in.

He stared in amazement. Clear water welled up from the very base of the hill, forming a small pool before disappearing back into the sand. The hill, he could now see, was in fact, an ancient sand dune, which had, over time, been overgrown with the hardy coastal scrub and grasses. He knelt and tasted the cold, crystal clear water.

It was the sweetest water he had ever tasted. It must flow through from the river Nicholas thought, and is obviously filtered by the sand and limestone.

Sweeping off his hat, he filled it with water and made his way back to water his horse, which was pawing the sand and nodding his head up and down in anticipation, he, having already scented the sweet water long before his master.

Looking up and down the beach, Nicholas could see no way through to the lagoon behind the reef from the sea, so decided that he must wait for a very low tide in order to spot a possible gap in the reef. Nonetheless the spring was a valuable find.

He mounted the grey and cantered back to the sand spit and the waiting ship's crew.

Peter Strudwich and Nicholas stood at the edge of the channel leading out to sea, it would be high tide in about fifteen minutes, this being the optimum time to make the passage through the channel.

'I have instructed them to row for the centre, before the river turns into the channel. The boats should be able to make passage quite easily.' Strudwich said. 'It should be a lot easier coming out on high tide than when you came in Nicholas, the undertow will carry them out.'

Nicholas stared at seemingly calm water hiding the undertow and said, 'I am in agreeance with you Peter, the swell is a lot less, but the undertow could still complicate things. Still, I think you should have a line from here to the bow just in case the boat slews toward the corner of the reef where the river enters the sea.' They both stared at the corner, the gentle swell lazily rolling around the edge of the reef, the high tide hiding the danger beneath. 'Can't do any harm,' agreed Strudwich.

They walked over to the boats, Nicholas leading his horse. At Strudwich's instruction, a long one-inch hemp rope was looped through the ringbolt on the bow of the first boat. The remaining seven seamen from Strudwich's own boat took the other end to the end of the spit, which tapered off into the corner of the river and turned into the channel. The man in the bow paid out enough rope to keep the tension off the bow until needed. The other end was now shortened to the pommel of the saddle on Nicholas's horse.

Strudwich looked at the channel once again, checking the tide, then, lifting his hand swept it toward the corner. 'Right lads let's go!' he called. The first boat was pushed off the sand and immediately the oarsman bent their backs to the task, rapidly drawing the long boat toward the centre of the river.

The boat began to pick up pace as the current seized it, almost lazily it seemed. The men on the spit, now rapidly moving with the boat to keep the slack on the rope whilst the man in the bow began to pay out as much as he needed to avoid dragging the rope.

The longboat was now nearing the bend of the river, 'Oars up!' shouted the man on the tiller, and they lifted clear of the water.

The heavy boat seemed to hold position for a second, then she came about to starboard and was quickly dragged into the channel, far too fast for the running men to keep ahead of it.

'Let go!' Nicholas yelled to the men holding the rope and spurred Stitch forward to keep pace.

They could see the boat begin to slew toward the ocean side of the channel and the reef. Peter Strudwich bellowed, 'Lash off that rope NOW!'

For some inexplicable reason, the bow man seemed to be frozen, he did not react, and Nicholas was unable to take the strain. 'The rope man! Lash the rope!' Strudwich was now screaming at the fellow.

The boat was now running perilously close to the reef and was rapidly bearing down on the vicious corner of the reef.

The man on the tiller bar screamed, 'Row! Row lads! Row!'

It was too late, the savage undertow had her in its grip and she bore down the channel, now only about a yard from the reef.

They all watched helplessly as the swell suddenly began to suck back to sea. Just as the longboat was about to pass the corner, the sea suddenly vanished from the port side of the boat, exposing the jagged fangs of the reef. The boat hung for a split second, flipped onto its port side and crashed down on the reef.

She shattered, long splinters of her blue and white painted planking shooting into the sea and air, the sailors were smashed into the reef and sea, their screams mingling with the sound of breaking, tortured timber. Mere puppets in the play, they were powerless to do anything about it.

The swell rose again and lifted the remains of the boat and some of the men, pushing them back into the channel and into the undertow. The screams of the terrified men galvanised the men on shore.

Strudwich was bellowing, 'Back to my gig! Go! Go!' They sprinted up the bar to the captain's boat, some three hundred feet further north.

Nicholas sat astride his horse, unable to do anything but watch the horror unfold before him. He had never felt more helpless in his life, and he watched in dismay as the current carried the men and wreckage out to sea.

Two men came and stood beside him, he glanced down. Tears were streaming down the face of the younger of the two as he pointed toward the mouth of the river. One of the unfortunate seamen, had his arm in the air, forlornly waving for help as he clung to a piece of wreckage, even from here they could see blood streaming down his face, and then, as they watched, horrified, he slipped beneath the dark blue water.

'God help them,' Nicholas said out aloud. The young man, now openly sobbing, dropped to his knees in the sand.

'''Tis 'is pa sir,' the other man said, squatting, his arm now around the poor lad's shoulders.

'I'm sorry son,' Nicholas said, and giving a great sigh, his own eyes misting, instructed, 'Take the lad back over to the other side of the bar, there's nothing any one can do now until the captain can get to them, no use upsetting him any further.'

'Aye sir, Mr Yuin sir? There was nothing you could have done sir, 'twas all too quick.'

'Aye, I know man, but...' He reached into his vest and pulled his flask of brandy out, handing it to the sailor, 'For the lad,' he said adding, 'Lad, I will talk to you after if you've a mind.' The young fellow could barely manage a nod and Nicholas spurred Stitch away up the sand to where the captain's boat had been, his heart twisting in anguish and helplessness.

Peter Strudwich had no time to lament as his sailors put an enormous effort into their rowing. There was no need to yell command for more, the gig cut through the sea as fast as humanly possible.

Peter could still see wreckage and he counted only four men in the water that he could see. 'Come about port, that's enough!' he called. 'Keep it up lads, we've about one hundred and fifty yards to go.

'Ease up lads.' They were rapidly bearing down on the first of the poor souls who looked as if he could not last much longer.

'Mr Anderson' He said to the second mate 'Let me have that tiller bar, grab the boat hook and get up in the bow,' Strudwich said. 'Call the directions, and two of you boat your oars and help him get the men on board.'

'Aye sir, we'd best be quick about it sir, they look to be just about knackered,' the mate said.

They came about and alongside the first of the injured and exhausted sailors. The poor wretch was hauled aboard as gently as they could, and he tried to hold the scream through clenched teeth, but the pain was too much and his cry could be heard from the ship and sand bar alike. The man's shoulder was broken, with the collarbone jutting through the skin. One side of his torso and hip had been stripped of skin where he had been driven into the reef. He lay in the bottom of the gig, shivering in shock like a leaf in the wind.

They rowed across to the next man who was waving weakly to them. Caught in the strong outflowing current, he was being rapidly carried out to sea, his terrified face and weak movements now foretelling a certain end if they did not move fast.

The man was lifted aboard, a long piece of the longboat's shattered timber, about half an inch thick, had been driven into his face. Entering just below his right cheekbone, it lay under his skin right up to his temple. About one inch protruded from his cheek, the splinter forming an ugly painful, blue and purple ridge. He was bleeding profusely from a dozen cuts and wounds caused by the barnacles and reef, and his left wrist was broken.

The second mate called, 'Stand to for a second.' He stood for a moment, one hand to his brow, then pointing to port, called, 'Over there! Can't tell 'oo 'tis suh. Be-Jesus! 'e don't look none too 'ot though! Tha' other's over there suh,' he indicated sweeping his arm to starboard. 'Which one first suh?' he asked. Peter looked to where his bosun was staring.

The first man was floating, almost full length on the sea, his attempts to keep his head above the water were feeble at best, and they were at least a cable length away.

Strudwich quickly searched for the other sailor, he was somewhat closer, about five hundred feet off, but off to starboard of the gig. He looked to be in better condition and appeared to be at least holding his head clear of the sea. He made the decision.

'That way!' he called, pointing to port, the boat began to pull away, the men putting everything they could muster into their effort.

They were about one hundred feet away when the wretched soul slipped from sight.

'Pull boys! Pull!' yelled Anderson. "'E's gone under!' He stood up and stripped off his tunic, he was poised on the bow ready to dive in as soon as they were close enough.

'Boat oars!' said Strudwich. The gig glided toward the spot where the man had disappeared. Anderson peering intently into the dark blue depths, the others doing the same on either side, the only sound was the constant groaning of the injured men lying in the bottom of the gig and the run of the sea against the hull.

They could see nothing.

Alan Anderson crossed himself and started to pull on his tunic, he and Peter Strudwich, realising there was no hope of recovering the sailor now.

Strudwich snapped. 'Look to you lot, one to go and we haven't a moment to spare, let's go!'

The exhausted sailors again called for one last desperate effort. Muscles screaming, they pulled away toward the last survivor, who was now some eight hundred yards away.

God let us be in time, thought Peter Strudwich. The reality that he had made the wrong decision weighing heavily upon him.

They rowed as hard as their weary bodies allowed, the outgoing current now began to assist them and they bore down on the helpless sailor.

Anderson and Strudwich could see that by some miracle the man, now only about sixty feet away, was still managing to keep his head clear of the sea.

'Hang on man we're nearly there!' yelled Anderson. Here, he observed, the sea seemed to calm and flatten out somewhat.

To their astonishment the sailor called back, 'I'm alright, by Christ, I be right happy to see ye' though. I was thinkin' ye'd never get 'ere in time Alan.'

The mate yelled excitedly. "'Tis Moylan by God!' Anderson's glee and relief evident as he recognised his friend and companion of many years.

'Ye crafty old bastard! Even the sea don't want ye!' he laughed.

Relief flooded over Strudwich, and the dreadful feeling that had gripped him began to abate as the minutes ticked by whilst they drew down on the man.

'Boat oars, well done lads!' said Peter with relief now evident in his voice.

Still grinning, Anderson extended the boat hook toward his shipmate. Moylan reached up and grasped the hook.

'Thank Go...' He never finished the sentence. 'Look out!' screamed Anderson as he saw a great grey striped shape flash out from deep beneath the gig. The boat hook was torn from his grasp, and he teetered on the edge of the gunwale, the gig rocking violently, then fell back into the gig on his knees.

Some of these men had fought in terrible battles at sea and thought they had seen and heard it all, but Moylan's scream was of an unholy and unbridled terror that would remain with them forever.

The huge tiger shark exploded from the depths and took Moylan around the waist. The massive jaws and rows of razor sharp teeth almost cutting the poor man in half, such was the force and power of the attack, gouts of his arterial blood spraying the surrounding sea.

The great shark and its victim, rose up out of the sea as if in slow motion, though in reality it was in seconds. The monster shook Moylan violently from side to side, foaming and spraying the surface to a broiling pink tinge then vanished with him through the dark stain.

Seconds later, Moylan's upper torso swirled to the surface, some twenty feet away. Doomed, his hand lifting toward the boat, he wailed softly, ' Help me,' then slowly sank from site.

Anderson screamed, 'Tommy!' and made to dive in after him, two of the sailors grabbed him and wrestled him, sobbing and fighting like a madman from the edge of the gig.

They sat stunned, some with hands over their faces, others with their heads resting on the gunwale, bloodied and blistered hands from the frantic rowing hanging limply by their sides.

Anderson now sat slumped at the bow, his hands covering his face, perhaps unwilling to share his pain or his blameless failure to save his friend. Tears ran freely from beneath his palms, pooling at his chin to drip onto his trousers, a forlorn rain of sorrow and heartbreak.

A groan of pain brought them out of their state of utter defeat.

'Come lads, we'd best get these poor buggers to the sawbones,' said Strudwich gently. He was having great trouble keeping his own emotions intact.

Six good men were drowned, two of whom vanished without trace, and he had to fight to keep his thoughts from turning in on himself. As captain he was responsible for each and every one of them.

The row back to the *Collette* was slow and painful for them all, physically and emotionally. The gig finally passing beneath the stern to reach the starboard side and the calmer waters in the lee of the ship.

Men clattered down the side to assist the wounded and the exhausted sailors.

Strudwich ordered a new crew be ready to row his gig ashore, then went below to offer encouragement to the two surviving sailors. He went down the companion ladder to the orlop deck where the ship's surgeon was attending to the two survivors' wounds. He spent a few minutes below, but neither man was in any condition to talk. The surgeon glanced up at him. 'They'll pull through sir.' Feeling helpless, he went topside, gave instructions to ready the ship for sea and returned to the gig.

They pulled smartly away from the ship and headed for the sand bar.

Ashore, they prepared to bring the other longboat through the channel. Not one man was enthusiastic about another attempt, but the change in tide would make it even more dangerous if they did not move quickly.

Whilst Peter Strudwich was attempting the rescue, Nicholas had time to reflect on what had happened and how. He came to the conclusion that it would be better if two ropes were used, one tied off firmly to the bow ring and another to the stern ring.

The lead rope would be manned and held by men on the sand spit, and the rear rope would be looped around the pommel on Nicholas's saddle. This way Nicholas and his horse could, to some degree slow the speed of the entry, enabling the men onshore to keep up and at the same time help to keep the boat from being dragged toward the reef. The men ashore would also be able to keep the tension on the bow for the same reason.

Nicholas could see Strudwich striding up the sand toward him, as he got closer he saw the strain on his friend's face. He chose not to say anything, allowing the man the option.

Strudwich looked at him and said, 'Six good men Nicholas, six.' Before Nicholas could reply he added, 'Do not blame yourself, the responsibility is mine and mine alone.' He spun on his heel and walked briskly toward the remaining longboat and its waiting men.

Gathering the sailors around he briefed them of the events and of the losses, then asked, 'Nicholas what is the plan? We must make haste, lest the tide turn against us as well.'

Nicholas explained, the captain nodding his head in approval. 'A better option, let's move!'

The operation went as planned, the longboat making the passage with no trouble, guided through by the men in front and further braked by Nicholas and his horse, leaving he and Strudwich to lament on why they did not think of the plan earlier.

Nicholas and Peter Strudwich said their farewells, there being little time left before the swing of tide began in earnest and Nicholas sensed Strudwich's urgent need to have his ship lively beneath him at sea.

Chapter 6

Inland – The first foray

Nicholas sat astride Stitch watching the *Collette* weigh anchor, the bellowing first mate's orders drifting back to him. 'Forecourse'l away! Loose heads'ls! Come on you lazy bastards! Loose tops'ls!' The men aloft hurrying to obey.

The ship stirred as the massive anchor cleared the sea. 'Anchors a'weigh suh!' was the last voice Nicholas heard as the *Collette* turned across the wind and picked up speed. Strudwich, at the stern rail of the poop deck, lifted his hand in farewell.

He watched for some time until the ship became a mere smudged triangle of sail on the horizon. He tugged at Stitch's reins and cantered toward the river, trying to wrench his thoughts from the tragedy and the sadness he felt in saying farewell to Peter Strudwich.

Nicholas trotted the horse across the sand bar and up until he was opposite the camp site.

Jack and Whip stood on the little beach – the huge Negro, naked to the waste with hands on hips, his black skin gleaming in the sunlight, and Whip, wiry as ever looking across the river toward him.

They watched as Nicholas, standing in his stirrups, pointed up river, then came back to his saddle. Lifting their hands in farewell, they watched as he cantered up along the sand bar and disappeared around the under-growth at the low hill opposite the northern beach.

The two men worked diligently at the tasks left for them, the number one priority being to finish the stockyards and the grain store and stable building.

Whip had found a deposit of broken limestone some two miles southeast of the camp, which would require transporting back to the camp site.

He and Jack had assembled the small cart, then turned their attention to the bullock. The beast had not fared well at sea, so they decided to use the bull instead. After some coaxing to get the huge creature in position, they attempted to harness the now ornery bull to it. This proved to be no easy task, as the young bull, after weeks aboard ship, was about as uncooperative as a Rabbi would be to accepting a pork chop on Passover.

First, the beast skittered all over the place, then it lashed out with both hind legs, catching Whip's shin – luckily for Whip a glancing blow, or lucky for the bullock as Whip put it. Nonetheless it was painful and in a short time produced a blueish lump about two inches in diameter.

It took almost an hour of hot sweaty work just to get the animal into the traces and by this time the men had just about had enough of its temperament. They lashed the bullock's nose ring to the stockyard fence, and with the beast swishing its tail in annoyance, went to the shade of the tent for a rest.

'Very 'ard animal, 'e no like the cart an 'e not for dis work, 'e is prince for breeding!' announced Jack, one of the few times he had spoken since arriving, his chest heaving from their exertions.

'Aye, an' I've just about 'ad enough of it dictating terms,' said Whip, mopping his brow.

'Bad things happen at sea,' Jack said, indicating with his left hand, at the same time eyeing the water pannikin in Whip's hand.

'Aye, I wonder 'ow many they lost, I guess we'll find out when Mr Yuin comes back,' Whip said, refilling and handing the pannikin to the Negro.

'Masser Yuin good man I think,' said Jack

Whip replied, ''E is at that, but listen Jack, I don't be thinkin' 'e will be likin' ye callin' 'im "Masser", but might be wise to wait an' see.'

'We must cover!' announced Jack, holding a dinner plate sized hand over his eyes and indicating toward the bullock. 'A blindfold you mean, aye! Good idea Jack, might just work at that! Worked on the ship didn't it!' said Whip. Rummaging around in one of the sea chests, he found some strips of calico. 'This'll do perfect!' he said.

The blindfold worked very well, calming the anxious animal almost immediately. Every now and then it let them know he was not happy, skittering sideways and spilling the load of stone.

They began the difficult task of carting the broken limestone back to the stockyards. Hours of back breaking work followed.

Whip marveled at the strength and stamina of the big Negro. Time and time again he had to stop and watch as Jack lifted massive lumps of limestone with ease, betting to himself that this time there was no way he was going to be able to lift the huge stones but lift them he did.

By two days end they had a substantial pile of stone carted and the next day they would start building the lower part of the wall structure. They would begin by breaking the stone into manageable sizes for the walls and grinding the smaller pieces into dust, mixing it with lime and sand to make mortar for the bonding.

It was late evening, the sky slashed with gold and orange in the west, heralding another magnificent display of Mother Nature's skill with her ethereal paintbrush.

Jack was tending the livestock, topping up feed and water for the coming night. He really enjoyed the task and seemed to have some affinity with them. He moved amongst them, talking to each in his deep soothing voice as if they were people instead of beasts. In particular he took a liking to the great bull and could stroke the animal's muzzle and neck. Almost everyone else was afraid of the bad-tempered beast.

He talked to the bull, running his hand down the massive head. 'I shall call you *Kubi*, he said soothingly. 'For you be big, bad, strong and intolerant of all other creatures, except perhaps your *nkomo*,' he continued, looking at the cows, the laugh rumbling in his chest. 'I think you will have many fine sons and daughters, hmm?'

The big man froze as he detected a sudden tremor in the beast, he looked quickly to the horses. Both had stopped feeding and were facing him now, ears pricked and standing stock still.

Jack continued to talk to the bull whilst slowly moving down its side, his hand running along the beast's sleek coat. The temptation to whirl around was great, but he continued and moved around the bull's rump.

There, standing not ten feet away, were two Blacks, both naked apart from loincloths. One, a young man, possibly about eighteen, and the other a girl, a few years younger he reckoned.

The young man was wiry and thin with dark curly hair and heavy brow from which tapered a broad flat nose. He had several scars cut across his chest in horizontal bars.

Across one shoulder lay the carcass of a small creature, many of which Jack had seen bounding through the scrub, its light brown fur ruffling in the gentle breeze. He held the animal by the legs, clutched together in one hand, in the other hand he held two long spears and what appeared to be a throwing stick. Jack could sense the fear in the youth as he looked at him.

Jack switched his gaze to the girl, she was shorter than the young man, slim and well proportioned with the curves of womanhood just beginning. Her facial features softer than the man's and he was surprised to see that she had reasonably straight hair which was also a little fairer than her companions. Her naked breasts were round and pointed and bore no tribal scarring that he could see. She was pretty, he observed, in her pubescent years.

She held a small elongated wooden bowl full of red coloured berries and some type of yellow grain.

As he looked at her, she giggled, flashed a brilliant set of white teeth and nervously stepped behind her companion, then peered, still smiling, around his shoulder.

Jack instantly realised that the young man, although terrified, was very protective of the girl, he could feel the affection.

Jack held his hand out, the palm upwards, a traditional greeting of friendship in Africa. He spoke in his native tongue of Zulu. *'Suwubuna,'* (hello) and took a step forward.

The youth trembled in fear but stood his ground. Looking down at them, Jack grinned at the young fellow's courage and was rewarded with the most radiant of smiles. The young girl, also still smiling, peeped shyly from around his shoulder.

Jack moved closer to the couple, still grinning, he towering over them.

The young Black swung the creature off his shoulder and laid it on the ground at Jack's feet as an offering to the giant Negro looking down on him.

'*Kaluwirri!*' said the youth, pointing to the furry bundle at Jack's feet and then to his mouth. Then swept his hand toward the camp, palm up.

Jack noticed that when he spoke the word, he had rolled the end of it, almost like a vibration of the tongue, and it was spoken very rapidly.

He was about to repeat the word and indicate his thanks, when he heard a familiar, but unwelcome sound,

He froze.

The click of a rifle's hammer was as obscene as it seemed loud to Jack and he spun, calling 'No! don' shoot!' and stepped in front of the Blacks, his arms akimbo.

'Jesus!' Whip cursed, jerking the rifle skyward. By some miracle it did not discharge in his haste. 'Ye crazy bastard, I nearly shot ye!'

'You don' hurt these people, Mr Whip,' he said firmly.'Dey's good people and only chil'en, an' dey give us a gift.' He pointed to the small creature. His voice was strong, bordering on a command.

'I wasn't plannin' on shootin,' ye bloody great galoot, just backin' ye' up,' Whip said, the look of concern creasing his face. The fierce glare vanished from the huge man's face, and his face split into a huge smile as he realised the Welshman had only been worried about him.

Still smiling he turned to the young couple, still nervous, who had no idea of the possible danger they had just faced. They immediately matched Jack's smile. Jack turned back.

'Mr Whip, don' look an' be worried like dat, Jack a very big boy now,' he joked, and his huge chest began to shake with mirth, then a deep rumbling laugh boomed among them.

Whip's scowl began to slide away. He put up the rifle as the big fellow's laughter got to him and could not contain himself at Jack's newfound cheek and humour and started laughing. Flashing their brilliant smiles, the two Blacks joined in as the most common language of all mankind weaved its magic among them.

As suddenly as the moment had come, it began to fade. The young couple, as if by some unseen signal, indicated with their hands that they were leaving and retreated toward the timber across from the stockyards, the young girl sneaking glances at Jack as they left.

Jack turned and looked at Whip. 'You like Masser Yuin Mister Whip, a good man,' he said.

Embarrassed, Whip said, 'Yes well, you need to…' turning to chide the big fellow about being more careful but stopped as he looked up at his face.

Great tears coursed down the Negro's ebony face, as he said, 'I never had no frien' for long, long time Mister Whip, all white men just want to hurt Jack, an' treat me like animal.' The tears continued. 'Never no laugh for long time either.'

Whip almost choked at the abject sorrow on the man's face. Trying to sound suitably gruff, and failing miserably, he said gently. 'Well now my lad, I figure ye've enough laughter in that bloody great chest of yours to keep us all goin' for a while, an' if ye want a friend, well then, I guess ye 'av one!'

Solemnly Jack said in Zulu, *'Yebo, si ngisaphila umngane.'* (Yes, we good friends.)

Whip looked at him, and although he knew nothing of the Zulu language, understood enough to know the two had formed a strong bond.

Changing the subject, he said, 'I heard them talking about these strange beasties back in the new harbour at Fremantle, they called them 'kangaroos or somethin' like. We'll take it back an' skin "im!'

That night they ate some of the *Kaluwirri*. Neither of them had partaken of red meat for some time, and although it was mostly tough and stringy, they relished the taste of the dark red meat, which they grilled over hot coals.

It had been an exhausting day, both men were flagging after their meal and lay back in their kits. They now thought it unnecessary to post a guard after the encounter today, feeling that no threat would come from the Blacks.

'I wonder 'ow Mr Yuin's doin',' mused Whip as he stared up at the stars and the black beyond. Receiving no answer, he turned to Jack, but the big man was already breathing heavily. Whip closed his eyes and was asleep in seconds.

Nicholas was now camped some four miles north-east of where he had left the river. He had stopped at the spring and filled his water bottles with the cool water, then continued on looking for some sort of trail inland, eventually finding a narrow trail if you could call it that.

It had been tough going, with very thick scrub causing many a detour. Both he and the horse became frustrated with the constant dismounts and back tracking. Most of the bushes appeared to be a variety of acacia, and whilst not a heavily timbered tree, were nonetheless growing quite densely together.

Finally, late afternoon saw them emerge into a more open area, with considerably less scrub. Nicholas could see many of the strange creatures he had heard about in Fremantle, kangaroos they had called them. They were either standing on their large hind legs and tails, and staring toward him, their ears swiveling back and forth, or bounding effortlessly away in groups.

Here, Nicholas observed, they appeared to be some of a light grey colour, and often had white tufts of fur on their chests. Others were of a red rust colour and were considerably bigger in size. This was in contrast to the smaller light brown ones he had seen around the river mouth area.

Watching one particular group of the creatures, who were closer than the rest, he observed several young ones grazing in front of the adults.

As he watched, he was astonished to see one of them fold over and disappear into the belly of one of the adults. Nicholas thought he was seeing things, then suddenly, the young one poked its head out and looked around. Fascinated, he watched the little head twisting and turning, its little body and legs distorting the mother's belly skin.

Suddenly, the animals all stood erect and as one looked, ears twitching, toward the far side of the clearing, all leapt into action bounding away with effortless ease to vanish into the scrub on the opposite side of the clearing to where they had been staring.

Nicholas looked intently toward the acacia and scrub hoping to see what had spooked them. He sat motionless for some minutes and was rewarded with only a fleeting glimpse of what could have been either a large dog of some sort, or cat, he was unsure which.

Stitch whickered, he too was staring intently toward the spot where the mysterious animal had appeared.

'Easy boy,' said Nicholas, patting the horse's neck, and squeezed his knees, moving him forward across to the spot where they saw the creature, drawing his rifle as he rode over.

Dismounting, Nicholas examined the ground for tracks, and found a medium sized paw print in the sand between two shrubs. Dog, he thought, counting the pugs.

He looked up, staring in the direction of the print. As he looked he was shocked to see, that not ten feet away he was staring into the face of a large dog or wolf.

The hair stood up on the back of his neck as he understood that he was unprepared, vulnerable and down on one knee. The animal stared unblinking at him with intense yellow eyes for a few moments. In a blink it was gone. All Nicholas saw was a flash of pale yellow fur then nothing.

Nicholas cursed himself for being so careless. Had he been in Africa, he told himself, or if the wolf had attacked, he would have been a meal by now.

Nonetheless the scare had its purpose and he would be far more vigilant from now on.

He left the clearing, wishing to find a spot to make camp for the night and headed east toward a flash of water shining through the trees.

He came upon a small outcrop of limestone running beside the river and rode up onto a flat surface backed by trees and sand. The sun was getting low in the sky and he thought this was as good a place as he would find for the night.

Nicholas rode up and down the river bank for about half a mile in either direction, satisfying himself that there was no immediate threat that he could discern. He had no idea if there were crocodiles in the river but he saw no sign of crocodile nests, slides or marks.

After watering his horse at the river, he stripped the bags and saddle from him, rubbed him down as best he could with an old curry brush he had. Tipping some of his feed bag out onto the ground he gave Stitch a small meal of oats. He hobbled the horse and laid out his kit for the night.

He was too exhausted to even bother lighting a fire, but reminded himself to do so before dark, the large dog still fresh in his memory. After a meal of salted beef and a pannikin of water, he lay back against a tree and made to enter into his journal the events of the day.

Sadness swept over him as he tried to write of the tragic events of the wrecked longboat. His quill poised over the paper, he recalled the screams of terror from the men as they were smashed onto the reef and remembered the gut-clenching feeling of utter helplessness as he watched the event unfold before him. Distraught, he could not bring himself to write anything of it.

Closing the journal, Nicholas got up and walked to the edge of the limestone where it jutted out over the water, he sat down on the edge and looked out over the river.

My God, why must things be so hard, he thought, remembering the young man whose father had perished before his very eyes, and of the others, swept out to sea to die, helpless in the clutches of the sea and its creatures.

There was nothing to be gained by reliving this – what's done is done. He chastised himself and forced the sadness from his mind.

The surface of the river here was calm, mirror-like even, the only disturbance the occasional dragonfly or insect, as it lightly touched the water in flight. The scene seemed to offer some solitude, and looking downstream, he saw small rings appear randomly on the surface as fish and insect alike went about their business.

The trees on the far bank were an almost perfect mirror image in the fading light, soft of colour and in different shades of greens – dark at the base and topped with an orange and gold halo. A small black and white fantail-like bird landed not six feet from him. Chattering away, its long tail swinging to and fro; it seemed to be a happy little fellow and somehow lifted his spirits. Springing from his perch of driftwood, it spiraled up into the air to snap at insects, and then flew chattering away across the river.

He was startled by the whirring sound of wings before he realised it was a species of wild pigeon landing some twenty feet away. He could see the bird standing almost stock still as it tried to sense danger, then suddenly it ran across the rock toward the water, halting just ten feet from him in the last remaining patch of sunlight.

Not daring to move, Nicholas was struck by the beauty of the bird's plumage as it stood sensing danger, but for some reason did not fly away.

The bird's wings were splashed with patches of metallic bronze, orange and green which shimmered in the fading sunlight and had thin white stripes running from its eyes down its neck before fading into chocolate brown and grey plumage on the back and breast.

Suddenly, the bird quickly ran to the water's edge, dipping its beak into the orange coloured surface, then with a clattering of its beautiful wings, whirred away into the bushes. It never ceased to amaze Nicholas how birds and butterflies could have the most outrageous mixes of colours, yet still look so beautiful.

The river was now an orange ribbon, punctuated with dark patches as it gently curved away to his right and to the west, a beautiful dappled surface with the sinking sun's bright tongue at its centre.

Sadness came to him as it reminded Nicholas of another place and time, when he had sat admiring a beautiful sight just like this. The difference being it was a lake, and he was in Africa with Victoria.

Chapter 7

The Amendsons, 1846

I t was a superb August morning as Nicholas rode along the rutted trail not one hundred feet from the edge of the great Lake Nyanza, which was later to become Lake Victoria, in Tanganyika.

He had ridden many miles from his prospecting area in the ranges to get here and had left his camp at the crack of dawn when the sky was a beautiful indigo and just beginning to lose ground to the orange glow heralding a new day. He was intent on arriving about midday at the home of his adopted family, the Amendsons. Having grown up for a good period of his life with them, he was looking forward to seeing them. It had been years since he had last visited, although he had written whenever he could, he was not sure if his letters had even reached them and his intention now was to surprise them.

Pausing about two miles from the house, he dismounted and went down to the shore of Lake Nyanza where, after checking the area for crocodile, he quickly bathed and changed, trading his sweat-stained khakis for an elegant white shirt, which he rolled up on his forearms, and drew on a pair of tan coloured breaches. A wide brown polished leather belt surrounded his waist and he now wore calf-length black boots, polished to a glossy shine.

As he dressed, Nicholas reflected on his childhood and how the chance meeting with Swedish doctor Ludwig Amendson some fifteen years earlier had occurred.

Nostalgia washing over him, he rummaged in his saddle bag finding the small hip flask of whiskey he always carried and sat on a large rock and reflected on how he came to be here sitting by this beautiful lake.

Nicholas was the only child of Robert Nicholas Yuin and his wife Teresa, a well-to-do family with a proud lineage and property investment history. Nicholas had already been placed at a fine English college for boys in 1823 when sadly, like a lot of the people in that county, his aristocratic parents had both perished with typhoid fever when he was but eight years old.

Nicholas was to inherit a considerable, though not vast, amount of property and financial gain when he turned of age. His father's brother and goodly wife came to the family home to comply with his father's dying wish – communicated by letter sent when Robert Yuin first became ill, he asking that they raise Nicholas as their own should he and his wife not survive the fever.

Nicholas was to be raised and educated in a manner befitting the family's standing and interest. In return, his brother and wife would receive a yearly stipend to ensure that they were compensated and made comfortable, and although entrusted to handle the family's interests, they were to use Robert Yuin's financial advisors when in need.

Nicholas's uncle bore no resemblance to his father as far as wealth and standing were concerned, although you could see a physical likeness. The uncle in fact had disappeared from the family when only thirteen years old over some dispute with his parents. He was a modest man with simple needs and carriage. He had however, kept in touch with his elder brother. He was generally a good honest man and he and his wife had owned and run a small sail makers store in Devonport.

It was a huge decision to sell up and take on the responsibility of raising Nicholas, but business was hard and was backbreaking work. Being childless they saw an opportunity to have a son and have some security. This was to eventually alter their thinking, but moreover, it was the decent thing to do. Another factor being that Nicholas was already in college and therefore the task was not as daunting as it may have been.

The couple had no idea of the actual wealth of Nicholas's family, although they must have been aware the family was quite well off before they arrived for the reading of the will. Thankfully for Nicholas, greed was not the motivator. His uncle and wife immediately set about helping Nicholas through his mourning. Later and during the breaks from college, he would spend hours with his uncle sitting in his father's study reading his books and especially examining the mineral collection his father had kept.

Nicholas, like his father, had at a very early age, become fascinated with geology and he himself had a large collection of all types of rocks and minerals which he treasured. His father could see the lad had a special gift for geology and all things associated with minerals, and gave Nicholas many beautiful specimens, some from other parts of the world. Young Nicholas could tell anyone who asked, at a glance what minerals they presented. So, it was his wish that Nicholas be educated with this as his chosen career.

Within a year the homely and loving wife of his uncle suddenly and inexplicably died of heart failure. His uncle, beset with grief, was unable to come to terms with his loss. He turned to drink and gambling, and over the next year or so sold off the considerable properties within the family, somehow bypassing the investment accountants. Within a short time, the family finances were in ruin and the once beautiful home was also eventually sold to pay gambling debts and taxes.

Nicholas, ensconced in the boarding college, had no idea of this, not that he could have done anything about it anyway.

It was mid-1824 and he was nine and a half when he was summoned to the dean's office one day to be informed he could no longer stay at the college as for almost one year no fees had been forthcoming. The college unfortunately had no choice but to end his tuition and boarding privileges effective on contact with his ward and uncle.

Three days later, Nicholas sat outside the great college building waiting for his uncle to pick him up. He sat there in the cold for five hours. His uncle finally turned up to take him home. He never uttered one word to Nicholas during the entire journey. Nicholas was very afraid but never showed it, he could hardly recognise his destitute uncle, fearing punishment if he spoke. His uncle was so different from when the lad had last seen him. He was unshaven, stank of rum and stale sweat, his clothes were threadbare and disheveled, and to Nicholas looked like a malevolent stranger.

At last they stopped at a dingy ale house and his uncle spoke for the very first time. 'This'll be where we be livin' now lad.'

In complete and utter confusion Nicholas blurted out, 'But where is my home!'

'Gone,' was the terse reply.

'Gone? Where are all my things and where are all of ma and pa's things!'

'I told you all gone, now ye'll not say another word,' and with that his uncle grabbed Nicholas by the ear and dragged him down the side of the house to a tiny room at the rear of the building. 'This is where you will stay until I decide what to do with ye lad. Here, this is your'n.' He thrust a calico bag into his hands.

Nicholas was pushed into the tiny room, which stank of mold, rotting vegetables and urine. Against one wall stood a timber frame with a filthy straw mattress, which was stained and rotting. Nicholas sat on the edge of it and cried until exhausted and eventually fell asleep. The next morning, he awoke, covered in lice bites and itching furiously.

He opened the bag and to his delight the first thing he laid eyes on, was his favourite piece of quartz crystal from his collection. A flawless specimen, it was about three and a half inches long and just over one inch in diameter. He held it up to the meagre light, and the perfect faceted point reflecting within somehow made him feel better. Also, in the bag were his Birth Certificate, a book of geology from his father's library, His father's signet ring and his wedding ring. There was a small brass cylinder about one inch long and three quarters of an inch in diameter with a small ring attached to one side, and a locket which belonged to his mother. There was also a coat and a pair of trousers.

Nicholas turned the shiny brass object over in his hands. It had two small rods on either side holding the end caps together and was engraved

Robert Nicholas Yuin. He pushed at the centre cylinder and it swung out from between the end caps to reveal a very powerful magnifying glass. Nicholas of course knew instantly what it was, having used it many times with his father. He cried tears of joy or sadness, either of which he could not tell. His eyes brimming with tears as he clutched the specking glass to his chest and remembering his Mother and of the fond memory of his beloved father.

For the next 15 months his life became that of utter misery, forced to do all manner of chores at the ale and doss house for his keep. He was subject to regular beatings by the owners for the most trivial of mistakes.

He never saw his uncle again and the one time he built up the courage to ask of his whereabouts brought only a furious beating and he was locked in the stinking little room for two days.

One evening when Nicholas was preparing to sleep, he held – as he did every night – his crystal until it warmed in his hand, then he lay down to sleep. He was almost asleep, when the door to his room suddenly crashed open to reveal the ale house owner and another man, a well-dressed gentleman.

'Come here you! the owner snarled, dragging Nicholas out of his bed and shook him like a rag doll, then stood him before the gentleman. 'Look at me boy!' the man demanded and reached out, pinching Nicholas's face in a bejeweled, white bony hand. Nicholas saw wet red lips and heavy jowls. Brown beady eyes were surrounded by a heavy brow and wild bushy eyebrows. Nicholas quailed at the site before him.

'He will do nicely, oh yes! Very nicely!' he cried excitedly. Nicholas was dragged inside the ale house and upstairs to one of the guest rooms. The owner flung Nicholas onto the bed and quickly pinned him to the bed across the chest with one arm. Nicholas had no idea what was happening and up until this stage had been too frightened to resist.

The fleshy faced man was now standing at the foot of the bed. Nicholas stared in bewilderment as he reached down and undid the thin rope on Nicholas's breeches and whipped them off before he understood what was happening. Nicholas was awash with embarrassment but still did not comprehend what was happening. He drew his legs up, twisting, and tried to turn on his side yelling 'Sir! Sir! What are you doing!'

'Be still boy!' yelled the keeper and with his free hand backhanded him so hard Nicholas was stunned to silence. Blood tricked from his mouth, his ears ringing and head spinning.

Nicholas stared in horror at the wet red lips which were quivering in excitement with little flecks of spittle clinging to the lower lip. Nicholas jumped as the man reached out and to Nicholas's shame began to fondle his genitals. 'P...please sir don't do this, this is wrong,' he cried, great tears running down his face.

The man stopped and said, 'It's all right my lovely boy, soon you will like it.' Nicholas screwed his eyes shut. The man undid his fly and his erect penis sprang forth, jutting from his breaches, he reached out and began to fondle Nicholas again. 'Come on, come on my beauty, turn him over now,' he cooed.

Nicholas's eyes flew open and saw the angry red staff sticking out of the man's crutch.

At the boarding school, Nicholas had often seen a few of the older boys engaged in sexual encounters with each other after the dorm curfew had begun and it was always something that revolted him.

He was shocked, and with a rush of comprehension realised what was about to happen. He means to bugger me! The thought crashed into his brain.

The keeper lifted his arm from Nicholas's chest to spin him over, in that moment Nicholas realised he still clutched his beloved crystal in his right hand. He swung his little arm up in an arc with all the strength he could muster and in that split second the point of the crystal struck the left side of the keepers head. The keeper crashed to the floor with a single cry and in the same instant – whether by accident or intent – Nicholas's bare foot snapped up into the slobbering pervert's groin. The man howled in pain and doubled over, staggering back into the wall at the foot of the bed, clutching his groin.

Nicholas looked down in horror at the keeper's limp form crumpled beside the bed and in sheer panic and fear, sprang off the bed and snatching up his breaches, pausing only to haul them on. Then still clutching his crystal, he bolted down the stairs and out through the rear door. Two steps from the door he ran straight into the keeper's woman, knocking her flat on her back and scattering and smashing the pile of dishes she was carrying all over the ground. She screamed a torrent of foul language at him. 'Ye clumsy little fooker!! Just wait until Oi' get me bleedin' 'ands on ye!!'

Nicholas had no intention of waiting. He scrambled to his feet, narrowly avoiding her outstretched claw and sprinted into his room, bundled his meagre possessions into his calico bag and by the time the fat woman had hauled herself to her feet he had fled into the night.

Nicholas had no idea where he was going, all he could think of was that he had killed the keeper and he would hang for it if he was caught. He had no doubt the pervert would have alerted the police by now and they would soon be in hot pursuit. When he stopped for a brief rest his skinny little legs shook in fear with a will of their own, and he had never felt so woe begotten in his young life. His short stuttering intake of breaths and tears came as one and his young head roared with confusion at what had transpired.

He had no idea who the slobbering dandy was, having never seen him before and so could not have known that the fellow was actually a magistrate of the Queens's own. The magistrate had no desire to be caught up in a scandal and the subsequent exposure of his perversion – let alone become involved in a death and subsequent investigation, which he knew, at best, was self-defense but could be construed as murder. The body was discretely disposed of and the man's wench well rewarded for her silence and moved far away to another county.

For two weeks Nicholas ran and hid, stealing what food he could in the dead of night and begging for the rest.

Eventually, he found himself on the docks at Devonport. There were four ships in the port, three at anchor in the middle of the harbour and one at dock.

Sneaking along the wharf at nightfall he knew that if he stayed in England he would never be able to live without fear of discovery and would in all probability, end up on the gallows. As he looked at the ships he made up his mind – he would stow away. Nicholas snuck into the open warehouse near the ship at the wharf and climbing on top of some bales

settled down to wait. Mercifully, sleep and shear mental exhaustion overcame him and he fell asleep.

His opportunity came around 1am when loud voices of indignation
and yelling woke him.

A ruckus had started on the wharf and sailors clattered down the gang
plank to separate two or three men brawling some fifty feet past the stern
of the vessel. He cautiously got down and positioned himself opposite the
gangway, then sprinted up the gangway and onto the ship and somehow
was not seen, eventually making his way down into the ship and hid
himself under some stairs beneath a pile of sail cloth. After some time had
passed and he had not been discovered, he again fell asleep. It was 1824.

The ship, a four-masted barque, a swift vessel and better rigged to rise
before wind. She sailed at four bells on the rising tide, bound for Cape
Town. Nicholas had woken to the creaks and sounds of pounding feet on
the decks above and shouted orders. He stayed under the sail cloth too terrified to move, and as the ship cleared the heads it began to pitch and roll.
It didn't take long before sea sickness clutched at him. The day, his first at
sea, was again turning into yet another nightmare, and as soon as he stood
he was violently ill. He struggled up and out from under the stairs and
had staggered only about two paces and straight into the bear like arms of
the bosun.

At first the bosun was furious and cuffed Nicholas about the ears.
Cursing, he dragged him up to report to the captain. Nicholas was still dry
retching and producing only a somewhat feeble spittle. It was as well that
he had not eaten for some two days or he would have been even sicker. He
was a picture of abject misery.

He was very lucky that both the bosun and the captain, although gruff
and stern, were of a kindly nature and managed to hear some of Nicholas's
story between bouts of illness.

On the captain's orders, the bosun took Nicholas under his care and
when he was well enough, he was set to work to earn his keep until he could
be dropped off at the nearest British outpost or colony. Nicholas adapted
quickly to life at sea and worked diligently, so much so that when he begged

the captain to be allowed to stay on board as part of the crew, the captain agreed. And so, for the next five and a half years he sought to learn everything he could from the friendly big bosun and the crew as the ship plied its trade up and down the west coast of Africa. Two years later and on another voyage south to Cape Town, they dropped anchor in the bay.

It was early 1830, and Nicholas with a little time ashore granted, began exploring the Cape Town docks and markets. After their difficult and very rough voyage around the Cape of Good Hope it was a welcome relief.

He was now fourteen years and one month old, but a far cry from the dirty, skinny half-starved lad who had stowed away aboard a ship in Devonport, England. He had grown quite a bit taller and now had some muscle on his frame, although he was still quite gangly.

He was always fascinated by markets, the variety of produce, fruit, spices, all different weaves of cloth, all manner of animal skins and weaponry that could be purchased at the markets up and down the coast of Africa. But this market was the most interesting he had ever seen. The smell of the spice was overwhelming but not unpleasant. He loved the bartering and haggling banter that the gatherings produced, it had an almost carnival atmosphere about it.

People were shouting out in many languages, most of which Nicholas had never heard before, let alone understood. Men and women were dressed in a huge variety of clothes, some almost naked, some in long flowing robes and others with cloth wrapped around their heads and even some women completely covered in long sheaths with only a meshed strip so they could see.

Men and women alike were of races from all over the known world, yellow skinned men and women from the Orient, Dutchmen, Americans, Irish, German, Indian and more. All seemed to be working together trading and bargaining on the markets lining the streets one street back from the wharf. Nicholas felt like he was in a completely new world and walked the market with fascination at every step. Then two things happened that would change his life and unbeknown to him, helped set the course for his future.

He came upon a slave auction and watched as the slaves were poked, examined and humiliated before the raucous crowd of bidders. He saw to his surprise that the slaves were of different colours – all were African, but some were of a lighter skin and others very dark. Some of them were very different in feature and stature. He was, of course, ignorant of the fact that these people had been enslaved from all over Africa and from many different areas, nations and tribes, and most people just thought of Africa as one nation rather than many different peoples, cultures and countries within.

As he looked, some of the young men and women showed utter defeat, some obviously shamed for the complete lack of modesty and others had the faraway look of hopelessness in their eyes. It was a very sad sight to Nicholas, and even at his young age, he felt indignant about the scene.

He stared at one young man, maybe about seventeen or eighteen years old, but he was a veritable giant of a man, way over six feet ten inches he reckoned, magnificently muscled and proportioned, like a finely tuned athlete. He had to be a warrior of some sort, Nicholas thought. He had a proud bearing, an almost regal carriage. The fellow had calico wrapped iron shackles about his ankles and wrists, and only a piece of cloth about his hips. As Nicholas stared, the only imperfection appeared to be from the cruel scars from the irons on his ankles, despite the wrappings. He suddenly locked eyes with the fellow. His stare at Nicholas was not that of hate or loathing but rather that of interest. Nicholas broke off the stare, wondering what had occurred, it was a strange feeling, something inside had shifted and he could not figure out what it was.

He looked up as the crowd roared their approval as the auctioneer gave the young fellow an almighty clout to the ear with his auctioneers baton, yelling, 'Keep your'n nigger eyes down you bleedin' 'eathen!'

Then to the delight of the crowd pulled up the fellow's cloth exposing his genitals, saying out loud, 'Now look what we 'ave 'ere, a fine young buck if ye ever saw one and 'ung like one o' them eliofants.'

"E will make fine breedin' stock. Open ye bleedin' mouth,' he commanded, reaching up and forcing the young man's mouth open with his stick to expose his teeth. 'A fine set of chompers on 'im as well! What do ye bid for this'un ladies and gentlemen?'

Nicholas felt a wave of shame and sympathy wash over him as the crowd screamed with laughter and began yelling out their bids.

He felt as if he was suffocating and could stand it no longer. He pushed his way back through the crowd, his head down in shame and disgust at the treatment meted out to these people. They were treated like animals, and it was so wrong he thought, lamenting the fact that he had no money to buy the young man's freedom.

As he finally got through the crowd he looked back, in an instant the young man looked up and stared directly at him again. He found himself gazing back with equal intensity at the man once more, but this time he saw a face taught with fury and tears in his eyes. The look in his eyes told of a deep and indignant rage and of helplessness.

Nicholas never forgot the immoral treatment of that day, nor the slaves shame and indignation, not that of sorrow, as one of the bidders reached out and fondled the fellow's genitals as he examined the young man. It was the beginning of a hatred for slavery that knew no bounds. The unfairness of it all weighed heavy in his heart.

He decided to head back to the ship. Nicholas had little experience in places such as this multicultural port, and certainly was unaware of the dangers lurking behind the bustling main bazaar. He forgot the bosun's warning to stay away from areas outside the market and in particular the narrow alleys running off the main market street.

He had decided to take a shortcut back to the ship and was almost at the dock end of the narrow alley he had chosen when he suddenly found himself surrounded by a gang of homeless youth. Nicholas had only a few pennies on him, which they took and then he was brutally beaten and thrown between the narrow walls of the shanty buildings either side of the alley.

He had no idea what time he regained consciousness, but it was now nightfall and he knew the ship would be sailing on the next day's evening tide. Panic slammed into him. He tried to stand, and as he managed to get to his feet, was hit by wave after wave of dizziness and he could not focus.

He had staggered out of the alley, his vision still blurred and groggy and was almost run down by Dr Amendson's flatbed horse and cart as he and his wife Lillian and six-year-old daughter were just passing.

Almost staggering into the horse, he again lost consciousness and collapsed onto the cobblestones.

The kindly doctor and his help carried him to his surgery, and after stitching up a nasty cut on the back of his head and wrapping his torso with bandages for his suspected broken ribs and other bruises as best he could, put him to bed to recover.

The next day he felt a little better, and as Dr Amendson sat feeding him some chicken broth to wash down the mild mix of laudanum and to build up his strength, Nicholas suddenly looked up at the doctor, and with tears rolling down his cheeks blurted out the whole story, right from the beginning back in England.

When he had finished, the good doctor simply folded him into his arms and held him until he fell into a deep sleep. A bond was forged right then, as strong as any parent's love.

Nicholas awoke early that evening still somewhat groggy from the laudanum and his ordeal. He suddenly remembered his ship. Panicking, he managed to blurt out that his ship was to sail on the high tide and he must get down to the wharf.

Dr Amendson argued and objected, then realised the young fellow, already distressed, would be in a state of despair and possibly be worse off if they didn't at least try to catch the ship.

The cart clattered onto the wharf just as the gangway was about to be hauled aboard. Still groggy Nicholas managed to haul himself up, and with help staggered toward the gangway. The bosun belayed the order to cast off and raced down the gangway to greet them, concern creased all over his face.

The good doctor explained what had transpired and Nicholas was assisted aboard, but not before Ludwig Amendson had made Nicholas promise to write, and with a gentle hug so as not hurt his ribs, thrust a bag into his arms.

It took a full two days before Nicholas recovered from the concussion and from his beating and then he was sporting some severe bruising around his back and chest and a cut over his right eye which was now puffed and a livid purple. Whenever he coughed or was made to laugh his chest felt like it was on fire. A further two weeks passed before he was well enough to be able to do reasonable duties on deck.

One afternoon whilst recovering, Nicholas opened the bag that the doctor had given him. There was a letter, pens, paper and envelopes. There were also some small vials of laudanum with instructions on when and how much to take for pain and infection should he need.

Opening the letter, he read an open invitation to visit Dr Amendson whenever Nicholas was in Cape Town. The doctor talked of how he and wife and daughter were making plans to travel to Tanganyika in approximately 18 months and how he had purchased land on the shores of Lake Nyanza, where he hoped to realise his dream of raising cattle. At the same time, he would open up a clinic to bring medical assistance to the northern tribes, a daunting task to say the least.

In the letter, he offered Nicholas employment to assist in the move and a chance to meet and talk to some associates of Dr Amendson who would also be travelling with them, the two gentlemen wanting to explore the area with a view to prospecting. Ludwig remembering Nicholas telling of how he dreamed of prospecting and his interest in geology..

There were also two letters of introduction, one to a Professor of Geology at the Royal Cape Town Geological Survey Department, asking if the professor could assist Nicholas with any geological maps of the area – actually a question more than a request – as he was reasonably sure that the area was unexplored as far as minerals went.

The other letter was to a Mr Peiter Villiers, who was a general store owner. The fellow had native people in his employ who were intimate with the tribes in the area – some were actually members of some of those tribes. He was a man with a vast knowledge of inland Africa compared to anyone else.

It would be just over thirteen months before Nicholas was to return to Cape Town and to his disappointment, the Amendsons had already moved to their new home by the shores of Lake Nyanza. Ludwig's friends, the prospectors, were however back in Cape Town for their next load of supplies, having lost almost all of their original equipment by marauding bands of warriors and a flash flood. They were now to sail to Mombasa on the east coast and after Nicholas had re-introduced himself, invited

Nicholas to join them. From there they were to travel directly inland to the Amendson property before setting off on their exploration once again.

That day was the cementing of Nicholas's own prospecting dreams and education in geology, and the stepping stone to doing what he enjoyed most – the excitement of a challenge and a lust for the new and unexplored.

So, it was with some trepidation that Nicholas stood at the door of an imposing building and grasped the heavy knocker and rapped.

Several minutes passed and he reached again for the knocker. Almost as his hand left the brass handle, the door swung open to reveal a portly man, with a long nose upon which perched a pair of the new-fangled glasses Nicholas had seen Mr Amendson wearing, his thin grey hair hanging in straight strands about his shoulders.

The man stared at him with a quizzical tilt to his eyebrow. 'Well boy, what is it?' he asked impatiently. 'Begging you pardon Sir, my name is Nichols Yuin and I have been told to ask for the professor of geology, I have a letter of introduction from Doctor Amendson,' he replied, handing over the letter.

Raising one eyebrow, the man tore open the letter and after reading it, said, 'Well you'd best come in I suppose.'

Nicholas was ushered into a long room. The room was furnished with row upon row of trestle tables which made him gape openly. On each row were thousands of mineral and rock specimens of all kinds, each piece sat upon a card with the description of where the specimen was found and its geological name.

'So, you want to learn about minerals young man?' he asked dropping his eyes to the letter adding, 'And, you would like some maps I see!' as he motioned to Nicholas to sit at an ornate old desk. 'If it pleases you sir. Ye… yes sir.' stammered Nicholas.

The old man stared intently at Nicholas for what seemed to be an eternity.

He abruptly said 'So what is it, learn Geology or take the maps and leave?'

Nicholas was a little taken aback. "Well?' Visser demanded.

'I would like to learn geology Sir, as a preference.' Said Nicholas, somewhat nervously.

'Right then, I am Professor Artie Visser,' he said as he stuck out his hand. The pair shook hands before the professor walked to a table groaning under the weight of books stacked a full three foot high.

He drew three large volumes from the piles and slid them across the table. 'Take these and study them well and I want them back in the same condition as they are now.' Nicholas looked at the dog eared and decimated state of the volumes and looked up at the old man, a scowl creased the man's face and Nicholas quailed. With a twinkle in his eye, the professor suddenly grinned and they both burst out laughing.

Nicholas sought out the prospectors and apologized, explaining that he had changed his mind for now.

For the next several months Nicholas studied hard, spending every night until late pouring over the geology books, the stack of three now growing monthly. During the day he would join the professor to examine the specimens, receive training in analysis, was tested and even yelled at when he got things wrong. He was taken to the adjoining building and shown how to build and operate all manner of sluicing, screening, crushing and mineral processing.

It was hard and grueling but learn he did.

Nicholas knew he could not possibly learn everything in the short time he had, so he applied himself with vigor, shutting out all his personal needs and distractions and often studying well into the night.

It was almost nine months to the day after his arrival, when Nicholas and Professor Visser were sitting at the old table taking lunch, when the professor suddenly pushed back his chair and went to a tall glass cabinet in the corner of the great room. He rummaged through the drawers and returned with two ornate wooden boxes, each about ten inches by six inches and about three inches deep.

'Harrumph,' he uttered. 'These are for you.'

'For me sir?' Nicholas said in surprise. 'That's what I said didn't I, are you deaf? Go ahead and open them before I change my mind.'

Nicholas stared at the beautifully made wooden boxes. On one, the initials 'AV' were inlayed in gold. He tentatively opened it. The box was lined in green velvet, but what lay in it took Nicholas's breath away.

It was a set of weigh scales, beautifully handcrafted in brass, and at the top of the box in small compartments were the weights.

Nicholas was stunned into silence as he looked up at the professor. He stammered, 'But sir, I...I cannot accept such a generous gift, they...they are beautiful...but...but they are your own!'

The professor looked at him, obviously pleased at the reaction.

'Well,' he said, folding his arms, 'too late, they are yours now and there is no argument about it. I will not have a use for them now, I am too old to go gallivanting about the countryside and you have earned them.

'Open the other,' he commanded.

Nicholas was in a world of incredulity as he opened the next box, this one was lined in red velvet.

In one half, lay a small book. The book was beautifully bound in burgundy leather and inlaid with a gold inscription.

It was titled, *Mineralisation and Geology of the World,* by Professor Artie Visser.

Nicholas reached in and opened the book. Inside the cover was written, 'To Nicholas Yuin, one of the most attentive and keen young men I have ever had the pleasure to teach. Go well young man.' It was signed *Artie Visser, December 1832.*

With tears in his eyes Nicholas flicked through the book. It had plates and beautifully hand-painted pictures of a vast array of minerals and a description and instruction on every type of method for the search of mineralisation. It was an invaluable geologists bible that few would ever be able to read, let alone afford. Wiping his eyes, Nicholas laid aside the book and turned his attention to the box again.

On the other side of the box laid out in special compartments was a full set of drawing equipment – ivory handled compasses, measures, ink, nibs, scribes and a magnificent magnetic compass.

Nicholas looked up at the kindly professor with red rimmed eyes and on impulse rose and threw his arms around the old man. The professor was taken aback, and gently lifted Nicholas's arms away saying, 'That's enough now, we now need to talk about your next step in life.'

When Nicholas had settled back in his chair, his eyes were drawn again to the gifts, still incredulous at the generosity and unable to stop his hands caressing them.

'Now!' said the professor, 'you, have a decision to make my young friend, and it is a decision only you can make.'

Nicholas looked at the professor intently as the old man said: 'You have learnt enough in this last nine months to leave here and become a very, very good prospector, maybe become one of the best.

'I believe you have learnt more than a lot of my students could possibly learn in that time. So, it comes to a decision, you can either leave now and apply what you have learnt to the field or,' he paused, "...you can stay here, further your studies with the aim of attending university and becoming a geologist. I will help you achieve this, but your decision is not to be rushed, I want you to think about this very carefully over the next few days.

'You will have my blessing and guidance whatever you decide to do.' Pausing, he said, 'Now it is late, best you go and get some rest.'

Nicholas was overwhelmed and left with his head whirling in euphoria. Over the next two days he agonised over the decision, but in the end the excitement of applying what he had learnt and the lure of adventure was too much to resist.

He returned to the professor and told him of his decision.

The professor looked at him and said. 'Nicholas, I think I already knew what you would decide, hence my gifts, and I remain immensely proud of you irrespective. He continued, 'The two prospectors you were to travel with to Lud's home have decided to prospect elsewhere!' He held up his hand, seeing the disappointment on the lad's face. 'Now, in one month's time Pieter Villiers is sending a party of traders up to Mombasa and four of his natives from the area. You are booked on the ship with them and once you have disembarked, you are to make your way to Ludwig Amendson's property on the shores of Lake Nyanza. Ludwig has two of his bearers there at Mombasa and you are to report to the trader in Mombasa. He has a horse and supplies for you for your journey."

Nicholas said his goodbyes to the professor with a heavy heart and made his way to Villiers' warehouse where the party assembled before making their way down to the harbour and boarding the ship for Mombasa.

He signed on to the passenger list, when he hesitated. Nicholas eyes fell on the date. With a jolt he saw that he would turn sixteen in three days' time.

What a gift he had been given he thought, and lifting his head, sniffed at the wind. It was pungent with adventure and the adrenaline surged through him like a wave.

Nicholas travelled around Mombasa and inland for three days after landing in Mombasa, after being told that the foray inland would not start for several days, he wanted to get his bearings and get a feeling for the land. He had quickly sought out the trader, chose a good horse and saddle and teamed up with the bearers, and subsequently introduced to a family heading west toward Lake Nyanza who would be in the party.

The place was a seething mass of traders from all over the world, but he did not like the cauldron of humanity, the stench of rotting animal and human waste and refuse was piled up everywhere.

Two months later he rode up to the Amendson's and the beginnings of what was eventually to be their home.

He stayed for over five years, and virtually became part of the family and was accepted as such.

He grew to love Ludwig and his beautiful and fascinating wife Lillian.

Little Victoria drove him almost insane with her constant questioning, but they grew very close as an elder brother and little sister would at that age. He spent most of his time helping Ludwig re-build the house and the outbuilding, stables, stockyards and fencing around the grand old house.

When he could, he spent many hours, exploring the surrounding district and was most interested in the mineralisation or the prospects of the ranges to the north-east of the property, although they were too far away to go to without spending some weeks getting there and back. Nicholas vowing that one day he would return and prospect the area in earnest.

It was 1836 and six months after he turned twenty-three years old, he was reading a newspaper that one of the neighbors had dropped off for them and he read of significant gold strikes in Canada and America and he often sat dreaming of going there, eager to test himself and his geological knowledge. He talked about nothing else for weeks. One day Ludwig called him into his study. After staring at him for some seconds, he silently slid a buff coloured envelope across his desk to Nicholas.

The envelope contained a ticket to Vancouver- Canada from Mombasa. Nicholas, dumbfounded, stuttered and stammered his thanks, scarcely believing what he held in his shaking hand, he hugged Lud with all his might until Ludwig said, 'Best you get moofing young man, an pack up ze belongs Ja?' Moisture glistening in both of their eyes.

Looking at the departure date on the ticket, Nicholas wasted no time. The next two days were hectic with Nicolas's packing and in between trying to placate Victoria who was sulking and would hardly speak to him, no matter how hard he tried.

On the day he was to leave however, when he had said goodbye to everyone else, she suddenly burst into tears and threw her arms around him. Lillian gently pried her arms away and Nicholas stepped into the saddle and wheeled away in a canter, tears in his eyes, but his lust for adventure consuming him like a raging thirst.

Chapter 8

Victoria

Nicholas stepped through the arch and onto the grassed area at the rear of Herrgarden Grande – Doctor Ludwig Amendson's sprawling home in Tanzania, Africa – inhaling the sweet scent of Japanese wisteria as he did so, its bunches of flowers draped over the arch like some sort of delicate mauve coloured cloak.

The area on his left was fringed with the most magnificent flowering white, pink and blue hydrangeas, whilst on the right, many exotic lilies and native plants bloomed in profusion.

The centre piece of the setting was an enormous old jacaranda tree, beneath which was a long, white-linen covered table. It was extravagantly laid out with a wide variety of meats, fruit and drink for the regular gathering that the farmers and cattlemen of the area organised almost religiously amongst themselves every second Sunday. Gathered about the table were about twenty or so people from the surrounding district.

Nicholas scanned the gathering, looking for Ludwig Amendson and his wife of thirty years, Lillian.

'*Mon Dieu!* Nicholas! What a wonderful surprise!' cried Lillian Amendson as she came through the arch behind him. Startled momentarily, Nicholas spun on his heel, and she gave him a hug, kissing him on the cheek, her genuine warmth and affection for him enveloping him as though he had never been away.

Lillian Amendson was in her late forties, perhaps forty-eight (no one really knew her true age, except Ludwig who married her at a young age). A striking looking woman, with large warm brown eyes over fine cheekbones, she had a cascade of sandy coloured hair, some of which was almost always gathered up high at the back of her head by some clasp or ribbon of sorts, the rest of which flowed down her back like a golden waterfall.

She was French, and despite the fact that she and Ludwig had now been living here, on the shores of Lake Nyanza in Tanganyika for some years now, and spoke several languages – Afrikaans, Zulu, Swahili and Bhantu dialects to name a few – she still had a delightful French accent.

Good God! Will she never age, thought Nicholas, as he looked at her.

'I have been away from here for six years and have been all over the known world, and you are, without doubt, still the most beautiful woman in the whole world. When are you going to leave Ludwig and marry me?' he asked, holding her at arm's length and looking at her, his own warmth and affection needing no spoken word. Her eyes sparkled. 'Oh, my Nicholas, still the cheeky one,' she cooed, running her hand down his cheek and linking arms with him.

'Ha! I 'eard zat young man, still trying to steal my vife, ja! After all this time!' boomed a voice from behind him.

Nicholas turned, beaming, to find Ludwig Amendson standing before him, a look of mock anger on his face.

'Come here you young devil, I zink I need to break you bones once again, ja!' he said wrapping a pair of massive arms around him and bodily lifting Nicholas off the ground in a bear hug from which there was no escape.

'Don't you dare 'urt him Lud! Put him down at once!' laughed Lillian, as he squeezed the very breath from Nicholas before eventually letting him go.

Doctor Ludwig Amendson had a great barrel of a chest and huge round stomach to match and was similar in height to Nicholas. The jovial face was ruddy, with fine, purple spider veins just visible on his cheeks. The chip-blue Scandinavian eyes had deep ingrained laughter lines etched into the corners. His once shock of yellow blond hair, now greying, was cut crew style. He beamed at Nicholas and said, 'Not too bad for an old man eh!' as Nicholas ruefully rubbed his ribs and inhaled deeply.

'Let me look at you!' he boomed. 'Hmmm, not quite the skinny little youth who left here years ago I am thinking…grown up to a fine specimen!' He turned to Lillian. 'Is true ja?'

"E is a very 'andsome young man,' she cooed.

'But come, come, we neglect our guests, come now Nicholas, we must introduce you.' Lillian added, and they linked arms and walked over to the curious guests.

'*Monsieur's and Mesdames*, may I 'ave your attention for a little bit *s'il vous plait*. I would like to introduce to you a very lovely man and friend of many years, Nicholas Yuin, 'e 'as been working in the mountains somewhere over … zere' Lillian twirled her hand in the direction of the distant ranges and proceeded to introduce him to each of the guests individually.

Nicholas of course knew some of the farmers and cattlemen from his previous prospecting excursions a few years ago. It was common courtesy to inform the landowners if you were to travel across their property, for whatever reason. Further, it made common sense for safety reasons.

Most of these people, generally, were only too happy to provide assistance and were genuinely pleased to see white strangers, and their hospitality was renowned. There were, however, always exceptions.

They were fiercely proud of their achievements and of their ability to survive in this often frustrating and heartbreaking country. Equally, they were fiercely protective of what was theirs, in particular their families.

The young prospector had made a number of friends among them, his honesty and respect for others standing him in good stead.

As Nicholas began to relax a little with the guests, chatting amicably and carefully fielding questions about his discoveries or prospecting successes, he had the distinct feeling there was tension somewhere in the gathering.

Several times he surreptitiously scanned the crowd but was unable to focus on anything, due in large part to the myriad questions the guests asked of him.

They were hungry for news of world events, some having not been away from the area for many years, particularly the women.

They found the young man had an excellent fashion sense and was very entertaining whilst adroitly describing some of the new fashions beginning to emerge in Europe. Peals of laughter tinkled out over the guests at regular intervals (mostly from the ladies), as they were both shocked and amazed at his descriptions, and he was aware that generally the ladies in these parts were ultra-conservative, particularly with regards to their dress sense.

Young Hymie Van Der Hoeke watched as Lillian Amendson made a great fuss over Nicholas, almost showing him off, he thought, constantly hanging onto the man's arm as she towed him around introducing him to the guests. Hymie was particularly annoyed by her familiarity with this handsome and dashing looking stranger, unaware that Nicholas had known the Amendsons since he was thirteen years of age.

Bigoted as he was, he thought it improper she should show such affection for this much younger man, particularly in front of her husband and their guests, who seemed oblivious to her behaviour! It was shameful!

Neither did he miss the fact that almost every woman at the gathering was on the point of swooning when introduced to this man. His confident and eloquent manner were offensive.

Jealousy and indignation burned within him. By heaven, he had better keep his distance from my woman when she arrives, he fumed inwardly.

Hymie was a hulking young man of strong Dutch parentage and born in Africa. Tough, stubborn, narrow minded, quick tempered and religious (when it suited him), he would be 20 years old in four months' time.

His family owned the adjoining property, Vryheid Plains (Freedom Plains), and primarily ran cattle. Like most of the settlers in this area, they had worked hard to establish their stake in the fertile lands along the shores of Lake Victoria.

They, like the others, had faced enormous odds against the British, Germans, natives, and all manner of hardship and isolation. This inevitably bred a tough, stubborn race of people who were, by and large, very set in their ways. The exception in this attitude being the Amendsons, but then they were not of the same heritage.

Lillian and Nicholas gradually made their way around to each of the guests until they came to Hymie Van der Hoeke. Nicholas instantly sensed animosity toward him and knew that this was the source of his previous unease. For the life of him he could not fathom why.

Lillian paused in front of Hymie and said curiously, ''ave you two met before?' cocking her head to one side, noting the scowl on the young man's face.

'I think not,' said Nicholas lightly. Locking eyes with the Dutchman, he held out his hand. The fellow hesitated, and seconds passed as he rudely dragged out his response. 'Hymie is the son of Johann and Ermina Van Der Hoeke, our neighbours from Vryheid Plains, '*oom* you '*ave* already met,' said Lillian, her eyes darting covertly between the two. Ah, who can work this young man out she shrugged to herself.

'Hymie!' she said somewhat sharply. 'This is *Monsieur* Nicholas Yuin, 'e is a very close friend of the family, or per'aps, is more like a son!' she said hugging Nicholas's arm.

Nicholas waited, knowing that when this rude and insolent pup gripped his hand, he would try to crush it. No matter, thought Nicholas, I too have played this game.

When the young man finally stuck out his hand, Nicholas was waiting for it. As their hands closed over one another, Nicholas's thumb immediately pressed hard onto the back of Hymies hand, preventing the fellow from gripping hard.

Nicholas, with seemingly no effort, squeezed his adversary's hand hard. The man's knuckles ground together painfully and the smirk vanished from his face as Nicholas suddenly increased the pressure, bringing an involuntary intake of breath.

'I'm terribly sorry, boy, I did not realise you had a sore hand,' said Nicholas, the amusement dancing in his eyes. Hymie made to rub his hand before coming aware of what he was about to do. He dropped his hand to his side, his eyes dark with resentment and embarrassment.

'Are you planning to stay around these parts for long Mr Yuin?' he asked bluntly.

'Oh, I'm not sure, it depends on many things,' Nicholas replied as he looked at Lillian, her eyes huge and questioning. 'Maybe a few years, I shall have to see.'

It was perhaps, the reason for the fellow's naked hostility. He decided to test the water.

Turning to Lillian he began, 'Lillian my dear, forgive me, but I have not even asked about our Victoria! How is she? More to the point, where is she?' He glanced at the young fellow, confirming his suspicions. Van Der Hoeke's face was red with anger and indignation. Nicholas went on. 'Come, you must tell me all about her, I imagine she has grown into an exceptional young woman, almost as beautiful as her mother! Ah how I have missed her, has she made acquaintance with a gentleman yet?' he asked, then tilting his head to one side he looked at Lillian's bemused face, and stroking his chin added, 'I think not, I fear they must be in short supply hereabouts.'

Hymie's face was now purple with rage.

'Well, very nice to make your acquaintance boy, perhaps I shall see you up in the ranges one day, or here,' Nicholas said, all but dismissing the young fellow. Taking Lillian's arm again, he walked her away toward the far side of the clearing to where Ludwig was in earnest conversation with one of the cattlemen.

Lillian had her hand to her mouth and was all but biting on her knuckles to stifle the laughter that was threatening to take over her self-control.

'Oh, you wicked, wicked man, *mon Dieu!* I thought he was going to *explosi-on!*'

Nicholas chuckled at her pronunciation, and then asked, 'Where *is* Victoria, Lillian?'

Lillian replied, 'First you must understand that Hymie is most obsessed with Victoria and considers 'er as 'own. Victoria does not want *zis*, but 'e will not listen.' She continued. 'As to 'er whereabouts, I am sorry, but she went riding just before the first guests arrived. She sighed and said, 'We argued, which seems to be every day now, even with 'er papa!' She looked at him, he could see tears threatening. Lillian took a deep breath and said, 'Can we talk of this later, darling, I fear I 'av been neglecting my guests.'

Understanding immediately, he said 'Certainly, off you go,' bending to kiss her cheek.

Chapter 9

Baba Joe

*T*he Amendson's guests began to depart, and Nicholas found himself wandering down to the stables. The white painted mud-brick building with its yellow-grey thatched roofs afforded excellent insulation for the horses against the African elements. Red geraniums grew in profusion from several half wine barrel tubs along the front and sides, while at the far end there was a trellis windbreak draped with vivid purple and white bougainvillea stretching out toward the house. The buildings and yards themselves were kept immaculately.

Lillian had told Nicholas that Victoria had made the stables her domain and it was she who kept the stables and yards in such pristine condition.

As he walked toward the stable hands quarters at the end of the building, an old white haired African gentleman stepped out of the first stable. He turned and looked at Nicholas. Recognition blossomed on the old face.

'Young Massa Yuin sah!' he exclaimed, dropping the wooden pail and broom he had been carrying.

'Huh, huh! I never thought to see you again sah! Welcome back sah, welcome back!'

Tears of joy ran down the old fellow's face as he grinned hugely and began pumping Nicholas's hand vigorously.

'I see you old friend, hello Baba Joseph, good to see you again,' said Nicholas. 'How many wives have you got now you old devil?'

The old warrior cackled, then said sadly, 'No more now Massa Yuin, same ones. Too much trouble in house and Joseph getting very old.'

Joseph had been with the Amendsons for almost all of their fifteen years in Tanganyika and was devoted to them. He was originally from lands near the southern border region of the ferocious Wahehe nation, a race of fierce warriors who were well organised and possessed an army and battle tactics that rivalled that of the Zulu even though they were of smaller numbers. The warriors were spread across the lands and tended to have small communities or out-villages, growing mostly maize.

From the early 1800s though, the tradition was formed that all young men up to about twenty-five were trained as warriors in the capital area of Iringa. The traditional belief of the 'power of the spear' originated from this.

This meant that about 20,000 fighting age warriors could be summoned within two weeks of a battle call if need be. They implemented well organised military and battle tactics, and the regiments were highly disciplined, able to run for two days without food and march straight into battle. Most of these tactics and formations were adopted over time from their traditional rivals, the Wasungu nation (Wa meaning group or a collective).

The name in English (Hehe) was thought to be derived from their war cry – *Hee twahumite...Hee twahhumite...He he he heeeeeee!* – which meant, 'We have come out!'

Joseph, in his prime, had been a forward scout for King Mumyigumba's army. These scouts were known as Vatandisi. Fierce and brave and adept at guerrilla tactics, they would penetrate the enemy's defences and kill anyone in their way before reporting back to their regiment commanders.

Ludwig had found him lying beside the track some one hundred and fifty miles south of here whilst travelling to the new property. He was emaciated and had been badly beaten and wounded by some of the rebellious young warriors of a neighbouring Wasungu tribe who had surprised the older man in a compromising position with one of their wives. They had dumped his inert form some miles from the track, no doubt thinking he was dead and that the hyenas and jackals would remove any evidence of their attack and murder. To ensure success, they had killed an impala and dragged it's still bleeding carcass in ever increasing circles around Joseph's inert form.

But Joseph was unconscious not dead, and although badly injured and cut and speared many times in the legs and arms, with one terrible wound in his back and another across his chest, he had somehow managed to crawl back to the edge of the bush track where he collapsed.

Ludwig, Lillian and little Victoria had tended his wounds as best they could and lifted him into the back of their wagon.

Under Ludwig's expert medical care, Joseph survived, although it was many months before he was able to recover fully.

He knew now that his warrior days had passed and felt in his heart he wanted to stay, believing he now owed his life to the Amendsons. But he knew, first he had to gain permission from his chief and his advisors.

Joseph knew this would be no easy task as there was deep rooted suspicion about the new 'settlers' and the German Army had been merciless in its quest for dominance and colonialism, slaughtering many of the people and burning their outlying communities.

One day Joseph simply disappeared. He reasoned he was returning, so there was no reason to say goodbye. Little did he understand the devastation the little girl would suffer.

After two whole months of negotiation and the subject of much discussion, permission was granted. This was, in no small part, brought about by Joseph displaying his now healed wounds and extolling the prowess of Ludwig Amendson's skill as a healer. The chief and his group of elders were astounded at the extent of the injuries and his survival. They were fascinated by the neat rows of stitches on Joseph's body.

The chief expressed the view that perhaps this knowledge and skill could help his people and so it came to be.

The Wasungu tribe who had inflicted the wounds, had been wiped out – every man woman and child – as punishment.

Little Victoria was eight years old at the time and she could not understand why her Baba Joe had vanished. She had been fascinated by the Hehe warrior, and she immediately adopted him as her own special friend.

One day she was playing with her doll on the beginnings of the new lawn, when she looked up and there standing before her was her Baba Joe. She squealed in delight and ran to him hugging him around his legs.

Lillian and Ludwig, hearing the squeal, raced for the lawn, Ludwig grabbing his shotgun off the wall as they went. They burst out onto the rear of the house to find a now angry little girl, with tears on her face and her hands on her hips berating Joseph. 'Why did you leave without saying goodbye, it isn't good manners!' she raged, stamping her little foot angrily. 'And!…you made me cry!'

Poor Joseph, with his very limited English looked lost and confused, although he knew that she really was happy to see him. He reached out his hand and gently stroked her face, wiping aside the tears and squatting down spoke to her in his own language, gently saying, *'Morwa di'* (little daughter). Victoria of course did not understand a thing he said. Lillian was about to tell Victoria to behave, but then to Ludwig and Lillian's amazement, she suddenly jumped into his arms, knocking him onto his backside. Both were now giggling and laughing, and the look on Joseph's face told of a bond that no one could deny, he loved the little girl as he would his own.

Lillian and Ludwig, at first a little apprehensive, began to see that Joseph, or Baba Joe as Victoria had named him, limped around and followed the young "Missy" around like a shadow and was very protective of their little girl. If he wasn't next to her, you could be assured he would be watching over her within easy reach. Visitors often came to the house, and if Victoria happened to be approached, Baba Joe would appear as if by magic, not intruding but within a protective distance of his little friend.

Joseph became a very loyal and special part of the family, and over the years he cared for and guided Victoria, teaching her everything he knew of the African way of life and its bush craft. Victoria, in return, taught Joseph the English language and some French, although it could be said he did not adapt too well to the French language.

Unlike a lot of the "boys" as the other farmers called their African help, Joseph was treated with respect and trust by the Amendsons, was given a job and wage. He was never enslaved and he responded in kind – mutual respect was triumphant here.

Chapter 10

Lion and Love

Nicholas glanced at the afternoon sun which was getting low over the ranges in the west and said to Joseph, 'Missy Victoria has been gone quite a while Joseph, I think she should have been back by now, don't you think?'

The old man snorted, 'Missy Victoria do what Missy Victoria want, she is like the wildfire, never no listen to Joseph no mo', biting head off when try to teach or be worry, even Lady A'menson and doctor!'

'Still, it *is* getting late, which way did she go?' asked Nicholas, grinning at the old man's rhetoric, but also seeing the hidden worry in the old man's face.

Joseph pointed south along the track on the lake edge, then turned without another word and went into the end stable, returning with Nicholas's horse. The bay mare had been rubbed down and her coat gleamed in the afternoon sun. 'Mus' be your horse Massa Yuin, doctor ask Joseph to bring from front of house and bed down,' Joseph said.

'Missy Victoria have beautiful gelding Massa Yuin, big one, black an' call 'im Bonito.'

Together they saddled Nicholas's mare. Nicholas was about to swing into the saddle when the Amendsons came hurrying down.

'Nicholas! Where *are* you off to! We've not even had a chance to talk man!' said Lud as he and Lillian stared at him. 'You are not leaving so soon, surely Nicholas,' said Lillian, a frown creasing her beautiful face.

The easy grin on Nicholas's face immediately putting them at ease, and not wishing to alarm them said, 'No, no, just thought I would go and meet Victoria as she returns, surprise her, and it will give us time to catch up. I'm not in a hurry to leave, we'll have plenty of time to catch up on events.'

'Ja! Goot idea and it is getting late, you can giff her a good spanking for being so foolish while you are about it!' Lud said, somewhat testily.

'Ludwig! Victoria is not ze little girl anymore, don't treat 'er so,' admonished Lillian, and rolling her eyes added, 'Little wonder she is so difficult these days.'

Nicholas swung up into his saddle and still grinning at Lud's instruction, said, 'I'd best get moving, see you both for dinner.' Waving, he trotted his mare out onto the track and down toward the lake. Turning south along the shore, he urged the mare to an easy canter, easily picking up the horse tracks ahead of him.

Quail whirred up and away off the track as Nicholas cantered along the wheel ruts cut into the hip high grass, which rippled in the wind like a green and yellow ocean to his left.

To his right and south-west, the mighty Lake Nyanza disappeared to the horizon.

Hippopotamus grunted and snorted as they sounded the alert, great crocodile, some, about sixteen feet in length, sprinted for the water at his approach. Half a mile further along, huge flocks of beautiful pink flamingo birds waded about in the shallows or stood on a sand bar, their din clearly audible even from a distance. On the immediate shore stood other flocks of yellow-billed stork, up to fifty of the birds either wading the shallows or standing together, and in amongst them darted pipers and stilts.

He could smell the special scent that lakes of size had. Teeming with marine life and animal alike, it was the scent of life itself, even more so than that of the sea at times.

About eight miles passed with no sign of Victoria. Nicholas was beginning to worry. Again, glancing to the west, he estimated there to be about two hours left before dusk, not a good time to be wandering about in this country on horseback, even worse if you were alone.

He stopped and drew his rifle from the long leather scabbard buckled to his saddle and checked it.

The rifle was a beautiful work of art and was custom made by Renette, a French gunsmith and inventor of some note. It was years ahead of its time in design. The stock and fore stock were of magnificent European walnut, exquisitely oak leaf carved, while the metal work was inlayed with silver and gold filigree, as was the breech area and trigger guard.

One of the first breech-loading, double rifles, it was based on the Swiss inventor, Samuel Pauly's breech-loading system, invented in 1806. Nicholas had paid a small fortune for it, some four hundred and eighty-eight pounds, and it had been worth every penny, it being powerful and very accurate. He slipped it back into its scabbard.

As Nicholas was about to set off again, he heard the muted roar of lion coming off the wind, which was cutting across from his left and to his front. They would be rousing for the night's hunt, he thought to himself. This is not good, he worried, where on earth can she have gone!

Nicholas slipped his boots from the stirrups and patting his horse's neck, stood up on the seat of the saddle looking around at the surrounding grass plains. God, perfect hunting cover for lion or hyena he said to himself.

He was about to return to the saddle when he spotted a dark shape some distance further up the track moving steadily toward him. He stared, apprehension gripping him, predator or... Minutes ticked by as the shape drew nearer. Relief flooded over him as he registered it was a horse, but then with a jolt saw it was rider less. Has to be Victoria's, he mused.

Nicholas slipped back into his saddle and cantered toward the approaching horse. The horse was trotting steadily along toward him, showing no sign of panic and responded calmly to Nicholas's 'Whoa there Bonito!' when he grasped the bridle.

The black was about seventeen hands high and was saddled with an expensive saddle, beautifully tooled and polished to a high gloss. Buckled to the saddle were a pair of equally fine tooled saddlebags, the initials **VLA**, clearly embossed into the flaps. Nicholas chuckled as he saw it was a man's saddle. Tch, tch! Shocking, he thought, imagining what the so-called well-bred ladies would think seeing Victoria riding this type of saddle instead of side saddle as was the ladies choice of the day.

Her rifle was still in its scabbard and there was a water bottle still attached to the horn. Frowning, Nicholas dismounted and soothingly talked to the gelding. 'Easy boy, let's have a look at you.' He ran his hands over the horse's withers and checked him out thoroughly for any injury – there was none, nor any sign of hard running.

Gathering the black's reins and remounting, Nicholas began to track back. Several miles further, he was still seeing two sets of tracks, one going and one coming. He would have to find her quickly he thought – she was obviously unarmed and may be hurt.

Two hundred yards further on he suddenly reined in. One set of the horse's tracks had disappeared, *Damn,* he thought, I've ridden over the split in tracks. He wheeled about and slowly walked the horses back, there! He saw the bent and broken grass stalks, almost invisible at the track edge, and further in saw hoof prints on an old game trail heading off on an angle. He stood up in his stirrups and scanned the grassy plains again.

About two miles ahead and slightly to the right he could see a low rocky kopje and a lone dead and broken tree atop it.

Staring at the kopje and thinking out loud, Nicholas said, 'I wonder if she rode over there? Bit bloody silly if she did!' Looking around apprehensively at the tall grass waving in the breeze, perfect territory for an ambush by a pride of lion, or any predator for that matter, he decided he had little choice but to check it out, time was running out.

A male lion's roar again rumbled across the plains, no closer than before he thought, but that did not mean the lionesses weren't already on the hunt and they, if hunting, would not be roaring at all. The horses skittered nervously.

This will be damn dangerous if something goes wrong, Nicholas thought. I will have just enough time to get over and back and make a run for home he thought, peering at the grass where Victoria must have ridden. He looked a bit further toward the kopje and saw the narrow game trail heading that way.

He decided to take only the one horse over, two would be almost impossible to control if a lion came upon them.

He took the rifle from Victoria's horse and her water bottle. Rummaging around in the saddlebags he found a leather cartridge pouch, checked the contents and also took this.

Looping the gelding's reins over the saddle pommel, then tying the thong of his hat to it, he slapped the black hard on the rump.

The gelding reared in indignation and bolted up the track in the direction of the house. At least they will see his hat and realise he had found the horse and was still looking for, or was with, Victoria.

Wasting no more time Nicholas headed for the kopje with its lone tree. He knew that if Victoria was all right, she would be smart enough to stick around the tree, it would offer the only protection for miles around and a good vantage point.

About a half a mile from the kopje, Nicholas again heard the male lion roaring and although it was not much louder, he knew the lionesses were the real problem and they would be out ahead of the male hunting, usual two or more of them, depending on the size of the pride. If Victoria was in trouble or they had spotted her then this was where the real danger lay. His horse skittered and danced around tossing her head. 'Easy, easy,' Nicholas soothed and stopped to calm the nervy and frightened mare. He checked Victoria's rifle, an American firearm. It was also a breech-loader but was of a smaller calibre than his at .456 and had only the single barrel.

Preferring his own, he drew his rifle from the scabbard and slipped Victoria's back into it. He looked around once more and then jigged the mare forward.

A flash of white suddenly caught his attention up on the kopje, by the base of the tree. He kept on riding, his senses on a razor's edge and very aware that in the long waving grass he would have little hope of seeing the big cats before they were upon him.

Victoria knew there were at least two lionesses stalking her, no matter how stealthily they crept toward her in the wind-blown grass. Joseph's teachings were serving her well and she could place the big cats perfectly, she did not miss the telltale flick of the ears.

They were about fifty yards from the rise in ground where she stood at the base of the tree. One to her extreme left, which was slowly slinking towards her, the other, on her right, had stopped and was just visible, she could just make out the top of its head and ears in the long grass at the edge of the rise.

She knew she was in big trouble – a sprained left ankle and a cut on her right knee that was still bleeding – as well as being unarmed.

She had tried for about an hour to climb the tree but had no strength in her left foot to enable her to reach the low broken branch that poked a mocking finger of false hope to the heavens. In any event, Victoria knew, contrary to popular belief, that some lions were actually quite good climbers and would have little trouble clawing their way up the trunk of this size of dead tree, especially since it was on a slight angle. Even if she could have climbed up, it would have given her only a slight advantage and temporary at that.

She cursed the black Egyptian cobra snake that had spooked her horse. It had been behind a flat rock when it suddenly moved and raised its head and the hood expanded out as it crossed in front of them just as she was about to dismount. The horse had reared just as she swung her right leg over, still with one foot in the stirrup. She had fallen and twisted her ankle, but thankfully her foot slipped from the stirrup or she would have been dragged along with her horse as it bolted. But now she was without water, her rifle and had no protection. She was helpless.

Tears began to well in her eyes as she saw both lionesses flatten to the ground at the edge of the rocks, now in full view and she knew they were about to come in for the kill. She knew that one would come at her on an angle and the other would hang back to cover her escape should she have been able to run. Fear clutched at her and she found it difficult to breathe. She wanted to pee, and her legs began to shake with a will of their own as she crouched and clutched at the tree trunk behind her.

Victoria had often seen prides of lions tear into carcasses and she quailed at the thought.

Oh God no! she thought in despair, her mother's and father's faces flashing into her mind and she sobbed in fear and sorrow. 'Please no, not like this!' she sobbed out loud.

The great cat on her left rose slightly as it bunched its muscle and made its run toward her. Bounding up the rock, she could clearly see its yellow eyes fixed on her and the ticks on the side of the cat's eyes.

A great boom crashed upon her, hurting her ears, she screamed, then saw the lioness suddenly stopped in mid-air, as if it had been slapped by some giant hand and was thrown back onto the ground. Seconds later another boom lashed about her ears and she spun her head toward the other lioness. It too was slapped down, although it was thrashing about at the edge of the grass. Before the echoes had finished rolling around the plains there was a snap of metal, another booming crash and it slumped to the ground, its legs rigid and jerking, then finally, gently shuddering to a halt.

Victoria's ears were ringing like a thousand bells as she stood stunned, too shocked to comprehend that she was safe, she stared at the dead lion, another click and snap brought her back to reality. She slowly turned to her right, the tears still rolling down her face. A man stood not twenty feet away, tendrils of blue smoke lifted lazily from the barrels of his rifle, which was now propped, butt down on top of his right boot, his right hand was holding the barrels out and angled away from his body. His other hand was on his left hip.

The tears still blurred her eyes and she wiped at them with her sleeve. She suddenly began to shake and the tears again began to flow, relief crashing upon her like a wave.

'Are you all right Vicky?' he asked.

Vicky? No one called her Vicky, except... 'N...Nicholas! Is that you Nicholas?' She tried to focus on him but the tears stung her eyes. She wiped her eyes on her sleeve. 'How did...I mean...' He at last came into focus.

'Dear God it *is* you!' Victoria's emotions overwhelmed her and the tears began again.

Nicholas walked to her, carefully laying his rifle against a fallen branch. He just caught her as she took a step toward him, her ankle giving away. He wrapped her in his arms.

'Now, now Victoria, it's all right, it's all right now.' He held her as she sobbed with relief, shuddering in his arms as the realisation that she was safe flooded over her.

When she had calmed down, he said, 'Come now, let's have a quick look at that ankle, we have no time and must get moving, it's getting late.'

'How did you? Where...' she started. Holding up his hand Nicholas said, 'Shush! Shush! We'll talk later, right now we have to get out of here, the sun will set soon and we don't want to be out here then.'

Nicholas sat her down on the fallen log by his rifle and went to undo the laces, she gasped as he began to unlace her calf-high riding boot. He stopped and said, 'Hmm, I think we will leave your boot on until we get home.' He smiled, reassuring her as he re-laced the boot.

Looking at the bloodstain and tear on her right knee of her riding breeches, he asked, 'How bad is the cut?'

'It's nothing,' she replied.

'Well now, hold my rifle,' he said passing it to her. He scooped her up in his arms with ease and began to make his way back to his horse.

'It's been such a long, long time since we've seen each other Nicholas, where have you been?'

Nicholas took some time to answer her and Victoria thought he was concentrating on carrying her down the slope. The truth was that Nicholas was intoxicated by her jasmine perfume and now acutely aware that Victoria was no longer a cheeky little girl, but a grown woman, and a very beautiful one at that.

To his embarrassment he found himself stuck for words, as he was consumed totally by her closeness.

'I have been to many places,' he finally answered, making a supreme effort to control himself. 'Canada, America, India, Argentina to name a few, but for some reason I always seem to come back to Africa.'

'Thank God for that,' Victoria replied as they reached his horse. I don't want him to put me down, thought Victoria. She looked up at him to find he was looking at her with a pained look on his face.

'Are you alright Nicholas?' she asked, her grey eyes still gazing at him.

My God, she is more beautiful than anything I have ever seen, he thought, and was unable to put her down or was reluctant to do so. He felt himself stir again and clearing his throat, reluctantly answered, 'I'm fine Vicky, I'll put you over here whilst I get the horse ready. Are you in pain?'

'Not now,' she answered but gave an involuntary gasp as her foot bumped on the ground as he lowered her to sit on a large rock.

It was as if someone was controlling events unseen as they locked eyes, and something shifted in each of them, their pulses pounding in unison. There was no physical touch, neither was there any need for it, such was the enormity of the moment.

Nicholas studied her, it was as if every minute detail of her face came to him without he having to break his gaze. Soft wisps of blonde hair curled at her temple, tinged copper by the looming sunset, while her grey eyes had tiny flashes of gold dancing within. Her nose, straight and narrow with a couple of faint freckles across the bridge, was now flaring gently with each breath and her lips were slightly parted. Nicholas could see an almost invisible, very fine down on her upper lip, and tiny beads of moisture glistened among the down.

Dear Lord, how can she be so perfect, he thought, and something squeezed his heart and his head spun.

Victoria was in awe of the feelings which swept over her in this so special a moment.

He is like a god, she thought as his amber eyes glowed with an intensity that was, she knew, reserved especially for her and this moment. She felt herself flush as his scent washed over her, and she was finding it hard to breathe. She dropped her eyes in embarrassment as she felt her long cherished self-control dissolve in an instant.

Nicholas knelt before her, she shivered slightly as he placed one hand gently upon her shoulder.

She felt the warm touch of his other hand as he reached out and gently lifted her chin, his eyes instantly captivating her and her heart leapt uncontrollably as she realised they were about to kiss, a mere half an inch and each other's warm breath was all that now separated their lips.

The kiss began gently and softly but with such fire and depth of feeling, it quickly consumed both and the world seemed to spin, sweeping them into the unknown. Nothing else existed in that moment.

They held each other in the afterglow of their shared and uncontrolled emotion, breathless and in awe of the feelings that flowed between them, foreheads touching, both concluding that this was a moment to be cherished.

Gently sliding his hand down her neck to rest on her shoulder, Nicholas shocked himself when he said, 'I am, from this moment, very much in love with you my Victoria.'

She pulled back from him and tears ran freely down her beautiful face and she said quietly, 'Oh Nicky, I feel such a fool. I never thought to look for what has been in my heart since I was a little girl, following you around like a puppy dog. I know now, I have always been in love with you, I just didn't know what was inside of me or what has been bothering me for such a long time. I feel like I have been freed from something.'

Nicholas simply smiled at her in reply and placed his open hand to the side of her face and was about to kiss her again when his horse suddenly danced around on its tether.

The muted roar of a male lion suddenly brought them out of their reverie. They suddenly were jolted out of their euphoria and could see it was getting darker, and the magnificent sunset turned a darker shade. Packs of hyena, African hunting dog and lions would already be on the hunt.

'We must get a move on,' said Nicholas, giving her a light kiss on her cheek, and suddenly was in command once more. He strode to his horse which was becoming skittish and knowing that this was no place to be after dark, he slipped the rifle over one shoulder, swung up into the saddle and nudged the horse over to her.

'Place your good foot in the stirrup and I will swing you up,' he instructed, then added, 'Easy though, it's going to hurt my lady.' He said, grinning at her.

Nicholas took Victoria's hand and half lifted, half swung her up behind him. She cried out a little as her ankle banged on the horse's rump, but she quickly snuggled into Nicholas's broad back and placed her arms around his waist, thrilling at their closeness.

Nicholas was getting worried as he heard the lilting gibbering of hyenas come in on the wind and he figured, not too far away at that. The biggest danger would be getting back to the road through the long grass. He swung his rifle off his shoulder, checked the load and laid it across the saddle in front of him and jigged his horse forward and into the grass.

For all the worry, they reached the road without trouble and Nicholas immediately kicked the horse into a canter along the road, now overcast with darkening stripes of shadow. He scanned the sides of the road and ahead, silently praying that he would not see any predator.

Victoria, despite the jolting pain from her sprain and the obvious danger, felt safe and happier than she could remember. The muscles in Nicholas's back, his scent and warmth filling her with a sense of awe and security that she had never before felt. She leant forward and lay her head onto his back and squeezed gently.

Nicholas was acutely aware of her warmth behind him and to his embarrassment felt himself stir involuntarily. His concentration on the road began to wander as he began to fantasise about them being together and what lay in the future.

With a shock, he suddenly saw that there was a dark object on the track a few hundred feet ahead. He reined to a halt, almost losing Victoria in the process. He cursed himself for not keeping alert as he began to register what the shape standing on the road was. 'What is the matter?' Victoria asked. 'Shhh, shhh,' he murmured.

It was a large female spotted hyena, but what worried him was he could see no others. Since hyena usually hunted in packs, he could assume the rest were already there, although it was now too dark to see into the grass at the edge of the track at that distance.

He had to make a decision and quickly. He knew that as soon as the animal on the road made a move toward them, the rest of the pack would explode into action – they would drag the horse down and they would be ripped to shreds within minutes.

He quickly and smoothly reached for his hunting rifle, cocking it as he threw it to his shoulder. He saw the hyena's ears flick in curiosity at his sudden movement. It was all the time he needed, he drew a bead on the animal's head and squeezed the trigger.

Victoria, peering around Nicholas's back, saw the hyena, and knowing how they hunted and the danger they were in, had just enough time to clap her hands over her ears before the heavy rifle's boom crashed around her. She saw the beast picked up off the ground a slammed some six feet away as if an insignificant piece of rag.

She had no time to even respond as Nicholas shouted, 'Hang on! Hee! Ya!' and spurred the horse to a full gallop, Victoria dug her fingers into Nicholas's waist and hung on for dear life as the mare exploded into action and quickly reached full gallop.

They bore down on the smashed almost headless carcass of the lead hyena. Nicholas could now see several other hyena scattering and milling around the edge of the road, gibbering in alarm. He knew that their hunting instinct and hunger would return soon, as would the threat, but the bay mare was now at full stretch and they sailed over the dead hyena and through the pack before they could get over the shocking boom of Nicholas's heavy rifle.

Nicholas kept up the pace until several miles had passed and only then did he begin to slow the mare to a trot.

'Are you all right Victoria?' he asked, turning around to her as best he could.

Victoria was thinking that she had never felt better, apart from her ankle, which was beginning to throb painfully. 'I'm fine really, that was close my Nicholas.' She looked at him, her heart hammering. 'My God that rifle is beautiful, what power it has, I should like to try it out one day.'

Nicholas laughed and turning, glanced at her. What a woman he thought. 'I think it would break that beautiful little shoulder of yours my love, my shoulder will be bruised even now!'

'Look!' said Victoria peering past him and pointing up the road.

A dance of lights had appeared some miles ahead as they stared. 'It must be a search party!' cried Victoria. Nicholas again spurred the mare forward.

The approaching lights were about two to three miles distant he estimated, still time for them to have trouble. He urged the now tiring horse forward.

One hundred yards was all that separated the converging horses now, and Nicholas and Victoria could make out four horsemen. All were carrying flaming brands aloft and the flickering orange light was a welcome sight.

Chapter 11

The Black Eyes of Death

The party was made up of Victoria's father, Ludwig, Hymie Van Der Hoeke, his father, Johann, and Joseph, who was leading Victoria's black. Joseph was bringing up the rear, his face joyous and almost consumed by the most magnificent smile.

Having heard the boom of the rifle, the search party galloped up to Nicholas and Victoria. Hymie Van Der Hoeke, on seeing Victoria still clinging to Nicholas's waist, flared, and his beefy face reddened with rage and indignation.

Before he could say anything, Joseph, tears of relief streaming down his ebony skin, cried out, 'Massa Yuin sah! I knew Missy Victoria be a'right with you looki'...

Hymie swung on Joseph. 'Shut your face! You no good black bastard! Know your place or I'll...'

'You will do nothing!' Ludwig snapped. 'Joseph works for *me*, is a *free* man and you, young fellow watch *your* tongue.'

Nicholas, locking eyes with the young Boer and slipping to the ground, said calmly, 'Joseph, it's all right, would you be so kind as to help me get *our* Victoria onto her horse please?'

He turned, reached up and grasped Victoria by the waist, gently lifting her effortlessly from his saddle. 'Lift your left foot up, that's it.'

Victoria slid her arms around Nicholas's neck for support and in doing so her face met the side of his face, she made no attempt to move away as Nicholas put her down, she gasped and stood on one foot as Joseph came around to help.

This was too much for Hymie; he leapt from his horse, threw his flaming brand to the ground, slammed the hapless Joseph to the ground and jumping toward them, reached out and grasped Victoria's arm, twisting as he did so. She cried out in pain as he dug his fingers into her arm.

'Hymie!' shouted Johann, 'Let her go!' and he swung down off his horse, but in that split second he knew his son had lost control, it was too late to get to him and stop him

'*Your* Victoria! By God I'll not stand for this!' he snarled. 'Get your hands off her you jumped up filthy cur!'

Something white-hot engulfed Nicholas, and in an instant all reason and rational thought vanished with it.

Despite his hype and anger, Hymie Van Der Hoeke never had a chance to react to the fury that suddenly fell upon him. Nicholas drove his right fist straight up between Van Der Hoeke's outstretched left arm and his reaching right hand. The vicious blow, swung with a roll of the hip, had all of Nicholas's weight behind it and it smashed up beneath Van Der Hoeke's jaw, slamming his teeth together with an audible sharp clack. Van Der Hoeke's left hand was torn from Victoria's arm. Two more crashing blows followed almost as one. One to his right eye, and as he began to crumble Nicholas's right fist again flashed in, smashing down onto the bridge of his nose. Struggling to keep upright, he hung for a few seconds, then his legs buckled and he crashed to his knees in shock.

The speed and power of Nicholas's reaction had stunned them all, and they stood in silence, not daring say a word. Nicholas's face was without expression, but they could feel the terrible anger emanating from him, his amber eyes glowing with frightening intensity as he waited for Van Der Hoeke's response. The only sound, however, was Hymie's panting and Nicholas's breath hissing out from between his clenched teeth.

Nicholas stood before him, the killing rage now just under control, but it took all of his willpower to stop himself from letting go and attacking again.

He waited, studying the Boer. Van Der Hoeke was already bleeding profusely from his mouth and nose, and a cut over the right eye, which was rapidly closing.

Suddenly, the silence was broken by an indignant growl of rage as Van Der Hoeke shook his head and made to power to his knees. Before he could get any further his father jumped on him and wrapping his bear-like arms around his son, he drove him back onto the ground. 'Enough! You bladdy damn fool! Enough!' cried his father.

Hymie was screaming, 'Let me go Pa! I'll kill the bastard, let me *GO!*'

The older man somehow managed to straddle his son's chest and pinned his upper arms beneath his knees.

'Don't be a damn fool! Listen to me! You had no right! You have shamed me in front of my neighbour!'

Hymie heaved and tried to throw his father off.

Johann Van Der Hoeke was a big man, strong and tough, he was no stranger to violence of the worst kind. He knew what would happen if his hot-headed son managed to break free, there was no question he would be badly hurt, perhaps killed. He backhanded his son across the face, hard.

Hymie was stunned! His Pa had hit him as well! 'I will kill the bastard,' he hissed through clenched teeth.

His father leaned down close to his face and said urgently, 'Now you listen to your Pa son. This man is dangerous and quite capable of killing you, even with his bare hands if need be, you have a lot to learn, now back off.'

The young man made a mighty heave and managed to push his father off and onto his side and now on all fours, started to coil himself for a leap to his feet.

The cold steel of Nicholas's hunting rifle appeared as by magic, the black eyes of the muzzles staring, then resting on Hymie's left cheek. The click of the hammers cocking was like a clap of thunder in Hymie's already ringing ears. He felt his sphincter loosen. With a supreme effort he stalled it but he could not control a little spurt of urine escaping, staining the front of his breaches.

He waited, terror upon him. In the orange flickering light of the flaming brands he saw their reflection dancing upon the shiny black barrels as his eye slid along the steel to the white knuckles of fingers curled around the triggers.

Nicholas's voice was flat and without emotion. 'Back down now! You ever lay a hand on her again, I *WILL* kill you son.'

Time stood still for Hymie Van Der Hoeke. He knew if he made one false move he would surely die as he slowly looked up to Nicholas's eyes.

What he saw was a mask completely devoid of emotion. The amber eyes, previously alive with the excitement of battle, were now glassed, flat and unblinking. He felt as though an icy hand was squeezing his heart.

His anger vanished as fear clutched at him, as the reality that his life hung by the merest thread hit home, another little spurt of urine escaped. His eyes slowly swivelled across to his father's face, and with a pitiful pleading in his voice, he croaked, 'Pa...Pa?'

Far in the distance of Nicholas's mind, he could hear a voice, but as yet he did not attempt to decipher who was speaking, or what was being said, such was his focus.

Suddenly, he heard Johann Van Der Hoeke pleading with him to hold and not kill his son.

The amber eyes suddenly came to life again but remained locked and unblinking on Hymie. Then, the stare of his rifles black eyes suddenly vanished as Nicholas lifted the heavy rifle away from Hymie's face, leaving two crescent shaped marks just below his left eye.

Hymie remained on all fours, an involuntary exhalation of breath escaped his mouth. 'Huh,' he managed softly as he dropped his head.

Nicholas turned to Victoria and said lightly, 'Well then, I think we should be getting along, don't you think? Poor Lillian must be beside herself with worry!'

'Joseph! Come, give me a hand if you please,' he said as if absolutely nothing had happened.

Joseph and Victoria just stared at him and were stunned when Nicholas suddenly turned and stood over Johann Van Der Hoeke, assisting the older man to his feet then stooped, picked up the man's hat and handed it to him. He walked over to the edge of the track and again stooped, picking up Hymie's hat, strode back over to Hymie, who was still on all fours on the track, and handed him his hat.

Hymie was too surprised to do anything other than to take the hat, and to his utter horror, found himself saying, thank you.

A brief twinkle of amusement danced within the amber eyes as Nicholas replied, somewhat tongue in cheek, 'The pleasure, is all mine sir.'

Nicholas went back to Victoria and Joseph. The old man was fighting a mighty battle within himself to stop himself from gleefully cackling out loud.

Nicholas put his arm around Victoria's waist and lifted her onto her saddle as Joseph, beside him, gently lifted and supported her left leg.

'All right?' Nicholas asked, one eyebrow cocking in query. She nodded in reply, and he did not miss the strange way she looked at him. It was as if she was studying him from afar, worry gnawed at his gut, but he gave no sign of it.

He knew he had exposed a side of him that she may not be able to accept.

They mounted and cantered back to Herrgarden Grande.

'I have lost her Pa, that bastard has stolen her from me!' said Hymie to his father as they cantered ahead of the others.

'Hymie, you never had her in the first place,' replied his father, sighing in resignation.

'What do you mean Pa?' Hymie cried, staring at his father in astonishment.

'I mean, son, that I have watched you chase after that young lady for nigh on two years,' his father said. 'And she, to her credit, has always behaved perfectly, has treated you with respect and honesty, but has always politely kept her distance from you.

'A blind man can see that she is not interested in you. Accept it, and end this obsession of yours, you cannot force your will and desires upon her.'

His father went on. 'She and Yuin have known each other for many years before you even began having thoughts about her. There is a bond between them man, and obviously a very strong one, she is not for you.'

The older man paused. 'You think about that my boy, don't be a bladdy fool, and let this be an end to it,' he said with finality.

Chapter 12

Wrench of Hearts

Nicholas stayed at the Herrgarden Grand for a further five days, during which time he saw Victoria only twice in the first two days, while she rested her ankle. Then, apart from evening meals, there was no opportunity to talk as she would excuse herself and retire straight after the meal. She made no attempt to contact him or ask for him. He tried to make excuses for her lack of communication but he could feel her difference in attitude toward him or thought he could. Considering the depth of feelings that had transpired between them previously, he failed to understand how or why she would not talk to him. Both times he had visited, Joseph and Lillian were applying Joseph's foul smelling poultices or some liniment to the badly swollen ankle. Their conversation whilst her ankle was being tended to, generally concerned her health and was at best restrained, so they had no chance to be alone when he could have perhaps explained his feelings and actions over what had happened, and in any case he certainly would not enter her bedroom without a chaperone.

All of this time, worry gnawed at Nicholas as he wondered if Victoria would understand that his response to Hymie Van Der Hoeke's actions were solely to protect her and he had instantly recognised that Van Der Hoeke was on the verge of completely losing control, such was his obsession with her.

He had asked himself over and over again if it was himself who had lost control, but the fact that Van Der Hoeke was still alive to talk about it, suggested otherwise. But did Victoria see it that way?

On the afternoon of the fourth day, Victoria sat with her mother on the front veranda, her ankle elevated. It was healing rapidly now, and with the aid of a crutch she had been able to take tentative steps after only two days, Josephs poultices that he concocted and applied to her ankle twice a day had worked wonders. She didn't dare ask what they were made of.

She was deeply troubled and confused, yet at the same time excited, an unnerving mix of emotion that she could not quite grasp.

Victoria had no doubt she was in love at last – it seemed her every thought somehow found a way to think about Nicholas. When she thought of him a wonderful feeling of euphoria washed over her and she felt a warm glow deep inside her. She was not however, aware that she was also talking about him constantly.

Many times she thought to ask for him, to talk about her concerns, but for some reason, kept delaying the talk.

What excited and troubled her was the Nicholas she saw on that early evening when he saw her under threat. Such power had emanated from him, physically and mentally, and she felt herself once again flush at the thought of it. She carefully stole a glance at her mother to see if she had noticed.

There was however, a moment when he was not the Nicholas she knew and remembered, and it troubled her deeply. He had been detached and seemed devoid of all feeling, and she knew with certainty that he would not have hesitated to kill Hymie had his father not begged for his life. She shuddered, remembering the unblinking lifeless eyes.

Lillian was studying Victoria, and knew, as mothers do, that her daughter was in turmoil and guessed what was troubling her. Ludwig had told her of the incident and they both noticed a marked change in their daughter. Lud remarking on the change first. 'What *is* wrong with the girl?' he had grumbled.

Lillian had snorted in reply, 'Men! It is obvious, no? 'E 'as been away! Now he is a very 'andsome and capable man, and she is not an annoying little girl any more but a grown woman!'

She instinctively had known that Victoria had fallen in love with their dashing guest and friend, and Lud was right – Victoria had changed and seemed at last somewhat settled, and despite her current trauma, a little calmer perhaps, if one could call it that. There was a visible lightness about her, but something else seemed to preoccupy her at times and she would suddenly seem sad and distant.

'Are you alright *mon cherie*?' she asked, noticing the shudder.

Victoria turned to look at her mother, so poised and beautiful as always, as warmth and concern radiated from her.

'Oh, Ma ma!' Victoria suddenly blurted out, 'I am so in love with Nicholas it hurts, but I saw something in him the other night that frightens me and I just don't know what to do!' Great tears began to flow down her cheeks and she twisted her hands in anguish.

Lillian smiled reassuringly at her. *'Ah oui!* she replied, nodding. 'I sensed something was bothering you my darling. Your Pa pa told me what happened with Nicholas and Hymie, and I *knew* you were in love!' She clapped her hands together in delight. *'Mon Cherie*! zis is wonderful, I'm so 'appy for you! Does our Nicholas feel the same I 'ope*?'*

Despite her troubles, Victoria was swept up in her mother's elation at the admission. 'Ma ma, yes! he loves me! We just, I mean something just happened between us, it just happened and we knew!'

'Well now Cherie, 'e is a fine young man and right for you, I think. But love must be the bond for respect, trust and friendship.' Lillian looked hard at her daughter and said, 'I see these things before you, why do you not tell me what is bothering you?'

Victoria looked at her feet and said, 'Ma ma, he was so cold, it was like the Nicholas I knew had been possessed by...by something...oh! I don't know! But if Hymie had moved just a little, I fear Nicholas would have killed him.'

She began to cry again, then said, 'Am I to see this unemotional person again, or was Nicholas right and just protecting me? Maybe he saw something I did not or he knows about these things.'

Lillian lifted her daughter's face with one hand and drew a lace handkerchief from her sleeve. 'Sometimes when a man thinks 'e is threatened or *sinks* '*is* loved ones are threatened, 'e, will stop at nothing to protect *zis*,' she said softly as she dabbed gently at Victoria's tears. She paused, thinking, then continued. 'To show weakness or waiver when faced with *zis* danger, 'e will instinctively know, just like the animals, *zat* all might be lost if 'e is not strong. '*Ard* to understand, no?' Victoria nodded in reply.

'*Cherie*, look at your arm!' she exclaimed looking at Victoria's arm where Hymie had grabbed her. It was an ugly mix of purple, yellow and blue with deep scratches raked across the flesh of her upper arm.

'I think Hymie *may* '*ave* '*urt* you both if Nicholas had been a lesser man, and '*ad* not reacted like 'e did,' Lillian said.

'All men '*ave* this in them, some are weak and some are strong.' She tapped the side of her head with one finger. 'Some are afraid of it and it never surfaces, some use and can control it, some cannot and '*ave* no control.' She paused, then with one eyebrow raised, looked at her daughter and said, 'Hymie is alive, no?'

Victoria nodded, then lapsed into silence, deep in thought as she considered her mother's council.

'One thing darling, it is unfair to keep our Nicholas wondering and worrying about your feelings, you must talk to '*im* – whatever you decide. The longer you leave it the more 'e will feel *reject'ion*.' Lillian bent and kissed her daughter on the cheek.

Lillian withdrew discreetly, leaving her daughter to sort her thoughts out. She thought to seek out Nicholas herself and offer some explanation for Victoria's somewhat distant attitude, but then decided against it, feeling that Victoria should be the one to explain herself to Nicholas.

That evening after dinner, Victoria excused herself and retired to her bedroom. She had mulled over things long enough, she scolded herself. I love Nicholas, that is certain and what Ma ma said makes some sense.

Suddenly, the euphoric feeling of warmth and good feeling washed over her and she knew that she must go to Nicholas and tell him what had been bothering her. God how I love him, she thought.

Lillian came to her a short time later and standing by her bed, said nothing, but simply raised an eyebrow in question.

'Don't worry Ma ma, I have decided to tell him all about my feelings, what you explained to me makes sense and I love him too much to let this stand in its way.

'Very wise, mon *Cherie* 'I detect that *'e is 'urting* very badly'

Victoria looked up at her and replied, 'I shall tell him first thing in the morning.' Victoria did not see the slight frown on her mother's face as she bade her good night, turned and left the room.

The morning came, with all of its African beauty, the pink and crimson tinted clouds splashed across the sky as if mother nature had wielded a gigantic paintbrush, breathtaking in its awesome spectacle.

An hour later, Victoria could wait no longer and she pulled on her dressing gown and limped to Nicholas's room. She tapped lightly on the door to the guest room.

There was no response, she tapped again, there was still no acknowledgement. Her heart thumping with expectation and thinking that probably Nicholas and her father had talked late into the night as they were prone to do, she bit her lip, and her heart pounding like a hammer, turned the doorknob and slipped through the door into his room.

He was not there.

Victoria, after her initial surprise, glanced around the room. Nicholas's duffle had gone, the bed was made and the room was tidy.

Fear and anxiety seized her like a giant fist as she saw the letter propped against the pillow.

She could see her name written on the front in an eloquent hand, but fear and dread prevented her from moving.

Eventually, she summoned up the courage to fetch the letter, and opening it, sat down on the bed to read.

My Darling Victoria,

It is with a heavy heart that I write this letter and no more difficult a task have I ever undertaken.

It has become obvious to me that my actions five days ago destroyed your feelings for me or at least have made you reconsider our compatibility.

I can understand that my reaction must have shocked you, however, the opportunity to explain has not been forthcoming.

I should like you to know that I acted the way I did out of my love for you and because I feared for your wellbeing, and that is all.

Having travelled to many parts of the world, I have mixed with, and have met all types of men. After a time, one hones a keen instinct to people's reactions in situations such as we unfortunately found ourselves in.

I could see that young Van Der Hoeke was incapable of controlling himself when the fellow perceived that you were attracted to myself, hence my reaction.

I beg of you, that, in future, you exercise great care when around this person and always have company with you when he is near, this fellow is not to be trusted.

I journey back to the ranges this morning and I guess that by the time you read this note, I shall be well on my way, for I shall leave before the dawn.

Understand, this is not my desire, however, after consideration, I conclude that this must be what you wish and so will abide.

I desire you to know that, no one time in my life have I ever felt love such as I do for you.

My love for always.

Nicholas.

PS: Please convey my apologies to Lillian and Ludwig for leaving so rudely and thank them for their hospitality.

18th March, 1842.

A loud ringing began in Victoria's head, and her emotions clawed at her chest as the enormity of what had happened hit home. She lowered her head to the pillow and could smell his scent. Overcome, and her heart breaking, Victoria sobbed into the pillow, 'No Nicholas...no!'

There she remained until Lillian found her.

Twenty-six miles away, Nicholas sat upon a rocky outcrop jutting out toward the expanse of Lake Nyanza, a magnificent sky heralding the dawn and reflected upon the surface in all its beauty.

Nicholas, his face pinched and his mind full of anguish, was in turmoil over his abrupt departure. He agonised over his decision, knowing he would never be able to erase his love for Victoria.

It was obvious, that she no longer felt the same! he angrily chastised himself. *The choice has been made and it's too late to change, time to move, look ahead not back,* he told himself.

He walked briskly to his horse, sprang into the saddle and spurred away without looking back, then turned and headed east for the ranges and his prospecting camp. But the ache in his heart was to remain with him for many years.

Chapter 13

Up River, 15 Miles

The twittering of birds and the scent of the dawn came to him first as Nicholas lay in his bedroll. He drew in the heady perfume of damp bushland. Birds were chatting away by the river and all around him as he slowly opened his eyes.

The sky was just beginning to glow with the coming of the sun, and turning to the west, the indigo void – sprinkled with tiny diamond pin-pricks – clung in vain to the night. Nicholas drank in the peace and began to stretch his limbs in contentment.

Suddenly, he started as a great whirring sound drew about him. He swung his head about wildly, trying to comprehend what the sound was but could not. As he was about to leap out of his bedroll and grab his rifle, which was loaded and lay within easy reach at his side, when he looked at the dead tree from which he had broken off branches for his fire the previous night.

The tree was green! What magic is this, he thought alarmed as he tried to clear the sleep and fuzziness from his head.

Focus came and he laughed out loud as he realised the entire tree was covered in small brilliant green parakeets, for all the world looking like leaves. At his laugh, they launched into flight as one, whirring away like a great bright green wave. He watched as they flew dipping and rippling in perfect unison, a high trilling sound coming from them as they rose up into the sky. As he watched their flight, dark one second, then shimmering green in the next, in the morning light. There must be thousands of them, he thought, such beauty! This country is so full of surprises! he reflected.

He lay back trying to remember when he had fallen asleep last night but failed. For after Nicholas had struck camp the previous night, he had laid in his bedroll and fell into a deep dreamless sleep, and now he felt charged and ready to move.

He banged his boots hard on the ground and shook them vigorously; a trick learnt the hard way after a scorpion had once crawled into his boots, no doubt seeking the warmth or protection during the night. He had pulled them on the next morning without checking and had suffered a painful sting. It had laid him up for a full day – headaches, aching groin and foot on fire. He now dragged on his boots, stirred the coals and threw a few pieces of wood on the embers of the fire he had lit the previous evening and then made his way to the river's edge.

Stripping off his shirt he checked for any tell tail sign of crocodile. Seeing none, he knelt and splashed the slightly brackish water over himself, gasping in the chill of the morning, goose bumps standing proud on his chilled skin. He then dried off using his shirt.

He looked around and drew in the morning scent and thought, Ah me! This is what the bushland was all about! He returned to the fire, propping a stout stick between two rocks before the fire and hung his shirt on it to dry.

After a scant meal of dried biscuit and a pannikin of tea, Nicholas saddled his horse, packed up his saddlebags and strapped on his bedroll, then mounted and began to pick his way through the sometimes-dense scrub which grew along this side of the river. He noticed that so far the scrub was a lot thicker on this side of the river although he could see no particular reason for it.

Nicholas decided that he would head north-east and away from the river and try to find higher ground to better gain his bearings. He reasoned that the river must soon narrow and be shallow enough to cross, the further he travelled upstream.

Nicholas found a sandy trail heading roughly north and cautiously made his way along the track. He had covered roughly fifteen miles, the distant ranges looking ever more inviting, when his instincts began prodding him that he was not alone, the horse was also a little jumpy. He slowed Stitch to a walk, and then stopping, slowly turned around.

He saw nothing as he scanned the surrounding scrub and looking back up the track could see no sign of anything.

Too wise in the way of the wild to ignore his instincts, Nicholas remained vigilant and undid the holding strap on his rifle and continued picking his way along the narrow track.

Cresting a small rise, he reigned in. Ahead in a depression, was a clearing about two hundred yards across with lush grass growing across it. To one side, was a small strip of orange coloured muddy water about thirty feet long and six to eight feet across, the banks of which were pockmarked with animal tracks.

Jigging Stitch forward, he rode to the edge and examined the tracks. Nearly all were of the kangaroo, but there were also quite a lot of dog prints, and strange three-toe prints which forked forward similar to the ostrich in Africa. Although he had yet to see any, Nicholas recalled being told of a large flightless bird common in Australia called an emu.

He again looked at the tracks, observing the distinctive prints of dog, some eight or so he estimated.

'I must be careful,' he said half out loud, wondering if the prints were all from the same species of the yellow-eyed animal he had encountered yesterday.

Awful quiet, he suddenly thought, his subconscious registering that there were no chattering of birds or any other of the myriad of sounds that normally would come to him. The hair prickled on the back of his neck.

Stitch suddenly whickered, his ears pricking forward. Nicholas looked up, and about sixty feet before him at the edge of the scrub, stood three of the dogs.

All were of similar colour, a light sandy coat and had erect sharp pointed ears. The dogs stood motionless, the occasional flick of one ear the only sign of movement.

Dogs and man remained frozen, examining each other.

What a beautiful animal these are, thought Nicholas as they stared each other down. The largest of the dogs cocked his head to one side slowly as if it had read his mind and seemed to telegraph that it was curious rather than a threat at this stage, although Nicholas had very slowly eased up his rifle, one finger on the hammers and the others ready to haul out the rifle.

The dogs had a wide deep chest with a white tuft of fur at the centre and a long-bushed tail, which curled up slightly.

The head was handsome with wide spaced yellowish eyes. They were not unlike the wolves Nicholas had encountered in North America, though definitely smaller and had their own beautiful sandy coloured coat. Then he remembered seeing similar looking domestic animals in parts of Asia and China when he had passed through the area on his travels, though they were not as big or handsome as these dogs.

Stitch suddenly snorted, danced his head and pawed at the ground. The dogs wheeled and vanished into the scrub. Nicholas reached down and patted Stitch's neck. 'Easy boy, easy,' he said soothingly.

Nicholas clucked his horse forward and trotted across the flat, picking up the faint track, which began to swing further east and away toward the ranges. He looked at them, now tinted with an orange hue from the rising Sun, and he could just make out the jagged bluff on the northern end and what appeared to be a hint of ravines slashing across the western side of the ranges.

Reaching into his pocket, Nicholas fingered the galena specimen. An uncontrollable urge to gallop toward the ranges fell upon him, but he knew that would be courting disaster, as few provisions and unfamiliar land were not a good cocktail for exploration.

He made good time now and the country had thinned out considerably making easy riding.

Nicholas was in awe at the variety of flowers growing wild across the low scrub and even amongst the thickets.

Strange mauve coloured flowers adorned shrubs around three feet high, the flowers, almost like an inverted trumpet, while others with blooms of orange, yellow and deep red were prolific. Small groves of low trees or bushes had bright red or orange blooms that were elongated with multiple stamens like petals, around which wild bees buzzed busily and small birds, with black and white plumage, slashed with yellow sides, hung sipping the sweet nectar.

Yellow, white and brilliant pink daisies carpeted the low rolling hills and plains, rustling in the gentle breeze, their faces turned to harness the mid-morning Sun.

Reigning in as they topped a low ridge, Nicholas looked around. As far as he could see, to the north-east to the foothills and west, the land was carpeted in colour, which rippled like wavelets upon a lake. My God he thought in appreciation and drew in the sweet scent of the wildflowers.

He had scarcely seen a more beautiful site and was moved to wish Victoria were by his side, sharing this magnificent artwork of mother nature, but the all too familiar feeling of deep regret and loss hung heavy upon him as her face danced before his eyes.

He was not to know that this beautiful site would transcend into the most hostile of lands come the summer months and become infinitely harsher the further one travelled inland.

Nicholas was about to nudge Stitch forward and cross the shallow sand-roiled river in front of him when he saw something move on the horizon. Reaching into his saddlebag he threw the glass up and focused, drawing the telescope barrel in and out.

A group of Blacks, about ten or so, were moving slowly single file to his left. Suddenly they vanished from his sight. 'Must have gone into a gully' Nicholas thought out loud.

He was about to lower the glass when a small black figure suddenly sprang into view and ran quickly to his right. Seconds later, a second figure, much taller, rapidly overtook the small figure. As he watched the larger of the two appeared to be shaking or hitting the other, but it was too far away to be certain.

The two moved back to the left and again vanished from sight.

Nicholas closed the telescope and sat chewing his lip, should he go and investigate? It was, after all, none of his affair. He decided that he would carry on and cross the brown sand rills of the river, which was slightly to the right of where the party had disappeared.

Kicking with his heels, his horse moved forward, he crossed the river, and had travelled almost a mile when he suddenly reigned in. What if the smaller figure was in trouble? he thought. So far the Blacks had been friendly so the chance of trouble from them seemed a little unlikely.

'Damn!' he said out loud, 'I can't just leave things alone can I,' and he turned toward the left, kicking Stitch into a canter.

As he drew closer to the spot where he thought the two Blacks had vanished from sight, Nicholas could see a deep gully running east to west. The growth in the gully was quite dense in patches and paper bark and gum trees grew amongst a variety of shrubs banked up along the sides and along its length.

Nicholas reigned in his horse and slid the long rifle from its leather scabbard and checked the load.

He sat stock still, slowly scanning the bottom of the gully for sign of the party of Blacks. He was about twenty or so feet back from the edge so he would not be not fully exposed.

There was no sign of them, and figuring they must be further up the gully, Nicholas squeezed his knees, Stitch moved forward and slowly made his way along the edge.

He was on the point of wheeling about and checking the opposite direction when he heard muffled voices coming from further up the gully. As he drew closer, a high-pitched shriek pierced the air, birds scattered from the trees and shrub at the sound and Nicholas reigned to a halt.

He dismounted quietly, dropping the reins to the ground and running his hand down Stitch's muzzle. Then, taking his scarf from the saddle bag, he wrapped it around the hammers of his rifle to muffle the sharp click as he cocked both barrels, he began to slowly make his way along the bank toward the sounds.

As he drew closer he could hear a man talking rapidly in short bursts, his voice raised to almost a shout, and a younger voice, perhaps a girl, whimpering and crying.

Nicholas froze as the sound of a heavy blow smacking flesh echoed up the gully followed by another sharp cry and wailing at an even higher pitch. He spotted a tall gum tree and made his way toward it, using its bulk as cover.

He peered through the gum leaves at the group now visible below him. He counted ten adult Blacks, six men and four women and a young girl. Nine of them sat cross-legged on the ground together, looking disinterestedly at the ground before them.

Some twenty to thirty feet further up the gully, another young girl, no more than ten to twelve years old, lay on her back, her upper torso twisted to the side, cringing from a tall naked black who stood before her. She was naked and blood trickled from her nose and lips, obviously from blows the man before her had inflicted, her skinny little arm raised up to try to ward off the next punch.

The man was thin though finely muscled and in prime condition. He sported an unruly mop of black curly hair and had a heavy black beard, he was completely naked save for a band of what appeared to be animal fur and feathers of some sort around his right bicep.

The naked man suddenly lunged forward and grasped the terrified girl's arm in his left hand and raised his right to deliver another blow. As he did so, Nicholas saw his erect member sticking out of his crotch.

Anger flared within Nicholas as he took in the scene, he stepped out of the cover and shouted, 'Hold!'

The tall man spun toward Nicholas, astonishment at the interruption and the shock of a foreign tongue momentarily rooting him to the spot, his hand still raised. The others still sat, gaping at this strange sight standing above them.

Nicholas had the rifle about half way to his shoulder, ready for the rapid movement he was sure would come any second. The tall naked Black was the first to move. He jerked the young girl toward him and leapt toward a shoulder of rock jutting from the left wall of the gully. Nicholas threw the rifle to his shoulder and aiming to the left of the man, squeezed the forward trigger.

Confined within the gully the heavy calibre rifle boomed louder than a close clap of thunder and a sizable chunk of rock burst into fragments a foot from the man's outstretched hand. With a cry, he let go of the girl and vanished around the rock.

Five of the group, three women and two males, now huddled shaking before him. The others had vanished to Nicholas's right. He glanced back up the gully but saw no sign of them.

The young girl lay whimpering on the sandy creek bed, her hands clasped hard over her ears and her bruised and battered little face pressed into the sand in sheer terror.

It was quite obvious to Nicholas that these people had either never seen a white man – or had never seen and heard a rifle discharge before. They were utterly terrified.

Nicholas swept his hand to his right and pointed up the gully. They understood immediately and bolted up the gully, the men gathering their spears and throwing sticks before Nicholas had time to stop them.

Nicholas made a double click with his tongue and a few seconds later Stitch trotted up behind him, and looping the reins over a branch, Nicholas warily made his way down to the still crying young girl.

He looked at the little naked body shuddering on the sand and anger rose within him again. Calming himself, he squatted down and gently reached out to touch her on the shoulder.

She recoiled as though his hand had burnt her. Terrified, she pedaled backward on the river sand then scrambled to her feet spraying sand everywhere. She leapt backwards, pressing her back into the rock face, her arm raised as if to ward off another blow.

He studied her as she stood before him. She had sand stuck to her face where the blood had trickled from her nose and to the trails of tears, which came down from two enormous brown eyes which stared at him as though he were some kind of ravenous demon. Her small pointy breasts, not yet fully developed, were also dusted with sand. She had a mop of untidy sandy coloured straight hair, which was sticking out at all angles, a dead leaf and small twigs caught up in it. Her hands were twisted together in front of her stomach in fear and she had the beginnings of hair between her legs. Nicholas, suddenly embarrassed by his scrutiny, softened his look.

In as gentle voice as he could, he held his hand before him, palm up, smiled at her and said, 'It's all right, don't be afraid, I won't hurt you.' She immediately began to cry again, this time the tears just flowed down her cheeks washing some of the sand away with them.

Nicholas slowly reached into his jacket pocket and drawing his scarf out, he slowly took a step toward her.

The poor child whimpered again and pressed back harder into the rock. He held out the scarf toward her indicating that she should wipe her face with it. She stared at the outstretched hand and suddenly snatched the scarf from his grasp and immediately held it over her loins.

Nicholas, choking back laughter, again smiled at her. She just stared at him, still terrified of this ghostly man before her, but for a split second a twitch of a smile creased one corner of her mouth.

Ah! Nicholas thought, breakthrough!

Now he had a dilemma: she obviously could not stay here alone, and somehow he had to gain some measure of trust. With what the poor lass had just been through, this was not going to be easy.

He stepped away from the girl and held out his hand. She stared at him, her eyes flicked to his hand and back to his face.

'Come on, it's all right,' he said and took another step away toward the bank of the creek.

Her eyes immediately darted around the scrub and she turned, peering around the rocky outcrop, no doubt even more terrified that the tall Black might return.

Nicholas now moved to the bank and made his way up to Stitch, who was standing, ears pricked staring at the creek beyond the rocks. He whickered nervously at Nicholas's approach.

Nicholas turned to check on the girl, she still stood where he had left her, tears again rolling down her cheeks. He extended his hand toward her, still she did not move.

A flock of grey cockatoos with brilliant pink plumage on their breasts suddenly swooped into the creek and settled in one of the gum trees on the far side, only to immediately scatter with loud screeching and clattering of wings.

The girl suddenly sprinted across the sandy creek and up the bank to the gum tree beside Nicholas, who had, with a blur of his hands reloaded his rifle and was scanning the far bank with intensity.

He could see nothing, and that worried him. I must get out in the open and away from the cover around the creek, thought Nicholas. He wheeled, snatched up the reins and sprang into the saddle, startling the girl.

'Come, quickly now,' he said holding out his hand. She stared up at him, still very afraid of him and no doubt of the horse. She quickly peered around the gum tree and raised her hand, biting on her knuckles, before again swinging around and staring up at him, her angst and indecision obvious. Poor little devil, Nicholas thought. 'Come on, I shan't hurt you, give me your hand,' he said gently, at the same time trying to keep the urgency from his voice. He held out his hand, beckoning with his fingers. She glanced around once more and slowly held out her hand.

Grasping her hand Nicholas lifted her up behind him. She wailed and was obviously terrified, whimpering and shaking like a leaf in wind.

The tall bearded Black appeared as if by magic, standing on the other side of the creek. He was now armed with spears and a throwing stick.

Nicholas wheeled Stitch around, lifting his rifle, cocking both hammers at the same time, the barrels now aimed unwavering at the Black. The click, although muted was quite audible and Nicholas knew the man would have heard it, but he did not even flinch, and quite possibly did not fully comprehend what it meant. They stared at each other across the thirty odd feet that separated them. Nicholas felt the girl's head scrape around to his left side, no doubt to see what had caused him to freeze. She physically jumped and began to shake violently.

The tall Black's chest was crisscrossed with many scars Nicholas could see, he was still naked and as they stared at each other the man slowly raised his right hand, pointing at Nicholas and the girl, two fingers tapping at the air, the threat obvious. He suddenly grinned, a flash of white in the dark face and vanished into the scrub.

Nicholas jerked the reins and wheeling, kicked his horse into a canter away from the creek. Apprehension gripped him taking a risk on turning his back on danger, but he instinctively knew to look back would be interpreted as weakness.

Three hundred or so yards from the growth by the creek Nicholas slowed Stitch and wheeled about.

He uncocked the rifle and slid it into its scabbard, then drew his telescope and glassed the area along the creek, seeing no sign of the Blacks.

He noticed the girl had stopped shaking and he now swung down from the horse. He reached up and lifted her down to the ground by the waist. Turning back, he undid the strap and buckle holding his water bottle and took a good pull from it. Eyeing the girl, he offered her the bottle. She simply stared at him not comprehending what he was offering. Nicholas tipped a little water into his hand and again offered the flask. The girl suddenly snatched the bottle from his hand and tipped it up to her face. Water splashed all over her cute little face and cascaded down her front, carving a dusty trail between her little breasts. She coughed and sneezed as the cool water ran up her bloodied nose and gushed down her open mouth.

Suddenly Nicholas said, 'Ah, hah!' and started to chuckle at the sight. She lowered the bottle, staring at him. An enormous grin lit up her face and she covered her mouth with one hand and started to giggle, her big brown eyes dancing with light and amusement, the tension of the trauma in the creek dissolving somewhat.

Small swarms of flies were beginning to attach themselves to the blood on her face, she made no attempt to shoo them away. Nicholas rummaged around in his saddlebags and found another piece of linen. Tipping some water onto the cloth he reached out and gently began to wipe away the blood from her face. This time he was allowed to touch her, some small gain of trust he mused – good!

Where to now, Nicholas pondered. As he looked at her, he pointed both hands to his chest and said, *'Yuin.'*

She stared at him, a blank look on her face. He repeated his actions. Still the brown eyes stared back at him.

Suddenly she grinned and said, 'Uin', and then imitating his actions said, *'Nimit'je'*, rolling the words together rapidly.

Nicholas grinned back and nodding said, 'Where are you from, I mean which direction,' sweeping his hand out in a semi-circular motion and pointing to her, then again the sweep.

She again stared at him, a small frown creasing her face. Suddenly, she spoke rapidly and pointed in a roughly south-westerly direction toward the coast.

'Ah!' exclaimed Nicholas. I wonder if she was taken from the people at the river, he pondered.

He took the bottle from her and secured it, then rummaging around in his saddlebags found a piece of dried biscuit and handed it to her, biting off a small piece before doing so. She took the biscuit but did not attempt to eat it. Mounting, he reached down to her and held out his hand. 'Come on then.' She looked at the horse and then back at Nicholas, then glanced back toward the creek. This must have frightened her for she began to shake again and then slowly held out her hand.

Nicholas easily lifted the skinny little waif up behind him and she clung to him as though he would vanish, still shaking like a leaf and starting to whimper in fear again. He spurred Stitch away toward the river.

As the miles fell away, Nicholas eased Stitch into an easy trot, he sensed the girl's tension begin to abate and she seemed to be getting over her terror of the horse. The little hands, which in the beginning were dug into his waist like talons, had now slipped down to his broad belt and he twisted in the saddle to check on the girl. A beaming little face greeted him, white teeth flashing on the dark skin. Nicholas smiled back.

Sometime later he felt her hands come around him again and the girl's head bumped into his back and stayed there. Asleep, thought Nicholas, well, that will do her good!

The plain began to gently slope toward a dark line of trees some miles ahead and a flash of water winked through the growth.

Glancing at the sun, Nicholas judged it to be about mid-afternoon. If I can find a place to cross quickly, I may be able to reach the camp by sundown, he thought.

Three kangaroos suddenly burst from a small grove of trees and bounded away to their left. 'Magnificent!' said Nicholas under his breath. They stopped about two hundred feet away and stood like sentinels, staring at them as they passed, their erect ears twitching in curiosity and fur rippling in the gentle breeze.

Away to the right a small rise ran toward the river and Nicholas swung toward this, thinking that if it ran to the river's edge he may be able to look down on the water and see a way across.

Stopping, Nicholas drew his rifle and cocked both hammers, not willing to take any risks.

Nimit'je, woken by the halt and the click of the hammers, began to tremble at the sight of the rifle. 'Shoosh, shoosh, it's all right little one, just being careful,' said Nicholas, reaching around and gently patting her on the shoulder.

He eased Stitch forward. Ahead, the ridge jutted out about a yard over the river, which lay supine in the afternoon sun some fifteen feet below.

Across the river, some fifty feet away, multi-coloured bands of limestone and what looked like iron, lay horizontal along the opposite bank, the strips of which forming a low ledge that gently curved away to their right. The banded ledge looked for all the world like laminations placed there on purpose, thought Nicholas. Not for the first time since he landed here, he was amazed at the contrasts the land offered. The river was shallow and clear, affording an easy crossing. Looking down he could see shoals of small fish darting about their business in the shallow sandy ribbons and pools of water.

Stitch suddenly danced about tossing his head as the sound of a bull-roarer, quite loud, buzzed from somewhere downstream.

Before he could stop her, the girl slipped from the horse and disappeared over the edge of the ridge, she reappeared, sprinting and splashing across the river to the other side, and vanished into the scrub and trees.

Well, goodbye! thought Nicholas with a wry smile and warily scanned the whole area. He could see nothing out of the ordinary and decided to cross the river, yet something made him uneasy about crossing – he felt exposed and would be especially vulnerable mid-stream. He hesitated.

Nicholas turned in the saddle and looked back behind him, he saw nothing that disturbed him and yet there was something tugging at his instincts.

He turned back to the river and was shocked to see an elderly Black standing, staring at him from across the river. He had grey hair and a long flowing grey beard almost touching his chest. Around his head was a dull red band and was naked save for a skimpy loincloth of some description, which actually covered nothing really.

In his right hand he held a clutch of spears and throwing stick, in his left he held a curved piece of wood.

He stood, motionless, his eyes locked on Nicholas. He seemed to have appeared out of nowhere, for where he stood there was no cover and certainly he could not have gotten to the spot within the time Nicholas had turned in his saddle and back again. They remained motionless looking at one another.

The old man shifted slightly and pointed to his right with his spears at the shallow water then swung his spears in an arc to his extreme right, indicating to Nicholas to cross.

Nicholas did not move for some minutes, digesting what this meant. Was he being tricked? Or welcomed, he thought. Reasoning that he likely would have been attacked already if there was a threat, he relaxed a little.

Looking down at the water he decided to cross and glancing up again was astonished again to find the old man had vanished. 'My God, these people are as good at vanishing as the Bushmen back in Africa,' he muttered. He tugged on the reigns and Stitch moved forward.

Chapter 14

The Nhanda People

Nicholas wheeled about and trotted back to the narrow path leading down to the water's edge on his right. The water slid lazily across in front of him as he tentatively nudged his horse into the river, his nerves taut and his senses screaming as he reached mid-stream. As the water rose to Stitch's withers, Nicholas was fully aware that this was where he was most vulnerable, and his eyes darted everywhere. His rifle, although already cocked, somehow felt to be just out of reach if an attack came. All looked normal. He reminded himself of his earlier assessment and he jigged Stitch forward and urged him up the opposite bank. Cresting the bank, he cantered forward and wheeled about almost on the spot but saw nothing out of the ordinary.

The scrub was relatively low as they cantered out of the trees and bushes lining the river bank and he allowed himself to relax a little, and his heart rate began to slow.

There was no sign of the elder – or anyone else for that matter. Nicholas scanned the ground where the old man had stood but saw no spoor at all. He jigged his horse forward and to his left, riding parallel with the river about 200 feet from the bank and headed downstream.

He had travelled about a mile when ahead in the distance he spied a grove of white trunked river gums. He instinctively moved toward the largest tree, magnificent in its sentinel duty. As he drew closer he observed that there was a dip in the terrain just behind the tree which sloped toward the river and then saw smoke drifting up behind.

Tension clutched at his chest like a vice as he suddenly saw that he was too close. Cursing his stupidity, he was about to spur away when suddenly he saw the young girl step clear of the great tree trunk. Nicholas froze and all of a sudden, there were about twenty or so of the Aboriginal people standing with her. All were looking at him with intent.

Nicholas was on a razor's edge of alertness when suddenly he saw that not one of the people carried arms of any description and his horse displayed no sign of unease.

The young girl stepped forward and was joined immediately by the old man, and together they beckoned him to come forward. Nicholas nudged his horse's flanks and slowly approached the group. Stitch whickered softly, and knowing the sound to mean no threat, Nicholas relaxed slightly.

As he joined the group, Nimit'je stepped forward and held onto his leg, no longer afraid of him or the horse. Her little head was held up proudly as she put her new-found courage on display to all of the others, old and young. She tugged at his leg and held her hand out to Nicholas, who reaching down, swung her up behind him. There was a collective gasp from the group and then they all began to chatter at once.

The gathering parted to let them through. Nicholas swung down from the saddle and lifted the young girl down, the people shrunk back as he led Stitch to the tree, little Nimit'je stepping proudly out in front of them. Some of the women whimpered a little in fear as he tied the reigns to a dead branch jutting from the tree and lifted his rifle from its scabbard.

Clipped and rapid murmuring rippled through the little group. Nichols looked back at them. He saw women of varying ages, all naked except for some who wore a small loin cloth covering their genitalia, as did the men folk. He saw five completely naked little children peeping around their mothers' legs, and many more little ones peeping at him.

The old man suddenly started to make a series of hand movements along with some rapid-fire words and several of the women immediately went to the fire and piled on some more timber. The people began to relax somewhat and approached him, tentatively at first, then bolder, touching him and gently tugging at his clothes and hair. Some of the bolder ones stood around Stitch and touched the saddle and cautiously touched his flanks. Stitch snorted loudly and jigged his head up and down and they scattered immediately, screaming and laughing at each other and prompting a burst of mirth from Nicholas.

The old man bade Nicholas to sit on a large fallen tree a little distance from the fire, he came to the conclusion, that Nimit'je must have told of his interference of her abduction and how he had rescued her.

The old man lifted his arm and pointed toward where Nicholas had rescued the girl and said, '*Wur'a, Watjari*,' and stroked his beard Then pointing again toward the area and shaking his head vigorously and scowling added, 'Mmmmm'. Nicholas understood he was saying they knew the man and he was no good. He nodded and said, 'Yes, yes.'

Suddenly four more men entered the camp and these were armed with spears and the strange curved wooden weapons. Nicholas slowly moved his rifle onto his lap, thumb ready on the hammer of the left barrel.

They stood together side by side standing on the other side of the fire. To a man they were as lean as greyhounds and exuded a proud bearing. Their chests were crisscrossed with great purple scars as were their upper arms. Around their right arms they wore a tightly bound band of what appeared to be the fur of the strange kangaroo animal that Nicholas had seen, but this fur was of a deep chocolate colour.

Behind them the sky was now shot with a deep blue and orange giving a magnificent backdrop to the four.

The man on the left was slightly taller than the others and he emitted an aura of authority, his chest was a network of scarring which far surpassed those of his companions. The man continued to stare unsmiling at Nicholas until Nimit'je suddenly began to chatter, so fast that Nicholas was amazed that anybody could possibly understand what she was saying. When she abruptly finished, the warrior swiveled his eyes away from Nicholas's face and looked down at the girl. Immediately Nicholas sensed a connection between the two, possibly her father. The man's face softened for a split second, she started to speak again but fell silent at the slight lift of his hand. At the flick of his right hand Nimit'je stepped back behind the old man, he then signaled with his right hand again, this time with two fingers curled.

Five women suddenly stepped out of the dusk, each bore a load of some description. Two of them had a small slain kangaroo on their heads, which they slung down before the fire. The others had several wild ducks and three very large lizards about three to four feet in length. These were brown and yellow speckled, and as they were placed by the kangaroo, Nicholas could see their long blue forked tongues hanging from their mouths. There were also curved shells of tree bark intricately carved with patterns resembling the ripples seen sometimes in clear water and punctuated with circles and wavy lines. These were filled with strange red berries about one and a half inches in diameter and some long tubers of sorts. Lastly, in a smaller bowl was a pile of fat white grubs about three inches long and a half an inch in diameter.

When the fire died down a little, the kangaroo was laid directly onto the coals to cook, and the ducks were also laid over the coals and turned until the feathers had all been burnt off, they were then scraped and one of the women produced a wooden bowl made from a type of tree trunk stub and was filled with some sort of clay. She began to coat the duck with the clay and then gently laid the duck down next to the coals until the clay hardened. This took about 20 minutes by Nicholas's reckoning. Once dry, a hollow was made with a stick in the coals and the molds were placed into this and buried under the coals.

Next, the large lizards were also placed directly on the coals and were turned a few times before being left to roast.

Nicholas watched in trepidation as the fat white grubs were lightly toasted over the coals on sticks, and suddenly all eyes were on him as one of the women offered him one. There was no way he could refuse, lest he offend, so he gingerly bit down on the grub. To his amazement it wasn't that unpleasant – it had a nutty flavour and was quite palatable. The people grinned and murmured amongst themselves as he boldly took a second offering of the white grub.

The duck molds were taken out next and Nicholas was served first. All watched for his approval. It was delicious and the whole gathering again grinned as one as Nicholas made gestures of approval. Next up was the large lizard. This held no real surprise for Nicholas as he had often eaten other types in Africa and it did not taste all that much different, a sort of nutty flavour, like a cross between chicken and fish.

The long tuberous roots were dug up from under the soil beneath the coals, brushed off with a small branch and placed on one of the hardened bark bowls. Two were set before him.

They were obviously very hot so Nicholas drew his belt knife and stuck one of them and blew on before trying it. It was a very similar taste to those he had tasted in some parts of Africa, very tasty.

Next came the kangaroo. An old woman pulled a large piece off and gave it him, saying '*karluwirri!*' as she pointed at the dark red meat. Again, using his knife, he carved off a piece. It was fairly tough but tasty, even though some parts were not well cooked.

Nicholas grinned and said, with his mouth full 'Gooda!' The group twittered and nodded their heads and smiled. He looked up at the girl's father, noting he was staring hard at Nicholas's hunting knife. 'Hmmm' thought Nicholas, an idea forming in his head.

The people just tore at the meat with their teeth and ate until there was nothing left. Nicholas himself ate quite a large portion of the karlu-wirri and found it extremely filling with little or no fat. Little did he know that it was extremely high in protein, and the next day his bowels would let him know just that.

The chanting and sounds from the "instruments" went on for several hours and Nicholas felt himself drifting as the monotone sounds vibrated the very air around him.

Small wooden bowls carved out into an elongated cup shape were produced. In each of the bowls was a different coloured powder, perhaps of stone or clay Nicholas thought, his mind slipping back to some North American and African tribes he had encountered. The women sat and added water and spat saliva into the bowls, mixing and stirring the powder into a thick paste. One by one they went to the other folk and began to paint all manner of patterns onto the faces and bodies of the group. The patterns most likely had some tribal significance Nicholas reasoned, but he had no idea what. The colours were red, yellow, ochre, white and light browns. Wavy lines, stripes, circles and dots were painted onto the legs, chest and arms as the women moved from person to person before painting themselves.

Many of the group then started to bang short sticks together in a regular rhythm and began a rapid type of singing which rose and fell over a constant range. Periodically one of the men's voices would rise in crescendo over the others, then fall back in rhythm with the others.

One of the men produced a long wooden tube about four feet long and two and a half inches in diameter. This was inscribed with many intricate patterns, and appeared to have one end darkened by something, although it was slightly bulbous and looked a little like it had been stuck on there as a type of gum, thought Nicholas.

The man sat down with the left leg tucked under him and the other extended out straight in front of him. One end of the tube was placed between the big toe and the next, while the smooth bulbous end was held to the man's mouth.

As Nicholas watched, he drew a deep breath and his cheek seemed to suddenly balloon out and Nicholas was amazed to hear a deep resonating sound issue forth. The sound seemed to vibrate the very bones in Nicholas's chest as the chanting and banging of the sticks blended into rhythm. The player would regularly change the sound with sharp punctuations, like a 'yow!' sound, blended into the constant monotone buzzing noise.

Several of the men were now dancing, the ornate patterns on their shiny black skin standing out in stark contrast in the firelight.

It was a surreal site, articulate and with purpose. Nicholas observed that the dances portrayed hunting and imitations of game, and all the while the people kept on tapping the sticks together. Each time the hollow tube changed note, so too the dancers made quick and definite movements. Dust rose from stamping bare feet and hung in the air about the fire, making the whole scene seem even more surreal. Eventually, Nicholas could not help himself and startled himself several times as his head began to hang down, heavy with fatigue. Try as he might to stay awake he fell into a deep sleep.

He awoke to the laughter of children playing nearby and the ever present little bush flies crawling over his face. Swatting at the flies he sat up and as he got his bearings, discovering that someone had covered him with his swag cover and placed a pillow of rolled up paper bark under his head.

The sun had painted the land a pale orange as it struggled to break the horizon. Tree and shrub alike looked to be an olive khaki colour in the pre-dawn light and there was a cool scent in the air.

A moment of panic hit him as he suddenly remembered his rifle, which late last night had sat across his lap, if for nothing else but self-assurance. He need not have worried, glancing around he discovered it laying on strips of paper bark next to him.

He roused himself and walked to the river's edge. Stripping off his shirt, he waded into the water to begin to wash. Laughter and shrieking giggles echoed about him. He turned and found about a dozen picanninies, naked, their skinny little bodies glistening with water droplets, pointing at him in amusement. As he turned, they, like the flock of little parakeets raced away over the bank out of sight. Nicholas laughed, thinking they must be laughing at his brown arms and white skin. He was possibly right, but then perhaps it was his wading in with his breeches that may have caused the amusement.

Not long after, Nicholas packed up his gear and made indications that he would be leaving.

The whole tribe gathered as he made to swing up in the saddle. Just as he put his weight on the stirrup, Nimit'je tugged at his shirt. He stopped and looked at her. The little girl handed him a necklace. It was made of gum nut tops, greens, oranges and reds, simple but beautiful.

Nicholas swept off his hat and bowed deeply to her, accepting the gift in silence and taking the gift tied it around his neck. He was deeply moved, but the best gift was the magnificent smiles the whole gathering gave.

The tall warrior came and stood beside Nimit'je, the same man Nicholas had earlier surmised to be her father and started to talk in rapid-fire bursts. Nicholas was completely confounded, so fast was his talk. Two more men suddenly came and stood beside Nimit'je's father. He said somewhat more slowly, pointing first at his chest and said *'Mumardie!'* then he put his arm around Nimit'je and said *'T"Thalbyina!'* and repeated it. Nicholas understood he was saying they were father and daughter. Nicholas nodded and tried to repeat the language. Laughing, the father said 'Gooda!'

Then, pointing to one of the young men he said 'Gnarlu,' and then to another said 'Yindu.' Nicholas repeated, *'Narlew* and *Yindu?'* Nodding vigorously, Nimit'je went and stood by Gnarlu and Yindu and the father said *'coodah'* and pointing to Gnarlu and then to Nimit'ji said *'thoodo'* before again pointing to his chest saying *'Mumardie!'*

'Ah, gooda!' said Nicholas, nodding that he understood. Father, brothers and sister!

An older woman stepped forward and shyly looked at Nicholas. Mumardie laid his hand on the woman's shoulder and said, *'Nungerdie!'* pointing to Gnarlu, Yindu and Nimit'je.

Then the father said, struggling, mumbled, then, pointing at Nicholas, *coodah* and swept his hand around all of them. 'Gooda!'

Nicholas gleaned that he was regarded as part of their family – *coodah,* he now realised, might mean "brother", a huge honour he was to discover later.

Mumardie then said, pointing to Yindu and Gnarlu, 'Gnarlu, Yindu, *coodah* – you!' as he swept his hand toward the coast.

Ah, so he had an escort thought Nicholas, very good! He did not register at that time that the two were to accompany him everywhere for as long as he wished.

Nicholas undid his belt and pulled his hunting knife off the belt. It was a Stanley Rogers, boasted an eight-inch razor sharp blade and had a well tooled leather sheath. The knife was one of four Nicholas had brought with him and was hollow ground and of good Sheffield steel. He handed it to Mumardie with both hands.

A collective gasp went around the gathering as Mumardie accepted the gift and drew the knife. The blade flashed in the morning Sun and he held the gift up for all to see, his pride and glee evident.

It was time to say farewell. Nicholas mounted and nudged Stitch's flanks, and as he trotted away up the bank he turned around for one last look. The only person to be seen was little Nimit'je, waving to him. He broke Stitch into a canter and rode up the bank. Not ten minutes had passed when he suddenly reigned in, in shock.

There, before him, stood the old man. At first he uttered not a sound but then smiled and pointing to his chest said 'Kalbarri'. Nicholas caught on and imitating the old fellow and pointing to his own chest, said slowly 'Ni-chol-as'. The elder repeated the name pronouncing the word slowly 'Nee-co-las'. Nicholas nodded his head. 'Very good!' and then said 'Kalbarri.' The old man laughed and said 'gooda.' There it was again, thought Nicholas, they must have been in touch with white folk some-where near he considered.

Then he remembered that he had been told that graziers called the Gregory Brothers were also prospecting further up river and may have had some interaction with these Nhanda people. Then he looked up as the old man pointed toward the west-southwest. Nicholas reckoned this would be the direction of their camp. He turned to give his thanks but the old man had vanished just as Gnarlu and Yindu trotted up beside him.

How in hell? Nicholas thought. It was impossible, but the old man had gone.

Nicholas saluted, shaking his head and grinning. He cantered away, still stunned at the old man's magic.

Chapter 15

The Wahehe, Maasai and the Amendsons

*V*ictoria was in despair. She could not come to terms with her own stupidity and taking Nicholas for granted.

It had now been a week since he had departed, and the ringing sensation and weight of what had happened had now formed into a heavy lump she carried around inside her which ached and pulsated like a living thing of its own, but never seemed to wane.

Two days ago, Victoria had run her horse hard to the kopje where Nicholas had rescued her from the lion. Nervously she had searched for signs of the remains of the big cats but found nothing, nor was there any sign of recent lion around the kopje. She knew hyenas would have eaten almost every last scrap, and what remained would have been dragged into the long grass by other smaller scavengers.

She had sat with her back to the tree and recalled the day's events, though mostly she dwelt on the overwhelming feeling that had swept her and Nicholas into the incurable and mystifying vortex of love.

As she sat by the dead tree, remembering, the sorrow came upon her like a wave, crashing in on her – she felt as if someone or thing had reached in and was squeezing her heart. The tears rolled down her cheeks and she never felt so devastated in her entire life. She let go and sobbed uncontrollably. In the end she could cry no more and finally rose to her feet and walked disconsolately around the kopje, remembering his touch, scent and tenderness. She resolved that she must at least try to find him, if for nothing else to let him know that she had made a stupid and imma-ture error in judgement and she loved him very dearly.

She mounted her horse and cantered back to the edge of Lake Nyanza and after scanning the area for crocodile, she watered her horse briefly and continued on home, pausing only at the spot where Nicholas had inadvertently revealed another side of his personality, a side she now knew was solely a reaction to protect her. She also knew that he was in fact mak-ing a statement – that he would do anything to protect her. She became angry with herself again for not recognising this in the first place.

Victoria made her mind up, she would organise herself and leave for the distant ranges to the east in search of Nicholas the very next day if she could and would leave without discussing this with anyone. She knew also how vehemently her mother and father would oppose her going. A young and attractive woman travelling alone in the area was at great risk – and she knew it. But her love and resolve burned within her with a ferocity that she could no longer contain.

As soon as she stripped her horse and had given Joseph the task of rubbing the mare down, she began to plan her trip, making a check list, gathering the things she would need and hiding her stores in the stables. One by one she took her supplies and necessities down to the stables when she thought she wasn't being observed and hid most items in the bottom of the chaff bin.

She cursed under her breath when Joseph would engage her in seem-ingly meaningless conversation about the weather and tales of the past, but she was careful not to brush him off lest he would think something was amiss – the old man missed nothing and was as cunning as a fox she knew.

She had no way of knowing that she was already being watched, or that she was about to embark on a journey that would alter her life forever.

Joseph knew his beloved Victoria very well and he had been studying her closely without her even being aware of it.

Three days ago, he had casually mentioned that the skies were very clear, and from the top of the ridge behind the homestead you could see very clearly to the ranges. Victoria had feigned indifference, but only two hours had passed and he had smiled as he saw her heading up to the crest of the hill with her father's telescope slung around her shoulders.

Today, Victoria had casually walked her horse into the stable foreyard almost as if she was trying to avoid attracting attention. He immediately knew something was being planned, for almost without exception, she always cantered or fast trotted into the yard. One look at the different set on her face told him she was up to something.

He studied her face covertly and could feel the determination emanating from her.

Little telltale moods and differences over the past week had told him she would do something, and he knew she would not mooch around for too long as she preferred action when things were not to her liking. So, it was just a matter of waiting. It came to him that the obvious thing she would do was to try to find Massa Nicholas, and from then on he had almost anticipated her every move.

Now she was going to and from the house in a most erratic way, and always into the feed store.

Joseph chuckled to himself. 'What power is this of the heart, which makes the young ones forget all about his teachings of stealth of the hunt and disguise of intention!'

Massa Yuin had left suddenly without warning. This too was strange. As strange as the feeling he sensed and shared when Massa Yuin and Missy Victoria were together, especially when they looked at each other.

Now Missy Victoria was so unhappy he too was hurting and sad.

What was this feeling that was so powerful? He shook his head at the wonder of it all.

He sighed. Missy Victoria was just as strong in reality, perhaps more so, and he wondered if he would be able to stop her from leaving if she really decided to go before his plan had time to come into effect.

He immediately prepared to send one of the young Maasai men and the two Hehe men on a stores run, telling Bwana Amendson he needed to buy stores for the stable and horse shoes, molasses etc.

This was not really a lie because they did in fact need these items. Normally this trip occurred every three months. They would harness a two-horse team, and either he and Missy Victoria or Missy and her mother would head south to the nearest landing in Mori Bay and the little trading post or stock agent on the shores of the great lake, or head inland to Kirugu, which was further and Joseph knew Mistress Lillian did not like to go there.

The Mori Bay post was a seven-and-a-half-hour journey from the homestead, or about 58 miles, and they would usually time it for when the supply boat came in. He would send the boys in a bit earlier, especially if he had heard that the supply boat may be early.

The cunning old man thought, when he got the opportunity, he would casually mention the planned trip to Maisy, the head housemaid, who he knew wouldn't be able to help herself and would have to gossip about the trip. Mistress A'menson would be bound to hear about it and this would pave the way for his request to go. It was very likely she would decide to come along, as was normally the case, then stay overnight at the Van Der Hoeke's property on the way.

This absence of Mistress A'menson would perhaps give thought to Missy Victoria not to leave whilst she was gone, although he knew that once she made up her mind she would go, even if she may later regret it.

He also knew that the hated Hymie Van Der Hoeke would not give up in his quest to possess Missy Victoria, and so the planned early trip was no mere whim but a part of the old man's forethought and cunning.

Mistress A'menson knew she was safe with the young warriors, who always wore their full fighting regalia when on these trips, partly to warn off anyone who might be thinking of robbing the group and partly to advertise their presence as the dominant tribes in the area. No one or any of the minority tribes in the whole of the country right through to the Iringa Ranges would dare to show any aggression towards the group with the two Hehe and one or two Maasai warriors present, for they knew the reaction would be swift and fatal, if not from the young warriors, then certainly from the highly organised and ruthless regiments of the Maasai and more particularly the Wahehe. And the response would not be restricted just to themselves, but their whole village could possibly cease to exist.

There were still considerable differences between the two races driven mainly by demarcation. For years there had been disputes of territory. It was as well that the Maasai were more interested in livestock, whilst the Wahehe mostly farmed crops. On these trips, the warriors dressed up in their regalia as a show of force and national strength.

Many of the Maasai and Wahehe tribes people had also come to revere Lillian as the doctor's wife and for the many times she had helped their people in times of sickness and hardship. The same now applied to Missy Victoria who often accompanied her mother. All that remained for his planning was for Mistress Lillian to decide to go this time.

The old man reflected on the beginnings of the relationship between the Amendsons and the tribal people.

The Maasai were the first people the Amendsons had encountered when they were first establishing the property, and they still had some considerable presence in the area.

At first the Maasai were suspicious and wary of the new settlers, having seen the encroachment of their territory increasing, and not all of the newcomers had been tolerant or respectful.

As was their standard initial response and retaliation against the presence of the settlers, they had initially claimed some of Ludwig's herd as their own as a statement and protest about the establishment of the cattle ranch, and they regularly stole cows and goats.

The Maasai, although somewhat nomadic, following the seasonal feed for their cattle herds, actually originated in northern Kenya. Traditionally, they did not graze their cattle much further south of here, and only began to drift down this far over the past fifteen years or so. Nonetheless, they still believed that they had a right to graze here and this was their land. Cattle was, and always had been to the Maasai, currency, a symbol of wealth, pride and the sustenance of their very being. In fact, a Maasai man was not recognised as wealthy until he owned at least 50 beasts and had a large family and many sons.

Ludwig had sat in council with Joseph and discussed the pros and cons of striking a compromise with the Maasai elders and chiefs. Although Joseph was adamant that this was technically Wahehe land, and even though he would not have dared speak of this in front of the Maasai, he had admitted that there were no better cattlemen in the land. Joseph spoke enough of the official language of the Maasai – Maa – to be understood.

Ludwig had struck a deal with them, offering a gift of thirty head of his own cattle if the thieving would stop and also offering employment to the young Maasai men as cattle hands – actually, they looked after their own herds but willingly kept an eye on the Amendson herd as well.

The Maasai culture was as traditional as it was ancient and had a solid structure and belief.

The young men and boys began life tending cattle almost as soon as they could toddle, and thus formed a bond with their beasts and there-after looked after the herds. Most other activities involved playing war games and acting out other traditions. On reaching puberty, generally between 12 and 18 years old, they would attend the circumcision rites. This was a sacred affair in which the young men would have the foreskin of their penis removed using a ceremonial knife, called the *emorata*.

They were made to wear a black robe and were isolated from everyone for about three months before returning to their village and family. When they did, they would go through initiation, tests of manhood and become warriors. During initiation they were to make no sound or flinch, as to do so would shame the family and lower their status as a warrior.

Part of the process of gaining manhood was rumoured to include the killing of a lion armed with only a spear. This was not true. However, sometimes lion hunting *was* carried out by individuals. Those who suc-ceeded gained enormous respect and standing within the Maasai nation. The skin of the slain lion would be given to the parents of the young war-rior and passed down through the generations.

In certain seasons, large groups of the Maasai would come down to the property and hold ceremonies. The Maasai loved to dance and sing and would perform the 'Up and Down Dance' or Adumu. Forming a circle, warriors would periodically enter the circle, springing up into the air some three feet on the spot for long periods whilst the women sang and men chanted.

Many times, they were invited to join the tribal people and observe these traditions and ceremonies, the deep resonance and the singing of the women a moving and beautiful thing to hear and see.

These invitations were restricted to the seasonal ceremonies and the 'sending off" of the Maasai youth, for example, though there were many other sacred ceremonies which were strictly Maasai only. Nonetheless, the family and Victoria knew many of the people, and she had played with and grown up with the young ones.

The Wahehe on the other hand would travel back to their own terri-tory on the Iringa Plains for their celebrations and initiations, and some-times would not return for two months or more.

To keep an even balance and to be seen as fair, Ludwig mentioned it might be a good idea that some of the Wahehe come for a visit and have talks. He would also offer employment and a fair wage should they wish.

Ludwig had sent Joseph to find out if any of the Wahehe would wish to come to the property. Three months later Joseph had returned from his journey, some four hundred miles south to the Iringa Ranges where the Wahehe ruled.

He returned to say that he was not at all convinced that the offer was accepted and though not overly hostile to the offer, the king had been somewhat indifferent.

It was many years before the first Wahehe people appeared. Ludwig and Joseph were standing in front of the stables in discussion, when almost as if by magic two Hehe men appeared in the driveway alongside the house directly in front of them.

These were magnificent young warriors, bedecked in full battle rega-lia. They held the long spears, the blades of which were blackened lest the shiny metal would give their position away. In their other hand they held shields of cow and buffalo hide while the handles of war clubs protruded over their shoulders. On their wrists were protective amulets of tough cow hide. They wore headbands bedecked with ostrich plumes spread out either side in a fan and were attached to a woven hide skull cap.

After the initial shock of the surprise appearance, Joseph had launched into a long questioning tirade when one of the two had silenced him with a sweep of his spear. The warrior had then replied in rapid-fire Bhantu and abruptly stopped, pointing at his companion.

Joseph explained to Ludwig what was said and that they had just run some 25 miles and sought help.

Ludwig had immediately turned and fetched water from the barrels by the stable wall and had brought it to them.

While they drank, Ludwig looked at the young man. He had a bullet hole in the shoulder which was swollen and weeping pus and blood. Joseph told him the serious wound in his shoulder just below the collar bone had been apparently sustained in an encounter with some of the German colonials who were moving into the area further south near the Wahehe homelands of the Iringa Plains. Ludwig at once saw that if he was not treated he would most certainly die.

Suddenly, the wounded man fell to his knees, either from shear exhaustion, the wound or most likely both. They carried the man into the room under the veranda of the house where Ludwig had his medical table and medicines etc.

After an hour and a half of convincing argument by Joseph, they conceded to allow Ludwig to operate.

Ludwig had dug out a large lead slug from the wound; luckily the bullet had not hit any bone, however it was lodged close to the main artery. The young man had hardly even flinched as Ludwig, delicately as he could, probed for the slug. He simply stared at Ludwig as he went about his work, the only sign of pain was an occasional hiss through his teeth.

When Ludwig had finished and cleaned and stitched the wound, the fellow had taken the lead ball, examined it closely then had solemnly touched his forehead and dipped his head.

The two stayed for six days whilst the young man recovered. Then they suddenly vanished.

Some two months later another two arrived, this time in simple traditional dress but still carrying their weapons. They had come to work and learn, and had brought gifts of a magnificent leopard skin, a decorated cowhide war shield and two beautifully carved and razor-sharp hunting spears, the latter highly prized in Wahehe warrior code. Their lives were built around their strength and the spear which was the Wahehe symbol of power. This gift came from the young man who had been wounded. Ludwig was not to know, but the story of his medical prowess had been fanned previously by Joseph on his visit, while the young warrior he had operated on – as it turned out – was the eldest son of a chief and was of royal Wahehe lineage.

Two beautiful young girls of no more than about 14 years old accompanied the young warriors. Both girls, Wasangu captives, were tall and lithe. The Wasangu were the Wahehe's traditional foe in these parts and they were traditionally given to important men among the Wahehe. It was considered a great honor to be given these captive girls. It was explained that they were a special gift from the wounded young man's father who was a provincial chief of high standing who thought that Ludwig should have two more wives.

Ludwig was very embarrassed, for Lillian was by his side when the girls were presented to him. He did not know what to do or where to look as both were naked except for the traditional loin wrap and an adornment of bead work around their necks and arms. As was the way of most of the tribal peoples around East Africa, they had shaven heads, accentuating the young beauties' elegant long necks.

When he looked at Lillian she was poker faced, although inside she was highly amused at his discomfort and this made Ludwig even more uncomfortable – as she knew it would.

Joseph came to his rescue, and after what seemed to be an eternity had placated the warriors, who became very animated and could not understand Ludwig's confusion, taking his reaction as rejection of the gift. Joseph skillfully renegotiated and had come to an agreement that the girls, rather than be Ludwig's wives, could be his adopted daughters.

The warriors very pointedly explained that the girls were chosen for their beauty and breeding. 'What were to become of them as there would now be no children?' they said. More discussion and argument had ensued. Finally, it was accepted that, since the girls were now to be his daughters, it was to be Ludwig who would assess other suiters given that he was now to assume the father figure role, and as their father would liaise with the chief before finalising any arrangement for marriage. This arrangement opened the way for the wonderful gift to be accepted and for the girls to be courted, as well as bringing the young ladies under his protection.

In addition, the girls were to be taught English and attend lessons within the household. This, it was explained, would surely be beneficial to the Wahehe nation. All was agreed.

Joseph had immediately offered to marry both of the young girls as an alternative. Lillian had eyed the old man with some distain and said this would certainly not be acceptable, and since the girls were now part of the family they would now, as daughters, be under her watchful eye. Calling Maisie, she abruptly gathered up the young ladies and vanished into the house with them.

The two young warriors were quick to catch on and started to hoot in fits of laughter until a withering glance from Joseph silenced them, but even then were having trouble stopping their snickering.

Joseph was mystified; he would never allow himself to be so obsessed with the likes of any woman, especially wives or intended wives, he reflected. They were as plentiful as wild berries he mused, but it had been a long time since he had seen maidens as beautiful as these young women. Women and wives were there to do his bidding and look after him.

The white man was very strange – they seemed to place great store in being as one with their woman.

Did they not know, that this could never be? Man was man and woman was woman, and the man must always be strong, the defender and take the lead.

There was nothing wrong with having two or more wives as was his people's custom – it made a man feel wanted and important and was also a sign of his virility.

Mistress A'menson, for all her femininity, was a very strong-willed lady and even Joseph would disappear when she was annoyed. Many times, he wondered how this was so, and why the doctor allowed this and would also disappear when she was angry. And why did he not take the very beautiful ladies the Hehe had gifted him, he mused. He was stunned when the doctor took them as only his daughters even though it was he who had suggested it. He ruefully remembered the look on Mistress A'menson's and her husband's faces when she had obviously silently warned him. Again, he seemed to do her bidding without argument.

Thereafter, two or three of the young men came to the property every four or five months to learn and gain some education in the way of the white man.

They were disciplined and dedicated workers, when tasked, but not one day passed when they did not practice vigorous and intensive training exercises with their weapons, sometimes not working at all but vanishing into the countryside.

Joseph told of how fully armed Wahehe warriors could run 40 miles without one stop and go straight into battle. The disappearance of the young men was merely part of their training and discipline.

Each time they disappeared, they would return in the late afternoon in their magnificent battle dress, carrying full weaponry, and although shiny with sweat and having been running most of the day, would be hardly breathing heavily.

At first the Amendsons were very worried over the apparent tension between the Maasai and the Wahehe – both peoples were proud and magnificent in their own way, and equally skilled in battle tactics and endurance. However, the trouble never materialised and they seemed to develop some measure of respect for each other and of their different cultures.

Periodically, Ludwig and Lillian would invite the Maasai and the Wahehe to join them for a Sunday lunch. On such an occasion they would slaughter a heifer and roast the beast over a pit of coals. The day brought much excitement and on these occasions differences were forgotten and laughter would punctuate the afternoon.

The system worked well and the Amendsons, the Wahehe and the Maasai worked carefully around each other's differences.

The young men were almost ready to leave when Lillian swept down from the house and announced that she would be going along with the young men on the stores run to the stock and station agents, and Maisie would be down shortly with her small travel trunk and some provisions for the trip. She announced she intended to stop off at the Van Der Hoeke's on the way, a good four hours travel south in the buggy.

As soon as she had gone back to the house a slight look of satisfaction briefly crossed the old man's face and he cackled inwardly at his forethought. He knew they would arrive at the Van Der Hoeke's around or just after noon, Mistress Amendson would be invited to stay overnight at the Van Der Hoeke home and would not refuse.

The cunning old devil had previously hinted to her that he was very worried about Missy Victoria and the fact that he thought Hymie might still cause trouble for Missy Victoria, especially now that Massa Nicholas had suddenly left and word of his parting would soon make its way to the Van Der Hoeke's via the staff who could not help but gossip. At best he figured it would be but a week before word got to the Van Der Hoeke homestead.

He called the eldest of the young Hehe men over, giving him explicate instructions what he must do when they and mistress Amendson arrived at the Van Der Hoeke residence.

One way or another, Joseph knew he must accompany his Missy on her quest to find Massa Nicholas. If his thoughts about Hymie Van Der Hoeke were correct, she was in grave danger.

The young Hehe warrior was to carry a message ahead of the buggy on the pretext of scouting. This was not unusual so he knew Mistress Lillian would not be suspicious. The stock and station agent was a further 12 miles from the Van Der Hoeke's property. About 10 miles from the homestead and just outside the Van Der Hoeke's property line, there was a Wahehe bush boma which lay on the original tribal path from north to the south and the Iringa plains. Here, the Wahehe king always stationed a number of his warriors.

Joseph's request was for four warriors to shadow Victoria when she left on her journey and this was also additional insurance should it come to pass that he was not to accompany her.

Now he must make plans to stall Victoria's 'secret' plans to run off to the ranges until his young warriors returned from the stores run.

Chapter 16

The Obsession

*H*ymie Van Der Hoeke had become a withdrawn and bitter young man and would not even try to reconcile the issue of the search for Victoria and his embarrassing behaviour of that night. His father tried everything to snap his son out of his moods, yet Hymie steadfastly refused to discuss it.

Three weeks had passed, and his obsession with Victoria, rather than abate, steadily grew to the point of fanaticism. The dreams that in the beginning, and prior to the night of the search, had been of blissful marriage and never-ending love, had now turned wholly possessive and a total imposition of his desire and will.

Hymie dreamt of Victoria almost every night and during the day she was never far from his thoughts.

All of the rebuffs that Victoria had given him in the past – they had started with polite refusals but as he had persisted had become downright blunt to the point of rudeness – were erased from his memory by his burning desire to have her. Nightly, he would dream of making love to her. She would, at first, resist him and then become overwhelmed by his manliness, and unable to resist, they would make love for hours.

Over the past week, reason seemed to slip from his mind as he realised, by his own actions, he now had no control over the situation, and it occurred to him that he most likely never really had.

This realisation frustrated him to a point of utter fury.

He ignored the fact that Victoria had always politely kept him at arm's length. Sometimes he would reflect and come to the conclusion that Victoria had always been in love with that cursed scum Nicholas Yuin and had not been decent enough to tell him. He decided she was a tramp. Thus, his dreams began to be punctuated with this imagined betrayal.

Increasingly, he would be overcome with rage and awaken during the night, his fists clenched and twitching, murder in his heart.

Later he would be overcome with remorse, and his obsession – which he deluded himself as love – would overwhelm him.

In his mind, he and Victoria were one, and always had been since they had met for the first time – they had always been destined to marry.

In his now very real fantasy, she would realise that it was he, Hymie, who was the one she really loved, and after they were married, life would be wonderful and contented.

Then things would twist, as his feelings of betrayal, egged on by his humiliation, marched into his mind. He would be coming home from working the cattle, looking forward to his Victoria standing waiting as he rode up, but instead of a warm welcome he would be greeted with silence. Entering the house, he would hear muted sounds, and then crossing to their bedroom he would discover to his horror, Nicholas and Victoria naked and entwined in a passionate embrace.

In the beginning in these dreams and thoughts, he would always be the one who was hurt and down in spirit, running away to loneliness, to the point where things would get desperately low and then Victoria would be sorry, and finding him, beg his forgiveness, and he would eventually forgive her. Hymie wallowed in this pit of woe and self-pity for weeks.

Eventually as the weeks slipped by, he grew tired of being down and consumed with this line of thought and the dreams began to take on a disturbing twist.

Hymie started to dream of revenge, and with this he began to be consumed with extreme and violent thoughts. The uncontrollable rage that was, in reality, never really very far away with this young man, started to blend into both his thoughts and dreams, and the humiliation of that fateful night burned like a raging fire in his gut.

In the dreams he would fight with Yuin and pummel him into submission, with Victoria watching and screaming. Now infused with power and control, he would turn to her as the victor and see the terror as she grasped that she was now at his mercy. The feeling of his power over her swept over him like a large dose of laudanum.

In his subconscious, the violent dreams began to take on a startlingly real clarity and became bizarre and shocking to the extreme.

He began to make plans.

Merely a week had passed and Hymie, unable to stand his frustration any more, began to ride regularly to the low hills which formed a natural backdrop to the Armendson home. The boundary between his father's property and the Amendson's was only eleven miles to the north and there was an outstation they used for branding cattle and general property repair only two miles from the boundary. He regularly rode the northern boundary and went there to visit the Amendsons' hills. This way he could come in from the east undetected – or so he believed.

He would dismount below the horizon then make his way to where he could look down on the homestead and spend hours looking through the spy glass in the hope of catching a glimpse of her. When he did see her, he would become so aroused his desire would bring him to extreme excitement, which was becoming unbearably intense. Barely able to control himself, he found he would have to leave and then it was not long after when the cycle of fantasy would begin all over again.

One day whilst he was lying on the hills behind the Amendsons' homestead, he was about to retreat after he had seen Victoria walking around the stables, when his heart almost leapt into his mouth. He could hardly believe his eyes as Victoria suddenly emerged from the rear veranda and began to stride purposefully up toward him. He quickly scanned the rest of the buildings, she was alone.

Hymie's body thrummed like a drum and his excitement ramped up to fever pitch as he stared through the telescope at the flash of her black, calf-length riding boots and sway of her hips beneath the dark brown skirt she wore, his breath now coming in short draughts. He squirmed back so as not to be seen, and as she drew closer almost stopped breathing at the sight of the bounce of her breasts beneath the white cotton blouse, a low groan escaping his lips. She was bare headed and her golden hair was gathered back in a bouncing ponytail.

She was now about three hundred yards away and he quickly analysed the situation, scenarios bouncing around his head like ricocheting bullets, all with evil intent.

He quickly retreated and hid behind a large granite boulder, the top of which was almost level with the hill crest some thirty feet away.

He knew she would be about ten minute's walk away by now given the steep slope and decided that he would wait until she turned and was looking back over the homestead and the beautiful waters of the great lake. He, of course, had no idea that Victoria would be looking in the opposite direction.

He was trembling in anticipation, the ache in his groin almost unbearable, and fantasised about what he was going to do to her. First, he knew he would have to disable her somewhat by perhaps hitting her in the head because he instinctively knew Victoria would fight like a cornered leopard if he didn't demoralise her first. This thought of his power over her caused his discomfort to heighten and he had to adjust his breeches. His trap was set and he grinned to himself. At last, he thought.

His arousal was now almost at bursting point as he imagined tearing and ripping off her blouse. Her breasts would be perfect and shaking as she tried to fight him off, then he would drag up her skirt ripping off her pantaloons, and then…

Hymie snapped to attention as he heard his horse whinny. It was tied to a stout shrub a short distance away.

'Shit!' he muttered. In his excitement he had forgotten the animal. It would be in full view when she topped the rise and she would recognise the pinto immediately. Cursing, panic now gripped him, but he was reluctant to abandon his plans, and his thoughts raced as he looked around for some cover closer to the top but found nothing.

She must be only about a hundred yards away by now, he thought, and he sprinted up to the top, flattening just below the crest. His heart pounded as he saw her heading almost directly toward him, but a little to his left.

He quickly realised that if he were to try to grab her as she neared him, she would likely try to run back down the slope before he could stop her and may scream. The old warrior had senses and eyes like a civet and was bound to hear her. Despite his age, he, the Maasai or Hehe warriors would be on him in minutes. They're like her bloody guard dogs! he thought.

In an instant the fantasy evaporated and he sprinted back down to his horse. Tearing at the reigns, he leapt into the saddle and spurred his horse into a full gallop toward the little hollow which was dotted with low acacia and shrubs.

Once in the heavier scrub he slowed and carefully picked his way along the centre of the hollow, the scrub and thorn bushes now screening him from the hills. He began to analyse the close call.

He must be more careful. A pathetic, almost whining sound rose from him – she being so close to him and he had been undetected. It was hard to comprehend that he had been so stupid as to forget about the horse. He ground his teeth in frustration, hardening his resolve to have her by any means.

'Damn it!' he raged, 'she was so bladdy close!'

Victoria reached the crest of the hill just as he disappeared into the hollow.

On the next rise slightly to her left and above the hollow not 100 feet from where Hymie had lain in wait, two figures in full hunting camouflage raised their heads slightly, their spiked grass headdress indistinguishable in the long waving grass as they stared down at the retreating Hymie and his pinto. They slithered back after about five minutes and then maintained an easy trot as they returned to the homestead to report to Joseph.

Victoria arrived at the top of the hill breathing lightly and swung the telescope up, focusing immediately on the ranges, as she slid the scope in and out to focus, suddenly some movement in her peripheral vision to the left caught her eye. She scrutinised the area of tall scrub then swung the scope to get a better look.

Nothing, but her instincts were heightened. Probably a little Duiker or something she thought, although she was now feeling a little vulnerable remembering the lion, and she had not brought her rifle.

Victoria reached behind her and tugging up her blouse pulled the small pistol from her waist band.

The weapon was a .31 calibre six-shot Allen & Thurber pepperbox revolver with a four-inch barrel. She had taken the pistol from her father's gun cabinet. It was almost new, only one year old, and had only had about 20 rounds fired from it. 'Nice little weapon!' her father had extolled. 'But useless past 40 foot.' He had not touched it since, so Victoria had decided to 'borrow' it when she left for the ranges.

She weighed the pistol in her hand and felt better before tucking it into the front of her skirt and returning to the telescope.

The distant hills were coloured with a mix of soft browns, greens and a blue tinge, but were too far away to see any distinct detail no matter how much she tried to will it.

The ranges looked so far away. As she carefully scanned every inch, she felt an overwhelming feeling of sadness wash over her and tears well up in her eyes. 'Damn,' she berated herself. 'Get a hold of yourself and just get going.'

Victoria spun on her heel to go back and instinctively her hands flew to her face, her heart hammering in fright as she saw a figure standing directly in front of her not six feet away.

It took a few seconds for her to recognise the man who was grinning at her.

'Joseph!' she cried. 'What are you doing here? And how did you… oh never mind.' Her heart rate slowed with relief and she remembered the old man seemed to meld into the countryside like some sort of ghost whenever he wished to.

He just continued to grin at her, knowing he was still the master of stealth.

'I just checking you safe Missy Victoria,' he said leaning on his short stabbing spear, his eyes glancing down at the pistol in her belt. 'Did you see what you wish for?' he asked with mischief dancing on his face and noticing the moisture in her eyes.

'Have your finished your chores yet Joseph?' she snapped, immediately regretting her tone and seeing the grin vanish from his face as he dropped his eyes. 'Oh, Baba Joe I am so sorry, I just don't know what to do, I made a terrible mistake, why was I so stupid,' she cried, the tears welling up in her eyes once again and running down her cheeks as she sat abruptly down on the dry grass.

Joseph looked down at his Missy Victoria with enormous warmth and sympathy in his eyes. She looked so miserable and lost and his old heart ached for her.

Joseph reached out and took the pistol from her waist band and slipped it into the small shoulder pouch he always wore, and then gently took her hand and led her back down to the house.

Halfway down he chanced a look at her face and saw the silent tears still rolling down her cheeks. 'You must be patient my little missy, all will come soon enough,' he said.

He steadfastly kept the lead in case she saw his own tears, feeling her pain as keenly as if it had been his own.

Much later, Victoria lay on her bed musing about her plans. She was now confused, she had a clenching feeling in her stomach which she became aware that she had been carrying around for days. She was beginning to have doubts – not about actually going, but about how quickly she was moving and preparing to leave.

Perhaps it was the strange sensation she felt when she thought she saw something up on the hill top, or perhaps of what Joseph had advised, being patient.

What if she did leave and just sneak off as she intended. What if something happened to Ma'ma or Papa whilst she was gone on her quest and she did not find out until too late? If this happened, she knew she would always carry the regret of her secret leaving like a stone in her heart.

Victoria suddenly registered that it was the fact that she was being deceitful by sneaking off that was causing her anxiety, and she was betraying the trust of her parents. Tears started again, and distraught and even more confused now, she got up and wandered back down to the stables.

Checking to see if anyone was around, she opened the chaff bin and cleared the chaff to one side exposing the slicker she had laid over her supplies. She was about to draw back the slicker when she noticed a piece of cloth protruding from the chaff where she had swept it aside. Frowning, she felt around and found a bundle wrapped in an oily rag sitting on top of the slicker.

What? she thought and picked up the bundle. It was quite heavy and she unwrapped it. In it was the pistol Joseph had taken from her on the hill.

She gasped and spun around looking for Joseph, he was nowhere to be seen. Then she started to smile as it dawned on her that he must have known her intentions all along, the cunning old fox! She should have known she could not fool the old man.

The guilt of her intention to sneak off began to weigh heavily with Victoria, and she finally decided she could not be so deceitful to her Ma'ma and Papa and just leave without telling them of her intentions. They would be devastated and hurt, although she knew they would guess the reason, and anyway Joseph would be sure to tell them.

She just could not hurt them this way. What if one of them became ill, was injured or worse while she was away, she knew she would never be able to forgive herself.

She would wait until her mother returned from the stores run in about three days and then tell them all of what she must do.

Immediately she felt better for her decision and went in search of Joseph.

'I wish Joseph could come with me,' she mused out loud. She would feel infinitely safer, being still mindful of her encounter with the lionesses.

She found him carrying buckets of feed over to the stalls. 'Joseph!' she called, 'Where did you put the pistol please?' effectively trapping him. Joseph looked at her with a solemn face, his mind racing for an answer as she stood before him, one hand on her hip and one eyebrow arched in query, there was the merest hint of a smile on her face.

Joseph knew the game was up and said, 'I cannot remember Missy,' a huge grin spreading across his face.

'Maybe you put it in the chaff bin,' said Victoria and burst out laughing.

The game over, they laughed until tears came, more out of relief than anything humorous said.

It felt so good to be laughing after the misery since Nicholas left and Victoria put her arms around Joseph and gave him an enormous hug. 'Whatever would I do without you Baba Joe,' Victoria said, releasing him, her love for him radiating.

Joseph snorted, there was mist in the old man's eyes, and he said, 'Missy should not be thinking of doing this thing, it is wrong and not good Missy. Much too dangerous when your head is not right, and to show no respect is worser and not good for Mama and Papa.'

Victoria was taken aback by the depth of emotion and feeling the old man showed.

'It's okay Baba Joe, I will not go now until Mama returns and I have had a chance to discuss it with Papa also.'

She knew she was in for a huge argument when her mother returned, especially with Papa, but if she could convince Joseph to accompany her it would be easier to convince her father and mother, after all she had been out with Joseph so many times hunting she could not count, sometimes for as long as two weeks.

The relief on Joseph's face was plainly evident, and the rest of his plan could now possibly come to fruition.

His mind turned to the hated Hymie Van Der Hoeke, and how he was going to keep the devil away from his Missy Victoria. The two young warriors of course had told him of Van Der Hoeke's presence up on the hill, and how close he had been to the unsuspecting Victoria. They also reported that there were previous footprints of the horse and man, at least six sets. He fretted about this and wondered just how long the man had been spying on her.

He had been so worried because the two had now left to catch up with Mistress A'menson and the others and would not return for at least three days. He feared Victoria was going to leave before he could organise things to keep her safe, and he also worried that the last piece of his plan had still to be fulfilled. This he would not know until the young man he sent on the errand returned with either what he wanted or news, good or bad. So, Missy Victoria's reversal of her decision to just sneak away was a huge relief.

He agonised over whether to tell Mister Ludwig of what had happened but thought he would be very angry with Missy if he did, and also Mistress A'menson was not here to keep things calm. Missy Victoria could be as stubborn and fiery as her father, and an argument might make her change her mind and go by herself anyway. He could not let that happen. Joseph knew that whatever Hymie Van Der Hoeke was planning was evil and he certainly meant to harm his Missy.

Lillian stayed at the Van Der Hoeke's homestead for a day before setting off the very next morning for the trading post.

After dinner on the night of her arrival, Lillian and Ermina Van Der Hoeke sat enjoying a fine Dutch De Kuyper butterscotch schnapps on the verandah. Looking out at the Sun setting across the lake, Lillian felt at peace, the cooing of the bar-shouldered and turtle doves, lulling her into a melancholy mood as the Sun began to slide below the waters of Lake Victoria. As it sank, an avenue of red ran across the water to its core, and Lillian thought one could almost walk upon the water to reach the warm glow.

She sighed and put her feet out in front of her in contentment, the superb schnapps lingering silken-like in her mouth,.

'Lillian?' Ermina said. Lillian turned to her and was surprised to see that Ermina was clearly distressed.

'What is ze matter Ermina?' she queried sitting upright. The woman simply bit her lip, shaking her head from side to side, her mind seeking an answer. Lillian's first thought was that perhaps it was the incident with Nicholas and Victoria that was troubling her. She was partly correct, or at least it was the catalyst.

The normally strong and stern woman suddenly started to cry.

'*Ach*, my son!' she cried in anguish, burying her head in her hands. 'We do not know what to do. Ever since that evening when he made a fool of himself when they were looking for Victoria, he will not speak to us. He is always moping around and now spends days away from home!

'He and his father have even come to blows!' She looked up at Lillian, the normally strong and stern woman's face was streaked with tears and Lillian saw the anguish twisting inside the poor woman.

Lillian rose and put her arms around the distraught woman's shoulders saying, 'Ermina, per'aps 'zis is your young man's part of 'is growing up, I zink in a little time 'e will get over 'zis, no?

'E will eventually see zat Nicholas and Victoria 'ave something very special between them, don't worry so much.'

'No Lillian, he is so different and as his mama, I know something is wrong. I think he is possessed by an evil force or demon!' She made the sign of the cross.

'He is saying irrational things and even talks bad of you!'

'Of me...?' Lillian exclaimed, 'But surely not! 'E as always been ze perfect gentleman! But what 'ave I done?'

Ermina looked at her, embarrassment reddening her face, and she looked down and said, 'He claims that you are...you are...'

'What?' Lillian asked, growing impatient.

'He says you are too familiar with Mr Yuin,' the poor woman exclaimed, wringing her hands.

Lillian covered her mouth in part amusement and part shock, she gave a short laugh.

'But zis is ridiculous, no? 'E is like a son to Lud and me. Why, we 'ave known Nicholas since 'e was only 12 or 13, you know 'e was a part of our family until 'e left to seek 'is fortune!'

Ermina looked at Lillian, '*We* know it is not true! But this is what I am saying, Hymie is not rational. When he said this Johann exploded and jumped the dinner table, they began to fight!'

The distraught woman resumed wringing her hands and broke out sobbing afresh.

"Then....then Hymie screamed out, he would have Victoria no matter what and ran out the door. We heard him gallop away on his horse. Oh, oh, oh, why is this happening, what have we done!'

Lillian was still in some shock, surely this was not happening. She stood there thinking furiously, and it began to dawn on her that Victoria may be in real danger.

Ermina broke in on her thoughts, reinforcing, if anything, her fears. 'Please be very careful, this is not the son I know and love. I feel something terrible may come of this unless someone can reason with him…I am worried about you and Victoria.'

Never one to overreact, Lillian, calming herself, thought for a moment. Hymie had never been anything but a perfect gentleman to her and Lud, and up until this incident recently, also to Victoria.

But still, she would take the advice and be careful.

In a moment of compassion and feeling for the poor woman, she said, 'When Nicholas returns, as I am sure 'e will, 'e will no doubt be by Victoria's side most of the time and I know that it will not be too long before they will make plans to marry.'

Ermina looked at her friend. 'He has gone? But so soon, where has he gone?'

The question in all its innocence, prompted a reply, but not wishing to speak of the rift between the two, Lillian said, 'Oh 'e 'as gone to the ranges to finish 'is prospecting for a while. Huh! ze men!' she concluded tapping the side of her head.

She had no idea at the time of the ramifications this last statement was to carry. Equally, she had no idea that Hymie had seen her travelling toward his parents' home, seen her arrive and at that moment was standing at the corner of the verandah behind a honeysuckle vine. He had heard everything.

Hymie's emotions were in turmoil. He switched between feeling betrayed by his family to the heavy weight of guilt of his own betrayal. A wave of emotion and regret swept over him, tears began to form in his eyes as he heard his mother begin to cry, he had never heard or seen her cry. His heart thumping hard in his chest, he was on the verge of rushing out to beg forgiveness, when Lillian mentioned the special bond between Yuin and Victoria and that they may marry when Yuin returned. Returned… returned from where? he thought. What was this? Had he heard right? Yuin had gone!

His glee at this news now crashed in on his thoughts. His emotions were now scrambling to react and find focus but try as he might he failed again to control them. The hatred, thinly disguised at best, won the struggle and soared to the surface in an instant. He ground his teeth in fury, the frustration fanning his jealous rage like bellows, the roaring in his ears drowning out any outside sound for an instant. Marry! It would not happen! He would not let it!

As he peeped through a small gap in the vine, he could see Lillian's face and rightly read the approval on her face. Harlot! he raged within, you are wrong and I will have Victoria!

He came back down from his rage to hear his mother ask where Nicholas had gone.

He strained his ears to hear Lillian reply that he had gone off to the ranges to do his prospecting. He peeped through the vine just in time to see Lillian tapping the side of her head and rolling her eyes.

He had, of course, no way of knowing where Nicholas was prospecting in the ranges, but he resolved to find out one way or another.

Victoria was sitting in the old rocker on the verandah when the buggy returned, her mother sitting proudly on the board and shaded by the parasol she held over her head. Victoria smiled. Her mother never ceased to amaze her – here she was, obviously hot and perspiring, covered in dust, yet still acting as though she was about to enter a social gathering.

As she was helped down from the seat, she glanced up at Victoria, and also quickly looked around. In that glance Victoria knew instantly something was wrong.

'Mama! Welcome back,' exclaimed Victoria, coming down the veranda and wrapping her arms around Lillian, then quickly followed the greeting by, 'What on earth is the matter Mama!'

'*Bonjour* my darling,' she replied offering her cheek. 'First I wish to take ze bath, zen, I will tell you. Can you please ask your Pa'pa to meet us in the drawing room? And also Joseph.' She whirled away calling Maisie to draw her a bath.

Victoria's heart sank. How did her mother know of her plans? It was impossible! Her ma ma knew! It was the only reason she could think of to explain her mother's strange attitude. To call a meeting was reserved for emergency only and very serious discussion. And to call Joseph as well! 'Oh bother!' she lamented, stamping her foot, 'I did not want a confrontation and argument.'

In all her years she could only recall twice when this happened before and that was when two male lions were terrorising the property and surrounding villages, killing several people and cattle in the process. They had leapt into the corral right next to the house, mauling and killing two horses. The second time was when a small band of renegade Wahehe warriors had been raiding in the area and had been seen not too far from the house. Although nothing eventuated, Ludwig had been prepared.

In due course they all gathered in the drawing room. Joseph looked extremely nervous, and catching Victoria's eye, he knew she was thinking as he was.

'Ma ma! I...' began Victoria, at the same time as her Father said, 'What is it my dear, you look very upset, I...' Lillian held up her hand to silence them.

'What is upsetting me is Hymie Van Der Hoeke! 'E is misbehaving badly!'

The relief on Victoria and Joseph's faces was palpable if anyone had looked.

Lillian continued. "Is mama and father think 'e 'as lost is mind, and from what zey 'ave told me, I think per'aps zey may be correct!'

She went on to relate all she had been told.

Ludwig was almost purple with rage at the insolence of the young whelp. 'He shows his face around here and I vil show him vot manners are made of!' he fumed.

'My God Ma ma, what is he thinking?' exclaimed Victoria, 'That I will just give in to his dreams and do whatever he wishes!' She stamped her foot, furious that he could show such disrespect for her and her family values, and even think that she was so weak.

'I will go and find him, and when I do he will be left in no doubt as to where he stands, which is nowhere! I love Nicholas, and that will be an end it!' she raged.

Joseph saw and loved the fire and rage that consumed his Missy. Eee! She is like the wind and storm! he thought proudly – a woman warrior! Eee! What a thought! But he knew now that his forethought was justified, she was in great danger.

'You will do no such thing!' said her father with finality. 'You will stay here, and you will not go running off by yourself anymore, you will always go with an escort, both of you!' he said looking at Lillian. 'Is this understood?' Both women looked at him, Lillian acquiescing silently, but Victoria had her head up in defiance, looking proud and angry.

The truth was, Victoria was on the verge of panic – she knew her father, and when he made these decisions, rarely would he be moved to change his mind, especially when it meant protection of his family.

Her mind racing, she almost blurted out what her intentions were, to ride off and seek Nicholas, but fortunately she first glanced at Baba Joe, who almost imperceptibly moved his head side to side.

She quickly concluded that to bring this up now would almost certainly blow up into a full-scale argument, and right now that would be unfair, given the worry her parents must be wrought with. She would not gain the result she wanted, better to take Baba Joe's hint and be patient. She again looked at Baba Joe, a tiny hint of a smile on his face told her he knew exactly what she was thinking.

It would be almost seven months before Victoria could put her plan into action. Ludwig quite rightly fretted for some time about her safety.

Chapter 17

Lungile (The good one)

Nicholas, rode into the camp about three in the afternoon and the first thing he saw was the giant ebony figure of Jack, standing with arms on hips and wearing a grin bigger than a split watermelon. Not for the first time Nicholas's feelings of familiarity rose to the surface, and it suddenly crashed into his head why this man seemed so familiar. Could possibly it be? he asked himself.

But for now, Nicholas saw only welcome and genuine warmth emanating from the big fellow. He would ask his questions later when the moment was right.

'*Sowubona, kunjani!* (hello, how are you) Massah Yuin!' grinned the giant, speaking half in Zulu and half in English.

'I see you Jack, *ngiyaphila wena,*' (I'm fine and you?) said Nicholas touching his heart in reply, noting that Jack had called him Massah. I must take him to task about that later mused Nicholas.

'*Kuhile,*' (good) the giant answered in Zulu.

'Was your journey pleasant Mas...Sir,' Jack stammered remembering Whip's word of warning about calling Nicholas massah.

'Jack,' Nicholas said in an even tone, 'there is no need to call me Master. I do not consider you to be a slave, to me you are a man, you do not belong to anyone! Understand?' he added kindly, looking at Jack.

Jack stood and his head dropped a little. 'Lift your head up man!' said Nicholas a little sharply. Jack did so and they locked eyes. Jack finally broke the deadlock and said, 'You a good man Mister Yuin, I knew first time Jack see you as young man, many years long go in Cape Town.

'I will call you Baba Nicho-las,' he said grinning from ear to ear.

Nicholas grinned and they shook hands. 'Best you make that a bit shorter Jack, how about Ubaba Nick!' Jack grinned in return and said, 'Ho kay, *Ngisaphila, Ubaba* Niclos!'

"Ubaba" was recognition and a mark of respect in almost all Bantu dialects in Africa and usually reserved for elders or revered men.

Nicholas was touched and elated, he was right, he had seen the man before! This *was* the giant young slave who he had seen treated so badly in Cape Town, amazing! After all this time and meeting here of all places!

Nicholas and Jack walked into the little establishment they had carved out of the scrub. Looking around, it seemed a lot of work had been achieved in the five days he had been away. The corral was finished and the limestone walls of the stockyard and dwelling were almost to full height.

There were water and feed barrels in the corral, and Nicholas was very pleased with the work Jack and Whip had accomplished.

Walking toward the dwelling he could hear the sound of timber being sawn, and rounding the corner saw Whip, one knee up on a timber horse and sawing a long piece of timber. There were about a dozen sawn planks standing up against the stone wall.

'Good afternoon Mister Yuin,' said Whip as soon as he spotted him. 'Ye had a productive journey I am a trusting?'

'More observation I'm afraid,' said Nicholas, 'but I will tell you about it over the evening meal'

'Very good Sir, we have a couple of would-be apprentices over there' He said indicating over his shoulder and there sat two young aboriginal men of about 18 years of age, Nicholas reckoned.

'How long have they been here?' he asked. 'They have come almost every day Sir and they just watch what I'm doing, just curious I guess.'

'Maybe at that,' said Nicholas. 'See if you can get them interested in helping Whip, it would be handy having extra hands, don't you think?'

'Aye, I'll see what I can do…might let Jack try, he seems to have a good rapport with these people, an' there is one young lady who seems fascinated by him, eh Jack?' He said cocking one scarred eyebrow at Jack with a mischievous grin.

A deep growling reply quickly put paid to Whip's attempt to josh the big fellow. 'No happen Ubaba Niclos,' he said glaring at Whip. 'My father choose me marry my girl since little, only first. When I go back to my people, she wait for me, and these people *no* Zulu!' he said emphatically.

Nicholas again reminded himself to see if he could get Jack to open up about his origin.

Nicholas began to make plans to make his expedition inland, and over the next few days he began to stockpile his needs, checking off things as he went – he reckoned he would head off within the week.

The opportunity to ask Jack about how he became enslaved came several days later when he and Nicholas were having a break from tilling the soil for a vegetable plot at the rear of the stone dwelling. It was tough work by hand and the day was hot. The infuriating little flies crawling all over them almost drove them to distraction, and many times they gagged and hawked up the pests after breathing them in – or snorting when they had crawled up their noses.

They had been at it for three hours when Nicholas called, 'Time for a break Jack!'

They sat in the shade, leaning back side by side on the rear wall sharing a ladle of water.

'We will gather the cow and sheep manure and make a pile in the garden Jack,' said Nicholas.

Jack had little idea about growing things or how to plant grain, for the Zulu people of his tribe, were for the most part hunters and cattlemen, the women did the cultivation, and warriors would never do women's work.

Jack cocked his head at Nicholas, his face bland and his hands out open in query. 'No understand Baba, what is "cow an ship nuer?"'

'You know, like that,' Nicholas said pointing to a pile of dung in the corner nearest to them.

'Ah, understand, you mean *kaka-shit*!' Jack roared with laughter. He would never have spoken so boldly when enslaved, but now he could feel his freedom it was good to laugh.

Nicholas had the feeling he had been tested, so he too started to laugh.

When they had settled, Nicholas thought now was the time to ask about Jack's past.

'Jack?' Nicholas began, 'I have never asked you, but may I know how you became a slave when I saw you in Cape Town?'

Nicholas watched as Jack stirred, scrubbing the dirt in front of him with one of his huge bare feet, noting now the slavery iron scars around the ankles, and glancing at his face, Nicholas saw the pain and sorrow flood into his big face.

There was a long silence in which the huge man appeared to be struggling with emotion. Nicholas waited patiently.

'My real name *Lungile* Ubaba, mean 'The good one' in my language. My line of people come from King *Dingiswayo*. He great king and we *Mtetwa* tribe before *Shaka* gather all people together to make one Zulu nation. I am to be next chief of *Mtetwa* people, but still now Zulu.

'Dey came just before the Sun come,' Jack continued slowly, speaking in a low rumble. 'All were sleep, because the *Impi* travel long way from battle with near tribe, enemy people, bad people. King order we kill whole village and take chief to him. We do dis, den return to king's village, big boma. Some of us go further, maybe running for half night to reach own small boma.

'Den we drink much and feast in salute.

'We are ten warriors, most young like me den, accept *Izinyosi* he is oldest and our Chief, and *Umkhandlu* and his son *Undwandwe*, dey great warriors from many battle for King *Shaka*.' The big man sighed then went on.

'But men with long dress, know now Arab men, come, kill listening guards and come into village, many, maybe three score, Arab and other tribe people, some *Nandi* from North, very bad people with many musket.

Dey kill all old men and women with sword and babies smash to ground or spear.'

Nicholas listened with shock and watched as great tears ran down Jack's face.

'I look and see *Izinyosi* with assegai try to fight, he spear many *Nandi* but many big boom and die with big hole in chest. But before dis, *Umkhandlu* tell me to take our family out away behind. I do as order, his family, my family.' He held his hand up with fingers outstretched. 'My mother and her mother and my betrothed and two brothers, also two other young maidens together and go into back away into dark and into hills, escape, I help but den run back to fight with my brothers.'

Den I see *Umkhandlu* and *Undwandwe* running and fight de *Nandi*. I join them, we easily kill many *Nandi* but soon dey also shot.'

Jack paused for some time and Nicholas could see he was struggling with the terrible and tragic memory, the tears dripping silently from Jack's chin.

'I see my father already dead, too old to fight, but he try, I ran back into boma, de killing rage upon me but knocked down like weak child from behind.

My head not clear. Suddenly, all noise go down and I look around all are staring.

'The chief Arab cut off *Izinyosi* head and hold up shouting, "*Si-gi- di! Niyabasaba Na?*"

'It is our war cry and dey asking if we are afraid in our own speak.

'There are many guns pointed at us and many swords. All de young maidens and young men, not yet initiated into manhood are held together in a circle of guns.

Not afraid, but we are lost and forced to put down our weapons for fear of dem killing all.'

Again Jack stopped for a while and after a time wiped his eyes and continued.

'De Arabs bring many horse and camel to de boma. Den dey put iron hoops on all legs and also on here he indicated his wrists and we walk north. Der are thirty-two of us and I am lead.

'Dey feed us and give some water, but always we walk north, stopping only at night.

'Women and children are always crying and wailing. At first I start to sing to dem to keep our spirit alive.

'I first sing about our mighty nation and de King Impi, and how we will be rescued. We all sing, de Arabs and Nandi let us.

'Den I make mistake, next day I start to sing about de Arabs and de Nandi,' he smiled at the memory. 'Sing about how dey *Kaka shit*, not to be fit to be in our presence, I sing dat dey is *Stabane*, mean faggot. De mothers are *Sifele*, mean whore. Sing dat dey father's balls are tiny, den all sing out very loud, *Tsa mor kaka!*' and dis mean' Go eat shit!'

Nicholas could not help but chuckle at this and Jack also managed another wan smile.

'De Nandi very angry, some speak Zulu, dey come down line of us, from each end, swing at Jack, but me duck but knobkerry hit young girl and smash skull, killing poor girl, I knew her as my mother's second cousin.' He dropped his head, 'I kill her.'

He shuddered and said, 'De Nandi keep hitting us, den Arab come. Shoot, kill two Nandi, he very angry, screaming a bring out whip an' hitting the Nandi many times. Dey take away dead girl. Den de Arabs come and look to mend wounds on us, it is strange, to be so cruel but dey also help us, I thought.

'Dey feed us well and give water, den we begin march north again. But I never no sing no more.

'We march for a full moon and slowly begin to turn to de east, never been dis far and wonder where we are.

'Many nights, de young maidens and sometimes our young boys are taken to de Arab masters' tents. De boys an' maidens maybe only ten years old, an others not more dan fourteen. We hear much screaming and crying and knew de 'masters' were ray-ped them. We warriors lay, burn with anger and shame at dis, de children's cries like de cut of assegai, an' also because we chained and can do nothing to protect dem.

'One day the *Nandi kaka* who killed my cousin come to me and he just stare at me. He has big burn mark on face, I know it is my mark to seek.

'I say "One day I will come for you and your people, all of you!" and I stare back. He laugh, but 'is eyes look all away an everywhere, I smell de fear and den he go away but also spit on Jack – no matter, I have de great burning in my chest, one day I will return and finish dis filth!'

Jack looked at Nicholas and Nicholas felt the power emanating from the big man, and thought, I would not want to be a *Nandi* when Jack comes for them.

'What is this mark?' Nicholas indicated, tapping his cheek.

'Is thorn when running at night,' Jack answered, hooking his finger at his cheek, before continuing.

'Den one day, dere is a strange scent in the air, it is damp, but not like anything we have ever smelt before. The trees and bush also look different.

'We have come to de sea and we stood in wonder at de huge sparkling water and of de strange big canoes. Der are many peoples, all kinds and all different ships, maybe ten. We told dat dis is Dar es Salaam.

'Dey keep us for five days, den we is broken up and some taken away. Der is much wailing and sobbing from de women and young boys as dey was taken away, but we can do nothing.

'Den one day, dey take four young maidens and de six warriors and put us on Arab ship and sail away to Cape town. We all very frightened and very sick and water very rough, but we survive.

'Den when we get to Cape town, dey take off the chains one day, one at a time, and wash and put oil on scars on feet and wrists. Dey wrap padding around den put different shackles on.

'We fed very well for two weeks, den dey take us to de market.

'Baba, you know what happen den, Lungile get sold to white man, English. He and wife not good peoples, try to make Lungile bed white woman but would not! Den dey beat me, den sell Lungile to Spanish man at French Guinea port. You know what happen next?

'I try to escape at port, but captured, den punish at sea. Capitan Studwish he come, capture Spanish and kill.'

He suddenly grinned as if wiping away the sorrow and bad thoughts. 'Now I am happy because I have Ubaba Niclos and Mister Whip, for fren! Very happy now!'

Nicholas was overcome with the tragedy of the story and he knew he had in all probability been told only half of the suffering that Jack and his people had endured.

They sat in silence, each in his own thoughts, Nicholas turned to Jack.

'Lungile,' he said. Jack swung his huge shiny dome to face Nicholas, 'Yes Ubaba Niclos?'

'I will arrange for you to return to your home as soon as the *Colette* returns. I will give you your papers of freedom and as soon as it is signed by one of the king's men in Geraldine you will be officially free for always, and then you can go and gather your family and people together once again.'

Jack stared in astonishment at Nicholas, and began to shake his head in disbelief.

'Ubaba, Lungile owe his miserable life to you, you are my brother now an' my family.

'Dis a wonderful gift you give me, but yet Lungile cannot accept!'

'What! Why on earth not Jack?' Nicholas asked, incredulous.

'Because Ubaba, it is my sworn duty to protect you and help you for always, dis is Zulu custom,' Jack said solemnly.

Nicholas thought about it, the silence palpable.

'Okay Jack, you are still a free man, this is my gift to you and I *will* make it official,' he said, and after a slight pause added: 'Now we are brothers, we will work together as family and you will help me and I will therefore help you, so when the time is right we will both return to Africa, and *then,* since you are working for me, I will send you to find your family. This is what is to happen, do you understand Jack?'

Jack was now thinking hard; Ubaba Niclos was very smart, and what he said was acceptable and he could not deny the gift now. The great warrior looked up with tears in his eyes and all he could manage was, 'Hokay Ubaba.'

They stood to continue working and were walking back to the tilled earth when something prompted Nicholas to ask, 'Jack, are you sure that your woman and family will still be alive, and how do you know?'

Jack fixed him with a stare and said, 'I know because she comes to me in my dreams and I know when she is in trouble, and if she is in danger she tells me Ubaba.'

A chill ran up Nicholas's spine as he recalled his own dreams.

Chapter 18

The Ranges, Early 1837

*V*ictoria and Baba Joe left the homestead at first light. They were mounted and led one pack horse. They were accompanied by the four Hehe warriors who trotted 200 yards ahead of them, their black and white ostrich feather headdress blowing in the gentle dawn breeze.

Victoria turned back and saw her mother and father standing in the yard, their arms around each other's shoulders. She felt a catch in her throat and knew they would be sick with worry of the unknown and of what might unfold in her search for Nicholas.

Her gut clenched and apprehension rose within her chest. She turned and faced the front, clenching her teeth in resolve and did not look back.

They had little idea where in the ranges to look for Nicholas's camp, but if anyone could track the sign to find it, Baba Joe was the one to do it. In addition, the Hehe were also experts at tracking, so the odds were very hopeful.

Months had passed before Victoria could no longer put off broaching the subject of her intention to leave and seek Nicholas and all the while she fretted.

Victoria had often argued long and hard with her parents about going to search for Nicholas and had almost ran out of reasonable argument, when one day Joseph had suggested he organise a search for Hymie to confirm at least that he had not been spying on Victoria. He had not been seen or heard of for some time now.

Ludwig had argued that he could not spare the manpower, and in any case, was not about to allow Joseph or Victoria to go galivanting off to God only knows where in the ranges by themselves.

This forced Joseph to reveal his plans, and the presence of his band of four Hehe warriors. They had, up until now been kept out of sight of all, even Missy Victoria. The warriors, although young men, had already been blooded and were all experienced.

Joseph, mindful of the fact that revealing the presence of the warriors might seem to Victoria's parents that he and Missy Victoria had been planning their trip for some time, he explained that ever since Hymie's loss of control Joseph had been very worried about Victoria's safety, so he took it upon himself to ask for some additional protection for her. This was half of the truth so he did not feel guilty about bending it a little.

In the end Ludwig asked if he could see these additional warriors, and with the appearance that very afternoon, he agreed to at least allow the search for signs of Hymie to go ahead. Ludwig knew it would only take these men about a half day to pick up any sign if Hymie had been nearby. They returned at dusk and had found no sign.

That evening, Ludwig reluctantly gave his approval for the journey, but only if they were accompanied by the warriors.

Ludwig had walked to the gun cabinet and opening the draw drew out the empty Allen & Thurber holster and a box of cartridges and came and stood in front of Victoria. She quailed, wracked with guilt.

'Ja, I vil allow your journey,' he said.

Victoria could scarcely believe her ears and quite literally was holding her breath when Ludwig capitulated. 'You know my darling, I vould haf given it to you if you had asked,' he said. 'Keep the pistol oiled and clean, it is now your own.' Victoria burst into tears at once and said, 'I am so sorry Papa, I did not intend to steal it, just borrow it until I got back.' With a shock she realised she had just admitted that she had intended to run off for some time now, dread fell upon her like a cloak. She looked up at her Father's face but he was just smiling down at her. 'Ja...I too vas once young and impetuous, but you have shown patience. Ve vill now start to make plans for your departure!' he concluded, and reaching down, gathered her to him, folding her in his great loving arms.

It is strange, thought Joseph, that they had not heard about Hymie Van Der Hoeke for months, since Mistress A'mendson's return from the stores trip. His scouts on their return had reported no sign of him being up on the hill. Indeed, there was no sign of him within at least 20 miles of the A'mendson property, not even at his own camp. It worried him and he resolved to be ever vigilant for any sign of the "piece of cattle dung". He then cackled to himself. No, no, no, cattle dung has uses, and he smiled at his own wit.

They made good time the first day, and although Joseph had told the Hehe to be very thorough and had them fan out across the front of the faint trail in at least a three-mile line, it was not in their training to cover ground slowly – until an enemy or hunting demanded it.

As a result, they were at times at least a couple of miles or an hour or so ahead of Joseph and Victoria, and they missed nothing.

Two days had passed without any sign of either Nicholas or Van Der Hoeke and the ranges continued to grow ever so slowly on the horizon. They could now discern patches of green amongst the valleys and rifts on the ranges, although it would be another two days before they would reach them.

They camped that night on the side of a small kopje but lit no fire and dined on dried antelope and fruit before collapsing from exhaustion, except for two sentries.

Earlier this day however, they heard the warbled cry of a grey Spur fowl come from the warrior searching on the far right. His name was M'uyinga and he was slightly senior to the others.

M'uyinga carried himself with authority and seemed to have much influence over the other warriors. Unbeknown to the others, he was to become a great warrior chief of the Bena Sangu people in the future.

M'uyinga had found an old set of horse tracks heading in the same direction as they were travelling. Victoria felt a thrill and she somehow convinced herself that they were Nicholas's.

After some debate, Joseph decided to join M'uyinga and widen the search. Victoria had retreated to the rear, but after a time found herself becoming bored. She looked over to the tree line and cantered up some distance until she could see Joseph.

Standing in her stirrups she whistled to Joseph and indicated where she was heading. After a slight hesitation, he waved back, and she turned and headed away toward the tree line.

Joseph was fretting that his Missy would be out of his sight, but then thought, no matter, M'hafi and M'fwimi would not be far ahead of her and in any event he would join her soon.

M'hafi was the youngest of the Hehe warriors and was working the extreme left flank of the forward scouting line, running effortlessly over the plain, intent on the ground in front of him one minute, the next, sweeping around as he had been trained to do.

On his left, about 300 yards away, was a line of green trees and he knew there was a stream running beneath the foliage. They had been running almost parallel with the line since early morning. Each day he had run alone, as did the others, but this time though, he had company. He had seen the woman they came to protect move in behind him, but she was some distance away on horseback.

Victoria rode at ease behind the warrior, and at times he disappeared for an hour, such was his relentless gait. She would have had to canter occasionally to catch up with him, should she choose to keep up with him.

She saw him moving way ahead and vanish over a slight rise.

It was good to have the warriors ahead of her and she felt secure with the thought. She had insisted on sweeping along the rear of the warriors each day and Joseph had convinced her that it was safer and less distracting for the warriors if she were to ride some distance back, almost out of sight. He in any case was always close by.

As she rode, her mind slipped back to her parting, when her mother had insisted that Victoria wear a light corset and undergarments on her trip. She had argued that it would be uncomfortable and hot and she hated the restriction.

Lillian's argument had been (as always) that if *she* could wear them then so could her daughter, and in any case, it simply would not do to forgo the garments in the company of men, even if they were warriors under Joseph's supervision – and that would be that.

Victoria had eventually relented, planning as she always did, to remove them as soon as she got out of site of the homestead. Her mother had given her three pairs of the very latest pantaloons and matching corsets which she had sent to her from France. These were really quite beautiful garments. The pantaloons, gathered around the waist, came to about mid-thigh, unlike the older styles which tied off below the knee. They were very daring for those times, even though no one could see them. They had pink ribbon ties around the thighs and around the waist. The matching corsets were even more elaborate but still with the same ribbon decoration.

They had not travelled more than three miles when Victoria called a halt and rode off the trail to some bushes to change. Joseph had cackled as he knew what she was doing. Nothing changes, he had thought, remembering how his Missy had been doing this since her mother had first insisted on her wearing these ridiculous things.

Joseph remembered little Missy stripping off all of her clothes as soon as she was out of sight of her mother and running around naked as the day with the other picanninies, and only a little loin cloth a bit later when she visited the tribal villages with him. In fact, she had only started to wear full clothing when she was approaching puberty.

As Victoria changed her clothing, she took off the corset, and was about to take off the pantaloons, when she looked down at her body. The feminine garment had actually looked very pretty and they were made of a light cotton, so were in fact quite comfortable. She wondered if Nicholas would like them and felt a rush of heat come to her as she thought of him. Glancing around in embarrassment, she decided she would wear them, but the delicious warmth stayed with her while she dressed.

Long ago Victoria had made her own shirts out of white cotton sheet, much to the dismay of her mother. The shirts were buttoned up the front, were long sleeved and had two breast pockets, male style. Her mother steadfastly insisted that she wear a corset though, and when her mother made up her mind about things like this, she would not move. In any event no one could ever deny that she was all woman even if she wore the shirts.

Victoria also refused to wear full dresses when she rode, preferring to use a long, belted skirt instead, and she rode her horses 'man' style instead of side-saddle.

This had caused Lillian much consternation until she finally relented when Ludwig had pointed out that they were living in a remote area anyway and most of the tribal women wore next to nothing at all.

She had wrapped the long brown skirt around her waist, knotted a red cotton bandana around her throat and did up the belt. Positioning the pistol in its holster at the small of her back, she then folded the corset away in her saddle bag, relishing the unrestricted feeling under her cotton shirt. She had swung up into the saddle and cantered back to the waiting men.

M'hafi, sprang from one boulder to the next, finally coming to a small rise next to a jumble of boulders. Jumping down, he landed on top of a large flat boulder about two feet above a clear patch of ground. Stopping for a brief moment, he then jumped down in front of the rock and onto the patch of earth in front of him. He scanned the ground ahead first, looking for tracks and then lifted his gaze to the plain ahead, propping himself on one leg as he did so and began his deep controlled breathing.

The black mamba was about ten feet long, near fully grown and in all its silvery scaled finery. It was a good three and a half inches thick in the body at its widest.

The snake had just come down from the side of the hill from amongst a stand of small trees and was just under the lip of the flat boulder on which M'hafi had stood, when the warrior suddenly dropped in front of it, the Mamba, sensing a threat, struck almost immediately.

M'hafi sensed the presence but he was too late. He spun to his right to face the snake, but all he saw was the silvery flash and a black gaping mouth as the mamba sunk its fangs into the top of his right calf, not more than a couple of inches from the back of his knee. He leapt away, terror upon him, but the mamba had, in an instant, lifted almost half its body off the ground for another strike. M'hafi, spinning, hit the boulder before him and crashed to his knees and on top of his shield, his assegai flying from his hand.

The aggressive snake's second strike came in a blur. M'hafi had no chance to avoid it as it hit him at the base of his throat and then struck again at his extended right bicep.

The Mamba dropped and saw an escape route to the left of M'hafi and quickly vanished into the rocks, leaving the stricken man clutching at his throat, his eyes bulging in terror.

The pain was immediate and unbearable. His blood rate, still high from running, was now increased by fear. Within minutes M'hafi was doomed, his throat constricted, he began to foam at the mouth as his nervous system began to seize. He tried to stand but collapsed, rolling over and into a deep gap between the rocks where for the next twenty minutes, convulsions and seizures wracked his body. Finally, shivering and trembling, his life ebbed away.

Completely unaware of the drama that had unfolded ahead of her, Victoria decided to trot over to the tree line to her left. She moved carefully, ramping up her concentration and senses as she approached the trees.

She heard a bark, not unlike that of a dog. Baboon! she thought. Something had spooked them. Suddenly she saw the tree branches shaking and the occasional glimpse of the troop of brown furry bodies as they retreated downstream. She reigned in her horse, a frown creasing her face. The tree line was still a good 150 feet away and the ground here was covered in low grass, there was no way she should have spooked the baboons she reasoned.

The baboons had vanished and she heard no more sound from them. Probably they had spotted a leopard, she thought. She slid her rifle out of its scabbard, checked the load and lay it across her lap before jigging her horse forward.

Victoria entered the cool of the trees with caution. It was quite dense and she glimpsed water glistening ahead. She emerged from the undergrowth and into the sunlight to find a small bubbling stream about 15 feet across. It was a beautiful spot, with multi-coloured, small moss-covered boulders and a small grassy clearing to the water's edge. Yellow butterflies floated around the edges and landed on the wet stone in some numbers.

She edged forward, and checking the area around, saw no evidence of crocodile or leopard, although it would be doubtful she would see a leopard should it choose to remain hidden, and rarely would they attack a human unless wounded or cornered. Nonetheless she was cautious.

She allowed her horse to drink then swung down out of her saddle and looped the reigns to a tree branch.

She was hot and dusty and thought, I have time for a quick wash and I can rinse out my shirt, then I can canter up and catch up with M'hafi.

Propping her rifle against a tree, Victoria turned and walked to the water's edge, tugging her shirt free of her belt and undid the buttons, pulling back one shoulder, when she suddenly remembered the tumbu flies.

The flies laid their eggs on wet cloth or clothing. When one put back on their clothes, the heat of the body hatches the eggs and they immediately begin to work their way beneath the skin. The saliva from around the tiny mandibles of the maggot had anesthetic properties. If undetected or untreated, they would feed and grow under the skin, creating a nasty boil-like lump, and can grow to one and a half inches in length. She shuddered as she remembered her father treating some of the people at his clinic with gaping holes up to an inch deep in their skin. She quickly re-fastened her shirt.

A horse whickered somewhere across the other side of the stream, her heart leaped.

'Nicholas?' she called, the excitement bursting within her. 'Nicholas?' she called louder.

Chapter 19

The Prospecting Camp

Still crouched behind the honeysuckle vine at his parents' home, Hymie could scarcely believe his luck. He had retreated from his parents' house and had run his horse hard to his out camp and immediately set about packing his kit for a journey to the ranges.

He resolved he would find Yuin, whatever it took, and he would make sure he never returned to the Amendsons again, ever. The hatred burned like a raging wildfire within his breast.

When Yuin did not return, he would then be free to pursue Victoria. Eventually, she would understand she had misjudged him and she would at last be his. It would take a while he reasoned, but he would win her heart – he would have her even if she did not give her heart, what did it really matter.

It never occurred to him that he had effectively destroyed any feeling she may have had for him in the past.

He left the next morning, riding hard to the ranges, but he headed east at first for some ten miles and then cut north-east to the southern tip of the ranges. Once there, he would cautiously start his search along the eastern face first. He, of course, had no clue as to where Yuin would be prospecting.

No one would expect him to travel east, and this way he would avoid both the Amendson land and the Wahehe dogs the old man had patrolling the property.

He spent almost four months searching the eastern side without finding even a single sign, and he started to panic about whether he had in fact chosen the wrong side.

He returned and began sweeping the western side.

Two months later, he had finally come across Yuin's deserted prospecting camp. He had almost ridden past it when he picked up some broken twigs and a very faint trail heading north and south along the edge of the range. There was a faint track heading up into a wide gully, and looking up the gully through the trees, he saw what looked to be a hut of some description. Looking down at the trail into the gully, he could see it had not been used for some while, maybe for a good two weeks or more. He could not know of course that the tracks were not even Yuin's.

The hut was quite sound and was surrounded by a thorn boma in good condition. The door was set in the back wall facing south-east to the ranges and was quite sturdy. Entering the hut, he found it also to be in good condition. The roof was supported by a sturdy central timber pole from which wooden pegs had been driven for hanging gear on. A timber framed bunk with canvass stretched across it lay to one side against the north wall, a three-legged stool lay upturned at the foot of the bunk. There was even a small table of about three feet by four feet against the front wall. A shelf had a few items on it. The hut had only one window facing west with a view to the gap in the boma.

Outside, there was a large cemented water storage barrel that could hold about forty gallons, Hymie reckoned, and was about half full of good water. That was a mystery – how could they have gotten the water to here? He climbed up the side of the gully with his telescope and began to scan the area. Aha! he said to himself as he saw a green ribbon of trees snaking away from the ranges some eight miles distance. That would be where they had drawn their water from he reasoned.

That afternoon Hymie backtracked some five miles and stalked and shot an impala and a young warthog. He dressed the meat and waited for nightfall. It would be stupid to light a fire in the day time – Yuin would possibly see it and his surprise would be lost.

Returning to the gap in the boma, he dragged the thorns across the opening.

He built a stone enclosure facing back into the gully, lit a fire within it and laid most of the meat out in front of a fire for some time before salting it and laying it out on the drying racks that were still at the rear of the hut, ready for tomorrow. He cooked the rest over the coals.

Hymie reasoned that perhaps Yuin had moved further up into the ranges as there were few items left, though he did not think they would be abandoned. There was some sluicing and a few other prospecting items.

No matter, this would make a good dwelling from which to be based, and if Yuin was to return he would be waiting.

He reasoned that Yuin would return here eventually, the camp was too permanent to just desert.

Tomorrow he would take his skin water bags down to the stream and top up the water barrel.

He laid out his swag on the bunk and closing the door lay down and was asleep within minutes.

The next morning, he was much refreshed and hurriedly wolfed down some of the cooked meat and began working his way along the escarpment.

Hymie checked every gully and opening he came upon with extreme caution, keeping to the thick tree line when possible and using his telescope rather than blunder into the gullies and any likely place that Yuin may have been working or frequented. He saw nothing except a very old trail running down along the ranges to the distant tree line that snaked out onto the plain.

He eventually came to the stream. It bubbled merrily out of the range through a well-worn opening in the cliff face. The water was crystal clear and icy, and he drank with relish.

Hymie began to scout around the stream in ever increasing sweeps. Finding nothing, he reasoned that whatever trail there may have been was either washed away by a storm, or had not been frequented enough, and he was about to turn back across the stream when his heart jumped.

There! He spotted a set of wagon tracks heading downstream and out into the plains. Looking back further along the ranges he saw the wagon had been back and forth a few times.

This must surely be Yuin's prospecting wagon! He was a ball of tension, and his instincts were screaming with excitement and fear of the pending confrontation.

He quickly backtracked across the stream and then, dismounting, crossed back and brushed away his tracks.

He could not know of course that Nicholas was long gone and that the tracks belonged to a peddler named Zachariah Ben.

Ben was a nasty little man who would steal from his mother if he had had one. He sported a thin pointy grey and dirty beard, stained yellow around his mouth from the never-ending chain of Mexican Santa Clara cigarettes he rotated between his hand and mouth. His teeth resembled a long-forgotten graveyard, with decayed stumps sticking up and down and scattered like grey neglected tomb stones. His breath too, should one be unfortunate enough to get too close, might be likened to the decaying bodies within the graveyard.

Zachariah Ben, was a cockney and had been run out of most settlements along the length of the East African coast, and now had come to the eastern shores of Lake Victoria. Card cheat, con artist and supreme pickpocket were his stock in trade and now he had turned to the homesteaders, tribes and inland cattlemen to ply his trade. He peddled anything from ladies undergarments, fine gowns and the latest lightweight dresses to coloured beads, 'magic' elixirs, pots, pans, herbs, all manner of trinkets, blankets and a whole range of other goods.

All of this was crammed into his little yellow and burgundy coloured wagon which was pulled by two sturdy little mules. His horse, a ratty looking dun, was the only other asset he had.

He had come from the north and had yet again burnt his bridges in a series of tribal villages and settlements from Kendu Bay, N'yangweso, Homa Bay and Muhuru. He came close to being killed in a small town called Woth Onger and continued fleeing further south after almost being tarred and feathered at a new German settlement near Migori after an attempted land swindle. He had now crossed into Tanganyika and decided he was far enough south to avoid trouble and pursuit when he came across the very stream that had Hymie intrigued.

He decided to rest for a few days. He had made camp some two miles north of the stream and had made two trips back and forth to it. Initially, he could not get the wagon close enough to fill the water barrels at the source – there was just too much growth and small boulders and rubble – so had travelled downstream for about six miles where the banks flattened out. Here he could fill his barrels and roll them back to the wagon.

Returning, he had found and made camp in a small natural cut in the rock face approximately 40 feet deep and some 30 foot wide with almost vertical sides. Perfect! he had thought, it would take little effort to hack down and drag thorn bushes across the entrance to keep predators out.

He had now been there for four days. The previous night he had heard lions roaring not far from his improvised boma and was concerned enough to stay put for the day, courage not being one of his stronger points.

Hymie decided to travel downstream until he could perhaps enter the stream and find out how far down or where Yuin had been drawing water. Here he would lay the ambush.

He easily found the spot on the north bank; skid marks of the barrels had left lines in the grass at the edge of the streams and again across the sand patches beyond that. He took his water skins and filled them, re-lashing them to the saddle, then turned to look for signs of Yuin.

He was reconnoitering the south side some 100 feet from the stream and was walking back to the tree line when he almost stepped on a Gaboon viper laying amongst the dead leaves. They were a beautifully marked snake, about four foot fully grown and roughly four inches across. When laying amongst the leaves they were almost impossible to see, the skin patterned like fallen leaves of dark chocolate, brown and fawn colours.

They were generally not an aggressive reptile, preferring to lay in cover – sometimes for days – waiting for its prey to come close. But when it chose to, it could strike with frightening speed.

It carried a formidable set of fangs around an inch and a half long, and if bitten, such was the amount of venom they could deliver with just one bite that any large animal or human for that matter was doomed. The fangs could easily penetrate a boot and once bitten you would be dead in about 15 minutes.

Hymie heard the warning hiss and leapt back with a forced exclamation of, '*Shit!*'

The viper had not moved, but Hymie, standing at least three feet away now and breathing hard, looked down at the broad flat head with its two little horns sticking up near its nose, it's forked tongue flicking as it tasted the air and temperature.

'Bladdy hell man, that was close!' he muttered to himself, his heart pounding. He knew how close he had come to dying right then and there.

Seconds later a male baboon sentry, hearing the hissed word, had focused on where Hymie now stood. From his vantage point up high in the trees he saw the human being and immediately barked a warning. The reaction was equally immediate and the troop swung into the trees and retreated downstream, quickly moving away out of danger.

Hearing the baboon, Hymie frowned – he did not think he had been heard, for his uttering had for the most been done through clenched teeth. Suspicious, he cocked his rifle and silently entered the fringe of growth and trees, moving carefully downstream.

About 200 feet further he came upon a small clearing on the other side of the stream and froze as he heard a horse approaching. He saw a flash of white through the green. Yuin! he thought.

He quickly stepped back into the growth and behind an old fig tree he was next to, then set himself. Taking his bandana, he wrapped it around the hammers to muffle the sound of the cocking. Then gently cocking his rifle, he removed the bandana and raised it to his shoulder.

Peering through the foliage he had a clear but disguised view and was ready to kill in an instant.

Hymie had most of the tension taken up on the trigger already and he was committed to fire. The figure on horseback was a blur, and he breathed out and held as he began the final squeeze. There was no way he could possibly miss once Yuin rode out of the foliage on the other side.

'Wait, wait,' he counselled himself. 'Not yet...wait.'

Something in the far reaches of his mind in that moment made him hold, or perhaps he sensed something. His awareness rushed back and so did his vision. Something was not right. With shock he lifted the pressure from the trigger. His head spun and his ears rang loudly. All stood still. The only thing he could hear was the thump of his heart beat, it was surreal!

He gasped, took a deep shuddering breath and lowered the rifle, his hands shaking. He could scarcely believe his eyes!

Victoria suddenly rode into the clearing across the other side of the stream and he had almost killed her!

My God, I almost pulled the trigger, he thought, his breath coming in short shallow draughts. He felt sick, and his knees were trembling. Bedlam was ringing in his ears and he slowly slumped against the tree, not daring to move.

Slowly, elation and thrill began replacing the shock, and he turned back to stare at her.

She looked exquisite as she sat on her horse in a patch of sunlight, her golden hair gathered at the back flowing down her back from under her dark brown bush hat that she wore almost without exception when riding. Her white shirt was tucked into a long brown skirt fastened by a shiny black belt, and she wore black calf-length boots.

The horse moved forward and began to drink. Victoria was alert and sat, sweeping her eyes around, her hands holding her rifle. She was now not more than fifteen feet from him. Hymie froze.

Clucking her tongue, she pulled the horse away from the water and dismounted, Hymie caught a glimpse of her thigh and white bloomers and the pink lace as she swung her leg over the saddle and slipped to the ground.

His mouth opened as the lust suffused his body and he felt himself harden as she turned and looped the horse's reigns over a small tree branch. He could see the outline of her breast as she turned, tying off the reigns then propping her rifle against the tree.

It was almost too much to bear and he found himself shuddering with excitement. Was this really happening? he asked himself with incredulity, and he almost ran out to grab her right then and there but checked himself when she turned back and began walking to the stream, almost directly toward him. His breath caught in his throat as months of frustration and want bubbled to the surface. She looked so beautiful he thought his heart would stop.

Memories of her scent, and the time when he had 'accidentally' brushed his forearm across her breast at the stables one day, rushed into his head. Another time when she had asked if he could untangle the thong of her bush hat from her hair, he had felt the skin at the nape of her neck – it was so soft and cool it felt almost as though it was not there!

His hand involuntarily crept down to stroke his erection through his trousers, and as he touched, his knees almost gave way.

She unbuttoned her cuffs then suddenly began to tug at her shirt, freeing it from the belt about her skirt and started to unbutton her shirt front.

Hymie gaped in disbelief as she lifted her left shoulder to shrug off the shirt, exposing her breasts. They were white, her nipples a beautiful coral pink.

Oh my God, he thought, gawping, his mind raging. She is so perfect! He stared fascinated at her breasts and he swooned as her breasts shook as she made to take off the shirt fully.

Suddenly she stopped, and after a moment pulled her shirt back on and buttoned it back up.

No! Hymie screamed inside, what had stopped her? He was trembling uncontrollably, his excitement buzzing like a swarm of bees.

Suddenly, his horse whickered back upstream where he had tethered it and he quickly stepped back behind the tree. Fucking hell! he raged internally, his excitement fading. Damn the bladdy horse!

His hand froze as he heard Victoria call out Yuin's name.

'No!' he almost whimpered. The anger and shame rose in him like a rapidly filling flask. He clenched his teeth, drawing his lips back in a snarl. A white hot and uncontrollable rage washed over him in an instant as he heard her call out Yuin's name again, this time louder, expectation ringing in her tone.

Love and hate walk a fine line for a person in Van Der Hoeke's state of mind, and he instantly wanted to smash Victoria down for violating his dreams and excitement.

The slet! he screamed inside.

Hymie heard Victoria splash across the stream and run up the gentle bank right past the tree he was standing behind, his face was white and a mask of fury.

She never knew what hit her as he reversed his rifle and smacked the butt hard into the back of her head with a sickening thud.

She dropped like a wet rag to the ground in front of him.

Hymie brought the rifle butt down again but pulled the blow up short in that last fatal second.

He took a great shuddering breath and looked down at her so still on the grass, blood slowly creeping from her hair at the back of her skull where he had smashed the rifle butt.

She lay face down in the grass. He stood over her and toed her head to one side, her head lolling over, lifeless.

It hit him like a ton of bricks. Christ I've killed her! he suddenly realised and remorse washed over him. He began to shake and emotion welled up inside him.

He was halfway down on his knees, tears coursing down his face. What he had done?

'No, no!' he screamed inside and thudded to his knees beside her.

Hymie reached out tenderly to stroke her colourless and beautiful face. Her skin felt somehow papery and cool and he snatched his hand away. His breath caught in his throat and he began sobbing in great shudders, rocking back and forth on his haunches.

He could not bear it and his head was ringing like a thousand cathedral bells tolling all at once.

Still sobbing and wiping away his tears, he again looked at her face but could not bear it and quickly shut his eyes, the sorrow welling up once again like a great wave inside him. He reached out and pulled her hair over her face and then stared in horror at the blood on his fingers, frantically wiping it off on his shirt.

He looked up at the sky and then around, back to where her horse stood. The blacks ears were pricked and it was looking straight at him. He recoiled as though slapped and staggered to his feet.

Reality rushed back into his brain as he considered how vulnerable his position was.

He glanced around quickly and then stood still listening. Nothing. Weaver birds were twittering across the stream. It meant there was no threat from that direction.

Gathering himself he thought, I must move quickly. Uncocking his rifle and slinging it over his shoulder, he took the little pistol from its holster at her back and shoved it into his breaches. Then he turned Victoria over and scooped her up in his arms and retracing his footsteps he made his way back to his horse. She lay in his arms like a dead antelope, her head lolling back over his arm, legs and arms flopping uselessly.

He laid her face down over his saddle and lifting her head saw no sign of life, he started to panic now, torn between checking her further and going back to cover his sign where he had attacked her.

He rushed away to carry out the latter, knowing that Joseph would not be too far away and likely would have his Wahehe dogs with him.

'Calm down!' he said to himself. 'She is dead and I cannot change that now.' He quailed again at the enormity, tears brimming again. 'Get a grip!' he yelled internally. I must use all of my skills to throw them off the scent. He stopped suddenly and went back to his horse as he thought of a way that may trick them.

Victoria lay exactly where he had lain her, and blood had now run down around her neck and was dripping onto the saddle and ground.

His heart pounded in excitement. 'She is alive!' he screamed inside with relief and reached out and felt for her pulse at her neck. After several attempts, finally yes, he felt a very faint thud beneath his fingers.

The relief was overwhelming, but he also knew she was badly hurt, so faint was the pulse.

Wasting no time now, Hymie whipped off his neckerchief and tied it around her head and over the wound, then led the horse back to the stream, entered and turned upstream some 20 feet. He tied it off to a low branch, grabbed his rifle again and began to retrace his steps again.

He went back farther to the wagon tracks and began to sweep the trail clear where he had left the wheel ruts, pausing only to remove any of Victoria's blood from the sand, which he tossed into the undergrowth. He continued, finishing up at the edge where he had hit Victoria. He paid particular attention to this area. Satisfied that he had covered his tracks, he walked over to Victoria's horse, and untying the reins, gave it an almighty whack on the haunches with his hand. The black bolted out through the thicket and beyond. Shit, Hymie thought, a mistake. The dogs or Joseph might see it rider less and come running. He should have led it downstream further. No matter, too late now. I must move, and quickly, he thought.

He was about to go when he spotted Victoria's rifle propped against the tree. Jesus, he thought, almost didn't see it. 'Bladdy fool!' he chastised himself and grabbed the weapon.

Hymie swept the tracks of the black, Victoria and his own from the east bank back to the stream.

He checked. 'Even the dogs will have trouble finding a scent with that job,' he giggled.

Returning upstream to his horse and Victoria, treading carefully so as to keep the splashing of his footfalls to a minimum, he hesitated for a moment, relishing the moment.

Sunlight streamed down in patches through the trees and onto the horse and its bundle draped over its rump. A patch of light played upon the back of Victoria's thighs where the skirt had parted. A lump came to Hymies throat as he stared at her legs and he stepped toward her, hand outstretched.

'Shit! not now!' he berated himself for letting his emotions control him. 'Move!' he almost yelled out loud.

He opened his saddle bag and taking out a coil of rope, quickly lashed Victoria to the rump of the horse. He checked her wound and noted the bleeding had slowed and was no longer dripping. Mounting, he turned downstream and very slowly walked the horse and his limp bundle down the stream, sticking to the middle where possible.

He travelled some two miles back before rock halted his progress and he left the stream, stopping some 50 feet from the stream and returned, repeating the sweep. He then, equally carefully, made his way east away from the stream and parallel with the ranges before slowly turning in an arc back to Yuin's camp.

It was getting late when they arrived back at the camp site, the shadows lengthening. After checking Victoria, he left her and the horse some distance back. She had not stirred even once since his blow, and he began to worry that he had hit her too hard and she may not recover.

He quietly scouted the area. Seeing no sign and no evidence of anyone's presence, he returned and led the horse behind the hut as the sky began to colour.

Hymie walked back about a mile and began to sweep the trail back to the hut. He got back just before night fell around him like a soft grey cloak.

He rummaged in one of the packs and produced a small paraffin lamp wrapped in cloth. Hymie hung the lamp up on a stick poking out of the wall inside and lit it, then untying Victoria he carried her inside.

Hymie laid Victoria gently down on the cot, rolling up a jacket to support her head, and gently turned her head toward him to keep the pressure off the wound.

He sat back and looked at her. There were rivulets of blood wrapped around her neck where the wound had bled and some on her cheek as well.

He reached over and ran his fingers gently over her lips; they were soft but becoming dry. He could feel her breath now, very faint and shallow. Hymie bit his lip in concern. He went outside to his horse and removed the water skins he had filled at the stream and began to empty them into the water urn.

As he waited for the water to drain, he reflected on the day and began to feel very pleased with himself, and the excitement began the buzz within him. Hymie began to relish the thought that he now had almost fulfilled his dreams – he had Victoria! It was unbelievable!

His breath began to shorten and the thrill coursed through him as he immediately thought of her legs and the sight of the little trail of soft fine blonde hair running up the back of her thighs, and her jiggling breasts when she was at the stream. His imagination and lust grew as his breathing became more rapid. 'Oh, how smart he had been!'

One thing left to do – kill Nicholas Yuin.

Wetting his spare neckerchief, he gently sponged the blood away from her cheek and from her neck, then moistened her lips with the neckerchief. She made a very tiny moan but did not move. His heart wrenched when he looked at her, then his eyes slid down to where her breasts swelled against her shirt. He reached out and unbuttoned the two top buttons of her shirt, then undid another.

Hymie closed his eyes, swallowed and slid his hand in and gently closed it around her right breast.

He gulped. It felt like nothing he had ever experienced, soft with a texture that seemed to be almost non-existent, and he rolled her nipple gently between his fingers, his breath now coming in short sharp gasps as he floated on a cloud of ecstasy. He could no longer stand it and frantically undid the rest of the buttons and laid back her shirt exposing both breasts. He stared in wonder for a few moments, then unable to control himself any longer began squeezing her breasts, holding and playing with them. He leaned forward and suckled on her nipples like a child.

He lifted his head and slid his hand to her belt, undoing the large buckle and pulling the belt from around her waist. It caught on something. Reaching around her waist he found the pistol holster, and guiding the belt through, pulled it free.

Hymie was trembling with excitement and his erection was now bent over hard in his breaches as it tried to rise. He reached down and adjusted himself, the touch almost causing him to lose control.

He waited a few seconds, wrestling with his heightened excitement. 'Not yet, not yet!' muttered, battling to control himself.

He unclipped the metal hook at her side and lay open the skirt, he stared in awe at her pantaloons and at the mound between her legs beneath the white cotton.

Trembling, he moved his hand over her mons before suddenly freezing as a lions roar came from the plains, followed shortly after by more.

'Shit!' he exclaimed, 'I haven't dragged the thorn bushes back over!' Still cursing, he stood, grabbed his rifle and strode out to attend to the task.

Returning, he began to get excited in anticipation as he walked back inside, closing the door.

As he turned to Victoria and went down on his knees beside her, ready to resume where he had left off, he ran his hand over her shoulder, marveling at the silkiness of her skin. Suddenly, she whimpered and then coughed softly and started to vomit, the spew running down the side of her shoulder and onto his hand.

Hymie leapt back to avoid the stinking mess. 'Damn it to hell!' Hymie groaned out loud. 'Not now!'

Victoria coughed once more and lapsed back into a stupor.

Hymie found a cloth and went outside to fetch water so he could clean up the mess.

He just got to the urn, when the roaring came again from the plains, he filled the small bucket and hurried back inside and began to wipe Victoria clean.

Unconscious and heavily concussed, Victoria lay unaware and inert as though she was not even there.

Chapter 20

The First Expedition (October)

Nicholas began to lay all of his provisions out in rows at the side of the hut. There was a lot of equipment, he mused.

Panning dishes, dolly, specking pick, small containers and bags for specimens, and all the other paraphernalia for his prospecting were set aside and packed into ships' calico bags.

For a good three hours the pile of equipment grew until finally he was satisfied.

Too much, he decided and cut out a number of things he had added just because he 'might' need them.

It was Nicholas's intention to take just one packhorse on this exploration, better for travelling and he would be more versatile in his wanderings.

Jack stood solemnly watching his preparations and was feeling a little more than envious that Ubaba Nic was going on an adventure. He also worried about Ubaba going by himself.

Later that afternoon Nicholas laid out his weaponry and began to clean each piece.

Fist he dismantled the .577 calibre Renette, carefully laying out each piece and cleaning them in paraffin. Then just as carefully, reassembled the beautiful weapon, lightly oiling each part.

Finished, he snapped it shut, enjoying the solid 'clunk' as it came together and threw it up onto his shoulder. Nicholas loved his rifle, not only because of the craftsmanship that it displayed and all of its magnificent inlays, checkering and engraving, but because it had never once failed him, and he had been in some fairly tricky positions over the years. Despite its heavy calibre, it was a very accurate weapon, even at some distance, due mainly to the long special heavy seven groove rifled barrel it had.

Next he turned his attention to the heavy brass cartridges. These were not found in use in any other rifle as far as Nicholas was aware, or at least hadn't been when he had purchased the weapon.

It would be about another twenty years before the new system of primed cartridges was finally refined and revolutionized the whole system of ammunition forever.

Taking a leather satchel from one of his packs, Nicholas removed all of his reloading equipment.

He then began to carefully weigh and mix the charges for the copper priming caps. This was a very finicky task and he knew he had to be dead accurate with each and every item.

Next he laid out his brass cartridges. Selecting thirty of them, he began the tricky task of inserting the primer caps in the end of each cartridge. Pressing down firmly, he pressed the primer home into the cartridge.

Finally, he charged each cartridge with his powder mix and with a special pair of piers squeezed the lead bullets into to the end of each.

Nicholas next turned his attention to touring the establishment and instructing Whip and Jack on what he wanted them to do whilst he was gone. The bulk of the work was to make plans and foundations for a decent dwelling of at least six rooms. The *Collette* would not return for many months and the timber and supplies Nicholas had ordered would be on board, but that would not stop the main structure from being built.

A day passed and early in the morning of the next day Nicholas, Jack and Whip began to load the packhorse.

Nicholas loved this time of the day, moisture in the air, the sky just beginning to orange, and this Australian bush had a special scent to it.

They finished the packing and now stood around the fire, drinking tea but saying little.

Jack rumbled at last. 'My fren, you must be careful on yor journey, an' if you do not return in three months Mister Whip an' Jack will come lookin' fo you!'

Nicholas looked up to the giant's face and saw moisture glistening in his eyes. 'I will be careful Lungile,' he said gently, 'and you had better make that time four months before you come looking for me.'

He glanced at Whip who was staring into the fire, his face set, and he suddenly said, 'What happens if'n the *Collette* returns Mr Yuin? I mean that bastard Birch will be gunnin' for us'n, what'll we do?'

Nicholas thought for a while before saying, 'You are right, I'd forgotten about Birch, hmmm…' He stared into the fire stroking his chin, then said. 'A question for you both to think about."

He looked at both men. 'Do you want to stay here with me until we have finished establishing this place, which could take at least three to four years? Or rejoin the *Collette*.'

Jack did not hesitate and emphatically stated, thumping his chest with his fist. 'I will stay here my fren!'

Whip took his time before answering, then said. 'If I be goin' back to the *Collette*, that mongrel will sure be 'avin me flogged an' what's left of me 'ide nailed to the yard arm.' He drew a great breath and said, 'I miss the sea for sure, but I be thinkin' that this 'ere is a good place an' I also will be stayin', because if I 'av to go back aboard the *Collette*, for sure I will kill that stinkin' piece of shite Birch.'

Before anybody could react, he went on, 'An if'n that same piece of shite comes ashore an even so much as thinks about causin' the big fella 'ere trouble, I'll 'ave 'im for sure an' this time 'e won't be gettin' back up – ever!'

Nicholas looked at Whip's face and was shocked to see nothing but murder on the man's face. He turned to look at Jack, the pride and gratitude palpable on the big man's face.

Clearing his throat, Nicholas said, 'I will write a letter to Captain Strudwich to arrange things with him. Since I most likely will not be here when he returns, you are to immediately give him the letter when he arrives, and to no one else, understood?'

Both nodded their heads.

'Now.' he said catching their attention, 'it is possible that the captain will send in Birch to fetch us all as he will not know that I am away. If that happens, I would suggest that you are not here either, find yourselves a place to observe from afar.' he added, jerking his thumb over his shoulder in the direction of the bluff. 'There is a spare telescope in the big trunk in the hut which you can use.'

Nicholas grabbed a small branch that was sticking out of the fire, and poking the fire said, 'Once the captain finds out we are all missing, I am certain he will come ashore to look for himself. Then you can just meet him at the hut pretending you have just returned from a hunt or something and you can deliver the letter. Birch will not dare try anything whilst he is there so you will be okay, understood?' Both murmured their ascent.

Nicholas watched them as they mulled things over and had already anticipated the next question.

They were all silent for a while then Whip said, 'But what if Birch does stay or the captain just sends him out searching?'

Nicholas looked him straight in the eye and said, 'It would not be your fault if Birch got separated from the others or lost out here, now would it Wilber? And whilst he was out there...' he waved the stick up river and out to the east. 'If the bastard happened to continually bang his head on your outstretched fist, no matter how much you tried to persuade him to stop, well now, that is not your fault either is it?'

Whip and Jack stared at Nicholas, the comprehension of what he had actually said slow to dawn on them both.

Suddenly, a ghost of a smile crossed Nicholas's face and they all began to chuckle at Nicholas's answer.

When they had settled down again, Whip was still not satisfied and said, 'But 'e will report to the cap'n an' for sure tell 'im t'was me, what then? I know Cap'n Strudwich, 'e wouldn't stand for it 'an they will 'unt me down for sure.'

Nicholas sighed. 'Whip, do I have to spell it out for you? If it gets to the point where either of you are in fear of your life,' he said rolling his eyes, 'and don't be fooled, that is a real possibility, make sure he doesn't make a report – it's a big country out there.'

They both stared at Nicholas, Whip's mouth had dropped open in shock. 'Jaysus!' he blurted.

Nicholas didn't say another word, but he was worried. He knew that Birch would either make Whip and Jack suffer terribly if they returned to the ship, even if by force. He knew Birch would stop at nothing to get at them and would fabricate any excuse to either kill them both onshore if Strudwich was not there to stop him, or he would find some way of getting them back on board.

All he had to do was to destroy the letter and there would be no stopping him.

It was for this reason that he had told Whip of the alternative. He knew it was wrong, but if it came down to it, Birch was a vicious, murderous individual and didn't deserve any compassion – good first mate or not.

The next day Nicholas left for his adventure, but he departed with worry about Jack and Whip's welfare gnawing at his gut.

Chapter 21

Death Adder

*A*bout six miles due north-east of the hut, Nicholas topped a small rise and stared at a faint grey smudge on the horizon. It was too early in the morning for enough of the rising sun to show any detail, the stars still faintly twinkling above him, but he reckoned what he was looking at was perhaps a distant range. Even with his telescope it was a long way in the distance, a good 30 mile he estimated, maybe more. Nonetheless, he decided to head for it and edged Stitch forward.

He reasoned that once he reached this, he would be able to climb up and then would be able to plot his next course and maybe even see likely prospecting grounds.

As he rode, Nicholas threw open his mind and absorbed the new scenes, scents and sounds. The sky was clear, and an orange glow just peeped over the eastern horizon.

The bush was alive with the sounds of all manner of bird life, sounds that were so different to other countries he had travelled. He stopped as he came down from the rise.

The rapidly advancing orange glow of the sun touching the lands features in some places with pink and mauve in ever an increasing brightness. Over toward the river on his left he saw squadrons of wild duck flashing downstream, although from here he could only now just see the line of trees which he knew hugged the river banks.

He stopped to watch as a little black bird with a white breast and long tail land not ten feet from him on a dry shrub and began a noisy chatter, swinging its long tail rapidly back and forth as it did so. 'Cheeky little sod aren't you!' Nicholas said out loud. Then suddenly, with a soft whir of wings, the little bird launched itself up about fifteen feet and snapped a moth out of the air before spiraling back and disappearing into the low shrub. Nicholas grinned and said, 'And quick too!'

He drew in the early morning moisture, intoxicated by the scent. Somewhere in the shrubbery, came the sound of a deep 'Whoo! Whoo!' not unlike that of wild pigeons in Africa. His assumption was correct as small birds chattered and sang in the coming dawn.

The sun was now on the climb as he continued in a north-easterly direction. He rode slowly, no urgency about him as he took in the extensive array of birdlife and animals that abounded in the area. Kangaroo stood about in groups of ten or twenty on grassy flats, some grey in colour and some a rich red.

The red kangaroo male was an impressive animal with a deep well-muscled chest, muscular forearms hanging wide from its square shoulders. He was amazed at the height of them when they propped themselves back on their tails to look at him, ears twitching nervously. He reckoned they must stand at least six feet tall, maybe more.

Small mice bounded from the retreating early morning shadow to hop across his trail on hind legs, much like the kangaroo, and larger ones about the size of a kitten hopped ahead of him and vanished down burrows beneath the shrubbery. These had pointed snouts and rat-like tails, except for a small brush at the tip, and their little ears pricked forward like that of a cat.

With a whoosh of wing, great flocks of some sort of cockatoo launched into the sky, and screeching raucously, swooped and rose in a dazzling display of light grey and bright pink plumaged breasts. As they turned, flashing their beautiful pink feathers in the dawn sun, they would suddenly vanish into the low grass across the scrub and perhaps feed on seeds amongst the grass.

It's nothing like Africa – or Canada for that matter, he pondered. The animal life in both of those continents was as fascinating as you could wish for, and equally as dangerous.

But here too was beauty. Totally different, subtle and very beautiful. It was as though nature had preserved all of the differences it could assemble and placed them here. The land did not seem to threaten, like Africa for example, where you had to be constantly on guard against human and animal.

But he knew he had much to learn about this land and reminded himself never to get too complacent.

Nicholas drew out his fob watch and saw that it was now eight-thirty. He reckoned he had now travelled about fifteen miles since his departure and the sun was now fully into the morning sky. 'Time for a cup of coffee!' he declared.

Dismounting, Nicholas went about starting a small fire and put the pot on to boil.

He took a small wrapped package of the rock cakes that Whip had made for his journey and selecting one, bit down on it.

Pain shot into his teeth and gums, as the cake hardly gave at all.

'Jesus Christ!' he exclaimed out loud, holding his mouth. He reckoned that this was the hardest thing he had ever bit on. 'Hell and damnation! Whip doesn't need to be a bloody boxer to knock people's teeth out!' he lamented, and pouring a cup of tea, he dipped the rock cake into it to hopefully soften it.

Nicholas doused the fire and packed up the kit into his saddle bags and continued on his way.

He made excellent time that morning as the country began to flatten out into rolling low hills, and the thorny scrub thinned the further inland he went.

Scattered groves of reddish coloured trunked eucalyptus grew randomly in groves around the area – so different to anything Nicholas had encountered in his travels – the leaves shining bright in the hot sunlight.

The low range he had seen earlier on turned into disappointment and was nothing more than a small run of hillocks, ironstone, gravel and low sharp prickly bushes.

Not much further beyond the small range however, Nicholas discovered a large gorge through which the river coursed.

The gorge was beautiful, and he descended the sides and walked along the river's edge. The western side from which he had approached had a relatively gentle slope to it, but the other side rose up to high jagged cliffs, the river meandering along the base of the cliffs.

Looking up he saw several layers of tumbled limestone and shale-like stone – mostly a light rusty red in colour, although on closer examination there were traces of jasperite and iron – stacked as if piled up by some ancient giant. Dense thickets of low shrub and many white trunked eucalypts similar to those on the riverbanks further downstream grew on the river's edges.

He rode some two miles upstream and finding a shallow point he crossed and headed back in a north-easterly direction, slowly ascending the rocky sides.

A few miles further along he stopped at the base of a high rocky range, some three hundred feet high he estimated. Seeking a better view, Nicholas tethered Stitch and the packhorse beneath a shady white gum sticking out from the rocks. He took a water skin, his rifle and telescope, and began the climb.

A full hour later he reached the top.

A fantastic formation greeted him. Jutting up from the top, nature had built a window frame into the top of the ridge.

The rock, over time, had fallen away or erosion had worked away a hole into the crested ridge, which itself rose off the rock shear at the top creating a window of about six feet in the ridge.

Through the 'window' Nicholas could see the river winding its way for miles south-west of his position.

He saw several small lizards and skinks on his climb. No harm there, he thought.

Nicholas knew from information he had gathered from a variety of sources, that apparently there were no natural predators in Australia that could threaten man or not that anyone had found yet, such as the great cats of Africa, so he was quite relaxed. He also knew there were many types of different snakes here. A lot were very poisonous, he was informed whilst in the port of Fremantle, and he kept a wary eye open but saw none.

In his climb he spooked some dark chocolate coloured kangaroos lying in the shade of the small caves interspersing the rocks. These looked different to those he had seen – blocky in appearance and shorter with larger haunches. As Nicholas headed back down he saw some smoke drifting up into the sky north of his position. Hmm, he thought, might be the other prospector's camp, and reminded himself to avoid it on his journey further north.

It was mid-afternoon and he reckoned he had travelled about 50 miles all up. The temperature had stepped up considerably, while the landscape and vegetation had flattened out and randomly scattered low shrub dotted the land.

Occasionally, Nicholas came across patches of a low spiky grass-like growth. The spiny bushes were unusual in that they often seemed to form a circle of sort and often had a dead centre of grey grass. He was later to find the shrub was called spinifex bush, and for the Aboriginal people this grass had many uses.

Around the central base of the clumps was found a very hard resin-like substance. The Aboriginal people called it *aywente*, which when heated turned sticky and when cooled became very hard again. This glue-like quality was used to secure the spear heads and twine, and also to affix the sharp spikes at the end of the Aborigines' throwing sticks, or *woomeras* as they called them, to which the end of the throwing spear was fitted. The *woomera* was also used for a variety of other uses.

He found his first sign real of mineralisation on an almost indiscernible ridge of brown and rusty quartz running across the side of a small hill. The hill was quite thick with growth and the small red trunked gums grew quite prolifically around the base and up the sides of the hill. A variety of other shrubs abounded all over the hillock and trailed off to one side into a small creek.

It was in this creek that Nicholas had ridden, seeking shade and the shrubs covered in lilac-coloured flowers that emitted a sweet and pleasant scent.

Nicholas was about to spur Stitch and the pack horse up the bank when he spotted the quartz through the shrub. Taking his small pick and a specking glass he made his way up to the quartz outcrop.

He spent about two hours prizing pieces of the stone away from the outcrop and found several interesting traces of mineral.

It was enough to make him decide to strike camp and to explore further the next day.

He made his way back down to where he had left his horses, and a short time later found a small sandy clearing in the creek bed and set camp. Taking the samples of the quartz, he took his dolly pot and began to pound the ore to a fine crush. Wetting it in the panning dish, he found traces of the galena he had expected and some minute traces of copper, but nothing significant. Oh well, better than nothing, he thought.

Scooping a body length hollow in the sand, he then cut some leafy branches from the gum trees and after running them over the fire to get rid of ants or insects, lay them in the hollow and spread out his swag over them. After stoking up the fire, he lay down and was asleep in minutes.

He awoke just before dawn hearing a distant howl of a dog. Must be the same type as I saw back at the river, he reasoned, and listened as the long drawn out howls continued, then suddenly stopped. Strange, he thought, but dismissed it after a few minutes.

He fed and watered the horses and continued his exploration.

That day he continued to explore the area. Finding nothing more at the small outcrop, he headed for a higher ridge some three miles distant. It rose abruptly from the surroundings and through his telescope he saw what appeared to be a dark grey streak down one face.

Interesting, he thought and nudged his horse forward to investigate.

He saw no sign of another human being but kept a wary eye out just in case.

Nicholas was halfway across the flat to the abutment when his instincts started to ring alarm bells. He could not say why the feeling came over him, but once before he had learnt the hard way not to ignore it.

He stopped and rose in the saddle, and after a swift look around began to quadrant off sections and studied each with care.

Nothing, but the feeling remained. Moving forward again he quickened his pace and about 100 yards from the rocks abruptly turned left and cantered around to the far side.

After checking the far side, he tethered his horses under a clump of the red trunked gums. Sliding his rifle and telescope out, he quickly made his way to just below the top of the ridge.

He panned the horizon first and within seconds spotted an out of place smudge on the horizon off to his right. The smudge was moving slowly to his left, which would place whatever it was on a collision course with his tracks. Man, or animal? he thought and silently thanked his instincts once again, remembering how the dogs had abruptly stopped howling just before dawn.

Moving his right leg to one side to steady himself he was about to reach for his rifle when he felt something hit his leg, just below the outside of his knee.

Looking down, he exclaimed 'Oh shit!' as he saw the blunt snout and triangular head of what looked like an adder of some sort just as it withdrew from its initial bite. It was about two and a half to three feet long with a fat body, in that moment it drew back its head, ready to strike again.

Time froze for a split second as Nicholas stared at the snake. In that moment, he saw it was beautifully marked with zigzag stripes – dark chocolate brown on a reddish-brown background.

His knee still within striking range, Nicholas suddenly jerked his leg up so that his high leather boot was in front of the snake. In doing so he nudged the snake. The desert death adder struck again with blurring speed and hit the leather near the ankle, this time causing no harm. But as Nicholas pulled his leg out of harm's way he knew he was in dire straits and his leg was already tingling.

Forgetting about the 'smudges' on his trail, he knew he must get back down to his horses with some urgency.

He started to make his way down the rocky hillside but his leg was becoming numb to his crotch and he was finding it difficult to keep upright. His breath was now rasping through his clenched teeth as he tried to control his anxiety.

By the time Nicholas had staggered another ten paces his whole left side was tingling and he was losing control of his limbs. Three times he fell on to his face despite leaning on his rifle.

Bleeding from several cuts to his face and hands, he eventually reached the small grove of trees beneath which he had tethered Stitch and the packhorse. Stitch skittered nervously as Nicholas reached him.

Nicholas was now becoming disorientated and had little control or feeling in his extremities. He was sweating profusely and had to fight – with little success – to fill his lungs. He made a grab for the saddle horn and succeeded in grabbing it with his left hand.

Spots danced before his eyes in brilliant orange and white patterns, and there was a roaring noise in his head. He hung on to the horn and tried to lift his arm to get to his water pannikin, but with the neurotoxin of the bite now gripping him and the spots now interspersing with black, he slowly slumped to the ground.

With paralysis overtaking his body, and with the struggle to drag air into his lungs, he collapsed under his horse like a piece of wet rag.

Gnarlu and Yindu picked up Nicholas's trail with ease and cautiously crossed it, giving the impression that they were heading away from the trail and perhaps had not noticed it.

They continued for about half a mile and reached two solitary sheoak trees. Here they sat down in the shade close to the trunks, blending in with the dark grey bark.

The old grey bearded elder had sent them to shadow Nicholas and to try to keep him from harm. The men knew every water hole and tree from which they could get water from in an area encompassing hundreds of square miles, whilst Nicholas could not know where to find water the elder had reasoned. They were told not to interfere or be seen unless absolutely necessary.

They sat in the shade, listening to the lulling sound of the light breeze as it passed through the long narrow leaves of the trees. Four hours passed and still the man had not emerged from behind the hill and outcrop.

Suddenly, Gnarlu made a decision and without a word they rose as one and trotted over toward the hill.

Rounding the northern side, they stopped. The white man's animals were tied to the trees and one was dancing its head up and down and pulling at the tether to the tree. Sometimes it nudged the prone figure of the white man lying beneath it. Somewhat nervous of the horses they tentatively approached.

Nicholas lay trembling below the animal, some white spittle at the corner of his mouth.

'*Djaning*,'(Death Adder) said Yindu emphatically, recognising the symptoms immediately.

'*War'u, war'u*,' (bad, bad) said Gnarlu shaking his head. 'Find the snake, quickly," Yindu said and pointed up the hill with his spears. Gnarlu began to track up to the top of the ridge. It did not take him long to find the abandoned telescope and the death adder.

One blow from the back of his boomerang was all it took to dispatch the reptile.

Yindu, plucking up his courage, approached the horse. Stitch stood motionless as Yindu knelt down at his master's body, which by now had begun to stop trembling.

'*War'u!*' Gnarlu said, still shaking his head and indicating the snake.

Gnarlu and Yindu looked at each other, they knew that this white man was unlikely to survive such a bite from this full-grown death adder, but they must try to help.

They quickly made preparations to move Nicholas to a better place where they could find water and traditional medicines, taking the dead snake with them, as they must use parts of the organs to make up an antidote

Chapter 22

Stream of Anguish

$\mathcal{I}$t had been almost two hours since Joseph had seen Victoria move off toward the tree line. He was still searching for signs with M'uyinga. They swept back and forth, crisscrossing on about 45-degree angles. They still had the single horse tracks, although they were sporadic and old.

Joseph suddenly realised his Missy had not returned and called a halt to M'uyinga. As he did so, he saw M'fwimi and M'risho trotting quickly across to them. He looked beyond them but could see no one else.

Fear clutched at his heart as the two warriors halted before him and M'uyinga.

The two explained that they had no return whistle or call from M'hafi for the last four miles and there was no sign of him or the Missy.

'Aye! aye! aye!' cried Joseph beating his chest hard with his fist. 'Quickly, we go back!' he said pointing with his assegai, trying to calm himself, but in his heart he knew something terrible had happened. As the warriors turned as one and started to run back, Joseph had to restrain himself from galloping for there were many ground squirrel and bush rat holes in the ground, and the last thing they would need was to snap the horse's legs. He looked to the sky, it was about mid-afternoon – not much time before nightfall, when they must stop for fear of spoiling the trail, and this area was no place to be stumbling around at night, let alone with horses.

They travelled back for a good hour, periodically one of the men would branch off toward the tree line, but would always return, and one look at them, even from a distance told the story, nothing.

Eventually, they turned toward the area where Victoria had veered off toward M'hafi and the tree line.

Joseph was beside himself with worry and his heart was as heavy as stone.

Suddenly M'risho called out, pointing to the sky. Two or three vultures were circling in one spot about half a mile ahead toward a jumble of rocks close to the tree line. Joseph's heart sank, and fear seized him as they hurried over to the jumble of boulders.

The three Hehe warriors began to search the rocks and Joseph circled the kopje of boulders, his eyes on the ground. He saw only one set of tracks, and jumping down from his horse, saw that it was made by a bare foot and was about three hours old. He backtracked for half a mile but found no horse tracks. Then he heard the whistle and went back to the boulders.

The three warriors were on the eastern side and standing together, they were all staring down at something.

Joseph dismounted and went up to join them, dreading what they might have found.

Steeling himself he looked down into the cleft.

M'hafi lay dead at the bottom of the gap in the rocks, his body arched in an odd shape, wracked and bent from the effects of the poison, dried white spittle still evident about his mouth.

So narrow was the cleft there was no way they could get him out. At least not without a lot of effort and time which they did not have.

M'uyinga pointed at the sign of struggle on the patch of earth and said, 'Mamba!'

They picked up M'hafi's shield and assegai and dropped them over the body, and turned and loped back down the trail, knowing now that soon it would be dark.

It would be difficult to find the horse's tracks, but if they did they may be able to ascertain what had happened. They would return to M'hafi's resting place later. Then they would fill the cleft with stone and camp the night.

Joseph was praying to his gods that she had been thrown from her horse or it had broken a leg and he would find her safe and well, waiting for them.

Tears began to mist his face as his thoughts began to conjure up worst-case scenarios and of how he would die himself if she was hurt, or worse, dead.

An hour later, they found the point where Victoria had veered off to the trees.

As they tracked toward the tree line they came across another set of hoof prints heading away from the trees, rider less, thought Joseph as he looked down at the spoor.

Panic teetered on a precipice in his mind and he immediately wheeled and trotted to the tree line.

'Missy Victoria!' he shouted. Silence was his answer. 'Missy Victoria!' he called again a little louder. Suddenly M'uyinga appeared at his side and touched his leg.

Joseph looked down at him and saw M'uyinga was shaking his head and pointing toward the direction of the kopje. 'K'uusa,'(come) was all he said and trotted off with the others.

Reluctant as he was to give up, Joseph could see it was getting very late. He was torn between continuing or returning with the others and waiting until the new dawn. What if she lay wounded or hurt somewhere in the tree line. The lion might get her and his gut clenched at the thought.

He also considered that he might destroy any sign if he continued, and more over it would be dark soon and too dangerous to stay out here alone.

They had heard hyenas and lions previously, and not long ago the roar of the lions seemed a little closer. He turned and trotted back toward the kopje.

It was an edgy and fitful night spent amongst the rocks. On return they had gathered smaller boulders and had piled them over M'hafi's body, satisfied that no predator of scavenger could get to it.

The ritual of Hehe mourning had to be shortened. Nonetheless, the incantations, songs and the ritual of spitting water took several hours. They then finally made camp.

In the middle of the night they heard the terrified scream of a horse and they all knew that Victoria's horse had been brought down – it would have had no chance against a pride of lions.

At least the lions would not be bothered stalking them that night.

It was dawn and the sky just beginning to colour when they set off south to the last spot where they had found Victoria's tracks and the horse's hoof prints heading away.

Joseph looked at the horse tracks, and said alarmed, 'No rider!'

They easily found the path, and now lead by circling vultures, quickly turned and began to track down the kill. Thirty minutes later they heard hyenas giggling ahead and knew they weren't far from it.

An angry muffled snarl reached them as they crested a small rise, and there below them lay Victoria's black. The horse was half-eaten already. What was once a beautiful animal was now a bloodied mess, part dismembered, its bones broken and stark against the gore.

It was a sad sight for Joseph who had looked after the animal since it was a foal and it was also his Missy Victoria's horse and so had received special attention.

There was one lioness still feeding and surrounding and harassing her were four full grown hyenas. She was, by the look of it, heavily pregnant which would explain why she was still feeding and also why she was the last to feed.

Barely visible in the long grass about sixty feet away lay a big male and two lionesses under the spread of an acacia. They could see their bloated stomachs, having fed well on the kill.

There was no real threat from the lions now they knew the beasts had gorged themselves. The beasts would rest, sleeping most of the day, but one never knew what temperament the lion may be in, especially the lionesses. Nonetheless, Joseph wanted to see if Victoria had taken her rifle so they had to examine the carcass.

They formed a line, and charging down into the hollow, began to shout their war cry in unison.

'*Hee twahumite, hee twahumite, he, he, he...heeeeeeeeee!*'

Running toward the horse, assegais banging on the inside of their war shields, they spread out a little as they ran.

Snarling, the big pregnant lioness laid her ears back and slunk away toward the tree as the hyenas scattered into the yellow veld grass to about 200 feet away, where they stood, waiting, knowing that sooner or later they would get another chance at the carcass.

The big male lion and his two lionesses were on their feet in an instant. They did not move but just fixed the group with their chilling yellow-eyed stare.

The rifle was nowhere to be seen and obviously Victoria must have taken it out beforehand or someone else had.

Hope fluttered in the old man's chest. They removed the saddle and bags, bloodied as they were and set off again to the tree line, picking up the spoor as they went. It went almost in a beeline to the stream.

They single filed into the tree line, silent and blending in with the surroundings.

They breathed in the scents surrounding them and absorbed the sounds and sights around them – skills born out of centuries of hunting in the land, from the northern boundaries to the far southern edges of the Iringa.

By not actually staring at any one particular thing but by expanding the awareness, they could pick up any tiny thing that was either misplaced or was foreign to the general pattern. They were aware that Victoria certainly, but possibly others, had definitely been here.

They became as one with nature, and not one thing went unobserved. Thus, the first thing they saw was Hymie's attempt to cover his tracks to the water's edge. Given this, it was very unlikely that anyone was still here, but a man without caution was a dead fool walking.

One slow hand movement and they silently fanned out either side, Joseph quietly sliding down off the horse and tying off to a broken stub on a tree trunk some twenty feet back amongst the trees. The packhorses were tied to his horse.

They crossed the stream and began the hunt for signs. It took a full two hours before M'fwimi, some way upstream on the farthest side, signaled with a click of his tongue that he had found something. They crossed over to him, and there on the broad leaf of a juvenile palm sat a tiny piece of soil and pebble, not more than one-sixteenth of an inch in diameter. It looked as though it was rusty, and they looked closer.

M'fwimi carefully plucked it from the leaf and rubbed it between his fingers. Blood!

Joseph's heart almost stopped in fear for Victoria. They found other bits of the same scattered around and after scanning the ground found where it had been scooped up and thrown into the scrub.

They discussed this in low tones and came to the conclusion that she had been wounded and captured, otherwise who would bother to go to such lengths to disguise the spoor.

'Van Der Hoeke,' Joseph concluded, nodding his head in realisation, and he suddenly felt a weight fall upon him like a wet and massive buffalo hide cloak. He blamed himself, he should have seen this!

'Aee, aee...aee! M'puva! M'puva,' (stupid person) Baba Joe lamented softly, beating his chest with his closed fist. The old man suddenly was bereft with woe and grief and an overwhelming feeling of failure.

The others left him alone for a while, respecting his feelings.

His friend M'uyinga suddenly appeared before him. 'Baba,' he said, 'this person who has her is a fool!' Joseph looked up at him in query.

'He covers the sign but takes the prize. If he has the Missy, they will be one horse, so easy sign somewhere eh?' He placed his hand on Baba Joe's shoulder.

'This foolish man not take *dead* Missy, if kill, leave here!' he said sweeping his assegai around. 'She not here!' he said emphatically.

'But then, she is perhaps alive!' Joseph broke in.

M'uyinga was right! His heart lifted and he took a deep breath. 'I must not give up,' he berated himself.

'Come, quickly now, we have much to do Baba!' M'uyinga said.

Rapping out commands, Baba Joe and the others immediately began to backtrack. Two of them to the stream and clearing. And two upstream to try to pick up where the outsider, whoever he or they may be, had come to this position.

It wasn't long before M'uyinga and M'fwimi cut the spoor of Hymie's horse coming down toward them. At the same time, Joseph and M'risho had picked up the sweep back to the water's edge.

Joseph's sharp eyes and experience served him well as he spotted a small gathering of ants tugging furiously at a squashed caterpillar, its guts squished out to one side.

Someone or thing had trodden on it. Bending down he saw what might be a partial boot print.

They entered the water and very slowly scanned the stream bottom, one upstream and one downstream.

Just as M'uyinga and M'fwimi arrived back at the clearing, Joseph clucked his tongue as he stared at some pebble in front of a larger rock under the water.

'There!' He saw an indentation in the pebbles. Taking a dry stick, he gently touched the pebbles in the little hollow under the clear water. Immediately fine mud bled from the indentation, quickly clouding and rushing on its way downstream.

'Fresh!' he cried to himself and looking around found the leaves of a small branch ever so slightly bent. He reached out and turned the branch over; the leaves and the thin bark on the branch bore marks. Bruised! he cried to himself.

There were no more indentations to be found, and just a few feet upstream there was a fine sandy rill across the creek angled downstream from the left bank. No tracks, he thought.

Looking carefully downstream, he expanded his awareness and as he did, very faint disturbances began to appear, almost washed away, and barely visible. But, they were there! A slight turning of small rocks and almost imperceptible colour differences where the rock and pebble had lain – the bottom section that had been resting down, was now turned somewhat and thus had a colour band exposed.

Very clever thought Joseph, but not quite good enough to fool us.

He and M'risho immediately headed downstream, with the others scanning the banks.

It was no more than another hour and a half before they picked up where Hymie had tried to disguise his tracks on exiting the stream near the beginning of some small rapids and shortly after they were heading east and onto clear spoor, made easier by the fact that with the extra weight of Victoria, the horses hoof prints were much clearer. It was now about three hours past dawn and they headed off at a good rate, worry gnawing at Joseph's gut as though he had a serpent within.

Chapter 23

Of Dreams and Fantasies

She lay naked except for her pantaloons and Hymie's neckerchief which, now washed, lay across her chest.

God, he thought, even in sickness she looked so beautiful.

He had let her be after he had cleaned her up. Something held him back from going any further with his molestation of her the previous evening.

It was not guilt, rather she was so still, like a limp rag. In the end he reasoned it was the vomiting that had made him stop, that and the fact that a wave of tiredness had washed over him after he had washed her.

He had picked up her shirt, it stinking of vomit and washed it in the bucket, then hung it out the front of the hut to dry.

Exhausted, he had rolled out his swag and slept with his back against the post initially, but eventually sliding down onto the swag and did not wake until after dawn.

As he opened his eyes the first thing he saw was Victoria, and the fact that she was here! She was *his* at last. Elation coursed through his body as though he was being immersed in warm water.

He rolled up to a sitting position and went to check her. A moment's panic hit him as he checked her pulse. Yes! It was a little stronger.

Opening the door, he checked around the inside of the boma. Seeing no sign of anything animal or human, he returned and propped open the door with a stick to let the fresh morning air in, although it was already beginning to warm up. He fetched the pannikin and tried to trickle a little water into her mouth but it just ran out.

Then suddenly she made a soft sound. 'Nnnnnmmm!' and turned her head slightly. Excited, he trickled a little more water into her mouth again. 'Yes!' he exalted, her tongue slowly moved and the water was taken in.

Hymie sat beside her on the stool for about an hour, gnawing at his lip as he stared at the inert form of Victoria, watching as she lay so still and so very pale, but then leaning forward, he noticed a very slight touch of pink on her cheeks now. 'That's better!' he said to himself.

Slightly relieved, he relaxed a little.

Hunger gnawed at his gut suddenly, reminding him that he had not eaten since yesterday. He reluctantly left her side and went outside to prepare some breakfast.

'Should he risk lighting a small fire?' he asked himself, wondering how successful his bush craft had been in throwing the old man and his dogs off his trail.

He knew sooner or later they would begin to sweep and would find the black and his trail further south.

It would not take them long to conclude he was carrying extra weight, but that weight could be water he reasoned, so relaxed a little.

They would not find his trail until at least mid-afternoon, he smugly concluded, and if they do track him to here, he would give them something to think about and a passage to hell.

He decided he would light a small fire and at least heat some water for a cup of coffee.

There was no sign of Yuin either and he reckoned that he would be prospecting far up the ranges, perhaps even on the other side.

The hot coffee was invigorating and the cooked meat from last night, although cold, was delicious. He looked at the fire, it had all but burnt down to coals. He turned and strode back into the hut again.

He had no sooner re-entered the hut, when a small piece of a branch that was lying on a rock to one side of the fire, suddenly tumbled into the coals, and shortly a thin wisp of smoke drifted lazily into the morning air.

Hymie stopped abruptly, gasping out loud as he took in the scene before him. The morning Sun was now slanting in through the open door, and warm golden light fell across the bunk bed and onto the unconscious Victoria.

The warm light giving colour and life to her. She is like a vision, he thought as he crossed to her.

He could not help himself and removed the neckerchief from her breasts.

They rose and fell with each breath, which now was becoming deeper. Reaching out he resumed caressing her breasts, squeezing until her nipples rose with the pressure.

He wished she were awake, fighting him, the vision of her struggling with him naked as he prepared to have his way with her triggered an immediate reaction in his groin and his heart rate increased.

He looked at her navel and saw a little fine line of golden hair running down into the pantaloons.

Unable to resist any longer, he drew the garment down over her legs and tossed them onto the floor.

He stared in awe at her mons, reddish golden hair covered it, and trembling he cupped her, pushing apart her legs with his other hand. Moving his hand up and down he could no longer stand the bursting lust within him. He stood and tore off his boots and clothes.

He stood over her, naked. His excitement now pulsing throughout his body.

He turned to get between her legs, when she suddenly moaned quite loudly compared to before and startled him.

He could not make out what she said and he bent over her to listen.

M'uyinga was in the lead. They had been running toward the ranges on a north-easterly angle when the trail suddenly vanished. Spreading out, they had difficulty finding it again.

Joseph fretted at the delay but knew it was only a matter of time before they found the now obviously disguised tracks – time they did not have. Joseph's instincts were screaming something very bad was happening, he could almost smell it.

M'uyinga suddenly stopped, staring at the ranges. Something did not fit.

The others also halted as he stared and they too looked ahead.

'What is it?' asked Joseph

M'uyinga pointed. Joseph looked but could see nothing, his eyes no longer as sharp at distances as the younger men. He suddenly remembered that Missy Victoria carried a small telescope in a pouch sewn into her saddle bag. He reached around and slid it out, then standing in the saddle he focused on where M'uyinga had pointed.

He saw a barely visible tendril of blue rising up from a gully in the foothills.

'Smoke!' he said out loud. M'uyinga had a huge grin on his face, and Joseph nodded in respect.

They now ran on. About a quarter of a mile from the smoke, Joseph called a halt, he again stood in the saddle. Glassing the gulch, he quickly saw the outline of the hut, the thin lazy finger of smoke now clearly visible. He turned to issue orders to proceed but stopped, chewing at his lip. Something made him turn back and look again.

'There!' His heart leaped as he saw the white shirt fluttering at the front. 'Missy Victoria's shirt!'

'Quickly!' he said. They fanned out a little and rapidly closed the gap to the hut.

Arriving at the edge of the boma, they saw the hut beyond.

Suddenly, they heard Hymie screaming in anger in Afrikaans and a sickening smack on human flesh.

Baba Joe quailed, then snapped 'Quickly! The rocks!' sweeping his hand in a motion around the hut. Holding his hand up he jabbed two fingers into his palm and said, 'No kill!'

Again, they heard Van der Hoeke scream out in Afrikaans.

M'risho and M'fwimi raced to the right of the boma and glided up over the rocks at the edge of the gulch and vanished behind the hut.

As Hymie looked at her, a single tear slid from the corner of Victoria's eye.

He hesitated for a moment, looking at her face, her slightly parted lips and her eyelids, her long lashes sweeping down toward the top her cheeks. The sight made his heart trip, she was so lovely.

He leant forward and wiped away the tear with his thumb.

Victoria was floating in a semi-conscious state and was still heavily concussed, unable to surface, although she was beginning to rise from the stupor in brief flashes.

The last thing Victoria was doing before the rifle butt had smacked into her skull, was running up the bank about to call Nicholas's name again. It therefore was the first memory that surfaced for a brief moment, right after Hymie had wiped the tear away.

He was about to resume his manipulation between her legs but froze when she suddenly cried softly, 'Nicholas?'

'Nicholas!' he exclaimed loudly. *'Jy fucking teef!'* (You fucking bitch!) he screamed in Afrikaans and back-handed her across the head so hard her whole body jumped and arched as if she had had a fit.

The blow sending her spiraling back into stupor again, blood now trickling from her nose and mouth.

Raging still, Hymie screamed, *'Ek sal jou wys jou slet!'* (I will show you, you slut!) and turning he yanked a length of hide rope from the centre post and lashed her hands together.

He dragged her off the bunk onto the floor, her head banging onto the dirt, starting the bleeding from the wound at the back again.

Grasping her hands, he slung her over his shoulder, and jamming his knee between her legs he lifted her hands up and over one of the wooden pegs driven into the post, and roughly let her go, jerking her limp body taught. The peg snapped with a loud crack and she collapsed in a crumpled heap to the floor.

'Fuck!' he yelled in frustration and dragged her up again and hung her onto another peg. Slowly, he lowered her until she hung helpless from the peg, her feet slightly splayed out at angles either side of the post.

Hymie was breathing hard; the fury now being replaced by a feeling of ultimate power as he looked at her now hanging naked and helpless in the flood of light spilling in from the morning Sun. An angry red mark across her face and eye. Bright red blood trickled from her nose and mouth, streaking her face and neck, somehow making it all the more exciting for Hymie.

He reached out and shook her breasts, squeezing her nipples hard, still furious. The rage upon him was like a fire and hate rampaging inside of him.

He was all powerful and in complete control of her, his mind now running on pure manic lust.

'Now is my time!' he snarled in English and stepped to her, his body cutting out the sun.

His desire at fever pitch, his head was roaring with lust and power. He gasped as he took hold of himself, stooping, he kneed her legs apart began to rub himself into her folds.

Hymie paused, hardly believing the moment. 'At last!' he exalted.

He was almost on the point of exploding in orgasm and his knees trembled. He had to stop, and gripping himself tightly, he fought off the passion that almost had him on the brink, trying very hard to divert his mind. 'Not yet, not yet, hold!' he willed himself, fighting for control, his legs shaking with a will of their own. Then he felt the intensity of impending orgasm fade away and again rubbed his erection between her thighs.

Then straightening and bringing his hands up to cup her face, he said viciously, 'Look at me! Now you are mine forever bitch!'

Closing his eyes, he readied himself to ram into her, savouring the moment.

M'risho and M'fwimi slid silently through the open door, their razor-sharp assegais ready, held at the hip and angling up. They moved as one and thrust forward.

Hymie could not comprehend what was happening.

All he initially felt were sharp pricks on the inside of his shoulder blades, then a shove in his back momentarily pushed him forward onto Victoria, dislodging his erection from her folds and his chest meeting her face. His body now flat against her, he thought in that instant, how soft she was.

Suddenly, he was dragged back by a terrible pressure in his shoulders, he felt a dull muted clicking as the long blades of the assegais cut into his collar bone, as though something massive was sitting on his chest. He screamed in pain as the spears cut into his nerves.

Hymie looked down and stared in utter disbelief at three inches of assegai blade poking through his skin just below his collarbone and on either side of his chest.

He dropped his arms and screamed again in agony as his muscle tore, partly severed by the razor-sharp blades. Trying to turn, he again felt the scrape of the blades as they were pushed up against the bone. Still screaming, his arms flopped to his sides uselessly.

He was hung, feet on the ground but held up and suspended on the assegais, grunting in pain. Joseph and M'uyinga stepped through the doorway and stood in front of him, the old man's eyes burning into him with a terrible intensity.

Joseph spun away from Hymie and quickly cut Victoria down, great tears running down his face as he saw the damage that Van Der Hoeke had done to her.

He gently lifted her, taking her weight. M'uyinga cut the ties at her wrists and carefully lifted her hands down before Joseph gently laid her down on the wooden cot.

'My Missy Victoria, what has he done to you?' He found it hard to comprehend what had happened, the tears continuing to slide down his weathered brown face.

A tap on his shoulder startled him. M'uyinga stood there with Victoria's shirt in his hand and the pannikin filled with water in the other.

Baba Joe took the shirt and lay it over her torso and lifted her skirt over her loins.

He bent, placing his cheek at her lips, detecting a very faint breath on his face. Joseph wiped his tears away and turned her head, examining the wound. He grimaced but noticed it was mostly blood apart from a sizable lump surrounding the cut.

Gently lifting her he started to clean her face and the back of her head. She whimpered, a soft childlike sound.

'Ah my Missy, it is all right now,' he crooned to her, 'Baba Joe is here, the pig will not hurt you again *Kw'eenda*,' (my love), he said gently wiping away the sweat that suddenly broke out on her face.

He felt her skin, it was clammy and hot, and she suddenly paled, her stomach heaved and spittle foamed at her mouth.

Joseph shook with worry, he knew she was in a very bad way. Laying her back, rage crashed over him in a flash and he turned and looked at Hymie.

He got slowly to his feet and walked over. Bending, he examined Hymie's now limp appendage.

Joseph could see no blood or any other evidence of fluid except for a single clear drop at its tip.

We may have gotten here just in time, thought Joseph.

No matter, he ground his teeth in fury, he would have his revenge.

'Get him out of here!' he snapped. 'But keep him hung...and give him water.' Then said, 'Hang over by the rocks in the shade – *pa-mafiga!*' (at the stones), he added in Kihehe.

Hymie heard the instruction in part between the pain and said, 'P... please,' then heard the Kihehe word for water and instinctively licked his lips.

Joseph looked up at him, Hymie's bowels almost let go such was the stare, a vicious grin devoid of any humour, slowly formed on Joseph's face.

Then Baba Joe added in clear English, 'I want him alive, and well. Then we make him pay for this!'

A chill ran up Hymie's spine as he looked back at the old man. 'No, please, I didn't mean her any harm, I just got carried away,' he wailed. 'I love her...please!' he pleaded.

The black eyes never blinked and the grin remained fixed and unaltered.

Joseph jerked his head toward the door.

Hymie screamed in pain as they dragged him – still stuck on the spears – over to the jumble of rocks and boulders, his bare feet feebly pushing, trying to take some of the weight.

M'risho and M'fwimi dragged him whimpering in agony up the boulders and wedged the assegais into the rock.

Hymie now hung, the balls of his feet just able to take the weight. Attempting to ease the pressure in his shoulders, he arched his feet down. As he tried to move the blades grated on his collarbone, and again he screamed in agony and passed out.

Joseph kept a vigil by Victoria's side, bathing her face and body to keep her fever down. The fever gripped her he knew, but she never moved a muscle. Her eye was now swelling rapidly where the *m'bwa* (dog) had hit her.

Many times, Joseph reflected on how he had allowed her to leave his side, he would never forgive himself for his error in judgement.

On the second morning he was elated to see that she appeared cool to the touch and he again placed his cheek near her lips. 'Ayee! She breaths deeper!' He was suddenly overcome with remorse and tears filled his eyes again.

Joseph and M'uyinga managed to gently prop her up a little and get some cool water into her mouth. Nothing happened and it simply ran out and down her chin. Then on the second try she suddenly swallowed. They looked at each other and both nodded and lay her back gently. Victoria began to breath deeper and more regularly, and she now seemed to sleep. The relief on Joseph's face was palpable.

Joseph got up from her bedside and glanced at M'uyinga. They both left the hut and strode to where Hymie, still hanging on the assegais, lay slumped against the rock.

Baba Joe stood in front of him. He saw that the thin trickles of blood that had wound their way down Hymie's chest had traces of clear fluid in with them. Soon it would *s'um* (poison), he noted.

'Water him, *m' beeta!*' (bucket) Joseph instructed moving his hands in a throwing motion.

Hymie jerked out of his stupor when the water was thrown in his face. He focused. Joseph stood in front of him, the vicious grin back on his face.

Hymie felt his bladder loosen and the yellow urine trickled down his thighs to pool at his feet.

'Huh! *Wiitete m'bwa k'oogopa!*' (You spilled dog, of fear) Joseph said in disgust.

'What are you going to do?' Hymie asked, a tremor in his voice.

Baba Joe, never broke his gaze when he suddenly said evenly, first in English, and added in Kihehe, 'Light the fire, we will cook. *Ly'aaka, tu' kaleka!'*

Joseph turned and collected a half dozen small round river pebbles, each about one inch in diameter from around the boma. He set them on a flat stone at the very edge of the fire and pushed the stone into it until the flames were licking at the small pebbles.

'What are you doing?' Hymie cried out, and he chilled to the core as Joseph slowly turned to look at him, the evil grin curling its way onto his face again.

Hymie stared, wondering what they were doing. Suddenly, it dawned on him that the hot stones may well be used on him!

'What? No! No!...I beg of you, please don't do this. I will reward you Joseph, my father will be most grateful! Please!' Sweat now poured down his face and trickled from his arm pits.

'Tie his feet apart. *N'goda!'* (Stick) Joseph snapped and pointed to the boma.

M'uyinga found a stout stick about four feet long and lashed it to Hymie's legs, spreading them.

'Put those under his feet,' he continued, pointing at two large stones about eight inches high.

'Please...No! What are you going to do?' Hymie squirmed, crying out as the blades once again grated inside his shoulders, fresh blood and mucus ran from the spear points and dripped onto his chest, matting in the tight curls of his red-gold chest hair.

Joseph and the three warriors squatted and began to talk amongst themselves, casually chatting and having the odd chuckle about something. Occasionally they turned and looked at him.

'Water, can I have water please,' Hymie gasped out.

Silently M'uyinga got up and fetching the ladle walked over to him, he held the water about an inch from Hymie's mouth, but no closer.

Hymie pursed his lips to receive the cooling fluid, but he was disappointed as M'uyinga kept the ladle away from his mouth by a mere

fraction, then tipped its contents down Hymie's chest and returned to his companions.

'*Ji* fucking bastard!' (You fucking bastard) screamed Hymie '*Ek sal jou doodmaak!*' (I will kill you!) he screamed in Afrikaans. He immediately screamed again in pain, the assegais once again doing their work.

Hymie was roused again by water being dashed into his face. He greedily ran his tongue around his mouth to gather as much water as he could from his lips and what remained running down his face.

He needn't have bothered, for there in front of him stood Joseph, with a ladle of water.

'Please?' he begged. Joseph raised the ladle and again the ladle hovered just out of reach, the water dancing in the bowl. 'Please, I beg of you!'

Miraculously the ladle came to him and he drank greedily. 'Thank you, thank you,' he croaked.

'More?' asked Joseph.

Hymie was stunned. 'Y…yes please,' he stammered, his voice still raspy from the dehydration and the pain.

Joseph turned, refilled the ladle, and again Hymie drank, the cool water invigorating him somewhat.

'Enough?' Joseph asked.

Hymie couldn't believe his ears, a suspicion began to gnaw away in the back of his mind, but he suppressed it. He told himself, if I am to get out of this, I will need every bit of strength I can get. He found himself nodding.

Again, the ladle was raised to his lips without trouble.

Joseph turned and walked inside the hut to attend to Victoria, a sadistic smile on his normally gentle face while his eyes were like chips of obsidian.

Hymie's mind began to drift, and despite the massive throbbing pain in his shoulders he retreated within his mind, seeking sanctuary in the thoughts of the past. He dreamt of his parents and of early days, passing in and out of semi-consciousness.

He dreamt of a time when his father had taken him to a special place in the ranges bordering the great lake, many miles north. He was sixteen years old. They had camped, then hunted the veld and fished in the stream.

It was the best time of his life and a time for father and son to bond before he entered manhood. In the evening they had bathed and splashed in a small waterfall, cool and fresh.

Hymie could still now hear the fall of the stream as it cascaded into the pond at its base. Hearing this in his mind, he felt he must pee and involuntarily rose out of his stupor.

He looked around to find that the Hehe were at the very front of the hut talking amongst themselves. Embarrassed at his nakedness, he hesitated to let go and pee in front of them.

He would wait he decided.

Thirty minutes later he could hold it no more and let go.

The hot urine thumped into the end of his penis, but no further. The burning was intense and he looked down to see why this was happening.

To his horror, a grass twine had been tied around the end of his penis stopping him from pissing.

Involuntarily, he let go again. Gasping, the burning intensified and his bladder felt like it would burst.

Joseph appeared in front of him again with another pannikin of water.

'More?' he asked, tilting his head in query. There was no humour on his face, just hate.

More pain assailed him and looking down to his horror he saw that now he almost had an erection! The end of his penis had swollen and had turned an angry and bloated dark purple colour, it bounced slightly with each pulse and the twine had all but disappeared within the swollen flesh.

He realised he was going to die in the most horrible way.

Hymie hung his head.

'Ahh, eh, eh, eh,' he began to quietly sob. 'P…please, I'm sorry, ahh, eh, eh, eh.'

Joseph still sat before him, not an ounce of emotion showing on his face and none was present in his heart either.

The old man rose to his feet and trotted back to attend his 'daughter'.

Joseph looked at Victoria, the concern creasing his face. She had not moved, but a little colour had begun to show on her face. She had taken several sips of water and had once wet herself, which he dutifully cleaned up and cleaned her with cool water before placing one of Van Der Hoeke's blankets on the bunk.

'Oh how he wished Dr A'menson was here!' Joseph lamented wringing his hands. He would know what to do. She was so sick, but what could he do?'

There was no way he could move her yet, at least not until she had gained consciousness, only then could he properly try to gauge her condition.

Joseph wondered if she would indeed gain consciousness ever again.

Anger rising again, he determined he must start work on Van Der Hoeke again lest she wake up in the middle of it.

He rose and went out to start the next stage of revenge on the *m'bwa* (dog).

Hymie was suffering the most intense agony, but even agony, like most pain, sooner or later can get a little accepted.

Water again was dashed into his face and he jerked awake.

Immediately the throbbing and sharp pains in his gut began again in ernest, and his penis now pulsed a painful tune with each beat of his heart.

Looking across, he saw one of the warriors poking at the fire with a flat piece of hard wood. The man suddenly turned and strode toward him, the flat stick held out in front of him, his feather plumes about his head blowing in the gentle breeze.

Hymie watched with trepidation as he saw blue smoke rising around a small pebble on the front of the stick.

The warrior halted right in front of him, expressionless, and just stared at him.

Suddenly, he reached forward and brought the stick and hot pebble straight up under Hymie's scrotum. It crackled and hissed as Hymie screamed and jerked in agony as the rock burnt its way into one of his testicles. The stone was withdrawn. Hymie had passed out.

M'fwimi went to him and none too gently, pried apart the flesh and cut the twine from his bloated penis with the edge of his assegai, the head now shiny with pressure and almost black in colour.

Nothing happened for a minute, then he jumped back as urine forced its way through the swollen tissue, splashing bright yellow urine all over Hymie's legs.

'*Eee! Ititeiitite!*' (He spilled all over the place) cried Mfwimi, wrinkling his nose in disgust and leaping back.

An hour passed and once more water was dashed into Hymie's face.

He came around slowly.

The agony slammed into him, jerking his head upright, his eyes bulging in his sockets, the veins on his forehead and neck stood out like great ropes, and sweat poured down his face and chest.

M'fwimi again stirred the fire with the blackened blade of the stick.

Hymie was barely conscious and his vision kept coming in and out of focus.

Yet another bucket of water was thrown into his face.

Gasping and fighting the terrible thud of pain in his groin, he eventually gained some vision.

Joseph stood in front of him, his face no more than a foot from him.

He stood staring at Hymie for a good two minutes. Suddenly, he said in English, 'So you see Massa Van Der Hoeke, even a "No good black bastard" has his time.

'But this is not for me.' He paused. 'Oh no, Massa Van Der Hoeke, this is for my Missy Victoria and is her payment for ruining her!'

The pain was immense and Hymie could at first only utter 'Uh, uh, uh, aaaah, uh, uh,' as the pain pulsed and flared with every beat of his heart. Finally, he slurred softly, 'N...n...n...no!' Somehow fighting the agony, he shuddered and drawing a ragged breath, said slowly, 'But...I, I did not, y...you stopped me before...' his voice trailed off.

Eee...this is a little good news! thought Joseph – if his Missy survived. The sobering thought once again fanning the hate within him for what this piece of shit had done.

The old man simply stared at him. He turned to Mfwimi, 'Finish it! The other one now...and put the twine strangle back on,' he said, firstly in English then in Kihehe. He walked away to the hut.

'Ahh, No! No! No! Please No!' yelled Hymie, his voice rising to a high pitch.

Baba Joe had no sooner sat down beside the bunk when Van Der Hoeke's guttural scream of agony rapidly rose to a high soprano pitch and echoed around the ranges as M'fwimi delivered the next sizzling stone to his remaining testicle.

Baba Joe wet the cloth again and gently wiped Victoria's face once more. He stroked her hair gently back from her pale face. Her left eye, now swollen shut, was beginning to turn purple and blue with the bruising.

'Baba Joe will never let you out of his sight again my Missy, no, no, not ever! Baba Joe is ashamed and cries in his heart for letting this happen,' he whispered. He looked at her and his old heart felt as though some demon was squeezing it. He lowered his head into his hands.

He jerked as she suddenly softly murmured, 'Baba Joe?'

'I am here Missy! It is me Baba Joe!' Ecstatic, he leaned over her, but she moaned and lapsed back into unconsciousness. His heart and spirit lifted as he knew she now had a little hope of recovery.

He came to the conclusion, she could awaken at any time and left her side almost running to the rear of the hut.

'M'uyinga, M'fwimi, M'risho! Come quickly! She speaks a little, but now she sleeps again,' he pronounced, a grin spreading across his face.

He then became serious again.

'Missy is not to know what happened – ever!' He stroked his chin thinking hard.

'Nandi bad man hit her with knobkerry, we kill, understand?' They all nodded, there was no need to repeat himself. He knew the warrior code would not be broken.

'What about this piece of shit?' M'uyinga said, jerking his head toward the unconscious Hymie.

Thinking furiously, Joseph said, 'Put his clothes on, we will saddle the horse and put everything on it. Take him down to where the water runs, tie the horse to a tree and leave him there, this far from the horse,' he added, pointing to the entrance of the boma.

'If the birds do not have him, tonight the hyena or lion will feast on them both.

'Clean any of our tracks back to here. M'uyinga and I, we will clean up all of his signs here, and ours. The Missy must not suspect.'

'What about the strangle Baba?' M' fwimi asked.

'Leave it!' snapped Joseph.

M'risho and M'fwimi dressed and lifted the unconscious Hymie onto his horse, none too gently tossing him across the saddle.

Twice he slid off the horse on the way to the stream, collapsing in a heap on the rocks.

By the time they got to the flats where the stream levelled he was bleeding from three or four cuts to his head. They tossed his limp body onto the ground as instructed and tied off the horse,

Good, they thought, the hyena will smell it.

They had been gone about thirty minutes and M'uyinga and Baba Joe sat with Victoria anxiously waiting for her to regain consciousness.

It appeared she was now in a deep sleep. They continued to keep her cool and tried to get her to take a little water, but to no avail.

Suddenly Joseph stood up. He had been thinking of the risk of just staying here and waiting for her recovery, but the more he turned it over in his mind, the less he liked the idea. He made a decision.

'We must get her back to Massa A'mendson!' he said emphatically.

'Quickly, we must prepare some cover and cut poles to carry her! We have maybe four hours before sunset, we will go until then.'

'If we can make a litter out of the bunk it will be easier for her, and we can make a cover from the plants at the stream,' M'uyinga suggested.

Joseph nodded in agreement.

M'fwimi and M'risho arrived back after about ten minutes, and they all immediately set about preparing to leave.

They had considered using the horses to carry her but reasoned that should the horses be spooked by lion or hyena they would not be able to stop them.

Forty minutes later they all trotted out of the boma. M'risho and M'fwimi in the lead and carrying the litter.

M'uyinga and Joseph checked the boma and hut, sweeping and clearing any evidence of theirs and Van Der Hoeke's presence. They then ran ahead with the horses and tethered them before returning and sweeping clean their tracks, continuing for some two miles.

Changing bearers every 10 miles, they made good time and covered about 25 miles.

They headed for an old cattle kraal they had passed en route, and on arrival quickly repaired what remained of the thorn boma, and after checking and attending to Victoria, they collapsed on the ground exhausted, too tired to even eat.

Four days later, exhausted, they trotted into the Amendsons' homestead, Victoria now restless and feverish.

Chapter 24

Zacharia Ben

Zacharia Ben looked at the vultures wheeling overhead as he nervously made his way down to the stream. He could hear hyenas gibbering not too far off and wondered why they were making a ruckus.

He was especially nervous because it was late in the afternoon, and although the sun was still shining and quite warm, he knew all the predators would be stirring for the evening hunt.

He cursed again the stubborn mule which had kicked over his last remaining barrel of water and so forced him to make this journey to the stream.

Suddenly, he heard what sounded like a man screaming. He listened and heard the scream again. Plucking up his courage he drew out his old rifle, an 1834, .653 calibre Baker flintlock, with a rifled barrel. Checking the load, he urged his horse forward, dragging the old mule with it.

Crossing the stream, he saw three spotted hyenas around the body of a man. As he stared, a large female hyena darted in, and great fangs bared, snatched at the figure of a man lying on the ground. Just as the animal's fangs snapped at the man's head, he jerked his head away screaming at the animal, but not before the great jaws ripped away some of his scalp and one ear.

Zacharia Ben didn't hesitate. He lifted and fired the old weapon, either out of fear or instinct.

The slug caught the hyena in the hip and spun it around before the others bolted back to the pack, the wounded beast squealing and limping back to the pack, now lurking some distance back.

Yelling wildly, he trotted up to the pitiful site lying on the ground. Zacharia's gut heaved when he saw the condition of the man.

The hyenas had snatched at the man's torso in a further two places, and the powerful jaws had ripped the bicep from the man's left arm and it hung only by sinew. There was another bite on the left calf, bad enough, although not as serious.

Hymie stared at him and it suddenly dawned on him that here was help. He collapsed back onto the grass and lapsed into unconsciousness.

Zacharia knew he would have to move fast before the pack, now scenting the blood, regrouped and came in for the kill. Looking up however, he saw that they were snapping at their wounded companion, and he knew the poor beast was doomed., but that may give him time.

Panting in fear, Zacharia went about reloading the old rifle first – hard enough normally, but with terror upon him, his hands were shaking with a will of their own. First, he dropped the wadding, then he could not hold still enough to wrap the patch on the bullet and insert it. Eventually, he succeeded and felt a little less vulnerable.

He next spent a full 20 minutes trying to lift Hymie onto the back of the mule, cursing and swearing at the top of his lungs. But the poor beast being too terrified and kept dancing about each time he approached it.

He finally managed to hobble the animal and eventually managed to heave the dead weight onto the terrified beast and lash the body into place.

The hyenas were now getting bolder – some were still attacking the female he had wounded, which was down on its back and would not last long he knew – but about six of them were now beginning to move toward him, sniffing at the air and gibbering amongst themselves. Terrified, he kicked his horse into a gallop, but the mule refused to gallop and all he could manage was a trot.

Zacharia found he was having difficulty in breathing and it felt like something was squeezing the life from him.

His horse had only had taken a few strides when he heard the frantic whinny of another horse. Looking a bit further upstream, he saw the man's horse about fifty yards away, rearing and dancing trying to tear off the tether from a thick branch, its eyes rolling and bulging in terror.

Whether it was greed for the animal or bravado no one would know, but Zachariah immediately headed for the horse, and reaching down, slipped the reins off the branch. Wheeling, he splashed straight across the stream, the sound of the hyenas spurring him along. He didn't stop until he reached the cleft in the cliff.

He dragged the thorn gate across and dragged Hymie under the wagon, before closing the barricade.

Suddenly, he knew he would have left a trail of blood, and now there was nothing he could do about it, there was no way he would risk venturing out of the thorny barricade again.

The man's clothes were soaked in blood and Zachariah, having spent too long in this country, knew that he must get rid of them and at least eliminate the source of the scent.

He quickly stoked up his fire and leaning over the now comatose man, commenced to cut away Hymie's clothing.

Zachariah wrinkled his nose as the strong smell of burnt flesh came to him. He sat back, puzzled over this because he could see no evidence of burns on the man.

Shrugging, he cut away the trousers. He sucked air through his teeth, staring at what remained of the man's genitalia. The penis was bloated beyond recognition, the head, black and shiny, while the shaft jumped with every pulse of the man's heart.

The testicles, or what was left of them, were blackened and burnt, lymph glistened on the burns and seeped onto the thighs.

Despite having seen many brutal things in this country, as soon as the stench of the mutilation reached his nostrils Zachariah felt his stomach heave, and clapping his hand over his mouth, leapt to his feet and ran to the edge of the thorns where he vomited violently.

When he had finished he returned, cutting away the remainder of the blood-soaked clothing. He threw them into the fire and went around to the other side of the wagon and splashed water on his face. Swilling out his mouth, he heard Hymie croak out, 'P,p,p...please.'

Mistaking the plea as a call for water, he filled the dipper and went around to the pitiful site of the man to try to trickle some into his mouth.

He was shocked at the reaction. The man shook his head violently, crying out, 'N,n,n...no, No!'

Hymie clutched at Zachariah's arm, and pointing to his ruined crutch managed to croak out, 'Cut...cut the twine!' before collapsing once again. Looking a little closer, Zachariah saw the loose ends of twine dangling from under the head of the shiny black head of the man's bloated penis.

'Oh, my Lord!' he exclaimed. Reaching for the knife at his hip, he used the back of the blade to push aside the flesh either side of the twine now sunken deep into the swollen flesh of the poor fellow's penis.

'Christ,' he thought as he examined the best way to cut it. 'This will be risky!'

The knife was razor sharp and Zachariah decided to try to cut the knot.

He pushed the swollen appendage down with a piece of cloth and touched the blade to the knot, one small stroke was all it took and the leather thong parted with a dull thud.

Nothing happened for a few seconds, then urine began to force its way through the swollen passage and quickly turned into a pulsing stream of bloodied golden urine. Leaping back, Zachariah tossed the cloth over the stream and went out to wash his hands again.

Screams of agony had him scurrying around to the man again. He lay writhing in agony, his hands clutched to his belly and crotch. Zachariah danced up the rear stairs of his wagon and pouring out a good portion of laudanum (made up of about ten per cent opium and ninety per cent brandy), he managed to get the fellow to swallow it and a cup of water. Ten minutes later, Hymie Van Der Hoeke lapsed, whimpering, into a drugged and merciful sleep.

Zachariah fetched his medical kit and began to clean away the gore from the other wounds.

He was unable to do much more than clean up the fellow's scalp and apply crude stitches. All but the ear lobe of the right ear was missing, so all he could do was bandage it to stop the ear from bleeding. Likewise, he could only cauterise and bandage the gaping wound where the left bicep had been torn away. Zachariah did not have the skills to attempt to reattach the loose muscle and so had to cut the remaining sinew and discard it.

The man's calf was not as bad as he first thought and he did manage to stitch up the wound quite well. He chewed his lip, knowing that the hyena bites would probably infect within hours.

Hymie slept for two days during which time he came to three times and sipped a little water, but fever gripped him and he was deteriorating steadily.

Zachariah carried jars of a new 'miracle ointment' under the name of Anderson's Dermador, one of many different types he carried. But this was new and seemed to actually work, unlike the other 'miracle cures' he offered to the unwary.

First invented in 1936 by Professor Homer Anderson of New York, this ointment was said to relieve anything from sprains, burns, bruising and all types of wounds – animals or human. This he applied liberally to Hymie's charred testicles and the head of his penis, to which colour had not returned. Zachariah noticed the wounds were beginning to exude a yellow pus and the skin was flacking away.

He kept up the drafts of the potent laudanum but in smaller doses, knowing the danger of the pain killer and its addictive side effects. Irrespective, the young man continued to deteriorate.

Zachariah stayed put for four days, unable to summon the courage to risk another attempt out of the thorn barrier. However, he had to fetch water, and this time he did so without any sign of predators.

The following morning found Hymie wracked with high fever. Zachariah made a decision and packed up hurriedly. He searched the man's saddlebags but the only thing he found of value was a small calibre revolver in a leather belt and holster, which he slipped around his waist. Not daring to head north, he headed south to seek medical attention for the young fellow who he knew would die if he could not find a way or someone to check the infection.

It was not that the evil little self-centered fellow really cared one way or another, but he considered that he might be blamed for the man's death, and in any case, there was a possibility that he might even be rewarded for his troubles if he could deliver the young man alive to someone who could help.

Unwittingly, he came upon the Amendsons' home first.

Chapter 25

A Conflict of Interest

J oseph was sitting on the front verandah with Ludwig Amendson watching the sun begin its journey into the great expanse of water that was Lake Victoria.

The sky was still blue and it would be tinted orange within the hour they knew. But still they sat in silence, the coming sight needing no conversation.

Joseph had sat in the same spot every day since returning, which was right between the front door and Victoria's bedroom window.

Ludwig knew and understood that the old fellow blamed himself for his daughter's attack by the Nandi warrior and so allowed him to stand guard duty. No amount of talking had convinced the old warrior that he was not to blame.

Ludwig had sensed something was missing from the old man's explanation of how his beloved daughter had been so badly injured, but when he had pressured Joseph he was met with a stony and somewhat chilling stare so did not pursue it. He was, though, confused by Joseph's reaction.

As they sat Joseph slowly rose to his feet, staring intently at the northern edge of the lake.

'What is it Joseph?' Ludwig asked. Joseph merely pointed with his long assegai toward the road, then trotting down to the gateway at the entrance to the house yard, he gave two short "yips", so much like a silverbacked jackal you could not tell if it were real or not.

120000

But two Hehe warriors heard it and within minutes had vanished toward the roadway coming from the lake.

Zachariah almost had a heart attack when, from out of nowhere, the two warriors materialised, as if by magic, beside his wagon, and they did not look friendly with their shields and spears.

Zachariah decided to continue without pause, and as he crested a small rise almost wet himself with relief as in the distance he saw what looked like a low building.

M'risho and M'fwimi instantly recognised Van Der Hoeke's horse tethered to the back of the little wagon, and before Zachariah was even aware of their presence, M'fwimi had lightly leaped up the back and had heard Hymie's tortured moans of fever.

It took all of his discipline not to open the back and kill the occupant, but it was not his decision to make and he leapt off the back. The Ubaba would deal with it.

Three hundred yards from the homestead, M'fwimi suddenly sprinted ahead and delivered his news to Joseph.

The moment the wagon drew up in front of the verandah, old Joseph was at the back of the wagon flanked by the two warriors.

Recognising Hymie's horse, Ludwig looked up at the terrified peddler, who stammered, 'I...I...tried m...my best Sir, but he is getting worse! Can you help him Sir? He really needs a doctor! he added, jerking his thumb to the rear.

'I *am* a doctor!' said Ludwig, who was staring at the pistol strapped to the man's waist.

'Where did you get that?' Ludwig asked, accusation clear on his face.

'Oh no Sir, I not be stealin' it,' Ben suddenly blurted out. "Twas in 'is saddlebag ye see, 'ere!' he continued, unbuckling the holster and handing it to Ludwig.

Snatching the pistol, Ludwig hurried around to the back of the wagon and was shocked at the look on Joseph's face. It was a mask of pure hate and murder and instantly some of the missing pieces fell into place about Joseph's previous explanation of what had happened to Victoria. He pulled down the rear steps and entered the wagon.

The stench of decay hit him like a wall in the confines of the wagon, and he stared in shock at the naked form of the threshing Hymie Van Der Hoeke and his horrific injuries.

'Fetch the stretcher and carry him to my surgery quickly!' he snapped toward Joseph and the two warriors.

None moved, the same murderous mask on each of their faces. They suddenly stepped back in unison a few paces.

Ludwig was furious but could see he had no time to waste arguing and shouted at two Maasai men working in the vegetable garden, who came trotting immediately. Together they carried the hapless Hymie onto the rear verandah and into the surgery.

Ludwig, with Lillian's assistance, fought for two whole days and nights to contain the infection raging through Hymie's body, and on the evening of the second night at 11pm Ludwig finally staggered into bed at Lillian's insistence, shaking his head at Lillian's query as to whether the lad would survive. 'God only knows,' were the last words he uttered before lapsing into an exhausted sleep.

On several occasions during the fits of fever, Hymie had deliriously muttered of his lust for Victoria. At one stage whilst Ludwig was applying cold compresses to his brow and Lillian had gone to make tea, Hymie had tried to sit up, the veins standing out on his forehead, and he had shouted in English, 'It's my turn now you fucking bitch!'

Ludwig went cold and he felt the full force and dreadful realisation of what had happened to his daughter and why Joseph and the Hehe had been so malevolent toward Hymie's arrival.

Ludwig was staring at Hymie with enormous rage clearly showing on his face. His ethics, principals and conscience tumbling before him as he sat trembling on the precipice of irrationality. Teetering on the edge, he picked up a large syringe.

Hymie's life hung in the balance when Lillian came quietly through the door to stand beside her husband. She had been about to enter and had heard the feverish rant, stopping her dead in her tracks.

She lent down to his ear and said in a whisper, 'No my darling Lud, you could not live with yourself,' and taking the syringe from his hand she held his head to her, hugging him as tears streamed down his face. She stood with him without another word until he gained control once again.

Later that afternoon he had Joseph walk with him and they sat down on a fallen tree some three hundred yards from the house. Ludwig told Joseph he was sure he knew what had actually happened and why Hymie had been mutilated, but now he wanted some straight answers.

For the next thirty minutes the old man relayed the events. Ludwig was somehow relieved after he had finished, but Joseph was crying softly and rocking back and forth, crying 'Ee...ee...ee, the Missy, the Missy!' Ludwig put a great arm around the little man and gave as much comfort as he could.

Finally, as they stood to go back, he said, 'Baba Joe, it is as well you found our daughter before the worst happened because I am convinced Hymie would have killed her, if not soon after he had what he wanted, certainly later.

'The Nandi story must remain Joseph. If that piece of *scheizer* ever recovers, he will be too afraid to dispute it.'

Several days after Victoria was brought home, Lillian had sent word to Ermina that Victoria was very ill – with a brief description of what had happened – but was slowly recovering.

The Van Der Hoeke's had arrived the very next day bringing food and gifts for Victoria.

They had, of course, asked if anyone had seen or heard of their son, and were clearly relieved when told that it was renegade Nandi who had attacked Victoria.

Lillian had dispatched a runner to carry the news of Hymie's arrival to his parents at daybreak on the second day, for neither she nor Ludwig had time to spare whilst tending to the young man.

Therefore, they were not surprised when around three in the afternoon one of the young hands called out that there was someone coming.

Johann and Ermina clattered into the yard on the two-horse wagon that Johann had recently bought, and they were immediately ushered in to see Hymie.

Hymie was still gripped in fever, his eyes wide open amid blackened sockets, shivering and drenched in perspiration at the same time.

Shocked at the weight loss and condition of her son, Ermina whispered, 'Will...will he survive?'

Ludwig said as gently as he could, 'You must realise ja? That Hymie has now been in a severe state of fever brought on by his wounds for over eight days now, and quite frankly I do not know how he has survived even up until now.'

'What are the wounds and how did it all happen?' asked Johann.

Ludwig had prepared himself for this question, and knowing that Joseph, still armed, would be outside the window of the surgery where he now had taken station, paused before answering: 'We think he was attacked by renegade Nandi warriors, possibly the same ones who attacked Victoria. They must have tortured him and left him for dead.

'Then hyena began to attack him, he has lost his right ear and some of his scalp through the bites and infection.' He continued, 'The beasts also tore away his left bicep and had bitten into his calf. He was saved by the peddler camped outside, he fought them off and brought him here.

'T...tortured him?' Ermina asked. 'What did they do?' she asked looking for evidence. 'And why?'

Ludwig coughed and said, 'My dear, you look absolutely pale, vy' don't you let Lillian take you into the house and you can rest, this has been a big shock for you and then Johann can tell you later, all right?' She acquiesced and left with Lillian.

In that moment Ludwig thought to tell Van Der Hoeke what had actually happened but decided to stick to the original story.

Johann Van Der Hoeke was no fool and Ludwig knew that he would put two and two together soon enough.

Ludwig lifted the cloth away from Hymie's loins.

Johann sucked air in through his teeth as he gazed at his son's mutilation. He staggered back and sat down on a chair with a thump.

'I did what I could Johann, but I am afraid too much time had passed before getting treatment,' he began. 'The burns were applied specifically and the head of the penis was strangled and past recovery. It was also poisoning him, so I had no option but to amputate it.'

Johann nodded slowly. 'Will he live?' he asked, looking directly into Ludwig's eyes.

'Again, I don't know, if we can break the fever, perhaps.'

He added, 'His mind also may have been damaged, you must understand.'

Having spent years in the area, Johann knew what this torture meant and why it was done. It was a Wahehe tribal punishment for rape, and not Nandi.

He looked up at Ludwig and from the tough old man's left eye dropped a single tear.

'I'm sorry man,' was all he said, and he got up and walked out and across the yard. Ludwig saw him striding toward the low hills and thought to go after him, but considered it best to leave him alone.

Two days later Ludwig came to the surgery at daybreak and was shocked to find Hymie sleeping deeply. The fever had passed.

A further three days passed and the Van Der Hoeke's returned home with their son.

Zachariah Ben was given instructions to follow the Van Der Hoeke's and he would be rewarded. Zachariah got his wish and was given Hymie's horse, Johann reckoning he had earned it, and he was given full provisions and left the next day, heading south to no doubt fleece more people on his travels.

Johann never spoke to his son, or about him, to anyone ever again.

When Hymie recovered enough, it was clear his mind had gone. He started to frequent the out camp more and more and eventually stayed there, preferring to be alone, and in any case, he talked constantly to himself. His only visible visitor, his mother, came once a week with food and love, as only a mother can.

Not that Hymie ever knew it but he was never alone. Two Hehe warriors were always camped on the Amendson's side of the small gully that separated Van Der Hoeke's hut and Ludwig's property, and always stayed just out of sight.

Nine months to the day and three days before Ermina's visit to the camp was due, the two Hehe trotted into the Amendsons' yard and went straight to Joseph.

'It is over!' the youngest said. 'B'cooh!' putting his finger to his temple.

Joseph nodded and went to Ludwig, and beckoning him outside, explained what had happened.

Ludwig relayed the news to Lillian and said he was going to the Van Der Hoeke's.

Johann knew Ludwig had the two warriors stationed nearby his son's out camp – and of course why. He never objected.

The two men left alone to travel to the camp and to confirm what the warriors had said.

Hymie lay on his back in the middle of the floor and his shotgun lay near him.

Mercifully, Johann had spared himself by allowing Ludwig to go inside first. He sat bolt upright on his horse some distance away. Ludwig came out and shook his head slowly from side to side.

'Let me clean things up for you Johann,' he said gently.

The big man nodded slowly, but Ludwig could see and feel the heart-break within the man even from twenty feet away.

Crossing to his horse Ludwig took a roll of bandage, a large piece of canvass from his saddle bag, a bag needle and twine, and went back inside.

He finished some thirty minutes later, emerging with the corpse draped over his shoulder and together he and Johann lashed the bag behind Johann's saddle.

They turned to take Hymie home when suddenly Johann, holding up his hand said softly, 'Wait.'

He walked back to the camp and finding a paraffin lamp hanging next to the door he emptied its contents along the front wall and set fire to the hut.

Mounting again, Johann kicked the horse forward and never looked back.

Victoria improved rapidly and appeared to suffer no mental distress, showing only annoyance that try as she might, she could not remember what had happened at all. She grilled poor Joseph mercilessly for hours, over and over again, only to receive the same story each time.

It wasn't long before she again began to think about Nicholas, almost daily.

Fourteen months later Nicholas's letter arrived.

Chapter 26

Shadows, Bush Medicine
and November Heat

Nicholas lay in the shadow beneath the brush humpy, a single walled affair, simple but effective against the elements and the dry heat of the day.

The voices in his mind chattered in nonsensical streams. He was not able to focus on anything, neither could he move nor make a sound as he was still gripped by paralysis from the snake bite.

Poultices of bark covered his leg under which was smeared a concoction of herbs and strange pastes that had an obnoxious odour to anyone not familiar with it.

He sensed rather than saw shadowy figures moving over him, it was as though he were suspended. His mind, unable to think rationally and frustrated at not being able to form any rational train of thought, ricocheted around his brain like a pea in a rattle.

One constant was of something familiar, but he was not able to absorb what it was. 'Clink, clink, clink,' it went on and on, while a type of monotone noise, also familiar, was always present.

Gradually, his mind began to catch some reality and he was able to briefly focus on some things. The most prominent of these thoughts was, 'What happened to me? Where am I?'

One time he began to work his mouth and his Adam's apple began to move up and down. He immediately felt the sensation of warmth.

Gnarlu and Yindu sat cross-legged on opposite side of Nicholas chanting in a monotonous drone whilst banging the beat sticks together, 'Clink, clink, clink!'

Gnarlu saw Nicholas's throat move and leapt to his feet, grasping a wooden bowl of bush medicine that was sitting on a rock in the sun. He rushed to Nicholas's side and trickled some of the green concoction into Nicholas's open mouth. To his delight Nicholas swallowed involuntarily.

'*Ku'arlu!*' (good!) he exclaimed, his white teeth splitting his face in a huge grin as he looked at Yindu, who also was grinning broadly.

Yindu said, '*Apa, apa*' (water, water) and they managed to get Nicholas to swallow a little more.

The next few days were a mish-mash of mixed thoughts for Nicholas as gradually he began to become aware of sensation in his body as more of his senses began to function.

One day he was particularly restless and began to move his limbs, albeit slowly, and began to mutter to himself. That afternoon, he fell into a deep even sleep and did not wake until mid-morning of the next day.

He lay without moving. It was the first time in seven days that he was aware of his body and could actually hear himself breathing.

Suddenly, the memory of the snake bite rushed into his brain and he struggled to sit upright. He was very weak and only managed to remain upright propped on his elbows.

He half lay like this for some time and struggled to open his eyes. Panic rose within him for a minute, he could not see!

Struggling to sit up, he lifted one hand to his eyes and he felt coarse material. Tearing it off, the sunlight instantly blinded him momentarily and caused him to cry out it hurt so much. Gradually, he began to reopen his eyes and found himself sitting under the lean-to.

Glancing down at himself, he discovered he was mostly naked, and looking up saw his clothes hanging from the peak of the staves on the lean to and his rifle propped against the upright. Around him were wooden bowls of water and some type of meat and what looked like some sort of root or tuber.

His leg was covered in some type of bark and he stank like nothing on earth.

Nicholas reached for one of the bowls of water and greedily drank it down. A short while later hunger pangs hit him and he tore at the meat, despite the fact that it was covered in the ever-present and minute little bush flies. His stomach suddenly heaved and he only just managed to hold the food down.

He was alive! Scarcely believing it, he suddenly rejoiced. Looking around again at the articles and lean-to he knew it was the Aborigines who had saved his life and had perhaps performed a miracle.

His eyes now gradually getting used to the glare, he again looked around. He saw no one and attempting to stand he promptly thumped back onto his backside. His head spinning, he lay back and tried to fight the wave of exhaustion that washed over him but failed.

Gnarlu and Yindu watched him from under the shade of a small kur-rajong tree from some distance away.

'*Ku'arlu!*' Gnarlu said, nodding his head. 'We go,' he said after a few moments.

They walked over the lean-to where Nicholas was now sleeping deeply. They refilled the wooden bowls with water and wrapping a small leg of cooked kangaroo in some bark, hung it on the stave in the shade and placed another two small bowls, containing small berries and leaves and some yams, next to the water. Then they stripped off the foul-smelling poultices and washed the scum of seven days off his body.

Yindu walked over to where Stitch was standing under a gum tree and stared at the animal. Five days ago, he had been terrified of the beast. But now was beginning to understand it a little and he thought how wonderful to have such a faithful animal and so clever. The other smaller horse, was docile and calm, Yindu making up his mind that the animal was stupid in comparison.

He thought back to the day after the white man had been bitten. The black maned and tailed horse had started to become agitated, jigging to the side and dancing his head up and down. Yindu did not know why this was so. Then he remembered when this man was at their camp, the man had reached under the beast and with a "clink" had taken off the hard seat on the animal and had brushed the animal's back.

The other horse was also shifting constantly and panting with loud noises, and he could hear the animals' teeth chewing. He could sense the distress of the beasts, and when he had plucked up enough courage he had walked slowly over and examined the big strap under the smaller horse's belly.

Reaching out he tried to undo the heavy metal buckle. The small horse stood passively and was clearly relieved when the strap suddenly loosened, throwing its great head up and down. The equipment slid to the ground with a crash as the animal suddenly jigged sideways. Stitch suddenly snorted and danced away. Yindu ran in terror with Gnarlu's screams of laughter echoing about him.

Finally, after staring at the buckle on the larger animal for a while and keeping a nervous eye on it, after several attempts he managed to undo the buckle and the horse immediately settled down.

Between the two of them they had lugged the saddle over to the back of the humpy along with the other equipment and returned to strip the blanket off Stitch's back and that of the smaller horse. In doing so the reins came loose and Stitch, sensing a bit of freedom, cantered off some distance.

The two men did not know what to do and could only watch as Stitch started to graze on some of the tufts of grass a little way off. They fretted that perhaps it would not return, but to their amazement, the horse was back beside the lean-to within an hour, and from then on never strayed further than visual distance, leaving only occasionally to go to the natural spring amongst the gums some four hundred metres away. They gathered bundles of grass for the animals which became quite used to the two men.

Also amazing was that every day the large horse came over to the lean-to and would peer in at the still form of its master. Sometimes it made a soft noise, then would retreat.

One day, the two men decided to hunt for some more food, after checking on Nicholas, they walked away to the northern tree line several miles distant. They hunted into the dusk and decided that they would return in the morning.

Nicholas woke early that next morning to the sound of Stitch's soft whicker and the horse nudging him.

'Jesus Stitch, lay off!' said Nicholas with a grin and reached out to stroke his horse's nose.

He felt much better and the massive headache had receded. He felt very weak though but managed to get to his feet. He stood swaying and looked down at his nakedness and was aghast at the amount of weight he had lost.

His ribs were clearly visible and his belly concave, but at least the awful stench of stale body sweat and the foul smell of some concoction had abated somewhat. He craved for a wash but dare not venture too far yet.

Then all of a sudden he knew he had to get moving and do something. Grabbing the bark parcel, he opened it and ravenous, tore into the stringy kangaroo leg meat and washed it down with some water. He then ate some of the yams and berries.

Feeling strength from the food flow into his body, he looked around at the surroundings. He spotted a grove of gum trees that looked much taller and healthier than their companions, running left and right, and thought it likely water was there.

He hauled on his breaches and boots, the effort causing him to reel. He clucked to Stitch and hanging onto the bridle he tentatively took his first steps in days toward the trees. His head spinning and the headache beginning again, limping heavily he managed to get to the trees and within the grove and shade. His leg was still numb and sore, but he figured that was a good sign.

He was delighted to find a small shallow pool about eight feet long and a yard wide at the base of a small rock overhang, the Sun playing on the surface through the trees. He peered into the pool – it looked clean and he could see no sign of any danger. The only thing he could see were small black beetles swimming up from the bottom. Their little appendages on each side 'rowing' them along, and there were tiny little black tadpoles swimming about. Good, he thought, if the water was contaminated there would be no life in the pool.

Stripping off his breeches and boots, he stepped into the water and almost swooned when he lowered himself into the water which was about twelve inches deep.

Nicholas could not remember a moment when he enjoyed the cool water so much and he scrubbed his body with the fine washed sand from the pool. It was rough on his skin but he did not care.

He lay back in the water and relaxed. Lifting his leg up he saw a slight swelling and dark discoloured flesh where the adder had struck him, a red streak still visible running up the inside of his thigh. Christ, I am so lucky, he thought.

He had just laid back again when a sharp snap made him freeze.

Slowly swiveling his eyes to his left, he was stunned to find a naked young Aboriginal warrior standing not six feet from him, a small broken twig in his hands and an enormous grin across his face.

'Jesus! Where did you come from, I didn't hear a thing!' he exclaimed. The grin remained.

It dawned on Nicholas that the young man looked familiar. 'Of course!' he said out loud, this was one of the warriors from Nimit'je's people.

Nicholas grinned back as it came to him, that this was what he had seen in the heat haze just before he was struck by the snake. Looking past the young fellow, Nicholas saw a slightly older man standing some thirty feet away. He too showed a wide smile.

He felt no unease about his nakedness, having spent a lot of his youth with the Maasai and Wahehe, and in any case, this fellow standing in front of him was also naked.

Nicholas realised it must have been these men who had nursed him back to life.

Yindu stared at the white man laying back in the pool, his white skin in stark contrast to the brown sand and black of the rock.

The white man had a lot of hair on his chest and belly but had no tribal scars to signify manhood. How strange he had wondered and yet he knew that this was indeed a man who had well and truly reached his manhood.

He was also fascinated by the many strange objects he carried. They were hard and cold to touch compared to his own tools and weaponry.

When he was much younger he had gone on a great and exciting journey, he recalled, and on the journey they had found a vast hill of very hard stone. This stone had 'clinked' when struck together just like the sound of this man's tools. Yet the tools here were shaped in specific detail and were strange indeed.

Nicholas was feeling remarkably better after his bathing and he was suddenly ravenous again.

Shakily. he started dressing but failed, since every time he bent over to haul on his breaches his head spun so violently he had to straighten. He gave up and made to move but as he started to walk his leg wobbled and he almost collapsed.

Yindu caught him before he fell, and putting his arm around him, helped Nicholas gather his breeches. Then they made their slow progress back to the humpy.

It must have made an odd sight, Nicholas was to reflect – naked white man and naked black man walking with their arms around each other.

They made it back and Nicholas ate some more of the food then collapsed beneath the shade and fell into a deep, deep sleep. The last thing he remembered thinking was that he was going to fully recover.

It took another full week before Nicholas was able to move about freely, and although he was still a bit weak, he was vastly improved.

Chapter 27

Aboriginal Bushcraft

*H*e began to walk with the two Aboriginal men and accompany them on their almost daily hunts.

He witnessed the most incredible display of hunting prowess he had ever seen, equally as good as the African San and Bushman of the Kalahari Desert, the Bushman ranging further into central Africa. He observed that there seemed to be the same connection with the land as the Bushman, perhaps not as ceremonial as them but the same respect for their prey and land nonetheless. Very little was wasted and almost all the parts of any kill were used in some way.

These people did not use bows and arrows or even blowpipes, preferring instead their long spears and throwing sticks which they could hurl over very long distances with unerring accuracy. They also used their boomerangs with the same incredible accuracy.

But for bird they used the throwing stick. This was a length of hard wood about two feet long and about one and a half inches thick. This the men threw with amazing skill at birds in flight, snapping the wings, and were onto the bird almost before it crashed to the ground.

The throwing stick was not as difficult to master as the boomerang. Nicholas spent hours trying to master these skills but failed every time, becoming disenchanted as he watched the Aboriginal men throw and hit their intended target as easily as drawing breath.

Then one day they were out hunting bustard, a type of wild turkey endemic to the area. They had long necks, stood about three-feet high, had a large wingspan of around four feet and a tuft of feathers at the back of the head. He had seen a similar type of bird in Africa but had not hunted them.

This day, he was copying the men, who were at pains to point out that he must mimic the gait and actions of these quite large birds. This they cleverly did by crouching down, holding one arm vertical, small feathers stuck in the back of the hand so as to appear like the tuft on the birds head and rapidly switching the bent over wrist back and forth. In the other hand they held their throwing sticks, ready for action.

Bustards were an inquisitive creature and would wander within throwing range to investigate.

The trick was, once within range, to suddenly leap up startling the bird, which immediately opened its wings to take flight and presenting a much larger target. The throwing sticks were thrown, the only sound a 'Whoosh! whoosh!' as the stick spun its way to the prey.

It was Nicholas's turn to try. The curious bird came closer as Nicholas tried to keep his adrenaline under control. 'Now!' he thought and leapt to his feet and threw in one motion.

He watched the throwing stick arch to his prey and to his astonishment, the stick cracked into the birds body and wing.

He was already running to the flapping bird almost as it fell, dust and feathers flying about. Snatching up the stick, he dispatched the great bird as he had been shown with one good whack to the head. The grins all round said it all.

That evening they roasted the bird. It was easy to pluck and then they covered it in clay and mud from the soak and placed it on the coals.

Nicholas had never tasted anything so good – it was as good as any wild game bird he had ever tasted.

He tried to learn the art of throwing a boomerang, and learnt that there were several types used, some for enemies and others for different types of game.

This alone was a supreme skill, and to the vast amusement of the two Aboriginal men, Nicholas managed to throw several boomerangs into the ground not ten feet in front of them, snapping them and creating a plume of dust in the process. Eventually, he managed to throw them with some success, but there was no way he would ever hit a bounding kangaroo, for example, as his companions could do, seemingly with ease. Nevertheless, he kept up his practice and was beginning to throw with some sort of accuracy after many sessions of trying, but he was still a long way from being able to hunt with it.

Under Gnarlu and Yindu's tutelage he began to gather a fascinating repertoire of bush craft and how to live and survive in this so vastly different land.

Although so very different to Africa, having no major predators or large animals, Nicholas was acutely aware that this land was very harsh and unforgiving by its very nature, although teeming with all manner of creatures. To the uninitiated, most people would walk right by the bush life without ever knowing it.

He was to learn the real meaning of looking and gain a fascinating insight to the true powers of Aboriginal observation and knowledge.

He observed and learnt the tracking skills of the Aboriginal, how a lizard's tiny tracks could indicate nervousness or fright and what was the likely cause, and how to tune in to the sounds of the bush, the cacophony of the bush orchestra and how each of the individual sounds had meaning.

He now observed and was aware of the many different notes of the birdlife, and how to listen beyond your immediate surrounds and to focus on insect noise and use it as your alarm against animal and man's approach.

The Aboriginals taught him how to differentiate between the non-venomous and venomous variety of snakes, of which there were many. He was shown the different marks made in the sand, and even marks on hard ground that he previously would never had noticed.

The habits, diet and telltale signs of other poisonous creatures, spiders and scorpions to name a few, and a list of edible insects almost too long to remember.

Gnarlu and Yindu took him to various places in the area, even going back to where Nicholas had been bitten. With seemingly nonchalant ease they located another death adder not far from where Nicholas first began to climb the outcrop of rock. Nicholas was no novice to bush craft, but these people were so skilled he could scarcely believe it.

One day, he and Gnarlu lay down face down beneath a grove of mulga trees on a carpet of dried leaves. Picking up a thin twig about twelve inches long, Gnarlu motioned that they keep very still and pointed to his eyes and back to an area immediately in front of them. Nicholas caught on that he was to watch.

As they lay there still and quiet in the shade, Nicholas began to see tiny movements among the leaves and bark.

First, a tiny head with disproportionately large yellow eyes poked out of the foliage. It was a gecko lizard. Almost at the same time different types of small beetles and ants began to emerge, scurrying about their business over and under the dry foliage.

Nicholas was astounded at the amount of life there was in this tiny patch of ground.

Gnarlu slowly reached out with the stick and slowly pointed at an almost invisible single thread of web, not more than two inches long on the trunk of the mulga bush. Then, gently lifting a piece of bark next to the base, revealed a spider about two inches across squatting upside down on the underside.

They were so close to it they could see the cluster of black eyes glinting back at them as the creature protectively sat across its white egg sack, the sack being woven flat onto the underside of the bark in a circular pattern.

Gnarlu gently lay the bark back down and reached over to another cluster of bark and twig. Lifting this, he revealed another type of gecko lizard, larger than the other with huge liquid dark eyes, about four inches long. It was beautifully marked, patterned in a brown and purplish hue with white markings. It had a stumpy fat tail and as they watched, the little fellow suddenly let out what could only be described as a dog's bark.

Suddenly, it's tail dropped off and it scurried under the leaves, leaving the fat wriggling tail behind as a decoy to whatever may have been thinking of making a meal out of it.

They backed out from under the tree, leaving Nicholas amazed and wondering what else was there to learn about this seemingly harsh country.

For four weeks Nicholas absorbed the bush craft. He learnt the Aborigines' tracking methods and a host of survival tricks that must have been passed down for centuries.

They would head out at dawn and walk the land for many miles, all the while the two Aboriginal men would stop and show Nicholas what they themselves knew from childhood. Nicholas observed that although he began to pick up the odd word in their language, they spoke so rapidly that he struggled to understand it. However, they began to learn English much quicker.

He also learnt that sign language was the preferred method of communication and the men seldom spoke whilst on their excursions, and never whilst hunting.

The three were one day walking across a flat plain of tufted hard grass and shrub some three miles from the camp. They were almost across, the grass and small shrubbery now thinning, revealing a red soil with scattered shrubs about three feet high punctuated by small red and grey trunked eucalypts. Nicholas was subconsciously thinking how lifeless the area appeared, but then chided himself that all was not what it seemed in this land, and sure enough he received a valuable tip on survival.

In this dry and dusty edge of the plain, he was shown how to locate a particular gum tree or eucalypt. Slightly different from others with a light red coloured trunk, it had glossy strips of thin brown bark hanging down the trunk.

It had bright green shiny leaves and stood alone, slightly apart from the other trees and shrubs. Yindu got down on his knees and began to scrape away at the soil with a wedge-shaped rock about three feet from the trunk. Soon he had exposed one of the roots which was about six inches down. He continued to scrape away the soil until he had exposed about ten feet of the root. The root was about one to two inches in diameter close to the trunk. Yindu cut off the root about a foot from the tree and again around six feet away from the first cut. Taking the length, he sat down with his back to the tree and stood it vertically in his cupped hand. After about ten minutes, a small pool of water formed up in his cupped hand. Not much, thought Nicholas, but enough to ensure survival if one was ever stranded out here.

Soon Nicholas began to seek these trees. There were not many scattered around, but from this day on he mentally logged each one he saw during his forays and exploration.

His new friends pointed out many types of food, silky pear vines from which elongated fruit pods grew, bitter sweet quandong fruit and nuts – a bright red berry about one inch in diameter, the red flesh quite palatable. These grew on small, light green trees which seemingly grew only in groves. The dried nuts on the ground were quite tasty when cracked open.

He learnt how to catch and eat the large lizards the Aboriginals called bungarra. These goannas grew to almost six feet, and when roasted on the fire were delicious, tasting like a cross between a chicken and fish. He was shown how to find the large fat "bardi" grubs, which he had now grown to quite like and how to find, and honey ants, their fat abdomens bloated and translucent with sweet amber juice tasting exactly like honey.

As the weeks passed, the Aboriginal pair continued to show Nicholas all manner of bush craft. Everything fascinated him as he absorbed it all and came to understand, that not only were they teaching him their bush craft and survival techniques, but he was being given a rare and precious gift in knowledge that few white men would ever be given.

Nicholas, now fully recovered, began to get itchy feet and his thirst for adventure began again to rise within him.

It was if the Aboriginal men knew in advance his thoughts and Nicholas woke one morning to find his companions gone.

He was at first a little upset that he had been given no chance for goodbyes, but then saw laid next to his blanket, a fine throwing stick and a hunting boomerang.

Somehow he knew there was to be no goodbye, rather they would meet again.

Little did he realise under what circumstances their next meeting would be.

Chapter 28

The Bush Copper and his Chains of Shame

*D*eclan McGuinness was a scrawny mean-spirited Irishman, unkempt with a great bushy black beard, his crown topped by receding lank and unwashed black hair. He had a rather prominent brow, from beneath which a pair of beady blue eyes stared out. His arms were covered in hair interspersed with red blotched skin, burned and ruined by countless hours under the harshest of suns, and his body odour was so rank it wrinkled even the strongest nose.

This individual unfortunately carried the rank of constable first class in the fledgling Western Australia Mounted Police Force.

He had started his career as a junior constable and stationed in the town of Ballyclare outside Belfast in Northern Ireland. McGuiness was an abrasive individual even back then and had no friends or family in the town and so was tempted to make the passage the new settlement of Fremantle in western Australia. On arrival, he immediately offered his papers to the local constabulary and on acceptance was stationed at the new town of York, some 70 miles due east of Perth, under Senior Constable John Drummond, a legendary figure around that time and area. Drummond was a fine and upright officer with a reputation for understanding the local Aboriginal people. He was of a fair but firm character, responsible for diffusing many a potential confrontation, and he was well respected by all.

McGuinness on the other hand was trouble. He fraternised with the local Aboriginal women, often plying them with sly grog to coerce them into having his way with them. He was cunning and managed to get away with this without arousing much of a fuss, although the local tribal elders were getting increasingly upset about his activities as he had been very rough with some of the women.

Declan McGuinness fell afoul of his senior officer when he was finally caught in an embarrassing situation with one of the local Aboriginal woman and later shot and wounded the woman's brother after the man protested about McGuinness's behaviour.

Trouble bubbled to the surface and the local people and elders of the Noongah tribal people of the area asked to meet Drummond. It was obvious to the senior constable that McGuinness was at fault and he had to act.

Drummond had already heard some complaints about the man's behaviour and rumours that McGuinness was apparently less than an honest man – not that he was a thief or any such thing as far as his record showed – with regard to telling the truth about his indiscretions, although there had previously appeared no solid proof about this either.

Not wanting to completely discharge an otherwise fairly good copper without any substantiated evidence, he had previously been asked by his superiors to examine the prospect of sending an officer to the mid-north of the state.

His hand now being dealt the cards needed, he sent McGuinness to the furthest place he could manage, the remote mid-northern region, and ultimately the new stock camp of Mullewa some 300 miles North of Perth.

This, possibly in the future, was to be a new police post, and at that time, the area was beginning to grow and needed a presence of the State law. The odd case of theft and some stealing of cattle by the local Aboriginals had been reported. And while a final decision had yet to been made to establish a permanent police station, Drummond wisely did not say any-thing about the future aspirations of the State Police to McGuinness.

Drummond knew that the one thing that McGuinness had going for him was that he was a tough, dogged and cunning investigator with very good bush skills. As his first ever duty, he was instructed to head north of York, travel on horseback alone and pursue four Aboriginal escapees from the Greenough River area, and if captured, bring them back by wagon to the prison compound at York. This he carried out to the letter.

McGuinness was summoned about one week later to receive an instruc-tion from Drummond. He was ordered to head north to the Mullewa dis-trict, establish and maintain a small police station and was promoted to first class constable of the district as a trade-off.

To say McGuinness was furious would be an understatement, and he hit the grog that night abusing all who ventured near him.

It did not occur to him until later that he would now be almost com-pletely independent and had only to answer correspondence and send reports back to headquarters in Perth. He could easily cover any 'misdemeanours', and cover them he did, as history would show.

As with many of the other pioneering forays by the white man, there were the inevitable clashes with the local Aboriginal tribes. In reality, who could blame these people for resisting the influx of these strangers on lands they had been custodians of for many thousands of years and there were quite a few of these new arrivals who were aggressive and belligerent.

McGuinness was as intolerant and mean spirited as he had always been, and when trouble arose he showed no mercy to the local Aboriginals and would clap them in irons, innocent or not, often travelling hundreds of miles in pursuit of the 'wrong'un's' as he called them. A lot of those he brought back were completely innocent, and almost no one spoke the Aboriginal language. Compounding this was the fact that there were many different dialects amongst the tribes.

The poor wretches, were treated appallingly and with McGuinness as the only "law" around, they often died without question or trial.

There was no one to curb McGuinness's cruel and vindictive streak – he did as he wished and he used this to his own advantage.

McGuinness did not care, he blamed his lot on them for being posted to this god-awful post, irrespective.

McGuinness didn't know, and moreover didn't care, about the history. He would return from his forays, men and women captives shuffling along behind his horses, chained hand and foot, blood streaming from the "iron bracelets", starving and dying of thirst. He would then chain them to the dead tree out in the sun at the rear of the shanty that served as a police station, again giving little food or water. Many of his 'prisoners' died at his infamous 'Mullewa Hitching Post'.

He also continued his liaisons with the local Aboriginal women, free or prisoner, more often than not by force.

It would be fair comment that the people who chose to live and attempt to build dwellings in the nascent community of Mullewa looked upon McGuinness with no small degree of distaste, not only because of his cruelty to the Aboriginal people, but because he had megalomaniac tendencies which many times had caused confrontation with the cattle drovers and adventuristic souls who were beginning to increasingly explore the northern regions.

He never did gain anyone's respect, black, white or in between.

The Mid-West Northern district was slowly attracting men eager to try their hand at raising cattle, and some drove up flocks of sheep from the Greenough River area. The Government was considering opening an inland Lands and Survey office to issue grants in the area, and so justification for a police presence was perhaps deemed necessary.

The establishment of the port of Geraldine was gathering momentum and the Lands and Survey office was based in Geraldine, or Champion Bay as it was first referred to.

These were very hard men, for not to be so, would likely mean failure. These hardy souls would venture far to the north and inland to the east in completely unexplored regions to seek new opportunity. Cattlemen, drovers, pardoned prisoners, investors and prospectors, all looking for their fortune.

They would let their hair down in the barely legal grog shanty, and Mullewa was about the only place available to get grog before the men ventured into further unknowns. McGuinness took it upon himself to police matters in a harsh and uncompromising matter, ending many a protest with the butt of his rifle when a quiet word would have sufficed.

But if the transient people of Mullewa Camp and the surrounding district regarded him with distaste, it was miniscule compared to the terror and hatred alike that he instilled amongst the poor Aboriginal people.

In typical white man's arrogance, to McGuinness, it meant nothing that these proud people had survived this harsh country for tens of thousands of years – without white man's advantages – so in the surrounding communities 'eyes, McGuinness was doing his job. They generally, also knew little of the aboriginal ways. In most cases, he therefore got away with his treatment of the traditional owners of the land, albeit so distasteful.

During his forays into surrounding districts, answering the call so to speak, McGuinness often would call in on the settlers' homesteads where he would filch meals and replenish his stocks.

Later, these visits were, by and large, the only times that he actually washed and had his clothing cleaned.

One of the first times this occurred, or one could say was actually forced upon him, was when he visited a small property owned and run by the Stokes family, which consisted of Robert Stokes, his enormous wife, Bethany, and two children Sandra, aged eight, and little Robert, four.

Bethany Stokes weighed every bit of three times McGuinness's weight, and four times that of her hard and wiry husband. Robert Stokes was no wimp though. It was said he once bit a man's ear right off because he had dared insult Bethany.

Bethany Stokes was somewhat of a legend in the area, equally respected and feared by most menfolk who came to know her, and if they did not know who she was initially, it wasn't long before they did, and they never forgot her.

Bethany Stokes stood about six foot, two, and had dead straight bright red hair, which when let down, covered her backside, though she always had it coiled up on top of her head making her seem taller again. She had arms like a tree cutter and hands to match, a very big woman, but she seemed to move as though she were a lightweight.

A scattering of freckles ran across her cheeks and nose, she had a livid and somewhat heavy scar which ran from ear to ear across her throat, possibly attributing to the slight gravelly edge to her voice, but no one was ever game enough to ask her how she came of it. Some wags said the government tried to hang her, but she was so big she broke the rope and in any event she couldn't have fallen more than a foot at the most given her height.

Bethany wasn't ugly at all, just big, and far from clumsy, when she was helping someone it was said she had a touch as gentle as an angel.

She was no wowser, and when she had a mind, could outfight and outdrink the best of them, and 'Cunnin' as a shite 'ouse rat', as someone had put it.

On the other hand, Big Beth (as she was called behind her back) had a heart of gold and stood up for any underdog, black, white or indifferent – if they needed help she would be there in an instant, often driving the horse and buggy one hundred miles or more. She was an excellent cook and no stranger to midwifery, as many of those in need in the area found out.

Some said she and her husband were both ex-prisoners of Mother England from Sydney town, and had been pardoned, but no one had ever dared to ask them.

So, it was with some trepidation that Declan McGuinness rode into the dusty homestead yard with three prisoners shuffling along behind him, his ever-present swarm of flies hovering about him like a black cloud. He was filthy, covered in red dust and the stench of his foul B.O. preceded him. He had little choice but to call in, having used his last stores two days hence, and he had but half a pannikin of water left.

Bob Stokes greeted the bush copper with his rifle in the crook of one arm.

'Greetin's to y'all!' McGuinness called in his most affable tone.

Before he could continue, Bob Stokes said, 'If'n you want to stay in one piece, ye'd best unshackle them Blacks copper, 'cause if Bethany sees 'em chained like that she will be on ye like a fallen 'ouse.'

Too late. Bethany came out of the house like all fires in hell and descended upon the hapless McGuinness and gave the constable a tongue lashing like he had never heard. Demanding he take the shackles off immediately, she grabbed McGuinness by the thigh in a vice-like grip and almost unhorsed him.

Now McGuinness had spent the better part of three weeks tracking the trio of Aboriginal men and had caught then red-handed spearing a calf, so he wasn't about to take the shackles off his prisoners easily.

Swinging down from his horse he tried fronting the irate monstrous women, but quickly understood he had made a mistake, was outweighed and felt miniscule in front of her – in fact he had to tilt his head back to look at her face.

'Ma'am,' he stuttered, trying to get a word in, 'these 'ere felons are cattle thieves an' oi cannot take a risk an' release 'em.'

Bethany Stokes stood over the skinny copper and stuck her great closed mit in front of his nose and demanded, 'Ye'll give me those keys right now Declan McGuinness, them poor creatures are no more danger-ous right now than my chickens, do ya hear me!' she shrilled. 'Oi will be lookin' after them until you leave, which will be none too soon 'cause ye stink loik me privy over there.' She swung her hand across McGuinness's face causing him to duck and flinch, and pointed at the ramshackle gim-let structure some distance beyond the house.

McGuinness, was not even a slight bit embarrassed by her pointed insult, having been the brunt of the same vernacular many times – he simply did not care about hygiene. But he was very thirsty and even more so, hungry.

'Ma'am all I be askin' for is some water an' maybe some tucker, Oi 'aven't eaten f' three days now, den Oi be leavin' ya foin company an' be on me way.'

She turned again on him. 'So, ye be 'ungry 'an thirsty does ya? Well Oi bet d'ose poor Blacks are worse off dan you! So if'n ye be wanting food an' drink, ye'll be takin' off dose irons and leavin' de poor devils to me lovin' God's care until ye go. Now gimme dose keys now or git!' she raged.

McGuinness was in a bind and she knew it. Damned fookin' ogre, he thought, Oi be fooked if oi go an' fooked efen Oi don't.

'All right,' was all he managed to get out before she was all over him in a flash. 'An' another thing, since ye have come to ya senses a wee bit, you'll not be enterin me 'ouse stinking and filthy loik dat.' She stabbed a long thick finger into his chest, almost knocking him to the ground. *'An'* another thing, ye'll be no cussin' in front o' me or especially me chil'ren,' she said jerking her thumb at the corner of the house where two small heads quickly vanished from site.

'Dere's a tub o' water out back and lire (a crude soap) and ye'll be washin' ye self, den ye can wear some o' me Bob's coveralls whilst Oi wash that filthy cursed copper uniform, now git,' she yelled, just about blowing his eardrums, snatching the key hook from his belt as he turned away.

'Bobby!' she yelled. Bob almost leapt into the air. 'Go git them coveralls o' your'n off the line an' give 'em to this piss-weak excuse of a 'uman bein'.'

Bethany looked at the poor Blacks' ankles and necks, bloodied where the heavy irons had chaffed the skin off, and to a man all had their heads hanging low. She visibly softened.

First things first, she thought, and lifting the lead chain she gently led them to the shade of the lean-to attached to the side of the house.

Shouting, 'Sandy, Bobbie! Bring me a pail of water and me medical box!' When the children came back, she gave each of the prisoners a pannikin of water, and while she watched them hungrily gulp down the water, she started to undo the neck irons. Anger surged within her and tears ran down her cheeks as she saw the raw wounds and imagined the pain these men had endured.

She opened her small box and took out her home-made balms, some ingredients made by local Aboriginal women who often came by to help Bethany, who while tough as nails, was respected by the women, and she learnt much about the land and its many things it could offer.

Gently she applied the ointments to the men's wounds and bandaged the worst of them.

Looking to the leg irons, she turned to her daughter.

"Sandy!' "Go fetch our Jannie from the crick"

Sandy ran as bidden and returned with skinny aboriginal woman in her 30's or there- abouts

Jannie could speak passible English. Bethany had Jannie tell the men she was going to help them, but they must not run away. They apparently agreed and remained after Jannie went back to her people.

As she did this she started to work out how she might get the men away from that bastard copper, because she knew sure as shooting, he would kill them one way or another.

Bethany bustled back into the bungalow and proceeded to make up a batch of mealy dumpling and some bread for the prisoners.

As she bustled back with the first of the small mealy dumplings, she almost collided with McGuiness as he returned from his washing.

McGuiness could not contain himself when he saw that she was feeding the blacks.

'Ye'll not be feedin' and spoilin' those 'wrong un's ma'am!' he said in an authoritive voice.

Robert was returning from the privy and was hitching up his dungarees when he heard McGuinness. 'Oh Jasus!' he muttered and quickly backed out of range.

Bethany froze, then slowly put the dish of food down and the next minute she had McGuinness by the shoulder straps of his borrowed coveralls, spun the copper around and slammed him against the side of the rough stone wall of the house. Robert later swore McGuinness's feet were dangling six inches off the ground. She grabbed him by the hair and twisted his head back and around about as far as she could. McGuinness squealed in pain.

'Don't you *ever* be comin' down here and be tellin' *ME* what to do in *my house* Declan McGuinness, not now, not ever!' She gathered up a great breath and snarled at McGuinness, her face so close he could see his own reflection in her eyes. 'You low life murderin' Irish piece of shite, you be a disgrace to the uniform ye wear and to be sure to ye county!'

She flung him to the ground and with that the monstrous woman stomped off back to tend to the prisoners.

It didn't matter to Bethany what race people were, and she could not see why people like McGuinness were allowed to treat these people the way he did and get away with it, policeman or not.

She wouldn't have it!

She knew well that McGuinness had arrested white men over the killing of Blacks, but no way did they get treated like animals like this. Bethany also knew that many of the Blacks McGuinness arrested, often over trivialities and sometimes innocent, had died at his hand, if not in violence then because of ill treatment.

It was just not right, she lamented.

Little did McGuinness know, but Bethany Stokes was to play a key part in his ultimate downfall.

Later when she got Robert alone she said, 'Git that no good rot-gut brandy ye have hidden away from me oiys in de back o' the lean to and get that bastard good an' drunk, an' oi want 'im out to it soon as we's 'et.

'But Beth...' he began but one look from her stopped him short and he just nodded in acquiescence.

After their meal, a slightly sweeter smelling McGuinness waited for his uniform to dry, not realising that Bethany had simply 'forgotten' to wash it.

Seeming to soften a fraction, Bethany grudgingly told Robert that he ought to offer McGuinness a rum. McGuinness's eyes lit up like beacons at the mention of a drink and accepted the 'gracious' offer with some degree of glee. He hadn't had a drink in almost two weeks now and dreamt of it almost nightly.

'First oi'm gonna check me felons are secure an' all!' he announced and went off to check they were secure. After checking to see if Bethany was out of sight, he gave each one a cuff under the earhole. Satisfied, he returned to the back of the homestead, already drooling at the prospect of a good drink.

Three hours later with the sky lit up in sunset, he and Robert sat out under a mulga tree, the only tree in the small fenced off rear of the house, drunk and dribbling nonsensical drivel.

Forty-five minutes later and McGuinness failed to conquer the savage liquor and collapsed sideways, out cold, narrowly missing the still half-full bottle of rum. Robert managed to stagger over to the house and crashed through the door onto the floor on his knees and somehow got himself onto the bed.

Bethany watched from the chicken pen and grunted in satisfaction. She walked over and took the half bottle to the stable and went to work.

Chapter 29

Hardy Men and Hardy Spirit

The country in the mid north area of Western Australia and beyond, tested the early explorers who travelled from Perth and north to the Mullewa district to the extreme. They had to be a tough lot to survive. They were mostly loners, often hard humourless men, though sometimes men of intellect or government employ could be found.

Nicholas was to meet quite a few of these hardy men during his forays inland and developed a huge respect for their sheer fortitude.

Possibly the most courageous and hardened of these new invaders to the land were the prospectors. They disembarked at the port of Fremantle at the mouth of the Swan River as free men from the other side of the world or were either pardoned convicts or escaped prisoners of Her Majesty, Victoria the Queen of England.

The wharves and shanty pubs were rife with rumours about gold strikes and other minerals to be found inland, and it was these very stories that dangled the bait to those who were eager to risk all to find their fortunes.

These men would invest all they possessed in water pannikins, sacks of flour, tinned food, pots, pans, panning dishes, a heavy steel ore dolly, picks and shovels and specking equipment and all manner of odds and sods and load it all into a heavy tin and timber barrow with a cast iron and steel wheel. They pushed these wheelbarrows laden with 200 pounds plus of equipment for hundreds of miles inland, with no real maps or knowledge of where they were heading, (save perhaps for some very sparsely marked government survey maps) and certainly did not know where the next water hole would be, let alone any shelter.

Those fortunate enough set out with camel and horses, but it was the tough hard men who did it on foot who, by and large, were the real heroes of discovery.

Western Australian was as diverse as it was dangerous and threw its harshest punishment at these stalwart men. Raging red-dust storms rolling ahead of massive thunderstorms, with their clouds like giant bruised fists, would be followed by lashing rain and lightning. In the hotter months, vicious great whirlwinds so strong they could flatten a man and send livestock running in terror. The Aboriginals called these whirlwinds 'willy-willies', and they tormented prospectors. These vortices of spinning high-speed winds sucked up anything in its haphazard path, forming great towering columns – some reaching thousands of feet in height – of stinging red dust, sand and a multitude of objects which could be seen for miles.

The ever-present swarms of little bush flies which never gave up crawling all over one's face and arms. Highly venomous snakes, spiders and scorpions were numerous and many fell victim to the bites received with no help from any quarter.

The land often went without any rain for up to seven years, so water was very difficult to find. There were no mountainous areas through the State that were substantial enough to sustain permanent rivers. The rivers that existed relied on storms and cyclones to flow, and then they would dry up within months, such was the heat.

Of the Aboriginal people encountered, many of the different tribes would have never seen a white man, and so speared many of the men to death, probably out of sheer terror than malicious intent. But then again, explorers, prospectors and white men of all kinds returned with stories of incredible generosity and kindness given by some of the tribes. These people often nursed men dying of thirst and starvation back to a condition where they could be carried hundreds of miles to help.

Many years later those who failed to survive, their skeletal frames or graves (had they been lucky enough to have been found and buried by other hopeful adventurers) were eventually discovered dotted across the vast inland of the Australian West – sometimes in places where even the nomadic inland tribes of Aboriginals chose their times to visit – a tribute to their pioneering spirit and courage in the face of the unknown.

Some called it foolhardiness or even stupidity, but no one could deny the sheer courage and toughness it took for these souls to attempt their forays into these desolate and always challenging areas. These men were a breed of their own.

Not to say that all parts of this vast State were harsh. There were many places of great beauty and serenity, although miniscule in comparison to the vast desolate area.

Magnificent gorges and water holes were scattered about the inland, fed by underground streams. They were sacred places with cultural significance to the Aboriginal people who had spent thousands of years as keepers of these natural gifts of nature.

Some would appear before the unwary as a great two to three-hundred-foot-deep slash in stony spinifex studded iron and stone plains. Water glistened deep down in the gorges like a diamond studded ribbon below canyons of iron and slate stone, riven into the earth as though some mystical giant had slashed the earth. There were long ranges of hills, purple, blue and splashed with reds and gold colours punctuated with small, stark, white-trunked gums. Great cuts were forged into the sides of these ranges and often water in abundance was found within these.

Other water holes could be found on vast plains of red soil, small shrub and dry creek bed. After crossing mile after mile of nothing except murderous heat and mirage, a green ribbon would appear like a phantom, dancing miles in the distance, waving and surreal in the extreme heat. Here, there often grew magnificent white and grey trunked eucalypts some up to thirty or even forty feet tall and many small bushes, shrubs and smaller trees.

Laying supine beneath the greenery, stretches of cool clean water sometimes lay. In these places the underground streams and rivers had surfaced through geological faults and created the water holes. Often, after good rains, they were a few miles long, but the heat and hot winds quickly reduced the overflow, or run-off, and evaporated the larger stretches of water to not much more than about one hundred feet long. Amazingly, they always eventually disappeared again, petering out to vanish beneath the sandy dry creek bed, leaving only the hardiest gum trees with their root systems reaching deep beneath the dry river bed and to the underground water flowing below to survive and telegraph what lay beneath the desert.

During drought years, some of which would drag out to seven or even eight years, the streams would shrink down to small pools or even dry right up, but always, not far below the surface there would be water.

These water holes usually formed up where the underground streams surfaced, some almost with permanent water.

However, no matter how small the water hole, they supported many species of animal. Kangaroo, emu, dingo and many marsupial animals were endemic to the area. Considering the near arid conditions, the bird life was as varied as it was amazing. All types of birdlife frequented the pools and they came in their hundreds.

Very few of the adventurers inland were ever privy to or were as fortunate to have gained the first-hand survival knowledge that Nicholas had gained, albeit, his knowledge had come out of his near-death experience with the snake bite, but a lot did survive.

When they ran out of food they had to trial most things by taste – being their own guinea pig so to speak – and many died trying to eat the native flora and fauna, not knowing what was poisonous and what was edible.

To the layman, the land was barren and useless, but it was in fact, teeming with life which with knowledge, could sustain life and nourishment indefinitely, the living proof being the traditional custodians of this vast desert land.

With guidance from the Aborigines or by sheer luck, the pioneers would find water in the most unlikely of places. Some of these were formed in granite hills, which were scattered around the land. These small water holes, replenished by unseasonal rain or thunderstorms, were often covered by large slabs of granite about three inches thick and up to two and a half feet in diameter, which the Aboriginals would place over the hole forming a natural 'bottle' in the stone.

These were called *gnamma* holes and were often up to six feet deep by four feet in diameter.

Over the years some of these watering holes became well known to the white man and in particular to the cattle drovers and stockmen, driving their herds of cattle all the way from the far north country to Fremantle.

Chapter 30

Ranges and Rogue Coppers

Some weeks after Gnarlu and Yindu had left, Nicholas had travelled about one hundred miles east south-east. He found a number of promising and potential mineral signs along the way and even found some traces of gold. There was not enough however to encourage him to stay and prospect in earnest, and he began to think that he should establish some sort of grid pattern in order to set up some loaming trails. Loaming entailed finding a trace of mineral, often in creek beds and working the land to establish the origin of potential minerals. One often did this by finding traces of gold for example, then working left and right to establish where the best concentration of gold specs occurred, panning all the way. At some point the gold would peter out and here you would dig down to follow the dip, in say a quartz reef.

Irrespective, his basic supplies were beginning to dwindle somewhat, but he now knew how to supplement his supplies with bush food that Gnarlu and Yindu had shown him. He wasn't overly concerned, and there wasn't a day went by when he did not practice the skills.

However, Nicholas began to consider that he should soon start making his way back to the river and restock his supplies. He was becoming increasingly aware of his surroundings the further he ventured inland, which was far more desolate than he had anticipated.

Feed for Stitch and the small packhorse was becoming very sparse, and he did not have enough regular water for his horses. This often forced him way off course to find enough water.

The days were now so hot that by midday he had difficulty moving, He had experienced many places of desert heat, but this heat was tinder dry, and mentally and physically draining.

There appeared to be numerous salt lakes, some vast, in the region making fresh water even harder to locate, and the heat that blew off the salt lake was akin to opening a blast furnace door, intensifying as the day wore on. Further, there were few or no places of shelter to get even a little relief. Even the swarms of infuriating flies that doggedly swarmed around them had the sense to largely vanish by about mid-morning.

Both horses had lost a lot of condition, and the normally stalwart beasts were showing signs of losing endurance. He reasoned he needed to find a place and put down a base from which he could rely on for feed and supplies, perhaps even bringing either Jack or Whip to maintain the base.

He reluctantly turned and began to head in a west south-westerly direction, reasoning he would find a decent place on the way back and return later with supplies and set up his base.

Nicholas was writing in his diary and with a jolt saw it was now almost three weeks into the month of February and since he had left the mouth of the Murchison months ago and wondered if big Jack would make good his promise to track him down if he had not returned in four months as he said he would. Nicholas smiled as he remembered the big fellow's devotion.

Then with a surprise, he saw he had missed Christmas – in fact he had not even thought about it. 'Oh well!' he sighed in resignation. It wasn't as if he had a family to return to, he thought ruefully.

He was also somewhat concerned that perhaps the *Collette* had returned, and perhaps Birch had somehow got back at Jack and Whip.

Although he knew Jack had natural bush skills, this was not Africa and he most likely would have difficulty surviving without some help, and it was as hot as hell.

He was not to know that Whip and Jack had received news that he was still in good health from Gnarlu and Yindu. Nicholas's attempts to teach the two English were good enough to give Whip and Jack the message that he was all right.

It took Nicholas three days to come to a range of hills which had gradually appeared to the south-west. The range ran east west and covered an area some five miles in length.

The ranges were made up of hard ironstone interspersed with some layers of very old limestone, an unusual combination that in its self, had piqued his interest. In fact, he was so interested he decided to set up camp on the western end, where there was better feed for his horses and he found a small water hole about three mile from his chosen camp site but further around the south-west end of the range.

He fossicked around for three days, finding some interesting varieties of ore and some interesting quartz protrusions, and so started sampling and prospecting around the southern side.

The area excited something within him, but try as he might, he could not figure out just what it was.

One day he climbed to the top for the second time with his telescope and sat watching as the sun began its journey to the horizon. Lifting the glass Nicholas scanned from left to right, searching for any ridges or scarps that might pique his interest. He saw two, a low rise to the west some thirty mile away he reckoned, and the other about ten miles to the north which looked as though it might be promising, the ground seemingly rose as a broken edge maybe a few miles long. He vowed he would examine this on the way home.

Nicholas snapped the telescope closed and began to make his way back down to his camp when suddenly he thought he saw movement out toward the west. He again opened the glass and focused on three figures. 'Blacks,' he said out loud as he saw two adult males and what looked like a young boy. It was hard to tell from this distance, given that they were still a good eight miles away, but they were heading toward his camp. Best get moving, he thought to himself, not because he was overly worried about the Blacks but because he did not want to get caught climbing down the ranges in the dark despite the fact that there was a three-quarter moon high in the sky. The memory of the snake bite was still fresh in his mind.

Nicholas had started his fire for the evening and tendered to Stich and the sturdy little packhorse when he sensed he was not alone. His senses were on high alert and his rifle lay within easy reach, fully loaded and cocked. He knew he was being watched but reasoned he would be in trouble already had there been any serious threat.

The trio of blacks cautiously approached Nicholas's camp. He had been right, one was a young lad of about ten years old. Both adults carried woomeras, or spear throwers, and long hunting spears, and also clutched a number of boomerangs.

They were extremely nervous and kept looking around constantly. This was making Nicholas somewhat edgy, so after a while he tried to say a few words that Gnarlu and Yindu had tried to teach him. This produced some laughter and grinning.

The older of the men cautiously stepped forward and approached the fire.

After a time, he indicated to the other two with a flick of his wrist and they came closer.

Nicholas had a haunch of kangaroo he'd shot that morning roasting over the fire on green branches and offered the three to join him. It took a little while, clearly they did not trust the white man.

Nicholas slowly got up and went to his saddlebag, and rummaging around found his spare tin mug, tins of sugar and black India tea. Pouring some water from his saddle pannikin into his blackened 'billy', placed it on the coals to boil. When the water boiled in about five minutes, he threw in a handful of tea leaves and made a brew. He poured two mugs of the tea and put two large amounts of sugar into each, then placed the second mug in front of the eldest man.

The Aboriginals had obviously never had tea before and did not touch the mug but watched with great interest as Nicholas stirred in the sugar, then lifted the mug up and blew into the mug cooling the tea as he did so. As he began to sip the tea, he made a point of slurping it loudly, much to the humour and amazement of the trio watching him.

The older man began looking down at the mug and slowly reached out and touched the side, instantly burning his fingers of course. Nicholas started to laugh as the old man hissed in surprise and he had to show him how to use the handle. The older man got the idea soon enough and blowing like Nicholas, took his first sip.

He froze. 'Oh oh,' thought Nicholas as he watched the serious look come over the old man's face.

Suddenly, he swallowed, smacked his lips and turned to the others and said something Nicholas did not understand. The young lad's face lit up in a grin, he frowned then suddenly said something, 'Thans'.

Nicholas was a little taken aback at the simple word spoken in English

They then started to pass the mug around between them, laughing then blowing and sipping as they went, leaving Nicholas wondering where they had come from.

Relieved there appeared no threat, Nicholas started to check the roasting meat. He knew the Aboriginals did not overcook their meat, so he cooked it lightly and distributed it to them all.

After they had demolished the small kangaroo haunch, Nicholas made another brew of tea and they again passed the spare cup amongst each other. Nicholas was vastly amused by the different looks on each of the trio's faces.

The other adult had just passed the mug to the young lad when suddenly he held up a hand and froze. He slowly rose to his feet and sniffed the wind, then proceeded to move in different parts of the camp site, always up wind of the fire. Eventually, he relaxed a little and sat down again, but Nicholas noticed he moved his woomera and spears closer to him.

Several hours later and tired of the concentration of trying to communicate, Nicholas rose and laid out his bedroll, the three Blacks watching him intently. Then Nicholas strode across the camp area and stepped behind a large boulder on the south-west side to urinate. He walked about six feet past and busied himself unbuttoning his breaches.

An almighty explosion fell on him and he pitched forward face first into the sand.

Chapter 31

Jack's Search Begins

Late January 1850

One early morning Gnarlu and Yindu had appeared before Whip and Jack just as they were washing before the day's work, startling them initially, but then Gnarlu suddenly spoke a little of the English that Nicholas had taught him.

'Fella belong big anmal 'orse,' Gnarlu expanded proudly to the two now astonished men, imitating a man riding.

'Be Jaysus, did 'e just speak English Jack?' said Whip as he looked incredulously at the Aboriginal man who was pointing to the north-east.

'This white fella, 'e gooda!' said Gnarlu, flicking his thumb up as Nicholas had taught him for all is good. ''Orses is gooda!' he added again stabbing up with his thumb.

It dawned on Jack and Whip that he was saying Nicholas was fine, but Jack chewed at his lip trying hard to believe what they were saying.

'I reckon Mister Nicholas is okay Jack, do ya think?'

'Hmmm, ma'be,' growled the big man from somewhere deep down inside of him, already making up his mind he was going to find Nicholas.

As suddenly as they had appeared, the two Aboriginal men turned and vanished into the scrub at the back of the stockyard.

After the two Aboriginals had delivered the news of Nicholas, the concern gnawing at Big Jack's gut had abated somewhat, much to Whip's relief.

Prior to this, Jack would climb the cliffs near the mouth every day and gaze into the distance for about 45 minutes or so, as if willing Nicholas's return.

'F' God's sake man!' Wilber burst out one day, 'e'll come back when he is good and ready, stop worrying! Ye are beginnin' ta drive me nuts climbin' up there every mornin!' Jack just stared at him and continued irrespective.

The truth of the matter and the reason for the outburst was that Whip was also beginning to get concerned. Whip knew from the reaction that Jack had made up his mind to go – it was just a question of when he would leave.

The next morning Whip awoke to find Big Jack gone.

'Ya stoopid big fooker!' Whip screamed into the dawn. 'I'll cut ya balls off if'n I ever sees ya agin!'

Whip sat down on the chopping block and allowed himself some sorrow for once in his life. He realised the big Zulu had become as much a brother as his own back in England, maybe more so. Tears rolled down his cheeks.

He looked up feeling very downhearted and suddenly jerked upright. Through his swimming eyes and right before him stood Big Jack, water streaming from his naked body and glistening in the dawn light and a grin as big as the sunrise on his huge face.

Whip shot to his feet in embarrassment, wiping his eyes with the sleeve of his night shirt shouting, 'Where the fook 'av you been?' Whip couldn't think of anything else to say as he was caught red-handed exposing his emotions.

Jack was shaking in delight and laughter at his friend's display, while Whip's temper, never far below the surface, exploded at being caught out, and the Welshman rushed at Jack.

Whip crashed into Jack who was weak from laughing, and the two fell to the ground, Jack still laughing and Whip trying hard to take a swing at his friend.

They scrambled to their feet. Whip swung a vicious right hook up at Jack but succeeded in only hitting Jack's left bicep. Jack suddenly stepped forward with speed and wrapped Whip in his huge arms. Whip felt his feet leave the ground as Jack straightened up, easily holding the now squirming Wilber.

'Let me go ya fookin' great prick, Oi'm gunna kill ya. *Let me go!*' he screamed.

Big Jack just turned with his struggling friend still locked in his arms and walking to the river's edge some fifty yards away tossed Wilber head-long into the river and was on him before he even broke the surface.

Jack, laughing even harder, shoved the hapless Wilber spluttering and still cursing under the water with one hand on his head.

The hopelessness of the one-sided fight soon dampened Whip's temper and then he too started to laugh as they splashed about in the river.

Eventually, the two friends settled down at the edge of the water with the rising Sun at their backs, chests heaving and not a word more was spoken as they simply sat and enjoyed each other's company and the dawn tranquility returned.

Later, Big Jack put his hand on Whip's shoulder and said, 'My fren', Jack not leave wit'out tellin' you, but...Jack going to find Mister Nicholas.' Whip slowly nodded his head but said nothing.

Jack, his hand still on Whip's shoulder said, 'Somethin' not right, is a feeling!' he said emphatically, his other hand thumping his chest. 'Must go!'

Whip had learned that the big Zulu had very strong instincts, and on several occasions Jack's feelings proved accurate. So, he nodded and said, 'Orright Jack, let's go an' organise your trip.'

Whip argued that Jack take the remaining horse, but Jack insisted he go on foot, and in any case he would be calling on the local tribal people to guide him. Jack was an adept tracker and to him spoor was spoor be it here in this land or back in Africa.

Jack kitted himself out with the bare necessities, a medium-sized water pannikin, some dried meat and some of Wilbur's 'Denture Destroyer' biscuits. For weaponry, he chose only a large Bowie knife belonging to Nicholas that he had left for their use whilst he was away, and a vicious looking North American tomahawk that Nicholas had given the big Zulu.

Nicholas had acquired the tomahawk whilst prospecting in the Canadian badlands. The tomahawk looked ridiculously small in Jack's huge hands, but it was finely balanced and razor sharp. Jack practiced almost every day and could hit a four-inch sapling square on at twenty-five paces with barely a glance.

'Jack leave tomorrow, dawn,' he said to Whip, looking at his friend for any sign of emotion. He was disappointed as Whip just gave a short curt nod of his head.

The next morning, they were both up before the dawn, Jack solemnly shaking Wilbur's hand and murmured, 'You be take good care of my lovely Kubi,' he said indicating at the great bull. Whip just grunted and looked away. 'An' you see, Jack be back soon with Mister Nicholas,' he added in finality, and spun away and trotted off at a fast clip before Wilber could see the tears in his eyes.

Wilber watched his big friend disappear into the scrub and he too now wiped tears from his eyes.

'Fookin' great galoot!' he said out loud.

Jack quickly fell into travel mode, born out of Zulu warrior training since he was old enough to learn to run, and he could run forty mile non-stop and not even raise a sweat. He headed for the last place he had visited the Aboriginal people to see if he could enlist the help of the two men who had brought news of Mr Nicholas. But he knew the tribe moved constantly and he did not know of the other places they could be at this time, other than two places closer to the river mouth, and he knew they were not there.

He needn't have worried, as about eight miles upstream of the river on the flat plains and in open country, he sensed he was not alone.

Suddenly he saw in the distance two figures. Although he could not see who it was, he continued to run toward them without breaking stride. The figures somehow suddenly vanished from sight and he slowed a little, veering toward the tree line of the river. As he approached the trees Gnarlu and Yindu suddenly appeared in front of him.

Jack slowed to a halt some six feet from the pair.

'*Suwununa!*' he greeted them in Zulu. 'Allo,' said Gnarlu in English. Jack could not suppress a chuckle and looked at the grinning men.

He pointed to the north and moved his hand between the men and himself and said, 'Fella 'orse,' imitating what they had told him earlier. With a wave of the hand they swung in beside him, Yindu taking the lead. An odd sight indeed – a black Aboriginal in the rear, a giant ebony Zulu in the middle, who towered eighteen inches above the others, and a thin black Aboriginal striding out ahead.

Jack thought as he strode along, that perhaps they had been waiting for him, which was correct, the elder foretelling that they would search for Nicholas.

They made excellent time, though Jack lamented that they could have covered twice the distance at his pace, but neither of the men would change their stride so Jack eventually gave up trying to push harder. He also had to respect the fact that they were in familiar territory, and he was not.

On the sixth day, Gnarlu in the lead suddenly stopped, waving his hand across and down indicating that they freeze.

He stood stock still for some time when all of a sudden there appeared three Blacks walking up out of a depression and moving toward them, some five hundred yards away now. Still Gnarlu did not move a muscle and neither did the others. Then Gnarlu lowered his spears, and looking behind him, moved carefully to his right, effectively lining up some dark undergrowth behind them in line with the approaching figures. Jack and Yindu followed suit.

Jack's eyes were darting left and right, tension building up in him.

Zulu warfare was formed out of a 'Cape Buffalo' head, whereby the centre of the head came in first and met the enemy head on. Once engaged, the Zulu generals would signal for the two horns made up of thousands of warriors to curve around and run into battle from the sides, a brilliant tactic which encircled the enemy. Not being aware that the Aboriginal people of Australia had no such warfare tactics like that of the Zulu – nor did they ever need such tactics – Jack was nonetheless wary.

The three approaching blacks slowed and approached cautiously. Jack suddenly noticed subtle hand movements taking place between the two groups.

As they got closer and they began to talk, greeting each other, he noticed the ankle bandages, which had slipped and exposed bleeding open wounds, as did the necks of the three men. Jack knew all too well what that meant and was baffled and confused by this. Nicholas had told him slavery did not happen here as far as he knew. A great and fierce frown creased his face as he tried to understand what was being said.

He needn't have worried. The three were the escaped prisoners from McGuinness's clutches, thanks to Bethany Stokes, and were unarmed. The three were also from a closely related tribe just north of Gnarlu and Yindu's tribe, a fact which Yindu later relayed to Jack.

After the group had come together the verbal exchange was so rapid that even if Jack could have understood some more of the language, he would have had no chance of following it.

Eventually, after much discussion, the three trotted off in the direction that Jack's group had come from.

'Bad man,' Gnarlu said in his extremely limited English, pointing in the direction from which the three had come and held hands around their necks and ankles, drawing rough chain links in the dirt. Gnarlu pointed east and holding his palm out, swept the other across it, he said 'Sssst!' made rapid movements of walking with his fingers. Jack nodded realizing he meant they must go quickly and they headed off at an increased pace. It was mid-morning now and the hot sun had yet to peak. They tracked into the night, a good sized moon now helping them.

They eventually saw a campfire burning brightly at the base of the ranges. It was after midnight and instinctively Jack knew Nicholas was close to this, if not at the camp. Excited, he was about to head toward the fire when Yindu caught his arm and pointed to two horses tethered on one side and another two tethered on the other. This was odd, thought Jack, grateful to Yindu for stopping him.

Yindu put his hand over his mouth and made a wriggle motion with his hand then pointed at himself. Jack understood instantly and Yindu vanished into the shrub and boulders.

He returned no more than twenty minutes later, and beckoning Jack to bend down, put his mouth to Jack's ear and whispered, 'Bad man,' Jack nodded, then Yindu patted the back of his head and indicated with both hands that Nicholas was lying down.

Jack, confused for a minute suddenly realised that Yindu was saying that Nicholas was lying down wounded or worse. A cold anger washed over him and he made the other two understand that he was going to investigate and they were to stay where they were and wait for him.

He crept forward and dropped in behind a large boulder and went closer. Just short of the boulder he saw a tiny glint on the sand in the moon light and bending down saw it was congealed blood.

Then he heard a man half speaking, half singing in an Irish brogue, almost unintelligible, but he was talking about his beautiful new rifle. Jack went closer and saw the scrawny copper holding Nicholas's rifle in one hand and swigging on a bottle in the other, Nicholas lying supine on the other side of the campfire.

Jack's rage boiled over and he simply walked up behind the man whilst he tilted his head back drinking, the moment the copper lowered the flask and started singing again Jack struck. Gnarlu and Yindu, waiting a short distance away, heard the Irishman's voice stop suddenly mid-sentence.

Chapter 32

Bethany's Scheme

ethany had worked diligently at her task, harnessing their horse and buggy, and picking up the unconscious McGuinness, she carried him over to the stable. Here she stripped him and redressed him in his filthy stinking uniform and pouring some of the remaining rum into a small cup with a pinch of laudanum, she propped him up and managed to get McGuinness to drink down the draft before none too gently tossing McGuinness into the back of the buggy.

Fetching a bottle of the 'Brady's' she stuffed it into one of the saddle bags.

Next she fetched the prisoners, still chained, but now bandages were wrapped around the irons so as not to aggravate their wounds. She got them to climb up onto the back of the buggy, hitched up McGuinness's horses and headed off east on the rough track to Mullewa.

Bethany found a good spot where she thought McGuinness might naturally stop, albeit drunk as a lord.

She unchained each of the prisoners and gave them water and some of her bread, then shooed them off. They were confused and just stood there.

'Ye are free to go! Go, go!' she waved her arms indicating they should move quickly.

Suddenly, they caught onto what she meant and turned as one and ran off in a westerly direction. They suddenly stopped about twenty feet away, turned as one and raised their hands toward her, grinning hugely, then spun and vanished into the night.

Big Beth snapped a branch off and began her set-up for whenever McGuinness woke up. Finally, she dusted off all trace of the buggy and tracks around the site and turned for home from about a half mile away from where McGuinness now lay slouched against the sheoak tree, his rifle against the tree next to him.

She was back in the house before her husband even knew she had left the homestead, while McGuinness couldn't even remember leaving the homestead. He had woken up about 20 miles east of the Stokes' property, his horses hobbled and grazing nearby on some sparse stubble, while he himself was under a sheoak tree, a quarter bottle of the rum on its side next to him.

He had opened his eyes directly into the morning Sun and it felt like someone had stuck a poker into them – the headache was immediate as it was massive.

'God!' he muttered, 'I am done over!' He had never had such a fierce hangover and it took him several attempts and some time to sit up, the nausea coming as soon as he stood, followed quickly by vomit. As the spasms abated and he finally got somewhat under control, he sat down but it took his wretched brain some time before registering that there was something not quite right.

Suddenly it hit him. 'The fookin' prisoners!' He shot to his feet, his headache almost knocking him down again. 'Shit!' the fookers are gone!' he said out loud, his stomach beginning to heave again with a will of its own.

All that remained were the irons, one end around a tree as was his usual practice of securing for the night and the rest strung out on the ground. Slapping his hip, keys – gone. Then he spotted them some six feet from the irons, and his rifle was propped up against the tree.

'Christ almighty!' he exclaimed. 'Dey's snuck up on me when I was drunk an' done a bolter!'

McGuinness had found an eight-foot tree branch with a broken off small branch stub on one end. "Tis how they done it!' he muttered between waves of nausea and the massive pounding in his head. 'Must 'ave snapped off the branch and hooked me keys, the cunning fookers!'

McGuinness was furious to say the least, torn between immediately mounting and giving chase or heading back to Mullewa to replenish his supplies. He raged at himself at first, then in typical fashion blamed the prisoners. Eventually, common sense somehow won the day and he decided he would set off back to Mullewa as soon as he could.

Head spinning and gut heaving, he was forced to sit down, and after a good swig of water, collapsed against the tree in the shade and fell asleep.

Two hours later he felt a little better and packed up, not even checking his back trail. As well he did not for he would have found something very odd about his horses' hoof prints, and had he tracked harder he may have found a set of buggy wheel marks.

By God that woman of Bob Stokes was a tough'n an' all, McGuinness was thinking, but she seemed to warm to him a little after a while.

Far from feeling well, he had taken two attempts to heave himself up into the saddle and had to sit still for a few minutes whilst his heart stopped pounding in his ears and his head stopped spinning.

With nausea rolling over him in waves and a cold sweat on his brow, he swore he would never touch another drop of alcohol. Eventually he kicked the horse forward and headed down the trail to Mullewa.

Chapter 33

Yuin and McGuinness

The copper walked his horse as slowly as he could, lest his head fall off, such was the ache pounding away like an angry blacksmith on his anvil. 'Good Christ that was some rum that Robert Stokes had,' lamented McGuinness. He was too hungover to even think about the escaped Blacks now and decided to keep heading east and head for 'Burro Rock', a low granite rise some twenty mile from where he was now. He knew there was a good *gnamma* hole there off the eastern side near the top which was quite large and had good clean water.

He got to the top of the granite rise just before dusk, having tethered his horses to a grove of sheoak and some mulga trees not far from the base of where he now stood. The hot sun had all but boiled the hangover out of him, and he had made his second trip up to the *gnamma* hole and filled the wooden pail he carried. He decided to sit for a while, a dull ache all that remained of his binge.

As the sun began to dip behind the granite behind him, he rose to return and make camp, when something caught his eye far off to the east. Something flashed for an instant, very faint but he saw it nonetheless.

Strange, he thought, it appeared to come from the far range. He waited but the flash did not come again. He decided to deviate a little tomorrow, even though he knew it would take almost a day in this terrain to get to where he thought it could have come from. It was not much of a deviation from the track back to Mullewa, maybe eight mile at best.

The next morning McGuinness felt much better and set out early in the direction of where he thought he saw the small flash of light.

The terrain started to deteriorate the further he went. Dry creeks riven into the soil, sometimes ten feet deep, meant backtracking and re-routing. The shrubbery was also harsh and prolific with many covered in thorns that when brushed against, festered within an hour. By midday he took a break and climbed a small rise to scan ahead.

Seeing nothing, except that he was actually about half way to the distant range, he picked out a reasonable route as far as he could see.

He was about to descend and recommence the journey when some small movement in the distance captured his attention.

He immediately swung the telescope to it and saw what he thought could be three black figures or maybe two, but he couldn't be sure at that distance. 'Aha!' he exclaimed, what luck! It had to be his escaped prisoners, he, not knowing that his escaped 'wrong'uns' had headed west.

He hurried back down and set off with renewed energy in the direction he had picked.

McGuinness made good time and although he could not find any decent sign to track, he reasoned if he could get to the foothills of the distant range, it would only be a matter of time before he found his 'wrong'uns'.

It was hard going, but five hours later he was a mere half a mile from the base of the ranges and got down off his horse and led it the final distance, hoping to pick a footprint. He had only gone about three hundred yards when he smelt smoke. It appeared to be coming from the north, so he tethered the horses to a small gimlet and gave them a little of his feed and some water.

Grabbing his rifle and several spare cartridges he set off on foot.

It wasn't too long before he spotted the glow of a fire. Elated, he spent a few minutes calming himself before reaching his all too familiar hunting mode.

McGuinness was an expert at stalking and he took a great deal of care in his approach to the camp site. Regularly stopping and glassing the site until he had a good view in order to do a head count. 'Dere!' he thought as he clearly saw the fire and almost reached for the rifle before realising something was different. He swung up the glass again. 'Damn me, dere's four of 'em,' he exclaimed to himself. He studied the four figures. One of them with his back to him, looked bigger and one looked smaller.

'Stuff me! If'n it isn't a white man!' he muttered under his breath. McGuinness was well aware of the fine instincts the Aboriginals possessed and also they could smell out a tit mouse from a hundred paces away, so he immediately backtracked and headed a bit further downhill so that the slight breeze was in his face. He then began to worm his way toward the camp site.

Luck was with him as the camp site was in amongst some large granite or ironstone boulders giving him perfect cover. He got right up to within twenty feet of the camp site without even disturbing the two horses he spotted north of the camp, having edged his way to where he now lay in the shadow of a large boulder.

'Patience now me lad,' he told himself and settled down to wait until later in the evening.

McGuinness heard someone approaching and coiled up ready for action. The white man walked straight past him and stood on a low slab of granite. McGuinness made a snap decision, considering that if the fellow turned he would likely see him, and as he did that, the three Aboriginals would hear him at the very least and would vanish in an instant. He waited until the man got busy with his ablutions then rose, stepping up onto the stone and smacked the figure hard under the right ear with his rifle butt, dropping the man like a stone. Then he immediately ran around the boulder and whipping the rifle up to his shoulder called, 'Hold! Ye black 'eathens!'

The three were already on their feet and in another second would have vanished into the darkness.

To his surprise they were not his escaped prisoners and one was a young lad.

McGuinness didn't really care who they were as no one in the community even knew who he had gone to arrest, so these would do anyway. He would deal with the lad tomorrow.

He went immediately to the older of the trio and struck the man in the face with his rifle, knocking him to the ground and immediately levelled the cocked rifle at the other two.

'Git down,' he yelled, one hand on the rifle and the other pointing down. Terrified, the Blacks immediately got down on the ground and McGuinness's boot in the back of each made it plain they were to remain belly down.

McGuiness spotted a coil of rope by Nicholas's saddle and gear, then gasped as he spotted Nicholas's beautiful hunting rifle.

Quickly, he lashed the three Aboriginals together, the young lad copping a none too gentle fist to the side of the face for whimpering.

That done, McGuinness went back to the rifle. He picked it up. Never had he seen such beautiful workmanship, nor had he seen an action like this. It was more beautiful than any woman he reckoned, running his filthy hands over the finely worked wood and its perfectly subtle carvings of oak leaf and swirl. He lifted it to his shoulder. 'What balance it had, perfect!' he said to himself.

Suddenly, he remembered the man he had hit earlier and quickly went to check on him. He lay as he had fallen. McGuinness dragged the man back to the fire. 'Jesus, but ain't ye the heavy one!' he exclaimed, panting with the exertion.

McGuinness checked the man. Blood had flowed from an open wound on the head where he had hit him with the rifle butt and he could only just feel breath coming from his mouth.

'Oi be thinkin' dis 'ere fellow won't be lastin' the night,' he said out loud. 'Ah well, looks loik Oi gets me a beautiful weapon and me prisoners!' he grinned to himself. 'Oi'l bury 'im in the mornin' an' no one will be the wiser!' he thought.

Next he got the three 'wrong'uns' together, the older man now having woken. 'Allo me sleepin' beauty, come to 'ave ya now!' he snarled at the old man. 'Come on,' he said and viciously jerked the lead rope and tied them off to a small tree just beyond the campfire. Then he went back to where he had tethered his horses, and bringing them back, he hobbled them and returned to the fire.

McGuinness danced a jig, one hand on the barrel of Nicholas's rifle and in the other he swigged on a bottle of the Brady's rum which he had found in his saddle bags after his visit to the Stokes' homestead, forgetting all about his vow of that morning. A powerful swill he reflected, gasping as it burnt its way down to his gut, with God only knows what alcohol content. 'An' me thanks to ye Robert an' Bethany Stokes!' he called into the night.

Back in Mullewa, the locals reckoned that if you left the cork out of a bottle of this stuff overnight, by morning it would've peeled the lime whitewash off the hessian walls of your house and killed every spider and snake within 40 paces.

One old soak reckoned he gave an Aboriginal man a swig and he ran off and passed two kangaroos and an emu before it wore off, McGuiness cackled at the outrageous exaggeration.

But McGuinness was a hardened drinker and his little beady eyes were as bright as the evening star as he stopped again to run his hands lovingly over the rifle's beautiful inlays.

He had dreamed of owning such a weapon since he was a child and now he had one!

And anyway, he had this stranger dead to rights; harbouring, aiding and abetting Aboriginal criminals, he chuckled to himself.

Forgotten was the fact that his new 'prisoners' had not even been officially charged, let alone been sentenced, and moreover, he didn't know if the Aborigines he had in custody now were even the same ones as he had seen from the rise.

McGuinness never even heard his assailant approach as a great vice closed around the scrawny neck of the Irish copper. McGuinness was slowly but steadily lifted off the ground, kicking and clawing at the great hands around his neck for what must have seemed an eternity as the life was being choked out of him. He tried in vain to prise away the hands from around his neck with his left hand. McGuinness began to lose consciousness, his vision blurred and tears started to run down his face as he began to spasm uncontrollably. He lost control and was about to let go of Nicholas's rifle when suddenly he was jerked up higher, spun around and held now by one hand. The assailant's other hand shot down enveloping the man's trigger hand, an audible but muted 'click' the only sound as the huge hand squeezed the man's fingers against the trigger guard and lock, dislocating two fingers and almost snapping the bones in the others.

'Mmmmmm uhh,!' was all the copper could manage as intense pain shot up his arm.

Declan McGuinness's eyes bulged as he tried to focus his eyes on who or what his attacker was, but all he could see was a large dark shape in the orange glow of the campfire behind. What he could vaguely see though was what looked like two great eyes bulging out with terrifying intensity. In his terror he couldn't tell if his assailant was human or animal and the eyes seemed to glow an orange colour.

'Oh God,' he thought as first orange spots danced in his eyes, then blackness enveloped him.

Jack flung the now still body away like a piece of rag and immediately went to Nicholas. Lifting him effortlessly he carried him to a large flat stone on the other side of the fire.

Turning Nicholas's head, he saw a large bump and gash on the left side behind the ear. Blood trickled easily from the gash as soon as he touched the wound.

Going to Nicholas's saddlebags, Jack found what he was looking for and returned with some water, white powder he knew Nicholas always carried for wounds, and a clean roll of bandage. He then dressed the wound as far as he could, the powder stemming the flow of blood somewhat. He took Nicholas's bed roll and laid Nicholas out again on the large flat rock and made him as comfortable as he could, then went to attend to the crumpled body of the copper.

He checked the man. 'Basta' still lives!' he exclaimed to himself.

Jack heard the soft foot fall behind him and suddenly spun around, the rage still bubbling within and ready to kill. The razor-sharp tomahawk came out of its pouch hanging down his back in a blur.

It was Gnarlu and Yindu. Both had a look of abject terror on their faces when they saw Jack's maddened eyes staring at them. He relaxed and grinned at them saying, 'Is okay now,' holding out his hand, palm up then returning the hatchet to its pouch.

Gnarlu and Yindu then brought the even more terrified three 'prisoners' into the camp site. They were trembling in fear as all had witnessed the great strength and murderous attack on the copper. They kept looking at the crumpled form of the now unconscious McGuinness.

Jack looked at the crumpled form and casting around saw McGuinness's tunic and went over to examine it, wrinkling his nose in disgust at the stink of it. He picked it up and quickly saw that this man was a police officer.

Hmmm, he mused and said, 'Not very gooda man dis one.'

Rummaging in Nicholas saddle bag he found some cloth. He took his knife and cut a strip off and tied tightly it around the coppers eyes.

Next he trussed McGuinness up like a turkey and propped him up in a cleft between two rocks and returned to tend to Nicholas.

Nicholas was beginning to improve, and now that he was not face down in the sand he was breathing evenly. Big Jack tenderly bathed his face and never left his side until the sun began to rise.

Jack dozed off for about an hour before the sun came, and when he awoke he saw the oldest of the new prisoners squatting in front of a slowly stirring McGuinness, who periodically would twitch as though he had been struck with a sharp instrument.

The old man was quietly chanting something, and in his hands he kept turning over two pieces of bone. He was staring intently at McGuinness; the low monotone chanting went on and on for almost an hour and a half.

Jack, being no stranger to witchdoctors in his own country, instinctively knew that this bad man had incurred the wrath of the old man and would pay dearly.

The old man was in fact preparing for a council of elders, McGuinness the subject.

The elders, if the crime warranted execution, would sometimes eventually summon a 'Kurdaitcha man' or 'feather foot' who would be the messenger of their decision and usually was an executioner.

Kurdaitcha meant 'feather foot', slippers that were made of feathers, bound with human hair and bonded with human blood. It was said that no visible footprint was impressed. It might take years, but eventually the *Kurdaitcha* would prevail in his task.

The Aborigines were, to a person, terrified of the *Kurdaitcha* men, and once sighted by these messengers – if they were sent after them – they knew they would die, not by violence, but by mind set. They often just died for no apparent reason or just gave up, knowing the inevitability.

As McGuinness would later discover this council decision would have a serious impact on his mental wellbeing no matter where he was, but other factors would play a part in McGuinness's fate, and not the least, Jack would be a contributor.

McGuinness began to come around and made a loud moan. Jack strode straight across to him and belted the trussed up copper so hard in the face, he lapsed back into stupour – out cold.

At Jack's direction, the young Aboriginal stayed with Nicholas after they had moved him under a makeshift lean-to in the shade of a small tree.

They fetched McGuinness's horses and carried McGuiness back to the trail to Mullewa. They searched and found a place well-hidden off the trail. Here they sat the still unconscious McGuinness against a dead tree, tying his hands behind the tree. They removed his hat, stripped off his shirt and removed the blindfold.

Big Jack placed a full pannikin of water just out of reach of McGuinness, so he could see the water, but could not reach it. They would return later in the afternoon.

They left to let the hot sun do its work.

It was late afternoon and thunderstorms were growing on the horizon when Jack, Gnarlu and the older man went back to where they had left McGuinness. It was still very hot and Jack wondered if the crooked copper had survived. He looked at the heavy dark cloud approaching and thought, 'Gooda, wash away sign.'

McGuinness had indeed survived. He sat, head down, babbling incoherently. His skin was bright red and great blisters had formed on his previously white skin.

'Auta, auta, auta!' he babbled, tongue beginning to swell. He was, no doubt, driven almost insane from staring at the just out of reach pannikin of water, and it had become the obsession it had meant to be.

They approached from behind and Jack's great hands again closed around McGuinness's neck.

The recollection was almost instant. With a half strangled and hoarse scream, McGuinness tried in vain to get away. 'Nah, no, no!' he managed as no doubt the image of the 'monster' came back to haunt him from the previous night.

Jack released his grip and applied the blindfold again. He took the pannikin of water, which had evaporated by some two inches and poured most of it over McGuiness's head, saving a little for the man to drink. He knelt down in front of the burnt and sun-struck man, examining him as if he were nothing more than the dead tree to which he was tied.

Although it was still quite hot, McGuinness was shivering from heat stroke.

Jack gave him a sip of water. 'More,' was all McGuinness could croak and he was given more.

McGuinness started to babble again, saying, "Elp me, de wrong'uns 'ave got me, dere's a big monster wit orange oiyes 'an e's fittin' ta eat me!'

Jack couldn't resist and he let out a low deep growl almost rattling McGuinness's chest bones.

McGuinness's reaction was predictable – he drew his knees up and screamed, a strangled terrified sound as his legs scrambled and he tried to retreat behind the tree.

Jack rose and indicated they were to leave. 'Tomorrow,' was all he said when they got out of earshot, and they turned away and trotted back to the camp.

Nicholas came to about three hours later, concussed and vomiting. He opened his eyes and saw the familiar face of Jack grinning at him. 'Jack? How come? What happened?' was all he could manage. 'Is okay Mista Nicholas, Jack here, I look after you, go to sleep now.' Then Jack managed to get him to sip some water and he lapsed back into a deep sleep.

The moon broke the horizon, bathing the land in a ghostly half-light and Jack could not sleep, so he sat thinking about what to do with the policeman.

It is quite beautiful, thought Jack, the occasional night bird 'woo, wooing' and the gentle twittering of some small bird or animal. But then his mind came back to tomorrow and the rogue copper tied to the tree.

His plan was to have the basta' lose his mind and so far it was working well. There was no way McGuinness would recognise him, but he might, if allowed to recover, come after the first three Aboriginals again.

'I will let the basta' cook more t'mora an' den, we will see.' Jack reasoned that if they put him on his horse and took him up the track a ways, cut him loose, he would either fall off the horse or stay on for a while. Either way, no one would know what had happened to him and would think he just ran out of water and supplies.

Short of killing him, there really was little else they could do. His mind made up, he decided that they would leave at first light, before Mister Nicholas woke up and started to ask questions that he knew he could not risk answering, reasoning that the less Mister Nicholas knew about the copper the better. He would just have to wait and see if Mister Nicholas remembered the bastard copper.

Gnarlu, Jack, Yindu and the younger Aboriginal man trotted off at dawn to attend to the plan.

McGuinness still lay where they had left him at the base of the tree. They quietly approached the blistered and heavily sunburned man. He was shivering uncontrollable in the morning dew, strips of almost transparent skin hung in small patches where blisters had burst, some beginning to turn brown from the previous day's vicious sun.

Jack again knelt down in front of the pathetic sight and again let out the ferocious growl from deep in his chest.

The reaction was again immediate. Screaming, McGuinness tried to get away, bringing up his knobbly knees yelling, 'Don' eat me, help me, Get away, Get away!' as he feebly bucked up and down before lapsing into wailing and sobbing. 'I, eh, eh, don', don',' he choked and mumbled.

Jack cut the now pathetic creature's arms free and stood back to assess the situation.

Then a strange thing happened. McGuinness suddenly snapped upright and said with some authority, 'Right now then me hearty, let's have ye, ye black thievin' bastard, Oi 'ave ye in irons in a jiffy.' Then he said, as if his mind suddenly changed direction, 'Ah, my loverly lady,' he crooned, 'Oi've ne'r seen such beauty ever,' and lifted his arms caressing something imaginary before him then just as quickly resumed blubbering.

Jack was satisfied the man was clearly losing his mind, and another half-day sitting on his horse in the sun would be certain to send him further into his own world – most likely never to return – or kill him, which was the intention.

They untied McGuinness and saddled his horse and fed and watered both animals with what remained of McGuinness's supplies and scattered the rest of his supplies, burying things which, if found, would raise suspicion.

McGuinness meanwhile alternated between issuing commands or swooning like a love-sick teenager and then suddenly crying in terror.

They sat him in his saddle, still blindfolded, tied his hands onto the saddle horn and headed off some two hundred yards parallel with the track toward Mullewa. They went about four miles up the track before finding a low strip of granite running toward the track. Here they turned and walked on the granite to the track. 'Gooda,' said Gnarlu nodding his black curly head, now catching on to what Jack had planned.

They untied McGuiness's hands and checked everything. Placing the reigns in McGuinness's hands, and purposely leaving McGuinness's feet out of the stirrups, Jack gently slapped the rump of the horse and it started slightly before plodding off on the familiar track towards Mullewa.

Jack didn't know that Mullewa even existed, all he cared about was that the horses were moving away from them and that the copper could not identify them. It really did not matter now how far it would take before McGuinness fell off the horse. They turned and swiftly made their way back to their camp at the ranges, Jack anxious to see how Nicholas was recovering this morning.

A stock and station agent found McGuinness's horses some 30 mile from Mullewa the next morning as he was doing deliveries, and six mile further on he came upon the figure of a man on the road.

McGuinness was in a bad way, his tongue swollen and blackened by the sun and great blisters and scabs covered his body under a swarm of flies that surrounded him. McGuinness's tunic was half stuffed into one of his saddlebags, he was near death.

The stock agent loaded him up into his wagon and returned to Mullewa as quickly as he dared.

McGuinness was eventually transferred by police wagon to Fremantle and spent months in the hospital there. The burns healed over time, but it took many months before he recovered some of his wits after his ordeal. However, his sanity, if one could call it that, steadily turned into an obsession about the wrong'uns with feathers on their feet who were chasing him, and he vowed to return to duty and hunt down the wrong'uns who tried to kill him. The police doctor who attended him through these times eventually passed him as fit enough to resume duty.

It was fair to say that McGuinness did not elicit much sympathy from the people of Mullewa when he eventually returned to duty and the local gossip and general comment was, 'The stupid bastard finally got 'is comeuppence goin' in off alone into Christ only knows where.'

McGuinness had almost died of thirst and drunkenness, this backed up by Bethany Stokes's testimony that he had left their homestead drunk as a lord and against good advice to the contrary.

Nicholas was wide awake by the time Jack and the others returned. They had the common sense to bring down a small kangaroo and a goanna with them, and so were able to explain their absence.

Apart from a massive headache, an equally massive raised bump, grogginess and a gash in his skull, Nicholas appeared none the worse for wear and so far had not asked how he came to be in such a state. The truth of it was that he was a little embarrassed about it, and in any case was fighting off the headache and nausea.

The two adult Blacks and the lad gathered around Big Jack and made clear their thanks, and again to Nicholas, then took their leave and continued in a northerly direction.

Some hours later Nicholas and Jack began to discuss what had happened at the river mouth during his absence, and they made plans to leave the next morning.

It was early the next morning when Nicholas, Jack, Gnarlu and Yindu began the journey back to the river mouth.

Chapter 34

Mombasa

$\mathcal{A}$s luck would have it, when the *Collette* finally called into Fremantle Port, there was a fast clipper at berth, the *Red Jacket*. This was one of the new steel hulled clippers, fast, topping 17 knots, and strong. She was built in the US in Maine, her keel layed in 1849. She was some 260 foot in length and had a 44-foot beam.

Red Jacket was named after a Seneca Indian chief named Sagoyewatha to whom settlers had given the name Red Jacket. The ship held the record for Atlantic crossings for some years before being purchased by English businessmen for upper-class immigration passages to Australia. Long, sleek and graceful of line, Captain Strudwich eyed her with no small amount of envy.

Red Jacket did not normally visit Fremantle, but had made a chartered stop to pick up English and Dutch gentry en route to Europe, via Africa of course.

Curious about the famous ship and hearing that the magnificent clipper may be sailing to Africa, Strudwich had approached the captain with the small parcel from Nicholas. In another positive twist of fate, the captain informed Strudwich that he was heading direct to Mombasa to pick up the Dutch envoy and return him to Amsterdam, and would be only too pleased to deliver the small package.

As it happened, the parcel was duly delivered to the Dutch embassy in Mombasa, however the envoy placed the small parcel on his desk along with other papers, and in the rush to get ready for his passage to Amsterdam on the *Red Jacket*, he forgot to mention it to his clerk.

The letter sat on his desk for six months before the clerk found it and organised for it to be delivered. Thus, it was almost ten months since Nicholas had given the parcel to Peter Strudwich before the Amendsons received it.

Lillian was on the front verandah of the house when the mail was finally delivered. After giving the travelling stock agent some refreshment and seeing him on his way, she sat down and sifted through the pile of mail.

Suddenly, she saw the brown paper package, and turning it over immediately saw Nicholas's name written on the back. Forgetting all of the other mail she opened the package and finding the letter inside began to read.

Lillian rose and walked to the end of the verandah and called, 'Victoria, Ludwig! Come quickly!'

Victoria and her father arrived at the same time and out of breath. 'What is it Ma ma?' cried Victoria, worry creasing her face. Lillian simply handed her the letter and sat down, watching her daughter's face intently.

She read the letter with trepidation gripping her. As she read, Victoria, was overwhelmed by a mixture of fear, heartache and guilt as she felt the loneliness and regret of Nicholas's letter.

Victoria brushed a heavy strand of hair from her face and slowly sat down beside her mother, the letter now shaking in her hand and tears rolling down her beautiful face.

'Oh Ma ma!' she cried and buried her face into Lillian's neck, sobbing as Ludwig picked up the letter and read, Lillian holding her distraught daughter.

'He…he, thinks I don't love him, what have I done!' she stammered. 'I don't know what to do Pa pa,' she said turning to her father. He looked down at her, his own eyes moist at the sight of his beloved daughter's heartache.

'Go and wash your face *mon cherie*, we will sit down and calmly discuss zis news,' her mother instructed.

Lillian, looking up at her husband after Victoria had left to wash her face, said with some edge in her voice, 'Darling Lud, she will want to go to Nicholas and very soon, we will not be able to stop her, any more than my parents could when they tried to stop me from marrying you and you taking me off to Africa.' She saw the fatherly anguish in his face and knew he would be thinking of all of the dangers Victoria must now face.

They sat at the dining room table, Ludwig quiet, as mother and daughter discussed – as Lillian had predicted – Victoria's decision to go to Australia and find Nicholas.

Also written on the back of the package was a small note, it read;

Sailing Ship, 'Collette', Captain Peter Strudwich, friend of Nicholas Yuin.

Estimate Departure from Mombassa Port on the tide – approximately 18th March 1850 bound for Fremantle Port via Goa India and on to Champion Bay, Geraldton.

Victoria turned to her father. 'Pa pa…' was all she managed before he held up his hand and stopped her. Ludwig stared at her, a stern frown on his face and she quailed in fear of what he was about to say. After a time he said, 'It is now the 2nd of February!' he said emphatically. He looked at her big eyes staring at him. God how I love my daughter, he thought and continued.

'My daughter, often in your lifetime you will find yourself in a position where you must make an important decision, as I now must, even though sometimes you will not enjoy it,' her father began.

Victoria's heart sank as she had convinced herself that it was her father who would ultimately make the final decision as to whether she could go. She also knew that after the last failed attempt to find Nicholas in which she was badly injured, he was not going to allow her to do this again without hard argument, especially sailing off to a largely unexplored land. She also knew that irrespective of Pa pa's decision, she was going to Australia to find Nicholas, even if it meant running away.

'Nicholas Yuin is as fine a man as you will ever find, and you know I regard him as the son I never had,' he continued. 'I know your depth of love for Nicholas is great, it is as my love for your mother and yourself, so I must inform you...' and he hesitated, stony faced, until he could no longer bear the devastated look on his daughter's face, '...that you are to immediately go and prepare for your journey lest you miss your passage to Australia!'

Victoria screamed so loud that Baba Joe came running into the dining room, assegai at point and a murderous look on his old face, only to find his Victoria kissing and hugging her father, and both in tears.

She turned and seeing Baba Joe cried, 'Baba Joe! I am going to Australia to find Nicholas!' The joyous look on her face did not lessen his devastation, and all he could manage in reply was a snorted 'humph' and walked back to his stables.

Over the next few days the house was a hive of activity as preparations were made for the journey to Mombasa. There was much to do and arrange as Ludwig and Lillian had decided to accompany Victoria to Mombasa.

Ludwig had considered sending Baba Joe with his daughter but did not think Baba Joe would survive the sea passage and he was too old in any case.

Baba Joe had talked little on receiving the news of Victoria's voyage and moped around as though someone had removed part of his soul, which in effect they had. He had sworn to never leave her side again, and now she was going without him. It was almost too hard to bear.

Victoria tried to talk to him but he was taciturn at best, offering only general comment. She was at first quite angry with him, although managed to keep that well-hidden as she knew the old man was hurting very badly.

One day not long before they were to travel, she went down to the stables to find something. She had just reached the stables when she heard the old man singing in the storeroom. He was singing an old song in Hehe that he used sing to her when she was a little girl and needed comfort. She went to the door of the storeroom and there he sat on the molasses barrel singing and tears streaming down his old face. 'Oh Baba Joe. I am so sorry.' she cried running to him and there they sat holding each other, he still singing softly and now Victoria crying also.

'Baba Joe, this is something I must do, please understand,' she sobbed. The old man simply nodded.

'Massa Yuin good man, love Missy Victoria very hard.' he said thumping his chest with his fist. and nodding vigorously.

'Come.' she said and took his hand. They walked arm in arm around the property and pointed out all of the places and talked of times when they laughed, got angry and played games when she was growing up. Baba Joe felt a bit better by the time they returned to the homestead, realising only death could take his special times with Victoria away. No one else had this, they were his memories and therefore sacred.

Baba Joe always knew his Missy would one day grow up and leave, but somehow he was not prepared for this to happen so soon, or so quickly. He also dreamed that one day Massa Yuin would return, and he and his Missy Victoria would settle not far from the homestead.

He knew Massa Yuin was the right man for her and had watched the two growing up together.

Nicholas the leader, always looking out for her even if he did not understand things between them were bonding – neither did his Victoria for that matter. But the old man could see the chemistry at work and secretly chortled to himself at the game play. In his culture, Missy Victoria and Massa Yuin would have been married the day she received her first moon time, even if she was only 12 years old and her titties had not fully developed.

The white people are different, stupid he figured to waste so much time when life can end any time. Why wait?

The activity on the day before they were to depart was frenetic. They would leave at daybreak the next morning, and one never knew what lay ahead on such a journey, the land full of threats from both man and animal.

Four Hehe warriors and four Maasai warriors, each wearing battle dress, were to accompanying the family. The posturing between the Hehe and Maasai was amusing, each trying to outdo the other, though both looked magnificent and equally fierce and threatening.

The Hehe would travel with them for about two hundred miles, which was as far as they would dare and the absolute limit of their national influence. After that the Maasai would negotiate for four more Maasai warriors of the area to join the group all the way to Mombasa.

There were many dangers, not the least of which were the Arab slavers – ruthless, unscrupulous and shifty – who didn't care who they captured for trade.

As it eventuated, they increased the party by eight men, for reasons that Ludwig could not fathom at the time, but the price was the same and he was grateful for the additional protection. He could not know, that on the return journey he was now bound to treat some sick people of the tribe, and it was for this reason that they inherited the additional men.

Traditionally, the Maasai shunned interference from the white man, especially medically. The sharmans had a powerful influence over the Maasai, but Ludwig knew that most of the sharmans were tricksters and magicians of a high standard. With this in mind he had learned to include them so as not to present a challenge, but sometimes he was greeted with open hostility.

This is not to say that they had no knowledge of medicine. They had vast knowledge of bush medicine amassed over hundreds of years, and he himself had learnt and used some of the 'medicine'.

The Maasai were magnificent in their battle dress and none of them was under six feet six inches tall. They lined up either side of the small caravan with two in the lead.

The journey was as direct a line as could be taken with some overland sections with no tracks at all. The intention was to try to stick to as straight a line as was possible to Mombasa, a journey of some five hundred miles. Ludwig had travelled the route to Mombasa several times and had, to a certain degree, blazed his own trail. He calculated that with the wagon and stops or delays it would take all of 45 days to arrive in Mombasa, arriving just under a week before the *Collette* sailed.

It was a sad farewell at dawn the next morning, and Victoria tried very hard to be brave about it. As she went down the line of people saying the goodbyes, she at last came to Baba Joe, standing aside with his head held up high, dignified, looking every inch a young warrior.

Victoria knew he was trying very hard to be in control, but head up or not, the tears were flowing down his face.

He said not a word until he reached out and placed a beautifully carved ivory talisman around her neck. Victoria began to cry and he reached out and cupped his hand under her chin, lifting her head. Then he said, 'This will protect you from all evil my daughter, has my spirit within,' he said thumping a clenched fist over his heart.

He wiped her tears away with his thumb and said with a finality and authority he did not really possess, 'Go now to find Massa Yuin and go well. Joseph will be waiting.' He turned and walked back to the stables, knowing that he most likely would never see her again – he was getting old, and now was the time for the young.

The caravan made good time and they covered almost fifteen miles in the first day, but this was the relatively easy part for most of the going was on flat grass plains, and they all knew it would get harder as the journey progressed.

Ludwig struck camp about an hour before sunset, finding a small gully dense with thorn bushes, and after inspection, ordered a thorn boma to be formed against an impenetrable dense thicket of vicious thorn behind them in the gully. The camp was no fancy affair, and Lillian and Victoria slept in the back of the flatbed wagon.

Two of the Maasai trotted into the camp with an impala, and they dressed and butchered it for the evening meal. This they cooked over a bed of coals and a specific type of 'green' branches that were placed around the bed of coals. Whilst this created a lot of smoke, which was the intention, it also disguised somewhat the smell of the cooking meat, an attempt to confuse any would-be predators. As a bonus, it smoked the flesh as well, tenderising and giving the fresh meat a pungent though pleasant taste.

As the evening fell, they could all hear the giggling of hyenas and the distant roar of the lion, reminding them of the dangers that lurked outside the boma.

Later that night, Victoria lay with her mother gazing up at the kaleidoscope of stars, the Milky Way stretching from horizon to horizon like a magnificent diamond necklace.

Closing her eyes, she could see Nicholas's face, the olive skin and amber eyes gazing back at her, and she remembered that first moment when she had been rescued by Nicholas and the powerful emotions that had engulfed her when they had kissed for the first time. They had been in another world, and the rush of feelings consumed her again as it had done that evening, and many times since.

Victoria squirmed and a small moan escaped her before she could stop it as she felt the rush of heat and emotion run over her body like a warm wave. She found herself taking short pants of breath until she suddenly realised that her mother was lying beside her. Lillian stirred and murmured, 'Are you all right darling?' If Lillian could have seen her daughter's face, she would have seen embarrassment painted all over it.

'I'm all right Ma ma, just wish I was in Mombasa already.' Actually, at that moment, she wished she was home alone in her bed with her privacy.

'Well, try to get some sleep darling, we 'ave a long way to go, and you will need all of your energy.' Her mother rolled away from her and soon was breathing deeply.

Ever since the moment when they first kissed Victoria fantasised about making love to Nicholas. No matter how hard she tried she could not stop the rush of blood to her senses and the glow of wanton desire that came with it.

It was not that she was completely naive about such matters. She had seen the young Hehe boys and girls flirting with each other when bathing, and young as they were, they still had gotten very excited, and the young girls were equally willing. Tribal customs forbade them from actually carrying out the act, but that did not stop them from sneaking off and simulating sexual play. She had no control over her desire for Nicholas. Why, she wondered, did she feel so excited by Nicky and only him?

It was strange, she had oft reflected, on how after only their brief encounter she could be so consumed with want for him, or at the very least transported to a dimension where no one else existed except she and Nicholas. Once they were in this space nothing else mattered to her, only the special feelings, and they were so powerful as to be all consuming.

Even now, laying here in the wagon, she was overwhelmed by the feeling, remembering his warm touch. Vivid in her memory were small things about him that to anyone else would be meaningless – the timbre of his voice, the fine stubble that had ever so lightly brushed her face when they kissed, and his scent, manly and strong. Oh God Nicholas, she moaned inwardly and had to clench her thighs tightly and freeze.

She remembered when Hymie had lost control of his emotions and common decency when she and Nicholas had met the search party that eventful evening.

My God, she thought, he had emanated such power, the burning rage in his eyes! She remembered well his face and his immediate instincts to protect her and the fury that raged within him like a rampaging Cape buffalo before he finally gained control of the situation.

It now came to her, that far from he disappointing and frightening her that night, he had displayed the very thing that attracted her to him, his strength of character.

Her hand, with a will of its own, found its way between her legs, and struggling to re gain control, she clamped her thighs hard and bit her lip in an attempt quell her feelings.

Dawn broke with the twittering of birds and soft grey skies.

They quickly broke camp and headed off on their journey, Ludwig wanting to gain ground and make the most of the cool morning.

They had travelled only a few miles when one of the Maasai scouts came running back to the party. He said there was a caravan of Arab slavers ahead and they must remain quiet until they had passed. Ludwig fumed as they waited some 4 hours before the Maasai scouts returned to advise it was safe to continue their journey.

The rest of the journey passed without any serious incident, apart from a cracked wheel on the wagon.

Overall, they had made excellent time and on the 42ⁿᵈ day since they began the journey, it now being March 1850, they crested the low hills on the outskirts of Mombasa.

Mombasa was a very busy sea port with the main city located on Mombasa Island. The port was a hub of the slave trade as well as all sorts of freight and cargo, ivory, gold and spices which came from the Orient, India and the Dutch East Indies. It had a tumultuous history, since its original establishment around 900AD. For the most part it had been under Islamic religious control and most of its rulers were Muslims.

Many other peoples had either sacked or claimed the city, the most prominent being Sudanese Arabs in 1151, then later the Imanate of Omani rulers took control until the intervention of the Portuguese, after a visit by Vasco Da Gama in 1498 (when he received a very frosty reception), the Portuguese returned and sacked or captured the city many times over the next couple of decades. Nonetheless, the city and port continued to be a major trading city.

To Victoria, it seemed a seething mass of humanity, and the threat of robbery, kidnapping and corruption hung in the humid and hot atmosphere like some evil stinking cloak. She hated it.

They finally made their way to the hotel in which they were to stay. The road was a sluice of stinking slurry churned up by horse and oxen drawn carts and humanity alike.

The Royal Victoria Hotel was a little way off the filthy road, and was in fact quite a magnificent building, very comfortable and beautifully furnished with artifacts and furniture from across the known world. The cobblestone drive up to the hotel was lined with a mixture of palms and multi-coloured bougainvillea as was the front of the property. On either side of a white-washed stone gate, two uniformed askaris stood at the gates. A wide verandah ran along the front and sides of the hotel, with great high-arched wicker armchairs offering a great view of the island and the sea beyond. Bright purple and orange bougainvillea grew in profusion at either end of the balcony, framing the view.

With no small amount of relief, the party entered the sumptuous interior which was of highly polished timber floor overlaid with a huge and magnificent silk carpet and scattered mahogany furniture. The walls were adorned with a variety of stuffed big-game heads mounted on plaques high on the walls. At the end, over the stone fireplace, hung a huge stuffed bull elephant head, complete with a pair of massive ivory tusks.

They signed in, retired to the verandah and ordered cold drinks while the porters unloaded the luggage.

'Very nice of them to name the hotel after me!' commented Victoria offhandedly, causing her mother to roll her eyes and coaxing a low chuckle from her father.

Ludwig sent one of the hotel's envoys down to the docks to find out if the *Collette* had made landfall, the envoy returned several hours later to inform that the Collette was indeed in the Port, although she rode at anchor awaiting a berth at the wharf.

Ludwig correctly assumed, as turned out, that it would only be a matter of days before the ship renewed its stores, loaded cargo and left Mombasa for the port of Fremantle, he sat brooding whilst the women chatted idly.

Lillian glanced at him and sensing he wished to say something to Victoria, she excused herself and disappeared into the hotel. At that moment Ludwig began to really feel the sense of loss of his daughter and he fretted about the dangers that she could face on her quest.

Ludwig left his seat and sat down next to Victoria and said. 'Daughter, you must promise to show every caution in your search for Nicholas,' he said with as much gravity as he could muster. 'This world you are about to enter is full of evil men, especially men aboard ships who have spent many months at sea cut off from family. Female company can twist a man's mind. Do you understand ja?' He went on. 'I know you will find Nicholas sooner or later, and your mother and I wish you all of the best and success ja?' Ludwig stood and reached into his coat pocket and withdrew an envelope, handing it to Victoria.

She saw it was addressed to Nicholas and looked up at her father in query.

'Giff that envelope to that cheeky young bastard when you see 'im *ja*? An giff him our love,' he concluded gruffly.

Victoria suddenly burst into tears and came into her father's great arms. They cried together and were soon joined by Lillian.

For the first time since Victoria was born, they were to separate as a family.

Chapter 35

The Discovery

The four men made a good start to the journey, Nicholas and now Jack learning that in this country the pace of travel was inevitably entwined with the land and its conditions.

They headed toward the low ridge that Nicholas had glassed and which he said he would check on the way back.

On the second day the dawn broke to a somewhat sultry atmosphere. Gnarlu stood sniffing the air before announcing it was to rain, twirling his finger skyward as he said it.

Sure enough, just after noon heavy cumulus clouds appeared to the west and it became quite hot.

They kept moving west-nor 'west, all the while watching the thunderheads grow in majesty. By mid-afternoon they could see lightning slashing down from the storms.

By the time they reached the low hill they were being lashed by thick red dust and stinging wind. They tethered the horses together, and Nicholas, grabbing his saddlebags and rifle, ran with the others toward the rocky outcrop. There were small caves or more like pockets in the rock just below the flat top, into which they climbed, one in each just as huge rain drops began to fall.

It rained hard for about an hour before a magnificent double rainbow heralded the passing of the storms. The afternoon sun lit up the rear of the storm clouds, highlighting the indigo and purple storm as it retreated east, while the magnificent roiling white and grey cumulus thunderhead up draught towers reached high into the sky.

Nicholas climbed out of his pocket, brushing off kangaroo or wallaby dung – obviously the wallabies thought the rock holes were good shelter as well, thought Nicholas wryly.

Looking around at the rain-washed outcrop, now glowing white and orange against the purple backdrop of the abating storm, Nicholas noticed a separate small mound with a strong spine of quartz running across and down one side of the slope. His interest suddenly aroused, he walked over to examine the white and rusty discoloured quartz.

This looks pretty good, he was thinking, when his heart suddenly leapt as he saw the yellow gleam of a speck on the side of a piece of wet quartz. It couldn't be, he thought. Getting down on his hands and knees, he scrutinised the piece of quartz. 'Jesus!' he exclaimed out loud.

Springing to his feet he sprinted to the horses, and grabbing his specking pick, bolted back up the spine much to the surprise of the others.

Nicholas swung the square end against the small slab of quartz shattering it. He held up the first piece to the light, nothing. Tossing it away he grabbed the next piece. Examining it, still nothing, and yet another piece. Then he saw it.

A newly exposed stone about four inches long and on the broken side imbedded in the quartz were not one but four small specks of gold about one-sixteenth of an inch in size.

'It's gold!' he shouted to Jack.

Nicholas turned and started to break up small piles of quartz at three-foot intervals as he worked his way down the quartz reef.

Next, he began to examine each pile, and using his specking scope examined every piece. The gold content rose steadily the further down the quartz outcrop he looked.

Big Jack sat with him at each pile taking a keen interest in every specimen Nicholas showed him. By the time they had reached the bottom of the reef and the ground began to level out it was nearing dark.

Gnarlu and Yindu had prepared the camp and fire. The fire was smoky as the wood they had gathered was damp, but soon the stacks near the fire started to steam as the fire took hold and dried out the wood. By the time Nicholas reached the flat and finished for the night, the fire was burning brightly.

As he and Jack were finishing, the ridge disappearing into the top soil at the bottom of the hill, Nicholas had prised out a good-sized piece of the weathered quartz and walked over to the fire. Smacking his prospectors pick against the side of the quartz to break the rock up, he held up a piece to the fire light and almost dropped it.

Laced through the middle was a thin vein of gold almost as wide as a quarter of an inch in one spot, and then thinning, it ran right through to the opposite side. 'My God!' Nicholas exclaimed. His hand shaking, he handed the rock to Jack.

Big Jack looked at the tiny ribbon of yellow and up at Nicholas's face, the grin saying it all as he asked, 'Is good?'

Nicholas stuck his hand out to his giant friend and said solemnly, 'Congratulations my friend, I think we may have stumbled onto a very good prospect! I think the indications are that when we dig down to intersect the reef out there,' he continued pointing to where the reef vanished into the flats, 'we should find good gold!' Jack did not yet see or really understand what Nicholas was so happy about – to him gold was stuff people with money wore for ornaments, not for him. But he could see how excited Nicholas was, and so he too was happy for Nicholas.

Nicholas, seeing some confusion on Jack's face said, 'Jack, this is a very good sign, understand?'

Knowing nothing about prospecting, Jack looked somewhat unsure if not confused, and shook his head.

'From up there,' Nicholas started pointing up to where he first found the specs, 'the gold specs get heavier and there are many more of them right to where the reef goes into the ground, understand? It means there is a very good chance we will find much gold down there but we won't know until we dig deeper out there.

'We will do some planning tomorrow and look at the resources we can find around the area, and then start the dig.' Nicholas could hardly contain himself, knowing this had all the indications of a really good find.

'Okay, ta'morra, we dig!' Jack said emphatically, spitting on his huge hands and rubbing them together.

That night, as they lay around the fire, Nicholas stared up at the perfectly clear sky and the myriad stars. Exhausted as he was, sleep would not come, he was too excited and full of enthusiasm. He could not wait to begin the new day.

Finally, after months of specking, he got the break he had been dreaming of, and he had enough experience to know that this had all of the signs of being a special prospect.

His mind racing, he started to mentally list all of the material he would need to start the prospect. A trip to the new port of Geraldine would be necessary, and there he would hopefully find all he needed. He would need to peg and register the prospect. By his reckoning he would need at least four wagon loads to start. The hardest part would be buying and transporting the mining equipment without arousing interest, and therefore sparking a stampede or gold rush to his area. The last thing he needed was to be hemmed in by rival prospectors. This would take some planning and hard thinking to come up with a solutioHis mind whirling, eventually sleep overcame him and he did not even know it.

The next morning, he was animated and was planning the best way forward. He decided it best to break up the claim into four or five sections, each claim under the names of Whip, Jack, the Yuin Scott Pastoral and Exploration Trust and himself of course. This way he could lock up large tracts of land and secure the area surrounding the find and moreover, spread the required stores amongst the four prospects without arousing too much suspicion. The first claim would be registered under the Yuin Scott Trust.

He would need survey pegs or staves to mark out the leases. Glassing around he spied a grove of small saplings, or gimlets, some distance north and noted that this might solve one small problem. First things first, he must peg the claim and the small gum would suffice for this.

Looking around, Nicholas noted that Gnarlu and Yindu had left. This was a common occurrence so he was not surprised – he knew they would return when they were ready.

After commencing the dig, Nicholas planned to make time to investigate several other areas he had spied from atop the small rise – after all, this prospect may yield little to sustain a good mine, even though his instincts and geological expertise were telling him otherwise.

Nonetheless, he cautioned himself over putting too much faith in the reef at such an early and unproven stage.

Nicholas had seen many a man broken after being unprepared for the disappointment of this type of exploration. Good mines were few and far between, and even fewer proved sustainable in the long term.

Prospectors often discovered good indications such as this, but there were too many 'true tales' of how men had gambled everything they owned only to discover the ore and gold ran out as suddenly as they had discovered it. Often, after only months of digging and shaft sinking, they gave up. Sometimes, even after years of hard digging and moving literally mountains of dirt, men possessed by the 'gold fever' would find less than what was originally discovered. Good men, some hampered by a lack of knowledge or dreams of riches, would become obsessed with the idea that the next blast or excavation would reveal a rich find. Some would remain at their prospect, lose sight of the obvious and never discover what they originally sought.

Gold fever was a reality, not a myth.

Very few prospectors around the world actually knew how the gold formed in the first place and thus could not discern when the gold would no longer be found. Many prospectors thought gold was formed as a natural molten substance and, when cooled, formed the nuggets and reefs. This misconception has led many a prospector astray.

Gold is formed in warm to very hot water deep in the Earth's crust. In most cases this fluid was forced, generally in an upwards direction, toward the outer Earth's crust by natural pressure and so was forced into various fissures and types of porous rock which ultimately would fracture by sheer pressure and heat. Any gold, sulphur, iron and silicone present is squeezed and sweated out through the fissures as a fluid and migrates through cracks in the rock under natural pressure.

The direction varied, either horozontal, or up, depending on your viewpoint – either toward the cooler outer Earth's mantle or to the surface where it would then begin to solidify and crystalise. More often it would form within white quartz, which by its very nature of being somewhat brittle, was often riddled with minute cracks. As the formation and land weathered over time, the quartz would be exposed to the surface and so would become the main indication for basic gold prospecting and geology alike. So, finding quartz outcrops would sometimes reward the prospectors with specks or even nuggets of gold, or more often than not, have nothing within it.

After all, the name 'prospect' was just that, the *prospect* of a gold find.

Nicholas's geological training and studies gave him a distinct advantage over many other prospectors, and he also knew that gold was also not necessarily only found in quartz. This was not to say there were no other good geologists out in the field looking for minerals with the same intent as Nicholas – more and more geologists were arriving in Western Australia almost monthly, some sailing from the east and many from overseas. Even the Chinese, who were as adept as any at loaming and specking, and sometimes far superior, were arriving in numbers, their history of prospecting going back thousands of years.

There lay many unknowns ahead, he knew: The possibility of bad ground, underground water streams or aquifers, and of course how far the gold actually ran in the quartz, or even in other gold bearing ore, which was possible.

Whether the quartz would widen or narrow was anyone's guess, but that challenge was precisely why men took up prospecting in the first place – adventure at the fore and perhaps find a fortune with it.

The only way for this prospect to be proven was to sink a winze, or shaft, down some thirty feet or more out from the reef's disappearance into the level ground at the base of the ridge. Nicholas looked long and hard at the positioning of the shaft and eventually chose to begin the dig alongside the quartz reef, some 25 yards away and roughly halfway down the slope of the ridge.

He chose this with good reason as he did not yet know enough about the prevailing weather and so decided to allow for the lowlands to flood at some time during the prospect, should it prove up. By his reckoning the shaft head or collar, should be at least 20ft above the level of the low ground.

The other reason for going to the side was so that they could sink the shaft and drive in at right angles. This would maintain the integrity of the shaft and also enable them to sink deeper if and when desired. One can dream, thought Nicholas, trying hard to keep a lid on his excitement.

Knowing he would have to get the first stocks for the mine sooner rather than later, and most of this he reckoned was going to be timber so that they could 'timber the 'collar' of the shaft – to say the first fifteen feet down from the top level, and enough lighter timber build some small buildings.

They would need the heavy timber and lots of it for the collar. Railway sleepers were a good choice, perhaps some would be available in the new town of Geraldine he thought. He of course had no clue that the town was now to be called called Geraldton. Nicholas thought he could possibly purchase sleepers or heavy timber planks as a new wharf and port was apparently to be constructed in the future.

When the *Collette* called in briefly to the new town site en route to the river, he recalled that two other ships were anchored in what was called Champion Bay, one of which was the HMS *Champion* herself. Aboard the 18-gun sloop were the first troops to be transferred to the area as well as convicts and ticket of leavers from the east to help build the new military barracks, police barracks, survey building and basic town buildings. The other ship was obviously laden with all manner of goods as they could see being unloaded onto the beach.

Amongst the beginnings of the new port, there were two makeshift ale houses already established, fairly rough affairs made of gimlet and white-washed hessian, and both of these were rife with gossip and talk about the whole area becoming a major pastoral hub.

Gossip was also rife about a mineral find – coal it was said – north of the new town, and that a wharf was to be built in this bay to service the area when developed. Perhaps if this was true, some enterprising person had started to stock mining equipment, thought Nicholas.

However, all that Nicholas could see as he walked around the area at that moment was a lot of activity and piles of cargo stacked up on cleared sections set back some 500 feet from the water's edge. When he returned to the ship, Peter Strudwich was eager to leave and catch the tide, so he did not have the time to find out what else might be available.

If he made a trip to the new port, this time hopefully there would be more opportunity. He would need to buy several iron kibbles for hauling the ore and mullock (worthless ore) up the shaft, a windlass and steel haw-ser, hooks, water tanks, oil, and hopefully later, a small Granby tilt trolley, or ore cart, which sat on small rail tracks and was pushed by hand. But that would come later if things turned out as expected.

Hopefully, he would find these things in stock agents at the port. If not, he would have to order them up from Fremantle by ship. Either way he needed to make the trip soon.

Later in the morning, he and Jack got ready to go out and cut some small gimlets. Nicholas had spied a grove of the small gum trees from the top of the ridge about five miles distant. They would cut down the tall skinny saplings, choosing those about one and half inches in diameter, and size them up for survey posts and pegs. They would also take the opportunity to look around to see if they could find any other material they might need.

Beyond the gimlet grove there appeared to be a line of larger trees which Nicholas knew would be one of the many dry creeks which meandered across the flat land. He was also thinking that there might be good river sand in the creek, which they could use to make concrete.

It took Nicholas half an hour of arguing to get Jack to try riding the small pony. He had never ridden a horse and was obviously nervous about it. He just kept saying, 'No neck'sary!' but Nicholas was insistent because he knew that one day Jack would need to ride a horse, and it just might save his life one day. Eventually, he won the argument and Jack climbed up into the saddle.

Glancing up at Big Jack sitting on the small but sturdy pony, Nicholas couldn't help but burst out laughing. The scene looked hilarious with Jack's feet almost reaching the ground when they were not in the stirrups, which they had to lengthen to the last buckle hole but this was still far too short.

Jack was complaining that the saddle horn was sticking into his balls, so they tried shortening the stirrups. This brought Jack's knees up to the level of the horse's back, if not above it, and the huge fellow looked bigger than his mount – and patently ridiculous.

They had not travelled more than 300 feet when Jack disentangled himself from the saddle and stood down from the pony.

'I run!' he said emphatically, thumping his chest to indicate there would be no further argument, and looping the reins of his horse over Nicholas's saddle, he loped away. Indeed, he reached their destination at the same time as Nicholas and wasn't even breathing that hard when they stopped.

Nicholas made a mental note to look for the biggest horse he could find when they went to Geraldine for equipment for the mine. It would have to be at least 18 hands high he reckoned, and a saddle without a horn he thought, chuckling to himself.

They started cutting the stand of gimlet, sizing and trimming the lengths they required. After about three hours of solid work, they stopped for a rest, Nicholas declaring they had cut enough for this trip and it was time for a bite to eat. It consisted of hard damper and the last two of Whip's dental breakers and a drink of water.

As they relaxed under the shade of the trees on the stringy bark carpet, Nicholas turned to Jack and said, 'Right, now tell me about how I came to be lying unconscious at the last camp by the rocks Jack. And don't tell me I fell over, there was no way that happened, I would have remembered tripping or slipping,' he concluded, fixing Jack with those burning amber eyes.

Jack was caught off guard. He had figured that Nicholas had forgotten all about it or had come to the conclusion that he indeed did trip over, hitting his head in the process.

He shuffled his feet, while Nicholas held his stare. 'Come on Jack, you have nothing to fear man, tell me what really happened,' Nicholas prompted.

Jack decided he had no choice now but to tell Nicholas the whole story as it happened. When he had finished, all Nicholas could think of to say was. 'Jesus Christ! A copper you say?'

Jack solemnly nodded his head.

'Did you kill him Jack? If you didn't, how do you know he didn't survive?'

'I don' know Mr Nicklas, him heading down track, crazy after sun!' he said twirling his great finger around his head.

'But you are sure he could not recognise you if he did manage to survive and regain his senses?' he asked

'No time did he see me gooda,' he said pointing to his face. 'No time,' he finished, shaking his head.

Nicholas was stunned about how things had transpired to say the least, but at the same time, full of admiration for Jack's cunning and handling of the situation. He had not only saved Nicholas's life and no doubt those of the blacks but had covered the tracks almost without flaw.

'Almost,' thought Nicholas, but for one small detail. The copper had seen Nicholas and he most certainly would remember Nicholas's rifle, and if he survived and recovered, most likely he would somehow put two and two together and come looking for Nicholas.

'I must keep very vigilant,' he reminded himself. He somehow knew that this situation would one day come to a head if the copper had survived. Severe sun stroke he knew, could often send a man insane permanently, but also the survival rate varied and he worried about it somewhat.

Seeing that Jack was feeling unsure, even on the edge of devastation about what he done, Nicholas suddenly held out his hand and thanked the big fellow, praising him for his intelligent handling of a tricky and bad situation.

He muttered with some evident relief, 'Thank you suh.'

'Jack, have you ever fired a rifle?' Nicholas inquired.

'No suh, no never fire gun,' Jack said.

'Well I am going to teach you how. If we ever have trouble, you will be of great assistance...help,' Nicholas added.

'Jack, having seen the devastating power of firearms, was enthusiastic. 'T'ank you suh, I like know dis,' he said.

Nicholas began to train Jack at every opportunity, and in fact Jack was quite good from the start, once Nicholas managed to demonstrate that if was not necessary to grip the rifle like it was going to run away. He also had to remove the trigger guard from the spare rifle as Jack's great fingers could not fit easily without discharging the round. Jack did however have trouble with ranging, but they kept at it until Nicholas was satisfied. In the end Jack was improving daily.

I will get him a good rifle if they are available in Geraldine, Nicholas thought.

Chapter 36

The Give-away Girl

Nimit'je sat daydreaming by the edge of the river about two mile from the tribe's main camp. She and Tjarlu had decided to sneak off and go hunting and fishing and managed to drift away from the main group without attracting too much attention, or so they thought as the young often do. Neither of them caught the knowing looks of the older folk as they observed the obvious attraction.

Tjarlu and Nimit'je had been best friends since they were old enough to start walking and were inseparable. As they grew they rarely went anywhere without each other and shared everything.

She often sat dreaming of the day when she knew she and Tjarlu would become a couple and marry under the tribal customs. This she knew in her heart would happen, because she loved him with all of her heart. He was her guardian and best friend, and although they had never coupled as lovers, they had played with each other and recently that play had taken another step toward adulthood.

The young girls of her tribe and indeed generally of all of the tribes, matured very early and it was not uncommon for girls as young as 11 years to reach puberty and be married not long after. Indeed, it was also not uncommon for girls of twelve years old to be with child after marriage. Tribal laws and customs lent to this as a natural order, hence the young girls were raised and were very much aware of the ceremonies regarding betrothal and marriage at a very early age.

Nimit'je had noticed that Tjarlu had changed over the past year. He often brushed her off when she tried to show him her affection and she had hurt badly every time it happened.

Tjarlu had his manhood and 'buckley' (circumcision) ceremony and feast a year ago, and she reasoned that this had changed him. In addition, according to tribal law, she was forbidden to look at his genitalia, however, her curiosity was at fever pitch and she had surreptitiously sneaked looks when she could and could not see any real difference, except it appeared angry in colour.

She did not understand that Tjarlu was becoming a young man now and his testosterone was beginning to affect him. She noticed also that he looked at her differently and often touched her hair, and his hand sometimes lingered, particularly on her budding breasts, which he had often done as they grew but more out of curiosity than anything sexual.

She could not explain it, but it felt different. Not that she objected, it felt pleasant, even exciting, and her nipples began to swell when he touched them.

Although only twelve and half years old, Nimit'je was not naïve about a man and woman having sex, as most of the girls were prepared for this by the women of the tribe and she had had no illusion what the evil man had intended to do to her before the white man 'Niclas' had stopped him.

Often, young girls were married off at her age and were 'available' as soon as they had their first 'bleeding'. Indeed, she also knew that she had been betrothed at the age of five. Nimit'je tried not to think about this although she knew her time for marriage through the betrothal was upon her, but she had heard the older women speak of the man to whom she was betrothed as not a young man, and the reason he had not approached and built his *youloo* (this was where the man took his new bride on the marriage night) was that he already had two wives and did not want another.

She also knew that Tjarlu's blood lines were a problem in their customs, but she did not care.

Nimit'je dug her toes into the warm dry sand and felt the pleasant sensation course up her legs. She shivered as again a strange feeling came over her as she remembered what had happened earlier.

It began in the morning, as she and Tjarlu had walked away from the camp. She was again subjected to Tjarlu's brusque mannerisms and sulking, and she was feeling a little hurt and confused.

Walking behind him, she started watching his body and the play of his lean muscles in his back and legs. She found herself mesmerised, and suddenly had a warm rush of feeling again.

She had not even reached puberty, but the different feelings within her built almost daily and she knew her time to bleed was only a matter of weeks away and she would become a woman.

They went to their 'secret' place by the edge of the river. This was a difficult place to see and they had to walk down a narrow ledge on the face of the rock overhang to reach a small sandy beach. It was hidden from view from above and from across the river. They had played here together as children for many years. It also had a quite deep pool at the foot of the stone ledge, always cool and clear.

Nimit'je and Tjarlu walked out of the secret pool and hunted fish as they had done all of their young lives. After an hour, Tjarlu had three good size fish and Nimit'je had a small wooden bowl filled with black shiny mussels.

Returning to the pool, they hung the fish off the rocks in the water to keep them cool and fresh then swam as usual, playing and laughing softly when suddenly they found themselves holding each other face to face. There was a sudden silence as they stood waste deep in the shallow end of the pool. Nimit'je could feel his manhood, now so hard, brushing against her belly and his hands on her waist.

Tjarlu was staring at her breasts, as he often did, but she felt a marked difference and involuntarily she felt a tingling in her nipples. There was no embarrassment only wonder as he pulled her close. Bending to her ear, he whispered his nickname for her, Nimmi, and she shivered and pressed her belly hard against his manhood.

Suddenly, Tjarlu spun away and swam to the other end of the pool where he stayed. She looked at him with a quizzical look, but he quickly looked away.

Nimit'je walked out of the water and lay down in the sun, water glistening on her dark skin and running down her face. She closed her eyes, confused, wondering what was happening. They had swum together as they just had so many times, but something had shifted, and why did Tjarlu swim away from her?

A little while later she felt Tjarlu lie down beside her, but he did not touch her. Opening her eyes she looked at his face and he smiled at her, her heart skipped a beat.

Nimit'je ran her eyes over his body, the black curly hair and developed muscle on his chest rose and fell before her. She looked at the line of fine hair as it left his chest and ran down to his belly.

She knew she was not supposed to look at his manhood, but she could not stop herself, her curiosity overcoming her caution, and her gaze wandered to his groin. His manhood stood erect before her. It appeared much bigger than before and she found herself noticing small details she had never bothered to look for before. Again, the warm feelings grew inside her. She forced herself to look away and found his soft brown eyes looking at her. She lay down beside him and they held each other, she with her head resting on his chest and sneaking subtle looks at his manhood, which still stood erect and bounced gently. She could hear his heart beating, and then after a while they dozed in the warm afternoon sun.

A little while later, Tjarlu suddenly rose, and gathering his fish spears, he strode to the end of the pool near the river. Turning, he gave her a beautiful smile and then walked into the river to hunt for fish.

Nimit'je was on a cloud of euphoria, all she knew was that something magical had bonded them and there she sat, in wonder.

The very next day, Nimit'je began to bleed and through her distress, her mother helped explain that she was now a woman and would soon be married, it was the sign.

In her naivety, Nimit'je had already decided that since her older betrothed did not want her, she and Tjarlu would marry. Little did she realise the devastating drama that single minded thought would cause later.

Organised some years ago, when she was about five years old, Nimit'je was betrothed to be married to an older man from a neighbouring tribe for important reasons. For many years there had been bad blood between several of the different tribal groups in the area, and occasionally fighting had broken out with deaths on both sides.

Fearing all-out war, the elders of several groups (including Nimit'je's father) had come to an agreement that blending the blood lines of the warring parties would be a wise thing and would possibly avoid war breaking out in the region.

This was a complex and difficult agreement because Aboriginal groups had rigid tribal rules as far as blending and marrying, bloodlines sometimes reaching back thousands of years.

Nimit'je was chosen as the tribal 'give-away girl', and her betrothed had bloodlines that would bond the parties into the future.

One week later, Nimit'je was summoned to walk with her father. She walked along behind him wondering why her father had asked her to walk with him. She had never been allowed to walk with him alone before and only ever was allowed to gather food with the other women of the tribe.

Hunting was strictly for the men folk, except for digging out lizard and goanna and other small animals they ate, and the women and girls always went out separately.

Mumardie stole a look at his daughter and he quailed at the thought of what he was about to tell her. He, of course, knew of the depth of feeling between Tjarlu and his daughter and knew also no matter how much they had tried to discourage the bond between the two, nothing changed.

This was going to be very hard. He took a deep breath and they stopped next to a large fallen tree. He said, pointing with his spears, 'Sit!'

Nimit'je did as she was told.

Her father stood before her and explained how the betrothal came to be and why it was going to happen. He also told her he knew about the feelings between her and Tjarlu. This was to cease from now on. She was the 'give-away girl' and would need to prepare herself for the marriage, and there would be no more discussion about it.

Nimit'je's world came crashing down. Her head was ringing and tears flowed as all she could do was shake her head. She knew that to offer argument would be met by fierce anger and maybe even a beating for disobedience.

She looked up at her father's face and was surprised to see a little moisture in his eyes. He reached out and laid his hand on her cheek, letting her know he understood. Then with a sharp command she was told to get up and they went back to the camp where she ran straight to her mother, her heart breaking.

Two days later the ancient marriage exchanges and customs began.

Chapter 37

Red River Gums and Gold

$\mathcal{J}$ ack and Nicholas decided to go for a walk along a large dry creek bed they had noticed running in an east-west direction through the middle of the gimlet grove. Most of the creek was in shade, for in addition to the gimlets, there grew great gum trees along the edge of and sometimes in the creek, their white trunks in stark contrast to the red soil sides and sandy bed of the creek. Some gums were almost three feet thick at the trunk and towered over the creek by about thirty feet in some cases. Later they were to find out they were called River Red Gums, named for the rich red colour of the wood under the white trunks.

Nicholas and Jack enjoyed the feeling of these creeks which criss-crossed this otherwise harsh land.

They are like veins in the land, Nicholas was thinking, knowing that these trees could only survive the extreme temperatures if they had water and so figured that there must be underground streams below the dry sandy creek bed. He made a mental note to do further exploration and perhaps some excavation to see if he could tap into a regular water supply, which could mean survival out here and may also help be of use to the mine if enough water could be harvested from the creek.

Eventually, they came across an area which was stony and hard for some fifty feet then rose up a few feet and built up to a shoulder jutting out into the creek. The rock was formed in slabs on the left side of an abrupt bend in the creek.

Here, the whole creek was heavily overhung with large white-trunked red gums, their long leaves hanging from sturdy branches.

Nicholas observed that the foliage here seemed much greener, and the noise of birds twittering in the shrub and trees was almost deafening. The gums were larger than he had seen in other dry creeks he had come across in his travels. There were bundles of dead twig and branches caught up about three feet from the base of the tree trunks and in some of the shrubs, indicating water must have run from left to right. High-water mark, thought Nicholas.

They made their way around the shoulder of the red, grey and ochre coloured stone slab.

They were surprised to find a beautiful body of water stretching out before them. It was about two hundred and fifty feet long and some thirty foot wide

Three or four teal ducks, surprised by their appearance, took off as they came into view with a clatter of wings and flash of green, quacking softly in alarm as they weaved their away up the creek before swerving over the bank and winging up past the gums to vanish. Two or three red kangaroos bounded away from where they had been resting in the cool shade of the great trees on the edge of the bank.

Nicholas and Jack grinned at each other in silence as they took in the beautiful scene before them, unexpected as it was.

'What a beautiful place this is Jack,' Nicholas said.

'I like here,' said Jack. 'Mebe gooda place for 'ut or 'ouse,' he rumbled.

They explored around the water course., the brown sandy banks and the dark water looked inviting, there was not a breath of wind and the tall stark white gums were reflected perfectly on the mirrored surface.

Black and white larks about the size of a small pigeons made loud calls from high in the gums. Sounds like 'pee..wit!' thought Nicholas.

Grey, black and light brown pigeons with curved crests on their heads, sat in pairs on dead branches jutting out over the water as several other varieties of bird flitted through the shrubbery. There were a great many insects everywhere around the area and the stream, if you could call the supine body of water that.

Despite the din of the wildlife, it was a peaceful place and one could easily be lulled into the harmony of it all Nicholas mused.

Nicholas dropped a couple of dried leaves off the top of the rocks into the dark mirrored surface of the pond. As he watched the leaves slowly made their way downstream. This must be an underground stream that has surfaced here, he mused as there was not a breath of wind to assist the passage of the leaves. Nicholas and Jack worked their way down watching the leaves as they steadily made their way along like a little flotilla until they eventually came to a stop against the wet sand at the western end.

The water seemed quite deep at the edge of the rocky outcrop they stood on, and testing the water with a gimlet, proved it to be about five foot in depth. It was clear and tasted quite fresh, certainly good enough to drink. This was a great find and would help them immensely with the mine and camp.

Nicholas looked at the sky and position of the Sun. If they did not start heading back soon they would arrive in semi-darkness, so they made their way back to the horses. They bundled up the newly cut timber into manageable pieces then lashed them to the two horses and started the walk back to the camp. Leading the horses across the flat stony plain, they arrived back in the late afternoon.

The next day Nicholas and Jack started to survey the area. Holding the compass, Nicholas started pacing out the claim. Each section they pegged they squared off by measuring and equalising the diagonals from each corner.

In all they pegged a full ten-mile tenement which included the water hole and beyond, and five separate lots. Then they went over the lot again with a sextant.

They carved and marked out the coordinates onto each stave and the relevant information required. Nicholas's intention was to buy lead tags and stamps when he went for the supplies.

Three days later, the leases pegged, Nicholas fetched his 'dolly pot and stamp', a bundle of small canvas sample bags and a small note pad, quill and ink pot and began to make a recorded sampling of the reef.

He had already sampled along the visible and exposed quartz and had been encouraged, even excited, about the amount of new indication he found. Now he wanted to get it all on record, complete with panning results. These he would send to Jonathan Trewellan and Sir Gregory Scott as soon as he was sure he had something viable to report.

The dolly and stamp consisted of a heavy iron pot, cylindrical in shape, about five inches in diameter and about ten inches long. This 'pot' had a heavy square end or base about one inch thick. The 'stamp' was a two-foot long piece of heavy iron bar about one and a half inches thick. One placed the ore into the cylinder and pounded the rock into a fine dust, or grains, using the stamp. The pounded product was emptied into a panning dish and sluiced in water, which was agitated back and forth by hand, all the while scraping off the mud and lighter stone until a small amount of fines remained. The sloshing back and forth would continue until the water remained clear, and gold if present, would sink to the bottom.

With some skill, the water was tipped in a rocking motion and the lighter and larger parts of the ore rilled away to one side.

A small indentation was pressed into the sloped rim about one inch from the base and ran the full circle of the dish. If any gold were present it would show in the small groove, what prospectors and geologists called a 'tail'.

Depending on the amount of gold showing in this final part of the procedure, it would either bring forth a groan in the absence of 'colour' (a frequent occurrence in a prospector's career) or great excitement and elation.

Nicholas was anxious to prove up his findings, and he knew by the visual presence of the gold in his ore sampling that he was not going to be disappointed, at least not at this early stage.

Starting at the top of the visible quartz reef, which was about 10 foot down the slope from the crown of the ridge, he began to break off small pieces of the quartz and bag them as he went, carefully marking each bag in numerical order.

This was hard going with his small specking pick and not for the first time he wished he had a decent crowbar and large sledge hammer.

The sample bags were about eight inches square and he sampled about every three feet all the way down to where the reef disappeared into the flat ground.

Whilst he was doing this, he had Jack down at the lower end digging out a costean. Nicholas had Jack two deep holes about of roughly four feet deep and eight feet out either side of where the quartz ridge disappeared, he then told him to trench from one hole to the other.

This costeaning or 'cross trenching' was used by prospectors so they could analise the width and depth of the ore body.

Jack dug with zeal with the only tools they had, a double-ended pick and small shovel, and by the time Nicholas had reached the flat he had been at it for four hours. The ground either side was softer than expected, probably from years of run-off from the small hillock and floods, but he knew it would get harder the further down they got. The next day the two men were at the costean just after dawn, the pesky swarms of bush flies already driving them to distraction.

The excavation was about four feet wide, ten feet long and was down to a depth of four feet. Still the reef ran on – in fact, at this point seemed to widen a little.

Nicholas knew that the width and depth would vary as they progressed, but they needed to continue excavating for at least twenty feet in total.

Nicholas estimated they would be about twelve to fifteen foot down and about twenty-five feet out in about four or five days' time when he expected they would finish this exploratory work, unless the reef took a sudden turn down, at which point they would be forced to stop.

He sampled the exposed reef as Jack continued to dig, then he joined the big man digging. It was hard going now because the ground, apart from being full of small stones up to football size, had quite a few porphyry-like interspersions running across and through the reef which took a lot of effort to excavate. Luckily, the larger pieces were riven with fractures so they were able to worry the rock into manageable pieces, but it was tough going.

The weather was getting hotter, and even though the two of them were now digging and were making steady progress, it was taking longer than expected. The ground became hard, difficult and fractured, and now after ten days had reached a point where the reef started to turn down, the deepest point around twenty-seven feet out and about eighteen feet down, the width had widened to about six feet at one point and they chased it up for about seven feet, then it dived again and narrowed back to about three feet on average. Nicholas thought to use this small chamber as a loading point when they got further in.

The ground appeared quite stable as they went down apart from the occasional patches where the ground seemed more compacted. Nevertheless, as before, they wedged cross-staves across the dig as they went, driving in timber wedges they had cut and shaped from some larger timber branches from the water hole earlier. As they progressed, the reef had not shown any sign of reducing in size or breaking up into small pieces, which was heartening although not conclusive proof of a good sized and sustainable load. The sampling and dollying would tell them that.

Nicholas sampled all over the exposed reef as far down to the base, again carefully numbering and recording as he went.

They started to drive in on a decline, descending on a reasonable ratio at about twelve feet out, now leaving an overhead of roughly four feet thick. This was necessary to keep on the run of the quartz and corrosive ore which descended before them and which was starting to deviate.

On the twelfth day, after digging for most of the day and making slow progress, the ground started to soften somewhat. Jack lay on his belly, reaching out ahead and digging with a small pick. He made steady progress, and as he went he shoved his diggings under his great biceps to Nicholas, also lying on his belly behind him. Nicholas would then scoop the dirt back and shimmy backwards, dragging the loose soil as he went into the second small loading chamber they had dug out. The chamber was just big enough to stand in but they would have to bend over nearly double to make their way toward the surface. They would crawl through the first turning chamber and start to haul up the diggings that Nicholas would load onto a wooden sled they had made. From there they would repeat the process, dragging up the samples to the surface on a wooden sled they had made out of a hollow red gum.

It was a lot cooler down at the bottom of their exploratory diggings and they both enjoyed the damp smell and the hard work now that the sun wasn't beating down on them.

But it was dangerous, back breaking and awkward work with only one way out and that was back up the small drive. Once they achieved digging out the small tunnel on their bellies to about three feet, they would come back and start to dig up to about chest height, following the reef width and three-foot tunnel, then start all over again.

Nicholas stood staring up at the reef face after chasing out yet another chamber and was thinking, we need to get some proper equipment before we go much further. He looked at the man standing before him and felt an overwhelming wave of affection for the big man who had become his closest friend and every day their bond grew.

Jack grinned back at Nicholas, lifting the small carbide lamp, exposing a dirt and sweat streaked huge shining face. He was enjoying the work. He turned and hung the lamp on a small wooden peg driven into a crack, then dropped to his knees and wormed into the hole and started digging a new cut.

Nicholas felt a trickle of dirt hit the side of his head and immediately looked at the north wall. Knowing instinctively what it could be he dropped to his haunches yelling, 'Jack, get back!' and grabbed the big man's belt and started to drag him back.

With a soft rumble the north wall suddenly gave way and buried Jack to his waist. Nicholas frantically tugged at Jack's heavy belt, his hands locked onto the stout leather. He leaned back with all of his strength, muscles straining, and managed to drag him back a mere two inches before being forced to stop as another shower of stone came down, although not as much dirt as before.

Dirt and dust in his eyes and mouth, Nicholas didn't even think as he attacked the dirt on top of Jack, trying to lighten the load on top of his mate's back. He knew he would have only minutes to get air to him and he tore at the dirt with his bare hands. Gritting his teeth, he felt the dirt grinding as he tried to fight the panic that was welling up in him.

Snatching up the small shovel he began again at the dirt. Nicholas's hands and fingernails were torn and bleeding as he moved the pile he had dug off.

As he dug he felt Jack's right arm was bunched up under his chest and his fingers were twitching at the left side of his chest.

'Air! air! I must get air to him,' he muttered and began to work the rubble away from under Jack's arm and hand. It was relatively soft and he was beginning to make progress.

'Jack! Jack! Hang on, hang on man!' he yelled. Suddenly, he stopped. He heard a faint and muted deep moan coming from his friend. He snatched up the sputtering lamp which then renewed its steady hissy and in the dim glow of the carbide lamp through the dust hanging in the air, he saw another slab hanging over them. A jagged, long narrow crack had appeared off the hanging wall. 'Jesus!' he said out loud, and ignoring the threat, redoubled his efforts.

Abruptly, his fingers hit something soft and rubbery, and realising it was Jack's mouth he dug his fingers in further feeling his nose. Nicholas wriggled his fingers against Jack's nose and to his immense relief was rewarded with a sputtering snort as Jack tried to drag in some air.

'Hang on Jack, don't move, you hear me! Don't move!, he shouted with great emphasis. A long moan rumbled from under the dirt.

Nicholas withdrew his arm, which was almost at full stretch. The small tunnel held, much to his relief, and Nicholas sat back and quickly took stock of the situation.

Wiping at the dirt and dust on his face and in his eyes, he tried to calm down and think.

Stop! he shouted internally. Slow down, think! he again shouted internally.

If he started to dig at the dirt on top of Jack's back he might take away the only support the hanging wall and dirt might have and it could all come down as he dug away at the base. They had cut stays and larger logs for uprights up at the surface, but he fretted that if he left Jack the dirt might fall whilst he was getting them, and he might get blocked out even further away. 'Jesus, okay, no choice!' he said out loud, and the decision made, he turned and made his way toward the light to get the thick support logs.

Nicholas had only gone up the slope about ten feet when he felt the rush of misplaced air against his bare back and heard the 'woomf!' of falling dirt.

'Jack!' he screamed and spun back down. But the dust was so thick he could not breathe or see a thing. Coughing, and panic now gripping him, he felt along the small loading chamber wall. The dust hung in the space choking him. He dropped to his hands and knees, and gagging and choking on dust, made his way forward.

He came to the place where he reckoned the first fall happened, but Jack's legs and feet were no longer there. 'Ah me!' he groaned out aloud as he felt it was fresh dirt from another fall he was feeling, 'Ah no, no!' he uttered and shimmied back a little to the edge of the chamber. Lowering his head to the dirt which now filled the start of the drive, he knew there was no way he could save his big friend now.

Nicholas lay prone, not able to move for grief, he sobbed, tears tumbling from his eyes. All he could see was Jacks great smiling face before him.

Something wet splashed down on the side of Nicholas's face, "What?" he thought, touching the 'wetness', it was sticky, like blood, he rolled over.

Nicholas jolted as if someone had kicked him.

Through the thinning dust and dim light from the tunnel leading out, looming over him, rivulets of blood running down his face and chest like some mythical monster, was Jack.

'Got a' water?' he croaked, barely able to get the words out.

Nicholas stared at Jack, unable to believe his eyes. He rose to his feet, too quickly and cracked his skull on the overhang, Wincing, Nicholas wrapped his arms around Jack and let the tears come. In that poignant moment, they stood, arms around each other, now forever bonded as brothers.

The dust continued to settle and some more light started to filter through.

'Water,' the huge man croaked again. Nicholas immediately dropped to his knees and felt around for the water bottle he knew was there.

Digging it out, he pulled the stopper and handed it to Jack. Jack dropped to his knees and took a swig of water, and turning to one side, spat the water into his left hand in which he clutched a large lump of mud. Then he drank, at the same time holding out his great fist to Nicholas.

Confused by the big man's actions, Nicholas looked at his hand and there in Jack's hand gleaming wet, lay a nugget almost two inches in diameter of near pure gold.

Nicholas stared in disbelief at the nugget, his mouth gaping and mind dancing between what he saw and the fact that the big fellow, so close to death a few minutes ago had had thoughts only to please him. Nicholas was touched beyond words and at the same time felt a heavy guilt weighing on him.

'Let's get you out of here Jack,' he said and pushed the big man out ahead of him and then led him to the small shady mulga tree growing on the side of the hillock.

Sitting him down on an upturned barrel, Nicholas started to wash away the blood and dirt from his friends face.

His own hands were stinging like hell, two of his fingernails had lifted and were bleeding as well.

'Bloody hell Jack, what a mess we are in!' he laughed. 'Look at us!' he continued as he held his hands and arms out in front of Jack. Jack looked at his hands then up at Nicholas and rumbled, 'Di'n need no nine tails eider!' his huge chest shaking at his own joke, though he quickly stopped as his bruised ribs protested but still managed a huge grin.

Jack was a bit of a mess with several cuts to the sides of his head and forehead where the stones had fallen on him. But the worst damage was to his back. Great scrapes of skin had been stripped off his back, almost as though he had been clawed. Agape at the damage Nicholas gently cleaned away the dirt and blood.

'How did you get out of there Jack?' Nicholas asked.

Jack turned from Nicholas's ministrations and said to Nicholas's astonishment, 'Stood up Niclas.'

'You what!' exclaimed Nicholas.

'Stood up!'

Christ! thought Nicholas. 'No wonder you cut your back like this, I don't know how you pushed up on all that dirt,' he said shaking his head in disbelief.

They rested up the next day, both men stiff and sore, the cuts and wounds letting them know how lucky they had been.

Nicholas decided that they had taken enough risks, and either way they had enough samples now to ratify the reef's value. They would rest up and do the sampling, then before leaving would peg the leases using the gimlet staves.

The next day, Nicholas and Jack started laying out and surveying the four leases Nicholas had decided to peg. They both were still very sore, so the pegging and measuring took another four days. This completed, they started to sort through the sampling.

Nicholas found a couple of two-inch-sized samples with ribbons of gold laced through the rusty coloured quartz, and big Jack began to show some interest in the gold, especially when Nicholas dollied up one of the pieces and panned it, showing him the beautiful 'tail' that was produced.

Nicholas showed Jack how to pan, and after a few days the big fellow was getting quite good at it and would spend most of his spare time during their breaks practicing his technique.

This afternoon, thought Nicholas during one of the rest breaks, he would lay out all of the sample bags and begin to dolly up portions of the samples. He decided that he would let Jack use one of the panning dishes, which would be a big help as he had two of these dishes, and further, it might get him to show even more interest in prospecting. Nicholas would record all of the data and send them back to Sir Gregory Scott, along with a couple of good specimens.

Jack and Nicholas sat resting under the sparse shade of a mulga tree which grew about thirty feet from the dig and where their stores were stacked.

It was mid-afternoon and a hot wind was blowing from the east.

'I am glad that is over,' said Nicholas, handing Jack his water flask. Jack just grunted and picked at a blister on the palm of his right hand about the size of a silver crown.

Nicholas stared out across the shimmering mirage. Witches' water, he thought.

'We will pack up and make our way back to the river after we have done our final sampling Jack,' Nicholas said. 'We need to check on Wilber as well,' he added.

'Yas, gooda see my fren' Whip an' my lovely Kubi. He might already make many of his wives with little ones!' he laughed.

Nicholas laughed as well, amused at the way the big fellow found great pleasure in things that others might find trivial. But Nicholas knew Jack had suffered terribly under his white masters and the slavers, and therefore possibly knew full well what was valuable in life and what was to be coveted. Not the least of those was friendship, either with man or beast. So, Jack's 'balance' was something special.

They both were silent, each with their own thoughts, and as Nicholas began to doze in the heat, Victoria crept into his thoughts.

Chapter 38

Richard Landale Beetson

*T*hey had been at the hotel for a day and a half when a fat and wheezing clerk from the shipping agent stumbled up the stairs to the hotel asking for Massa Ah…Mendson. He carried a note informing that the *Collette* was indeed in port and was now loading cargo. The note was from Peter Strudwich asking if it would be possible to meet.

Ludwig immediately sent word back to Captain Strudwich and an invitation to dine at the hotel that night at 8pm.

Strudwich arrived with five minutes to spare. He was immaculate in a navy-blue seaman's coat, white spats over black shiny boots, cream seaman's trousers and a white shirt.

Around his waist hung his military service sword on a highly polished black leather belt with equally polished brass buckles and chain. On his head he wore an embroidered navy captain's bicorn.

He was accompanied by a gentleman by the name of Richard Landale Beetson, a Government Salt contractor under the Indian regiment control of the East India Company, or EIC as it was commonly known. The gentleman was equally resplendent in a long beige frock-style coat, with black lapels and a white ruffle blouse adorning his upper torso.

He was tall, about six foot two, fair of hair, his face was finely chiselled and clean shaven except for a thin mustache enhancing his upper lip. He had fair hair, braided and as was the fashion, long and tied at the back with matching black bow. A sash of white polished leather ran over his right shoulder to his sword belt, from which hung a beautiful ornate sword buckled over a wide black cummerbund.

His trousers were stove pipe straight, also white, with a thin red stripe sewn into the seam. Black highly buffed military-style calf-length boots shone in the light, and he wore a black and fine gold braided Albert Shako military-style hat.

He was a very handsome man with good presence of character and stood a clear foot over Strudwich.

As the introductions began, Victoria and Lillian were sitting together on one of the high-backed cane lounges observing the men as they exchanged the usual pleasantries. Lillian, in particular, could not help but notice the tall colonel's eyes flicking toward her daughter more than once, and sneaking a peek at Victoria, saw her openly looking at him.

As he approached and courteously took Lillian's hand, he informed her that he was en route back to India from England, where he had been tending some business interests and would sail on the *Collette* as far as Goa in India. Finally, he turned to Victoria and immediately locked eyes with her. Victoria could sense the authority and power emanating from those stone grey eyes. Oh my! thought Victoria, catching her breath and immediately plunging into embarrassment as a vision of Nicholas flashed into her mind. She flushed as she felt a feeling of betrayal wash over her.

'Richard Landale Beetson,' he said to her, his eyes never leaving her for a second as he proffered his hand.

To her further embarrassment Victoria found herself unable to break the man's gaze, and then to her horror, she had involuntarily offered her hand to him, which he took with a firm grasp, and bending at the waist, smoothly raised her hand to his lips.

She was in a panic and her heart was pounding, but she seemed powerless to do anything about it.

Observing the proceedings with her famous raised left eyebrow, Lillian watched the exchange with some interest, if not amusement.

Mon Dieu! but 'e is a magnificent specimen of man, she mused, and looking covertly at Victoria, almost burst out laughing at the look of awe and embarrassment on her daughter's face. Ah to be 'er age again, she thought.

'Captain Strudwich informs me that we are to be travelling companions aboard the *Collette*, well, at least as far as Goa…at least,' he explained.

Beetson immediately turned to Lillian and Ludwig and said, 'You can be assured I will make it my mission to keep her from harm Madame and Monsieur Amendson…'

Lud winced at the statement knowing what his daughter's reaction was likely to be. Victoria was furious. How *dare* he assume I cannot look after myself and act as if I am not even here!

She interrupted before Beetson could finish. 'Thank you sir, but that will not be necessary. I assure you I can look after myself!' she said abruptly.

'Victoria!' exclaimed Lillian, sliding a look at Ludwig, who had a hint of a smile on his face, which vanished as soon as Lillian looked at him. Strudwich did not bother to hide his amusement, his face a wreath of smiles.

Somewhat stunned by her reaction, Beetson stammered, 'I apologise mademoiselle, I meant no insult, nor impropriety.' But Victoria had already risen and was striding across the verandah to the interior of the hotel.

Lillian's eyes bored into Ludwig until he coughed and offered, 'My apologies sir, but Victoria is obviously still tired after our long journey… she is also very independent having been our only child and quite used to standing on her own two feet so to speak.' He grinned and added, 'The word headstrong comes to mind, and sometimes where we live, that can be advantageous.'

He could see Lillian rolling her eyes at his statement and weak offer of an apology.

'It is quite all right monsieur, it was insensitive of me to assume the responsibility. Your daughter is a very impressive young woman if I may offer the compliment, and I apologise.' He held up his left hand showing a sizeable gold wedding band, and added, 'I am, after all a happily married man with several children.'

'I think perhaps it is Victoria who should receive your apology Richard,' Ludwig said.

'Of course, of course, I will do so immediately I have the chance,' Beetson quickly replied.

Peter Strudwich laughed, saying, 'Be sure to wear some warm clothes colonel!'

Ludwig could not help himself and burst into a deep rumble of mirth.

Lillian rose and said, 'I think I will go to freshen up before ze dinner gentlemen…no no, please do not get up.' She swept from the verandah as only Lillian could and vanished into the hotel.

Once inside she made a beeline for Victoria's room and tapped lightly on the door. '*Cherie*? Are you there?' Victoria opened the door.

"I want to talk to you my *Cherie,* do not worry, but it is important, *no?*'

Victoria and Lillian sat at the small bedroom table and Lillian began, 'I do not want you to think that I am '*ere* to lecture you about *Monsieur Beetson Cherie*, and I am not. When you '*av* been raised as you '*ave*, you do not '*av ze* opportunity to interact with many other people outside of the few who we live with, *no?*' Victoria nodded, wondering what her mother's angle was.

She went on. 'We all know '*ow* much you love Nicholas, *zat* is obvious, *no?*'

'But out '*ere* in the world,' she swept her hands around, 'no one else knows about it, or even should care if they just meet you.

'*Ze* gentleman '*e* is but one of thousands of attractive men oo' will be drawn to you,' she said waving her hands around, indicating Victoria. 'Whether you know it or not *Cherie,* you '*av* grown into a very attractive lady and men will want you for a variety of reasons, not all good intentions either.'

Victoria looked at her mother and said 'What on earth do you mean Ma'ma?'

'*Mon ami* Victoria! Take your pick! Rape, blackmail, ransom, slavery, use you to make someone jealous or just charm you, give you fine wines and dine you then take you to bed and then just discard you! You must be very careful, it is a long way to this new land and to Nicholas and *'e* is not *'ere* to protect you like *'e* did before with Hymie.'

Victoria was a bit more than shocked. 'You mean the colonel?'

'*Oo* knows my darling, but I do not *zink* so, *'e* is already married!' Lillian said.

'What I am trying to say is *zis*…I watched you, and you were affected by monsieur Beetson's presence, *'e* is very handsome and charming, *'owever,* *'e* is but one of thousands of attractive men. *'E* is most likely a gentleman of the highest order, nonetheless you were affected, and zen, you felt ashamed because of your love for Nicholas and you felt guilty, and *'e* took that as though you were attracted to him from your blush and stare!'

'But Ma ma…" Lillian waved her hand to silence her and said 'Wait! Then you snapped at *'im* a little too *'arshly* because you felt *zis* guilt, again *'e* thinks you are reacting to his approach, no matter what *you* think. Some men do not take rejection easily and you must always be cautious and do not ever lose control, understand?'

Victoria nodded, and not for the first time her mother's knowledge and forethought amazed her.

'Now, I want you to prepare and come down to dinner with me. You should act as…as though nothing happened at all, be charming and polite but keep your *'ead* up and show pride. *'E* will take it as though you are still very independent and proud. *Zis* will either fascinate *'im* or make *'im* more cautious in *'is* approach, which is what you want, *no?* 'Question Captain Strudwich about Nicholas, *'ow 'e* is going, is *'e well*, what is *'e* doing etc, etc.

'You will be in control of the conversation and *ze monsieur* will soon get an idea of why you are travelling 'alf way across the world to find Nicholas, and anyway, *'e* will get off *ze* ship in India, problem is gone…poof!' she clapped her hands together. They laughed together and prepared for dinner.

But alone, Lillian wondered if the handsome Richard Landale Beetson would be put off so easily, and she gnawed at her lip as she pondered the question.

Later that evening, they all sat down to dinner in the dining room, Lillian making sure Victoria did not sit opposite Richard Beetson and was separated from him by Peter Strudwich, thus avoiding any meaningful eye contact the gentleman might have designs on making, while she herself kept up a constant dialogue with the handsome man.

This was not difficult and Beetson was quite forthcoming of his adventures, the wars in India and of his plans. He was interesting, and both Lud and Lillian were happy to hear his stories.

He had been very astute and had amassed a fortune when he sold his salt holdings and business in Cattuch in Orissa Province to the East India Company and Government in England.

He also talked of taking up landholdings in South Australia that the new Government and settlement was offering in approximately ten months' time, at which time he would have his family sail from England to Adelaide.

Victoria kept the conversation well in her control and made the most of her enquiries to Peter Strudwich – in any case she was genuinely interested in where Nicholas was, what he was doing and what the Murchison River was like.

'Well I am afraid we must part your delightful company my good people, we have a big day tomorrow,' Strudwich announced standing and bowing to the group. 'We will sail on the next decent tide and that will be at eight bells the day after tomorrow.'

Turning to Victoria, he added, 'Miss Victoria, if you would choose to have your luggage, apart from your personal items, delivered tomorrow afternoon, I will personally see it stowed safely for you, and please could you be on board by no later than seven-thirty the following morning?"

Strudwich and Beetson bade them all good evening and departed.

Victoria felt her stomach clench with excitement, soon she would see Nicholas again.

Victoria tried everything to find sleep, but eventually gave up, she was so excited. She packed and unpacked her valise several times before Lillian, woken by her daughter's movement, came to her with tears in her eyes and they held each other, crying as only a mother and daughter could, and talked long into the night.

The next morning the family travelled down to the wharf to where the *Collette* sat moored at the southern end of the mercantile section.

Having already said the goodbyes at the hotel, soon Victoria stood by Captain Strudwich at the poop waving goodbye, tears rolling down her face as she saw her father place his great arm around her mother's shaking shoulders as she dabbed at her face with her small kerchief.

The bosun shouted orders as the sailors scrambled aloft and the great canvas sails snapped full with a good breeze behind them. The ship quickly picked up speed and they were soon heading into a moderate swell, the land mass of Africa steadily becoming but a smudge on the horizon which they kept to port as they progressed up the coast.

Chapter 39

Mombasa to Goa, March 1850

Three days out of Mombasa and the weather conditions remained favourable, a steady southerly breeze off the starboard stern side. The *Collette* kept a steady course and was making good time in a moderate easterly swell.

The voyage first took them up to the trading port of Malindi, where they loaded bales of ivory, leather and African hard wood. From here they steered nor' nor-east with the intent of catching the summer monsoonal winds and currents which would carry them across to India. Strudwich explained that the voyage to Goa could take up to a month and a half depending on what conditions they would encounter, and storms could be a severe hazard at this time of the season.

Victoria noticed that Strudwich had the crew carry out almost daily gun drills since leaving Mombasa and she asked why he drove the men so hard at this.

He explained that to the north along this coast there were many pirates and slave ships traversing these seas and they must be alert and ready for anything. So as not to alarm her, Strudwich explained that in the last three voyages they had encountered no real problems other than the last voyage when a fast dhow started shadowing them, however it had eventually drifted off. The *Collette* was also very well armed and in fact carried quite a number of the latest rifled cannon, with a longer range and greater accuracy.

As they sailed along the east coast, it was a good time for Victoria to gain her 'sea legs'. Luckily, she did not seem to have any immediate effects of sea sickness although she was warned that when the conditions turned rough she could well suffer. Strudwich explained that any seaman that bragged he did not get sea sick was a liar.

Peter Strudwich kept her well entertained with his tales of the many voyages and perils he had faced over his many years at sea.

He was immensely proud of the *Collette* and showed almost every part off to her with pride, and he kept the men busy at all times, scrubbing, oiling and painting. At dinner one evening Strudwich gave her the history of how the three masted Blackwall Frigate was built and the many changes he had made to her to make the ship faster, and how he had improved the armament. He had the company fit sixteen of the new breech loading 'Armstrong' rifled bore cannons to the *Collette*, eight a side. The new cannon had thirty per cent greater range over the old muzzle loading cannon and at least twice the accuracy. Combined with the ships' speed, they made the ship a formidable foe.

Strudwich explained that although the class of ship was named a Blackwall frigate, it was not actually a frigate and gained the title partly because the shipwright did produce frigates originally for the Royal Navy. In fact, the Blackwall class had similar lines from a distance, but a Naval Forth rated frigate carried about 56 cannon and was about 20 feet longer but that being said, it was fitted exclusively for war and carried a minimum of 420 men.

The Blackwalls and other such named vessels were not actually owned or built by the English owned East India Company, nor by the opposition, the Dutch East India Company, and in fact neither of the trading conglomerates owned ships for that matter. They actually leased the ships either from privateers or shipping companies, the exception being war ships, which in turn were often crewed by her Royal Majesty, Queen Victoria's First Royal Marines and sailors.

The *Collette* was a fast ship and was purchased by Sir Gregory Scott's company, GA Scott investments. Scott had had two such ships commissioned, the *Collette* and her sister ship, the *Cirrus*. The company lost the *Cirrus* with all hands in late 1848 off the Cape of Good Hope during a storm, so of the company owned Blackwall Class Frigates, the *Collette* was now the only one.

Peter was at pains to explain that he had once been caught in a major cyclone just west of the Indian coast when he was racing to beat the blow. The ship incurred serious damage and almost foundered.

Strudwich and his crew managed to nurse the vessel – either by luck, skill or fate he could not say – into a ship building port off the west coast of India, not far from Goa.

He found the Indian shipwrights to be first class and were contracted to build a number of East Indiamen ships for the Dutch and the English, but these were banned from sailing to Europe and restricted to the Japan and China trade.

Touring the yards, Strudwich was taken by the Indian timbers they used, Indian cedar and teak.

These were lighter and stronger than the European timbers, and the craftsmanship was equal to any he had seen, if not better.

He had the *Collette's* uppers and decks which had been damaged by the cyclone stripped and replaced by the stronger and lighter Indian timbers, except for the mast steps.

The Indians finished the refit in record time and included some fine carving into the bargain in the stateroom, the forecastle and poop deck. In addition, they made a new figurehead at the bowsprit, even more beautiful than the old one, which had split during the storm.

As a result, the *Collette* had shed about thirty ton in weight, bringing her overall weight to 1240 tons, and at one 174-foot feet in length, she was stronger and faster. She now had many improvements for stowage, particularly in the gun galley.

Far from being bored by all this information, Victoria found herself fascinated. It was a new and exciting adventure to her and she found confidence in knowing all about the ship.

'Tomorrow I shall show you the workings of my ship,' Peter said with a broad smile.

The more I get to know this girl the more I like her, he thought. She has spirit and is very intelligent, little wonder she and Nicholas are attracted to each other.

By Victoria's observations, she found Strudwich to be a deeply principled man with a sense of fair play that rivalled that of her father, and she warmed to him as a dear friend and almost as family.

He spoke unbidden of his fondness for Nicholas, and thus was forthcoming on many things that may well have taken her years to extract from Nicholas herself. He told her of Nicholas's travels, his fierce determination when it came to accomplishing a task or standing up for justice, or anything he believed in.

What affected her most of all though was Peter's observation of Nicholas's love for her and how he carried his departure from her like a lump of lead in his heart. She explained that she too carried a heavy burden about the events leading up to his decision to leave.

Peter told her he knew all about what happened on that early evening by the great lake, and he explained as best he could how a man will put his life down to defend those he loves.

With tears in her eyes, Victoria told of both the fear and the feeling of awe she had felt on that night. She saw some part of Nicholas she had never seen, much less understood. It was not, she explained, him beating Hymie the way he did, it was when he drew his rifle and placed the barrels on Hymie's face. He was, she said, almost a separate being as he stood over Hymie, his face was a mask devoid of any emotion or anything at all and it had frightened her, but most of all it was the change in his eyes.

The sparkle that he always seemed to have in his eyes had been replaced by flat emotionless discs, like obsidian, and she knew he was within a hair's breadth of killing Hymie.

As he looked at her face, the tears of confusion wet upon her cheeks and her eyes moist, Peter felt her pain and confusion as acutely as he would his own and had looked down to contemplate how he could explain Nicholas's reaction on that late afternoon.

He thought about what she had told him for some time before answering, and he had to tread carefully for he too had seen this manifestation in Nicholas, remembering the incident with his boson. He knew Nicholas could be a dangerous man.

But how to explain to her how such a man can elevate his senses and focus to a level where he can kill or commit to any such action that leaves no room for error? Dangerous ground for him to explain as she was hanging on his every word, most likely because she needed to accept this part of her man out of sheer love for him.

He cleared his throat and began to explain to her that sometimes when a man reacts in this manner, it is often partly born out of some primeval instinct, be that self-preservation or a decision to carry out whatever was necessary in a certain situation, and those actions sometimes left no room for emotion. This was possibly a result of his past experiences, and in this case, experience had made Nicholas very aware of what could evolve.

Events in life, past or present can shape one's life persona and sense of values, sometimes for the better, sometimes not. In the case of Van Der Hoeke, Nicholas had recognised immediately on meeting that the angry young man was teetering on the brink of manic obsession, and proven right when Hymie reacted the way he did. He was, in fact, about to step completely out of control, and the flash point was right there in front of them.

Peter saw he now had Victoria's complete attention and he continued.

'In life, there are some men and women, when faced with crisis, opt for hesitation instead of action. In a life or death situation the hesitant are no longer with us, do you understand?'

Victoria nodded slowly, thinking about it.

'Be it a wrong decision caught up in the moment, or afterwards proven right if you survive.

'It is the quickness of mind and the ability to assess and act that makes a good leader, or even a general if you like, and I think Nicholas's actions that day are commendable for whatever the method he chose to use. He avoided a situation that could have harmed you and even your father should he have sprung to your defence physically.

'And Victoria consider, *if* he did not care deeply for you he possibly would not have reacted in this manner, his sole instinct was to protect.'

As she thought about Peter's words of wisdom, she began to understand that she was very naïve when it came to situations like that of which had occurred. She had never been exposed to any threat of this magnitude.

She had reacted too quickly in her assessment of Nicholas's actions and been too judgemental. Her heart pounded at the full realisation of why Nicholas had been quick to defend her. Thinking about it, he had always sprung to her defence and had always been there for her as her protector, right from the beginning.

Peter looked at her as she thought things through, praying he had said all that she needed to hear.

Victoria looked up at him and with tears brimming in her eyes once again, slipped her arm through his and rested her head on his shoulder.

Thank God, he rejoiced inside and squeezed her arm to let her know he understood.

'Are you prepared at all for what this new land is like my dear?' he asked, as it suddenly dawned on him that she probably had no idea what to expect.

'No, or just a little,' she answered, 'but I really do not care as long as I am with Nicky, it cannot be any harder than home surely!' she countered.

Peter thought for a minute before answering. 'Victoria, we don't know a great deal about the land where Nicholas is exploring, what I have seen so far is only the ports and the mouth of the river where Nicholas had begun to build a dwelling and establish a cattle farm.

'Me thinks Nicholas will be exploring inland such as is his passion for minerals and I am told it is a very harsh land with extreme heat in the summer months and freezing desert cold in the winter. There are also problems with a lack of water in the summer.'

Seeing he had her full attention he continued. 'The mouth of the Murchison River appears to be quite pleasant, but has no tall trees or green grass, well at least at the time of the year I was there, but I imagine there will be good water at the river.'

Victoria seemed to contemplate what he had said. 'I don't expect it to be easy captain, but I feel that Nicholas and I will endure no matter how hard things are.'

Well, he thought, she appears to have the gumption for the venture at least, and he saw first-hand how she could be very independent, chuckling to himself whilst remembering how she put Landale Beetson in his place.

Turning as if something had suddenly called him, Strudwich suddenly began to bellow orders, having the sails trimmed and altering the rigging. Victoria watched in fascination as the captain strode among the men rapping out directions, changing this and that, having things retied and telling the bosun and first mate to rearrange crews so that bucket gangs could remove water ballast from different chambers.

Landale Beetson appeared beside her and asked, 'What is happening Miss Victoria?'

'I don't really know monsieur,' she replied. 'The captain was just talking to me and suddenly broke away and started shouting orders.'

Beetson looked around and scanned the horizon, seeing nothing out of the order, he shrugged.

Strudwich ran up the poop stairs and said casually, 'We will have heavy weather in less than an hour, I suggest you both go below and secure any loose items, this blow will be hard.'

In half an hour they both returned to the helm on the poop to find the captain and the helmsman lashing heavy sisal to the deck cleats either side of the helm.

Strudwich looked up, and without a word but grinning pointed off to the north-east. A thin smudge had appeared on the horizon and the sea had changed colour. Ten minutes later the 'smudge had developed into a bank of rapidly growing cumulus cloud. Great streaks of cirrus cloud spread out from the centre like sharp fingers, some right over the ship.

A calm came over the area but fifteen minutes later and the wind from the north-east had increased and was beginning to blow hard in their faces. The clouds were building rapidly, and they could see lightning stabbing down, brilliant against the now indigo storm.

Strudwich, still grinning, saw the fear on Victoria's face and stepping closer said, 'Don't worry, we are going to have a hard time, but this ship is an excellent sea boat and we will be okay, all right my dear? If you were ever going to get the sea sickness, now is the time,' he laughed. 'Now will you both please go below and secure yourselves.'

Within ten minutes the storm hit them and the wind began howling like a banshee as it tore at them. The captain, knowing Victoria and Beetson had gone below, proceeded to lash himself to the poop rail in front of the helm alongside the helmsman.

The storm was on them for five hours, and the wind and rain never let up even for a second. Lightning lit up the cabin like day and the ensuing claps of thunder were so loud it hurt the ears.

Victoria clung to the edge of her timber bunk, feet wedged into the corner with her head hanging over the side. Her stomach constantly heaving and spasming even though there was nothing left to vomit. In her life, she had never felt more wretched than this moment. The floor of her small cabin area was awash with her vomit and the smell gave her stomach a message to heave each time the odour assailed her. The wind howled unabated as did the pitching of the ship, which seemed so insignificant and danced to the whim of the storm. Eventually, exhausted from heaving and fear, she slept.

She awoke the following morning, still groggy and feeling decidedly ill. She noticed that the floor of her cabin had been sluiced down and the curtain over her bunk had been drawn. A large wooden pail of fresh water sat by her sea trunk.

Stripping, she washed herself and changed into clean clothes, a black ankle-length skirt, wide brown belt and pale blue short-sleeved blouse. Suddenly, she needed to feel fresh air on her face, a prickly heat flushing her, and as quickly as she could she made for the companion way and up onto the deck. The effect was immediate and she instantly felt a little better, a cool breeze cleansing her.

She climbed the few stairs to the poop where Captain Strudwich stood at the stern, arms clasped behind his back gazing at the distant storm as they sailed away from it.

He turned as she reached the deck and said, 'Ah! Victoria, looking much better now you are. I hope you can forgive me, but I took the liberty of washing your face with a cloth late last night after the storm abated somewhat and drew your curtain and sluiced the deck in your cabin.'

He wrinkled up his nose and added, 'Sea sickness is often joked about but it is no fun as you found out. I have even seen good sailors die from it, poor souls.'

Victoria waved his apologies aside and thanked him. He said, 'You will no doubt feel better from here on, we suffered no real damage and we are now making excellent time.'

Victoria looked at the captain with some interest and said, 'I have never, never, *ever* felt so sick. Do you ever get sea sick?'

'Not anymore,' he replied. 'Touch wood, but if any seadog ever tells you he has never been sea sick, he is a bona fide liar!'

For his part, Landale Beetson was a perfect gentleman, and not once during the voyage did he ever give Victoria any cause to show umbrage.

She considered he had concluded that she would never look at another man, so much in love with Nicholas as she was.

It was not that she disliked attention from other men, far from it, she found it flattering, however it did not take long in any conversation before her thoughts always strayed to Nicholas. She found that when this occurred, she became very protective of her thoughts, and thus sometimes a little too short with any would-be admirers.

Seven weeks and two days later at ten bells they dropped anchor in Mormugoa harbour in Goa, a week or so late due to the storm taking them further south than anticipated and they had to tack for some time north to regain the currents and had navigated some fairly rough waters.

Victoria looked up in awe at the magnificent fortress of Agoda, and even higher up at a castle and battlements bristling with cannon and complete with lighthouse. From the ship the island of Goa, if you could call it that, looked quite beautiful with many trees. The island in fact sat between the mouths of two rivers, the Mandovi and the Zuari. The island was wedge shaped and quite hilly. The indigenous peoples called the island

Choddnnem, which is Sanskrit for 'the most beautiful diamond'. Legend has it that Yashida, Lord Krishna's mother, threw her diamonds away here.

The Portuguese called it Ilha dos Fidalgos after the noblemen living in Goa. Mormugoa was an excellent sheltered port and they relished the calm waters after the rough waters they had encountered.

Landale Beetson explained that the Portuguese *conquistadors* actually claimed and built the forts and church on the island, later followed by palatial buildings to house the noblemen who eventually lived there, until the British captured it.

'It is here that I must bid you all farewell, at least until we meet again,' said Beetson.

Looking over the side he saw an East Indiaman boat gliding up to the side, oars shipped and vertical.

'The pleasure has been all ours Richard,' Captain Strudwich replied. 'We hope to see you again and I am glad to have of been of service,' he said saluting. Beetson returned the gesture.

Beetson turned to Victoria. 'I am very pleased to have made your acquaintance Miss Victoria. If I may say so, Mr Yuin is a very lucky man and you may tell him I said so ma'am.' He lifted her hand and put it to his lips, bowing deeply from the waist. 'I wish you every happiness,' and clambered down the side to the waiting boat.

'A fine young gentleman Miss Victoria,' Strudwich commented as he watched the skiff pull away to the landing.

Before she could answer he added, 'We will be here only two days hopefully, enough to unload some of the cargo and gain some and will sail at the next available tide.'

It was hot and humid and Victoria was feeling very uncomfortable. She went up to the poop deck where the crew had erected a canvas awning. Here at least it was cooler and she and the captain talked of his adventures at sea.

A shout went up and a seaman was pointing away to the landing. 'A skiff Sir, looks like 'tis the Beetson's boat Sir, but 'e ain't in it.'

A smartly dressed cooly clambered over the side and made his way to the captain. Saluting smartly, he handed Strudwich a letter.

Reading, Strudwich looked at Victoria. 'It seems the good fellow continues to be a gentleman Miss Victoria, he asks that if it please you, he has arranged for you to be taken to a friend's house on the island to take a bath and attend to your needs. Indeed, the lady of the house would find pleasure also to join you in afternoon tea.'

Noticing the slight frown appear on her face, he hastened to add, 'The man has left to attend to his business matters further north, and I am to escort you to the house.' He smiled down at her.

She smiled and accepted the offer. Oh, to have a bath, she swooned to herself and wash her clothing in something other than salt water and hard lyre. She ran to gather her bag and clothing.

Victoria spent a delightful two hours in a magnificent hot bath and her clothes were whipped away by the servants for cleaning.

The lady of the house was a Mrs Anderson Smithe, Juliet, and she and Victoria had an outrageous afternoon as they swapped stories. Juliet was especially interested in hearing all about Africa and about Nicholas. Thanks to Lillian, Victoria was able to provide details of the latest fashions from France as best she could.

Juliet's husband was a major in the East India Company and a good friend of Richard Beetson and was currently on campaign at the border somewhere and had been away for fifteen weeks.

It was 5.15pm when Peter Strudwich sent a message to say that the ship was only just now being berthed at the landing and they would be unloading that evening. He tentatively asked if it would be possible for Victoria to stay overnight as he was not comfortable in fetching her at possibly midnight.

Mrs Anderson Smythe was delighted to keep her guest for longer. Later that evening, they enjoyed a sumptuous meal and talked long into the night. Peter was relieved because his shipment of cut Indian teak timber and mahogany logs had yet to arrive, and this had to be loaded. The mahogany logs were ordered by Nicholas. Typical of the man's forward thinking, mused Strudwich and remembered the small trees around the river mouth which were not robust enough for what Nicholas and his men needed overall. In addition, some of the teak shipment was also for Nicholas.

The bulk of the teak was for a fledgling shipwright currently in Fremantle, a Thomas Moray, who was shortly to take up residence in Geraldine. The man was a very good carpenter and not without ship careening experience.

Julia, who was enjoying the young ladies company immensely, insisted Victoria stay the night and immediately sent a message back to Strudwich.

Peter Strudwich came to fetch Victoria the next morning informing her that they would sail for Australia at 12 noon. Victoria bade her new friend goodbye and they clattered away in a little donkey drawn cart to the landing.

Right on time they were towed away from the landing by four large boats, four oarsmen a side, until they reached the westernmost tip of the island beneath the fort, sails cracking and the sailors and bosun shouting. The ship picked up speed and headed down the coast before she would turn south-east to Australia.

Excitement charging through her veins, Victoria stood at the bow dreaming of Nicholas.

Chapter 40

Meeting the Stokes

$\mathcal{J}$ ack and Nicholas finished their sampling, and reducing the samples to a manageable size, they commenced packing up the site and getting things in order. They formed up three squares of stone about six feet across on the higher slopes of the hillock and built the sides up to about one foot in height to keep the equipment above any minor flooding.

On top of each square they laid the remainder of the gimlet staves side by side to form a rough platform and stacked the material and stock that they were to leave behind on top of each square.

They covered each of these with some bushes and dead trees so as to look as natural as possible from a distance. They stood back to study their handiwork, walking back and forth and adjusting the cover, then Nicholas rode out some three hundred yards to see if they were blending in with the other shrubbery. Satisfied, he rode back. Gnarlu and Yindu suddenly appeared, as if they had sensed their departure was imminent. The two men examined what had been done and removed some of the brush, replacing it with their own choice. Nicholas had to admit they were better at disguising the platforms than he or Jack. Nicholas and Jack had built these platforms on the north side of the small hill so as to hopefully shield them from the casual observer who may pass by on the opposite side of the flat. Not that they believed anyone was likely to venture so far off the nearest track which was at least eight miles south of the claim, and barely visible in any case. But better to be cautious, Nicholas reasoned. The last thing they needed was someone poking around the excavations and perhaps specking up some gold and thereby starting a gold rush in the area. That would come soon enough, he reasoned, once he had staked his claim and assayed the samples in Geraldine or Greenough.

Nicholas was understandably nervous about leaving the site unattended, but then he reasoned that they had seen no one at all in the time they had been there.

Nonetheless, the four of them swept away all tracks as they retreated in the direction they had originally had come to the flat. This took them a day and a half, even though it had rained a couple of times with quite heavy afternoon thunderstorms, and most signs of their original deviation to the hillock had been washed away by now. Nevertheless, they erred on the side of caution.

They headed off in a west south-west direction and meandered as they went, swinging east for quite a few miles then coming back southwest, Nicholas wanting to give the impression that they had come from a more easterly direction rather than from the north.

By midday it was so hot and dry it took their breath away, and the sun bore down with an intensity that was akin to hammer blows on the skull.

So, it was that they approached the track running from Bethany and Robert Stokes' homestead to Mullewa, and exhausted, began to look for a place to camp.

They camped that night at the foot of a huge granite boulder about 200m wide and at least double that in length. Gnarlu and Yindu led them to the top of the boulder and there, slightly off to one side, Yindu pointed to the flat rock surface. Following the pair, they walked until they came to a fold in the rock before coming upon a pile of flat granite slabs stacked overlapping each other. The two Aboriginal men carefully removed some of the slabs until, to Jack and Nicholas's amazement, exposed a deep dark pool of water, 'A *gnamma* hole!' exclaimed Nicholas recalling the name

Gnarlu had taught him. After filling a couple of small buckets of water for the night and eating some roasted Pigeon and a small goanna Yindu had killed with his nulla nulla throwing stick, they fed and watered the horses and then too tired to talk, all collapsed into sleep.

The next morning, they set off again while it was still quite dark, but they could however, see faint traces of light in the east. Eventually, they swung onto a track which ran roughly east west and turned to the west.

After about 12 miles, Gnarlu trotted up alongside Nicholas and, pointing down the track, said "Nungerdie" throwing his hands out wide and up. 'Bigga 'ooman,' he continued, pointing down the track. 'Gooda!' he exclaimed.

Nicholas stared at him, confused and having no idea what the man was talking about – superstition, danger? But Gnarlu was grinning, so obviously it was unlikely that there was any threat in what he was trying to say.

'Come,' Gnarlu said dropping two fingers and trotted ahead.

I have no idea what that was all about, thought Nicholas as they nudged the horses forward.

Bethany and Bob Stokes were going about their daily chores when Bob, splitting gimlet at the side of the house, was startled by the magical appearance of Gnarlu, standing almost directly in front of him on one leg, the other propped against his knee and supported by his clutch of long hunting spears. A huge grin of white teeth sparkled on his face.

'Jaysus!' Bob cried as he jumped, his heart pounding. 'I wish ye would'na sneak up on me like that ye bladdy scoundrels,' he exclaimed as he saw Yindu in a similar pose about fifteen feet behind Gnarlu. He too was laughing and giggling. Grinning back at Gnarlu and Yindu they shook hands. They always took great delight in sneaking up on Stokes, and they never once failed to frighten him. It had become a game to them both over time.

'Bet'ny!' he yelled, 'we got us visitors!'

Bethany came out of her kitchen, hair tied back and wearing an apron covered in flour and wiping her brow with a large red and white checked kerchief.

She had just baked a dozen kangaroo pies, six were cooling and she had just placed the remainder into her oven, an early model American Montgomery Ward wood fired stove. It had three ring-tops with removable inserts and a good sized oven. It was her pride and joy, even though it radiated a fearsome heat into her kitchen as most of it was inside the kitchen and the wall behind it was only beaten iron plate.

Her Bobby had discovered it by the side of the road on one of his rare trips to what was originally called Geraldine, though he had heard that the Government had renamed it Geraldton. The stove lay with a variety of other goods, timber, some flue stacks and the like.

He had spent the day using the timber and some ingenuity and managed to get it onto his flatback. He continued onto Geraldine and had taken it to the army barracks in Geraldine where, at that time, the police constables were housed, to ask if it had fallen off someone's dray.

The copper informed him that they knew of it, but it had proved far too difficult to move, and was amazed he had managed to get it onto the flatback by himself.

The constable was a decent sort of fellow and after some thought said, 'That bloody great thing has laid on its back out there for at least four months Mr Stokes, since the wagon it was on lost a wheel. Tell you what, you donate a pound to the local school dat's gonna be built, I mean when it eventually gets built, and ye can 'ave it 'an all of the other stuff, 'ow about it?'

Bob couldn't believe his luck and told the copper that whenever they passed by his place he would be sure to get Bethany to cook a meal for them.

'Ye mean ye will ask her politely from a safe distance,' chuckled the constable. Bethany's fearsome reputation as someone you didn't mess with was widespread, and the constable had met her once before doing his duties.

Gnarlu was greeted by a great bellow of mock indignation. 'Ow is it that we don't see you for months yet every time I bake kangaroo pies ye turn up outa nowhere?' Bethany asked.

Gnarlu's grin again split his face, his white teeth emphasising his delight at seeing her. He had already smelt the pies cooking at least a mile back. Bethany bustled off to the kitchen and returned with pies for the warriors.

Gnarlu, pointing back up the road, said, 'Gooda man coming, 'Uin, and bigger man, Jack, come soon.'

Even though Bob and Bethany understood a little of the broken English, they could only guess at what he was saying, but following his pointing arm, they saw through the shimmering mirage some movement on the trail.

Bob immediately grabbed his shotgun which was leaning on the wall. 'Looks like two horses,' Bob muttered. 'Maybe three.' Bethany added. They waited as the figures drew closer.

'No, definitely two hor...' Bob didn't finish as he suddenly saw that there was one man on a horse leading another and a huge man walking beside the mounted horse!

Bethany, being a good foot and a bit higher than her husband, suddenly cried, 'Jesus Christ! Will ye look at the size of that Black!'

A more unusual sight they had never seen – Nicholas sitting tall and easy as he always rode, his African bush hat pulled down low on his brow and cradling his rifle across his thighs. They could see he would be tall, and appeared to be lean and fit.

Striding alongside, easily matching the horses' stride was Jack. Impressive enough just from his size, the big Zulu was barefoot and had stripped down to a pair of frayed cut-down seaman's trousers which were held up by a broad black leather belt Nicholas had given him. His skin shone like polished ebony and the great slabs of muscle across his chest and stomach rippled in unison as he strode beside Nicholas.

A more magnificent specimen of man both Bethany and Robert had never seen, and a giant of a man by all reckoning.

Sensing no threat, Nicholas called out in greeting, 'Good morning to you Madam and Sir,' as he easily slipped his leg over and dismounted.

'May I present Jack, my assistant, and myself, Nicholas Yuin,' he greeted, sweeping his hat from his head and extending his hand to Robert.

Bethany, finally tearing her gaze away from Jack, swung her attention to this well-spoken gentleman and began her appraisal.

She got only as far as Nicholas's eyes, and for the first time ever Bob was astounded to note that Bethany's usual gruff vitriol and suspicion was replaced by a stammer as she locked gaze with this Yuin, who without any waiver, held her gaze. Clearly flustered, she murmured, 'Uh, uh, pleased to meet you sir,' and gave a slight curtsey. Bob stared in disbelief at the little pantomime.

Snorting, he proffered his hand, first to the huge man standing beside Yuin, as he was closest, noting that all of his hand and wrist almost disappeared in the man's firm but controlled grip. Then he turned to Yuin, and as they clasped hands he looked up and discovered some explanation for his wife's odd behaviour.

It was the eyes, burning bright and of a deep amber – quite unnerving, he noted, but sensed something genuine about the man. As they shook hands, a lifetime of friendship began for the four.

After calling in vain for Gnarlu and Yindu, for they had taken the kangaroo pies Bethany had given them and as usual had vanished, Robert and Bethany Stokes showed Jack and Nicholas around the little homestead.

Nicholas was impressed at some of the ingenious little inventions that Bob had come up with to make life a bit easier for his wife and family. For example, an irrigation system, where no water was wasted, enabling the little vegetable garden to grow. It was a system of charcoal filters and containers all gravity fed.

'Where do you get your water from Bob,' queried Nicholas, noting only two 50-gallon galvanised and riveted tanks to the side of the house.

'I carts it from the soak about 10 mile west of 'ere, said Robert pointing at the twin cart tracks heading away from the tanks and adding, 'Every two days usually. But's gettin' dry now, soon I'll probably 'ave ta drive ta Mullewa for it,' he said sadly. 'Got 'nother two tanks out back though.'

They retired to the little verandah and long table by the kitchen, but not before Bethany had shown them her pride and joy, her oven.

Two children suddenly appeared in the yard accompanied by a young Aboriginal boy of about thirteen and a scrawny little girl of about four, her hair, brown and sticking out in all directions. The oldest of the white children was a girl of about eight years old, with bright red hair like her mother's and a cheeky face. The lad, about four and skinny, looked just like his Pa.

'This is Sandra and young Robert,' Bethany said. 'Say hello to our guests and watch your manners you two. Now scoot!' She waved the other children off. 'Dey's from a camp over dere,' said Robert waving his hand south of the house. 'Dere's about twenty of 'em dere, but dey's good folk we reckon.'

'Ow do you do sirs,' Sandra curtsied, a twinkle in her eye. The little boy was unable to take his eyes off Jack and said, 'Youse be a giant sir!' Standing up straight he looked up at Jack's face with wonderment written all over his face.

'Robert! Mind your tongue!' Bethany chided. 'Go and wash you pair, an' I mean all over, an' ye better not use any more than that 'alf a bucket of water out there.' The two scampered.

'We's got another 'in, Adam, 'e's older,' said Robert. 'We's adopted 'im some time back. 'E's a good boy, but right now e's down by the creek digging up some gravel stone,'

In no time it seemed, Bethany had amassed more of her kangaroo pies and produced some ears of corn that Bob had managed to grow, albeit pretty scrawny. Nevertheless, the corn was appreciated by Nicholas and big Jack after being away prospecting for so long. Jack took an immediate liking to the kangaroo pies and polished off at least four, Nicholas noted. That said, they were delicious.

The Stokes observed that Jack, despite his intimidating size, seemed a likeable fellow, and once he began to relax, the Stokes got over their awe at his size and warmed to him. Meanwhile, Nicholas kept prompting Jack to tell a little of his Zulu heritage and his people.

Bethany fussed about the table like some teenager Bob noticed – she was even pleasant to *him*! not once trying to dominate as she usually would do or ordering him about. It was, 'Me Bobby this and me Bobby that.' She hardly drew breath about how he had slaved, building their home from nothing to this. Maybe this Nicholas Yuin and his giant friend should come and visit more regularly, he mused wryly.

Gnarlu appeared at the door along with another black they had not seen before who was standing some ten feet back. Gnarlu beckoned to Robert to come outside. After a few minutes Bobby came back in and said to Bethany, 'Ye favourite person has seemingly recovered, or at least in part, and 'e's back in Geraldine on light duties. Now dere's a new copper in charge at Geraldine, Drummond oi think 'e said, or sumthin' loik thet. The people are worried.' he added waving his hand toward where Gnarlu and his friend had been standing. 'And dey say McGuinness, 'e is not the same,' he continued, tapping his head with one finger. 'Keeps on about Kadaitcha men, monsters, wrong'uns and visiting us.'

Jack rumbled "What be dis 'Kadaicha person?' Robert replied, 'E's a tribal disciplinarian or excecutioner, de tribal elders summon 'im and dey sometimes make a curse wit bones at a ceromony, den people of'in die. 'De Kadaicha man 'e does it, sometimes dey call i'm the 'Feather foot, as 'e wears shoes made outa 'umin 'air and feathers, so 'e leaves no trace'.

Bethany stared at him, her face growing dark, and said, 'N'eber mind dat Robert, the copper, McGuinness, ain't at the Mullewa camp?' He shook his head. 'Dey's temp'ry closed the police camp dere,' he replied.

Her demeanour changed and all grace vanished from her face as she snarled, 'That no good cruel and crooked piece of shite need not show 'is face around here agi'n. I was hopin' he would stay in that mental place in Fremantle forever, damn!'

The Stokes then told Nicholas and Jack all about McGuinness and how he treated the blacks with such cruelty, and how he was completely dishonest and scheming. They told the story of how he spent an evening with them about eight months ago, albeit self-invited, and left after filching a bottle of rum and apparently fell off his horse and lay for days concussed by the side of the track. His main mount making its way back to the Mullewa camp by itself, an' just turned up standing outside the gimlet and whitewashed hessian camp the copper called his 'station'. A day later the local Stock and Station delivery man apparently found McGuinness's packhorse by the road, and then further on found McGuinness, near death from dehydration on the track.

Apparently, the Stock and Station man loaded McGuinness onto his wagon and returned to Mullewa camp where McGuinness recovered somewhat, albeit babbling incoherently. When he was deemed well enough, he was transported eventually to the Mercy Hospital wing for the insane in Fremantle. No one thought he would ever return.

'Humph, should have shot the bloody 'orse and thet stock'n station fella for aidin' and abettin' an arsehole,' fumed Bethany.

They all laughed at her venomous quip, and she relaxed once more and started laughing.

Through all of this, Nicholas slid a look across at Jack's face and was relieved to see he was poker faced.

Again, he reminded himself he would have to be very careful should this copper and he ever cross paths again. One thing was for sure, he would act first should the need ever arise.

It was decided that it would be a folly to attempt to continue their journey back to the river that afternoon, and besides Nicholas was enjoying the Stokes's hospitality. They would leave at first light the next day.

Bob had produced a bottle of the Brady's rum after dinner. Jack refused and Nicholas explained that he only drank maize beer and then only on a very special occasion back in Africa.

Nicholas, however, did join Bob in a glass, and at the first mouthful exclaimed, 'Jeeesus Bloody Christ!' his eyes watering and spluttering as the liquor burnt first his mouth and then all of the way to his gullet. 'What in God's name is that made of!'

'I dunno,' Robert admitted. "'Tis made in Fremantle or Mullewa or somewhere,' he chuckled.

'Bet'ny cleans 'er copper ladles and pans with it and dey come up like new, maybe a plumber makes it outa that camel's piss, sal ammoniac 'n acid!' he exclaimed laughing. ''Tis true! She *does* use it fa' cleaning!' laughing even louder when he saw the bemused look on Nicholas's face.

'Oi been meanin' ta ask, beggin' ye pardon Nicholas, 'tis none o' me business, but 'ow is it that you and your men come ta be at the river, Oi mean why an' all?'

Nicholas did not reply immediately, mainly because he was struggling against the severe heartburn Robert's rum had given him. Then, with his hand rubbing his chest, he took a deep breath and said, 'Well, when I was in Fremantle, I went to the governor's office and was granted a concession, two actually, of sixty-six thousand acres each, or one hundred and thirty two thousand acres running north and south for about forty miles inland over the river.

'We are going to run cattle and the name of the station is Yuin Scott Station.'

Robert whistled. 'That's a big parcel of land ta handle Nicholas. 'Ow many head are ye planning on runnin?' Nicholas took a small pull of the rum, and coughing, he managed to gasp out, 'Around a hundred and fifty to start, then we will see about increasing the herd,'. Robert could only manage to shake his head, which was getting heavier by the minute.

Nicholas struggled through the remainder of the glass, and refusing any more, excused himself and headed for his swag, the stench of the rot-gut rum pungent on his breath and still burning like hot coals in his gut. His head was spinning. 'Jesus!' he said to himself, 'I can't even feel my tongue. That stuff is a deadly brew, and I will have to be really desperate before I ever touch another drop of that!'

They were awakened pre-dawn by the clatter of pots and pans emanating from Bethany's kitchen as she busied herself baking and preparing their early breakfast.

She had been up since 2am, baking bread and preparing food for their journey. So, it was that they breakfasted on fresh eggs and steaming slices of bread and lard washed down with hot mugs of black Indian tea even before the sun had appeared.

They took their leave with some sadness but glowing in the fact that they had formed a good friendship with these hard but generous couple.

Bethany handed Jack a parcel wrapped in calico cloth and the smell of fresh baked kangaroo pies wafted around Jack, who just stared at her for a minute in obvious appreciation.

Big Jack suddenly bent down on one knee before Bethany saying in Zulu, '*Bekumnandi ukuhlangana nawe hamba kahle bukekayo inkosi-kazi*,' then rose and held his fist to his great chest. Nicholas swore he saw moisture glistening in his eyes just before Jack turned to Robert and said '*Hamba Kahle*, umm, Englis is, go well Inkosi fren!' He beamed and they shook hands.

Bethany, touched by Jack's obvious affection, turned to Nicholas in query and asked, 'Nicholas, what'se he say now?' Slightly embarrassed, Nichols replied, 'Jack is Zulu royalty Bethany, or his family is very high in their kingdom, and the Zulu people of high rank normally do not show much emotion to anyone let alone go down on one knee, especially to a woman, and even then it would only be in private.

'You have been honoured, because what he said was, "It is good to have met you, farewell beautiful lady". Bethany blushed to the roots and placing her hand over her mouth said softly, 'Oh my!' She looked at Nicholas and back to Jack and said, 'Thet there big fella loves you, ye know, reckon 'e would do anythin' for ya.' It was Nicholas's turn to colour, she catching him off-guard with the comment.

Nicholas hugged Bethany and shook hands vigorously with Robert before swinging up into his saddle. 'Wait, I almost forgot,' cried Bethany and she ran back to her kitchen and returning, passed up another calico parcel. 'Some loaves of bread and biscuits for ye journey Nicholas.'

'Thank you both for your hospitality, we will see you on our return in about three months.' They headed off, anxious to get back to the river camp and see Whip and organise their trip to Geraldine.

Chapter 41

Young Adam

Nicholas was reflecting on their meeting the Stokes family, when he thought of the young lad Adam, and how warm and open-hearted the Stokes were. Robert had explained how it was the lad had become family.

Robert told Nicholas, that once when he had gone into the Mullewa Camp, about 50 miles east-south-east from the homestead and which consisted of about 30 tents and two or three very rough shanties, one of which was a grog shop, he had intended to pick up and buy stores which had been brought up by wagon from Fremantle. Unfortunately, he fell afoul of a couple of Irish rogues who lured him away with the promise of grog and some special deal at the back of the rough and ready meeting place. This consisted of a series of gimlet poles and a roof of brush, but attached to the rear was a hessian and lime-washed walled room, with a door and one window and an iron roof. It was about as good as the camp had in the way of buildings, apart from the questionably legal grog shop.

Spiking up the alcohol level in his drinks, they got him to sign away his and Bethany's holding, which was not an insubstantial amount of acreage, and then beat him within an inch of his life whilst they were about it.

Unfortunately for them, they stayed with their victim and continued to hit the grog in celebration.

When he didn't return by the next morning, Bethany was getting really worried. She waited another hour, being unable to stand idle any longer, and went to the Blacks' camp where her two children were playing. She was assured they would be looked after until she returned.

She then saddled up their draught horse, a great black and white stallion they called Brutus – possibly the only horse that could carry her – and headed off to town to find her husband.

She rode all day and half the night and got to town that night at eleven o'clock. She apparently found Robert's horse and flatbed still tethered up outside the grog shop, the load of stores still stacked on the tray. No way would Robert have left the stores like that. Foul play was afoot and she was going to find out what had happened.

Pulling a stout nulla nulla from her saddlebag she went straight to the little tavern.

Bethany didn't know what to expect, of course, but she did know this was not like her Bobby to just decide not to come home, not like him at all.

Ducking down through the door, and without any hesitation, she walked straight up to the barman and owner and said evenly to him, 'Where's me Bobby at!' The unfortunate man, who knew the Stokes quite well, as did most folks hereabouts, took a bit too long to answer. Whacking the nulla nulla on the bar top with an almighty crack she shot her left hand out and dragged the poor man across the bartop. 'Where is 'e!' she snarled in his face, not a half inch in front of her own. He stammered that he hadn't seen him for a good day and didn't know where he was, adding that he was with two shady looking Irishmen when he last saw him leaving the grog shop.

Bethany was about to crack the fellow on the skull, when a young lad standing behind her piped up and said, 'Oi' knows where dey is M…Missus.'

Apparently, the lad had been running the grog for the two rogues, who had also given him a good too many cuffs behind the ear for his trouble, and they hadn't paid him either.

Bethany let the barman go and he fell backwards behind the bar almost sobbing with relief. Swinging around, she looked down at the skinny lad, who quailed at the huge woman standing over him.

Bending down and in a soft and kindly tone Bethany apparently had said to the lad fishing a coin out of her vest, 'Well, now me lovey, why don't ye jest show me and I'll give ye' this nice shiny shillin'!

'What's a young'n like youse doing 'angin' about the grog shop anyways boy, an' where are ye parents?'

She looked him up and down. The boy was filthy and his clothes rags that hung on his skinny little frame.

'Oi's an orphan ma'am, I ain't got no none.'

'Ow old are ye boy?' Bethany asked.

'I be six years, I tink ma'am,' he stuttered.

'Huumph! It just t'aint right boy, 'angin' about there, lot'sa bad fellas come there, evil buggers ye know,' Bethany said.

'Yas'm,' said the poor lad as he stared up at this huge woman in awe.

The lad led her to the back of the hall, and on the way told her of Bob's beating, adding that he didn't look too good now. They had crouched at the side of the lean-to off the back of the hall and she could hear them laughing and talking. They waited.

As soon as the door began to open Bethany had moved like greased lightning and was on the rogue before he even knew what hit him. The lad saw a full arm swing at the man's face with the nulla nulla, dropping him like a stone. Then she burst straight into the room, and a great ruckus ensued. Even though the lad dare not enter the room, he knew who was on the receiving end of it and could hear the other Irishman screaming. By the time people had come to see what the trouble was all about, all they found was the first rogue still laid out cold outside the door and the other inside whimpering like a baby, a bloodied gob with no front teeth, a broken nose and one eye smashed. It looked like he might have had an arm broken as well.

From that time on no one messed with Bethany, and the young lad wasn't ever seen around there anymore either.

Bethany drove the cart as Robert lay in the tray, propped up as comfortably as Bethany could make him. The young lad sat astride the great draught horse, looking for all the world like a pimple on a rock.

'What's ye name lad,' Bethany called out to the boy.

"Tis Adam ma'am,' he called out twisting toward her. She pondered this for a while, then, 'Adam what, what's ye surname boy?'

He looked down, and mumbled, 'I don' really know ma'am, never had one I guess.'

'Well,' she said brightly, 'we'll 'ave ta see about one for ye, orright!'

'Yas'm.' he said quietly turning back.

A year later, the lad was still at the Stokes's property, and Robert and Bethany took the boy in and gave him a home, and for the first time in the lad's life he dared to think he was wanted. Moreover, he now had a surname. 'Stokes be ye surname now me boy,' said Robert one afternoon as they sat down after their chores. 'An' as soon as Oi be gittin' ta Geraldine, Oi'll be seein' the magistrate about an adoption. Ye be happy with that?'

Adam choked, unable to speak and the tears fell down his freckled cheeks. He could not answer, but Robert's heart nigh on broke for the boy, and he reached out and pulled the boy to his chest and held him until the lad stopped shuddering and settled.

Bethany, watching from the kitchen, wiped the tears from her own eyes as her Bobby and young Adam got up, and hand in hand walked over to the stockyard. 'Good, good,' was all she could manage, catching her breath.

Nicholas was to hear other stories of the couples' generosity and how they had often turned up when someone was in need of comfort or had trouble, often travelling long distances to help those in need, even if they didn't know the people.

Good people, Nicholas mused, and he suddenly hit on an idea to give some reward for this dedication to helping others, which could work to his own advantage as well.

Nicholas thought, I will give this some planning later, opportunity has more value than a gift.

Chapter 42

Back Home Again

On average, the group covered about thirty-eight to forty miles per day, forty on a good day.

The terrain was the biggest factor and one had to consider the heat and available water for the horses.

Nicholas figured the camp to be about 125 miles from the Stokes's house which he gleaned from conversations with Robert Stokes and his excursions to Geraldton.

Considering that they had two horses, Nicholas reckoned it would take two or even three days to get back to the river mouth and what they now called home.

As the miles ticked by, Nicholas had time to reflect about the friend-ship gained. The Stokes sure did things tough, but they were also smart, he reflected. By befriending the Aboriginal people and treating them with respect, they gained eyes throughout the region, learnt bush craft and how to read the weather, all of which was a huge advantage in this tough land. Bethany, in particular, had taken it upon herself to become the Aboriginal peoples' champion, and many a person who stepped outside her code of ethics and sense of fair play had found out to their cost that she could be a formidable opponent, physically and mentally.

They topped the small rise to the north of the homestead late on the third day and stopped to scan the area surrounding the yards. They had made good time but were very tired. Nicholas drew out his telescope and glassed the yards and house and was shocked to see that the house was now much bigger. A sizeable stone chimney now protruded above the gabled roof, and a verandah about ten feet wide he reckoned, swept right around all sides. There was a long, low stone building where the rough timber shelter used to be at the holding yard. 'Wilber, my friend, you have been very busy,' Nicholas mused. He could not, however, see any sign of the man. He turned to comment to the others, but Gnarlu and Yindu had, as usual, done their vanishing trick without them even noticing. Jack stood staring down at the yards and he turned saying 'Kubi!' pointing toward the yard with a huge grin. Nicholas swung the glass and sure enough there stood the huge beast, he looked even bigger, thought Nicholas.

They started down toward the homestead and got about halfway down, entering the last dip in terrain about 400 yards from the corral, when Jack, in the lead, suddenly held out his hand indicating stop, and he cocked his head and slowly turned back, gazing behind the horses. Sensing something was not right, Nicholas was about to reach for his rifle. The big Zulu was already crouching to fling himself face down in the spiky grass when they heard an ominous click.

'Ye both be getting slack, Oi could'a blown youse arses orf easy loik! An' it be about fookin' time ye came home an' all!'

They whirled around to see Whip arising from the grass off to the left behind them with his rifle half-cocked.

With a great bellowing whoop, Big jack covered the twenty foot before Whip could even react and was on him in a flash, lifting him into the air as if he weighed nothing, then whirled around in a circle, Whip's legs flyng out about horizontal with his chest.

'Let me down ye fookin' great galoot!' he yelled as he lost his grip on his rifle. It spun away into the grass, he being unable to hold onto it due to the speed which he was being spun around. 'Let me *down*, fook ya!' he screamed.

Nicholas was doubled over laughing, and as he lifted his head he saw Gnarlu and Yindu both sitting cross-legged not thirty feet away, both laughing hard.

Jack suddenly let Whip down and they both began to join in the laughter. Whip massaging his ribs and arms where the big fellow had grabbed him. 'Fookin' idjit,' he complained.

The comradeship bubbling over, they all headed down to the homestead. It was good to be home!

Jack disappeared out to the corral as soon as they got to the house, heading straight for the bull pen.

'Dis'l be interestin', the bull is as testy as a cut snake an 'e won't let anyone near 'im,' said Whip, rubbing his hands together and they hurried after Jack.

Jack went straight up to the pen and vaulted over the fence, walking straight up to the huge animal.

'But Jesus 'e has balls!' said Whip in admiration as they all watched astounded as Jack wrapped his massive arms around the great bull's neck and nuzzled his ear. Kubi let out a huge bellow and Jack grasped his nose ring and walked back to them all watching in amazement as the bull just walked along behind him as docile and meek as a newborn lamb.

'Oi don't fookin' believe dis!' muttered whip. 'Dat bloody mean bad-tempered bastard 'as chased me outta there every day since youse left.'

'You take good care of my Kubi my fren, Jack thanks you veeery much!' Jack grinned down at them. 'Now he is the big prince!' he said eyeing the bull's massive balls.

'Well ye 'ave a big surprise comin', but let's get every thin' unloaded an' ye's can tell all about what 'appened out dere tonight over supper,' Whip declared.

Whip had baked a good sized fish he had caught, and complimented it with a couple of good sized roasted ears of corn he had grown and some boiled potatoes he had also grown.

They talked about the journey and by ten o'clock that evening had to end the story, exhaustion after their push to return catching up with them.

Whip had built two rooms inside the main walls, one small and a larger one, all of stone and limestone, and had walled off a long room onto the verandah facing the cattle pen and barn shed. This room he had allotted to Jack and had an extra long palaise, or platform bed, on a wooden frame to cater for Jack's massive frame. He had even managed to make an extra high door, however Jack still had to dip his head to get through.

It wouldn't have mattered where they slept in truth but they were grateful nonetheless and fell asleep immediately.

The next morning, before the early morning damp had even dried, Whip and Nicholas were woken by Jack's bellow of joy as he came into the yard in front of the barn. 'Oh ho!' he was shouting and Whip and Nicholas scrambled out to see what the commotion was all about.

There stood Jack cradling a new brown calf about four months' old in his arms. The poor little calf was bellowing for his mother and struggling to get out of Jack's embrace but to no avail.

'Are now, so ye've discovered ye surprise 'av ye?' laughed Whip. 'Kubi did well 'e did. An dat's not all big fella, 'e's done it agin, the other cow is big in belly also!'

Jack put the calf down and it bolted back to its mother, bellowing and eyes bulging, its little back legs kicking out in protest.

Jack jabbed his thumb at his chest, and beaming said, 'Ohhh, we be very rich now, Kubi has used his balls an' he da papa! He make many babies now you see!'

'Come on then we best have breakfast then,' said Whip laughing at his friend's gleeful observation, and went to the kitchen to prepare some tucker.

Nicholas sat down at the table after breakfast and began to add to the already extensive list of material and some machinery they would need to fit out the mine. There was also quite a large amount they needed for the homestead now.

As he pondered the problem of keeping the transport of mining equipment low key, he came upon a possible answer. If he sought their permission, perhaps Robert and Bethany may let him send two wagons to them, thus breaking up the train of freight, and he had just the disguise he needed for the large wagons.

Into the bargain he could carry out his gesture to the Stokes for their generosity to all as well.

The more he thought about it, the more he thought it a good idea. The budget would take a good hammering, but he had no doubt it would be worth it.

As he wrote, he began to think about how to move the material out of the port without arousing too much suspicion of a strike.

For a start they would need at least four large wagons, and given the weight they would carry, they would need substantial teams to pull them, probably oxen. How to hide the mining gear was the problem, if indeed it was to be found at the port.

Maybe if they stacked the gear inside the timber, he mused, but then he was not expecting his timber shipment he had asked Strudwich to bring to have arrived as yet.

He ruled out having the *Collette* bring the gear to the river mouth as getting it there was no problem but unloading it into small boats rather than a decent sized barge from the ship was. At any rate he thought negotiating the river mouth would be very risky indeed, especially with a towed barge given the current that had already wrecked havoc with the long boats.

Nicholas was in deep thought when a small soft whimpering sound came to his ears. He got up and stalked about the house trying to identify where the sound was coming from. Sounds like a small child, he thought. Looking out of the window, he saw Whip and Jack working on something, but they were a good hundred yards away. He went outside and walked around the rear of the building and stood by the stack of timber piled up against the back wall. The soft whimper seemed a little louder here. Then he saw a small brown foot sticking out from behind the pile of wood near the tall cupboard which stood next to the door.

Getting down on his knees, he peered into the shadow to discover Nimit'je with her arms wrapped around her skinny little knees and crying softly.

'Hey, come on little one, what is the matter now?' he said gently reaching out with both hands.

She immediately came to him and he lifted her up and carried her inside, she, still crying.

Nicholas sat her down at the table and drew another chair up beside her. He examined her for any signs of violence or injury but could see none. 'What on earth ails you little Nimmy, hmmm?' She looked up at him. She was shuddering as she tried to catch her breath, little sparkles of tears on her dark lashes, and then started to sob and talk at the same time. Such was her misery that Nicholas found a great lump forming in his chest. 'Wait, wait girl, let me get some help here,' he said. Nimit'je did not understanding a word of what he was saying.

He got up and poured a cup of black tea from the fire plate and loading up the mug with five or so sugars which he remembered she liked, he gave it to her.

Nicholas went outside and called Jack over. 'Will you go and see if you can find Gnarlu or Yindu please Jack. Our little friend Nimit'je is in there, she is very upset and I need to know what ails her.' Jack stuck his head in the door and saw Nimit'je look up at him with tears running down her face. 'She no hurt my fren?' he asked in query. Nicholas looked down at her and said, 'No, she seems all right I think.' Jack had learnt quite a bit of Nhanda, as had Whip, and he spoke to Nimit'je gently. But she just wailed louder and shook her sandy hair.

'Okay!' Jack rumbled and ran off toward the last place he had seen the family.

Nicholas went back to the poor little girl and put his arm around her as she sipped her sweet tea.

After about fifteen minutes, she laid her head on his chest and still shuddering, went to sleep.

A good hour and a half passed before he heard someone coming across the yard. Nimit'je was still sleeping softly when Gnarlu and Yindu both appeared at the door with Jack.

Nimit'je suddenly woke up and seeing her brothers immediately started to wail.

'Jack, take the girl out to the yards with you and send in Whip and see if you can stop her misery a bit until I find out what is the matter. Here, and give her one of these,' he said getting up and opening up a tin. He drew out one of Bethany's biscuits and handed it to him.

Whip came and sat down. In their absence, Whip had become a lot more fluent at the Aboriginal language, or at least able to decipher what was important.

Nicholas stared at the two and said sharply, 'What is the matter with her? Can you ask please?' They both looked at each other as Whip started to translate and tried his best to explain, although somewhat reluctantly.

It came to Nicholas after some time, and with some respectful prompting, discovered it was a tribal matter and he should not interfere, it was tribal law.

Bloody hell, thought Nicholas, this was like trying to draw teeth! Fearing the worst, he asked, 'Whip, what tribal law are they talking about, are we even allowed to know?' It took another fifteen minutes before they finally worked out the answer.

It was about a gift of bethrothal. The tribal elders and her father would decide who was to be betrothed, and in the case of a girl, it was usually the most prized and precious to the tribe based on bloodlines and attractiveness who was chosen. Once the decision was made, as in this case, it was final.

Although she knew of the betrothal she only recently was given to understand the real reasons for it. Nimit'je quite obviously was not happy about it, but there was little they could do to help her. To try to intervene would in all likelihood be viewed as gross interference and cause a lot of trouble and most likely alienate them from the people.

'Jesus wept!' cried Nicholas, 'she is only about thirteen, if that even!'

That was, however, the only information they could extract from her brothers. They would speak no more about it. Nicholas and Whip could sense that they were approaching territory that was simply out of bounds.

Both Nicholas and Jack were familiar with arranged marriages and betrothals in cultures throughout Africa, and in Nicholas's case, other countries as well. Often, as Nicholas suspected was the case here, it was an arrangement to keep bloodlines and a way of avoiding wars between tribes and clans. Better this than dozens if not hundreds dying in war and battles. Just the same, their hearts went out to the bright young girl whom they had come to know, and all of them gave her a lot of affection. So, this betrothal that Nimit'je did not want did not sit well with any of the three.

Gnarlu and Yindu left with Nimit'je, she looking back at them with a forlorn look that nigh on broke their hearts, powerless as they were.

Nicholas made up his mind. He would leave alone for the buying trip in the next few days, first travelling back to the Stokes's homestead, and trusting his instincts, put his proposal to them. Depending on their decision, he would then head back to the homestead. From there he would head straight to Geraldton and organise the equipment and shipping.

Nicholas told Jack and Whip of his intention that night and that he would prepare for the journey the very next day. Fielding the questions as they came, eventually they all knew what was expected.

'What about the young lassie?' Whip suddenly asked, fixing Nicholas with an unblinking if not fierce stare. Nicholas paused before he replied evenly and in a tone that made what he said very clear. 'You are not to interfere in any way Whip, either of you! Not now, not ever! Is that understood?' he said flicking his gaze between the two.

"Tain't right, she's only a lil' girl fa' Christ's sake!' fumed Whip.

'Listen hard. We interfere here, we run the risk of...' here he held out his hand counting off on each finger, 'number one, undoing all of the good work we have done to befriend these people.' He paused. 'Two, we would shame Mumardie and his family, they possibly would face spearing, death or banishment including Gnarlu and Yindu."

Wagging his finger, he said with some force, 'Three, what would you do with the girl, she would be an outcast at the very least but more likely her own people, or perhaps the betrothed's tribe, might hunt her down and kill her, you too most likely. Do you want that? We are the interlopers here and we know nothing about these people's customs and tribal law.'

There was a palpable silence as this was digested.

'Orright,' said Whip shaking his head. 'Oi sees what you say, better she does what her people want, that way at least the little'un stays alive.'

'What about you Jack?' Nicholas asked. Jack looked at him. 'Yaas my fren, Jack understan' an' sees what you say is true, in Africa the same in many places,' Jack replied nodding his great shiny head.

'Good, let that be an end to it then!' Nicholas concluded. 'One more thing Whip, I take it the Collette has not returned?' Whip frowned and said 'No Nicholas she has not, 'tis a bit strange loik in'it?

'Hmmm, maybe, but a lot could have changed I guess, I'm not too concerned, she wasn't due for a little while yet actually' he concluded.

Nicholas left for the Stokes's the day after. It was still quite dark, the sunrise a faint glow on the horizon.

Chapter 43

A Generous Opportunity

*H*e rode at a steady clip in the early morning cool, hoping to cover a good fifty mile on the first day.

Nicholas loved this time of the day, the cool air, damp and fresh, brushing his face as he cantered along. The bush was alive with birds, and kangaroos would stand and stare, and there was always a special feeling about the early morning.

Soon the sun cracked the horizon and the warmth steadily grew, and it all changed again as the bush started its preparation for the new day.

Nicholas especially enjoyed the fact that there were no natural predatory animals in Australia, at least not to man.

Nicholas kept the canter up until mid-morning before bringing Stitch down to a walk. He stopped and watered his horse from a small billabong near the upper reaches of the river. As soon as he stopped, the ever present little bush flies swarmed in on them, covering his back in their hundreds and crawling all over his face as they sought the moisture of his sweat. At first the flies had driven them all mad, but in time they came to accept that they could do little to stop them and ignored them.

As he started off again he picked up one of his trail markers and was pleased at his progress, they had managed to cover a lot of miles and as the heat of the day started to climb they steadied down to a walk.

He set camp late that evening, confident he had achieved what he set out to do that day. A couple of hours after, as he sat at his fire preparing his meal, Yindu walked into his camp without a sound and sat down at the fire opposite Nicholas. He seemed troubled and never said a word despite Nicholas trying to start a conversation and he refused an offer to eat. Nicholas figured it may have something to do with Nimit'je's pending betrothal, but he purposely never broached the subject.

Nicholas knew that Yindu and his little sister were very close, so wondered if there was trouble, why he was not with her, or at least nearby.

Sensing the subject would be closed, he purposely did not ask where Gnarlu was.

The next morning Yindu was gone and Nicholas picked up his spoor heading in the direction of the Stokes' homestead.

It was again very early as Nicholas started off again, Yindu joining him late afternoon. He again was somewhat sullen and the usual flashing white smile was absent.

They made camp under a bright moon and continued the next morning, arriving at the Stokes' homestead mid-morning.

Nicholas was looking forward to seeing the Stokes' reaction to his proposal.

Robert and Bethany were understandably surprised to see him return so soon, albeit welcoming.

Over tea, Nicholas immediately got down to business, explaining the reasons why he had to get things moving, he had much to do and would be asking a favour.

He explained that what he was about to tell them was to be kept in strict confidence, no exception he said.

They looked at each other and agreed. Nicholas instinctively knew they would honour his request.

He told them of his discovery and how he thought this to be a very profitable prospect, placing a good-sized piece of quartz with a healthy ribbon of gold running through it in front of them.

The collective gasp and bright eyes made him smile as they turned the specimen over and over.

'Beautiful, beautiful!' was all Robert could say. Nicholas purposely did not show the large nugget Jack had produced, the quartz being enough he reckoned. Nicholas had already made up his mind that he would keep the nugget in memory of that day underground and of the friendship between he and Jack.

His proposal was that Robert act as a front man for him. 'You will need to come to Geraldine with me tomorrow with your flat bed and assisting me with the purchases Robert' he said to the open-mouthed Robert, who slowly nodded his head. He explained that they would stay two weeks buying, then would mix the mine machinery with building materials, roofing, corrugated iron, timber, water tanks, tools, fixings etc. They would buy two more flat beds, as large as they could, and drays to pull them. One was to stay in Geraldine and the other two to be loaded with equipment. Robert and another driver were to drive Robert's wagon and one of the new wagons, fully loaded, back to the Stokes homestead, two or three days apart. This way the lead wagon would always know it had backup should there be a breakdown.

From then on, the relay could begin with Robert and an assistant driving to and from the homestead, and in this way they would always have fresh teams and keep inquisitive minds from what was the real intent.

Then came the sweetener. Nicholas's company would buy enough material to build a large fully covered shed, at least one hundred feet long, large stockyards and a dry room for perishables at the homestead to store equipment and stores. The shed and dry store were to be wholly owned by Robert and Bethany. In addition, Nicholas would buy up enough stock to enable the two to start up a stock and store agency which would be theirs. They should begin to stock a good variety of items and the essentials – medicines, flour, sugar, tea, coffee, tobacco, tinned food, spirits, rope, cloth, firearms and ammunition etc.

They were to always, as a priority, stock supplies for the mine or any expedition that might occur, this always to be kept as the property of Nicholas's pastoral company and include keeping enough as a backup for the homestead at the river mouth.

The arrangement was to continue for two years, by which time the Stokes should be able to stand in their own right financially. A clause was to be included, that any decision to change and alter, would be subject to discussion with Nicholas.

He also would arrange for tests to be done to see if there was water in the homestead's immediate area and surrounds, explaining that they would need a lot of water as backup during the summer for the mine. The spin-off was that Bethany and Robert would always have water if enough water was found in the immediate area. He would bring in a small rig to drill pilot holes.

If this produced favourable results, he would hire in drillers and larger rigs and place windmills and tanks.

Robert broke in at this point and said, 'I 'ave some experience in makin' cement tanks Nicholas. Gimme a couple a good hands and we can put in underground tanks out by the sheds, they's a lot more practical an' keeps the water cooler as well! We can make'em as big as ye want as well!' he concluded, his eyes bright with enthusiasm.

'Excellent Robert! But first we have to prove the water below.'

He explained that once word got out about his find, and it would, the area would be flooded with would-be prospectors seeking their fortune. They would need stores and rather than travel back to Geraldine or Mullewa, they would, no question, use the Stokes agency. They should be able to make a good thirty to forty per cent profit on all goods. Nicholas, as the financier, would require ten per cent of the profit, but would still buy all of his needs through the agency, except any heavy machinery.

There will be many opportunities to provide the locals, old and new with everything they needed, variety was the key to success he explained.

Whilst setting everything up, and from the moment he and Robert left for Geraldine, he would pay Robert a wage and until further notice.

'Phew!' he said finally, smiling and focused on the two.

'Well, what do you think, do we have a deal? Or do you need time to discuss this alone? he asked.

The silence was deafening as he looked at Robert and Bethany, both of them with mouths open, no doubt not believing what they had just heard.

Bethany was the first to speak, but all she could manage was, 'Oh Lordy, Lordy!' and shook her head in disbelief.

Robert stammered, 'Sir, me 'n Bet'ny been stomped on, cheated and shite on as long as we's can remember which is why we's out 'ere. Every time we's look like gettin' ahead, sumpthin' slams us down a'gin.

'Oi wanna know why's tis' us'n you wants to be so generous to, sir. An' we don' know if'n we's, deserve it anyways?'

Nicholas looked at the two, Bethany had great tears flowing down her face and at that moment Nicholas saw a beautiful woman with love and decency written all over her, the 'tough as nails' mantle and hard mask had dropped, and Robert, radiating honesty and dedication, complimented his wife's persona.

'Because,' he started, 'I need people around me I can trust and have no doubt about their loyalty and friendship, and here, with you two, my instincts tell me, I have found it.'

'Oh Bobby!' Bethany began, wringing her hands, 'I do'n know what ta say, Nicholas…' she spluttered but couldn't continue and began to dab at her eyes.

'Well then I guess you could start with a *yes*!' said Nicholas with a devilish twinkle in his eye, a grin to match and knowing full well he had what he wanted. But not the least of his euphoria was that he had just given two people he cared about a great gift.

He remembered a wise old Chinese man once telling him, 'There is no greater feeling as that of sharing and giving!'

'You must also consider the three children. Who knows, if things go well and there are significant discoveries – and therefore many more people and families – you might attract a teacher with a little bit of help. And the young Blacks could benefit as well!' Nicholas added with a wink and a twinkle in his amber eyes.

That did it.

'Yes sir! is'n the answer!' said Robert with some emphasis. 'We'll never, ever let youse down! Not ever!'

Robert sprang up from the table yelling, 'Adam, c'mon lad we got us'n some work to do!'

He stopped at the door and said "Nicholas, you would'n know I be guessin', but tha' new town at Champion bay she be now called *Geraldton*, official loik, by der Gov'ment

That afternoon, Bob and young Adam assembled the traces to the wagon and readied the horses. Bob packed wagon spares, spare axle and grease and his travelling kit, which consisted of mallets and various tools for maintenance and repair. Next he set about grooming Stitch despite Nicholas telling him that he would do it. Bob would have none of it saying, 'From 'ere on Nicholas, 'tis my job, 'tis the least I can do after ye generosity.'

Bethany bustled about her kitchen baking all manner of things he imagined, suddenly grinning at the thought of her cleaning the pots etc in Brady's rum. He shuddered, remembering the taste of the rotgut. 'I must remember to buy him a decent stock of rum, should sell well if the Brady's rubbish was all one could get around here.'

Thinking about it, as he sat down at the back table and proceeded to strip his rifle and clean it.

Chapter 44

Goa, Colombo to Geraldton begins May 1850

*V*ictoria sat in the bow with her back to the sprit, willing the ship to go faster as it dipped into each wave.

'Miss Victoria!' yelled one of the crew from the rigging above, breaking her out of her reverie. She looked up to see him pointing off the port bow. 'She blows!' he yelled to her, a grin on his face. She scrambled up, and there, not two hundred feet away hung a plume of mist and she just caught sight of the massive fluke sliding beneath the waves. Then, another broke the surface, closer this time and she could clearly hear the great whoosh of air it expelled, the great shiny back glistening in the sunlight as it curved through the sea to slide below with barely a ripple.

Victoria marveled at the graceful creatures, so enormous it was hard to grasp the size, and yet it cleaved the surface like an animal a quarter of its size. In all she counted nine whales of varying size as they broke the surface.

Suddenly, a huge whale about eight hundred feet away smashed through the surface of the sea, spiralling up and out almost to the length of its body before gracefully turning and crashing back into the sea with an enormous splash. Victoria, hands at her mouth and so thrilled, could only manage a shout of wonder. *'Mon dieu!'* what a wonderous site to behold, she thought.

She was later to reflect, having never seen whales before, that she had taken whale oil for granted, and had never thought about whaling and the killing of these magnificent animals. They somehow instilled a feeling within her that they could almost communicate with her. The whales stayed around the ship for almost fifteen minutes before they vanished as silently as they had arrived.

Victoria was beginning to marvel at the sea, and from here on she took a keen interest in everything maritime.

Peter Strudwich, noticed her keen interest and provided a never-ending stream of facts and figures for her to contemplate. She learnt how to read maps, plot courses and use a sextant. Strudwich showed her how to read the weather and what changes to look for, like the type of clouds, their movement and speed, and sea colour changes, and he spent hours explaining the moods of the sea.

Soon Victoria began to test herself when topside, telling Strudwich what she saw and her analysis of the conditions. A good little student, he thought, and not for the first time considered what a fine couple she and Nicholas would make.

The lessons helped keep her occupied during the long voyage, and the days slipped by bringing her ever closer to Australia.

The next port of call was Colombo, the main shipping port and city in Ceylon. Here they would perhaps take on some minor freight and spices and replenish food and water stocks for the long voyage to Fremantle. From there they would sail up the west coast of Australia to Geraldton.

During one of the many 'lessons' on navigation, Strudwich was studying the prevailing wind charts which were sketchy at best for that section of the ocean and he muttered, 'I am concerned about picking up favourable winds from here.' He ran his finger across the map from Ceylon toward Fremantle at a point about two thirds of the way across the Indian Ocean and tapped the point on the chart. 'It can be quite fickle at this time of the year as we approach the Australian coast. Hmmm' he mused as he traced the route up the West Australian coast toward where Geraldine was inked in. I wonder if it might be quicker to sail direct to Geraldine instead of

Fremantle, he thought, picking up his mapping pen, and now tapping the chart in thought. After all he thought, he had Nicholas's shipment of teak and mahogany on board. If he could pick up cloth, grain and spice from Colombo, unload the heavy timber at Champion Bay he could then sail from Geraldine and onto Fremantle with a lighter load.

'Can we not sail direct to Geraldine instead of sailing to Fremantle first?' Victoria asked as if she had read his mind.

Peter looked at her, her eyes wide as she waited with bated breath for his reply. He almost laughed at her naked want for the suggestion. Stifling the laugh, he managed a faint hint of a smile before turning back to the map and answering, 'We shall see, it all depends on wind.'

Just on three weeks passed and the *Collette* dropped anchor in the port of Colombo in Ceylon.

Colombo was a thriving and fast paced port, with at least fifteen ships of a variety of flags lying at anchor, and the long wharf was packed nose to tail with many ships loading and unloading freight.

Freight was traded from as far as the Americas and all the way up to Japan. Silks, cottons, wool bales, spices, timber, ivory and many more goods were traded and loaded here, as well as opium.

At the entrance to the bay, lying somewhat distant from the main dock and on the sea side, were three 56-gun Royal Navy ships of the line. These were strategically moored so incoming and outgoing ships had to pass between them. Strudwick noted the positioning, a frown creasing his brow, that was a lot of firepower he mused.

He also observed two military East Indiamen moored at the docks, increasing his consternation.

The East Indiamen could only mean an even heavier military presence and that meant trouble of some nature.

Peter glassed the rest of the wharf, and he could see the dark blue uniformed armed marines with their white crosses stationed on the ships and also assembled on the wharf.

The other shipping was varied, Dutch and Portuguese, and some privateers amongst many others.

There was even two of the new steel hulled sail rigged steel 'steamers' at the wharf.

'Ugh!' Strudwick grunted. 'Bloody ugly looking contraptions they are!'

The wharf and city was one seething mass of humanity and Victoria wrinkled her nose in distaste at the stench wafting across the bay.

As soon as the ship was secured, Strudwich left to attend to the docking and loading formalities in the port authority offices, which at this stage were under the complete control of the Royal Navy.

He returned, hot, sweating and grumbling some five hours later.

'Damnation!' he raged once ensconced in his stateroom. 'We have to wait until tomorrow to berth and load our cargo!' He drew a large breath, no doubt seeking to calm himself down.

'I was hoping to catch the tide swing tonight, but now I will lose the day, maybe more!'

Victoria did not understand how one day was going to make a difference. What she did not know was that the ships of the line were not sitting off the port for no particular reason – quite the contrary – and it was this observation that had Peter Strudwich concerned.

He had heard rumours of substance whilst ashore, that the British Governor of Ceylon, Viscount Torrington had executed many of the chieftains and religious leaders and priests, this included a well revered Buddhist monk. The people were planning a rebellion against foreign powers, and Strudwich had been told that the ships were there to blockade the port if necessary.

As it evolved, they were to be delayed six days in total while the Royal Marines attempted to put down the rebellion.

Strudwich fretted whilst they remained at berth in the port. The freight had already been stowed and all was in readiness for their departure. If the situation deteriorated, they may all be in some danger.

On the sixth day he requested a meeting in the port with a Major General Ronald Curtis,who was the officer in charge. Strudwich decided to bring Victoria along with him, hearing that the major general was something of a ladies man. Strudwich explain his intention to Victoria and she raised one eyebrow in mock indignation at him, before smiling at him.

She said if it got them sailing out of this hot box sooner, all the better. She dressed in a simple but fashionable white flowing dress trimmed in royal blue quarter-inch silk ribbon, looking cool and beautiful. Strudwich hoped that he may gain some advantage with her presence as the general was reputed to be an uncompromising and stubborn man. They were kept waiting for well over an hour, sitting at the harbor office in sweltering heat.

Finally, a commotion ensued at the building's entrance with half a dozen ships' captains all clamouring for the attention of a short, though immaculately dressed full major general who strode out of the sun and into the building.

As soon as his eyes adjusted to the room, He stopped dead, holding up his hand for some quiet and he openly gaped at Victoria, then strode across the room and immediately swept his hat from his head and bowed at the waist before her.

Victoria looked at him. His eyes were beady and close together, as for his stature, he was of average height, paunchy, balding and had a massive handlebar moustache, which was waxed at the tips and curled upwards. Ugh, she thought, but managed to give a radiant, almost devastating smile. The general was smitten immediately.

Curtis stammered, 'I am terribly sorry mademoiselle, captain, I had no idea you were here waiting in this heat. Come, come, you must come into my office, it is much cooler there. Burns!' he snapped to his aide, 'Bring some lemonade for my guests please and get those coolies in here with their palm fans' and ushered them into his office, closing the door behind them. He rushed to his desk and drew out a large chair for Victoria. Strudwich noticed the general's hands were shaking a little as he held the chair for her.

'Got him!' Strudwich thought gleefully, noting also that Curtis could not take his eyes off Victoria, and stepped forward. 'Allow me to introduce myself major general. My name is Captain Peter Strudwich of the Indiaman *Collette* en route to Australia, and this, turning and holding out his hand to Victoria, who took his hand and he hesitated for a poignant moment, before saying 'is my daughter Victoria!' neatly sliding in his protection with perfect timing.

The now red-faced Curtis was saved further embarrassment of his naked ogling by his manservant who brought in a tray of lemonade. 'Please, please,' he said ushering them to the lemonade.

After some light banter and exchange of the customary latest stories and news, Curtis turned to Strudwich and asked, 'What can I do to assist you captain?'

Within an hour, they had secured permission to sail on the evening tide, the major general finally convinced that by letting the *Collette* sail, he had one less ship to worry about. Playing no small part in his decision was Victoria's presence.

So, it was that they cleared the bar and set sail for the West Australian coast at midnight.

Victoria stood beside the captain as they swung east around the southern shoals running along the west coast of Ceylon.

The scene before them was wonderous as a great silver moon hung just above the horizon, casting a silver ribbon right to the ship. The weather was fair and the *Collette* dipped into the silvery sea, as though the moon had given them a marked passage.

Victoria sighed deeply and felt as though she could almost reach out and touch Nicholas, and again remembered when Nicholas had rescued her from the lionesses, their first intimate touches and the power he emitted when protecting her. She sighed again and a single tear rolled down her cheek.

Peter Strudwich slid a glance at her and saw the wet trail down her face. 'Patience little one,' said Strudwich kindly as he put his arm around her shoulders, 'we have a ways to travel yet.'

Attempting to change the subject, he added, ''Tis nights like this that keep me coming back to the sea. Have you ever seen such beauty!'

They stood together in silence, listening to the hiss of the sea and the creaks and murmurs of the ship as she cut her way along the shimmering road and east to Western Australia.

Some three weeks into the voyage, Peter Strudwich gave orders to head further south, as he knew from his previous crossings that the winds could rapidly change from the westerlies they were running before, albeit off their port quarter and enjoying at the moment, to strong south-westerlies which swept up along the coast of Western Australia. Coming in too far north would see them fighting and tacking back against this to get to Fremantle.

One week later he decided they would head for Champion Bay first, not wanting to risk a weather ridge changing the winds, his experience and instincts at work again. He gave the order to change to a west-nor 'west direction three degrees in order to intersect with the change.

Victoria, who was in the stateroom studying maps when she felt the *Collette* slowly, almost imperceptibly heal over, clattered up onto the helm station. Smiling, eyes wide and breathless, she exclaimed, 'You have changed course!'

Strudwich laughed at the look on her face. 'Yes! Geraldine ho!'

Another agonising four and a half weeks passed as the *Collette* steadily sailed her course, the winds, whilst not strong were at least steady and from the south-west.

One morning at six bells, on the 26th June 1850, the lookout yelled from above 'Land Ho!' the cry drifting down faintly.

Victoria frantically got dressed and rushed across the deck to the bow and up the stairs to the forecastle to find Strudwich standing, as always, with the glass up. Turning to her and offering the glass, he said smiling, 'Geraldine or maybe Geraldton as it is now supposedly officially called!'

Victoria could just make out through the sea mist some blurred multi-coloured difference and a pall of smoke on the shoreline.

'Finding the exact whereabouts of Nicholas, Jack and Wilber, could be difficult, although they did establish a dwelling and stockyards at the river mouth, so it is likely someone must have crossed paths with them,' Strudwich said to her.

'The town is very new Victoria, in its infancy. There was only a newly arrived regiment, the 99th commanded by Lieutenant Elliot, and crude barracks sent up from Fremantle by the Governor to liaise with the local

Aboriginal people, with whom there has been some violent trouble. There is a variety of traders, pastoralists and others who mostly have travelled overland from the south.

'There is a police station manned by a newly arrived senior constable, name of Drummond, two junior constables and two Black trackers. They are good men but stretched to the limit as you can imagine. We will check with them also.

'All of this was just starting when I was last here, ye understand lass' He said.

He went on. 'The governor had directed that work start on a wharf next year, and there are large stocks of timber, steel plates etc. already ashore.'

'There are quite a few of people here, all types, some ticket of leavers, and a contingent of convicts sent up with the regiment. Ye can be sure there will be entrepreneurs and all sorts of other rogues all trying to make their fortune.' He turned to her, concern creasing his face. 'Be careful and do not trust anyone lass. I will be here for about a week, me 'be one and a half weeks, all being well, and will accompany ye whilst we establish the best way to find Nicholas. If you decide to ride North, then for a start ye will be needin' supplies a small wagon and 'orses to pull it, an' a good strong 'orse for ridin'

He added 'Despite the fact that I intend to sail to the river, I don't know the situation at the river mouth Victoria and I will *not* allow ye to be landed off my ship with no supplies, horse or some knowledge of what has transpired there, do you understand?' Victoria looked at the man with fondness over his obvious concern for her, and said, 'But how will we find out about Nicholas? I mean who will know about him since he was landed at the river mouth and not here, except for he stopping here for a short while, before sailing north to the river with you. No one would know him. Perhaps he and the others have never been to Geraldton or Geraldine?'

It was a fair question, to which Strudwich replied, 'Well, there would not be a great deal of people moving around inland as yet, and those who do or have would likely report either to the magistrate, the constabulary or the Government surveyor or surveyor general if he is here, so that is where we will start.'

Strudwich went on. 'Last time we were here, we were told that land concessions for grazing had been granted further north, and some graziers had undertaken to drive their sheep up from the south-west, the Burges family and the Gregory's I think were the names. I tell you that would be a very risky trek to undertake alone,' he concluded, shaking his head.

'Is there anyone else we can ask outside of the soldiers and the police?' Victoria asked.

Tugging at one of his bushy eyebrows, Strudwich replied, 'There is one such fellow who may know something. There a man known as Tommy O'Farrell, he is somewhat infamous in the town as a shrewd and cunning businessman and would know almost everyone I should think. Despite what a lot of people think, I met him when we were last here, didn't seem like too bad a fellow if I am any judge. And that is something I am very good at!' he said with a chuckle. 'They call him Tommy the Chip, so we will try to locate him once we anchor, get ashore and tend to the documentation, and have met the welcoming committee.'

Victoria asked, 'Why is he called Tommy the Chip?

'I don't really know young lady, but best not to inquire I think... nicknames come in many forms and some are not too flattering from my experience,' Strudwich concluded.

Strudwich turned to his bosun and barked, 'Trim 'er down mister as soon as we get clear of the reefs by the point. I want everything stowed below and the decks sluiced and ready for arrival.'

Four hours later, after a fair amount of tacking against a stiff southerly breeze, the sails came down and they fired an arrival cannon and glided into a calm Champion Bay and dropped anchor. It was early April and the weather was calm and warm, although some chill was beginning to creep in at night.

Strudwich and Victoria stood on the poop whilst he glassed the town. 'Hmmm, he muttered. 'Looks like things are moving along quite quickly, much different from when I was here last, a few business shanties have sprung up and, oh yes, I can see the military tent barracks have been erected. That is all from I can see from here. Wait, there is a dwelling next to the barracks, must be officers and administration quarters. He swung the telescope slowly along the waterfront. 'Plenty of timber and logs and fittings but no sign of any start on a wharf though,' he said.

Swinging up onto the railing on the bow, he pointed the telescope further toward the north. 'Ah, there are quite a few more shanties and buildings further up and looks like a smithy and a corral of horses. That's something at least. Wait a minute, I can see the roof of a fair-sized house further north, interesting!' He said and seeing that Victoria was almost exploding with excitement and curiousity, he played a little game.

Stroking his chin in thought, he suddenly said, 'I don't think we will go ashore for a couple of days yet, just let things settle down first.'

He looked at Victoria's face with a deadpan expression and was rewarded with a look of abject woe. Instantly, he regretted his play and added quickly, 'But then you would probably try to swim ashore!' He laughed at her. Victoria dug him in the ribs with her elbow, hard, winding him. 'Ooff!' He gasped in a lungful of air. 'All right, all right, we will go ashore within the hour,' he said, now laughing with her, her excitement infectious.

Peter swung up the glass and slowly panned west and suddenly exclaimed, 'Well bless my soul, there is a man true to his word!'

'What is it!' Victoria said sensing the excitement in Strudwich.

'When I was here last, I pointed out to the surveyor general, Mr John Roe, who was here on government business, that the reefs at the western tip of the point we went around on our arrival were a death trap for the uninitiated seaman,' he replied. 'I suggested that they consider building a lighthouse on the point as it would not need to be a very high light and would not cost that much. He said he would consider it and seek permission from the Governor.

'Now look, it looks like they may have built a keeper's dwelling out there, or have started it, and there is some stone material stacked up.' he added handing her the glass.

Victoria looked and saw a small dwelling with a verandah jutting out to the west. 'I should like to live there,' she said.

'Hmmm, maybe, it gets mighty windy in the summer months around this coast and these parts,' Strudwich muttered.

In actual fact the dwelling was built for Surveyor General John Roe for his visits, and he had ordered it built on the auspice that it would eventually become the lighthouse keeper's dwelling. Unfortunately, it would be many years before the new lighthouse would be funded and built. Then again, the tower was to be of cast iron and shipped from England and there was at present no facility or ship able to carry such a weight let alone unload it at Champion Bay without a wharf and cranes.

The current tower atop Flagstaff Hill would suffice for a long time yet.

True to his word, Strudwich and Victoria were rowed ashore about an hour later.

As they rowed across to the shoreline, Strudwich pointed to the assembled party on the beach waiting to greet them.

'Ah,' he said, 'we have a full welcoming committee. That is Augustus Gregory on the right, the surveyor general's man. The tall fellow with the grey beard next to him is the surveyor general himself, Mr John Septimus Roe, a marvelous man, he is a devout Anglican stalwart, his father was actually a minister, and our Mr Roe has been involved in more adventure, war and discoveries than you could ever imagine. Then next to him and in uniform, we have Lieutenant Elliot who is now the temporary town and district magistrate and also the commander of the 99th Regiment.

'Next to him, judging by the uniform, I think is Constable Drummond. I have not yet met him but will soon enough. Last but not least is Mr William Burges, the government magistrate and native liaison officer. I've not had much to do with him,' he concluded.

As the long boat touched the shore in the curve of the headland, Strudwich grabbed his dispatches and leapt ashore and turned as the sailors helped Victoria to dry sand.

The long boat immediately pushed off to commence the unloading of freight.

After shaking hands all round and introducing Victoria, the party walked up to the military barracks as there was not at this stage any other buildings that could give some shade and somewhere to sit and discuss news and plans.

They all sat on benches and chairs under the small verandah at the front of the building.

Victoria looked at the building. It had what looked like long dried sticks for the main construction and was over washed with lime. However, the building was neat and quite strong looking.

Victoria sat patiently awaiting her opportunity to speak. The men, after some discussion and talking about the plans for the new town, gave leave to ask Victoria why she had come to Geraldton. At last, Victoria had the opportunity to ask of Nicholas.

To her dismay, no one had even seen or heard of a Nicholas Yuin. She felt like crying and was having difficulty controlling the urge, and she bit her lower lip, hard.

In the uncomfortable silence that followed, Peter Strudwich slid a glance at Victoria's face. He knew she was devastated and his heart went out to her as he saw her struggling with the disheartening news. He couldn't even imagine how she must be feeling.

Peter thought the better of letting anyone know that it was he who had set ashore Yuin and his two seamen, lest they read something into the motive and Nicholas had not wanted anyone to know of their arrival. In addition, Burges, the Aboriginal liaison officer may take umbridge to the fact that he had not been informed. He had lectured Victoria about saying anything about it unless they asked her directly. If that should happen, he would offer the explanation.

'Please excuse me gentleman,' she said standing, her voice quavering. They all stood at once.

'I wish to gather my thoughts and thank you all,' was all she could manage, the tears suddenly starting to run down her face with a will of their own. She turned to go.

'Just a minute my dear, if you please,' said the surveyor general suddenly, holding up his finger. 'Please sit down,' he added, his stern demeanour brooking no argument.

Victoria turned dabbing at her eyes as Peter put his arm around her and pulled out a seat for her.

If she could have been anywhere in her life right now it would not have been here.

She looked up into Mr Roe's clear, piercing blue eyes, and the merest hint of a smile tugged at the surveyor general's normally taciturn demeanour, then vanished as he said to her, raising one finger, 'I just remembered, I am sure, I have in my dispatches, a registering of a pastoral concession of some 132 thousand acres at the Murchison River.' He looked at the attractive young lady with tears in her eyes and such woe upon her, and slowly as if he was forcing it, smiled at her.

'It was registered under the name of Yuin Scott Pastoral Company. One moment and I will see if I can locate it.' Turning, he entered the building behind them.

The group, one and all, were staring at her, awaiting her reaction, and to a man they were all smiling.

Victoria's head was spinning, she could not believe her ears. Her mouth was open and she placed her fingers over her mouth and held her breath.

'Ah, yes here it is,' he said on his return, extracting the document from a pile in his hand and laid it before her. Victoria read it and there it was, the title Yuin Scott Pastoral Company in bold flowing hand.

'You…you mean he *is* there?' she asked, swivelling her gaze from one person to the next then looking up into Roe's face for confirmation. 'I really cannot say Miss Victoria, but it does seem awfully coincidental that the name Yuin Scott is here,' Roe concluded, tapping his long finger on the title.

Augustus Gregory broke in. 'Miss Amendson, my brothers and I hold a mining concession at the very beginning of the Murchison River, some 60 miles inland, the Geraldine Mine, and we *have* heard of the establishment of buildings and some white men constructing something at the river mouth or near it. We have not had the time to investigate as yet unfortunately, which is why I did not mention it.'

He went on. 'Sometimes we have some interaction with people from the Nhanda tribe, the tribal chief elder is called Kalbarri and he was the one who indicated this to us. So, it is possible, I suppose, that this Nicholas Yuin is one of the men, or of the same party, although we have never met any of them, though this is not surprising. As I said, we have been traversing mainly back and forth from here to our mine, organising equipment. We also have pastoral concessions at Northampton, a little south and inland of the river mouth, so have been extremely busy.'

Victoria stood once again, but this time her head was up and she wore the most radiant of smiles.

There was nothing on Earth that was going to convince her that this was not where Nicholas was, and she was almost giddy with expectation.

She looked at Surveyor General Roe and Mr Gregory. 'I cannot thank you enough gentleman, you have given me hope and something to aim for once again,' she said in all sincerity.

Roe felt compelled to caution her and said, 'Young lady, I am not being negative but remember, that is largely uncharted territory, none of us have seen Mr Yuin, so you must be prepared, you understand?'

But nothing was going to dampen either her determination to find Nicholas or her buoyant spirit.

She curtsied. 'Thank you for your words of caution, Mr Roe, I shall keep them in mind.'

'Go with God young Lady,' he said, nodding again with the hint of a smile. 'But one moment my dear. 'Before you trip over your enthusiasm, this occasion calls for a little toast I think. It is not every day one has the unlikely task of shattering a beautiful young lady's dreams, then in the next minute resurrecting her heart and smile!' Roe said.

'A round of rum for everyone is in order, and I think I may have some sweet sherry my dear, if you would care to partake?'

The drinks were poured and they began to chat about the exciting things and experiences, but mostly about the dreams and aspirations they all had in common- the north-west. It was all so exciting, thought Victoria. She felt as though she was on the precipice of a whole new world and she was having great difficulty curbing her impatience.

'I must find a good horse, no, two, and buy supplies. I will need another rifle and ammunition and supplies!' she excitedly told Strudwich. 'And also, I will…" Peter Strudwich held up his hand, laughing. 'Whoa there my princess, slow down now,' he said. 'Let's make a list and form a plan, you must heed John Roe's words and be careful, yes?'

As it happened, Augustus Gregory was standing back to back with them, and stroked his long beard in thought when he overheard Victoria's enthusiasm boiling over.

Sometime later he approached Peter and Victoria and put an offer to Victoria, obviously wanting Strudwich's approval as well.

'Er, excuse me Miss Victoria, if I may have a moment?' Peter and Victoria looked at him. He went on. 'My brothers and I are assembling wagon trains at the moment. We are loading up to transport our latest shipment of equipment up to the mine, and we intend to leave in about three days' time. 'If you are in a position to purchase a good robust small wagon and dray, you would be welcome to join us.

Although I personally will not be joining the wagons, my brothers are, and they could offer protection. I really would not like to think of you attempting this journey alone or with people you know nothing about. It can be dangerous with some of the indigenous tribes causing quite some bother on occasion.'

Victoria almost forgot herself and threw her arms around him. She checked as Strudwich said 'What is she to do once your trains get to the mine Augustus?'

Augustus had obviously thought about this and replied, 'She would be welcome to stay at my sister Letitia's home in Northampton. It is not much as yet, but I am sure Miss Victoria would be comfortable enough and Northampton is on the way.'

Nodding, Peter turned to her knowing full well she would go either way, and she had that radiant smile back and her eyes sparkled like diamonds.

Whilst chatting over their drinks, Victoria thought to ask why the mine was named after a lady and, if so, who was she.

Augustus laughed and said, 'My dear, the name is not that of a woman, it is in fact named after the governor of what is now Western Australia, Governor FitzGerald, and in addition this town has been gazetted with that same honour, Geraldton.'

Augustus was expansive with his information and his knowledge of the new area was extensive.

By the time Peter and Victoria bade their goodbyes and thanks, they both had valuable knowledge that would be invaluable in the future.

Three days later at dawn the three wagons left Geraldton. Victoria now had her small covered wagon loaded with her luggage, which wasn't much – four large trunks and two soft travel bags, so she offered to carry the light stores for the Gregory's.

In their generosity, they even provided one of their workers to drive the wagon, leaving her to break in and ride her flighty new gelded horse, a dark chestnut with a vivid white blaze on its nose and white socks. The man who sold her the horse said he purchased it from an American in Fremantle and he said the animal had quarter horse in its blood lines. Certainly, the horse was well muscled and quick off the mark she observed. She had also purchased another sturdy horse as back up should she need. The horse was a bit 'Roman nosed 'and wasn't a particularly attractive animal but appeared as though it would be strong.

Eight miles due east, they turned north and picked up the trail to Northampton.

Chapter 45

Destiny or Chance?

*V*ictoria sat astride her horse about 500 feet away from the heavily loaded wagons and watched as the Gregory brothers, Henry and Francis, and the hired help went about setting camp for the night and pegging out the graze lines for the oxen and donkeys.

The countryside was fair, slightly undulating with sweeping grass shimmering light green and silver in the breeze. In the distance she could see small table top mesa's rising above the grass plain. She breathed in the warm afternoon air – it smelled of raw nature, she mused, but was different in that it was missing the ever-present animal smell of Africa.

They were three days out of Geraldton and the going had been hard. Twice they had stopped to tighten wheels on the long and large freighter wagon, and to check and grease the axles. Heavily loaded on high with stout timber and stay poles, the wheels were under a lot of strain as they traversed the rough track, which was inundated with hard stone ridges, large holes and deep wheel ruts.

Pulling the front wagon were ten large and strong oxen. Each day had been punctuated by the bellowing of the oxen, the crack of stock whips and cussing by the men as the poor beasts strained to pull the overloaded wagon through the worst of the potholed track and deep wheel ruts. Many times, the wagon bottomed out and required digging by hand to free them.

The Gregory brothers had purchased the equipment, mostly freighted in by ship from Fremantle, and hired the wagon trains from local contractors for their new galena and copper mine north of Northampton, and everything they could possibly carry of their immediate needs was being hauled.

A second flat bed, in contrast, appeared slightly lighter, and this was pulled by a donkey train of sixteen animals. The donkeys seemed to pull more in unison and their wagon carried most of the mining equipment and stores, although a lot of it was not heavy major equipment.

The variety of stores they carried seemed never ending, thought Victoria, and now they had broken an axle in the late afternoon, they would now have to partly unload the lead wagon to enable the axle to be replaced.

At least they did not have to worry about predators such as lions, she mused.

As Victoria sat watching, a strange feeling she could not identify came over her, not unpleasant, but disconcerting nonetheless. Maybe someone was out there, she pondered. Undoing the thong from the rifle scabbard she slid her rifle out and checked the loads. She wheeled the horse around and scanning the horizon westward, she saw nothing and jigged her horse around so she could cover the land to the south-east. Nothing.

'What is it!' she thought out aloud, shaking her head as the feeling persisted.

Well versed in the African bush with its variety of predatory animals, she had been well taught not to ignore her instincts. Sadness came over her for a moment as she remembered Baba Joe's teaching and the tears he shed when she parted. Her heart caught for a moment and she bit her lower lip, missing terribly the gentle old man and his wisdom.

Nicholas, Robert and the boy Adam arrived at the river homestead in good time. Having no load on the wagon made it somewhat easier, But they were dragging a log on chains behind the wagon to blaze a bit of a trail where they could and Nicholas had chosen a fair route for the future having traversed the land north several times now.

Without preamble, they checked the wagon and made ready to depart the following morning, Nicholas deciding that Jack would accompany them. Apart from the obvious help, he was determined to find the biggest horse he could for the big man, and he also had to find the magistrate or the governor's representative to register, or prove, Jack was a free man.

Having never been south overland, he was looking forward to it. They had not seen Gnarlu or Yindu since their return and Yindu had not accompanied them on the trip from the Stokes' property either. The land to the south, or the red bluffs, was another tribe's area (Watjari), so in any event he had not counted on them accompanying them south. Still, there must be some trouble, Nicholas considered, maybe with Nimit'je and the betrothal given the odd behaviour of Yindu and the absence of Gnarlu.

This section of their journey would take longer, and he decided they would cut across south, then east, and find the main track to Geraldton. Robert explained that he had once blazed another trail. This, he said, ran roughly parallel to the main track on the west side of the main track by some two mile and eventually it melded with the main line just north of Geraldton.

If it were in good enough condition, it would be preferable to use so as to avoid meeting other wagons on the main route, especially on their return with hopefully their load of mining gear.

On discussion, they concluded that in reality, if they found the goods they sought, no matter how hard they tried to disguise it, such a large amount of freight would still prompt curiosity.

With Robert's direction, Jack was to scout ahead as they progressed.

On the fourth day Jack was scouting some two miles ahead of the wagon. He was roughly in the middle of a shallow valley when he suddenly stopped. Cocking his ear, he was sure he heard the faint lowing of a bullock. He thought the other main route must be, at this point about one and a half miles to the south east, at least that was according to Robert. Hearing the sound again he trotted off to the stone ridge to investigate.

Jack stood just below a ridge of limestone and saw the wagons below. Only half of his head was exposed – he had picked a large jumble of stone atop the ridge in his line of sight where he knew he would be silhouetted against the stones, effectively blending in with it. He was some 400 yards or more west-north-west of Gregory's outfit. With the sun over his right shoulder, it would be very hard to define his head against the stones.

He saw first a lone rider, somewhat closer to his position, and then swung his attention to the wagons and studied the men working below him. Checking the wagons, he saw they were unloading the freight. The lead wagon was twisted at an angle and he saw that they must have some trouble with the rear axle. He counted seven men down at the wagons, eight including the horseman before him. He swung his attention to the lone horseman. As he did so, his keen eyes picked out the butt of a rifle strapped to the saddle at the rider's left hip.

Almost as though he sensed Jack was now looking at him, the horse-man suddenly and rapidly drew the rifle out and laid it across the saddle. Then just as suddenly wheeled his horse about. Jack was surprised to see it was a woman, her profile clearly showing a breast line in silhouette as she spun around and stared directly at him. Jack knew that even though his head would be indiscernible at that range, he froze.

After staring in his direction for a few minutes, the rider suddenly jigged and spun around facing the south-east. Jack instinctively stepped back below the ridge and thought as he grinned in appreciation, 'Huh, the woman has good instincts and was not afraid! *Yena ezihlakaniphile!*' he nodded, speaking aloud in Zulu.

He looked back to the north to see the wagon just appearing along the low and shallow valley before him, with Nicholas and Robert driving. He could just make out young Adam's head bobbing up and down where he sat at the rear of the wagon.

Jack trotted back down the side of the ridge and stood waiting as the wagon picked its way slowly toward him.

The going had not been too bad up until now and 'Robert's Route', as it came to be known, was proving to be a wise choice. In any event Robert had heard that the main trail had deteriorated badly due to some rains and an increase in traffic to the new settlement of Northampton. It was rumoured the Government was planning to survey for a railway line connecting Geraldton to Northampton in the future, but most people thought it a long way off because the new town had yet to prove itself.

The whole area was being sectioned into grazing rights, and granted lots were up for auction. Some of the lots were of considerable size, up to sixty thousand acres. Several mineral prospecting rights had also been granted and the people building the new town were hopeful of a major strike in their area.

The wagon hit yet another soft hole and jarred their teeth and now Robert was wryly thinking it would be debatable as to which was the worse trail, the old trail or the new!

Jack explained what he had seen, and Nicholas sat stroking his beard, which he had not cut since his snake bite episode, and it was thick and straight to almost his collarbone. He did not mind the beard; however, he was quite fanatical about keeping it clean and many times almost cut it off.

Looking at the sky and then pointing at the jumble of odd shaped stone about a half a mile distant he said, 'It's getting late, we will camp up over there.'

Pointing ahead, he added, 'Perhaps these folk might need some help after we set up camp and if we have time before dark we will go and see.'

Unfortunately, it was after dark by the time they made camp and reasoning that the other party would be bedding down, they decided not to go over to offer help and risk injury to the horses in the dark.

As it was, the Gregory's worked through the night by carbide and paraffin lamplight to remove most of the freight, they then had to jack up the bed and get the broken axle out, the deep wheel ruts in the trail making it very difficult. As one of the men exclaimed, it was 'A fookin' bitch to get out!'

The sun was well up when, a small cheer rose as they finally slid the broken axle out.

Their relief and satisfaction vanished when, to their consternation, discover that their replacement axle was a different size.

The silence was profound as they gathered around and looked. The new axle was slightly smaller in diameter and certainly shorter in length by some three inches and quite obviously from another type of wagon.

The tired men were furious, tempers snapped and things were becoming very heated as the blame was bandied back and forth.

It was now nine o'clock and Victoria had just made a large pannikin of black tea for the men and had only just placed it on the tray of the freighter, when the discovery was made.

Sensing that she may be drawn into the dispute somehow, Victoria decided to leave them to it until some rationality returned.

She went to Henry and quietly told him she was going to scout ahead a little way. He nodded hearing the cussing and agitation escalating, and added, 'Good idea, please don't stray far off the main track Victoria. I don't see any immediate danger but if you do stray too far we may have difficulty finding you, just be careful'. He said, 'Actually, there is a soak not far up, on the right-hand side. Ye'll know it because it has a prominent hill behind it and if you look, ye can see some large gum trees at the base of the hill, that's where ye will find the soak.'

'Make sure you scout the surrounding area before you go in, there might be some of the local tribesman there, but I very much doubt it.

He drew on his ever-present pipe and puffing, continued. 'There was a tribal skirmish there quite a few months ago we's were told and an elder died at the water hole during the argument. The Blacks usually don't go back to the places where someone dies for some time after, sometimes never, depending on the circumstances, but be careful though,'

'I will be careful and thank you Henry,' Victoria said.

She saddled her horse, checked her rifle, took a leather purse of cartridges and the bone handled hunting knife Nicholas had given her from the saddlebags and threaded them onto her belt. Then she went to her wagon and drew out one of her trunks onto the backboard and retrieved her bed roll.

Unrolling it, she placed a clean beige coloured skirt, fresh under clothing and a clean white long-sleeved blouse within the centre of the roll. There was not much privacy during their trek north and she hoped the water hole was unoccupied and had some clear water so she could wash and change. She rolled the bedroll up and tied it behind her saddle.

Last of all, she topped up her water flask and then on an impulse unbuckled her saddlebags and hung them at the seat of the wagon, reasoning she would not need them, and in any case they were full and quite heavy. 'Would you mind if I borrowed another water flask?' she asked Henry. 'Good thinking young lady,' said Henry fetching another slightly larger flask, tying it to her saddle.

'I need to calm things down, sort this out and find a way to get things moving again,' he said nodding toward the now shouting men.

She swung up into the saddle, turned to wave goodbye, but Henry was already striding toward the arguing men shouting, 'Hey! Hey! Hey! Calm down now lads!'

She jigged forward and headed to the far rise ahead and north along the track.

Topping the rise, she stopped and looked back at the wagons, then turned to scan the land in front.

Some miles away and on the horizon she could see a darker patch against a backdrop of two low hills, which she reasoned would be the soak.

Patting the gelding's neck, she kicked her horse into a canter. The quarter horse was proving to be quite a find and he was now getting used to his new owner. I suppose I should give him a name,' she thought but nothing came to mind. Oh well, she thought, something will come up if he continues to improve.

Nicholas was woken up the next morning by Jack nudging him and handing him a metal mug of hot black tea, a boiled egg and a large meal biscuit and then he moved off toward the others.

Jack was now rousing the others in the same manner and they all set about cleaning things up and getting set for the new day's travel. It was quite late and they had all slept late, exhausted after the hard push began from the homestead. Not wishing to push too hard today, they went about checking the axles and greasing them.

When all was ready, and Nicholas had saddled up Stitch, Nicholas turned to Jack.

'We are a bit late but Jack, you and I will go over the ridge and see if we can be of assistance to those other waggoneers, that is if they are still there,' he said.

'Still there Niclas, work all night on wagon,' Jack rumbled. 'Must have big trouble with axle maybe.'

'Very well,' he said and turning to Robert said, 'You carry on with Adam, Bob, and we will catch up with you later on in the day. Jack says the ground is not too bad for several miles so you should be okay. Well then, let's get cracking!' he added, clapping his hands together and mounting, he and Jack trotted off to the north-east.

An hour later Nicholas and Jack came over the ridge and made their way towards the Gregory's' wagons.

Realising they may look a little threatening as they made their way straight to the wagons, they split apart a little.

They need not have bothered, because the men were all grouped at the opposite side of the broken wagon, and Jack and Nicholas could hear raised and indignant voices from two hundred yards away.

In fact, so engrossed in their argument were they, that they had not spotted Nicholas until he reigned in at the end of the broken wagon, Jack standing beside him.

Seconds ticked by and they actually stood there unnoticed, so engrossed were the men in their discussion. Waiting for a slight lull in the angry exchange, Nicholas coughed.

Several of the men physically jumped when they saw the giant Black, barefoot and clad only in his cut-off trousers and a checked shirt with the sleeves torn off, and beside him a lean black-bearded man still mounted on his horse, his hat pulled low over his eyes.

There was a palpable silence, before one of the men managed to exclaim, 'Fook me, where did you come from!'

Nicholas pushed his hat back. 'We are travelling to Geraldton, over there a ways,' he said pointing to the west. 'Late last night we were scouting ahead and saw you were in trouble and thought perhaps you may be in need of some assistance as you seemed to be struggling a little with that axle. We came to see if you needed help.'

A well-built man with a large pipe stuck in the corner of his mouth and a battered felt bush hat perched on his head with the forward brim pushed up, stepped forward and stuck out his hand. 'My name is Henry Gregory,' he said and they shook hands. 'I and my brothers are freighting this gear, or we were, to our grant north of Northampton. That's a mighty kind offer from you sir.'

Nicholas, not forgetting there may be racially prejudiced opinion amongst these hard-looking men which he may need to nip it in the bud, immediately swung around to Jack and said, 'This is Jack, he is a free man and my good friend.' Jack immediately stepped forward and held out his hand. '*Sawubona*,' he said and Henry shook his hand. He grinned up at Jack. 'Ye got to be the biggest man I's ever seen man, bloody hell!' Jack looked down at him and grinning, rumbled, 'Very good, you down dere, 'an I's up here den, we shall be fren then Mister 'Enry Gregry.'

There was a ripple of laughter and everybody visibly relaxed a bit as the others stepped forward and began to introduce themselves.

Nicholas turned back and was about to tell Henry who he was when his eyes fell upon the front of the wagon seat. He stopped dead, mouth open and staring incredulously at the saddlebags hanging on the seat post. The initials **VLA** were clearly embossed onto the flaps.

They all saw the look on his face and turned as one to see what had caused it.

As in some dream, he slowly made his way through the throng and across to the bags and layed his hands on the initials.

Nicholas stammered, 'C...can I ask where you got these, I mean are they yours?' and turning to look at Henry, thinking perhaps he had purchased them somewhere.

Henry shuffled and said, 'No they are not mine Sir. But perhaps you would be so kind as to tell me *your* name?' he asked suspiciously.

His heart hammering, Nicholas was quite shaken and confused, but managed, 'I am terribly sorry Henry, forgive me, how very rude of me,' and removed his hands from the saddlebags and again held out his hand.

'My name is Nicholas Yuin.'

Henry looked at him. 'Hey, that's who...' began Henry's brother Francis. Henry held up his hand and stopped him before he could finish.

'Nicholas Yuin, eh! Hmmm, seems to me I have heard of that name recently,' he said smiling and scratching his head. Nicholas looked hard at him wondering at this turn of events.

'The saddlebags Mr Gregory, how is it you have them?' Nicholas asked pointedly.

'I don't *have them* Mr Yuin, they belong to our travelling companion, and *she*, is the rider coming in from the north right now,' he said pointing up the trail with his pipe.

Nicholas spun and faced north. A rider had just appeared atop a ridge about a mile distant.

The realisation swept over him, and with ears ringing he grasped that it must be Victoria!

Nicholas moved so fast he caught everyone by surprise as he spun around, tore the reigns off the wagon and bodily vaulted into the saddle. 'Yee-haw! he shouted and spurred Stitch into a furious gallop toward the distant rider.

'Appears he is somewhat happy, Jack,' Francis said with a chuckle.

Jack had an enormous grin on his face. 'Is his Victo'oriaah!' he said proudly.

Victoria had travelled only some five or so miles north, before veering off to the south-east, the tall gum grove now clearly visible.

About a mile and a half from the soak, she drew out her rifle and as always checked the load then laid the weapon across her thighs.

Remembering Henry's advice, she headed south east first and made her way around the two hills at the juncture of which lay the soak.

Victoria scanned the area right around the hills and came around on the northern end. She had seen nothing to arouse her suspicions and no sign other than an ancient campfire. Looking at it, she considered it had to be at least a year old.

She now cocked her rifle and cautiously edged her mount forward to the soak. There was no sign of anyone near or on the approaches so she uncocked the rifle and slipped it into the boot.

Dismounting, she looked at the pretty little soak and walked around the edges. She found the soak got deeper at the base of the rocks where the water ran in during the rains. It was about three feet deep and a rock ledge sat just above the level of the water next to it. 'Perfect,' she said out loud looking around.

It was a beautiful place, sheltered from the wind and calm. Small bright green parakeets and many other different types of birds twittered amongst the shrubs and trees. She looked at the stone above the pool and marveled at the painted layers of colour – orange, greys and whites all blended to give this wonderful backdrop.

Fetching her rifle, she again checked the load and re-cocked it, and leaned the rifle against the stone. She then stripped off her clothing and waded into the cold water. 'Heaven,' she swooned, then shivered as she sank down into the water feeling her nipples harden like buttons in the cold water. She tried to relax fully but understandably was still a little nervous.

An hour later, she had washed out her dirty clothing with lemons she bought in Geraldton and climbing out of the water, sat on the ledge, combing and cleaning her hair with the juice of the lemons.

The early morning sun shone down on the rocks and as she sat naked on the rock, she began to relax somewhat as the sun warmed her. Gathering up her wet clothes she walked to some small shrubs gathered at the base of the rocks still bathed in the sun. She wrung them and draped them over the small shrubs to dry.

Unrolling her bed roll Victoria sat back down, enjoying the sun, and began once again to wonder about Nicholas.

How long she wondered before she found him. Would he still have the same feelings? She thought he would, a belief bolstered by the stories Peter Strudwich had told her.

What would he look like now? Had he been involved with someone else? Anxiety gnawed at her and she fretted. But then as always a warm glow settled about her. She had no control over it and it just seemed to descend on her like some secure mantle and she sighed deeply.

Victoria examined herself for any flaw that Nicholas may not like, running her hands over her smooth legs and then up to her breasts, weighing them in each hand and looking at her nipples, now soft and normal again in the warmth. She began to daydream about Nicholas as she had done a thousand times, with no power to control it. What would he look like naked she pondered? He always had an aura of power about him, which she now recognized, he had always had since he reached his teens. Was his manhood big, or small? She did not know. And how would she react with him when they made love for the first time? What was she supposed to do? She felt a flutter of panic at the thought and at the same time as she felt excited by the speculation of what it would be like.

Suddenly, a flock of grey parrots swooped screeching into the eucalypt tree beside the pool and Victoria jumped in fright, then somewhat embarrassed, looked up at the birds.

There were eight of them all lined up on a dead branch. They had bright pink breast plumage and light grey everywhere else except for the face. 'So beautiful!' Victoria exclaimed and stared in wonder.

With jolt, she thought she had maybe spent too long at the pool, but quickly glancing at the sky, saw she should have plenty of time and relaxed again. She dressed in the clothes she had brought, feeling refreshed and clean.

The wet clothes had dried in no time and folding them she packed up her gear, mounted and headed back to the trail.

Victoria was a little worried she may have over stayed at the soak and she really did not want to exacerbate Henry and Francis's problems any more than they were, and so was relieved when she topped the higher of the two rises and saw ahead of her the cluster of wagons about a mile ahead, one of them still slightly askew.

Chapter 46

Serendipity

*N*icholas was at full gallop laying down on Stitch's neck for several hundred yards before the ground began to deteriorate and he was forced to slow down to a good canter, weaving around holes and ruts which would surely break the horse's legs should he step into one.

The impatience burning within him like a wild fire, Nicholas tried to collect his thoughts.

What would he say? he mused. God this might be awkward! What if she did not know him anymore? Maybe she thought badly of him still? We haven't seen each other for years and he had never received any correspondence from her, so...? The doubts roiled around his head threatening to overwhelm him. At that moment, had he been thinking clearly, he would have assessed she had not come all the way from Africa for any other reason than just to see him, as logic would dictate.

'Stop it!' he raged. 'What is the matter with me!' He forced himself to concentrate on the trail and curbed his impatience somewhat, but as soon as he reached the top of the first low ridge, he reigned in, staring down the rise. It was her! He felt her presence like some palpable presence. It surely was his Victoria, he could see the golden hair even from here. A wave of feeling like he had never experienced rolled over him, rising in his chest akin to a dam about to burst. Glancing forward he could see that the track was flatter and smoother and he galvanised into action again.

'Hee-Yaaaa!' he yelled and he kicked Stitch into a furious gallop, dust and stone flying up from his hooves as they bore down on her.

Victoria had just reached the bottom of the high ridge when she heard someone yell.

Looking up at the top of the ridge she saw a rider galloping toward her as if the devil himself was chasing him, dust swirling around him as he raced toward her. She quailed, suddenly frightened, but soon sprang into action.

She barely hesitated and hauled her rifle out and cocked it. She jigged her horse around on a slight angle and got ready to aim at the rider, who was now only about one hundred and fifty yards away and closing rapidly.

Nicholas, shrouded in dust, hauled back on the reigns as hard as he dared barely twenty feet from Victoria.

The boom of a heavy bore rifle at close range shocked him as the bullet cracked past his right ear.

'Bloody hell!' he exclaimed, struggling to hold Stitch as he reared and then wheeled around dancing his head. 'Easy, easy boy,' he patted Stitch's neck trying to calm him, who was very agitated and still huffing rapidly from his hard gallop. He heard the metallic 'snap' as the breach on her rifle closed.

'Jesus! She shot at me!' he gasped with increduality, and then for some insane reason saw the humorous side of it and started to laugh.

He held out his arms to show his submission. Still chuckling he stared at her. She was frowning at him over the sights of her rifle.

God, is there anywhere a more beautiful woman! he thought. She wore a white blouse, beige skirt and black polished calf-length riding boots making a picture that caused his heart to falter. He looked at her, her face in shade under a neat flat brimmed black hat from under which her blonde hair tumbled down about her shoulders.

How I love this woman, he thought, his heart rate now increasing by the second.

Victoria's rifle was a single barrel breech loader, but she had reloaded the rifle with practiced speed and she was now pointing it straight at Nicholas's chest.

'That will be close enough Sir,' she said in a calm and even tone.

She looked at the stranger starting with his face, but he had a sweat stained brown cattleman's Stetson pulled low over his eyes and all she could see was a glimpse of white teeth through a jet-black beard which was well down to his collarbone. She frowned as, to her astonishment, she saw he was laughing at her.

'He's laughing whilst I have a rifle aimed at him?' she muttered, incredulous, before anger began to flare as she studied the stranger further.

He was lean and well-muscled and quite tall by the way he sat in the saddle, and now as his mirth subsided, seemed to have a calmness about him.

He made to move, hesitated, then dropped his outstretched arms. She flinched and he held up one hand and simply said, 'Easy now,' and to her chagrin, he started to chuckle again.

'Is this any way to treat a man who rescued you from lion a few years ago Vicky?' he said pushing his hat back and fixing her with his amber eyes.

Her mouth dropped open as what he said hit her like a brick wall, and her head started ringing so loudly, it was all too much. 'N... Nicholas? How..?' She made no further sound but the tears welled up spilling down her face and her heart pounded. She tried to draw a breath but could not.

Her rifle began to slip out of her grasp and she was swaying in her saddle. Nicholas was at her side in an instant. Taking the rifle from her hands, he uncocked it then lifted her down from the saddle. She could barely stand and she felt light-headed as he suddenly scooped her up, his arms under her legs and shoulders and he walked to a large rock and sat down with her on his lap.

She wrapped her arms around his neck and shoulders and cried softly, sobbing into his neck, mystified and overwhelmed all in one. After a while, and when she had calmed, he gently put his hand under her chin and lifted her face to him so he could look at her.

Nicholas examined her as only a lover can. Her eyelashes, wet from her tears, glistened in the morning sun, and he reached up and pushed aside her hair from her cheek, stuck there by her tears. He bent and kissed the tears away.

In a daze himself now, he drew in her scent. She smelt faintly of lemons as he gazed down at her, the faint sprinkling of freckles on her face bringing back memories. Her translucent eyelids, darker and contrasting with her facial skin, caused him to catch and hold his breath.

Her eyes fluttered and she looked up and smiled at him. 'My Nicholas,' she sighed. He drew back slightly and his heart skipped as he bent and kissed her. The world spun as the kiss and emotion carried them on a plain belonging only to them. Breathless, they said nothing for quite a while as the enormity of their being together after so long apart overwhelmed them.

Their heads touched and they could feel each other's breath. Nicholas cupped her cheek in his hand and said, 'I love you my Vicky.' She hugged him and murmured softly into his ear, 'I love you too. Now at last, I am so happy,' and the tears began to slide from her eyes again. There was nothing more to say at that moment and they just held each other.

Nicholas suddenly recalled Victoria shooting at him and said, 'Lucky you missed when you took the shot at me!' and he started laughing.

Victoria looked at him, trying hard to be stern and stop herself from laughing. 'It wasn't lucky, and I didn't miss, it was just a warning shot,' she said and began to giggle at the absurdity of the scene that had unfolded, finally seeing the humorous side of it.

Nicholas suddenly thought that the men at the wagons would have heard the shot, Jack in particular.

He looked up at the trail where it came up over the ridge and sure enough there stood his giant friend with his hands on his hips looking down on them.

Jack had indeed heard the echoing thunder of the rifle and was up and running up the trail before any of the Gregory's or their men could react. He was nigh on two hundred feet up the trail, tomahawk in hand, before someone muttered, 'Bloody hell! Will ye look 'ow fast 'e can run!'

Jack skidded to a halt just before the top of the first ridge, expecting the worst. He scanned the view ahead and went forward again, taking small slices of view as he inched forward. All he eventually saw was Nicholas sitting with his arms around the woman Jack now knew must be his Victoria. Their heads were touching, and they appeared to be laughing.

The two horses, reigns hanging, grazing unconcerned nearby told him all was well. Although the couple were still several hundred yards away, Jack relaxed and he grinned in contentment, his friend was safe and happy and that was all he cared about.

He was about to turn away, when the two below him stood, and Nicholas was waving him down.

Jack didn't need much encouragement and bounded down the hill, the tomahawk vanishing back into its pouch behind his neck as he ran.

Jack stood towering before the couple, and before Nicholas could introduce Victoria, Jack held up his hand and making a great show, walked slowly around Victoria, examining her from all angles.

He made a full circle, and then standing beside Nicholas and bowing before her and looking straight into her eyes, said in his deep rumble, '*Ngiyakwemuela Inkosazana Victo'oriahh!*' (Welcome Miss Victoria.)

Then without breaking his gaze and nodding his great head said, '*Yebo Ubaba Nicalas, Inkosazana Victo'oriahh bukekayohle umfazi!*' (Yes Nicholas, Miss Victoria beautiful woman.)

He continued. '*Futhi Lungile ukuvakashela umfazi inhliziyo ngoba wena.*' (Also Lungile see heart only for you.)

'My name Jack, I Lungile, I Zulu, Niclas my brother an' bes fren! Now I have the sister an' *two* bes fren also!' he rumbled, beaming, and held his clenched fist to his chest.

Victoria was touched by Jack's sincerity and his obvious affection for Nicholas.

Of course, Victoria understood everything Jack had said, she having been taught Bhantu very well by Joseph. Zulu was a little different, but only in the phrasing.

She replied in Bhantu, trying also to incorporate a little Zulu. *'Ngiyabonga Lungile, wena hle indola, umuntu-hle, umngane!'* (Thank you Lungile, I see you are a good man and good person). Victoria placed her open hand to her chest.

'Ho!' he said excitedly. 'Jack knew you inteelgint, now speak Bhantu as well! Oh ho! Hle, hle!' (good, good.)

Chapter 47

Young Hearts and the
Price of Forbidden Love

Nimit'je's head felt heavy and ached terribly and she just could not understand why she had to marry this other horrible old man. No matter how much she was told the reasons, she just could not accept it and had been crying on and off for several days now, and an ever-increasing ringing in her head, compounded her woes. She was miserable, and no matter what anyone said or who tried to console her, they all failed to lift her spirits.

The tribe knew she was different. From the time she was born she had an attitude toward life that stood out from all of the other children. She had an indomitable spirit that seemed to lift all around her, and thus was much prized by the whole tribe. But seeing her now in such devastation affected everyone. It appeared as though some evil demon was stealing her spirit.

Her father, now shamed in front of the people by her behaviour, did not handle this well at all. He knew that her world was turned upside down, but there were many things to consider other than what Nimit'je wanted, and it could even mean the very survival of the tribe and people.

One day, after days of hearing the crying and sniveling, and possibly to hide his own hurt, he did something he had never done to any of his children, he lashed out at her.

Hearing another wail of woe, he threw down the piece of meat he had been eating and strode up to the humpy she was curled up in and seizing a handful of her hair dragged the hapless girl out before the tribe and slapped her across the face, hard, knocking her to the ground.

Blood trickled from her nose and her ears was ringing from the blow. She struggled to all fours, wailing softly and waiting for the next blow, but it never came.

'Nimit'je, this has to be done,' he growled. 'It is arranged and cannot be undone, you must accept this! And you have been told of the reasons why.' He looked down at her, spun away and stalked off, leaving her whimpering and stunned.

Ashamed of himself, and of what he had done, it wrenched at his heart, and gathering his spears and woomera, he left the gathering and vanished into the scrub to be alone.

Two days later, her mother and two other women rubbed Nimit'je's body and hair with emu fat, and later that afternoon her mother, Gnarlu and two other women escorted Nimit'je to her betrothed's camp.

The camp was especially formed for the marriage and was called a *youllo* (camp for the marriage). Once there, they placed her in the marriage bower to await her husband.

She was alone in the *youllo*, the only sound the chirping of the crickets and the occasional "woo hoo!" sound of the boobook owl.

Her mother had left with the others, and Nimit'je felt she had now been abandoned by her mother, father and family, and had been left alone to await her fate. Nimit'je knew that if she ran away and left the *youllo*, she would create shame and possibly start a war. She was trapped.

'Tjarlu,' she murmured in her utter misery, and with a great sigh fell into silence, her young mind swirling with confusion and hurt. Finally, she accepted there was no way out of this horrible predicament.

Accepting now that everything was out of her control and the consummation of the marriage was inevitable, Nimit'je retreated into a trance-like state, and save for the roaring in her mind, she systematically blocked out everything until she no longer thought or cared about anything and she finally drifted into a deep sleep.

Tjarlu had been taken away from the tribe several days ago until the marriage was completed. All of the tribe had known about he and Nimit'je all along it seemed, and Nimit'je's father, fearing that Tjarlu and his daughter might try to run away together, had ordered he be taken far up river and beyond the range north of it. He was to remain there until summoned.

He was accompanied by one of the young warriors who was about six years older than Tjarlu.

Tjarlu and Nimit'je were not related directly, however, had things been different and Nimit'je not been betrothed, and she and Tjarlu decided they wanted to marry, great complications would have stood in their way.

Tjarlu was on the wrong side of the bloodline tree. The process to gain permission to marry was a very complicated and long process, and was not a simple matter of changing the laws but needed agreement from all, especially other members of both families. And since some of the family members on both sides had passed on, it would have been a very delicate matter even if the union were to be considered. Apart from the betrothal that had been in place for years, this was the other reason why Nimitji's father Mumardie had ordered Tjarlu away from the camp and any temptation to elope.

For days now and tortured by the injustice of it all (at least in his mind), Tjarlu could not stand it, neither could he get the image of the older man deflowering his Nimit'je out of his mind or how terrified she would be. 'My Nimit'je!' he fretted. He spent his days in isolation dreaming up different ways on how to save Nimit'je.

Becoming frantic as her time drew near and starting to panic, he could no longer stand it. It was now only this day and by tonight, it would be too late, he had to do something.

Tjarlu knew if he went near Nimit'je and was caught he would be speared, maybe even killed. If he and Nimit'je ran away together he knew they both would be hunted down and most certainly killed.

That morning Tjarlu made up his mind, and his youth overriding common sense, he set a course that was to change all.

Ignoring his own cautions, and knowing the ramifications if caught, he decided he had to act, and set his plan in motion. Sneaking up behind his companion was easy, and he cracked a good-sized stone into the back of his head, knocking him unconscious. After making sure the unconscious man was in the shade and had water, he ran toward the place by the river he knew Nimit'je would be taken tonight.

Several hours later, he stood surveying the *youllo*. Seeing no one, he chose a place to hide himself, and now lay waiting, concealed well under a stand of mulga trees and covered in leaves directly behind the *youllo*.

He was confident he had not been seen and knew it would some time before his guard woke up and ran back to their tribe to raise the alarm. In his youth and excitement, he did not consider the tracking skills of his guard.

The guard had received a heavy blow and did not come to for some three hours. He was heavily concussed and did not regain all of his faculties for a good five hours after Tjarlu had escaped. When his head stopped pounding and he began to think clearly, his immediate thought was to track and find out which direction Tjarlu had headed. And track him he did.

Although he did not actually see Tjarlu and Nimit'je escape and was careful not to be seen at the *youllo* or anywhere near it, it was obvious what Tjarlu intended to do. He knew it would be only a matter of time before someone discovered Nimitji's absence. He retreated and ran back to the tribe to report to Nimitji's father.

Tjarlu had worked out the escape route. Once they had run from the *youllo*, he would take her upstream in the river to conceal their tracks. The river actually ran east for quite some way from here, and if they continued it did a sharp turn south before turning around the range and heading north-east in roughly the opposite direction. At this time of the year, the upper river was not very deep. At its deepest it would be about three feet deep so it would be relatively easy to walk in.

Tjarlu knew the river path well, as did all of the tribe. The river formed part of the tribal folk law or the 'Dreaming'.

The Dreaming told of the Rainbow Serpent coming down from the inland on its way to the sea, and the river was actually the tracks of the serpent. It left the water as it slithered and carved its way around the land on its way to where the river mouth is now.

Right at the mouth of the river, the serpent met the evil spirit 'Gabba Gabba' who lived at the vast red bluff cliffs, and a fierce battle ensured. Gabba Gabba won the battle and the Rainbow Serpent, wounded, retreated and made its way north along the coast. On its way it created the line of cliffs at the shoreline.

They would leave the river at the point where the river turned north-east, and if they were extremely careful and stuck to the rocks at that point, any pursuers would likely assume they were still heading upstream. They actually would make their way back to the river mouth to again confuse anyone tracking them. He considered that no one would think they would backtrack to the river mouth and near where the Gabba Gabba resided.

After a few days and when things looked clear, they would make their way south, then eventually turn and come back up the coast along the base of the cliffs passing east of the Gabba Gabba forbidden area and ending up at the river's last bend. He considered that the searchers would not expect them to return so close to the river area tribal lands.

It was a good plan, Tjarlu thought, and in his naivety believed he had covered all that was needed.

Now all he had to do was wait for nightfall. He was trembling with excitement, love and want for Nimit'je, and knowing Nimit'ji was in the *youllo* so close by was almost unbearable.

Nimit'je, now in an exhausted sleep, hadn't even heard one her intended husband's wives walk into the *youllo* clearing with a glowing stick and start a fire just as the sun disappeared below the horizon.

However, Tjarlu saw her from across the river, and saw that the fire was directly in line with the *youllo*, casting some shadow behind the small bower. He watched as she left for the camp, which was some two miles away upstream. He could see one or two people further up the track and knew they were there to make sure no came down the path to the new bride.

His timing had been good, and he quietly slipped into the river, and crouching in the shallow water with only his head showing, crossed the river. He had only just burrowed down into the leaves beneath a mulga tree and sprinkled leaves on his hair when Nimit'je's mother and two others holding Nimit'je arrived. His young heart saddened when he saw his normally smiling and happy Nimit'je looking so forlorn and sad, her eyes puffy and swollen. He wanted to run to her and tell her that he had a plan and all would be fine, but knew he had to be patient.

He had watched as Nimit'je's mother and the other women left, leaving Nimit'je in the *youllo*.

An hour later it was dark, and Tjarlu knew he must make his move now or risk the husband coming to claim his bride as would be his right. He knew that the man could come at any time, or even not at all if he chose. Irrespective, he was now the husband the moment Nimit'je was placed in the *youllo*.

He rose and carefully brushed off the leaves and rubbed his thigh where ants had begun to bite him. Tjarlu's senses were on full alert as he slowly rose and stood motionless under the mulga tree, listening with his mouth open, which enhanced his hearing, and drawing in air through his nostrils to pick up anyone else's scent, but could sense nothing.

He quietly made his way to the back of the *youllo* and parted the bower branches.

Nimit'je lay with her back to him, breathing regularly. He watched the rise and fall of her rib cage for a moment, trying to find a way he could wake her without her panicking.

He decided he would just call her name softly at first then gently shake her if she did not wake.

He leant into the *youllo*. 'Nimmi,' he whispered. She did not stir. 'Nimmi!' he whispered again, this time a little louder and with some urgency to it.

She moaned and slowly rolled over toward him, and murmured, 'Tjarlu.' She said his name with such tenderness he almost lost control of his emotions, but gathering himself, he reached out and gently shook her shoulder, again whispering with a little more force, 'Nimmi!'

Nimit'je suddenly jerked awake in alarm and her mouth opened as he came into focus. Tjarlu quickly clamped his hand over her mouth and said, 'Quiet Nimmi!' Her eyes were wide and he added, 'Quickly, we haven't much time, come, come.'

As if in a dream Nimit'je climbed through the opening in the bower and they stood, listening for any sound. Tjarlu's hand came over her mouth again. Hearing nothing, they quickly made their way to the river, Tjarlu brushing sign as best he could and then entering the water from the rocks. Lying still in the water at first, they then quietly made their way upstream, keeping as low as they could and sticking to the shadows where they could.

They silently and carefully approached where the camp was. A corroboree was under way in the camp, which was not far off the river bank, and the noise of the sticks, singing and didgeridoos covered any slight noise they may have made. The tribe was singing about marriage and young maidens, leaving no doubt the corroboree was in celebration of the marriage.

Her indomitable spirit beginning to return, Nimit'je giggled at the thought. Tjarlu turned, the whites of his eyes flashing, and held a finger to his lips. 'Shhh,' he said quietly.

The biggest danger was if someone came to the bank of the river, but they were in luck – no one was there – and they covered a good half a mile before stopping for a rest against some rocks and stood up to their chests in a deeper pool which was at the foot of the rocks.

Nimit'je moved herself into Tjarlu's arms. He was warm, and she wriggled against his body and hugged him, she didn't want to let him go. But Tjarlu came to his senses and gently pushed her away, whispering into her ear said, 'Come Nimmi, we have a long way to go and must hurry.'

They quietly walked up out of the deeper pool into shallower water and sneaked slowly along the river and continued on their journey. They left the river some eight miles up from the camp, climbing out on rocks so as not to leave any tracks on the shoreline.

It took three days of hard travel in a meandering great loop, hardly stopping before they finally reached the river mouth, sweeping sign and trying to remove all trace of their flight.

Nimit'je and Tjarlu stayed at a little cove under the flat rocks at the foot of the red bluff where it tapered down to the river's edge. They were careful not to light a fire during the day lest smoke attract the searchers, who no doubt would be vigilant in their search, and the young lovers knew in their hearts that the searchers would not give up either. Their only chance of survival was to leave the tribal area completely but this was going to be very difficult.

Tjarlu was so tense and wary, he appeared almost aloof to Nimit'je. Each day before dawn, he would silently rise from Nimit'je's side and climb up the side of the red bluff on the ocean side out of sight of anyone looking at the cliffs. He would then slide his head slowly up so he could scan the surrounding bushland and up toward the bend in the river where it turned north-east. The only sign he had seen was a small tendril of blu-ish smoke coming from the white man's camp. Here he would remain for a couple of hours. The only other sign he had heard on the first day was that of a *coolardie* (bullroarer), but it was a long way away and he could not hear what the message was.

Tjarlu went to extraordinary lengths to sneak back to the little cove undetected and he was sure they had yet to be discovered. Each day they sat under the little overhang, sheltered by the branches of the tea tree he had gathered and placed over the entrance.

Nimit'je understood the tension in Tjarlu and she tried hard to give him comfort and make him relax, but he was like a cornered wild animal and the slightest sound made him tense up.

The truth was that his gut was clenched in fear for most of the time. In his mind he knew that they would be very lucky to escape their pursuers.

He whispered in her ear that tomorrow evening they would sneak away south. They had stayed here too long and they could not survive cramped up in the little overhang, too frightened to even move about in the day, so they could not even hunt or find a decent source of fresh water. As it was there was only a small patch of seepage they used for water, but it was brackish and with little flow.

Tjarlu speared fish in the deep pool which was next to their overhang. He would sneak down at dusk and making sure he kept his spears low and below the rim of the rocks surrounding the pool, would make his way carefully back to Nimit'je. They would light a small fire once it was dark and cook the fish he had speared.

It was on these last two nights that Nimit'je became so overwhelmed with love for Tjarlu that she wished they were far away from here, and on hearing that tomorrow night they would leave, she was as happy as she could be, despite the threat of discovery. She wished Tjarlu could relax just a little but he was wracked with doubt and fear for them both she knew.

At dawn on the third day Tjarlu lay by Nimit'je's side where they had slept beneath the overhang. She lay with her head in the crook of his arm and he looked down on her face. He was overwhelmed by his feelings for her as he looked at the little highlights of her dark honey-coloured skin as the faint coming sunlight grew on her cheeks. Nimit'je was sleeping lightly and he watched her face. He loved the darkening sideburns that came down in front of her ears in delicate little wisps, and her eyelashes were soft, dark and long. Tjarlu knew he had been taciturn and distant, and he suddenly felt a wave of love fall over him. A single tear rolled down his cheek as he let the feeling wash over him and he leant down and kissed her nose, the tear falling upon her cheek as he did so.

Nimit'je woke, sighing gently as she felt the tear fall on her face and looked up at Tjarlu, eyelashes fluttering to focus. Seeing the trail of moisture on his cheek she threw her arms around his neck and held him tight as though she would never let go. There was nothing sexual about the embrace, just overwhelming love between the two. Eventually, Tjarlu eased them apart, and reaching over picked up his barbed spears. He stood, hesitating, undecided. He had left it quite a bit later to climb to his vantage point, and he gnawed at his lip.

Whether it was because they had decided to leave that coming night or he just relaxed a little, he decided to spear fish that morning instead of carefully climbing the cliff as he always had done.

Tjarlu made his way down to the ledge at the edge of the deepest part of the pool. He could see several large fish swimming just below the surface, and he lifted the spear and prepared to throw. Focused, he lifted the spear in his right hand and was about to throw it when he inexplicably and suddenly hesitated. He looked over at Nimit'je and smiled at her.

The spear was a momentary blur, and with a sickening thud it disappeared into Tjarlu's left side beneath his armpit and protruded a foot on the other side, the momentum knocking him flat onto the rock and almost off the ledge into the water.

For a second Nimit'je sat incredulous, then screaming, she sprang out of the overhang toward Tjarlu.

Before she could go further, she heard a thud behind her and instantly a massive explosion into the back of her head, the blow splitting open her skull and knocking her onto all fours. Blood pulsed from the wound. Her head ringing and her sense of being already fading as she struggled to focus, a bright white light was all she could see, and it seemed she was rushing down a tunnel toward it.

Nimit'je tried to force it away. In what seemed an eternity she finally succeeded and managed, fighting against the blurred vision, to focus on Tjarlu. He lay on his side facing her, blood forming in a great pool around his chest. He coughed and bright red frothy blood ran from his mouth.

He suddenly smiled at her, his teeth stained red from blood. She tried to smile back but she had no control and the white light returned, then began to get brighter and she again seemed to be rushing toward it. Her arms began to shake and then gave way. She pitched forward, the white light still before her.

Then strangely, things slowed down, though many things were whirling about her as though she was in a hollow. The things slowly began to take the shape of people's faces. They were happy and laughing. Then, still spinning although much slower, they all began to sing, and as they sang the voices and singing seemed to blend into the most calming and beautiful music, and soft colour began to whirl around the vortex. It was so beautiful she thought. The white light now began to fade away and she felt a warm calmness come over her, the happy people and everything else now beginning to fade. She was being carried amongst the happy people, and ever so slowly the beautiful colours swirling in the great vortex around her started heading toward the centre.

The hunting parties had almost given up on finding the 'Giveaway Girl' and her abductor in the river mouth area and they had swept in from two directions.

Each tribal hunting party had spent days tracking and backtracking and finally both parties had converged on the area.

They were of course aware of each other but did not interreact in any way. Either way, the die was cast – both parties were intent on ending the pair's lives.

Of the Nhanda, Gnarlu, his father Mumardie and three other warriors searched along the south bank toward the river mouth and had carefully avoided any contact with the white man's dwelling but not before they had ascertained that the runaways were not being sheltered there.

They were some distance from the final bend at the river mouth and had camped at a small stone outcrop the previous night about halfway between the homestead and the river mouth, a distance of about one and a half miles.

Gnarlu had scouted further inland that evening and had reported that the other search party belonging to the Wajarri was camped on Nhanda *barna* (land), some distance south of the river near the base of the red bluff cliffs on the inland side. However, they were slightly closer to the final bend, and there were four warriors.

They rose early as the sun pinked the river and slowly headed toward the river bend, tracking as they went and hoping to get there ahead of the other searchers.

Mumardie and Gnarlu were torn apart inside by anxiety, and each step they took in the search was taken with dread as they knew what had to be done, and it was imperative that they reached the run- aways before the other tribe's party did, because this was Nhanda *barna*.

Even though the intent was to be the same, if the Watjari tribe killed the couple first, there would certainly be a vengeful war until only one tribe was left standing, if at all. The victor could take all of the women and kill all of the vanquished tribe's children, as was the custom.

They advanced parallel with the river when Mumardie saw something move about 200 feet ahead of them by the edge of the river's first bend. He held up his hand, the others now saw it too. It looked like the end of a spear sticking up vertical and slowly rising.

They all saw another figure rise above the rock line off to the left and saw the sweep of the arm and woomera flash down. The spear snaked through the air and disappeared right at the point where the upraised spear poked above the rock. As the spear vanished a terrible agonising scream came to them before being abruptly cut off.

They all knew it was Nimit'je and were sprinting over the rocks toward the place.

They saw four Wajarri warriors appear, running toward the edge of the rock shelving.

Two of Mumardie's warriors skidded to a stop and threw their spears. As the Wajarri turned toward them they made to throw their own spears, but they were too late. Two of the Wajarri warriors fell, but one managed to throw his spear. The barbed war spear whistled past Gnarlu and hit the warrior behind him, felling him, speared high through the thigh.

Mumardie and Gnarlu ran straight ahead and Mumardie's war *coyley* (boomerang) whistled out of his hand and struck another warrior in the side of the face with a crack they could clearly hear.

They burst upon the scene and saw a black-bearded warrior poised over the prone figure of Nimit'je with a large nulla nulla raised over his head. 'Wur'a!' exclaimed Gnarlu, recognising the warrior, and he threw down his woomera arm with all of his might and the barbed war spear came to the black-bearded warrior like a slithering brown snake.

It struck the man high on the left side, and about two hand widths appeared through his back just below the shoulder blade, the nulla nulla spinning away onto the rocks.

The impact spun him around and knocked him onto the rocks, snapping the spear off and he rolled off the rock ledge behind and into the swirling pool below.

Mumardie ran to the edge of the rocks and ran looking for the black-bearded warrior they knew as Wur'a, who had attacked his daughter, but he could see no sign of him or a body.

Gnarlu leapt off the ledge to his little sister and fell to his knees beside her. He gently turned her head a little and saw the terrible wound on the back of her skull.

Turning her over and cradling her in his arms, he turned around to see his father standing behind him, scowling fiercely, but tears were scouring tracks down his face. They both knew she would not survive the wound.

Gnarlu watched his little sister's left foot quivering and shaking until it finally stopped. He looked at her face as she drew in a shuddering breath and then, she sighed her last breath and was still.

He placed his head on her cheek, softly wailing as tears rolled down his face, rocking backwards and forwards.

The 'Give-away Girl' was no more.

Chapter 48

Back to Geraldton

Victoria, Nicholas and Jack made their way back to the Gregory's broken wagon and spent the night at the camp. During the evening they discussed what to do and it was decided that Henry would accompany Nicholas and Jack back to Geraldine to purchase another axle and hire another wagon and team – to get through the rough track ahead they would have to spread the load.

After she and Nicholas alike, had spent a restless night, Victoria was going wherever Nicholas went, and she stated emphatically that, 'I have not come all of this way to find you just to sit here waiting again and that is that!'

The next morning, after lashing the broken axle to one of the mules, the four set off to catch up with Robert and Adam.

Nicholas knew Robert would have stopped for the night and figured that he would be about four or five hours ahead, depending on the trail condition.

It was not the time for talk and they all hastened along to catch Robert and Adam as quickly as they could.

Victoria, however, was riding along as if she were floating within an euphoric cloud and constantly stole looks at her Nicholas. He rode with such ease in the saddle as though attached to the horse. He looked so handsome and wild she thought, her heart rate immediately escalating uncontrollably, with his black hair wafting about his neck where his braid had loosened a little and his equally black beard waving about in the breeze. She stole yet another look at his strong straight back. She remembered the power he had displayed in the incident with Hymie and suddenly felt a rush of warmth come over her, an all-consuming wonderful feeling of love.

Nicholas sensed she was looking at him and he turned and grinned at her before she could turn away, he was also thinking about her and wondering when they could be alone. It was then he began to think about what people might think of her now that they had found each other and the inevitable was going to happen sooner rather than later. He knew neither of them would be able to control the buildup of feelings bottled up inside each of them, they both were carrying a veritable dam of emotion that was so intense as to be almost overwhelming.

Since they were not married, she could very well be the brunt of vicious gossip and people could be very cruel in isolated places like this, especially since Victoria was so independent and beautiful with it.

He thought, I'll bet she has already raised eyebrows and been the subject of many a 'tch, tch' in the settlement, and they would certainly have been shocked seeing her not only riding a horse in a man's style instead of side-saddle like a lady should, *but she also* carried arms! 'Shocking,' he chuckled. Not to mention her wearing calf-length skirts and simple thin cotton blouses *and* having her hair down rather than in the so-called modest tight buns and high gatherings favoured by English ladies.

Nicholas was still grinning at the audacity of his Victoria and loving it at the same time when Victoria saw him and said, 'What is so funny?' Caught off guard he managed, 'Oh nothing, just remembering how you took a shot at me,' he grinned, which was a little of the truth anyway.

Thinking about the rules of society and women's fashion in particular, Nicholas could never understand the ridiculously tight bodices and corsets the English and French women wore, not to mention some of the floor-length dresses, high necks and caked on face paint and rouges, which he detested. Bloody hell, he thought, must be as hot as hell in this country.

He considered that most of the women he had met in the so-called higher bred section of society, particularly in Europe and Britain, were no ladies when it came to fidelity and loyalty, and when it suited wore extremely low-cut bodices as well.

Nicholas wondered how they could avoid the harsh gossip and cruel assumptions that would come if they were not very careful. To marry was the obvious answer, but finding an appropriate cleric was another matter as most likely the closest would be in Fremantle.

They caught up with Robert and Adam some four hours later as predicted and they all continued on to Geraldton.

Victoria and Nicholas had no real opportunity to be alone during the remainder of the journey and it was as frustrating as it was necessary, as they both knew they had to be a little more patient. But it was so hard, as every touch and brush against each other started a maelstrom of barely controllable feeling.

They spent another three days travelling, and on the afternoon of the third day topped a wind-swept rise and could see in the distance smudges of smoke from what could only be Geraldton.

Robert had not been to Geraldton for almost six months, and as they got closer was surprised at the rapid pace of development.

The road from the north now appeared to enter the town site further toward the coast Robert explained, and 'Thank God for that!' he exclaimed, the old road was as rough as hell he told them.

Scattered along the sides of the new approach were all manner of shanties and budding businesses, several grog stops, a bakery, a milliner's and a butcher shop to name a few. There was even a smithy, complete with a stockade of horses.

'Where did the people come from?' Nicholas asked.

Robert explained the constables at the police house had told him last time he visited that around forty ex-British Army servicemen and their families were arriving in Geraldine to start up the new port. They were each to be granted lots of land in areas to be measured up by the surveyor-general's department.

The smells of the new establishment wafted over them – baking bread mingled with freshly sawn timber, smoke, livestock and a hint of rotting waste. A cacophony of noise rose around them; the laughter of children, harsh outbursts of anger and shouted orders to man, woman and child assailed their senses. Children danced in front of them, pointing and laughing at Big Jack as the huge man strode ahead of the party. Jack wrinkled his nose in disgust at the close proximity of the buildings and smells, and wished he was back at the river. He glanced back at his friend. Nicholas saw the look of disgust and nodded his agreement back to the big man with a grin.

Nicholas spotted some large horses in the stockyard, perhaps above 16 hands. Remembering Jack's hilarious attempts at mounting a smaller horse, he made a mental note to come back and check the stock out before leaving. Jack, his senses ever sharp, turned to see Nicholas staring across at the horses and instantly read Nicholas's thoughts. Scowling and muttering, he turned his attention back to what lay ahead.

It was at this point that Henry decided to seek out his brother and find a spare axle and another wagon and team before heading back.

'It is here I must part your good company Nicholas,' he said drawing alongside and shaking Nicholas's hand. 'Thank you again for your generosity and assistance, I am sure we will meet again, if not here, then up a ways' He jerked his thumb toward the North. Turning to Victoria he smiled and said, 'Good luck to you both,' before waving and riding off toward the military barracks.

As the party progressed into the settlement around the bay, they were confronted with a scene of frenetic activity. Lines of men carrying bundles of all shapes and sizes loaded long flat freight wagons with multiple draw teams of either horse or oxen tethered to them. Vast piles of timber were stockpiled further up the beach, some cut and semi-dressed and others at least two foot in diameter. Must be for a wharf,' thought Nicholas, eyeing the timber and noting that most had one end painted with pitch. Indeed, several men were doing just that. He wondered if some of it would be for sale, unlikely as it was.

Foremen and seamen alike bawled out instructions, and whips cracked like rifle shots across the draw teams. Soldiers were patrolling in pairs throughout the landing and Nicholas noticed some sort of barracks had been established on the low hill overlooking the bay with a couple of build-ings already built. One in particular was set aside and was made of similar stone to that of a house they saw coming in. Must be for an officer, thought Nicholas.

A parade ground had been cleared and he could see about twenty marines in tight formation on the ground.

Further up the hill, the ever-present Union Jack was fluttering in a light breeze. The flag staff was placed in the centre of a four-sided timber tower some twenty feet high. The structure was about ten feet square at the base and four feet at the top and was fixed on top of a low sturdy stone base. There appeared a ladder affixed to one side.

The Union Jack was positioned as the most prominent feature in the new town.

Nicholas reigned to a halt and standing in his stirrups began a sweep-ing look of the scene, concluding as he took it all in that it was indeed a fine place for a town and port.

Out in the bay three ships rode at anchor, and fully-laden barges fer-rying goods between the ships and the shore were pulled in by teams of mules and several block and tackle pulley systems, and back out by long boat, the sailors' backs shiny with sweat under the hot sun.

There was even one ship being careened. She was lying on her side in the cusp of the beachhead at the point. Suddenly, with a shock Nicholas realized it was the *Collette*. She was propped over by large staves and sail-ors swarmed around the stern and along her sides.

Victoria exclaimed, her hand to her mouth. 'Nicholas, look it's the *Collette!* She was to supposed to sail several weeks ago, I wonder what has happened?'

Nicholas did not answer and merely shook his head, they continued toward the point, a frown upon his face as they drew up adjacent to the ship and almost immediately saw Peter Strudwich striding out to meet them.

Victoria stood in her stirrups and cried out, 'Captain!- Mister Strudwich, sir, hello!' clapping her hands together in glee and springing from her saddle.

Strudwich's face was adorned in a magnificent smile as stood before them, and much to Victoria's embarrassment, exclaimed out loud, 'Uh-ho! the lioness from Mombasa finds 'er shaggy maned lion!'

Leaping from his saddle, Nicholas embraced his friend. 'So good to see you Peter! What a surprise!'

'Indeed Nicholas!' Turning to Victoria, he lifted her hand, then hugged her before holding her at arm's length and saying, 'You look more radiant than ever me' dear, and I see great happiness in your face!' Victoria beamed at him, and somewhat overwhelmed by emotion, kissed the captain on his cheek, moisture in her eyes.

'You must tell me why the *Collette* is careened and why you are still here?'

'Ah well now, that is a story. We hit some reef when we departed, but I will explain all in due course,' he said with a twinkle in his eyes, and well aware of Victoria's impatience. 'We must organise dinner tonight and I will tell ye all about it,' he concluded.

'An excellent idea Peter. I have much to discuss with you, especially with an eye to the future,' enthused Nicholas, looking down at Strudwich with that unblinking stare which Peter had come to know. But a slight twitch of a smile on Nicholas's face gave the game away. Ha! He means to marry the young lady! the canny older man concluded, nodding.

Studwich turned to Jack. 'Good to see ye haven't been shot yet Jack,' he laughed. At first Jack was somewhat confused by the remark, then remembered Strudwich's parting when he "sentenced" he and Whip to take station with Nicholas ashore at the river. 'You have permission to shoot either of them if they step out of line Mister Yuin!' Strudwich had boomed out in front of the whole crew, with a serious look on his face. Jack grinned hugely and they clasped hands and shook.

Introductions were made to Robert and young Adam and Adam plucked up his courage and asked 'Beggin' ye pardon are ye really a ship's captain suh?' his eyes darting back and forth between Strudwich, the ship and the braid on Peter's shoulders. 'Is that your ship?'

'Why yes, young man, would you like to come and see her?' Peter asked.

Adam's eyes all but popped out of his head and he excitedly replied, 'Would I? Could I really?'

'Of course, come along then,' and Strudwich put his arm around the boy's shoulders and began to tell him all about the ship and other tales of dubious truth, as seamen are wont to do when they have a willing audience.

They all began to move along the shoreline, Nicholas and Jack in the lead while about thirty paces behind, Strudwich, Victoria, Robert, young Adam and the rest of the party followed. When they were about 15 hands from the stern of the *Collette,* several sailors yelled out 'Oi Jack! Mr Yuin sir!' waving to them. Two large staves were angled either side of the rudder to support it while cross clamps held the rudder in position. Leaning on the staves was Birch, a murderous gaze locking onto Jack and Nicholas as he tapped his dirk repeatedly on the nearest stave in obvious threat.

Jack instinctively stepped ahead of Nicholas, his hand instantly reaching for the tomahawk behind his neck with the intention of protecting him.

Nicholas placed his hand on Jack's arm and said, 'Easy Jack, he wouldn't dare try anything.' With that he quickened his pace before Jack could react and called out loudly, 'Why Mr Birch, how very nice to see you again!' and he strode straight up to the man, thrusting out his hand.

Confused, Birch instinctively and to his horror, almost stuck out his own hand. Nicholas grasped Birch's hand anyway and shook it with such vigour that Birch had trouble stopping his head from shaking. Several guffaws echoed around the ship as many of the sailors knew of Birch's hatred for Yuin and the big Negro. 'Doing a fine job I see,' Nicholas called out, slapping Birch hard on the bicep causing him to stagger a little.

Birch now yanked his hand away and snarled quietly, 'Oi'l ave both of y's guts before Oi leave, make no mistake 'bout that!'

Nicholas, still enjoying the exchange, and knowing he had infuriated and embarrassed the evil bastard, looked around, and seeing they had the crew's undivided attention, said out loud grinning, 'That's twice now we have your invitation Mr Birch, perhaps we will meet up and enjoy a drink or some other order one day. Jack and I will look forward to that day, will we not Jack?' he exclaimed cocking his eyebrow at Jack. With that he abruptly spun on his heel and turned his back on Birch to show his disregard for Birch's threats and walked off.

As soon as Nicholas walked off, Jack took a step toward Birch and began to tap his razor-sharp tomahawk on the stave, cutting off small pieces of timber and mimicking Birch's tapping of his dirk. Leaning down, he said in a menacing growl from deep in his chest, *'Ngilindele ntoni inja wena,'* (I wait for you dog!) and he too suddenly turned his back on Birch and strode off after Nicholas, grinning.

Birch looked around at the crew and saw the amusement on their faces. 'Back to work, all of you,' he snarled.

Strudwich, let out his breath in relief as Jack and Nicholas joined him. 'My apologies Nicholas, I forgot to warn you he was at the stern. You watch yourself with that cove, he talks often about what he will do to you and Jack one day, despite my threats to close his mouth.'

'Ah, don't you worry yourself Peter, he will get his one day and not necessarily by Jack or I. The poison bottle always gets spilt sooner than later, it's just a question of when the stopper get loose enough, if you know what I mean.'

Peter pursed his lips. 'Hmmm, just the same, watch your back.'

Strudwich turned and strode back to the stern. 'Mr Birch, a word if you please.'

Birch came to him, a scowl still on his face. Strudwich said to him in an even tone, but nonetheless with some force behind it, 'If you cause any trouble with Mr Yuin, or Big Jack, or even if I find out you instigated it, drunk or sober, I will arrange a meeting with the 'cat', are you clear on this?'

Birch, keeping his eyes down, growled to himself.

Peter snapped at him, raising his voice with some force. 'Look at me man, are we clear?'

Birch lifted his gaze and locked eyes with Strudwich, and after holding the gaze Birch said with some impudence, 'Aye cap'n, as you wish.'

Furious at the thinly veiled challenge, Peter Strudwich turned and walked quickly back to join the rest of Nicholas's party.

Nicholas took one look at his friend's face and knew instantly that there was unfinished business between Birch and the captain.

"Well, Robert and I have to seek out supplies Peter, we have much to do, so we will part company until this evening, unless you have a will to join us of course?' Nicholas said.

'Aye, I would like nothing better than to join you,' he said, rolling his eyes toward the ship, 'but I must keep an eye on what is happening back at the ship. Thank ye anyway, we will catch up later as ye say.'

He turned to go, then had a thought. Turning back and squatting down in front of Adam he said, 'I am sorry I did not get the chance to continue your tour of my ship young fellow.' Seeing the look on Adam's face, he added, 'However...' and turning to Robert said, 'If your father agrees, you could come with me now and I could bring you back this evening?' Peter saw the slight nod from Robert and turned back to Adam. 'Would you enjoy to accompany me young man?'

Adam was stunned and couldn't believe his ears. 'C,c,can I please Suh?' he asked Robert. Robert tried hard to answer in a gruff fatherly manner but looking at the beaming face before him he failed miserably and merely said, 'Off you go then,' grinning to himself.

'Victoria, would you care to join us instead of running hither and there looking at supplies and mining equipment?'

Victoria was reluctant to leave Nicholas, even for a moment, but then considered it a good opportunity to ask Peter about some subjects she needed answers to, now that she and Nicholas were finally together. 'Yes, I would like that captain, thank you.'

Nicholas and Robert were thankful they had a free reign now and could concentrate on establishing contacts. Further, both had been a little concerned about who they would meet, the town being full of new folk by and large and who knows whether they may come across unsavoury people, Victoria would no doubt attract some unwarranted attention. They waved and watched the three walk off hand in hand to the ship, Strudwich's arm up and pointing, already telling Adam about his ship.

Chapter 49

Tommy 'The Chip' O'Farrell

*T*ommy O'Farrell, had first arrived at Champion Bay around December 1848 on horseback accompanied by several of his Irish employees, arriving about a year before the Crown's regiments.

They took their time, taking some three and a half weeks from Fremantle as Tommy's natural curiosity of all things diverted them many times – he did not miss very much on the journey. On arrival and after several days of appraisal, talking to the constabulary and some surveyors, he quickly came to the conclusion that the area was going to boom and hurried back to Fremantle, by ship, where he began to buy up all manner of stock for his intended business.

No one knew where he got the money from to buy the considerable amount of equipment, but the strongest rumour was that he was part of the Irish gang culture back in Belfast which was now very strong in Fremantle, and all the staff he employed at Geraldton happened to be Irish.

Rumours and innuendo aside, he was an immaculate, charming and witty gentleman and soon had all at the new town happy to call him friend.

In stature, O'Farrell was not a large man by anyone's standard, but that being said he made up for it by sheer force of character. Standing about five foot ten inches, he had a slight stomach, but underneath his shirt sleeves he was powerfully built. Either way, one knew not to mess with him. But all that aside, it was his generosity that won most people over. If some poor soul was in trouble or down on his luck, he would be the first to lend a helping hand.

Tommy knew that to befriend people and help them built loyalty, and that loyalty could be very valuable in building an enterprise.

After his return to Fremantle, it wasn't long before he was back in the area bringing in a vast array of equipment. Most of the equipment came by long sturdy wagons he had specially built in Fremantle. They were longer than usual and had larger diameter wheels. Some were fully hard covered in lightweight timber for protection of perishables and the finer items, and for the next six months the wagon trains rolled into Geraldton once a month.

Some said Tommy got his nickname "The Chip" from some dastardly gang related deeds back in Belfast where he was born. Some of that may well have been true, but not accurate as far as the nickname went.

Tommy's father was a Belfast man through and through with his lineage stretching right back to the 15th century when Ireland was under the rule of the hated English King, Charles III. His hatred for the British was ingrained into his soul after the British threw his beloved 'Da' (Tommy's grandfather) into prison, where he died.

It is said that true love will conquer all, so whether this was the case when Tommy's Da was about to burgle a British nobleman's home on the outskirts of Belfast at 1am, who could say. As it was told, he was caught in the act by a young serving maid. She was a pretty young lass with long blond tresses and warm brown eyes. As he crept toward the rear door, he literally banged into her as she suddenly swung open the door and stepped out. Both collapsed to the ground in a noisy clatter of pots and pans she was carrying.

There was no time to speak as they scrambled to their feet before the gentleman of the house and a soldier, who were at the kitchen table, suddenly appeared at the door loudly demanding an explanation as to what the ruckus was about. The soldier had his bayonet affixed and musket cocked.

Tommy's Da, apparently, was about to go for his knife, when the girl, knowing what was about to happen, stepped in front of Tommy's Da and stuttered that this was her chosen man and she was sorry but they had fallen over. She copped a crack in the face for her indiscretion.

Then, with no small amount of luck, or perhaps an overindulgence of wine, the gentleman suddenly saw the humour in the situation, and smiling, sent Tommy's Da on his way.

It was not the last time Tommy's Da sneaked out to the farmlet.

So began a romance, a British-hating Irish lad and a smiling English maid.

They later married and when Tommy was born, much to his father's horror, his mother insisted on Thomas's second name being Charles, after King Charles III and her father's, and so it was that Thomas Charles O'Farrell was christened.

In Tommy's youth, despite all of his efforts to keep the name buried, his mates finally discovered his second name and for the next few years he endured beatings and bullying on a daily basis. They cruelly nicknamed him 'Tommy the Chip', a short insult to the hated English king and a derogatory name oft used by Irish gangs.

One day Tommy had had enough and for a couple of weeks he dreamt of a variety of ways of smashing the biggest bully of all. He snapped during one such beating, and going berserk, bit off the bully's left ear then switched to the fellow's nose, almost biting it off.

Tommy whipped out an old worn kitchen knife he had honed razor sharp and drove the blade into his opponent's throat with such force it apparently came out of the back of the lad's throat. Standing over him, the rage subsiding, Tommy had calmly watched the bully's life ebb away and turned to the shocked circle around him and waved his knife at them in challenge, they all swayed back, they all got the message loud and clear.

No one ever picked on Tommy again and no one was game to ever call him 'The Chip' either.

Tommy used that terror to become a much feared gang leader.

The strange thing was, Tommy quite liked his nickname even though no one was game enough to speak it to his face. He knew they used it behind his back and actually thought it some measure of respect, so he kept up the pretense that he hated it.

O'Farrell knew that as a rough-edged Irish gang leader, he was never going to succeed in the world while the English ruled over almost everything and every country, so he studied constantly, learning politics and business from every avenue he could as well as Queen's English. He became quite eloquent and used it when it was needed, although with an Irish lilt. His thirst for learning never waned and he read almost every day.

So, it was no surprise when he learned of new opportunities arising in the new colonies in Australia that he began to reason that here was an opportunity to start an enterprise with little competition in comparison to what he was used to. He assembled his belongings, a crew of artisans and an equal amount of tough Irish enforcers and booked passage to Western Australia.

They spent two years in Fremantle, establishing a variety of small businesses, all complimentary to building and supply. Tommy heard about 'Geraldine and after weighing up the available facts, he and four of his men voyaged to the new establishment to appraise it for opportunity.

They returned to Perth and made their move.

O'Farrell was no fool and had squatted on land outside of the new town boundaries, he and his gang of artisans built the house so quickly it was too late by the time the town authorities could do anything about it and only nine months passed before he went before the new Magistrate William Burges with a document laying claim of forty acres of land some four miles North of the new town boundary.

There was technically little the magistrate could do as the document was actually signed by the Governors department in Perth, in any case, Tommy 'The Chip' O'Farrell had broken no law. It was rumoured that O'Farrell also now ran the only brothel and the illegal games in the area, since those establishments were run by Irish overseers all seemed quite obvious but no proof could be found, and in any case they were well run, clean and there was never any trouble (not that anyone heard of at any rate).

Thus, O'Farrell began trading as the first and only stock and station agent in what was to become the town of Geraldton. Although he insisted he was just a general trader, Tommy was, and became much more than that. There wasn't much the agent didn't carry in the way of farming equipment, and on hearing rumours of mineral prospecting starting to the north, carried quite a lot of general mining and prospecting equipment.

To date, not much of this mining equipment had turned over as he had expected (exorbitant pricing had a lot to do with it), but he kept it irrespective, hoping things would improve.

The only prospectors of note in the area were the Gregory's and they had most of their equipment shipped in themselves, much to his chagrin.

Despite his reputation as an Irish rogue, Tommy was a likeable fellow and a very astute businessman.

Nicholas, Robert and Jack drew the wagon up at the gateway at O'Farrell's allotment and looked up at the house.

Lifting his rifle down from its place in the back of the seat, he placed the weapon under the wagon seat and passed his leather satchel to Jack. Turning to Robert he said, 'We will first make contact with Mr O'Farrell, Robert and if all is fine perhaps we can bring the wagon up onto the property. Could you wait here until we come back?'

'All will fine Nicholas,' Robert said patting the seat.

Nicholas and Jack proceeded up the rough drive toward the house.

They were within 20 yards from the stoop jutting out from the front verandah when two men appeared from either side of the verandah. They were dressed almost the same with grey flannelette shirts, small grey striped vests, dark grey trousers and grey felt bowler hats.

Nicholas had no doubt that there would be weapons just out of sight around the corner, and he figured it had been a good move to shift his rifle in full view of the house and it showed Mr O'Farrell that he was a cautious man.

One of them said politely in heavy Irish brogue, 'Top o' the mornin' sirs. What do ya be tinkin' we can do for ye's?' A huge open smile cracking his face, but Nicholas noted that the man's grey eyes were as hard as stone and they never left the pair.

Nicholas said, 'Good morning gentlemen, we have come to make contact with Mr O'Farrell with a view to business. Is he by chance available?'

The ornate dark green door swung open before the guard could reply, and through it strode Tommy O'Farrell.

'Welcome Mr Yuin and Big Jack, or is it just Jack? Come up, come up,' he announced as he beckoned them onto the verandah.

'Tommy O'Farrell,' he said his hand extended.

Nicholas was a little taken aback as he approached O'Farrell, his own hand extended. 'You are well informed sir...Nicholas,' he said as they shook hands.

O'Farrell grinned, a cheeky smile, then immediately turned to Jack and offered his hand to him and said politely, 'Welcome Sir, my men helpin' careen the ship were right! But ye's be the biggest man I have ever seen, so forgive me if I am a little in awe, 'an may I 'ave what is left of me hand back?' he concluded laughing, making light of the fact that Jack's hand-shake had all but squeezed all of the blood from Tommy's hand.

Massaging his hand behind his back, he said, 'Please come in,' and he ushered them both into an open sitting room. The room had highly polished Oregon floorboards, but was sparsely furnished.

One wall was taken up entirely by a floor to ceiling bookshelf abso-lutely full. There was a simple fireplace and fire tools in brass trim beside it, and a large sideboard of mahogany lay against one wall.

They sat on leather lounge chairs and were served tea and biscuits.

After some banter Nicholas came straight to the point and asked about the stock Tommy had, his ability and timelines to bring in freight.

'Ah, finally I meet a man who knows what he wants!' said O'Farrell. 'Can I be askin' what it is that ye be wantin' this equipment for, apart from the obvious fact dat you are minin', or goin' ta be?' Tommy had uncon-sciously slipped into his Irish brogue. 'Or am I to be mindin' me own busi-ness Nicholas?'

Nicholas locked eyes with O'Farrell, looking for any deception. He knew that sooner or later his discovery and the building of the mine would become public knowledge but did not want that to be so yet. He also realised that to gain trust and thereby cement a future business arrangement with O'Farrell he would have to give the man some incentive. O'Farrell was no novice and had already done well, was well informed and further, he had the resources, so in all probability it could be to Nicholas's advantage to be somewhat more forthcoming with his intentions.

O'Farrell, seizing back the moment said, 'Forgive me Nicholas, that was rude of me, I meant no disrespect. Sometimes I am too direct for my own good, eh.

'Perhaps we should get to know each other a little better first, and perhaps your man might like to bring the dray up alongside the equipment near the barn, for safe keeping?' he added jerking his thumb toward Robert sitting on the wagon.

Jack rose and went down to Robert.

'Let us go and inspect what equipment I have while your man brings in the wagon,' O'Farrell said.

Nicholas and Tommy walked through the house toward the rear.

Nicholas noticed at least eight rooms built into the house, and they passed through a massive kitchen in which several cooks were hard at work.

'You have a fine home Tommy.' commented Nicholas.

'Yes it is, I think, but a bit too large,' he said. 'Sometimes I get lonely in it, especially at night, the men have their own barracks back behind the barn and I have yet to find the right woman to share things with.'

Turning to Nicholas, he said, 'Generally, Oi don't trust em, only trusted me Ma, an' she's passed,' devilment dancing in his eyes as he laughed along with Nicholas.

They walked all over the yard, inspecting the rows of equipment. Nicholas could see that O'Farrell, or someone in his employ, must have knowledge of mining for there was a lot that Nicholas could use here. All the while the men played the game of getting to know each other – a question here, either loaded or straight, hints or deft diversions. The pair's negotiations and verbal sparring were on a par, and throughout they began to warm to each other's intelligence and character.

They had much in common, although treading different paths. Once a path or object of desire was chosen, both men brought the same focus and drive to achieve these desires, come hell or high water.

Both men had a similar sense of values in honesty when dealing with like-minded souls and preferred to give the benefit of doubt before judgement. Neither intentionally went purposely out to hurt others, but once crossed, never forgot it, and both were men of action when needed.

A bond began to form, and though strange, it seemed to Nicholas that he somehow may have found a true friend, not unlike the feeling which came over him after first meeting Gregory Scott. Little did he know it, but Tommy O'Farrell was thinking exactly the same thing, and for the first time in his life found his iron-clad guard lowering somewhat.

Robert, Jack, Tommy and Nicholas continued walking amongst the equipment, Robert noting the items Nicholas needed as they walked. It was past noon when they completed the yard inspection, and they went back to the house and sat at the great long Huon pine table in the kitchen.

Sandwiches and lemonade were served and the cooks departed for their afternoon break. Drawing up the list and correcting some of Robert's terrible writing and spelling, they began to go through the list with Tommy.

'Now,' Nicholas said to Tommy, 'we should like to go over your hardware and grocery stock if possible,' and with that, reached into his satchel and brought out an extensive list that he, Bethany and Robert had compiled.

O'Farrell took the list and studied it for some minutes. It comprised of many items from spices to firearms and even feed for stock.

Tommy looked up, switching his gaze between Nicholas and Robert and asked, 'Be' Jasus, ye'll not be tinkin' o' startin' in opposition ta me now would ye's?'

'No Tommy we would not!' laughed Nicholas and Robert. 'At least not here in Geraldton!'

O'Farrell cocked one eyebrow in query at Nicholas's add on, all of his self-protection about to snap shut.

Nicholas saw the veil begin to slide over Tommy's face and held up one hand. 'Wait a moment Tommy, let me explain and come clean with you with regard to our aspirations.'

Tommy stared at him, momentarily caught off-guard.

It was then Nicholas decided to tell Tommy about their plans to operate a small northern stock and station store to service the northern needs of cattle and sheep properties and general folk, including prospectors' needs, in particular his own. They wished to negotiate with O'Farrell as to price and availability, and with a view to he being the prime supplier.

'In addition,' Nicholas continued looking around the room and decided to take a calculated risk. 'To demonstrate my trust, and I hope cement our confidentiality in each other…' he paused to reach into his satchel and placed a two inch-sized lump of quartz before O'Farrell.

O'Farrell, stared at the gold-laced piece of rock, not daring to even touch it. Suddenly, he reached into his coat and withdrew a large kerchief which he threw over the specimen.

'Christ!' he exclaimed, glancing furtively at each of the two large windows facing the rear.

'Christ!' he said again, 'so dis is why ye are in such a hurry ta buy the minin' equipment.

'Have you even showed this to anyone as yet?' he continued, switching from his Irish brogue to cultured English.

Nicholas solemnly shook his head and simply held out his hand to O'Farrell across the table.

Tommy looked up at Nicholas and looked into his eyes. They had changed, he realised with a shock, the amber glow had vanished and now were as dead as a viper's as he shook hands with Yuin. B' Jasus, Oi'll not be the one to ever be crossin' this man, he thought.

He shook hands solemnly with Nicholas. 'Ye secret 'tis safe with me Nicholas. Dis is great trust ye have placed wit me an' Oi'll not be the one ta be breakin' it now, d'ye be hearin' me 'den?'

Nicholas slowly nodded his head.

'Trust once given, should n'er be broken,' said Nicholas. 'In Oliver Cromwell's words'

'We have a bond,' and gave a final shake of the hand.

They talked for another hour as Nicholas explained how he wanted to proceed with his plans.

Tommy 'The Chip' was most helpful and suggested many helpful ideas, not the least was the offer to initially use his large fleet of covered wagons to transport the mining equipment to Robert and Bethany's home.

This, of course, would be under a contract basis and include manning. He also offered to supply and build the warehouse and anything else, also under contract.

This was welcoming news and no doubt they would have to settle on the costs, but either way this could get things moving faster than Nicholas could have hoped for.

They decided that there had been enough spoken today, and Nicholas had many other things to deal with, so he suggested they discuss contracts and other items at a later date.

As they rose to part company, Tommy suddenly said, 'Ah me, what am I tinkin', where would it be ye'll be stayin' whilst ye's are in Geraldton?'

Nicholas, Robert and Jack looked at each other. They were intending to set up their tents a way out of town, but it obviously was too late to do that now. Nicholas suddenly remembered Victoria and Adam were still down at the ship. Guilt fell on him like a cloak.

Before they could answer, Tommy said, 'Dat's settled den, ye'll be all stayin' 'ere wit me in dis 'ouse, an' for as long as ye be likin', an' Nicholas, I see dis mornin', ye 'ave a very beautiful lady with ye. She'll be needin' some privacy and clean sheets 'n beddin' an' all ta' sleep in.

'Oi've even got a bath an' a boiler, she is welcome ta use – it's never been used! Well, we all, dat is the men 'n I, use the drop tap at the water tank, back o' the barn as usual.'

Before they could even answer, Tommy laughed. 'At last Oi 'ave some company in dis big ol' 'ouse o' mine!'

Off he went, shouting 'Seamus, Seamus! Ye be getting ye arse in 'ere, we got guests fo' a while.'

Nicholas looked at Robert and Jack, grinning. 'Looks like we are staying here!'

They went out to the barn and Robert and Nicholas retrieved the horses. Jack handed Nicholas his rifle and they trotted off to find Victoria and Adam, Jack as usual jogging ahead of them.

Chapter 50

Love, an Epic Journey

*V*ictoria sat 25 yards or so from the west side of the ship on a blanket atop a small sea grass hill overlooking the *Collette*. She was shielded from the sun by a large oriental parasol that Peter Strudwich had by some miracle produced, along with a pitcher of lemonade and some sandwiches. He had given her some time, sensing she was somewhat in turmoil, before returning to sit with her for a while, and so, as it now turned out, had far from been wasted.

She and the captain talked at length about what to do now that she and Nicholas had finally found each other. She was concerned, since they were not married, about being branded 'A loose woman' should she return to Nicholas's home at the river mouth or mine. Strudwich advised that she should not worry about this, and time and planning would solve that issue.

They talked of many other things that she knew Strudwich would keep in confidence. For example, where they could get married if that was Nicholas's intention, and could he, as master of the *Collette* marry them aboard the ship? Peter Strudwich laughed and said, 'Whoa up lass, it is not true that a captain can legally marry people aboard a ship, ye must find out if a cleric or ordained minister is to visit here and when,' he concluded.

Strudwich answered her querie with one of his own, asking whether she had had a chance to discuss it with Nicholas. Of course, she had not was the reply. Strudwich said to her, 'Well m' dear, I think number one ye should slow down a little, and two, ye need to let Nicholas know your concerns and I am sure ye will find he has the same concerns, yes?

'Ye two have much to organise and discuss to avoid these types of problems. He has not, as yet, had a chance to talk to ye in private has he now?' She shook her head. 'Well then, softly, softly little Princess, all will come with patience.'

'If Nicholas asks me to marry him, I will surely say yes, but afterwards, where exactly would we stay? Victoria asked. 'How would we find out about the minister or cleric?'

Although Strudwich had no immediate answers he said, 'We will make some inquiries lass, don't fret so.

'Now I apologise m'dear but I must tend to my duties and to the repairs to the keel and rudder,' and he strode away to the ship.

Victoria was still confused and worried, however it was good to have him listen to her concerns and she felt somewhat relieved.

She decided to walk to the site of the lighthouse to while away some time, thinking Nicholas would return soon.

Victoria returned some time later but there was no sign of Nicholas.

She was now getting concerned as it was now past noon and still yet no sign of him, Jack or Robert. Worry gnawed at her belly as she fretted. She looked to the *Collette,* again seeking some sign of the captain and lad. She pushed aside the worry, and as she often did let her attention wander and began to observe her surroundings.

It was strange to look at the *Collette*'s deck on such an angle after so many months of walking her decks on the passage to Geraldine, '*Geraldton*' she corrected herself.

Peter had explained to them that when the *Collette* departed just after she and the Gregory's had left to travel north, they were gripped by a fierce current that had caught all unawares, and just as the *Collette* had unfurled full sail, the aft section of the keel had clipped some reef. Although they had not taken much water, Strudwich decided to head back to Champion Bay and careen the hull and assess any damage. It was to be a wise decision as they discovered that one or two of the large aft keel bolts that anchored the rudder had been damaged, as well as some of the great timbers.

Seeing some movement beside her, she looked down at the sand beside her and a saw a large caterpillar covered in black ants as they tried to move the struggling creature to their nest. Looking up she suddenly compared the *Collette* to the caterpillar as the sailors and workers swarmed over her. The ship, out of water, was no different – helpless.

She looked again at the ship and saw Peter Strudwich finally appearing over the side of the ship, clambering down the rope and slat ladder, young Adam hard on his heels. The boy's face was round with wonder and excitement as they carefully negotiated the sloping deck to the sand.

As Strudwich walked toward them, a soldier marched down the track and called out to the captain. Strudwich stopped and waited for him. The soldier said something to Strudwich and he nodded. The corporal saluted and walked away.

'Well, that puts paid to dinner tonight at the barracks,' he said as he came up to Victoria. 'Yesterday afternoon, John Roe, Constable Drummond and Judge Burges went to investigate something at the planned Lynton Convict Depot up near Port Gregory. Some trouble with the Blacks I am told. Never mind, we shall have to make other arrangements.'

Victoria looked up at Strudwich and said, 'I am worried, Peter, Nicholas has been gone some six hours and we have yet to establish a place to stay.'

Peter looked at her, worry etched on her face and said with a confident air, 'My dear, of all of the people ye should *not* be worried about, it is Nicholas, *and* Jack for that matter, hmmm!' he said with one raised eyebrow and a smile on his face.

'They will be along directly and I am sure they would have made the necessary arrangements.'

'Work is progressing very well on the careening and repairs thanks to some of the excellent artisans Tommy 'The Chip' has hired to us,' Strudwich said running his eyes over the ship.

'Why have you removed all of the cannon from the ship, and all of the other items captain?" Victoria asked.

'I wish you would call me Peter, I think we are beyond formalities, don't ye think my dear?' he said , looking down at her. Victoria smiled and nodded at him.

'Well, in answer to your question, we lifted all of the cannon and ammunition off her and anything else we could , except for a few items that were too difficult without a wharf, so as to lighten the ship.' He went on, 'Anything else of weight from the topsides was taken down, sails, mid-masts, spares and storage containers. If we did not do this, we would never float her off the sand when we have finished, you understand?'

Victoria looked at the rows of black cannon stored up further along the shore and the stacks of rigging and containers and said, 'Yes, it is quite obvious now that you have explained. How will you float her again, I notice you have not taken off the masts, why is that?'

'Good question young lady,' he replied with a hint of a smile. 'We leave the masts in place because it will provide good leverage when we try to right her, just before we do the refloat, understand?' Peter drew a sketch in the sand showing how by using braces and cantilevers this would be done.

Strudwich explained that there was to be an extra high tide due with the new moon. Before that, they would, on the low tide, excavate the seaside of the ship as far as possible, then on the high tide all hands would man the long boats and hopefully they would float her off the sand.

Victoria nodded, hardly imagining the hard work that would entail.

Not twenty minutes passed and over the ridge came the trio, Big Jack in the lead, his head shiny with sweat. Whooping, Jack ran straight into the sea to cool off as Nicholas and Robert cantered up to Victoria and Peter.

Jack came out of the sea and walked around the stern, wary of Birch and ready if he gave any trouble. Birch of course had seen Jack dive into the sea but went back to work and so was surprised when Jack came around the stern and rudder where they were replacing the lower rudder cleat bolts, Jack walking not six feet from them as he made his way back to Nicholas.

As he walked by, Birch began to mutter, just loud enough for Jack to hear, 'Oi'm gonna kill that there nigger if'n it's the last thing Oi do.'

Jack stopped and glancing up the hill saw Strudwich and Nicholas staring down at them. Jack held his ground and grinning, repeated his earlier statement, *'Ngilindele ntoni inja wena,'* before striding off.

Birch, fuming that he could not understand what Jack had said, muttered, 'It don' matter whatever 'e said, Oi'm still gonna get im.'

One of the sailors, Johann De Freys, was a man of solid build who carried himself with dignity. De Freys, who was of South African Boer origin and a tough man to boot, said , *"E said,* in Zulu, that 'e'll be waitin' fo' ya, ya filthy dog. Want ma' advice man, leave well 'nuff alone, e'll tear ye's in 'alf, make no mistake boarty. Dem Zulu boys don' know the meanin o' stop when de' get riled, an 'e's bigger than most!'

The men in hearing distance chorused, 'Wooo 'oooo! Pins be fallin' Birchy, Wooo 'oooo!'

Birch's face was purple with rage and he snarled, 'Get back ta work ye fookers or I'll have ye all flogged.' There were several snickers up and down the lines of men. Clearly, Birch had lost what was left of their respect.

Adam rushed to Robert as soon as his feet touched the ground, and dancing from one foot to the other in excitement said, 'Pa, I's seen mighty cannon, great big n'mighty powerful bullets and cannon balls 'n grape shot, I's been all over the ship with Cap'n Strudwich an' now I knows everythin' about it. I's gonna be a captain one day...' They all laughed as Robert said, 'Whoa boy, calm down!' and laughing, he ruffled the lad's hair. 'Calm down now.'

Nicholas and Robert were obviously quite excited by the day's events. 'We have stumbled upon a good supplier who has many of the items we need to start the mine operation and the store at Robert and Bethany's place,' Nicholas said.

He told of the meeting with Tommy 'The Chip' and how he and O'Farrell had sized each other up, and how Nicholas was quite confident they could trust each other.

Nicholas and Robert told them of the other events of the day, and how he, Nicholas, hoped they didn't mind but he had already accepted that they would all take lodgings at Tommy O'Farrell's house.

Before he could get a response an Irish lad came cantering up on a large grey Clydesdale mare to inform them that Mr O'Farrell had heard that their dinner engagement at the barracks had been cancelled, adding that Mr O'Farrell also was to have attended. The boy continued, saying Mr O'Farrell now insisted that they all join him for dinner tonight at his home. Besides, it would be more convenient since they were to lodge at the house.

They all accepted, and the lad, grinning, trotted away.

'Aye, well,' Strudwich began, 'I have been told O'Farrell is a decent sort and very helpful to the local folk. Before we head away, do ye think I could have a word with ye both?' he said turning to Nicholas and Victoria.

They looked at him quizzically and followed him some distance away from the others.

They were about one hundred feet from the others, when Strudwich suddenly turned and faced them. 'Now,' he said, 'if ye be beggin' me pardon, but ye's two I think of as I would my own children, if I had any now, so I'm hopin' ye will take my advice now.' Seeing he had their attention he went on.

'Since I have known ye Nicholas, I have watched and listened to ye talk about, write letters and know in my heart and mind that there is a very special person who has been in ye's thoughts for too long.'

He then turned to Victoria. 'Young lady ye are and have been that special someone all along, and during the voyage I have watched and listened to ye, all with the same intention.'

Victoria suddenly jumped, for at that moment she remembered she had a letter from her father for Nicholas.

'Now, ye's both have to sit down tomorra' and talk about your future, for God's sake.' he pleaded.

'I have spent almost all of me' life at sea. I married a beautiful and lovely woman in England, someone I had known since childhood, and I carry to me' grave the fact that I left on a voyage not one week after our marriage. She died whilst I was away at sea. She died alone giving birth to a little girl and I never got the chance to even tell her how much I loved her. I was away for three years, that was me' own choice. I took her for granted, understand?'

The look of pain on Peter's face brought tears to Victoria's eyes, and Nicholas sat silent, listening. 'What of your daughter now Peter?' Victoria asked.

'Another time lass,' he said quietly.

Strudwich had never talked of his life in England and Nicholas knew this moment to be especially poignant. There was a slight pause whilst Strudwich let his statement be absorbed, then he continued.

'Now, that gold mine of yours will still be there Nicholas and so will the equipment here. This lass has come halfway around the world to find you, so ye's be two,' he motioned at them both with the stem of his pipe, 'Take the time tomorrow and make ye plans for ye future.'

'T''is far more precious than any gold, let me tell you now!' he concluded and stalked off back to the others, leaving Nicholas and Victoria staring at each other.

Nicholas put his arm around Victoria's waist, feeling a great lump forming in his throat as he steered her back to the others. Victoria said nothing, but she was in a world of emotion herself and she hugged Nicholas's arm to let him know she understood his anxiety and somehow knew why he had not addressed the situation that Peter had spelt out. She had sensed his excitement and could see he was overjoyed to see her and of what was to become, but she also knew he wanted to get things moving. No doubt he was torn between action on two fronts, and there were so many things to consider.

She knew Nicholas had hard traits and loved to be in command of his destiny, and she knew not to question this. I must give him some space, she instinctively knew and she would allay his turmoil somewhat tomorrow, but tonight, she *must* give Nicholas her father's letter.

The evening meal was sumptuous by anyone's standard that night. Tommy had produced a veritable smorgasbord, chicken, suckling pig and a variety of vegetables and fruit and some very fine wine with it all.

The conversation was light and entertaining, and as a group of people, all from different walks of life, there was no shortage of interest.

The food was laid before them and they all began to enjoy Tommy's fine food.

Jack however, sat in silence and barely touched the food, a look of sadness upon his face.

Nicholas stared at his friend, thinking the big man was perhaps unwell. 'Jack, what is the matter fellow?' he asked.

'I feels bad Nicl'as, my fren Whip is no here to enjoy dis,' Jack waved his hand across the table. 'He alone wit nobody but my Kubi and m'be Gnarlu or Yindu, I don' tink I…is not fair!' Shaking his great head slowly, he looked up at them all, and his sad big eyes made them all pause. A moment passed as they did not know how to respond to what he had said.

'Well den, Oi'l be sure to make him an even bigger feast when Oi be meetin' 'im Jack, don' cha be worryin' 'bout that my friend', Tommy proclaimed with a warm grin on his face. Jack grinned back, obviously feeling better and thanked him. Jasus, 'e is but a big'un dis bloke. thought Tommy. Tank da good lord he's friendly! he chuckled to himself.

Jack, satisfied now that he was not being selfish, began to eat with relish, consuming almost double what anyone else could.

After dinner, they all retired to the front verandah. The sun was setting across Champion Bay splashing an orange glow across the sea and onto the verandah. It was truly a beautiful scene; patches and ribbons of blue sea draped in orange. No one said a word as they all were caught up in the moment.

Seamus produced a tray with coffee, sherry and shortbreads as they all lapsed into silence absorbing the warm sunset.

Chapter 51

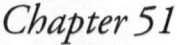

The Letter

*N*icholas announced that tomorrow he was going to seek out the officer of lands and survey and register the claim. He was about to go on, when he felt someone was staring at him.

Nicholas glanced up and was met with a fierce glare from Peter Strudwich.

Guilt washed over him as it dawned on him that once again he was making plans that did not include what had been discussed with Peter and Victoria. The truth was he was in unfamiliar territory, and for the first time in his life, felt he was not in control of his direction and so almost unconsciously sought to avoid what he must do.

There was so much to consider and *all* of it very important. Nicholas's impatience and drive to complete what he had decided did not help him, and he felt that *all* of the tasks demanded immediate action and *all* were very important.

Nicholas fretted, for example, that someone may jump his claim. He needed to establish the mine and have a permanent presence there, and the freight was urgently required to be loaded and transported for the mine and to start Bethany and Robert's enterprise.

And now, he was wracked with guilt because he found it difficult to find the time to spend with the greatest love of his life.

Normally, Nicholas could organise what was required to establish the mine and all of the other things with some ease and would and could do it by himself – it was just a matter of prioritising the needs and making a plan. But here he was hesitating. So many things to do.

With Victoria it was a whole new situation, and nearly all of it new territory for him. He worried about not applying himself correctly and about making sure Victoria was not subject to gossip or innuendo, especially since they would be living away from the general population.

His mind swam in an ever-increasing swirl of doubt about how to achieve all of this.

They must get engaged but he had no ring for her; she had no wedding dress as far as he knew. What about Ludwig and Lillian? He had not sought their approval and they would marry without them present. How would that effect Victoria, and who would officially marry them in the new colony?

All of this whirled about his head and he seemed unable to grasp even one of the things to begin. Ahhh! he raged internally in frustration.

He did not consider for even one minute that he needed help, nor had he recognised that this was not just about himself organising things as he was used to doing, but Victoria also needed to share the wedding plans. Marriage is about sharing, and Nicholas, despite his love for Victoria, knew nothing about sharing with a woman.

He was about to discover that he did not have complete control in this situation, and he was going to marry a very determined and intelligent woman. Victoria was not just a beautiful girl but a grown woman now and she had a similar drive to his own. When Victoria chose a course, she did not waiver until it was achieved, not unlike Nicholas for that matter.

Victoria appeared at Nicholas's side and bending down, placed the envelope from her father before him, kissing him on the cheek as she withdrew. Although she knew nothing of its content, knowing her father and his prudence in all situations, especially with regard to his only daughter, she could guess what had been written and the reasons.

486

Nicholas turned the letter over to see that it was from Ludwig and almost opened it right then and there but resisted the impulse, considering he would rather wait until he was alone or with just the two of them present.

He was not to know that it contained a solution to one of his concerns.

Early the next morning Nicholas rose, and taking Ludwig's letter, made his way out onto the verandah. He sat at the northern end where the rising sun warmed a small corner and propped the letter against the pitcher of water in front of him.

He stared at it almost willing it to open, wondering what was written.

Seamus appeared with a large mug of his Irish coffee, which consisted of a very strong black concoction, certainly coffee, but laced with whiskey and strong enough to give a ninety-year-old an erection, Nicholas thought ruefully as he sipped the brew.

He reached for the envelope and opening it, began to read.

My Dear Nicholas,

I hope this letter finds you in good health and if you are reading this letter then I know you will be of happy countenance, as Victoria would have delivered it to you.

Lillian and I will miss our only daughter very much and I counsel that you will only know of the depth of this when you eventually have children of your own.

We still reflect on that day in Cape Town when we first came upon you, covered in blood, bruises and barely conscious. How time moves! After that, you came back to live with us at Herrgarden Grande.

Nicholas, you are to Lillian and I, like the son we never had, and we watched you and Victoria grow up, you always there to protect her.

We are also aware of the circumstance which unfortunately estranged the pair of you, and I'm referring to Hymie Van Der Hoeke's indiscretion.

Lillian and I both know, you were only demonstrating that protection.

We ask that if you still feel mystified by her reaction, please do not judge her too harshly. She has only ever seen your care for her when growing up together, and at that age you would have been viewed by her as her big brother.

Remember, Victoria has had little interaction with men her own age, knowing little of a man's natural protective instincts over loved ones, and she certainly has had no romantic involvement with any man, despite our neighbour's obvious intention. She did not understand how some men can become obsessed, and with that obsession, sometimes dangerous.

When you first left Herrgarden Grande to follow your prospecting and adventuristic dreams, we think Victoria suddenly discovered that her feelings for you were a great deal more than she realised. You left a void within her that could not be filled, neither could she fathom what was actually missing until you returned. However, she certainly changed, even more so after your last involvement with each other. Lillian and I have both explained to her the reasons for your reaction.

Our daughter, as you now will no doubt be very aware, has been in love with you for a very long time, and as we have observed over time, you in love with her.

You both are now a very long way away and we consider it a possibility that we cannot be with you when finally, you both take the step that will bond you forever.

Nicholas, I cannot possibly wish for any man other than yourself, to take my daughter's hand in marriage, and since I cannot be with you in person, offer you my permission and blessing to marry Victoria.

You have our heartfelt best wishes and love to you both.

Ludwig and Lillian
14th March 1850.

Nicholas stared at the letter, then re-read it.

He looked up as Peter appeared on the verandah. He had a stern look on his face. Nicholas held up his hand to halt any conversation as he drew next to him, and holding out the letter to him said, 'Would you be so kind as to read this please Peter.'

Frowning, Peter took the pages and quickly scanned the letter, the word 'permission' catching his eye.

'I'll be back in a moment,' he said and went back inside, leaving Nicholas somewhat bemused.

Peter returned a few minutes later and sat to read the letter in front of Nicholas. When he had finished, he handed it back and he said, 'Hmmm, well that is one hurdle out of the way Nicholas and it will bode well for when we find a cleric to marry the two of ye.'

'It certainly allays some of my guilt for want of a better word, out of respect for Lillian and Lud, you understand,' Nicholas said.

Peter stood and looked at Nicholas, his affection overriding and cancelling out the lecture he had intended to give. He reached into his coat pocket and withdrew a small dark green leather-bound box. The box had gold filigree edging embossed into its lid and a black silk ribbon secured it.

Nicholas looked up at Peter's face in query. He saw only warmth in Peter's expression as they locked eyes. Peter placed the box on the table and said, 'This is my gift to ye and Victoria, Nicholas, and I do not want any argument, understand?'

He reached across and pushed the little box to Nicholas.

Nicholas was touched and hesitated before saying, 'I thank you Peter, but perhaps I should wait until Victoria is here to open it?'

'No, I think not Nicholas, please open it now' Peter said, glancing nervously toward the door as he said it.

Nicholas took the box and carefully undid the ribbon, then removed the lid.

He gasped, standing in the white silk interior were an engagement ring and matching wedding band.

Nicholas was speechless as he stared at the most beautifully crafted setting he had seen.

The engagement ring was adorned with a large single white diamond that even in the early morning light sparkled like the Sun itself. The stone was at least a carat in size and was surrounded by eight pear-shaped pale emeralds to complete the flower design and set in rich yellow gold. The wedding band itself was delicately set with four round-cut emeralds alternating with white diamonds, carefully sized so as not to divert attention from the engagement ring, simple yet beautiful.

Nicholas's mouth opened and shut, but before he could respond Peter said, 'These rings I brought for my wife as a token of my love, but I never got the chance to give them to her, she passing before I returned home as I told you previously.' He went on. 'I found the rings in Spain, but actually they were made in France I was informed, but it did not matter.

'The setting was what caught my eye and the emeralds were my wife's favourite stone and a close enough match to the colour of her eyes.

He again held up his hand, as Nicholas was about to speak and continued. 'I look at Victoria, and like her, these rings need to have sunlight and their beauty shown not locked away in the dark of a little memory box to be eventually forgotten, stolen or lost at sea. Ye understand what I am telling you Nicholas?' He stared at Nicholas with some intent and was rewarded with a slow nod of Nicholas's head.

'Ye and Victoria both have become as close to my heart as if ye be my own children, and so I want ye to have them because I know I have family once again now.'

Nicholas looked up at him and was a little surprised to see the beginnings of tears in Strudwich's eyes.

Nicholas stood and embraced Peter, each patting one another on the back. No further words were necessary.

The door suddenly swung open and Nicholas snatched up the box and put it in his pocket as Victoria and Tommy came out onto the verandah.

Victoria saw the quick movement by Nicholas but could not see what he actually did as Peter partially blocked her view, however she at once saw that something emotional had occurred and she looked quizzically at each of the men.

She looked radiant this morning, her hair was tied back in a ponytail, but she had also raised a bundle above it which tumbled down on top and fell to her shoulders. Victoria had chosen to wear a pair of large three-inch round gold earrings her mother had given her the night before she departed Mombasa and they shone in the morning sun.

Nicholas looked at her as she now sat down at the table, the morning sun behind her. She wore a short sleeved pale pink blouse, which flayed out over her hips and a beige pleated skirt.

He saw that she had placed a small sprig of jasmine flowers behind one ear. Victoria had picked the tiny sprig from the bush at the water tank at the rear of the house.

His emotions were in turmoil and his heart thudded out of control in his chest. He did not know whether to show her the letter first and then get down on bended knee in front of the others or wait until they were alone and propose then. Then he thought, that all he really wanted at this moment was to be alone with her.

They breakfasted all together in the great kitchen and moved outside after they had finished, Tommy shouting at the men to get cracking and start loading. Nicholas also gave directions to the crew loading.

Tommy, was chatting to Peter as Nicholas joined them just in time to hear Peter say he had to return to his ship. 'Tommy said he be havin' everythin' under control here Nicholas, why don't ye...' he said jabbing his thumb over his shoulder toward the house where Victoria stood watching the activity, and he turned on his heel and wandered back to the house. Nicholas watched him enter the house, then getting the message he went and drew Jack and Robert aside and asked them to saddle Stitch and Victoria's horse. 'Very, good!' Robert said, nodding his head vigorously and they turned away to do his bidding.

Going back inside he asked Tommy if he could have some sandwiches and a bottle of wine.

Tommy smiled and turning, gave the direction to Seamus.

'Ye know Nicholas, I know of a beautiful little glen not even six miles from here upstream of dis little river up the road, an' I be tinkin' that dis would be a crackin' place to take the young lady for ye picnic an' all, what does ye tink man? We's an' all can handle all o' dis,' Tommy concluded sweeping his arm at the loading and looking at him, one eyebrow cocked.

Nicholas felt somewhat foolish at being outmaneuvered but agreed and accepted Tommy's proposal.

Shortly after wood, Nicholas and Victoria rode out of Tommy's yard and turned north along the wagon ruts running out of town.

Tommy and Peter Strudwich came out of the house and onto the verandah to watch them go.

Peter shook his head and said, 'At last! It sunk in, I be thankin' ye now for helping Tommy.'

Tommy danced a little Irish jig, hopping from foot to foot, and turning to Peter with a wicked grin said, 'Ain't love grand now.'

Victoria and Nicholas walked their horses along the faint track, which ran roughly alongside the stream slowly meandering down between the low hills toward the sea. The sun was shining and it was a near perfect morning.

They began talking of the events in their lives since Nicholas left Herrgarden Grande, Victoria eventually telling of how she left home with Baba Joe and the Wahehe warriors to search for Nicholas not too long after he had left, and of how she was injured by the renegade Nandi near the ranges. She told him of Hymies passing and how he had been shockingly injured and could not face life. Nicholas was shocked and said to her with a frown, but then a grin, 'You're not impulsive by any chance now my dear?' Before she could answer he added, 'First, you almost got eaten by lions by riding off by yourself and now you tell me you ran off to strange places and get attacked by renegade Nandi?'

Victoria's reaction was exactly as he had anticipated, hot denial and anger.

She was furious and rounded on him. 'How *dare* you call me impulsive, when on both accounts it was *you* who caused my situation!'

He started to laugh. 'Me? How so?'

She snapped, 'I only went to the ranges to look for you! In any case it was a well-planned expedition and I had Baba Joe and the Wahehe with me, it was *NOT* impulsive!' She went on, still fuming, 'And...and the lion situation, was because...because,' her voice faded away as she saw he was grinning at her the same way he used to when they were growing up. He was teasing her.

He just grinned at her and spurred his horse up the trail laughing. Angry again, she chased after him as best she could.

When Victoria finally caught up with him he was sitting cross-legged on his saddle, completely at ease, holding out a water bottle to her – and still grinning.

She thought how ridiculous her outburst was, and try as she might, couldn't help but start laughing herself as she took the water bottle.

Victoria was uncomfortable with the corset digging into her ribs. Damn the stupid thing! she thought and excused herself and rode off behind some low shrubs beside the track. Nicholas, sneaking a look at her, could partly see that she was doing something to her blouse. Ha! He knew exactly what she was doing, knowing of her hatred of corsets and such modern women's paraphernalia. He laughed to himself. Ah, my free and lovely lady! he thought. He was still grinning when she came back. She looked at him and at his cheeky grin. 'What Nicholas? I hate these things!' she said, waving the rolled-up corset and stuffing it into her saddlebag.

They continued, side by side, Nicholas telling her of his leaving the ranges, confused by her reactions and unhappy because she gave him no opportunity to explain. He told of his frustrating attempts in London to finance the adventure to the Murchison. He told her about his meeting with Sir Gregory Scott, of Scott's financial backing and their partnership. He told of how Sir Gregory had directed that the *Collette* and her master Peter Strudwich be at his disposal. He further described the voyage and the risky business of landing at the Murchison River mouth, with the angle the river entered the sea. He told of how they built the homestead and the discovery of the gold much further north.

Victoria asked why the landing at the river was so dangerous, although she said she could imagine, considering that it was uncharted.

Nicholas described the river in detail, telling of the vicious cross-currents partly caused by the river's outflow and the swell which battered them. He told of the lives lost and of how they had transported the livestock across the river once on the sand bank. There was so much to tell her and it came to Nicholas, until just now, of just how much had been achieved in the time they had been in Western Australia.

They began to talk about growing up together and both felt even closer as they rode, their legs occasionally touching and their mutual anticipation of the next 'accidental' touch.

They talked, remembering the days at Lake Victoria, a special time, and laughed often at incidents remembered. But now they could both feel their emotions building slowly around them as they reminisced, a familiarity belonging to themselves and no one else.

It was good to be away from the others, and the anticipation began to rise between them causing the occasional involuntary shallow breath.

An hour later, they came upon Tommy's "Little Glen" as he had called it.

They tethered the horses and laid out a calico sheet and a horse blanket and Nicholas rummaged around in his saddlebags producing a bottle of sweet Spanish red wine and the sandwiches and some other little things Tommy had organised.

The Little Glen was a pretty little pool, clear and surrounded by snake bush and a variety of other shrubs, most of which were in bloom at this time of the year, so there was a sprinkling of yellow and mauve flowers, and a pleasant faint scent drifted around the area. They sat in dappled shade beneath a white trunked snappy gum.

Nicholas could stand it no more and moved slightly behind Victoria and encircled her in his arms. Nuzzling her hair, he smelt the jasmine and the cleanliness of her hair. She leaned back against him, and turning, looked up at him.

Their breath came in short pants as they stared at each other. Nicholas smiled at her and saw every detail of her face. He loved the golden little wispy sideburns and the almost invisible fine hair fading away from them down her jaw line.

He examined everything he could see, the slight bow of her mouth with fine hairs on the upper lip. He saw the tiny little freckles on her cheeks and the sprinkled few on her nose. He looked down to see the slight swelling of her breasts against the pink blouse and the rising and falling of them as she breathed.

Victoria wore no make-up except for some dark tint on her eyelashes. Her lips were naturally pink and slightly parted and he could just see two of her front teeth. He loved the little bow her upper lip formed.

God she is so beautiful, he thought and felt himself harden under Victoria's forearm which had been resting on him. This time he was beyond caring about it and everything seemed so natural, warm and relaxed, he was floating in a cloud of bliss.

Victoria, feeling emotional, stared up at her Nicholas, and his smile lifted her into a special place. She too examined his face. Such a strong chiselled face she thought, so full of character. She reached up and stroked his beard, deciding she did not like it as it hid parts of his face she loved.

It was Nicholas's amazing eyes that had always captivated her. They could, she knew, turn from warmth to unbridled menace when challenged. She suddenly shivered and came out in goosebumps as she again remembered the power she witnessed that evening by the lake when Nicholas had leapt to her defence. But now, at this moment, they showed only love and warmth, and she felt drawn into them and powerless to resist, even a little.

Nicholas's lips were suddenly almost touching her own as they felt each other's breath and gently began to kiss.

The kiss left them both breathless, as whilst it lasted quite a long time it was monumental in its feeling. It was impossible to describe the moment but it was as if some being held the two of them in its hands and gave its blessing, and neither could escape the euphoric swirl that surrounded them.

They did not move and simply looked at each other. Victoria suddenly felt Nicholas's hardness under her forearm. She was not embarrassed – in fact wanted to explore him more but she had never touched a man before and so was a little shy to make any further move. My God, she thought, it is so hard! The thought thrilled her and her heart accelerated with a will of its own. She unconsciously began to breathe quickly and felt a rush of heat come over her. They kissed again, their tongues flickered together as they swam in the pleasure of it all.

Nicholas was also having trouble controlling himself. He slid his hand up from her waist and gently cupped her breast. Victoria felt the rush of heat come again and she moaned slightly. He then undid one of the buttons on her blouse and slid his hand between the buttons to hold her breast. He could feel her nipple on the palm of his hand and he gently rolled it between his fingers, feeling it rapidly swell at his caress. He bent and kissed her neck, then blowing his warm breath into her ear, nibbled it. She shuddered and felt herself lose all control.

Victoria lifted herself away slightly and lay her hand on his hardness, rubbing it up and down.

Nicholas sat up suddenly and undid the side buttons of his breaches and lay down with her again. Victoria undid the buttons on her blouse.

Her blouse now hung off each shoulder, and as she turned to him one side slipped off her shoulder, exposing first one then the other breast. She made no attempt to cover herself, and Nicholas gaped at her purity, her white breasts and perfect dark pink nipples. He could see the blue veins running through them. He nipples were erect and stood out swollen and hard. Nicholas reached out and held both of her breasts, they shook slightly as he bent and took one nipple into his mouth.

Victoria began to slide her hand into his breeches and she thrilled at the thought in anticipation.

Suddenly, a dozen or so beautiful pink and grey birds flew screeching into the glen, to land at the edge of the water not six feet away, then instantly seeing them, flew away, screeching in alarm.

Nicholas and Victoria both jumped, startled by the raucous noise, their hearts pounding, caught in embarrassment, Victoria clutching her blouse together.

They both laughed at the absurdity of it all, the moment passing as did the passion for now. They rested in each other's arms for a moment, enjoying the closeness. No words were spoken and both were a little relieved in some strange way, and they both began to dress.

Nicholas then remembered the letter and delving into his waistcoat passed it to Victoria just as she fastened the last button on her blouse.

As she read the letter, Nicholas opened the package of sandwiches. There was also a small jar of olives, some cheese, and the wine. He also found Tommy had packed a chamois and two fine crystal glasses.

She was still carefully reading the letter when he poured a glass of wine and handed it to her.

Eventually, she carefully folded the letter and handed it back to him. Victoria did not speak, just sipped her wine and looked at him over the rim. She was smiling he could see yet wore a slight frown. He was anxious – undecided whether to ask for her hand right then and there or wait until everyone was present.

Nicholas gave himself a mental slap on the face and said to himself, Christ man, make a decision!

He decided to ask her now.

He stood and withdrew his bandana from his vest pocket and said, 'Vicky, close your eyes please.' She immediately said with surprise, 'Why, what for?'

Nicholas said, 'Please my Lady, close your eyes,' as he shook out the bandana. She looked at the bandana dubiously and closed her eyes. Nicholas had no sooner draped it across her eyes than she sniffed and baulked, wrinkling her nose saying, 'It stinks Nicky, what are you doing?' and pushed it away.

'Sorry,' he laughed, and turning went to the stream and vigorously rinsed his bandana out several times, examined it and wrung it out again. Satisfied, he came back, waving it to and fro to dry it. 'Now, is that better?' he asked. She examined it, and giggling nodded her head.

Nicholas kneeled down in front of her as he tied it around her head and over her eyes, and said, 'No peaking now.'

Nicholas took out the box, undid the ribbon and opened it. The diamond and emeralds flashed in the dappled light. God almighty! He was suddenly seized in panic – he had not checked the size! What if it was too small? He hesitated, too late he thought, and continued.

He took her left hand and kissed it, placed the open box in her palm and whipped the bandana off.

Victoria blinked, and as she got used to the light, her eyes dropped to see the rings glinting at her from the white silk.

She gasped and cried, 'Oh Nicholas, they are beautiful!' tears brimming in her eyes and her right hand at her mouth.

Nicholas took the box from her and gently lifted the engagement ring from its place and taking her left hand looked at her. The look on her face was burned into his memory forever in that instant. Holding his breath, he slid the ring onto her ring finger. Thank the Lord, he said to himself, it was just a fraction large but that did not matter at that moment.

'Will you marry me my Victoria,' he asked her gently.

Victoria looked at the ring and then back to him and threw her arms around him and burst into tears.

'Oh Nicky, yes, yes of course, I love you more than life itself! Yes!'

It would be hard to describe the feelings that now formed between Victoria and Nicholas. Every time they thought to speak, something forestalled them. It was as though some mental process over which they had no control was manifesting itself.

They walked around the Little Glen, arm in arm, Victoria laying her head on his arm as they walked, and Nicholas, lifting his arm around her shoulders and gently squeezing her, felt as though he was holding a fragile presence rather than a beautiful woman.

They eventually returned to the horses and Nicholas said, 'It's getting late, we better head back.' He bent and kissed her forehead.

They packed up the remains of the picnic and Victoria stepped behind her horse and put the corset back on announcing that she wanted to ride with Nicholas. They hooked up her horse's reigns to Stitch, and Nicholas swung her up behind him and they headed back, Victoria's arms around him.

Chapter 52

1850, Changing Priorities

July1850 found the new town bustling with activity. Augustus Gregory had at last finished his survey and the layout of the town. It had been announced that some forty lots of land were being released within weeks.

Under the new survey, only a few of the existing buildings were to remain. All the temporary shanty-style dwellings and businesses were to be replaced with solid buildings and placed on the newly surveyed town lots. Stored on the beach at Champion Bay were large stocks of stone, timber and roofing, all available to the new settlers at a minimum price, either cash or low interest government loans. The settlement was abuzz with rumour and gossip.

There were many so called Pensioner Guards and their families and ticket-of-leave convicts amongst the new population, all scrambling and keen to establish a new life in the new town. It was a period of great excitement for the people, and a place where a man could make a new beginning.

Tommy 'The Chip' had been lobbying for months to have his block of land included as part of the town's new boundary, however it was too far outside of the new town limit and so it remained as a semi-pastoral/rural and stock and station business, independent but still subject to Crown Law. Tommy did however secure freehold ownership of a further 300 acres north of the town abutting his existing landholding, this grant running within ten chains of the surveyed coastal line but was, at that time, somewhat isolated.

In the end, this land proved to be an important and profitable acquisition for the Irishman and, unknown to Nicholas and Victoria, important to them also.

There was talk that a Pensioner Guard and ticket-of-leave township was to be established at the Lynton site near Port Gregory, north-west of Northampton, to assist in building both Northampton and Geraldton. Some of the more astute businessman in the new town called it crazy to start this depot so far from both towns, a plan doomed to failure they said.

They were eventually proved correct.

Tommy, Jack, Robert and young Adam were on the front verandah after a particularly tough day loading when they saw Peter Strudwich coming up the track from the bay. He sat in the back of a small dray with his legs hanging over the back. It had been a long hard day for Strudwich, and he had endured more trouble from his first mate's abuse of the men. Strudwich was in dire need of a drink as he trudged up the path to greet the others.

He did however, have some good news for Nicholas and Victoria – John Roe and Augustus Gregory had arrived back from the Lynton site, and as they had encountered some resistance from the Blacks whilst trying to negotiate the establishment had returned early.

The other news was that it was rumoured the Anglican reverend, Charles Clay, might be coming to visit Geraldton sometime soon, but apparently only John Roe knew when, he and Clay being close friends.

The ride back to Geraldton was that of easy conversation and light-hearted banter. Victoria loved sitting behind Nicholas, she could feel the play of muscle in his back and she frequently hugged him. She was rewarded with occasional smiles and she was already scheming about when they could be alone again.

Nicholas was telling all about his foray into the Murchison River area and beyond. Victoria sat fascinated by his tales and enjoyed this intimacy with her man. He had just finished telling Victoria about the multi-legged 'spider' when they first landed at the river. Victoria was laughing, and all assembled on the verandah heard her as she and Nicholas appeared around the bend.

'Ah mercy now, dat's a welcome sound now! Thanks ta God someone is happy!' said Tommy as he looked at the row of stern and exhausted faces around him. 'Seamus!' he shouted, 'get some lads ta come an' grab the horses, there's a good lad, an' I be tinkin' we'll 'av another two tumblers as well.'

Victoria jumped down from behind Nicholas, sprinted up the steps and threw her arms around Peter Strudwich and cried out, 'Peter, we are engaged to be married, Nicholas has asked me to marry him!' She stepped back and proudly showed her ring to all of them. Nicholas had naturally told Victoria about Peter's gift and now she linked arms with the captain and reached up and kissed him on the cheek. Not wishing to embarrass him she whispered in his ear, 'Thank you, thank you, you wonderful man.'

Peter looked at her and the happiness was hard to ignore. Nevertheless, he managed a gruff reply saying, 'We shall talk about that later young Lady,' and tapped one finger gently on her nose. He did not, however, succeed in hiding his delight from either Victoria or Nicholas.

Handshakes and congratulations came from one and all, the news quickly spread up to the store shed and accommodation building and all of Tommy's men joined them. Tommy produced several bottles of French champagne and rum from his cooler under the house.

Someone produced an accordion and a fiddle, and some of the Irish lads had very fine voices and sang anything from traditional Irish folk songs to beautiful and moving ballads. Amongst them were the twin brothers, Sean and Michael McNab, and the pair moved some to tears with their heart-rending harmony and ancient ballads. The brothers entertained the group for most of the night, hardly taking a pause save for quaffing rum.

Needless to say, there were a few sore heads the next morning at the breakfast table.

After breakfast, Tommy, Robert, Victoria and Nicholas walked up to inspect the progress made loading the previous day, and Nicholas was elated at the amount of work done.

'Where is Jack?' he asked, suddenly noticing his absence.

'Ah, 'e's up with the teams and da 'orses, 'e goes up every morning, just loves dem bullocks, 'e 'as a way with 'em dat fo' sure,' Robert said.

'Aha, that's why Seamus is complainin' then about 'is sugar lump stock!' Tommy said. They all had a laugh.

He had already told Tommy about how he had intended to transport the equipment up to Robert and Bethany's and store it there until he was ready at the mine site. He had also discussed what he wanted built at the Stokes', and had drawn up plans for the store and barn etc. He and Tommy had examined and discussed the plan in detail.

He was lamenting that there was so much to be done and was wondering how he could make it all happen in time, especially the transport.

'Well then,' said Tommy, switching to his cultured English voice with a twinkle in his eye. 'If I may be somewhat presumptuous Nicholas, why don't you let me send my team of artisans back up with you when you go back? I mean they can start building as soon as they arrive old chap and you would be well advised to have the extra hands with you for a number of reasons, you understand.' He went on, 'Also, we will, at some stage, have to drive the teams back for the next load once the buildings have been completed because apart from the rest of the general material, the stone blocks and glass will not be arriving for at least three weeks.

Victoria giggled at Tommy's switch to a cultured voice, though he could not completely erase his Irish lilt.

'Further, they could offer some protection whilst you and Jack went onto your claim, for the lady you understand,' he said.

'Hmmm, might not be a bad idea Tommy. We will discuss and go over the financials when I return from my meeting today, if I can manage to steal some of John Roe's time.

'We must also discuss our wedding plans Vicky,' Nicholas said, placing his arm around her shoulder. She smiled and said, 'I can do most of that Nicholas, I need to organise catering as soon as we know when a minister can come. Oh, and I may need a dressmaker. Oh, did I tell you Mama gave me her wedding dress before we left Mombasa?'

'Most presumptuous lady our Lillian,' laughed Nicholas, shaking his head and rolling his eyes.

'If ye be wantin' any help, just ye be askin', you 'ear?' said Tommy.

'Surely now ye'll be wantin' to 'ave the weddin' 'ere…I mean there's no other place now is there? 'An, dat bein' da case, ye's will all be stayin' 'ere, I means, ye's all already 'ere yes?

'Please,' he added, the devilish twinkle in his eyes and laughing.

Victoria looked up at Nicholas to gauge his reaction to Tommy's offer. She personally thought it a great idea.

'Are you sure Tommy, I mean you have been so generous to us, I for one fear we are putting you out almost everyday,' he said.

'Don't cha be worryin' ye selves 'bout t'ings like dat, tis an honour, an' what a thrill ta be 'aven Geraldton's first grand weddin!' Tommy was jumping from foot to foot at the thought of it all. 'De ta de, de ta de,' he broke into his little Irish jig. 'It'll be so grand!' He laughed excitedly.

Caught up in his glee, Nicholas saw an almost imperceptible nod and smile from Victoria.

Chuckling Nicholas said, 'How can we resist Tommy? Thank you, we both accept.'

The following morning, Nicholas went to meet John Roe, or perhaps William Burges, and lodge the documents he had written up for making his claim for the prospect at the new mine.

As far as Nicholas was aware, at that time in 1850, one only had to give the coordinates of the leases required to prospect. One did not have to report a development until the new mine reserves were proven, and if the intention was to process any ore. This applied to any mineralisation of consequence that may be found on that lease.

He was in luck. John Roe was there and agreed to his request for a meeting.

Nicholas had to wait a little as Roe had business with another supplicant, so he sat on the little verandah that jutted out the front of Lieutenant Elliot's little house, which doubled as the administrative office of government officials, and watched the soldiers go through their drills on the sandy parade ground. Not long after a shabbily looking fellow exited the office, followed by a tall well-dressed gentleman.

'Ahh, the mysterious Mr Yuin I presume.' said John Roe as he came from the open doorway with hand extended.

Roe was impeccably dressed with long grey coat, dark grey trousers, a black pin-striped vest and full shirt and ribbon tie, despite the warmth of the day. Nicholas noted the firm handshake and the direct gaze, a mere hint of a smile at his mouth. He had a neatly trimmed grey beard and moustache in the Van Dyke style but had full side hair on his cheeks.

Nicholas subconsciously rubbed his hand over his newly clean-shaven face with only the moustache remaining.

Victoria had let him know none too subtly two days ago that she did not like his full beard, and had wrinkled her nose saying, 'They stink Nicky.' And so, the moustache was his last vestige of defiance in that matter.

'I am honoured to meet you Mr Roe,' Nicholas said, and with that Roe said 'Come, come', and led the way to his desk in the sparse room. 'Please sit down Mr Yuin,' he said with a wave of his hand. Nicholas sat and glanced around noting the cot against one wall and the rudimentary timber desks, of which there were two, and three wooden chairs. There were stacks of documents and maps neatly stacked on the other desk set against the wall.

'How is the charming Miss Amendson may I ask Mr Yuin?' Roe began. 'She is, I presume, well and happy now that you two have at last found each other once again. An amazing story of love and devotion I think?'

'She is fine thanking you sir, and very happy as, in fact, am I,' Nicholas replied. 'We became engaged to be married only the day before yesterday.'

Roe clapped his hands exclaiming, 'Excellent, excellent!' and stood and extended his hand in congratulation. They sat again and John Roe nodding said, 'There will be much to do Mr Yuin. You will marry in Geraldton I presume?'

'Yes sir, we will marry here, but as yet have not set a date.'

Roe steepled his hands and took pause before he said, 'Hmmm, then you will, I presume be in need of a minister or cleric in the near future?'

Nicholas had already been informed that Roe was a staunch and religious man of the Anglican denomination.

'Yes sir, you would be correct. In fact, that is one of the reasons I have come to meet you, to seek knowledge of, or perhaps you may be able to advise, of a minister who may be visiting the area in the near future?'

John Roe looked at the man before him, studying him as subtly as he could. Roe was an excellent judge of character, and the more he spoke to Yuin, the more he liked the much younger man. Roe thought, I can see why Sir Gregory has a bond with this young man. He has the same fire in his eyes as Scott had when he and Scott first met.

Nicholas, aware that he was being scrutinised, waited a moment, then continued. 'In the interim, I have urgent need to return to the Murchison and beyond as quickly as possible, and I shall explain shortly sir. However, I do not wish to spoil in any way our intended plans for marriage.' He withdrew the claim letters from his satchel, placing them before Roe and went on.

'We had considered accepting Augustus Gregory's generous offer of lodging my intended at his sister's abode at Northampton until arrangements could be made for our marriage, but now that the *Collette* is being careened here at Champion Bay, this means our great friend Captain Strudwich will be here for possibly two months, perhaps less, and I find it to be a more appropriate arrangement to have Victoria stay here.'

Roe immediately said, 'Mr Yuin, there is a cottage being built at Point Moore for the lighthouse keeper. You are aware that the light is incomplete, however the abode will be shortly available. It already has four walls, a roof and verandah, and you are welcome to make use of it.

Nicholas said, 'Sir, I thank you for your most generous offer, however, Tommy O'Farrell has provided lodgings for us all at his house, and we have made business arrangements using O'Farrell as our source of supply. It is far more convenient since I will be traversing back and forth to Geraldton.'

'Quite, quite, best not to place yourselves in the path of vicious rumours, I agree!' said Roe.

Suddenly he chuckled, 'Aye, aye, our Mister O'Farrell has a rodent's nose for business that I cannot help but admire.'

Roe placed both hands on the table and standing rang a small bell. In an instant a young private appeared at the door, saluting smartly. 'Yes sir?' Roe ordered two cups of tea and some biscuits without bothering to ask whether Nicholas wanted any and remained standing with his knuckles on the table. Locking eyes with Nicholas he said, 'From what I know, Tommy the Chip is a good and straight man and very generous with it. However, as you would well have observed, he is a very astute man.

'I counsel that you tread carefully, as Tommy will either be your best friend for life, or should you two cross each other, a hard enemy.'

Roe added, 'Tommy is offering his generousity either because he sees his meeting you as an excellent business opportunity, or it is because he believes you and he will be the best of friends for always, perhaps even both, in which case you will never have anything to worry about, especially his loyalty.

'Now, getting back to your enquiry with regards my knowledge of a minister to perform the marriage, you are in luck sir! There will be an Anglican minister arriving here on or about the 13th of September. He is the Reverend Charles Clay, a personal friend and an ordained Anglican minister. He is based in the settlement at Northam, east of Perth, a good man, and I am sure Charles would be delighted to perform the ceremony. With your permission, I shall send a letter to him, I am not sure whether it will reach him before his departure, but no matter, I am sure he will be delighted irrespective.'

Nicholas's head was spinning, it was all happening so fast.

Nicholas was about to thank Roe for his counsel and information, when he was interrupted by a loud and frantic knocking on the door.

Someone called out, 'Mr Roe sir, my apologies, but I have information of an urgent nature.'

'Come man,' Roe said with some annoyance.

A hot and sweaty man in rough mining flannels entered the room and stood there for a moment, obviously exhausted, mopping his forehead with a sweaty bandana and taking deep breaths.

'Yes, yes, man what is it?' Roe asked.

'Sir, 'Enry Gregory, 'e 'as sent me to inform you that the blacks are fightin' an' killin' each other at the Murchison.' He gulped and proceeded. 'So far as 'e can tell it is a' inter-tribal dispute an' 'as not spread further than the Watjari to the south an' the Nhanda tribe at the river.'

Nicholas went cold and said, 'Ahhh, no,' knowing immediately it had to be over Nimit'je and her betrothal.

Roe thanked the man who turned to go when Nicholas said, 'Excuse me my man, do you know of Tommy O'Farrell's establishment?' The man nodded. Nicholas asked, 'Would it be possible that you give this information to him, and also, there are a couple of my people with Tommy at this moment, Robert Stokes in particular. Just ask that they prepare to move, and inform that I will join them soon, that is if Mr Roe does not mind?'

Roe nodded in confirmation and thanked the man again, telling him to go to the mess tent and get some refreshment. The man bustled out of the door and was gone.

Nicholas, worry about Whip churning at his gut like acid, told Roe of the situation as he knew of it. He told of his own interaction with the Nhanda and why he thought the war would have started. Nicholas took a deep breath and calmed himself. He thought it best to be straight and inform Roe of his intentions, including his prospecting and mining intentions. He presented the documents to stake the claims he wanted to prospect.

The four claims were under the names of himself, Wilber Wilberforce, Jack Lungile and Sir Gregory Scott and himself, he being the agent for Sir Gregory's claim as an equal partner in the Yuin Scott Pastoral Company.

He did not, however inform Roe of his gold discovery, considering it wise at this stage not to risk the information leaking out. First he needed to establish the load, and he did after all have the advantage of time on his side in that matter.

Roe said, 'You are in partnership with Sir Gregory Scott?'

'Yes sir, he and I met in London and established our arrangement. He is a fine gentleman and I am fortunate that I have his complete trust and respect,' Nicholas answered.

'I know Sir Gregory well Mr Yuin, and you are right, he is a fine gentleman, you could not have a more respected man in all of England than Sir Gregory,' Roe said.

Nicholas told him of the intended establishment of the store and general stock agency at the Stokes' and of the homestead being built at the Murchison.

Roe was impressed and said he was very pleased that he was helping the community expand, noting the considerable financial commitment. He said he thought the northern establishment of the Stokes' enterprise would serve the exploration and the flood of prospectors and pastoralists well into the future.

They talked for a further hour and discussed many topics, Nicholas warming to the taciturn man, appreciating the man's keen intellect.

Suddenly, John Roe stood and said, 'Well I can see that you have much to do Mr Yuin, as have I.

You will be wanting to get moving I presume to see what effect the tribal war has had at the river. If I can be of any assistance, now or in the future, please let me know.'

They shook hands warmly and Nicholas strode out into the sunlight, squinting. He saw a man in police uniform leaning on the verandah post. He was a scruffy looking fellow, with unkempt hair sticking out from under his police cap and was sporting a dirty black beard.

The copper was staring straight at Nicholas as if he knew him. Remembering the conversation at the Stokes' house about the copper from Mullewa, he put two and two together – McGuinness!

Nicholas chose to act as if the man wasn't even there. He leapt into the saddle, spurring Stitch to a gallop down the track to O'Farrell's.

Chapter 53

War at the Murchison

It was late afternoon, and Tommy, Robert and Jack were sitting on some barrels in the shade at the store shed at the rear of the house, enjoying a well-earned mug of water. Young Adam had accompanied Strudwich down to the ship today, a pastime the lad grasped at every opportunity.

They had achieved a lot today with four of the long beds finally loaded and sides fitted. They had also loaded Robert's wagon with some of the smaller goods, tools and personal items for some of Tommy's men accompanying them. They had all started at dawn and were feeling the effects of the early start.

Their conversation was interrupted when a man came striding up the path toward them, having left his horse at the front hitch.

'Now what'll dis fellow be wantin' fa' God's sake.'

The fellow was somewhat portly and was fair blowing by the time he came up to them.

He was red faced and sweat ran down his face in rivulets. 'Beggin' ye pardon Tommy,' he wheezed.

'God's sake man, 'ere now, 'av a drink of water before ye blow ye bloody pooper valve!' laughed Tommy, handing him a mug of water.

'Thank ye, thank ye,' the fellow said grasping the mug in both hands and scoffing down the cool water.

'Now den, what's the big fuss me hearty,' asked Tommy.

'I's just come down from the barracks Tommy. Mr Yuin is up there with John Roe, an' 'e, Mr Yuin, told me to 'urry down an' tell ye's dat der's a tribal war 'appenin' up by Northampton, at the river!'

'What!' Robert jumped to his feet as did Jack, Robert immediately thinking of Bethany.

'I's just ridden down from Northampton wit' a message from 'Enry Gregory to warn everyone thinkin' o' goin' up there,' the man, somewhat calmer, continued.

'Yes'ar ! The Blacks are killin' each other, dozens of 'em apparently already dead!

'Mr Yuin said 'e be comin' down 'ere as soon as 'e's finished 'is meetin'. An' to tell youse an' Robert Stokes to get ready to move.'

The fellow asked for another drink and said, 'I'll be 'eadin' back den Tommy, thanks to ya, good afternoon,' and he doffed his hat and hurried away.

There was stunned silence. Jack said, 'Nimit'je an' Tjarlu, Robert, dey's done an' escaped, big trouble, I be thinkin' dis why.'

Robert hardly knew of Nimit'je and Tjarlu but knew all about the young couple and the unhappiness over the betrothal from Jack, but now he was really worried about Bethany.

'Christ almighty! What about Whip, 'e'll be right in the middle of it an all!' said Robert.

Jack was already pacing up and down, fear for his friend gnawing at his gut.

'Well now den, we ain't gonna panic now are we, we'll all be waitin' till Nicholas comes back an' see what 'e tink's before runnin'off 'alf cocked,' Tommy said, reading Jack's reaction and anticipating what Jack was about to announce which, however predictable, was to immediately run to his friend's aid. 'After all, it's too late to leave t'day anyhow!' he added. 'Now come on, we'll go wait fo' Nicholas on the front verandah.'

Peter Strudwich and young Adam arrived just as they were walking down from the shed. Robert quickly told Strudwich what had occurred. Young Adam wrung his hands and said, 'Pa, what about Ma?' Robert looked down, and squatting in front of him said, 'Now don't ye be worrying 'bout ye ma now boy, she bein' a long way nor north - east o' the troubles, an' at any rate, them's people love her, they'll not harm her, understand son?'

Adam looked at his adopted father, tears in his eyes and managed, 'Ma would fair whup 'em anyhows, if'in theys caused any trouble wouldn't she Pa?' They all laughed at the lad's statement and Robert held the boy's shoulders and said, 'Ye can bet on that son! Come on then,' and they all went on to the verandah to wait.

In the meantime, they discussed the war and speculated why it had started.

Big Jack was still pacing up and down, a great frown on his forehead.

Peter said, 'Jack, come and sit down for Christ's sake, ye'll be worn out before ye even start ye hear!'

When Jack reluctantly complied, sitting on the stoep, Strudwich said, 'I don't think Wilber will be in any danger lads, unless 'e interfered with what was 'appenin'. From what youse is all sayin' it's all between the two tribes and the betrothal trouble.'

'Big Jack suddenly sprang to his feet and said, 'Nic'las come,' just as Nicholas appeared some 300 yards up the track. Minutes later he galloped into the yard, going straight up to the shed at the back.

Nicholas had already decided what to do and how they would proceed. He strode straight into the kitchen and got a large tumbler of water downing it in one long draught.

Victoria and Tommy appeared at the doorway, and she came to him, placing her arm in his affectionately before seeing the frown on his face and asked, 'What is the matter Nicholas?'

'Tribal war at the river area has broken out I am afraid,' he replied turning to Tommy and asked, 'Could we get the fellows who are going to accompany us to the north to join us on the front verandah Tommy? I'll tell you all about it when we get assembled.'

Tommy went straight out the back door shouting as he went.

'Come Vicky, once we are all together I will tell everyone what we are going to do and discuss how it is to be done.' She had never seen Nicholas project such a commanding demeanour. He is like a general, she thought giggling to herself, but proud of him anyway. They walked through to the verandah and sat down with the others.

They all started to talk at once, Nicholas held up his hand for quiet and said, 'You all know what the situation is from Henry Gregory's man yes?' They all nodded in unison.

'Well, here is what we are going to do!' said Nicholas, taking charge. 'As I see things, I do not think we will be in much danger. The war is between the Nhanda and the Watjari, and unless Whip has interfered, and I don't believe he would do that – he is not that stupid – he likely is at the homestead and fine, understand Jack?'

The big fellow slowly nodded his head.

Nicholas continued. 'Something else other than Nimit'je and Tjarlu's running away – if that is what happened and those two broke the betrothal – must have happened. We do not know what that is so we must be careful as we enter their respective areas. The war means tribal boundaries between the two will now be blurred. Depending on the victors, or what has evolved, that *could* change our standing with, for example, the Watjari, if they have the upper hand. To get to the homestead we must first cross Watjari land.

'The war and dispute, whatever it is, I think will be restricted to the Watjari and the Nhanda lands and I do not believe will affect any other tribes or settlements, but we must be alert nonetheless. Is everyone clear at this moment?' Nicholas asked. There was muttered agreement punctuated by 'Aye' and 'He is right I reckon'.

'How are we going to travel Nicholas, all together or do we separate?' Robert asked.

'Good question Robert. First, I want to move quickly before those up the hill,' he jerked his thumb toward the Army barracks, 'decide that no one will travel north until they investigate, which would take weeks.'

Placing his hands on the table he added, 'I want to be on the trail with the first trains by no later than mid-afternoon tomorrow even if we have to work all night.'

This drew a whistle from Tommy and mutterings of disbelief from others in the group.

'Tommy, after this meeting I want to ratify a deal with you with regards to the extra men we discussed. Is that convenient for you?' Nicholas said.

Tommy was impressed with the way Nicholas took control of the situation immediately, leaving no doubt about what was expected, 'Dat'll be no problem Nicholas,' Tommy replied. 'We'll discuss that later. Under da circumstances, all Oi'l be askin' is rates ta cover me boys' wages n' keep, an' we'll be leavin' it at that.'

Nicholas thanked him and made a mental note to return the favour in the future before starting again. 'Firstly, Bobby, what is the latest status with regards to the loading of the wagons and how many can we get rolling by mid-morning tomorrow. Consider first, which of the wagons will be slowest, if you will.'

'We's got two long beds loaded an' ready ta roll,' Robert replied. 'Tha' first two 'ave the 'eavy minin' gear in 'em, dey's loaded in the order ye be wantin' Nicholas, an we's already, or I should say Jack 'as, already had the two teams for 'em 'arnessed up ta check, so dey's can be ready no problem. Dey's bein' tha 'eaviest, an' slowest o' tha' lot.'

'Good, good,' said Nicholas.

'The other two, well dey's got the foundation stones and mortar lime bags, timber, iron, forge 'n smithy's tools, rivets an' nails along with paint, water troughs, four 1000-gallon water tanks, ¾-inch 'awser's, 200 yards, 500 yards o' ¾-inch 'emp rope, six boxes of square shank bolts 'n nuts,' he paused, eyes cast skywards as he tried to remember what else they had loaded.

'Ahhhm, der's about 400 lengths o' ½-inch water pipe, some o' the new galvanised stuff, some copper n'lead, dey's all be about 15-foot lengths... oh and seven boxes of brass water taps, couplins etc, but those last two are still bein' loaded. Each wagon 'as feed an' water for the trains an' also spare axels, wagon wheels and jackin' equipment Nicholas.'

Nicholas broke in before Robert could launch into more detail again and said, 'Excellent, that's almost four wagons, you have been very busy!'

"Ang on, der's still quite some loadin' to do on the second two as I mentioned Nicholas,' Robert continued. 'Oi dunno 'ifin we c'n get it all done by tomorra afternoon, but we's can try.

'We have also loaded up my wagon, an' it 'as all of tha' small store stuff an' also the bedding, tools etc for campin' on tha' way. Young Adam can drive it, no problem, since 'e 'as bin loadin' it, right Adam?' He winked at the lad. Adam thought his head would explode with pride and replied, 'Yes sir, I can do it!'

'Couldn't 'av done wit out Tommy's lads,' Robert continued. 'Worked like nig..ohhh,' his voice trailed off as he quickly looked at Big Jack, who had rolled his great eyes in Robert's direction, and mumbled, 'Sorry Jack, Oi' wasn't thinkin', I's sorry.' He was so embarrassed he actually shuffled his feet back and forth under his chair.

Before anybody could react, Jack, who fortunately for Robert, was feeling in much better humour now that Nicholas had taken charge and he knew they were moving quickly, took two great strides around to Robert, and grabbing him, chair and all, lifted him clean off the floor. Robert went grey in fright and could only manage a shrill 'Sheee..it!', thinking he was going to die. Jack looked at him, then gave him a huge smacking kiss on the cheek and said, 'Dat's all right, *Ikosi umlungu akunandaba,'* and dumped him back on the floor with a bang.

Victoria, clapping her hands together, burst out laughing, as did Nicholas and the rest of them.

Robert, highly embarrassed and now even more so, was vigorously scrubbing his cheek.

'Wha'did 'e say, wha'did 'e say,' he pleaded.

Victoria, still giggling, said, 'He said it doesn't matter boss white man. He was making light of your utterance Robert.' She started to giggle again at the audacious big man.

As the laughter died down, Nicholas was thinking good timing as it had lifted the gloom from the group.

There was still some light ribbing going on when Nicholas said, 'Peter, Victoria and Tommy, can I have a word please? Turning to the rest of the men he said, 'Excuse me gentlemen, we won't be a moment.'

Once inside Nicholas turned to Victoria and placed his hands on her shoulders. 'Vicky, John Roe informed me today that the Anglican minister, Charles Clay, will be in Geraldton on or about the 13th of September. Are you happy to have him marry us around that date, or near to?' He grinned down at her, watching her face soften and then smile at him. She gave a little jump and hugged him in answer.

Nicholas fought to keep his composure. 'Good, good, that's settled. That's about 7weeks from now and I will be back in about 6 weeks. Tommy, is that all right with you?'

Tommy answered with his little jig, 'De, ta, de, de, ta, de,' before saying, 'O' course it's foyne, it'll be a joyous day! An' don'cha be worryin' 'bout a thing you two.'

Nicholas turned to Peter and asked, 'Peter, our dear friend, would you give Victoria and I the honour of giving away the bride since Ludwig cannot be here?'

Peter, stunned, then swept low and bowed before them and replied, 'This is a great honour, of course I accept,' and received a huge hug from Victoria.

'Now the bad news. Victoria, I must leave tomorrow to check on Whip and the Nhanda, I am the one who has the closest relationship with old Kalbarri and his tribe, and especially so with young Nimit'ji.'

Victoria silenced him with two fingers to his mouth. 'Of course you must go Nicky, I understand completely, its fine. Nothing is going to upset me and I have much to organise here,' she said bravely, despite the fear she was feeling for him.

The relief on Nicholas's face was palpable as he had been expecting a hard argument with Victoria insisting on accompanying him north.

Victoria then, trying to put a stern voice on said, 'But you had better be back here 6 weeks my man, and in one piece!' Despite her attempt at levity, worry churned at Victoria, and a wave of emotion suddenly overcame her and she started to cry. Everything seemed to be happening so fast.

The relief Nicholas had felt vanished and turned to woe as he looked at her.

She apologised softly and went to her room.

Excusing himself, Nicholas went and tapped lightly on her bedroom door. 'Vicky? It is me, can I come in?'

A faint 'yes' came to him and he entered to see Victoria sitting on the end of the bed, tears running down her face as she looked up at him. She looked so sad, his heart almost stopped.

'I am sorry Nicky, but everything is happening so fast, and we have spent so little time together and now you have to go up immediately and might be hurt, maybe even killed!' she burst into tears.

Nicholas's heart broke and he rushed to her, holding her tight as she sobbed quietly into his chest.

He thought, this is not fair, why did all of this have to happen now. He could find no words to say to her at this moment, trapped by what had to be done. He just held her and tenderly stroked her hair as she calmed down.

Finally he quietly said to her, 'I am sorry Vicky, you are right, everything is happening so fast and all at once. These last few days have been frantic, hardly having spent any time together. The situation at the river, is not as bad as it seems, I think. Most people around the area have only had contact with the tribes randomly, and that is not the situation with Jack, Whip and I.'

Nicholas then began to tell her of Nimit'je's near rape, his bonding with the Nhanda and how old Kalbarri saw him as a friend and even placed Gnarlu and Yindu with him to help guide and teach him about the land. He told of how Gnarlu and Yindu had saved his life when he had been bitten by the snake. He continued talking if only to make her feel better.

When he had finished, she seemed somewhat calmer and he could sense that he had at least succeeded in allaying a lot of her fears. 'Fear is usually bred out of the unknown,' he said, recalling one of Ludwig's sayings.

'Tonight, we will have dinner together, just you and I, would you like that?'

She nodded. He knew it wasn't much, but given the time was all he could do.

Victoria was feeling much better now that she understood Nicholas was quite close to one of the tribes and was seemingly well regarded by most of the people up there.

'I am all right my Nicholas,' she said reaching up and kissing him. 'You must go and attend to the men, I will be fine, I think, everything just rolled up on me.'

Nicholas kissed her back and rose to join the rest of the men.

'Robert, Tommy and Peter, a word?' They came to him and he began, 'All is as okay as it can be. I really think Victoria needs to have another woman to talk to. I wish Bethany could be here, do you think she would be happy to come down Robert?'

Robert nodded in agreement. 'Yes, she be 'appy, no problem Nicholas'

'But there is no way we could get her down here so quickly,' Nicholas continued, 'And I will not contemplate bringing Victoria with me at this stage, so what is, is what is, unfortunately.'

He told of how they were going to have a special dinner tonight. Tommy immediately told him that he would organise it for him. 'Don' cha be worryin' 'bout that me hearty! An' we will bring in extra hands tonight to finish loading, okay!'

Nicholas, relieved, now turned to the rest of them.

'Right gentlemen, we will proceed as follows.' Nicholas told them that Robert, Adam and Tommy's crews were to proceed direct to Northampton with the two heaviest long beds and Robert's wagon. They would be followed up by the other two slightly smaller wagons that would finish being loaded tonight, one of which would eventually deliver part of its load to the river homestead.

Nicholas, Jack and two of Tommy's trusted men would accompany them to where the main trail to Geraldton branched off. They would then peel off and head straight to the river to check on Whip. If all were well, Nicholas, Whip and Jack would leave Tommy's men at the river homestead and head straight to Robert's homestead to organise the work for Tommy's artisans.

Jack and three of Tommy's men would immediately take the two trains (including the drivers) loaded with mining equipment and stores straight to the prospect, leaving Whip and Nicholas to organise the layout and survey for the new buildings. Then he and Whip would hurry to catch up with Jack at the granite dome.

Once they got to the mine the next day, they would unload all of the mining equipment and show two of the artisans, each skilled in stone masonry and basic carpentry, what was to be done until they returned.

That done and the camp set up for the men, they would leave two horses behind and drive the two long beds back to Robert and Bethany's and check all was in order with the building. Bethany, Robert and the children would join them, and as quickly as possible all would head back to Geraldton via the river dropping off the last remaining freight at the homestead for Tommy's lads to unload. Once the livestock was checked and they were happy with the two Irish lads caretaking abilities, they were to head on to Geraldton.

'Now gentleman, any questions?' Hardly giving anyone time to respond, he snapped, 'Right, let's get cracking lads.'

Tommy stood watching Nicholas organise things. 'Well if I's ever 'ad any doubt about 'is leadership qualities, dey's all been skittled!' he cackled to himself.

Tommy had one of his men harness his jaunting cart to his favourite horse, a little grey mare which he called Pintess because she was quite small but sturdy. He did not really like riding, having been thrown off a horse and landing on a hard cobblestone street in Belfast when he was young, so had acquired this single seat Irish-made jaunting cart to get around in, ideal for this country as it had the new leaf spring suspension.

Tommy headed to the barracks, his intention to ask if he could set up a table and chairs at the keepers cottage for Nicholas and Victoria, either tonight or tomorrow night. Permission was given, so Tommy headed back. On the way, he thought to have a look at how the *Collette's* repairs were proceeding.

He had just turned toward Point Moore when he heard a ruckus at the ale house, in which he happened to have an interest. It was the last shanty before the beachhead with a rough wooden sign at the front reading, "The Champion Bay Inn". Two sailors were hard at it, one of whom he could see was the *Collette's* first mate, Birch. He was getting a bit of a flogging from a slightly smaller man as far as Tommy could tell.

Tommy's men had kept him up to date about the first mates behaviour and his open threats to Yuin and Big Jack, so from their reports he was not surprised to see him in a fight. Tommy saw two of his men he had directed to shadow Birch watching the proceedings.

Making a note to let Peter Strudwich know about the fight, he had a look at the *Collette* noting work at the rudder had progressed well, but the rudder itself was still standing upright against the hull instead of in its brackets, or whatever they were called, thought Tommy.

Turning for home, Tommy drove up to the storage shed and saw Nicholas and Robert deep in discussion. Dismounting from his buggy he wandered over and said, 'Anythin' I can 'elp with gents?'

Nicholas frowned and said, 'Looks like we may have been a bit ambitious trying to get everything done by tomorrow morning. Robert thinks we are courting disaster to attempt it, what do you think Tommy?'

Tommy walked around the wagons noting quite a few items lying on the ground around the wagons still to be loaded. He answered, 'Aye Nicholas, I be tinkin' Robert be wise, 'tis a bloody rough track an' all, why not give it another day. The men can all work tonight till late and take it easy on the 'morrow, den, all can be checked an' deys can leave early the following' morning, at sunrise if need be, but all fresh loik. Ye'll not be loosin' anythin Oi reckon man.'

Nicholas thought for a moment, still fretting about Whip's welfare, then nodded. Robert rushed off calling to the men as he did so.

'Now den Nicholas, Oi spoke ta John Roe. 'E says we can use the light 'ouse building for ye dinner with the *beee-utiful* Victoria,' he twirled his hand in the air. 'No problem, an' dis can now take place tomorra' at sunset instead! Dis' will also give me an' Seamus time ta do dis properly, so dis delay is fortunate, yeh?'

Nicholas looked at the Irishman, grateful for his thoughtfulness – he just went out of his way to help without even being asked and had great consideration for others with everything he did. 'Thank you Tommy, I am ever so grateful for your care and assistance. I really don't know what I would have done without your generosity.' He placed his arm around the man as they walked back to the house.

Peter Strudwich was in the kitchen chatting to Seamus when they both walked in and Tommy said, 'Ah Peter, can I 'ave a word, I saw somethin' on the way back from the barracks dat Oi be tinkin' ye should know.'

He relayed to Strudwich what he had seen and added a few other bits of information about Birch gathered from his men, especially about his constant threats to Nicholas and Big Jack.

Peter shook his head and muttered, 'Enough is enough, he is destroying the morale of the crew. I will deal with that troublemaker tomorrow, one way or another, good bosun or not.'

Chapter 54

Elusive Passion

*N*icholas headed straight for Victoria but she wasn't in her room, nor was she on the verandah. Puzzled, he asked Seamus had he seen her.

Seamus said she had walked out of the front yard about thirty minutes ago.

Nicholas, panic setting in as the sun was fading, walked down and saw her tracks heading north toward the Chapman River where it crossed the north track. He found her some twenty minutes later sitting on a small hill looking over the sea, her arms around her legs, her chin on her arms and gazing out to sea.

She waved to him and he climbed up and sat beside her. He kissed her on the cheek, and placing one arm around her, hugged her close.

Before he could say anything, she looked at him and said, 'You have come to tell me that we cannot have dinner tonight because the trains are not ready yet, haven't you?' She smiled at him.

Nicholas felt terrible, as she was right of course. 'How did you know Vicky?'

'Oh Nicholas, I knew you had set an enormous task, but in truth Tommy told me he doubted if the wagons would be ready almost an hour ago.'

The cunning bugger, Nicholas thought, he had taken advantage of the moment. But again, before he could comment, Victoria said, 'Tommy said it was a good thing because you had now arranged a special evening for us tomorrow night and now it would not be rushed, so I am happy because I get to have you two days instead of one!' She put her arms around him, kissing his cheek. 'Mmm, no nasty, smelly beard, much better,' she murmured.

'Bless him,' thought Nicholas, and he kissed her forehead.

'This is a nice spot here Vicky, a good place for a house I think, what do you think?'

'I agree, it's lovely, but I want to live by the Murchison River so I can be closer to you, and also I will be able to help with the mine, yes?'

'I was only thinking of the future,' he said a little defensively. 'I didn't actually mean now.'

'Our future is being together, at least most of the time. And after all of this time apart, I want to share life together as it was meant to be!' Victoria said, giving him the hint that his days of just up and leaving whenever he felt like it were now numbered.

He nodded, thinking of how her parents shared everything, and smiled at her strength of will.

It was late afternoon, and Victoria and Nicholas walked arm in arm along the shores of Point Moore. The wind had dropped to a zephyr and the late evening sun had begun to colour the sky, the early evening blues of the sky reflected on the water as the sea began to flatten out – it was the beginning of a beautiful evening.

They had taken off their boots and relished the feeling of the gentle warm water as the small waves curled to the shore, swirling wet sand onto their feet.

They stopped on the top of a small sand spit, saying nothing as they gazed at the rapidly changing light on the water. Nicholas sat on the sand and drew Victoria onto his lap. She laid her head on his shoulder and sighed, happy in the simplicity of the moment.

Nicholas looked over toward the lighthouse keeper's building. Seamus and another fellow were busy at the makeshift stove and wooden trestle table they had set up earlier at the rear of the dwelling. Earlier, Seamus had shooed them away and said he would signal them when he was ready.

They noticed Tommy even had his men move the two-seater couch from his verandah to the front of the keeper's dwelling for their comfort.

Victoria turned slightly and looked at Nicholas. In the fading orange light, the outline of his face was clearly defined, the high cheekbones now prominent in the orange glow and his ever so slightly slanted hazel eyes gazing back at her. She thought him to be the most handsome man on earth and her heart began to pound.

Nicholas looked back at her, mesmerised by her fine features as they gazed at each other, the sun's glow turning her hair into thick strands of orange gold as it tumbled about her shoulder and down her left side. She is perfect, he thought, and marveled at the warmth and softness which rose from her like some warm and welcoming mist, and he could feel the love radiating toward him. He moved his head down to her and gazed at her for a moment. Suddenly, they were kissing, and she felt the familiar flush and a grasping at her heart, making it hard to breath, but she did not want the wonderful feeling to stop.

Eventually, they broke the kiss and Victoria became aware that her hand was lying across his groin and he was now very hard. She did not feel embarrassed and neither did she remove her hand.

She began an almost involuntary movement of her hand up and down the length of him, thrilling at his strength as she explored him. She froze when Nicholas let out a groan. She could feel his hardness was now pulsing under her hand, and suddenly Nicholas, with a little urgency, undid the clasps of her blouse and slid his left hand in to fondle her breasts. He found her nipples and gently squeezed each one, rolling them between his fingers then sliding his hand under each breast as if weighing them. Victoria was rapidly losing control and found she was moaning and panting as Nicholas began to draw up her skirt with his other hand.

She did not stop him and gasped at his touch on her thigh.

Nicholas ran his hand gently up between Victoria's thighs with an almost impossibly light touch. He thrilled at the skin, so soft it was almost beyond any feeling, as though it was not actually there. He found her softness beyond belief, and slowly ran his hand up and down, feeling the edge of the silk French knickers she wore, and then gently cupping her. Victoria gasped softly, and involuntarily her thighs opened slightly. She moaned, her hips trembling, punctuated with little jerks. She had no control and arched her back as he began to caress her.

Victoria's hand was now stroking his length with some urgency as each time she squeezed, he sucked in his breath and raised his hips, and she felt, with a rush of heat, that she was now beyond caring about anything as he continued an up and down motion between her legs. The feeling was delicious and she began to float in a world of pleasure she had never experienced.

She was flushed with love and pleasure, and surrendering to the rising feelings, she turned to him and their lips just touched as they felt their warm breaths.

'Mr Yuin Sir?' They both jumped in fright as Seamus hailed them from up on the point. 'Beggin' your pardon, but dinner is ready.' Even though, Seamus was some 200 yards away and could not have seen anything, both were a little embarrassed as they straightened their clothes and brushed off the sand. Then with a girlish giggle, Victoria took Nicholas's hand and they stood and walked back in silence, still a little overawed by the passionate moment.

Coming around the corner of the small verandah, Victoria exclaimed, 'Oh Seamus, it's so beautiful, how romantic!'

Seamus had laid a special table with a white tablecloth, cut crystal glasses and fine silverware. A lit candle in a glass holder and a small vase with pink and white daisies shared the centre of the setting. There was even a bottle of Tommy's special Madeira open beside the table.

Seamus, grinning from ear to ear, held her chair out for her. Nicholas sat opposite and said, 'Well done man, magnificent!'

Seamus said, 'Oi'm gonna serve youse during the meal, an' den Oi'll be leavin' youse both an' will be a'comin' back later with young Billy 'ere to clean tings up den.

'Now den, Oi'll foist be servin' ye's wit me own special pumkin an' onion soup, an den Oi'll be bringin' out da main dish.' He poured each of them a glass of the Madiera then vanished through the doorway.

'Oh Nicky, this is such a special night, I'm so happy, and look at the colour on the water! Oh look, there, dolphin!' Victoria cried, pointing. A pod of dolphins surfaced not fifty yards away in the channel between the shore and the reef, breaking up the blue and orange reflections on the water, their backs glistening black as they cleaved through the water. Nicholas and Victoria could clearly hear the 'phhhh' of air being expelled as they broke the surface.

It was a truly magnificent evening, almost magical Nicholas thought as he was swept up in her excitement. They raised their glasses and staring at one another wrapped arms and sipped the superb wine.

Dinner was perfect. Seamus's excellent soup for starters was followed by grilled whole fish topped with a sweet and spicy sauce as the main and finished off with a dessert of crepes with strawberry conserve topping.

After thanks were given to Seamus and Billy, the pair departed, leaving Nicholas and Victoria alone at last. They decided to walk off their meal and strolled back toward the settlement before returning.

Nicholas was starting to think about being alone with Victoria at the cottage, and his excitement grew as he remembered her touch and warmth.

As they sat on the couch Victoria lay her head on Nicholas's lap and he slowly caressed her back and arm, excitement building between them. 'I cannot wait until we are married Nicky, I dream of looking after you and living by the river at the Murchison,' Victoria said.

The river mouth and Whip were things Nicholas had tried to push from his mind for tonight, but now the worry began to gnaw at him and he forced his thoughts back to the present. 'Yes my sweet, it's the same for me, I have often sat at the homestead and dreamt of the very same thing. Whip and Jack have built quite a building there, or should I say mostly Whip, we even have our own master bedroom!' She giggled and said, 'I hope so my Lord, it would be very embarrassing if we shared a room with Whip and Jack,' sliding her hand up to his groin and squeezing him.

'Ahem Nicholas and Victoria, may I intrude for a moment,' John Roe called out as he approached the corner of the verandah.

Victoria snatched her hand away as if she had touched a hot stove plate and sat up, while Nicholas physically jumped and answered, 'Of course Mr Roe please,' gesturing for Roe to sit as he came around the corner and stood before them.

'I am sorry to disturb, but I understand you intend to leave for the Murchison tomorrow?'

'That is correct sir, we will leave at dawn. Jack, two of O'Farrell's men and I will split from the main train just before Northampton and head to the river mouth to check on the well-being of our man there and of the condition of the property. All being well, we will leave Tommy's men there to care take, Jack, my man Wilber and I will then rendezvous with the wagons at Robert and Bethany Stokes' property before guiding the remaining wagons with the mining equipment on to the prospect site and unload the equipment...' He faltered, realising he had offered too much information about the mining intention.

Roe looked at Nicholas and said quietly, 'Mr Yuin, do not worry about any indiscretion on my behalf about your mining intentions, and I have already worked out that you have already had some luck with that.' He paused as Nicholas looked at him quizzically before adding, 'Your mining purchases sir, are a little hard to keep secret in such a small town.' He gave a rare grin.

'Now,' he said, opening his satchel and withdrawing a sheath of papers, 'these are relevant extracts of the Abolition of Slavery Act, applicable to slavery in England and her colonies, including this land, in case anyone attempts to advise otherwise with your man the African.

'This copy has my signature and seal on it for the big fellow's keeping.

'Some further information, it appears the fighting between the tribes at the Murchison, *is* restricted to the two tribes as originally reported. This is confirmed by one of my police constables. There are however many casualties on both sides, men, women and children, and as of yesterday they were still at it, so please be very careful young man.'

'Thank you so much for this sir, we appreciate it very much,' Nicholas said. 'In return, if you yourself ever need assistance in any way please let us know, we would be more than happy to oblige.'

With that, Roe excused himself and departed.

Victoria peeped around the corner of the building, and seeing Roe walking some distance away, turned to Nicholas and started laughing.

Nicholas looked at her quizzically. She said, 'Oh Nicky, first it was the parrots who interrupted us at the pool, then Seamus calling us right when...when...you know,' she looked down coyly and giggled again. 'And... and now, we were about to get all romantic on this beautiful evening and *voila*, Mr Roe turns up. It is as though no one wants us to be intimate before we marry!'

She started to laugh again then suddenly stopped and started to cry. 'And now you are going away tomorrow morning for God knows how long and I am really worried something might happen to you, before.... before we...!'

Nicholas gathered her in his arms and hugged her tight.

'Now, now sweetheart, all will be fine, and before you know it I will be back and helping you get ready for our wedding.' She calmed down somewhat and looked up at him, her eyes wet and glistening with tears. Nicholas felt his heart tremor, she looked so sad.

He kissed away her tears and sat on the couch with her in his arms. They sat holding each other, she feeling more secure, albeit still upset, and Nicholas, in turmoil about leaving her, but knowing he must. It was near midnight when they reluctantly headed back to the house.

Chapter 55

Heartbreak and the First Freight North

The sun had not yet risen but Tommy O'Farrell's yard was a scene of frenetic activity as at least 20 men went about their tasks doing final checks and harnessing the oxen and mule teams to the four wagons. The larger wagons were teamed by Oxen, fourteen beasts to each and the smaller wagons teamed up by mules, some 20 a team. The morning was quite rowdy despite the fact that it was only 2 am. Bawling animals, whistles and shouts rang out as first the oxen were led out of the yards and trained up to their harness and yokes, then maneuvered into position. They would be the first to leave, being slower than the mule trains.

Strips of orange light from several oil lamps hanging high on the storage shed wall imparted an ethereal glow to a pall of fine dust hanging over the yards. Jack could be seen moving like a giant ghost amongst the bullocks, talking soothingly to the most stubborn animals.

Another hour and a half and all were harnessed. One by one the teamsters and leaders came to where Nicholas stood watching, reporting they were ready to leave. Fortunately, three days ago, two of O'Farrell's oxen trains had arrived from Perth, which was fortunate because after resting them, it gave the option of another thirty beasts to choose from for the teams heading north.

Nicholas smiled thinking about the teams and could not help but compare the dangers ahead with those of Africa, with its plethora of large predators, while here, there were essentially none to worry about.

Nonetheless, the excitement of adventure gripped him and he eagerly grasped the feeling.

As he stood there, Jack came up with Stitch and a packhorse and tied them to the fence rail beside him. 'I 'av checked everythin' Niclas, all be good, an' Mr Tommy has gived you two rifles, dey's a' new ones, an' two undred 'cart...cartregis', dey's looking like fine rifles,' he said, stumbling over the new words.

Before Nicholas could reply, Jack's eyes slid to his right and he said, 'Don' you worry *usisi* Victoria, Jack will guard 'is fren' with 'is life!'

Nicholas turned to find Victoria standing beside him, worry etched on her face.

He reached out and put his arm around her pulling her close.

He turned back to Jack and grinning said, 'And where is *your* horse Jack?' Knowing full well that Jack would refuse to ride one even if he did have one that was big enough.

Jack looked at him and said, *'Dey'* are my 'orses Niclas,' pointing at his huge feet. He laughed, then turned away still laughing at his own joke.

Victoria could sense the nervousness and excitement in Nicholas and knew he was very worried about this man Whip at the Murchison River homestead and was keen to get moving.

Nicholas had told her of Whip's anger at the tribal laws and Nimit'je's forced betrothal. Nicholas was hoping his last very pointed instruction about interfering in any way at all had been heeded but knowing Whip's affection for Nimit'je – he often said Nimit'je was a special little girl – he wondered if Whip had been able to restrain himself.

About an hour later, Robert and Adam came to say goodbye to Victoria and Peter Strudwich, who by now had joined her at the rear of the house.

The sun was just beginning to pink up the sky. Perfect timing, thought Nicholas.

Robert strode up to Victoria and Peter. He shook hands with Peter and made a huge show of kissing Victoria's hand, grinning at her as he said, 'Well, we will be gone then, an' don' cha be a' worryin' any then okay? All will be good, an' I can't wait till ye be meetin' me Betny. Oi reckon ye'll be gettin' along real fine there missy. Come on then me lad, we'll be a goin'.'

With that they climbed up on their wagons, and with a shout and a crack of whips, Robert in the lead, they all filed out of the yard and turned north.

Tommy, Nicholas, Victoria and Peter watched the first two large trains head out, young Adam driving his father's wagon was next followed by a dozen spare oxen. The young lad, excitement beaming from his face as he turned out of the yard, waving furiously, until they were out of sight of the front verandah.

They resumed getting the remaining two wagons moving, and two hours later, they too turned north up the track.

Peter and Tommy went back through the house, leaving Victoria and Nicholas alone on the verandah.

Nicholas wrapped his arms around Victoria and said, 'Time for me to go my love,' and he reached down and lifted her chin and kissed her. He could feel her trembling and sensed she was teetering on the brink of crying.

She said nothing but he knew she was fighting for control. He said, forcing some lightness into his tone, 'I will be back before you know it. Don't worry, nothing, but nothing, will stop me from getting back for our wedding day!'

'Oh Nicky, just be careful please,' she murmured.

Nicholas bent and kissed her again, and they turned to the rear of the house.

Jack stood holding Stitch's reigns. He handed them to Nicholas and stood before Victoria. Touching his heart he said, '*Hamba kahle udade isisi, sizobonana* (Goodbye sister, see you soon.)'

Nicholas swung up into the saddle, checked his rifle was there out of habit, then gave her a grin and a wave and kneed Stitch into action, Jack already loping off in front of him.

Tommy, Peter and Victoria sat at the kitchen table, or more appropriately, a bench. They talked about the general advances being made in Geraldton since Constable Drummond and John Roe had arrived. Conversation was deliberately steered away from Nicholas's departure as they could see that Victoria was extremely fragile at the moment.

Tommy said, 'Well den, tomorra, I's be going down to the Greenough station to greet one o' me trains comin' up from Fremantle, dere's four big wagons, pulled by some sixty beasts . Would ye be tinkin' Victoria, o' accompanyin' me self an' all?'

Before she could answer, he continued, 'Der's a lot of livestock comin' up on dis train, including Jack's 'orse an' a dozen other good 'orses, an' Greenough is quite a nice place wit green plains an a river.'

'Jack's horse?' Victoria asked, one eyebrow raised in query as she recalled Jack's banter with Nicholas before their departure.

'Aye, Nicholas asked me ta find the biggest 'orse ta be found, an' luck be 'avin it, some Frenchies brought out this 'orse, Oi, be tinkin. 'E said it was a Percheron or some such 'orse and a few other good 'orses, but dey – the Frenchies – fell ill an' sold 'em ta me man in Fremantle before dey's left to go back ta France.'

'It had better be a big horse Tommy,' Victoria said telling Tommy about Nicholas's previous attempts to get Big Jack to ride a horse. She and Tommy laughed and then said, 'I would like to accompany you Tommy, and it will take my mind off things, thank you.'

Tommy turned to Peter and asked, 'Ow about you Peter?'

Strudwich was about to answer when one of his sailors came running into the kitchen, red-faced and breathing hard.

'Captain, please come quickly, someone 'as damaged the rudder spike Sir, an' now there is a fight startin' between Birch and De Freys.' The man took a great gulp of air and continued, 'Birch, 'e's threatenin' everyone an' tried ta take the cat to De Freys, blamin' 'im fo' the damage, an' De Freys reckons Birch did it 'imself because 'e 'ates ye sir an' said 'e was gonna cut ye!'

'Okay, calm down man, we will go and see what this is all about. Get ye self a tumbler of water now, good man,' Strudwich said.

'Well, there ye have my answer Tommy, but thank ye anyhow, I must sort this out. Incidentally, a Percheron *is* a very big horse usually, from France and the Perche Province of long ago.'

He continued. 'Yesterday I had a heated discussion with Birch, tellin' 'im to alter his attitude. He was most belligerent and uncooperative. I told him I had had enough of his disrespect and I would be contemplating his future as crew, and now this. It is the end now,'

Tommy said, 'That's foin Peter, but Oi'm gonna send my man Isaac along wit ye, just for protection loik, okay. He be full of 'ate, this man Birch.'

'That's very thoughtful of you Tommy, but there's really no need thank ye, I can 'andle things myself.'

Strudwich left with his sailor, but Tommy called up Isaac regardless and quietly spoke to the man. Nodding gently, the man left.

It wasn't long before Jack and Nicholas caught up with the wagon trains, which was as well, because the further north they travelled the drier the ground became, and dust was being churned up by the wagons and teams creating a choking grey cloud.

Twenty miles later, Nicholas and Jack, now joined by two of Tommy's men, veered off the main trail and headed for the river.

Ten miles passed and Nicholas was feeling uneasy. It was not that he had expected to see any of the Watjari, even less so the Nhanda, but the unease at entering Watjari land remained.

Jack also was feeling apprehensive and had slowed his running gait to almost a walk. Something was wrong and neither he, with his normally sharp instincts, nor Nicholas, with his good instincts, could place the reason.

As far as they knew they were now quite some way into the Watjari lands and were entering an area of low scrub and occasional patches of small gums.

Suddenly Jack stopped and signaled for them all to stop. He was sniffing the wind, turning his head this way and that, his hand still up halting them. He trotted back to the others and said, 'Something wrong Niclas!' and pointed ahead at a line of gum trees about a mile ahead. The wind was blowing straight in from the north. 'I smell de dead men,' he said drawing his fingers across his throat.

Nicholas drew his glass from its leather tube cover at his saddlebag, and focusing on the tree line ahead, slowly panned the line. He initially saw nothing and was sweeping back when he saw a single dark line standing almost vertical against the green of the background. He refocused the telescope and studied the line. A spear!

Still locked onto the spear, he said to the others, 'Arm up men! I think there's trouble up ahead!'

Reaching down, he passed the glass to Jack and said, 'There, to the left of that dead tree Jack.' Jack took the telescope and squinting through it said, 'Strange Niclas, no moving, an' if ambush, why show!'

'Good point my friend, good point.'

Jack said, 'Wait, I look,' and before anyone could react or argue, he peeled off to the left and was fifty feet away in an instant, running like a great cat across the scrub. He disappeared down a low gully running toward the creek.

One of the Irishmen, named Patrick, exclaimed, 'Fa' fook's sake man, 'e'll get kilt fa' sure an' certain, 'im bein' by 'imself like!'

Nicholas drew his own rifle out and checked it, before saying, 'That man would take some killing my friend, and he has amazing abilities for tracking and stalking, despite his bulk. We wait!'

Twenty five minutes passed whilst Nicholas and the Irish lads waited.

Nicholas, still using the glass, caught sight of Jack only once before the fleeting form was off to the right of the supposed standing spear.

Ten minutes later, Jack appeared next to the spear. 'Let's go,' said Nicholas and they cautiously moved forward to Jack.

The spear was embedded in the back of what Nicholas assumed was a Watjari warrior. Jack said,

'He crawl from dere. Many more dead peoples over dere, ma'be twelve or more, mostly men.'

Nicholas looked at the dead man. The corpse was crawling with ants and blowflies. 'I reckon this one's about four days' old Jack, what do you think?' he asked. 'Yaas, I think too Niclas,' he said wrinkling his nose at the smell.

They inspected the other men and one woman, concluding that there was a battle from either side of the creek, culminating in the middle of the creek.

They moved on, heading nor, north-east, which would put them in line with the Nhanda's tribal area where Nicholas first met Kalbarri and his people after rescuing little Nimit'je. A feeling of dread hung heavy upon his shoulders as they found yet another battle scene on the way. This area was especially heartbreaking as the dead were mostly women and children and only three Watjari warriors lay scattered around. Jack said, 'Dey come from dere, an' dey are running dis way,' he said indicating a southerly direction. Nicholas wheeled Stitch around. The horse, and indeed the others including the three packhorses, were skittish at the carnage. Nicholas leant down and patted Stitch's neck. 'Easy boy, easy,' then he stood in his stirrups and spotted some more corpses some distance away.

Cantering over to them he discovered four more warriors. He couldn't tell for sure but reckoned two of them were Nhanda and the other two Watjari. There were peculiar markings on two of the shields which matched the one given to him by Gnarlu.

An eerie quiet surrounded them, the only sound the slight breeze blowing through the open grass land surrounding them. There were no bird calls or other sounds other than the buzzing of the flies at the corpses.

Nicholas shivered at the feeling. 'Let's go!' he said with some urgency, and fretting now about Whip's welfare, added, 'We move quickly from now on and change direction at my signal.'

Two hours later they came to the track leading to the river where Nicholas had first met Kalbarri's tribe and families.

He turned to the group. 'We will keep together until we reach the big bend in the river. If we come across any activity, we will fan out ten chains apart on my call, understood?' They all murmured in agreeance. 'Right, come on,' he continued, 'we will scout well ahead before we cross the river. We will head upriver first to the bend Jack, that's about an-hours ride, maybe two with caution.' Nicholas turned to the two Irishmen. 'Patrick, Michael, we will take time because from there, we can sweep back toward our homestead.

They nodded. Both the men were tough and hardened to fighting, which was why Tommy had chosen them. That being said, they had had little to do with the local tribes and their methods of fighting – though neither had Nicholas nor Jack for that matter, knowing little of the tribal battle strategy here – but Jack, in particular and Nicholas both knew of tribal war methodology in Africa.

They came upon a long creek running south-west that joined the main river about three miles from the big bend.

Jack and Nicholas noticed the birds first, great wedge-tailed eagles perched up in the river trees lining the creek. The birds got their name from the way their tails formed in flight, fanning out as normal, then tapering to a wedge point. There appeared to be some fifteen of them that they could see, spread out over a couple of hundred feet. There were also many dozens of the ever-present black ravens, cawing their mournful rasping call, which set alarms off in Nicholas and he held up his hand to halt them.

Nicholas knew eagles were generally solitary or in pairs when a kill had been made. At the very most there would be five at a kill. But there were so many here that there had to be a lot of food for them, he reasoned. Further, normally they would have taken flight by now but they all had, as far as he could see, heavy crops.

Their reluctance to move and fly off also signaled there was no body there as far as human beings went, or at least who were alive, thought Nicholas. Cautiously, they moved forward spreading out in a line.

'Bloody hell!' said Patrick, closely followed by Michael, who said with a catch in his voice, 'Dis be a right terrible thing lads'. They both crossed themselves and stared in disbelief at the butchery.

Above the dull hum of the thousands of bluebottle flies, the ravens lifted like a black cawing cloud on their approach and another three or four eagles bounced along the ground, their great wings beating as they struggled to gain flight.

The scene that unfolded before them was horrifying, and they silently and slowly made their way into what had obviously been a main camp. Nicholas knew it was a Watjari camp, having been told before by the Nhanda and Mumardi of its approximate whereabouts.

The area was littered with at least fifty or sixty dead, warriors, elders, young men, women, young girls and piccaninnies, no one had been spared. The flies and ants were crawling all over the scattered corpses like some moving blanket as they went about their macabre business, swarming about the heads and crawling around any opening they could find.

The slaughter had been complete and they could see that there were both Nhanda and Watjari warriors, distinctive by their different chest and arm scaring's. All were daubed in war paint, and woomeras, spears and nulla nullas lay scattered amongst them.

It was the sight of the women and children that wrenched Nicholas's heart. Babies with either spear wounds or crushed skulls, some still in their mothers arms, and many other children up to their teens lay scattered amongst the women folk like gruesome rag dolls.

Patrick and Michael looked down at the children, Michael making the sign of the cross, and with his hat in his hands wept openly.

Nicholas, with tears in his own eyes reached over and patted Michael on his shoulder. 'Come Michael, there's little we can do now man,' he said, fighting the well of emotion in his own chest. 'Dey be fookin' butchers man, de little'uns, s'not fair, not fair at all,' Michael said shaking his head.

Jack came and stood silently at Nicholas's side. He looked up at Nicholas with great sadness on his face, and pointing down the river said, 'You must come Niclas.' Looking in the direction Jack was pointing

Nicholas saw another grim site. More dead; He again stood in his stirrups and saw they all appeared to be warriors.

Feeling sick to his stomach he kneed Stitch forward and he and Jack slowly made their way over to the group. There were about twenty dead warriors scattered over an area of roughly twenty to thirty yards.

Jack strode ahead and stood near two more warriors, about twenty feet further toward the north-west. Both had died in combat with one lying half across the other with a broken spear protruding from his back. Looking at the group, Nicholas figured they had been dead for about two days, with some beginning to bloat. Strange, thought Nicholas, looking back toward the camp site. He considered that the main group of dead were about three days old at least. Nicholas rode Stitch over to where Jack stood.

Jack pushed the top-most man off the other, the corpse rolling off half onto its back with a thud.

With a jolt, Nicholas sucked in his breath. It was Yindu.

'Ahh, Christ no,' said Nicholas out loud and clutched at his head.

Nicholas did not know whether he was feeling sadness or anger the most. So much carnage of mostly innocents. He looked again at the children, then back at Yindu. All he could do was hang his head in great sadness.

There was no way they could bury any or all of them, they did not have the time, and now they were really worried about Whip.

'Niclas, now we must hurry and find my fren' Whip, yes?' said Jack.

Without waiting for a reply, Jack took off sweeping for signs. First he went about two hundred feet to the left, and then running fast went to the extreme right, but always heading toward the Nhandas' main camp about fifteen miles from where they now were.

'Let's get out of here,' Nicholas said quietly to the others.

Fifteen minutes later Jack came back, and halting them, reported, 'De big battle, mostly at all together, some Nhanda runnin' back to de river!' pointing to the north-west. 'Den come dis Watjari,' he pointed at the site where Yindu lay since most of the dead were Watjari. 'From dis way,' he said pointing toward the Nhanda camp direction.

Nicholas stared at his friend as he realized what Jack was saying, and a feeling of great dread suddenly enveloped him.

What Jack was pointing out was that this slaughter here may have been in retaliation for a similar attack on the Nhanda and may have been the last battle. Yindu may have led the retaliatory strike, arriving here before the Watjari raiders came back.

Sucking in a great breath, Nicholas slowly let it out and said again, 'Come on then you men, be alert now although I have a feeling we have arrived some days too late for the Nhanda after all of this has concluded.'

The further they travelled that day the more he knew he really wanted to get to the homestead before nightfall, and now very worried about Whip's welfare, he thought to himself, thank God he did not entertain bringing Victoria here at this time.

Turning his attention to the present, his mind full of images of the picininnies, their white teeth flashing as they played giggling and laughing at him when he was first invited to Kalbarri's camp. Seeing the broken little bodies behind them, his feelings of dread intensified. Shaking his head in dismay he said, 'We walk in single file, arms up and ready, okay? Patrick, right behind me, then two packhorses, then you Michael and the last two packhorses. You all know what to do if there's trouble, okay. Make sure you have your ammunition handy, now let's move.' They all moved off, while, Jack, anxious to get to the homestead, was already running ahead.

They came across the river crossing where Nicholas first crossed with little Nimit'je and where Kalbarri had appeared as if by magic.

Chapter 56

The Last of the Nhanda

They stopped at the river crossing, Nicholas holding his finger to his lips, and they all listened in silence for any sound of human presence. The silence was all they received, chilling under the circumstances. Like the other scenes they had come across, there seemed some sort of void in natural sounds, and again there was little, if any, sound of bird life.

They crossed the river together, bunched up tight, senses on high alert. Again, Nicholas called a halt and they listened. Nothing.

Preparing for the worst, they fanned out a little and slowly picked their way forward toward the Nhanda camp.

Fifty feet from the camp, they came across three dead warriors and one dead Nhanda woman.

The warriors were all Nhanda. Nicholas looked down at the bloated four, covered as the others in ants and crawling blow flies. He recognised none of them.

The scene which greeted them as they came to the edge of the Nhanda camp was shocking beyond belief. Nicholas counted about thirty women and children and close to the same number of warriors, Watjari and Nhanda. The corpses were in a more advanced state of decay, but even so Nicholas and Jack could recognise many of the Nhanda people. Speared and bashed, the women and children were covered in red and black meat ants and bluebottle flies, or blow flies as most called them. Ravens cawed loudly as they approached and flew up to the trees, where they stared down silently at the intruders.

It looked like the Nhanda had been surprised by the way the corpses were scattered about, and perhaps outnumbered Nicholas observed. As if to confirm this, he found Mumardie lying next to the big tree which had offered shelter to the people. Mumardie was not armed and his spears and war shield still lay vertical, stacked up against the tree to his right, he had a spear sticking out of his chest and a massive wound to his forehead.

Mumadie's wife had similar wounds and two other young men in their teens lay dead beside each other, although it looked as though the lads had tried to put up some resistance.

'Gnarlu and Kalbarri,' Nicholas said to Jack and they both split up to look for them.

Thirty minutes of checking found no sign of the two.

When they finished scouring the area for Kalbarri and Gnarlu, Jack said to Nicholas, 'Mebe dey escape, or fight somewhere else Niclas.'

Nicholas slowly nodded his head but dared not build up his hopes.

'Right, let's get to the homestead,' he said abruptly and kicked Stitch up over the ridge. They all followed, anxious to get away from the grim scene.

They had not gone thirty feet, when Jack skidded to a halt in front of them, holding up his hand. They all wheeled about, horses snorting and whinnying, as they fought to hold them.

'Fook me! Are you crazy man!' Patrick called struggling to hold both his mount and the pack horses.

Jack strode back past them all, a great frown on his face, and then cocking his great head to one side, he turned back to them holding up one finger and said urgently, 'Shhhhhh!'

Nicholas was about to ask what on earth was the meaning of the halt, when he heard something as well.

It was a very faint call. What was it, he thought, trying hard to think what it was that he heard. Was it a bird call? But there was something different about the sound.

They waited but no further sound came. Nevertheless, Jack stood still, his great head cocked on an angle as he listened, mouth open but otherwise stock still.

'There it was again!' Jack was off and running, downstream of the slaughterhouse that had been Kalbarri's camp, with Nicholas in hot pursuit.

They skidded to a stop some ten feet from the river bank. Nicholas leapt from the saddle, rifle in hand. Jack again lifted up his hand for silence.

They waited. The cry was slightly louder this time. It was a baby's cry they both recognized with a shock as they looked at each other.

Jack slowly moved to the edge of the river and started down the embankment. 'Careful now Jack,' warned Nicholas, cocking his rifle.

There was a small sand rill at the edge of the riverbank, with a deep pool overshadowed by a slab of rock. At the upstream end lay a young girl of no more than fifteen, naked. One of her feet lay in the pool and they could see she had been struck a terrible blow to one side of her head and they could clearly see the grave indentation to her skull. Blood had congealed over the wound and down across her breasts. They could see she was near death, her breath coming in short shallow puffs.

Nicholas registering that he had seen the young Nhanda woman before, on one of his visits, nursing a small girl child.

She was clutching a small kangaroo fur bundle with her left arm, the other arm was dangling, useless, by her side. A small pitiful cry suddenly echoed around the overhang, and a small brown fist suddenly rose out of the bundle.

Nicholas and Jack instantly moved as one to the pitiful young woman's side. Jack knelt in the water, one hand under the little bundle in case it fell into the pool, while Nicholas, propping his rifle against the rock overhang, squatted down before her.

Jack pulled aside the fur and peeped inside. The baby's face was screwed up in obvious distress, possibly sensing her mother's own distress.

The young lady suddenly made to move and fixed her gaze on Jack and then slowly turned her head a little and saw Nicholas. She strained and managed a hint of smile, recognising him.

The sight was so heartbreaking Nicholas felt his emotions boil to the surface and he bit his lip to hold them back. 'Ahh my God, this is all so wrong,' he murmured.

The young girl suddenly tried to lift the little bundle toward Jack and turned to him. Jack held out both of his hands, taking the baby's weight. Still the girl held her little smile. No sooner had Jack taken the baby than she tried to speak but could only manage a gargled 'Huck!' She arched her back and collapsed back on the sand, her head lolling to one side, and she breathed her last.

The baby began to cry in earnest, but Jack now had her in his arms and crooned to her in his deep rumbling voice and soon she quieted somewhat.

'Come Jack, bring the child, we must get out of here and get to Whip,' Nicholas said reaching for his rifle.

'Yas Niclas, we must go, I fears dat dis little one mebe all that is left 'ere now.'

They made their way back to the others. Nicholas secured the baby across his back with help from Jack after cutting up a small horse blanket, and placing the kangaroo fur about the child, they knotted the blanket over his shoulders and across Nicholas's chest.

Jack handed Nicholas his rifle and they moved off toward the homestead.

They moved quickly toward the homestead, all of them with senses heightened, but they saw nothing that would cause alarm. In fact, it was eerily quiet whenever they paused to take stock on their way and scan their surroundings.

On the last stop before the homestead, they paused on the low ridge just north-east of the homestead. Positioning himself back far enough below the ridge so as not to expose too much of presence, Nicholas stood in his stirrups and began a slow and wide scan with his glass.

The homestead came into focus and Nicholas studied the buildings and yard carefully. He could see the cattle and sheep slowly moving around their stockades with no apparent sign of alarm, and smoke curled lazily from the stone chimney. All looked normal.

Jack said, 'I go Niclas, wait.' Nicholas nodded as the big man vanished into the low scrub on their right.

Chapter 57

Whip's Dilemma

$\mathcal{F}$our days after Nicholas, Jack, young Adam and his father had departed for Geraldton, Whip was up at the crack of dawn. His morning habit was to sit on the corral fence with a cup of tea and watch the sun as it rose behind the buildings before attending to his chores around the homestead. There was much to do for one man – vegetable garden to tend, produce to pick, feed preparation for the stock as well as doing general repairs. However, on this day, Whip couldn't explain it, but something was bothering him and he had awoken with the feeling. Wilber was not, generally speaking, a man who dwelled on superstition or even religion for that matter, but something wasn't right.

After he had fed the stock, collected the eggs and checked and watered the vegetable patch, he was still feeling uneasy. He returned from the stockyards and went to the gun rack just inside the door of the homestead, and selecting his rifle loaded it. He seldom left the house without it from that day forward.

The feeling continued for the next two days, and pondering, he realised he had not seen either Nimit'je or Tjarlu or Gnarlu and Yindu since the latter pair had taken Nimmy, as he came to affectionately call her after Tjarlu had also called her that. That was a full six days ago now.

He worried at this and began to fear for Nimmy's welfare, knowing of her defiance of the proposed betrothal, and he still fumed at the injustice of it all.

Remembering Nicholas's very firm instructions on the matter only increased his angst as he daren't try to leave the homestead to find out what was happening.

Trying his hardest to get the little girl out of his mind, he wondered how Nicholas, Jack and the others were faring and if Nicholas had secured his equipment for the mine. The morning was beginning to warm, and he went and made his second mug of the strong black tea he liked, laced with at least five lumps of raw sugar. Juggling the rifle and the mug, he made his way back to the corral.

He was sitting on top of one of the timbers surrounding the corral, nearest the grain store, when Nimmy crept back into his thoughts. As he sipped the brew he chuckled as he remembered the first time he had made a cup of tea for her. He had a mug of his sweet tea in front of him as he was doing his laundry and periodically took sips of the brew. Nimit'je was watching him with interest, then said 'Me?' pointing at the mug.

He had handed her his mug and she took a tentative sip of the now cooled liquid.

'Gooda,' she had said nodding her head in approval. Whip went back in to the house and made her a mug of tea, adding a sizable amount of sugar as he did so.

As soon as he placed the mug in front of her, she had grabbed the hot tin mug in both hands, burning them of course. He had burst out laughing and she had stared at him, an angry frown on her face. He showed her how to use the handle and said, 'Careful now Nimmy, it's h...' was as far as he got as she lifted the hot tea and took a sip, burning her lips. 'Wishhh, wishhh!' she had said putting down the mug and fanning her face, and then she giggled. Whip showed her how to blow on the liquid so she could sip it.

From then on, as soon as she came to visit, she would say 'Me, tea, gooda!' and make a tipping motion mimicking drinking. So off he would go, dropping anything he was doing to make her a brew of the sweet tea.

Oh well, I hope she is alright, he thought and again began pondering the events when Gnarlu suddenly appeared like a wraith in front of him.

'Jesus!' Wilber exclaimed almost losing his balance, the contents of his mug flying, spilling hot tea over his leg. 'Bloody 'ell man, ye frightened tha' shit outa me,' as he clutched wildly at the posts to keep his balance and clutched at his trousers where the hot tea had splashed.

Whip looked at Gnarlu's face and at the multitude of cuts on his forehead, the blood caked on his head. But despite the wounds, he immediately saw the sadness and pain in his eyes.

Gnarlu said to him, 'Come, 'ilber, come!'

Gathering his composure, he asked, 'Come where Gnarlu? What is it ye be wantin' man?'

Gnarlu walked to the hay cart, tapping it with his spears. Wilber suddenly noticed that he held three war spears, and there was blood on the spear tips, fear for Nimitji suddenly clutched at him. Staring at Gnarlu, he said 'Nimit'je?'

Gnarlu looked at him stoically but then tears came into his eyes, confirming the worst. 'Ahh no please,' said Wilber and he nodded and walked to the donkey pen, got the animal, which he called 'Ears', and harnessed him to the cart, Nicholas's instructions vanishing from his reason.

Wilber went into the house and fetched the leather ammunition pouch, then grabbing his rifle that was leaning on the stock pen, he grabbed Ears's halter and walked slowly off behind Gnarlu toward the river mouth.

As decreed by tribal law, and specifically because of the significance of the killing, no Nhanda or Watjari would ever come to the area ever again. Gnarlu knew this, just as surely as he now knew there was going to be a terrible and vengeful war of which there would be no quarter given by either tribe.

He was torn on what he should do. His grief for Nimit'je lay heavy on his heart, and despite the tribal law, he could not just leave Nimit'je and Tjarlu out on the rocks even though they were now forbidden to even touch them, let alone bury them.

Gnarlu, his father and Yindu had already begun their mourning by banging their heads on the sharp flint stones embedded into their woomeras.

Before he had come to Wilber, Mumardie, Gnarlu and Yindu knew what they wanted to be done. Knowing Nicholas's tribe and how they had shown great affection toward Nimit'je and Tjarlu, in particular to his sister, they reached out to Wilber for help.

Wilber climbed up the rocks and the first thing he saw was Nimit'je, lying on her back, a great pool of congealed blood about her head. He swung a fierce look at Gnarlu. Gnarlu however was crying and slowly pointed to a dead warrior sprawled nearby. He spat out the word as if it were poison, 'Watjari!'

Wilber went to Nimit'je and gently scooped her up in his arms. 'Ahh, my little Nimmy, no, no no, no!' he said softly as he walked back to the cart and ever so gently laid her limp body in the tray.

He was wrenched in sadness and of the futility of it all as he trudged over to Tjarlu, placed his foot next to barbed end of the spear and grasping the shaft, withdrew it from the lads chest and he threw it into the river with some fury, then picked up Tjarlu and lay his body beside Nimit'je's.

Tjarlu's arm had flopped over Nimit'je's body as he laid the lad down, almost as if he were trying to protect her, thought Wilber.

Wilber was in a quandary as to what to do or how to bury the two, let alone where. So, he headed back to the homestead, covered the two with a calico sheet and backed the cart into the cool inside the grain store.

He drenched some hessian cloth with water and lay this across the bodies and cart sides.

Wilber knew that normally bodies would begin to stiffen anywhere from four to six hours after death, maybe a little longer if he could keep them cool. He reckoned the cool breeze flowing over the wet hessian and through the grain store would lower the temperature somewhat. But, he sighed, knowing he would have to move quickly.

Gnarlu, somewhat more composed, came and stood before him.

"Ilber, down!' he said reaching down and digging a small hole in the dirt. 'No down- out!' he said sweeping his arm up high and around and walked over to the edge of the homestead clearing. Again, pointing with his clutch of spears, 'Bad, na, na!' and shook his head.

'Down!' he walked back from the scrub line, stamped his foot and again swept his arm around.

Whip looked at him, trying to understand what Gnarlu wanted. Eventually, Whip understood that he must not bury Nimit'je or Tjarlu outside the homestead area. Most likely because the two had been killed for breaking tribal law or some such superstition he thought.

Whip walked over to the natural outcrop of rock that Nicholas sometimes liked to climb to sit and think. It was almost a pyramid shape. Perfect, thought Whip, and he walked around the outcrop until he found the right spot, somewhat away from the rock and near a good sized white trunked gum. He turned to Gnarlu. 'T'would dis be a good place man?' he asked Gnarlu. 'Gooda!' said Gnarlu, nodding. He then turned to the south-east and pointing two fingers to his eyes then pointing them to the south-east, he suddenly squatted down in an upright foetal position, clasping his arms around his knees and looking to the south-east.

Wilber nodded. 'All right Gnarlu, I understand.' He walked back to the shed, sloshed some more water onto the hessian and gathered his pick and shovel.

It took Wilber and Gnarlu a full four and a half hours to dig the grave. Thankfully, the ground was firm and not too hard and they encountered only a few manageable sized rocks.

He had decided it would be better to bury the two together, mindful of the time now passed since they had been killed. There was no time to dig two graves. Whip remembered how this had all happened and how Tjarlu's arm had flopped over little Nimmy when he had placed them in the cart.

Finishing the hole, they went back to the shed to fetch the bodies. Returning with them, he discovered with a jolt a large pile of paperbark had been deposited by the hole. Casting around, he saw no sign of anyone else but guessed it was Mumardie.

Whip moved quickly but had to do the preparation of the bodies himself, as Gnarlu shaking his head vigorously had backed away when he brought the bodies out.

First, he lay a bed of the paperbark in the hole at one end, then shuddering he lifted Nimit'je's little frame off the back of the cart and struggled down into the grave with her over his shoulder.

The body was just beginning to stiffen as he bent her into the upright foetal position that Gnarlu had shown him. Wilber was openly crying when he emerged from the deep hole to fetch Tjarlu's body.

He positioned Tjarlu's body next to Nimitje's and entwined Nimitje's left hand with Tjarlu's right hand and positioned their heads together. Both were facing the south-east toward their camp site and what was their home.

Whip looked up at Gnarlu before he placed the remaining paperbark over the two.

Gnarlu was also now weeping, but managed a 'Gooda, 'Ilber' then backed away. Wilber lay the paperbark over them and climbing out, he stood by the grave. He tried to think of some words to say but nothing seemed appropriate, and in truth, he was too upset.

Whip grabbed the shovel and furiously began to fill the grave. His anger and helplessness spurring him, he did not stop even once until he had almost filled it. He took a large swig of water from his pannikin and went at again until it was finished.

The next day Wilber started to build a cairn over the grave site. Using mortar and the stone from the hill, it ended up sitting about three and a half feet high, with sloped sides on a rectangular base and facing south-east as he intended.

He stood beside the monument, his head bowed, sadness weighing heavy on his soul.

Wilber suddenly felt some presence, and turning he found Mumardie, Gnarlu and Yindu standing behind him. They were daubed in fresh war paint, blood from their mourning blows across their foreheads mingling with the paint, and they each carried their war spears and shields. Whip knew what that meant, all-out war.

No words were spoken as they stood there each with his own thoughts. Then one by one each of the men touched him on the shoulder and nodded. Finally, it was Gnarlu who touched him on the shoulder. 'Gooda man you 'Ilber! Mumardie, Yindu thank you,' Gnarlu said touching his own chest, and nodding he walked away to vanish into the scrub with his father and brother.

Whip went about his chores each day following the burial, but in truth he did them with no enthusiasm, he just could not shake the sadness of his little friend's passing and the manner in which she had been killed.

Whip was no stranger to violence and the horrors that went with it, but had not ever felt loss like this, such innocence and gone with one blow. He wished he had Jack or Nicholas to talk to and get it all off his chest.

Nicholas kept the glass up to his eye, looking for Jack, but he didn't appear. Lowering the glass, he rubbed his eye with his fist, then lifted the glass to his eye again sweeping across the homestead again. 'There!' he exclaimed. Standing by the back verandah was Jack.

The big fellow beckoned to them and they started forward in single file, walking down the final dip in the terrain before the buildings. They got within about 250 yards, Jack clearly in sight, but he was still at the corner of the verandah. Jack held up his hand to stop them.

To Nicholas's immense relief, Whip suddenly walked out from the other corner of the verandah, heading for the grain store.

Jack, moving like a great cat, was on him in a flash and lifted the hapless Whip clean over his head, a dish cloth flying out of his hands. It took a few seconds for Whip to realise it was Jack who had grabbed him. Screaming and fighting like a cornered wild dog he was furious. 'What da fook do ye's think ya doing ya fookin' big id'yit!' Jack let his friend down none too gently and Whip came up with a vicious right hook that whistled past Jack's chin. Jack grabbed Whip in a bear hug. There was nothing Whip could do and he went limp, and tears began tumbling down his cheeks as all of the emotion of the past week burst its banks.

Jack was still holding him when Nicholas and the others rode up. 'My fren Whip, it's all right, I's sorry my fren, I's sorry. What's the matter my fren, I's very sorry,' Jack kept repeating.

Nicholas swung down from his horse gently so as not to awaken the now sleeping baby strapped to his back, and while he was overjoyed to see Whip, he was worried about the Welshman's distressed state.

Whip managed to struggle gruffly out of Jack's encircling arms, furiously knuckling his eyes dry and mightily embarrassed by his lapse in control.

He stood back a little from Jack and apologised to his giant friend, and stuck out his hand saying, "Tis so good ta see ya my friend, so sorry, but…a sad thing has happened an' I don't seem ta' be able to come ta' terms wit it,' he stepped back shaking his head.

Nicholas stepped forward and said evenly, 'Well then Wilber, it's so good to see you unharmed, we have been very worried, what with the war and everything happening.'

He and Wilber shook hands warmly. 'Sorry sir, I didn't mean ta show such weakness.' He paused and took a great shuddering breath and was about to go on, but Nicholas sensed he was teetering on the brink of an emotional meltdown again, so he forestalled him. Placing his arm around his shoulders he said, 'Wilber, this is Michael and Patrick they've come to help us.' Nicholas looked at the two. 'Best you call him Whip, its what he prefers,' he added, and they all shook hands. A couple of hours later and knowing that the others were bound to talk about what they had seen, Nicholas decided to tell Whip about what they had seen.

Wilber stood stony faced at the news of Yindu and Mumardies deaths and of the slaughter and he uttered not a word. Nicholas knew that this was possibly too much for the already distressed Whip and he quickly thought to break up the somber mood. Just as he was about to take control and change the subject, the baby let out a wail of distress from her wrap at Nicholas's back.

Whip nearly fell over in shock and yelled, 'What the fook! Dat's a baby!'

Jack stepped forward and began to untie the sling as the baby was now screaming in anguish.

No sooner had he untied the straps than Whip had taken the child and announced, 'She be all wet! We needs to dry 'er!' He took off into the house cooing and speaking gently to the little mite.

'Bloody hell! 'He's like a clucky hen and only after two minutes,' said Nicholas, grinning and standing with his hands on his hips looking at Jack's incredulous expression and he now being conscious of his wet back.

A few seconds later, Whip was yelling, 'Jack! Fetch me that ship's duffle, tha' one wit all da flannel and soft cloth, an' dere's a real soft woman's dress in dere, bring it 'ere an' a knife.

Jack didn't move, not believing his normally rough-edged mate could suddenly behave like this.

'You had better move man, before *Mrs* Wilberforce skins your hide!' Nicholas said and they all laughed as the giant man went to find the duffle bag, muttering and shaking his head.

'Well that's a tailor-made distraction for our friend's woes, that's for sure,' Nicholas said.

'Let's get stuck in and unload everything, it's been an unsettling day for all of us and its getting late. We can catch up on -all that's happened over dinner. Who wants to prepare dinner?'

'I'll be doin' it, I 'ave some meat 'n vegetable 'ere,' said Whip as he stuck his head out of the door, yelling, 'Jack! Where be dat stuff!' He again disappeared into the house, wondering how he could break the news about Nimit'je.

'Right lads let's get stuck in!' said Nicholas, and they all set about unloading the gear.

After they had finished, Nicholas looked up and saw that the sun was just about to slide below the horizon. Seeking to lighten the mood, he called out, 'Right fellows, let's go and wash up!'

'Ho! Whip, come on, we are going down to the beach, an' bring that gallon of rum with you and some tumblers! They all followed him down to the little beach behind the homestead, stripped off and plunged into the river, scrubbing their clothes as they splashed and fooled around in the cool river.

"Tis real noice ta be a'washin away the stench o' death, what do ya's be reckonin'?' said Michael as he furiously scrubbed his body with the river sand. They all murmured agreement.

Not long afterward, Whip arrived with the rum and tumblers in a basket, his rifle under the other arm. He set down the rum and laid out the tumblers, filling each and handing them around, then said to everyone's amazement, 'I's goin' back ta look aft'a the little one,' and he strode away before anybody could comment.

The baby was now crying a lot, and no matter what Whip did, she continued to cry. Whip, in his ignorance of baby care, could not understand why she wouldn't drink, no matter that it was just plain rain water.

Patrick, returning with the others, stuck his head around the door jam and said, 'Whip, me lad, Oi's 'ad some experience wit da little tikes like, me Da' bein' a horny bastard n' all.

'We's n'us'n' 'avin thirteen kids in de family, back in Ireland. We'd a had fourteen, but me Ma died givin' birth ta the fourteenth, an' the baby died too! 'We all 'ad to 'elp, us boys an' girls, so I's know'd 'ow ta make feed, cause dat little tykes 'ungry man, not so thirsty, what do ya tink?'

Whip looked from Patrick and back to the distressed little girl and nodded. 'I's not be knowin' nuttin' 'bout babies Paddy, so I's be grateful fo' any 'elp ye could give.'

'Roit now den me lad, let's get at dis,' Patrick said 'Ye got any milk? Cow or goat will be good?'

Whip, as it happened did have fresh cows' milk from that morning stored in the stone cool safe by the hearth.

'What about grain?' Whip produced large tins of maize (corn), meal wheat and millet.

After setting some milk on the stone oven to boil, they ground a small amount of maize meal into a fine powder and mixed it into the boiled milk with a small pinch of sugar.

They gently fed the mixture to the little one After a few splutters, crying and pushing the spoon away, she started to take some of the mix. Hesitating, to give her time to digest the food, she started to cry for more. It took a good hour but she eventually drank down about four good spoonful's of the milk and dropped off to sleep.

'Now me lad, we must always be sure ta boil the milk, an' don't be usin' much o' tha' maize meal, or ye'll bind 'er up.

'An ye'll be needin' ta tink up some way ta be makin' a teat o' some sort to give 'er a drink o' tha' milk, maybe make it outa wood or sumtin', otherwise ye's gonna be up all night wit 'er screamin', Patrick concluded.

'Thank ye Paddy, Oi'l whittle one up outa some dat dry mulga bush an' lightly cure it in tha' fire,' he said pointing at a stick leaning by the hearth.

They all sat around the dining room table and Whip served up a good meal of stewed kangaroo, carrots, potato and some native yam, which he had learned how to find thanks to the Nhanda women.

After the meal they started to discuss what had happened, and Nicholas, who was about to speak, was forestalled by Whip who held up his hand and quietly said, 'Oi got somethin' to tell ye Nicholas an' Jack.'

He gathered up his emotions and bit his lip, then blurted out, 'Little Nimmy and Tjarlu is all dead!' I'se buried 'em out by the stone hill, da Watjari killed 'em, 'cause I guess she an' Tjarlu must 'av run off together.'

'I's so sorry Nicholas, I got involved like ye said not to, but Gnarlu, Yindu and Mumardie came an' wanted me to, cause dey was just lyin' out on the rocks an', an', but now she's dead, so ye's know why I be so upset, okay.' 'Dat liddle girl was special I reckon, an', an', me'be 'er killin', that's why the war started, I guessin', it bein' Kalbarri's land 'n all. He could go on no longer and sat, battling to hold onto his feelings, which again threatened to boil over.

Nicholas and Jack sat in stunned silence, their original fears now confirmed and knowing now why the war had started. Nicholas, thinking hard about their position as it stood now, sighed and cleared his throat. 'The circumstances as I see it Whip, are that I said not to interfere as I recall, and as I now see it, you did not, alright? The Nhanda elders asked for help, in particular Nimit'je's father and brothers and that is the difference,' Nicholas said, adding, 'Have you seen Kalbarri at all?'

Whip shook his head. 'No Sir, I ain't seen 'im, but den Oi wasn't really thinkin' straight. 'E might have been 'ere, I dunno Sir.'

'Well, tomorrow, we must first get ready to travel to Robert and Bethany's to meet up with the freight, that's you, Jack and me. But first thing in the morning, you, my friend are to show Patrick and Michael all they will need to know about looking after this establishment for a while, and I have a few alterations they will need to start on. They are both skilled artisans, like yourself, I might add. Alright Whip?'

'What alterations Nicholas?' Whip asked.

Nicholas, seeking to buoy Whip's spirits, stood and said to him with a grin, 'I don't know whether you have heard from the others Whip, but I have found Victoria, or should I say she found me!

'We are engaged to be married! And you, as I just said, will come with Jack and I to Robert and Bethany's tomorrow and *then* on to the mine, after which we will all go back, via here, to Geraldton where I am to lose my freedom!'

There was a chuckle around the room. Whip just sat there with his mouth open as he digested what Nicholas had just said, before leaping to his feet and vigorously shaking hands with Nicholas. 'Congratulations Nicholas, congratulations!' he said with genuine warmth. 'Oi couldn't be happier for ye's, 'tis wonderful news! Phew, just when Oi' was thinkin' der would never be any good 'appinin' agin 'ere.'

Dawn of the next day found Jack, Nicholas and Whip standing at Nimit'je and Tjarlu's grave site. No words were spoken, each of them had their own thoughts and they stood with a hand on each other's shoulders.

With a huge sigh, Nicholas said softly, 'Well, little Nimit'je and Tjarlu, your place of resting is here with us now and we will be sure to remember you both forever. We hope you are happy together where ever you may now be in spirit, Amen.'

Jack stepped to the cairn and said, *'Hamba kahle Nimit'je, hlanzeki-leyo inhliziyo,'* then turned with the others and walked toward the homestead. Halfway there Whip suddenly stopped and said with finality, 'The little piccaninny!' He jerked his thumb toward the house. "Er name is "Nimmy", seein' as 'ow she come to us as Nimit'je 'as just passed.'

Chapter 58

Greenough and the
"MNYAMA UBABA"

*T*ommy and Victoria left for Greenough River Station and registry
office at 5am the next day. Tommy said he was expecting the wagon
train of freight and his contingent of men around ten in the morning.

They had a leisurely trip accompanied as always by Isaac. The man
was devoted to Tommy and had been his constant shadow since his days
in Belfast. Isaac was tall, possibly several inches over six feet, and appeared
lean, it being a little hard to tell as he always wore his long black and
grey coat and always buttoned up even in the hot months. He had a long,
mournful clean-shaven face, that is, what you could see of it. On his head
he wore a battered and bent tall black stovepipe hat, and a dark brown scarf
was always wrapped around his neck.

He gave Victoria the shivers because he never smiled and spoke only
in a whisper and then only to Tommy. He seemed to just float along as the
coat was so long it ended just over the top of his boots. That aside, what
struck Victoria, and others, was the aura of menace that hung over him.

'Tommy, why doesn't Isaac ever talk to anyone except you and never
smiles?' Victoria asked.

Tommy looked at her and said, "Tis a long sorry tale miss. Me'be I will tell ye 'bout it one day. Fo' now all ye be needin' ta know, is dat while ya' be wit me, or 'e's wit ye, ye need fear nuttin'."

Victoria looked over at Isaac riding beside the cart, and in that instant he turned to look back at her, the deadpan face and pale blue eyes equally lifeless staring back at her. Victoria quickly looked away.

Some four hours later they were crossing the last grass plains before the river mouth and the station. It was quite beautiful, Victoria thought, the long spear grass waved and shimmered in the morning sun, almost rippling like water she noted, and patches of small yellow flowers swept in and out of the little gullies. In the background beyond the river they could see some huge white sand dunes. They appeared to have been just painted there, thought Victoria, as they glinted in the morning sun.

Tommy steered the buggy off to a small track on their left and continued for about four miles before eventually stopping on a small rise looking over a part of the shallow river.

'Dey can't surely be very far now, Oi be tinkin' Miss Victoria. 'Tis a beautiful morning, Oi tink we moit be 'avin' a cuppa tea while we wait, what do ye say Miss?' said Tommy. Victoria nodded and he opened the cabinet behind the seat and getting down, set about making a fire and boiling the water.

'Ha, dat fella Seamus be a good lad, 'e 'as even packed us some scones as well as sandwiches!' he exclaimed.

Tommy and Victoria sat up in the buggy, chatting mostly about Africa, Tommy wanting to know all about it, especially the wildlife.

Victoria told him all about life at Lake Victoria and growing up at Herrgarden Grande. She talked of the lions and when Nicholas had saved her and of Nicholas's confrontation with Hymie Van Der Hoeke. She described the crocodiles in the lake and how the hippos were more feared than the crocodiles and why. She also mentioned that she had an expert teacher in Baba Joe.

Talking about Baba Joe brought a lump to her throat and she hesitated during the talk. Thinking about him and her parents made her a little homesick, but she sighed and carried on and told Tommy all about the Wahehe and the Maasai.

'Facinatin' tis all o' dis Miss Victoria, Oi be wishin' I could go dere one o' dese days an' see it an' all fo' meself loik…'

A low whistle from Isaac stopped Tommy's chatter, and they both looked at him. He was pointing at the low ridge some distance away.

A pall of dust was all that could be seen at first and then not long after they could see the wagons and several men on horseback appear through the dust.

'Well, dere day are den Miss, our wagon trains!' Tommy flipped open his fob watch and added 'An' right on time an' all!'

Now they could hear the whistles and shouts punctuated by the crack of the drovers' whips. Two of the heavily loaded long bed wagons drew up at the southern side of the shallow river and the men went about unhitching the wagons and watering the oxen.

Whilst that was happening another pall of dust appeared up over the ridge. It was not a wagon train however, it was horses. Victoria could see, even from here, that they were moving excitedly and eager to get to the water. She estimated there were about 30 in the herd and four stockmen with them.

She was about to comment to Tommy, who had his glass up, when he said excitedly, 'Will ye look at that now!' Even without the glass Victoria could see a single black horse with two stockmen appearing over the ridge some two hundred yards behind the first herd. Unusual as it was to be separated, it was nothing compared to the size of the black horse – the animal was huge and dwarfed the two stockmen and their mounts trotting either side of the black.

Tommy handed her the glass. 'Oh Tommy!' she exclaimed, 'It looks magnificent! I've never seen such a huge horse! Look at the way it holds his head, wonderful!' She handed back the telescope and clapped her hands together in delight.

By the time the Percheron and minders got to the river, Victoria and Tommy were down by the river bank opposite, watching as the black stallion came to drink.

The other two wagon trains arrived over the next couple of hours, and the men made bivouac by the southern bank of the river.

'Dat's the biggest 'orse I's ever seen to be sure, to be sure!' Tommy said. "E's a bit like Jack in a comparative way, meanin' no disrespect o' course, just huge!'

'Yes, I was thinking the same Tommy,' Victoria said. 'Now all we have to do is get Jack on him. Does he have a saddle Tommy? It will have to have been especially made to sit on that back, an enormous one in fact!' She and Tommy laughed. 'I dunno Miss, der'e might be one wit 'im, we will find out soon, 'ere comes the team captain,' Tommy said. A lean wolfish faced man came splashing across the shallows toward them on a chestnut horse, reigning up beside them.

'Afta' noon Tommy,' he said in broad Irish brogue, and immediately switched his attention to Victoria. 'An oo' might Oi 'ave the pleasure of meetin 'ere', such a beauty I's never seen in all o' me loif like,' he continued as he swept off his hat and bowed as low as he could in the saddle.

'Now Declan, don'ch ye be forgettin' ye'self now, be lookin at 'er left hand me son, she be engaged to a friend o' mine, and a very fine fella, an' 'e would eat ye fo' breakfast make no mistake!' he laughed.

Turning to Victoria, Tommy said, 'Miss Victoria, this cove an' God's gift to women and regular ratbag is wit'out question, the cheekiest Irish bastard ever to come outa Ireland, and that's sayin' sumpin since we's all cheeky bastards from over dere. 'E is Declan McNalty,' he concluded with a flourish of his hand.

Victoria laughed at the friendly insults and inserting a little French accent into her voice said, 'Pleased to meet you *Monsuir* Declan McNalty.'

McNalty clutched at his chest and pretended to sway in the saddle. 'Jesus Christ, an' a Frenchie accent an all, oi's gonna 'ave me a 'eart attack. 'Oi'm in love to be sure an' certain!'

'Bloody 'ell, cut it out Declan, ye'll be makin' me throw up!' Tommy said laughing with Victoria.

'Ye's made real good time Declan as always. No trouble?' asked Tommy.

'Only wit that big black bastard, pardon me miss, 'e wouldn't run wit t'other nags, so we put 'im up front, den 'e bit two o' th'others, so den we put 'im back some an' 'e seemed ta calm down a bit, but 'e sure is a beeeutiful big bugger. Question bein', 'oose gonna be a ridin' 'im?'

Tommy said, 'Wait until ye sees 'is owner! Did 'e come wit a saddle man?'

Declan shook his head. 'No 'e did not, only a bleedin' great hackamore and some special bits n' bridles. We was wonderin' 'bout that, so we bought a couple of good hides o' leather wit' us Tommy, 'ope ye didn't mind. Maybe dey can find a saddler somewhere?'

They crossed the river and Victoria jumped from the buggy and went straight to the giant horse, 'Careful miss! 'E's a bit flighty, despite 'is size!' McNalty called.

She walked straight up to within about six feet of the black and stopped and stared up at the great head. His great big brown eyes stared back at her, she then slowly walked around him. He did not have another mark on him, no white flash or socks, just ebony black all over. He towered over her. 'My God, what a magnificent powerful beast, you are, you are like royalty!' she said to him as she looked up at his enormous head.

Victoria, held out her hand to him and he snorted and pawed the ground. Suddenly, he took a step toward her and sniffed at her hand, allowing her to reach up and stroke his muzzle, then he snorted and danced his head up and down in front of her. She turned to the others grinning, and said quietly, 'He likes me! Have we any chaff Declan?' 'Aye we 'ave,' he answered and turned toward the wagon nearest them. 'Peewee!' he shouted. A skinny young lad scrambled out from behind the wagon and said in a shrill nervous voice, 'Ye called Sir?'

'Get a bucket o' tha chaff for the miss 'ere…no, get that big wooden pail.' The lad bolted out of sight and was soon back with the wooden chaff bucket.

Victoria soon had the black munching happily from the pail.

'What's his name Declan?' she asked. 'I dunno miss, no one knew it. 'Tis a shame though, wonderful 'orse loik dat needs a grand name, don'cha be tinkin'?' he said.

'Well then, we will have think of one that his owner might like then,' she said.

An hour later Tommy, Victoria and Isaac headed back to Geraldton, Victoria silent and wracking her brains for a suitable name that Jack might like.

Suddenly it hit her. Royalty, she thought. She suspected Jack's lineage must have had some standing in the Zulu nation before he was enslaved and considering the Zulu people did not ride horses as far as she knew, Jack's learning to ride was going to be unique and very interesting, so she thought a fitting name would be, *MNYAMA UBABA* - Zulu for BLACK LORD.

Chapter 59

Whip, Nimmy, Bethany and Gnarlu

As usual, Nicholas was up at the crack of dawn prowling around while it was still semi-dark.

Wilber came out to him, bringing two pannikins of hot sweet tea for them and they stood together in silence at the edge of the river. The river was dead calm and tiny wisps of mist ran traces across the surface, broken only by the tiny ripples of small fish and insects. A small bird called its cheerful song heralding the orange dawn.

'I been meanin' ta ask Nicholas, what did Jack say at Nimit'je's grave yesterday?' Whip asked.

Nicholas looked at him and said softly, 'He said, "Goodbye Nimit'je, pure of heart".'

Wilber just nodded his head and drew in a great breath. 'Aye, she was that, 'tis 'ard, real 'ard!'

The day was full and there was much to do, with Whip and Nicholas showing Michael and Paddy what they wanted done in their absence and how to maintain the homestead. They packed the saddlebags ready to load onto the horses and stacked them up on the table outside the grain store.

When all was ready, Nicholas took Patrick out on a hunt for meat. He shot and killed a small kangaroo and demonstrated how to dress the animal, wasting nothing except the gut and intestines, which he explained were often worm ridden, so care had to be taken not to perforate the large intestine when gutting.

He showed Patrick how to draw out the sinews running the length of the tail and how to hang them in the shade to dry. The sinews, he explained, once dried, could be moistened again and could be used as a good bind for many things as well as stitching.

Whip and Michael milked one of the cows and mixed up some of the feed for Nimmy, who had woken all of them twice during the night. They fed and changed her, and once she was asleep, Whip took Michael around the stockyards and showed him what had to be done daily and how to maintain the stock.

Before they realised it, noon was upon them and Nicholas knew it would be pointless to leave now as they would have to break for the night after a short distance and so announced that they would leave tomorrow at dawn.

The next day, Nicholas, Jack and Whip headed off at dawn to Robert and Bethany's home, little Nimmy now strapped to Whips back was asleep, they had two packhorses in tow and Jack had already disappeared up the faint trail.

On the way, Nicholas was thinking about how Bethany would react to little Nimmy. He reckoned she would take instant charge of the little one and he wondered how Whip would react to that.

One thing for sure, there was only going to be one winner in that debate, and it wouldn't be Whip, he concluded chuckling to himself.

As they rode, Whip was a little concerned about Nimmy. She had been restless all night and she had some stomach trouble for sure, cleaning her was very messy and too liquid, as Patrick had pointed out. Thankfully, she was now sleeping, he figured the rocking of the horse had sent her off. He was in a quandary on what to do and was already thinking that this woman Bethany might know how to help.

It was good to get away from the homestead, Wilber was thinking, like some weight had been lifted, and he began to enjoy the journey and the cool of the morning. The little warm bundle at his back felt comfortable and somehow pleasing.

They had been travelling for about three hours and the sun was well into the sky when Jack suddenly appeared in front of them.

He pointed at the trail at his feet.

'Blood,' he said. Looking down they now saw the small swarming of tiny bush flies and a distinct spatter of dried blood on some dried leaves.

Nicholas dismounted and stooped to have a closer look. He poked at the leaves with a stick. 'Maybe a day and a half to two days old Jack?' he looked up asking. Jack nodded. 'Yas Niclas, 'bout a day an' a half I think. Headin' to da north-east also, but 'e is alone and carryin' a spear I think,' he added pointing to the regular dents in the ground beside a very faint footprint.

'Dis man, wounded bad. See how de left foot mark draggin' de toes.'

'Hmmm, yes, okay, well we best be alert then, we've still a way to go so we will head to the *gnamma* holes and camp there tonight' he said, and they continued on their way, alert and rifles drawn.

They approached the *gnamma* holes which were on a great low granite dome rising some thirty feet above the surrounding land. There were 3 on this particular granite rock. In a cleft on the eastern side of the granite, the natural holes, roughly five feet deep and about one and a half foot in diameter. One of them was slightly open and the water lay about two and a half feet from the top, it contained cool clear water, fed by the rains running down the granite face, the others were only about half full.

Except for one, they were covered by stout sticks and a slab of granite about two feet in diameter and three inches thick, while smaller rocks covered any gaps to stop animals from falling in and contaminating the water.

Jack and Nicholas had been shown the location by Yindu and Gnarlu on one of their excursions north and this and two others provided a vital lifeline, especially in summer, when the temperatures could reach one hundred degrees or more on some days.

Scouting around the great weathered rock they discovered more blood stains, the dark drops plain to see on the granite, some next to the exposed hole.

They made camp at the base by some of the mulga trees and after attending the baby's needs and rocking her to sleep, they all slept.

The next day they re-placed the rock slabs over the gnamma hole and they again set off toward the Stokes' homestead.

The blood stained tracks disappeared after several miles and they assumed that the wounded man had either died or had taken a different route.

They made good time and late that afternoon they arrived at the Stokes' homestead yards. A stream of yelling children swarmed out of the scrub led by the Stokes' two children, along in their wake, the shyer aboriginal kids joined them. Young Robert sprinting ahead reached them first, and in an instant was swinging by Jack's huge hand and then a half a dozen more black children joined, all of them laughing and yelling at once.

'Bloody hell, der's no chance o' sneakin' up on this 'ere mob,' Whip said, raising his voice over the excitement and chuckling.

The first thing Nicholas noticed was that Robert and the teams had arrived. The yard was filled with the wagons and the oxen were strung out behind the small barn structure in Robert's makeshift enclosure.

As they walked the horses closer to the house, Bethany appeared from around the rear of the house, as ever wiping her hands on her apron, a huge welcoming smile on her face as she placed her hands on her hips and yelled 'An' it's about time!' Nicholas reckoned she would be in her element cooking for all of the crew.

'Hello Nicholas and hello Jack!' she boomed as she waited for them to dismount.

No sooner had he dismounted than Nicholas found himself in a great bear hug and was subjected to a smacking kiss on his cheek. 'Me Bobby tells me 'tis congratulations Nicholas, I's bein' so 'appy for ye's an' I cannot wait ta meet ye Victoria!' she added letting him go.

Jesus this woman has some strength, thought Nicholas as he finally managed to breathe again.

Given the size of Jack, she couldn't give him the same hug but she grasped both of his arms in affection. Jack looked down at her and said, '*Sawubona hle inkosikazi uma.*'

She turned to Nicholas but before he could translate Jack said in his deep voice, 'I say, Gooda day beautful lady,' and he took one of his hands away and closed the fist over his heart.

Embarrassed, Bethany shuffled in the dirt and said, 'Aww com'on you cheeky devil.'

She turned to Whip and said, 'An' you must be Wilber, ye be welcome Wilber...what...!

The little baby let an anguished cry just as Whip was about to acknowledge Bethany's welcome.

A momentary look of shock, then Bethany was at Whip's side in a blink, her eyes shining like beacons and her face creased in a great warm smile. She was at the bundle on Whip's back peeking down at the little screwed up face of Nimmy.

While Whip was struggling with the straps Bethany had the baby out and was cooing over the child as it were one of her own. It made no difference to Bethany, it was a beautiful little baby and therefore deserved all the care and warmth the enormous woman could muster. 'What's its name Wilber, an 'ow come you ave it?'

"*Er* name, is Nimmy,' Wilber said with emphasis, fearing he was losing the child already. He felt uneasy and nervous, and he was thinking, bloody hell, dis woman is a force!

'Nicholas and Jack now forgotten, Bethany, the child cradled in one arm, suddenly said, 'She wet an' messy! Pwaa! What 'ave ye been feedin' 'er!'

She suddenly grabbed Whip by the arm and dragged him along to the house. 'Come on then, ye can be tellin' me all about 'er while we change an make up some feed fo' 'er!' she ordered, and still yapping at poor Wilber, marched him into the house.

Nicholas stared at the pantomime. Whip looked for all the world like a puppy being led on a lead, dancing and looking for a feed. Grinning, Nicholas turned to Big Jack, who was sputtering to hold in the laughter. He and

Nicholas suddenly burst out laughing and made their way over to the activity by the barn, horses in tow, but not before they caught the murderous look from Whip as he was propelled through the back door into the house.

Robert scrambled out from under one of the wagons and they all shook hands. It wasn't long before the whole crew surrounded them peppering them with questions about the war. 'All right you lot,' Nicholas said holding up his hands, 'let's quieten down and I will tell what we saw and maybe why it happened.'

Nicholas began with the first sighting and left no detail out. The silence was palpable as he continued, finishing up with the story of little Nimmy.

'I don't think the war will affect us more than what we saw, and only Whip has seen any of the Nhanda people since before we arrived back at the river, sadly. In any case it was a fair way south of here, but I fear we have in the little baby girl, the only survivor of the Nhanda.'

Nicholas noted a few of the men glancing at each other and there was a little muttering amongst themselves. He cocked his head in query.

Robert said, shaking his head, 'Nicholas, lemme' see, before we arrived, yesterday mornin', Betny an' tha' kids woke up ta' find Gnarlu lyin' in the yard 'ere.' He pointed to a spot halfway between the house and the shed. "E was badly wounded, a big hole in 'is leg an' a piece o' spear in 'is back and almost through 'is gut. Betny cleaned 'im up, cut in through the stomach and got the spear out an' e's over dere in tha' shed. 'Es not lookin' good, Oi dunno whether 'e be gonna survive dis.'

Nicholas stood in shock for a moment. The blood stains, he thought, then walked briskly into the shed, Jack by his side.

Gnarlu lay on his back on a makeshift cot in the coolest part of the shed. He was almost grey in pallor and barely breathing, but his eyes were open and swiveled to Nicholas as soon as he was at his side. Nicholas saw he strained to smile. 'Ahhh, my friend what have they done to you!' said Nicholas stroking his forehead. He was burning hot, despite the cooling wet hessian, strips of which, had been placed over his thighs and across his chest and, young Adam now laid a cool wet piece across his brow.

A dark almost black poultice of what looked like some charcoal mix was smeared over the wound in his stomach, flecks of some green leaves and some blood were visible in the concoction.

'Robert, have one of the men rig up a swinging fan off the roof, like this,' Nicholas said, 'And umm, find me a piece of charcoal please.' Seeing the puzzlement on Robert's face he sketched a rough design on the foot of the bed. Peering over his shoulder one of the Irish lads said, 'Gotcha sir,' I's seen dese befo' in India, Oi'll build it, 'tis easy man!' and he rushed away to gather the material.

They all walked outside again. 'Well Robert what do we start with?' Nicholas asked.

'I thought first we's oughta be buildin' a row o' 'uts fo' da men Nicholas and build a small tank stand at one end just lower than da wagon bed, we's can then put one o' the thousand-gallon tanks on it for the men.'

Nicholas nodded his head in approval. 'Good, good, let's get to it men.'

Nicholas walked along the length of the shed and said to Jack, 'I don't know whether Gnarlu will live through this Jack, but we have got to try! Other than Nimmy, he now might be the last of the Nhanda left alive.'

Jack rumbled, 'Yas Niclas, but dey is tough people, an' we's seen many times dat dey can survive many wounds wit dere bush medicine, just like the African people, an' Umame Betny knows much 'bout the bush medicine, so we will see, neh!'

Jack and Nicholas entered the house, the first thing they noticed as soon as their eyes adjusted to the light, were the bundles of flowers hanging upside down from the roof beams, there were bundles and bundles of white, yellow and pink everlasting daisy's everywhere.

Jack could not help himself and stood, his huge chest shaking with mirth as he looked at Whip. Whip was sitting right under a huge concentration of the drying flowers and sat rocking Nimmy in Bethany's rocking chair, a crude affair, but strongly built by Robert. It was, however, also very big and Whip looked miniscule sitting in it. But that wasn't what made Jack laugh.

Whip sat with a now properly nappied, but otherwise naked little Nimmy cradled in one of his tattooed arms, the other awkwardly holding a feed bottle at which Nimmy suckled greedily. The arm holding the bottle was adorned with a rather explicit tattoo of a voluptuous naked woman, from elbow to wrist. Jack's eyes flicked from the tattoo to the bottle to the delicate flowers and back again, finding the scene most amusing.

He rumbled, 'Good afternoon Mrs Wilberforce, mama and de' baby are dey well?'

Nicholas now laughed out loud as well, but one look at Wilber's face saw only an embarrassed and furious stare, they backpedaled out of there very quickly.

That evening they sat around the table for the evening meal, including Tommy's young engineer, Petey Galvin, and foreman Finbar Conner. Galvin had come to look at the water supply and possible wells and would move out to the mine site later. The meal, whilst not sumptuous, was tasty and hearty, a fine stew of beef that Bethany had somehow obtained from the blacks, she not asking from where they obtained it for obvious reasons.

They were all sitting down having a rum after the meal – not a Brady's but one of the new flagons Nicholas had procured from Tommy's stock, a vast improvement. Most of the men though had bivouacked out by the shed.

Bethany quizzed Nicholas about Victoria, the wedding being the main topic of conversation and she asked one question after another.

She sat quietly for the next ten minutes or so whilst the men discussed the pending trip to offload the mining equipment, which was to begin perhaps tomorrow, and plans to transform the Stokes' homestead.

'So Nicholas, 'oo is keepin' your Victoria company while y'es are up 'ere settin' all this up?' Bethany asked.

Nicholas fell headlong into Bethany's trap when he replied, 'Why, she is staying with Tommy O'Farrell at his house, and she also has Peter Strudwich to look out for her, who also is staying at Tommy's.'

She stared at him, long enough to make him feel uncomfortable.

Robert knew his wife, and could sense she was aiming at something, but he couldn't think of what that could be.

Bethany said, rather pointedly, 'Ye's gonna get married as soon as ye get back, yes?' Nicholas, still unaware of where she was heading agreed of course.

"As she got any women folk in Geraldton, tha' she could talk to, I mean 'bout, tha' weddin', the dress…things tha' women talk 'bout on such an important day Nicholas?'

He replied, 'Well no, but Tommy…' She pounced. "*E* is a man! and unmarried, so what would 'e know 'bout weddin's,' Bethany cut him off. 'So you mean ta tell me dere's no one the poor girl can talk to and 'elp 'er, I mean a woman!'

The silence hung over the table, and no one dare speak, as Bethany glowered at Nicholas.

'I guess not,' answered Nicholas, now feeling guilty as hell for not considering this earlier. Once again he had focused on what *he* wanted and what *he* organised, forgetting or not even considering what Victoria's part in this was.

He was having visions of Victoria, sitting alone on the verandah waiting for him night after night, with, as Bethany had snorted, "no one to talk to but bloody men!" 'Sorry Nicholas, Oi be meanin' no disrespect, but some advice from a woman's point of view, *sometimes,* in tha' future, ye'll need to be considerin' ye wife a lot more.'

An uncomfortable silence now hung about the room.

Suddenly Bethany scraped back her chair and stood, knuckles on the table.

'Right, Bobby, ye'll be getting our wagon ready *tonight* an' tomorra, Oi'l be packin' up tha kids, includin' Adam an' we's 'eadin' off to Geraldton ta be with the poor lass, at first light!'

They all stared at her as she stabbed her finger onto the table with a force that made the cups jump, 'Any arguments?'

Whip cleared his throat. 'What about Nimmy, will ye be leavin' me some ideas for lookin' after 'er Betny? Oi means iffin' it pleases ye?'

She having already made up her mind about this, replied, 'No it don't please's me Wilber. Ye'll be 'eadin' off to the mine tomorra or tha day after, an that'll be no place to be takin' tha' poor little mite, likely her 'ealth be at

risk, so Oi'l be takin' 'er wit me ta Geraldton, 'iffin that'll be fine wit ye?'
Bethany stared at him, leaving no doubt she was daring him to disagree.

Whip, looking at her, nodded his head, knowing there was no avenue
for argument, and moreover, she was right. 'Yes well, I was going ta suggest it be dis way of course,' he said.

Bethany rolled her eyes and addressed the table again.

'Right, dat's settled den, now 'bout Gnarlu. Nicholas, what do you have
in mind?

'At this time, as far as we know, Gnarlu might be the only survivor of
the war and the only male Nhanda alive, so we need to do everything we
can to help him, without going into the main reasons for this, that's the
fact of the matter,' Nicholas replied.

'Well, e's too sick ta move,' Bethany said, 'so one of the Irish lads or
someone 'as ta be appointed to look after 'im, alright? I'll also speak to some
of the tribal women about 'elpin', dey's fantastic wit' the bush medicines.'

She got up. 'Right now, dat's the most important t'ings taken care of,
and now you'se men can discuss all o' the other t'ings ye might tink is important. Now, I's got cookin' ta do for the trip tamorra' so I's best be getting at
it,' she concluded and stomped off into her kitchen. Soon they could hear
her out the back of the kitchen calling for the Aboriginal women to come to
her. A short time later the pots and pans were banging away in the kitchen.

'Jesus Christ almighty!' said Petey, 'ye wife is a force 'urracane Bobby,
but she's right every turn Oi be reckonin'.'

Nicholas was left wondering how he had been so inconsiderate of his
wife-to-be, and how selfish for that matter.

The next morning, Robert and Adam led Hercules out and put him
in traces, and after putting on his huge nose bag went and selected a good
packhorse, a little bay mare to the wagon and proceeded to load up the
saddlebags, mostly with light things, the bulk of the items Bethany had
requested were loaded onto their flatbed.

In one long box, she carefully loaded bunches of the dried everlasting daisies, fretting that they might shed all their petals before she got to Geraldton,
she placed sheoak tree branches amongst them to provide some cushioning.

Bethany then went to Gnarlu, changed his dressing and poultices then gave instructions to the Irish foreman to make sure he kept an eye on Gnarlu's temperature and make sure he was cleaned. Two of the local Yamatje women were there, and Bethany and Robert translated as best they could.

She then went and checked the kitchen and laid down the law to the new cook, who was given permission to use it whilst she was away.

Coming out again, she yelled at Sandra and little Robert to get up on the dray. Adam was already up on the wagon, reigns in hand.

'Ye got that shotgun Adam?'

'Yes ma, I got it, an' the shells, all under the seat!' he called out

'Well it's not gonna be any damn use under the seat if'en we needs it now will it!' she said. 'Git it out, and the shells, an wrap it up in tha' blanket between us!'

The big woman turned to her Bobby, visibly softening. Hugging him she said, 'Now don'cha be worryin' 'bout me an the chil'len Bobby, I knows this 'ere track well, an we go the same way down as you'se all come up, so it be all good!' She stooped and kissed him on the cheek.

She next turned to Nicholas and Jack. 'Be safe you two an ye's better be down there in one piece in a few weeks or I'll be askin' some severe questions,' she grinned. 'Don'cha be frettin' now Nicholas, dis'l be a good thing, the poor girl must be goin' outa' 'er mind tryin' ta do everytin' by 'erself!'

She looked around at all of the building material and equipment, and nodding her head, said, 'Excitin' ain't it all! Thank you Nicholas, good things will come our way I reckon wit all o' this. Oi can do some real good when dis is all finished, especially wit de' poor black chillen. Oh, I's made a big batch o' me pies for you'se all last night, dey's in the kitchen safe.'

'Bethany,' Nicholas said, 'if your heart was any bigger you would have to have a cart to carry it around. Thank you and we will be there, don't worry.'

Lastly, she turned to Wilber. Her big arms reached out and she took little Nimmy, who was fast asleep, wrapped in a calico and blanket lined rucksack that Bethany had used for her own children.

'Wilber, Oi'l be takin' good care of 'er,' she said peeking down at the little peaceful face. 'Ye've done a marvelous job wit' 'er, ye should be proud 'bout it, despite tha' ignorance of some others!' She flashed a glance at Nicholas and Jack. 'But soon, we'll all be together at the wedding in about 5 weeks, won't we!' she finished glancing pointedly again at Nicholas and Jack.

Handing the rucksack up to Adam, she climbed up onto the seat, snatched up the reigns and yelling 'Git 'ercules!', they moved off, all waving and shouting goodbye as they headed off through the mulga trees.

Nicholas watched them disappear from sight and chuckled to himself at the way Bethany took charge of all matters. However, she also knew what lines not to cross. A rare woman indeed, he thought.

Chapter 60

Hard Graft and the New Venture Begins

The next two days were frantic as foundations were surveyed around the Stokes' property and the building lines were pegged out.

Some of the artisans started on the Stokes' house, adding another two rooms and expanding Bethany's kitchen. The kitchen was to be a surprise for her when she returned, and they were to lay a water pipe from where the tank stands were to be built, on the end of the shed, into the kitchen as well.

The young engineer proved innovative and energetic, and encouraged the men as he went about his craft.

Nicholas gathered the rest of the men and split them into two groups. He instructed one group that after they had started the quarters and had fixed the roofing in place, they were to start on the shed as a priority.

'Lads, we want the shed up and the roof on, including the guttering and pipes to the water tanks as number one priority, because when the rains start we will be able to fill the tanks ready for summer, all right?' he said. They all nodded that it was understood.

'Now, we'll be heading off to the mine tomorrow with those two wagons,' he continued pointing at two big wagons loaded with the heavy equipment and timber. 'So tomorrow we will get them ready, I want the wagons checked, greased and the beasts fed and watered early tomorrow. Okay let's get to it!'

The next morning, they awoke to some light drizzle and a complete overcast sky, the cloud moving in at some speed from the south-west.

'Damn it' Nicholas exclaimed, and muttering out loud said to Robert, 'Jesus, I hope this doesn't set in Robert!'

'Oi don't reckon it will Nicholas, should clear by mid-morning. If a breeze starts up within the hour it'll soon be over,' Robert said.

As Robert predicted, the rain soon cleared and the two wagons rolled out by mid-morning heading north to the claim and driven by two of Tommy's most trusted men and two others for the return journey.

The journey to the claim passed without incident, and progress, although not breaking any records, was steady. They travelled the same route that Nicholas, Jack, Gnarlu and Yindu had used coming back to the Stokes' homestead.

The rain had been light, not even enough to form puddles, but it did dampen the dust.

The bush after the rain smelt wonderful, and the air was fresh and clean.

They set up camp again beside what they now called the 'Northern Granites' late in the afternoon. The rock mound was smaller than the others they encountered on the trail- south side of the Stokes homestead and this formation had many tumbled and large granite boulders scattered around one side. It was amongst these boulders that they set up camp.

Nicholas showed Whip and the Irishmen the *gnamma* holes atop these rocks and advised that the holes were not for just for general use and were to be used sparingly as many of the Aboriginal people relied on the holes for survival. He gave strict instruction that the water holes were not to be used for stock water, especially the animals pulling the wagons and in any case, they carried quite a lot of stock water on the flatbeds.

Nicholas and Whip walked around the rock as the light was fading when Whip said, 'Dere's somethin' 'bout this place Nicholas, don'cha think? Oi means it's quiet, but just the same, 'tis buzzin' wit' life.'

Nicholas paused and listened. Whip was right, all that could be heard was the cooing of the topknot pigeons and the twittering of some smaller birds, and there was a low, almost indistinguishable hum all about them. 'You are right Whip, it is soothing and peaceful, why even the oxen are quiet!' Nicholas said.

'This is a magical country alright, 'tis 'ard an' bleedin' 'ot, but some 'ow I's getting' ta like it 'ere, even better than the sea maybe...don't get me wrong, I's still miss tha' sea, but still?' He let the question hang, then went on, 'Fo' example like, I's already missin' the 'omestead an' our cows'n sheep, an' I's frettin' about them Irish boys lookin' after me garden an' our animals.

He sighed and continued, 'I never planted anythin' in me miserable life before, but der's somethin' 'bout watchin' things growin', I dunno.' He took a deep breath and he went on, 'Fo' the first time in me life, I's thinkin' maybe I'll be likin' it here enough ta stay maybe, an' I's got you an' the big fella's as me best friends now, 'tis like a brother 'ood!'

Nicholas knew not to interrupt as he was getting a rare glimpse of Whip's innermost thoughts, rare indeed.

They climbed up almost to the top and sat down on a small fold in the granite, feeling the heat from the rock under their backsides.

Wilber went on. 'I's 'ad a hard life Nicholas, an' now I's tinkin' maybe I can be content 'ere. Dat's why Nimmy's passin' in such a murderous way 'as affected me so much now. I thought, she was becomin' like a daughter ta me, the skinny little t'ing was special though, 'er an young Tjarlu, dey, was so bonded an' in love, an' so smart, why, I was teachin' the pair so much every day.' Nicholas could hear the heartbreak and frustration rising in Whip's voice.

"'Twas wrong what was done to 'em, includin' tha' bloody betrothal which started the whole fookin' trouble in the first place!' The anger now rising to the surface. 'Ahhh fook me, 'tain't right! 'It took all o' me will power ta stop me'self grabbin' me rifle and 'untin' down the bloody murderin' butchers, let me tell ya! But I remembered ye instructions, an' after a while I seen tha' sense o' it all, so I did nuttin' but it don't sit well on me conscience Nicholas.' Wilber was quiet for a while, no doubt fighting the emotion boiling within him but failing as the moisture crept into his eyes and he stammered, 'An' now she's gone, p…poor little Nimit'je.' He hung his head in sorrow.

Nicholas could feel the anguish tearing his friend apart, so he put his arm around his shoulders and said, 'Listen to me Whip my friend, you must not blame yourself for not being able to save her and Tjarlu. I reckon the die was cast about their life, long before we ever set foot on this land.'

He gripped Whip's shoulder, shaking him gently before continuing.

'Remember that Nimit'je was betrothed to that other man in the Watjari long before she and Tjarlu really knew what the feelings between them was! These betrothals are commonplace among tribes and there is always a reason for it, in this case it was to try to stop what eventually happened here between the two tribes. Both Tjarlu and Nimit'je knew what would happen to them if they were caught, and they knew that it could start a war as well! They knew Whip! But they chose their own way out of love for each other. They were young and impetuous for sure, but they did know the risk they took *and* what could happen to everyone.'

Whip sniffed and wiping his eyes, nodded vigorously.

Nicholas could see he was struggling with it, even if it was true.

'Look at me my friend!' he said demanding Whip's attention. Whip looked at Nicholas.

'Listen now Whip,' he said lifting his finger to make the point, 'most importantly, *you* had no idea what had taken place until Gnarlu came to you, and by then it was too late, understand what I am saying? So, if you had run off after and killed the warriors who did this to Nimmy and Tjarlu, what good would that have done? What would it have achieved? Nothing but more anger and trouble, and maybe even your own death! It was already too late, yes?'

Whip sat silent for a while, then he said, 'Ye be right Nicholas, I's being foolish 'bout it all.'

Nicholas locked eyes with him and said, 'No my friend, when things hurt, your reaction was, well, it was just normal, okay?

Wilber looked at him and Nicholas saw he had taken the point. Wilber drew in a great breath and sighed.

'Now we will move on friend and keep that little girl's memory alive by remembering that huge smile she always had every time she saw us,' Nicholas concluded.

'Come on, we had best get back, it's getting dark.'

Mid-morning the next day saw them arrive at the mine site. Nicholas had the trains drive several miles north before instructing then to turn back south in a large sweeping U-turn just shy of the creek, then approach the site from the west.

Jack was already there waiting.

'What keep you? You'se *toooo* slow fo' ma' big foot!' he boomed laughing. 'I's faster than de 'orses!'

"E's gettin' cheekier by tha' day the big bugger is!' laughed Whip.

'Right men we need to get into unloading the equipment quickly!' said Nicholas striding off with them and pointing out where he wanted each piece offloaded.

They rigged up three of the long timber poles, drilled one and a half inch holes in the ends and bolted on the steel plates over the holes. A two and a half foot long, one and a half inch thick steel bolt was driven through the plates, holes and through a large double-sided horseshoe eye bolt which straddled the centre pole to which a snatch pulley and ropes were hung. That done, the tri-pole gantry crane was final lifted up.

It was hard work and took a lot of effort to get upright and secure, and not one of them was without splinters and blisters.

The heavy machinery, or rather those pieces which could not be rolled or pushed off, were lifted off and placed on gimlet staves to keep them off the ground should it rain.

It took a full week to finish the unloading and assembly.

Whip and Jack took one of the shortened trains out to the stone deposit and collected and cracked two full wagon loads of hard weathered stone for building, in particular to reinforce the shaft 'collar' once they began to sink the shaft.

Next they went about building a shed on one side of the existing entry to the mine drive that Nicholas and Jack had driven down.

This was to be the men's dwelling until Nicholas, Jack and Whip returned after the wedding.

At the rear of the building, they were to build a lean-to, a forge and a blacksmith's workshop, next to which was to built a small corral for the horses, of which there would be two for a start.

Nicholas then explained to the two artisans what he wanted built by the time he returned. He knew he was asking a lot, however, should they be delayed by weather or whatever, the men would be left with plenty to do.

They toured the claim area and he showed them the water hole and the outcrop of weathered stone they could use for building purposes.

The last thing he showed them was the claim cairns so they knew the area of the claim.

Nicholas, Whip and the two wagons left about ten thirty the next day, Nicholas well satisfied with what had been achieved in just over two weeks.

Whip was feeling much better after his talk with Nicholas and they could see he was back to his old self, ribbing Jack on a daily basis and copping a fair bit of the harmless barbs back in return.

Jack's grasp of English was now well advanced, thanks to almost constant tutoring by Nicholas, who found the more he learnt the more affable the big fellow became and a wicked sense of humour developed with it.

After camping at the *Granites* again, they arrived at the Stokes' homestead late that afternoon and light rain was again falling.

Tommy's work foreman, Finbar Conner, stood in the middle of the yard to greet them, his hands on his hips and worry creased all over his face.

As Nicholas drew up, he said, 'Oi be real sorry Mr Yuin, but the Black, 'e's gone.'

Nicholas's heart wrenched and he lowered his head and said, 'When did this happen Fin?'

"'Twas last night we be tinkin', well ta' be honest Mr Yuin, we's don't rightly know, but we be tinkin' maybe between ten o'clock or me'be sometime in the early mornin'. Braden, dat's one tha lads assigned to look after 'im, was sleepin' right beside 'im, but when 'e woke up, 'e was gone, 'e never 'erd nuttin.'

Nicholas nodded his head. 'Did his health improve at all, before…?' he asked.

'Well, we reckon he didn't much change, cept 'e was takin' in some o' dat broth Mrs Stokes made up for 'im. An' 'e kept sayin' sumpin' loik "Kalballage" or sumthin' loik that.'

Nicholas looked at him and said 'Kalbarri?'

'Dat's it! Dat's what 'e was on about. What's it mean sir?' asked Fin.

'It's the name of his tribe's chief elder, we haven't seen him since they started the war, but now that Gnarlu is dead, well, Gnarlu may well have been the last Nhanda man alive…'

Fin broke in. 'Wait a minute Mr Yuin, Oi be sorry fo' not explainin', the Black's not dead, least 'e didn't die 'ere. Loik Oi sais, 'e disappeared last night, we's woke up this morning an 'e's up 'n gone!'

'Gone? How…Jack, have a look around will you please,' Nicholas said.

Jack turned and started checking around. 'Me'be, four or five peoples come I reckon Niclas, an' dey carry Gnarlu away, dat way!' he said pointing east as he came out of the shed. 'Ye want me ta follow dem Niclas?' Nicholas shook his head. 'No Jack, if they wanted us to be with them they would have come in the day I reckon, leave them be.'

The relief was enormous, but somewhat tempered by the fact that they didn't know whether Gnarlu had been taken away to be tended by his own kind, or taken away to die in some tradition. Thinking about the situation, Nicholas thought it strange that Gnarlu was calling Kalbarri's name, albeit softly, and wondered if Kalbarri has survived the massacre.

'Well thank you men for looking after him, there's nothing you could have done I reckon to prevent this, maybe it's for the best, he now being with his own kind, and he is a tough man, don't you worry.

'All right Finbar, show me what's been happening.

Work had progressed well, with some of the timber wall frames either lying on the ground or already upright in position, albeit supported by stays. Several low stone and mortar bund walls about twelve inches high had been placed around the perimeter of the soon to be erected buildings. Nicholas was pleased to find that Bethany's new kitchen was well under way. The stone foundations being well progressed as was the stone alcove where Bethany's prized oven would sit. As he watched the two men laying the stone he thought, these men are excellent at what they do, and were very hard workers. He made a mental note to discuss their full-time appointment for Yuin Scott with Tommy.

The pressure was now considerably reduced with the additional workers and things being under way at last, and Finbar had proved to be a good foreman.

Nicholas began to daydream about his intended, despite trying to stop himself, but he missed her greatly and was therefore anxious to get moving again. He left instructions for the empty trains to make their way back to Northampton, and once there, to check with the Gregory's in case they needed anything and then carry on to Geraldton.

Jack, Whip, Robert and Nicholas headed off to the river homestead the next morning.

They stopped for a cup of brew about halfway back to the homestead and during the light chatter, Nicholas mused out loud, 'I suppose we had better think about a name for the homestead, what do you think my friends?'

Whip said, 'What about "The River" or maybe "Murchison Homestead"?'

'Hmmm maybe,' said Nicholas now deep in thought, names tumbling around in his head, quickly analysed and just as quickly rejected for one reason or another.

Suddenly, Jack said, 'I thinks it shoulda be de "Kalbarri Homestead", cause it's 'is land anyway, ifin 'e is still 'ere dat is, but any 'ow, still 'is!

'Sounds good ta me,' Robert chimed in, ''Tis like respect, kinda.'

'Kalbarri Homestead Nicholas repeated out loud. 'Yes Jack, I think that is good, and as you say Robert, it shows respect for the poor souls who have died here in this horrible war and especially to Kalbarri himself, whether he is still with us or not.'

So it was decided, the name Kalbarri was to be the homestead's name in honour of the land and the sad event that befell the Nhanda, the custodians and Aboriginal people of the area around the Murchison River.

Arriving at Kalbarri Homestead they were greeted by Paddy and Michael. They toured the homestead to see what had been done in their absence, except for Jack, who, as usual went to inspect *his* cows, especially Kubi.

Paddy reported that everything was fine and they had started to extend the homestead as instructed. The livestock were all fine with the exception of one chicken which died mysteriously yesterday, with no sign of any trauma. 'Not even a mark!' he said, shaking his head in wonder.

'We's plucked it an findin' no marks on 'im, we's den boiled it Nicholas, not wantin' ta waste it loik, so we's ate it, last night in fact.'

Nicholas looked at him, with one eyebrow raised and a frown now creasing his brow. 'Bobby, wasn't it you that told me that you and Bethany lost some chickens this way?' he said, winking at Robert as soon as Paddy had turned his attention to Robert.

'Yes Nicholas, exactly de same way, terrible it was,' he said, dead pan and shaking his head.

Paddy looked at him, the puzzlement clear on his face. 'Twas only a chicken man, what be so terrible 'bout that?'

'Oh, the chicken was nothing at all,' Nicholas said, but it was the visitors that got...ah best you tell him Bobby.' Whip, hearing the talk, sauntered over to listen in.

Robert was loving this and he launched into a vivid explanation of what happened.

'Well,' he began, 'just like you, we couldn't find nuttin' on 'em, not even a scratch, but dey just dropped dead! So's we plucked 'em both, dere was two of 'em, an Betny boiled 'em up same as you'se did. We's 'ung 'em out ta cool a bit so's we could 'ave a special meal wit Betny's sister an' 'er 'usband that night.

'An' dat's when we found out about the disease!'

Paddy, now joined by Michael who said, 'Never! What disease be dat den? Oi never 'eard nuttin' bout no diseases in chickens, lessen dey be rotten an' dis 'ere chicken was fresh.'

'Makes no difference, we's found out from tha copper from Mullewa, 'e come visiting after the death.'

Paddy went white. 'Waah, what death?'

'Well dat's why ye don' see us eat'n them there chickens in this coun-try. The copper tells us dat dere's dis bug ere in dis country, looks loik a flea mind, dat bites de chickens, right near its beak puttin' a poison in the chickens' blood like,' Bobby said shaking his head.

Nicholas had never heard or seen a better storyteller than Bobby; his hands were gestilucating emphasizing every word, but he was struggling hard not to laugh, and the expressions on Paddy's and Michael's faces were priceless.

'But it was too late, one day later poor Jane was dead. On dere way back ta Mullewa, she had a fit and died right there in the wagon. 'Er husband Phillip, barely got back to Mullewa alive. 'E survived, but 'e's stuffed now, all para…paralysed loik this!' he said curling his hand to his wrist and drag-ging his leg. 'Dat's why de copper come out ta warn us 'bout tha' disease.'

There was silence, then Michael said, 'Well 'ow come you'se did'n' get sick Robert, Oi means, ye ate it too roight?'

Waiting for this Robert said, 'Nah, de sister an' 'er 'usband arrived late, an we's all eaten already, had ta, ya know kids an all can't wait, so we's thankful to the good Lord fo' 'is mercy.'

'Dere's no cure fo' dis poison is dere?' Michael asked, his face a picture of fearful hope.

'Aye, der is, an ye's be in luck lads, I's just 'appened ta have a bottle of tha' stuff wit me now, 'tis good fo' a lot o' tings mind, but tastes pretty 'orrible loik.'

'Well, you can give it to them later Robert, we've got things to do first-that can't wait! Nicholas said sternly. 'Come on Robert, let's go!' and he swung up into the saddle, Robert doing the same.

Whip, almost choking, now mumbled, 'I gotta go an' see Jack, excuse me lads,' and he walked away rapidly, faking a coughing fit as he tried to stop himself laughing.

"Ang on now Nicholas, this 'ere could be a matter o' life n'death. Me an Michael 'ere might get sick while ye's be gone fa' fooks sake!' The fear, naked on both of their faces, almost made Nicholas break the pantomime. 'Oh you should be okay for a while yet Paddy, we won't be long.' With that they spurred away before either of the two Irishmen could put up further argument.

As soon as Nicholas and Robert got over the rise, they collapsed in laughter. 'Jesus Christ, did ya see the fookers faces!' said Robert wiping the tears from his eyes, his chest heaving in merriment.

Nicholas shaking as well said, 'Serves the lying bastards right, died mysteriously my arse!

'Now what's this "medicine" you've got Bobby?'

Bobby turned in his saddle and withdrew a bottle of his dreaded Brady's Rum.

Bobby said, 'This 'ere bottle has been left in the 'ot sun for a day. Betney 'id it from me, she put it on top o' the water tank, but I's found it anyway, an' it's fair rank Oi can tell ya, but Oi've 'ad a swig or two, ya know, just ta test it,' he said grinning. 'Woo, ee, it's got some bite, tastes like paraffin an' tar! Now all we gotta do is get this bloody label off'n it!'

Twenty minutes later, they rode back to the homestead, arriving just in time to see Patrick and Michael poking their fingers down their throats at the back of the grain store and vomiting their hearts out.

Putting on stern faces and yelling out for the two to run and get a couple of glasses, Robert produced the black bottle of the "over-fermented" Brady's.

'Right lads, take a full glass first,' he said. 'Then another every 30 minutes, that should clear up any o' the poison.'

Michael grabbed the glass and downed his in a gulp followed quickly by Paddy.

There was silence for about thirty seconds, then with a huge gasp, Michael grabbed the side of the store and managed a rasping, 'Fook me! What 'tis dis camel piss! He took a great shuddering breath, his gut, already torn by his dry reaching, was racing up and down like a woman's washboard.

Paddy had much the same reaction, managing, 'Jesus Christ an' 'ail Mary, dat's fookin' awful shite!'

'Now lads, ye must be waitin' about another twenty ta thirty minutes, an' 'ave another glass,' Bobby instructed.

Twenty minutes later Paddy got up and poured himself and Michael another glass.

Paddy said to Mick, 'That's the most god-awful shite Oi ever be drinkin' Mick, but I gotta say, Oi, don' feel too bad now, tha' shite must be doing sumpin'.'

'Aye, 'tis a powerful brew. Ifin Oi didn' know better, Oi reck'n it's makin' me pissed already!' Fifteen minutes later they were halfway through the third shot and were feeling the effects of the 'Christ only knows what proof' Brady's rum.

As they looked up Robert, Nicholas and Whip walked up. 'How are you feeling fellows?' Nicholas asked.

'Well Nicholash, Oi's orright so far, we's reckon this'n be all mighty strong medicine,' Paddy slurred.

Michael said, 'Jassus, ye be fookin' roight dere an' beggin' ya pardon Ro…Bobby, but what 'n the fook is dis 'ere shite?'

Bobby looked at Nicholas, a grin starting on his face. 'Well now me lad, let's see, some call it *Anti-Bullshit Mixture*, an' some call it *Anti-Chicken Thief Mixture!*'

There was stunned silence for a minute whilst Paddy and Mick digested what Bobby had said, then they both looked up at Bobby, Nicholas and Whip who were all beginning to shake with laughter.

'Fook me Paddy, we'sh been 'ad good 'an proper,' wheezed Mick adding, 'me 'ead don' seem to straight.' Paddy nodded, trying hard to focus on his mate, and his tongue was feeling numb. Suddenly, he fell sideways, out cold.

The next day, Nicholas was loading his saddlebags and checking his rifle when Paddy and Mick approached him. He turned and faced the two shamefaced Irishmen.

'Well then boys, what have we to say?' he said to them

'Ah, we's be very sorry Nicholas, we weren't honest an' dat's bad. So, we be wantin' ta apologise and 'ope ye can be forgivin' us, loik. We's shittin' ourselves dat ye be tellin' Tommy an' all.'

Nicholas let the silence hang as the pair shuffled in the dust. Finally he said, 'Ahh, what the hell, it was worth watching you being had. In future you don't have to hide anything, okay? So, what chicken? All right?' He clapped both of them on the back.

The four of them left early the next morning for Geraldton.

As they rode off, the two Irish boys waved them off. Paddy said to Michael, "E's a fair man dat Nicholas, an' we won't be trying nuttin' loik dat agin...oh bloody hell, here Oi go agin!' and he rushed over to the bushes frantically tugging at his trouser belt.

Chapter 61

Bethany and Victoria

Victoria sat in the wicker chair on Tommy O'Farrell's front verandah, sipping a cup of tea and enjoying the morning before tackling the mammoth task of preparing for the wedding.

She dreamt almost every day about Nicholas and also fretted for his safety and return.

Tommy had been wonderful, putting himself and all of his staff at her beck and call, a warm and generous man she was thinking just as he walked out to join her.

"Tis not long now Victoria and Nicholas will come galloping over that hill there, you'll see!'

Switching to his Irish brogue, he added, 'Den me lass, we'll all be makin' merriment, an' you two will tie der knot an' be a marryin', 'twill be the first grand weddin' in all o' Geraldton an' we will make it all 'appen, ta be sure an' certain, oh yes! A grander weddin' ye'll never see!'

'Oh Tommy, you are such a delight, every day you lift my spirits and make me think positive whilst my Nicholas is away.'

'Ah me lady, 'tis you who bring family to me home. So we work well together, eh!'

'Well today, I am going to seek out the Chinese family, the Wu's, yes? And also, I am looking forward to meeting Mr Wu and his wife and his daughter who Seamus tells me are very good seamstresses.'

Tommy nodded and said, 'Well, if Seamus says so, it must be so, his father was a top tailor in Belfast before they blew 'im to pieces 'e tells me, and 'e uses the Wu's as tailors for me!'

'Very good, but I am now worried about flowers for the day Tommy. I really don't know if we can get any out here.'

Tommy agreed, and said, 'Don't be worried Victoria, somethin' will turn up I'm sure,' though he was thinking, Jesus, I dunno about flowers, nothing would last a trip up from Fremantle, even if they had any to begin with.

Victoria excused herself and went back to her room to get ready for the day. She dawdled, idly filling in time, she was hesitant to even look at the list she had made of things to do for the wedding, she finally sat down at the small desk in her room and picked up the list. Looking at it, she suddenly wished her mother was here helping her.

She looked up into the mirror and started to cry, home sick and missing her mother's guidance, then looked at the list again. It was twenty odd items long but may as well have been two hundred as far as her hoping to achieve it. Everything was so hard, and whilst Tommy and Peter Strudwich had been very supportive, she really needed another woman around helping, but she was alone. Even Nicholas being here would have made it easier, and again she put her head in her hands and cried in helplessness.

Sniffing, she said to herself, 'Stop it! Ma ma is not here, and neither is anyone else!'

She went to stand and reached for a small kerchief when she jumped and stared at the mirror.

An enormous woman stood in her doorway. All Victoria could say was, 'Oh,' the tears still wet on her face as she dabbed at them. She turned and faced the woman, it could only be…she asked, 'Are you Bethany?'

Bethany opened her arms and said in a motherly and gentle voice, 'Yes honey I's her! Now come here lovey, ye look like ye could do with a hug, I'm 'ere ta 'elp ye.'

Victoria found her legs moving with a will of their own as she came to Bethany and was immediately enfolded in Bethany's great arms. 'I damn well knew it!' she said with some venom, 'bloody men! Them buggers got no idea 'bout a woman's needs, none at all!'

Victoria disentangled herself and said, 'Nicholas, is he all right?'

'To be sure he is fine lovey,' Bethany answered. "E an Whip'n Jack an' me Bobby must be 'eadin down 'ere in about a week or so 'Oi reckon, and don't ye be worryin' now, dey's all safe.

'Now den, ye get yourself together an' we'll start getting things movin' fo' tha' weddin.' With that she vanished from the doorway and stomped toward the kitchen, calling out, 'Now where's dis nice man Tommy I's bin 'earin' 'bout.'

Victoria came out to the kitchen to find Tommy, Seamus and Bethany all chatting about the wedding and quite clearly Bethany had taken charge of the planning. She was shooting questions rapid fire. 'What about the flowers, what about the invitations, 'oo was gonna perform the ceremony, 'ow many guests, what food was to be served?'

Tommy and Seamus could hardly get a word in before Tommy, not used to being quizzed like this, suddenly held up his hand and said firmly and with authority, 'Whoa 'dere ma'am, let's take a deep breath me lady. We will plan this thing out *together*, but first we had better get you and the children cleaned up an' settled into some accommodation an' den, we will all sit down with the list and make a plan, understand?'

Bethany, likewise, not being used to being told what to do, locked eyes with Tommy and saw quiet intelligence and also strength in the chip blue Irish eyes. She smiled and nodded, quite taken with the man. 'Yes of course, we'll all be workin' on dis, 'tis tha best way o' course.'

Victoria was feeling somewhat light-headed after the planning meeting as things just seemed to start happening.

A small cry came from Bethanies room, Victoria called out 'I'll get her Bethany!'

Bethany came out a little while later and stood next to her, she said 'Aint she just beautiful my lovey?' Victoria was cradling Nimmy in her arms as she rocked back and forth in the wicker rocker chair. The little baby was quite exquisite she saw as she examined the sleeping child. The little bow lips slightly open as she slept as only babies did. One day I will have a baby with Nicholas she thought and with that thought a contended glow washed over her.

Victoria murmured 'Yes Bethany she surely is and special as well, maybe the last of her people, which is really sad.'

Bethany coughed and said, 'Well we will see I guess, now I's got work to do, so ye be all right Lovey?' And she swept away to the kitchen.

The normally quiet kitchen was abuzz with activity, with Seamus and Bethany working together like a well-oiled machine, with nary a disagreement. Together they had worked out a system for when they would start cooking before and during the wedding.

Tommy was organising the hand press printing of the official invitations and seating for the guests. In addition, he had a special wagon train coming up from Fremantle, and he was fretting about it arriving on time, though he knew there was nothing he could do but wait.

Victoria went about getting ready and doing sketches of her mother's wedding dress and how she wanted it to be altered to suit her own style. She now had the time and so figured it a good opportunity to meet the Wu family.

One morning she mentioned to Tommy that she was going along the street (if you could call it that) to see the Wu's and arrange the alterations to her mother's wedding dress.

Tommy frowned a little, and standing came to her and put his arm around her and said, 'That'll be fine by me lovely lady, but ye'll be accompanied by Isaac at all times, fo' protection loik, alright?'

'Really Tommy, that's not necessary, I am perfectly capable of organising my own wedding dress!'

'Oo aye, that may well be my lady, but seein' as 'ow Nicholas is not 'ere, an' you are guests in my 'ouse, den ye be my responsibility until Nicholas returns, alright? So, Isaac *will* be accompanyin' ye, an ye well know that dere's been trouble wit dat first mate Birch threatin' people,' he said with finality.

Seeing that Tommy was not going to be swayed on the matter, she nodded, but Isaac still gave her the shivers. That being said, she did feel some kind of protective presence when he was around she had to admit.

Further, all of Tommy's men seemed to speak of Isaac with some kind of awe.

Tommy watched them go. He would not generally be worried about Victoria being alone, however, since Peter had discharged his first mate, Birch had been constantly causing trouble in the township, not to mention his utterings of revenge on Nicholas, Whip, Peter and Big Jack.

Lao Wu (old Wu) was a skinny little man with a sparse goatee-type beard – a few long strands of chin hair about three inches long – but he did have a thin moustache of sorts.

He and his family all came out to meet Victoria. Although his English was nowhere near perfect, his wife Chen and daughter Meili were somewhat better at English and they quickly established a rapport. They explained that they did the laundering for the town, and recently were approved to do the laundry for the military as well, courtesy of Mr Roe, of which they were very happy and very grateful.

Victoria was invited inside the little whitewash plastered hessian front shop and was served some excellent Chinese green tea. The Wu ladies examined Victoria's dress and very quickly picked up what Victoria wanted, the sketches helping, and after some intense chatter in Chinese, they knew exactly what to do.

Turning to her, Meili said quietly, 'This ah, shoulder, off ?' she drew a long finger nail across from shoulder to shoulder, looking up at Victoria in query.

Victoria looked at Meili and saw a beautiful elegant girl of around eighteen, though in fact Victoria was to discover later that Meili was actually twenty-three years old. Her skin was flawless white and her face had a perfection that was hard to describe, framed in jet black dead-straight hair which fell to her hips.

'Yes! Exactly!' said Victoria, smiling at the girl. Meili smiled back. Neither of the two could know that the Wu's and the Yuin's lives would become intricately entwined in the future.

Victoria departed the Wu's and left her dress with them for the alterations, happy in the knowledge she was another step closer to marrying her Nicholas.

She stepped out into the street and as if by magic, Isaac materialised beside her. She turned to him, and smiling looked up at him and said, 'I am sorry it took so long Isaac, but there was quite a lot of fine work to be done.'

Isaac looked down at her giving a slight nod, and she was surprised to see the merest glimpse of a smile on his face, which quickly fell shut like a steel trap as he switched his attention across the road to an alleyway.

Possibly no one else would have seen the person standing in the shadows who had been looking at the odd couple, but with Isaac it was more an instinct than a visual thing that had caught his attention. On passing the alleyway his eyes swiveled right from under the brim of his tall creased stovepipe hat, and he confirmed what had piqued his attention.

Unaware of what had transpired, Victoria thought, he likes me.

Birch ducked back into the afternoon shadow, wondering who the long streak of a man with Yuin's intended was. Still, he was sure he had not been seen, and the two walked past giving no indication of spotting him. 'E looks like a fookin' undertaker! he mused and shuddered. He headed back to the ale house, hatred stirring in his gut.

When Victoria and Isaac got back to the house, Tommy was nowhere to be seen, so Victoria headed back to the kitchen. She heard movement out on the back porch and went out in time to see Bethany and young Sandra, hanging the last of the dozens of bunches of the everlasting daisy's.

'Oh, aren't they beautiful!' cried Victoria, gasping at the pink, white and yellow flowers. She reached out and gently touched them, they rustled like fine paper at her touch.

Bethany was beaming at her and said, 'We's not 'aven a flower problem now! 'Tis solved, dey's called 'Everlastin' Daisies'. Every year in spring, if'n, tha rains come, dey come up, covering great fields of the country where our 'ouse is.'

'They are wonderful,' cried Victoria, clapping her hands. 'Perfect colour for my dress and all, there's pink and white edging of small flowers on the wedding dress!'

'Every year, me an' the kids collect bunches of 'em. We's tie 'em off an' 'ang 'em up in the shade, an' deys last about nine ta twelve months, an' we's got some from last spring an' just gathered these ones,' she said pointing to a section at the other end. 'So you'se be lucky, 'cause this year 'as been very 'ot an' not much rain! Now all we need ta do is get every thin' done in time. Let's go look at our list again lovey.'

Bethany and Victoria worked together at organising the wedding and they soon became good friends. Bethany was quite taken with Victoria and was excited about having another woman who would be closer than those at Mullewa, and she spent what time she could telling Victoria about many of the things about living in the bush. She cooed about her Bobby and told her all about Nicholas's plans and his generosity to the Stokes.

Tommy came back sometime after lunch and asked for a 'little' meeting in the kitchen because he had some news from John Roe. He said in his educated English, 'I hope you will not be too upset Victoria, but John Roe informed me today that the minister, Mr Charles Clay's arrival has been delayed by about five days due to some other commitment upon which Mr Roe did not elaborate.'

Victoria sat, taking in what Tommy had just said. Her head was in a whirl for a moment, they all sat watching for her reaction.

'Well Tommy, this could be a blessing in disguise,' she began. 'I mean, we are struggling to achieve everything in time by the 28th of the month. That means, if we make the wedding date the 15th of September, we have another week to prepare, yes?'

Tommy, already sweating on his 'special' wagon's arrival was delighted at her easy acceptance, but he kept a poker face and answered evenly. 'Well yes, since you put it that way, and Nicholas has yet to return,' but quickly added, 'I mean he may be another week or so yet, what do you think Bethany?'

Bethany said staring at Tommy, 'Well first, 'ow come ye be speakin' like an English toff one minute an' a bladdy Irish low-class sailor the next?'

Tommy and Victoria laughed at Bethany's blunt question. 'That's a very good question my dear,' he replied before switching back to his Irish brogue and saying, 'Oi'l be sure ta tell ya one day me lovely lady, 'tis a mystery ta be sure an' certain!' His eyes sparkling with mischief.

They all laughed. 'Oi be tinkin' it be a right big advantage, ta be sure an' sure,' Bethany said, mimicking Tommy's accent nigh on perfectly.

The immediate pressure off, things started to happen. They decided to hold the ceremony and reception at the back of the house, on the sparse lawn, and John Roe had called in to offer the lighthouse dwelling to Nicholas and Victoria for the wedding night. 'It now has doors, windows, a lounge chair, a bed and some other furnishings. Also, some heavy curtains, as well as a fine fire grate in the hearth as well. You and Mr Yuin are welcome to it,' he had said.

Victoria graciously accepted the offer, another thing to tick off the list, and she was delighted as the dwelling was somewhat isolated from the town and she had not been looking forward to spending their first night as a married couple surrounded by guests, children and God only knows how many of Tommy's men. Perfect, she thought.

She was beginning to like John Roe, his stern exterior and how he always carried himself, a decent and grand gentleman and so full of mystery she considered.

Several weeks had passed by and still Nicholas and the men had not returned. Victoria was starting to worry once again about Nicholas, although she managed to keep her thoughts hidden well. Bethany was not fooled though and kept up a constant barrage of diversion tactics.

Two days later, at around eleven in the morning, Victoria, Bethany and Isaac were returning from the Wu's after another fitting (the third) and she and Bethany were chatting about how skillful Mrs Wu and Meili were, and how they were so spotlessly clean and meticulous in every detail.

They stopped to look at the small bakery that had opened, chatting with the baker. Before long people started to gather around, all asking Victoria and Bethany questions. The pending wedding was certainly no secret and the women in the new town were as excited as anyone.

Suddenly, Isaac took two steps toward Victoria, the crowd parting as if he were a shark in a shoal of fish. He reached out and gently tapped her on the shoulder.

Victoria turned to look up at him and was stunned to see a half-decent smile on his face. She smiled back at him and said, 'Yes Isaac? What is it?'

The smile had vanished, but he put his hand back on her shoulder, turning her gently round and pointed north.

Four figures were appearing over the rise up the road, three riders and one running. It took a minute before the appearance of the men registered.

'Nicky!' she cried out and lifting up the hem of the cotton shift she was wearing ran up the road toward the riders, her blonde hair streaming about her head as she ran.

Chapter 62

Bliss and Hearts to Beat

Nicholas jumped from the saddle as Victoria came running up the road and as soon as she was within arm's length, he swept her off her feet, laughing and spinning around as she hugged him.

He put her down gently, swept off his hat, bowed grandly and said half mockingly, 'Love of my life, 'tis I who have returned to marry thee! He said dramatically. 'Ha! I told you I would return with all haste!'

Victoria just hugged him and said, 'I am so happy you are back safe and everything is happening! Bethany is marvelous and I have the alteration of the wedding dress organised, and, and...' Nicholas held two fingers up to her lips and said still laughing at her excitement, 'Whoa sweetheart, whoa! Let's go up on the verandah and have a cold drink, we have been riding hard and we are all fair exhausted, and then you can tell me all about it.'

They all walked up to the verandah, where Nicholas introduced Wilber to Victoria.

Whip said softly, one hand on his heart, "'Elp me Christ! 'E said you were beautiful, but I never thought...' he trailed off and went down on one knee and lifted her hand to his lips. 'Oi'm mighty pleased ta meet ye Miss Victoria, an' Oi'm in love wit ye already!'

Victoria giggled and said, 'I have heard so much about you Whip, we were all very worried about you with the fighting up at the river, but here you are, safe and sound!' Whip got to his feet. 'Well aye, but in truth Oi didn' see any of tha' war, only some of da cause and result.'

Victoria turned to Jack, and looking down at his huge feet, said to him, '*Sawabona Ubhuti* (Hello Brother), I see you haven't worn out your two horses yet Jack?'

He grinned at her, '*No, Usisi, unyawo- hle!*' (No Sister, feet best!), and he walked away to talk to the others.

Seamus and Tommy came out with drinks, followed by Bethany with little Nimmy asleep in one arm and a plate of cookies in the other. She was followed by the two children close behind, who immediately ran to their father. As usual he was gruff but fooled no one.

Bethany went straight up to Wilber and Jack and passed Nimmy to Jack first, saying, 'She is all content now Whip, 'ere.' Jack passed Nimmy to Whip, who gently took the babe, as though she was fragile porcelain, he had a grin on his face like a Russian clown.

They all chatted as the four new arrivals cooled down with cold drinks.

Victoria whispered in Nicholas's ear, 'Jack's horse is out in the back paddock, a black, he is the most magnificent animal you have ever seen, a huge horse and I have chosen a name for him, if Jack likes it, I thought *Mnyama Ubaba?*'

'That, my love, sounds excellent! Black Lord. We will have a look later,' Nicholas said nodding his agreement.

There was some somber moments as they relayed the sad events at the now named Kalbarri Station and of the killings. There was a quiet reflective moment and no small amount of sadness within the group as they digested what had occurred.

Nicholas said, 'Well now, the whole situation seemed as though it had been ordained years ago, so in reality, we could not have been able to interfere in any way, nor stop it from happening.'

Seeking to lighten the mood Nicholas said, 'Well, tell us all about the wedding plans, what has been happening?'

Everybody started to talk at once, and Nicholas laughed and relaxed as they all told of the preparations. But Nicholas found he was in a bit of a dilemma as he listened to the banter. They had asked Peter Strudwich to give away Victoria, and that was fine. But who to ask to be the best man?

He could ask Jack, but thought maybe the big fellow would be uncomfortable, he not being remotely familiar with the wedding plans white men had. Then there was Whip. He could do it, but Nicholas did not consider he was as close as say he and Jack were.

Finally, and the last person he could consider was Tommy. He had been marvelous and was becoming a close friend, but not quite as yet. He decided to talk to Victoria about it later.

Shortly, Victoria tugged him away with the intention of showing him *Mnyama Ubaba*.

Nicholas was dumbfounded when they approached the rear stables of Tommy's allotment. The huge Percheron stood stock still in the centre of the stockade, staring at their approach.

The stable hand called out as they came to the fence of the stockade. 'Be careful, 'e's gotten very testy 'e 'as to be sure an' certain Miss Victoria. No one can get near 'im 'cept when ye pick up the groomin' gear, 'e likes ta be groomed ta be sure, 'tis the only time 'e stands an let's ye touch 'im!' But still, be careful!'

As if to confirm this the black pawed the ground and let out an indignant whinny, tossing his great head up and down.

Nicholas said, 'My God, aren't you the most beautiful beast I have ever seen! Vicky you have chosen the perfect name for him, The Black Lord, indeed! Good God he's huge!' The black suddenly sprang to the left and ran a full circle, then to their surprise stopped and trotted over to within six feet of Victoria and danced his head up and down at her. She looked at him, his coat was glossy and shone like he was oiled. He *is* magnificent, she mused. She looked up into the brown eyes.

'Ha, he recognises me!' she said with triumph in her voice.

'Give me some oats please,' she asked politely. 'Yas'm, but please be careful,' said the nervous stable boy.

After a little coaxing the black came over and tentatively snuffled up her offering of oats.

Nicholas, still in awe of the horse said, 'Now all we have to do is to get Jack to accept him and learn to ride!'

I wonder if he has ever been ridden, Nicholas pondered.

They left and returned to the house.

Peter Strudwich had heard Nicholas had returned and left the *Collette* mid-afternoon to greet him. He and Nicholas had much to discuss regarding current events, and Peter was looking forward to meeting again.

Peter found Nicholas, Victoria, Tommy and Jack at the rear of Tommy's store building. They were discussing riding lessons with Jack and he was proving as difficult and stubborn about riding a horse as always.

'I all ways run, since I's been born, we trainin' to be de warriors and run to de battle!' Jack boomed. He thumped his great chest and said, 'No ride around on de liddle 'orse's back!'

He held both hands up mimicking holding reigns and clucked his tongue, then pranced around on his toes as though he were riding, bringing peals of laughter and giggles from them all. He looked ridiculous, which was his intention.

"Orses too liddle Nicholas, I's would be needin' some orse' too big!' He threw his arms up above his head saying, 'I's don' need 'orse, I's *run*!'

Victoria leaned over to Tommy and said quietly, 'Tommy, where is the black?'

'Just a minute,' Tommy said as he motioned to one of his men and quietly said something. The fellow nodded and disappeared into the stable area. Minutes later he rode out on a horse and cantered over the low ridge toward the back of the property. Tommy turned to Victoria and said, "E's comin', I 'ope!' winking at her.

Nicholas said to Jack, 'But Jack, maybe you could try! If we did get a big horse for you, yes?

'I worry about you may be getting hurt whilst we are away or bitten by a snake, or needing a horse when we explore further north?'

'Hmmm, only 'urt, I's 'member is bloody saddle sticking me ball...' he stopped mid-sentence. 'Sorry *Usisi*, I's forget manner.' She giggled, remembering the story.

'Why everyone worry 'bout Jack ridin' 'orse when I's jus' don' want to!' he said with some emphasis. Suddenly he had had enough and was getting angry, and with that he turned and walked toward the back of the yard.

He got about 20 feet from them. There was a deep drumming coming from the ground, stopping Jack in his tracks. He stood, one ear cocked, trying to identify the drumming.

First the head appeared over the ridge, Jack snapping his own head up as soon as he saw it.

Mnyama Ubaba, at near full gallop crested the rise, running straight at Jack, but slowed down as soon as he saw the huge man come into full view, He walked a little toward Jack, and standing about thirty feet away, snorting, he danced his great head up and down. He stopped and stood motionless, his ears pricked as he stared at the big man. Jack stood staring back.

Jack said, *'Ukusa'* (Come) – it was more of a gentle command – and he held out his hand. The horse pawed at the ground and whickered slightly. Much to the onlookers surprise, *Mnyama Ubaba* slowly walked straight up to Jack and tossing his head up and down bent and snuffled Jack's hand.

Victoria and Nicholas looked at each other, not quite believing what they were seeing.

They heard Jack say, *'Sawabona Bukekayo-hle'* (good morning handsome) followed by, *'Ukusa wena unjani,hmmm?'* (How are you hmmm?) as Jack reached out and gently stroked the animal's muzzle, rewarded with a gentle wicker.

He walked around the horse, his left hand stroking the neck and then running along the horse's flanks to the rump. Everyone held their breath as Jack walked around the rump of *Mnyama Ubaba*. They all, contemplating what devastation would happen if one of those massive hoofs connected with a kick. But Jack continued running his hand around the rump, close, brushing the tail, all the while still talking to him in his deep soothing voice.

Jack instinctively knew he had the animal's confidence, just as he did with his great bull Kubi, so he did not fear him and the horse sensed it. He continued and came back to the head and stroked the mane gently.

They stood, Jack murmuring softly into *Mnyama Ubaba's* ear, as he ran his hand up and down the velvet-like ear.

The big fellow turned and walked back to the group by the fence, and to everyone's surprise, the black followed, nary a pace behind.

Jack stopped and turned to them and said, 'Dis is *real* 'orse!'

He looked at Nicholas and then to Tommy and asked, 'Dis 'orse, 'e belongs to you Tommy? Where 'e comin' from?' Tommy shook his head and said, 'No big fellow, 'e is not mine,' smiling at Jack.

Before anyone else could say anything Nicholas said, 'His name is *Mnyama Ubaba*, Jack.' He is a Percheron breed and he comes from France.'

There was silence as Jack, nodding, digested what Nicholas said. Turning and stroking his huge head, he said slowly with a deep frown on his brow, 'Dis a fine name for 'im,' as *Mnyama Ubaba* nudged him none too gently against the fence with his head. Jack looked at Nicholas, perplexed.

Nicholas said, grinning at him, 'He belongs to you, he's *your* horse Jack.'

Jack stared at him, confusion on his face. Now he understood why the horse had a Zulu name.

'My 'orse?' he asked, pointing at his chest, looking at the black and then back to Nicholas.

'Yes Jack, my gift to you.'

There was silence as Jack took it all in. He knew that this animal would have cost a lot of money and he was struggling at the enormity of the gift. He looked up at the huge brown eyes staring at him and turned back.

'Niclas, I…' Jack started, but Nicholas, Victoria and the rest had started to walk back to the house, leaving no time for Jack to argue, he stared after them and *Mnyama Ubabe* again nudged him hard against the fence.

Nicholas looked back at Jack and the black as they reached the back door of the house.

'Look!' he said to them.

Jack was standing next to the horse and even from there they could hear his deep crooning voice as he talked. He was running his hands over the horse again and the black just stood there.

'Ha! Seems dey's got a bond now Nicholas, to be sure! Ain't love grand,' cackled Tommy.

'Oh yes, I forgot, we are to be arrangin' a saddler to come ta town, 'Mr Roe asked us to bring 'im up, e' will be 'ere ta service the army as well, an' pe'raps 'e can make the special saddle, maybe without a saddle horn!' cackled Tommy.

Laughing, Nicholas said, 'Well thank you Tommy, all we have to do is convince Jack to get on him and learn to ride!'

Later that afternoon, Nicholas and Victoria decided to take a walk down to the point, the weather was warm and a gentle breeze blew from the south-west, so arm in arm they strolled down the dusty track toward the *Collette* still lying on her side.

Peter Strudwich had been called back to the ship for some reason, so he and Nicholas didn't get the opportunity to talk as yet, but this afternoon Nicholas was content to spend the rest of the day with Victoria.

Nicholas was a little surprised at the warm welcome people of the community gave them, many coming out to wish them well as they walked by. It seemed the whole town knew about the wedding coming soon, thought Nicholas, not realising that his upcoming nuptials was the first wedding to ever happen in town, so of course everyone was excited.

In fact, for the first time in months he was feeling relaxed and happy, everything was now coming together and the future was looking good.

He ticked off some points in his mind.

Peter had said the section to replace the damaged rudder had arrived aboard a survey vessel out of Fremantle and was in the process of being fitted, and he was fairly certain the *Collette* would be back at sea some days after the wedding, perhaps before even, and would head to England via Colombo.

He finally had obtained a horse for Jack, and Jack and the big black had some kind of bond by the look of things. Convincing Jack to get up on the horse was another matter.

Wilber seemed enamoured with the little girl survivor of the Nhanda as though she was his own daughter, and the gruff, normally taciturn man, had changed for the better. Perhaps Wilber thought the little babe was the reincarnation of Nimit'je, Nicholas wondered.

And soon, he and Victoria would marry at last. He looked down at her and slid his arm around her waist and immediately thrilled at the firm slimness beneath his hand. She looked up at him with her grey eyes and smiled at him as she lay her head against his arm as they strolled.

As they approached the Wu dwelling, Victoria was telling Nicholas what a wonderful job the two women of the household – Chen and her daughter Meili – were doing to the dress for her, when there appeared to be some kind of ruckus in front of the Wu household.

'Oh no, it's Mr Wu and his wife. Nicholas, help them Nicky!'

Lao Wu was standing with his back to his wagon's street-side wheel, his left hand held out over his wife's body in protection. In front of him, stood three drunken louts who were hurling abuse at the old man and were poking a stout stick at him.

'Ching, Ching, Chinie' man! Ye be stinkin' little yella man,' the tallest lout sang and he stabbed again at the old man, who quite surprisingly easily brushed aside the stick as though it were a toothpick. Huh! thought Nicholas noticing the speed and precision of the movement.

Nicholas suddenly took several rapid steps toward the scene, and just as the lout began to swing a roundhouse blow with the stick it was snatched from his grasp. Nicholas, still in motion, whirled and cracked the stick down on tall man's skull, breaking the stick and knocking the fellow down onto all fours.

Still holding the broken staff, the end of which was splintered into a sharp point, Nicholas had the sharp point at one of the other's throats before the man could react.

Nicholas said evenly, 'Well now, this not very fair you bunch of pansies is it? Three grown men against an old man and an old lady?'

'Now how about you pick up this piece of dung!' he turned and drove his boot into the man's gut hard, bring a loud whoosh of air and a shrill cry of pain from the coward, whose head was now dribbling blood. 'And get out of here! That is unless you would like to stay and take me on! Three against one with you piss-weak pieces of shit is fine by me!'

The two still standing, hesitated a bit, then not taking their eyes off Nicholas for a second, carefully bent and lifted up their moaning friend and staggered off down the road.

The had gone less than 10 yards when Senior Constable Drummond and his junior constable grabbed two of them by the scruff of the neck and none too gently threw them down onto the ground on top of their still gasping friend.

'Well, well you three, appears you don't listen ta advice now do ye's now? Only thirty minutes ago I told ye to lay off the grog an' go 'ome!' With that he lent down and cracked the top two men's heads together, hard. 'Ow,! Jesus! Ow!' the pair yelled out.

Nicholas winced hearing their heads clash. 'Ouch!' he grinned, turning to Victoria, but she was with Mrs Wu and the old man. Turning back, Drummond called out, 'You or'right Mr and Mrs Wu, an' no need to ask 'ow you are Mr Yuin, I seen it all anyhow?'

Nicholas waved and turned to the old man. 'Are you okay Sir?'

The old fellow turned from his wife and grinned at him. '*Sie, sie*, sank you, sank you,' he repeated in heavily accented English.

Mr Wu turned and waved at Drummond, calling out *'Meiyou gwan-see'* (It doesn't matter) and bowed first to Nicholas and then to Drummond.

'C'mon you three pieces of rabble,' Drummond boomed out, 'a night in me 'ot box'll do ye no 'arm now will it.'

Victoria introduced Lao Wu and Chen to Nicholas, and after much bowing and curtsies alike, Lao Wu and his wife said, *'Ni hao'* (hello) before repeating *'sie, sie'* several times in thanks to Nicholas for his interjection. Several times Chen Wu said to Victoria, *'Hen Hao'*, indicating toward Nicholas.

When Nicholas and Victoria left to continue their walk, he asked Victoria, 'What does *"Hen Hao"* mean Vicky?'

'I don't really know, but I think it means "good", they approve of you!' she replied laughing and hugging his arm.

'I bet that fellow will have a pounding headache tomorrow morning!' Victoria said.

Nicholas sighed deeply. 'I wonder if I will ever go anywhere without getting set upon by trouble.' he lamented and shook his head.

'Never mind Nicky. Oh look, there's the *Collette*! She looks all new and clean!' she exclaimed.

As they drew near they could see that the bulk of the men were beginning to dig a deep trench from the hull to the water's edge, and already the ship's stern had slewed a little toward the sea and she was more upright.

The water seeping in was proving difficult though, and men shoveled the sand out frantically as even more moved the piles of sand further away as fast as the men in the water shoveled it out. A dual pump was removing water and sand near the stern, the two men on the pump's handles glistening with sweat as they rapidly lifted the draw bar up and down.

Two longboats were out in the bay, most oars up with long hemp hawsers attached to the boats and the ship's stern as they awaited De Frey's orders to row. As they watched two more of the longboats arrived. Two men, one from each boat, dived overboard, with light painters around their waists and empty barrels as floats. The pair kicked toward the ship and the shore, no doubt preparing for a major tug operation to drag the ship back into the water.

Nicholas and Victoria walked past the stern where half a dozen men were applying pitch and nailing square copper plates onto the hull behind the rudder, which was now in position. Another group was nailing more copper plate down at the keel where the plates had been stripped off during the repair. They watched as the men rapidly brushed the boiling pitch to a section of the hull and almost immediately the next two men fixed the copper plate – one placing the plate and the other driving in long bronze spikes or nails through the plates and into the timber beyond. It was back breaking, strenuous work and the men, up to their thighs in the sea, stripped to the waist, gleamed with sweat.

Peter Strudwich emerged from the group waving and came over to them.

'Hello ye two, beautiful evening for a walk, yes?'

'Hello Peter,' Victoria said, 'It is lovely. Looks like you will have her back in the water soon?'

'A couple days I reckon my lass, maybe sooner. You see I 'ave them working flat out ta finish the final platin', an we's been waitin' for the king tide, which according to my nose, will be at eight bells tomorrow night, so they have much to do. We've still got to screw the stern around an' try an' get 'er more to the vertical, which will not be easy.' He grinned at them.

Strudwich looked keenly at them both and said, 'I can be lookin' forward to ye's comin' down to watch 'er float off then now can I?'

Nicholas answered for them both and said, 'Wild horses couldn't keep us away Peter!'

'That'll be something ta see! After that we'll check her all over, do a sea trial, load an' we's be off to London Town! We have dispatches and mail to deliver for John Roe an' Mr Burges,' he said, his eyes sparkling beneath his eyebrow verandahs at the thought.

He added quickly, seeing the look on Victoria's face, 'That'll be after the weddin' of course my young lady.'

'No more trouble from your Mr Birch I take it Peter?' Nicholas inquired.

'I laid him off Nicholas, as you no doubt heard, causing too much trouble and demoralising the crew. I promoted Johann De Freys to first mate, 'es a 'ard man to be sure, but don't 'av the vicious streak in 'im like Birch 'ad.' He added, 'The men respect him as well.

'But that brings me to what I wanted to tell ye Nicholas, an' you also Victoria. That mean bastard is still 'ere, an' although the coppers are keepin' an eye on 'im until 'e gets passage outa' here, an' that I am told will be next Friday or Saturday mornin', I'm still 'earin' that 'e's 'ell bent on getting revenge on you, Jack and Whip – an' now me as well.

'So, please be very careful. 'E will fight dirty given the chance, so keep your eyes open!' He concluded.

'Thank you Peter, we will be extra careful, we knew he wouldn't let the incident on the ship go easily, and we are aware he has been still making all kinds of threats. Tommy's men have been keeping an eye on him as well, and when I am not around Tommy has his man Isaac accompanying Victoria.' Nicholas said.

Peter raised his eyebrows and shuddered when Nicholas mentioned Isaac. 'My men an' 'alf the colony are afraid of that man,' Peter said. 'They say 'e's like Doctor Death, or the Grim Reaper or somethin', e' gives me the shivers.'

'Isaac likes me,' Victoria said somewhat smugly, 'why, he even sort of smiled at me.'

'Everyone likes you sweetheart,' said Nicholas bending down and kissing her cheek.

Strudwich added, 'Ye'd be possibly the only person who's ever seen 'im smile then Victoria. You know, he is absolutely devoted to Tommy the Chip they tell me. I wonder 'ow come that's so?' He paused. 'Ah well 'tis none of our business at the end of tha day!'

A shrill voice suddenly called out, 'Cap'n Strudwich suh!' Young Adam Stokes' torso was sticking out of one of the master's cabin windows. 'I's cleaned out ye cabin as best I could suh, what do ye be wantin' me ta be doin' next sah!'

Suddenly, noticing Nicholas and Victoria, he cried, 'Oh hello Mr Yuin suh an' Miss Victoria!' Young Adam waved to them vigorously.

Strudwich said, 'Ye can wipe down the ceiling lad, an' I hope you 'aven't placed ye bloody dirty feet on my writin' desk young fellow?'

Adam near fell back inside. Regaining his composure, he replied, 'Ahh, no suh, I's got the old blanket on it.' With that he vanished inside the cabin again, no doubt only now placing the blanket on the desk.

They all laughed. "E's a good lad that one,' Strudwich said. 'Ye know 'e wants to come with me when we sail but I 'ad to say no because 'e's just a wee bit too young at heart yet, an' first we'd 'ave to get past Bethany.'

'Good luck with that!' Nicholas said chuckling. 'Maybe next year you might have a chance, that gives you a year to work on her, or Adam will.'

'I don't think anyone will be able to stop him when the time comes, he's pretty determined, an' if my instincts are correct, 'e's a natural,' said Peter.

'Best I be gettin' to know Bethany a bit better, would ye help there you two?' he asked, one great bushy eyebrow cocked in query.

'I dunno, Peter, you being a known pirate and all, she might object!' Nicholas laughed. Peter shook his finger at Nicholas, 'Now, now young man, don't ye be startin' up any rumours ye hear!' Strudwich chuckled, the twinkle in his eye would give anyone who heard the banter pause to consider.

'What are those men doing there Peter?' asked Victoria, indicating a couple of sailors standing by a fire on which sat a large copper kettle of boiling water, the steam swirling around them. They started to walk over to the fire and kettle.

'The lads 'av discovered a lot of crawfish or some such thin' livin' in the reef over yonder,' Peter said, jerking his thumb toward the reef. 'They are delicious after they boil 'em up. Come, ye's can try some!' Peter picked up a square of calico and took two of the now red and cooked crustaceans. He expertly twisted the tails off them and cracked the side of each tail's shell with a belaying pin, prising them open to expose the succulent white flesh within. He twisted out the tails, placing them onto the calico, he sprinkled a little salt over them and handed them to Nicholas and Victoria.

Victoria took a small bite and was delighted with the sweet taste. 'Mmmm, they are delicious!' she said. 'I have never had anything like this and so sweet tasting, have you Nicky?'

'Not as good as this! But I have tasted similar, in fact, I ate my first in the Cape in Africa when I was studying there and again in Canada by the coast. They were bigger, but these are by far the sweetest I have ever had!'

Still chewing on the crawfish, they gave their thanks and continued their stroll out to the point.

Sitting down on a grassy knoll by the sea, Nicholas said, 'I have a dilemma Vicky, I just cannot decide what to do with regards to selecting a best man?' And he told her of who he considered and why it seemed complicated.

Victoria smiled at him and said, 'My love, the answer is simple, don't have one! I am not having a maid of honour either. I did consider Bethany, but she…ahh…is too big, and further to make such a dress for her would take too long, and anyway, she will be up at dawn preparing things on the day and will be so busy, it would be impossible!' She looked at him. He was nodding his head in agreement. She added, 'And really, I don't know her well enough to be honest.'

Nicholas said, 'It's the same with Jack, I mean he is so huge, and the same also applies to clothing him!'

He looked at her and started to chuckle. Victoria also started to giggle as they imagined what it would look like, two huge people and Nicholas and Victoria in the middle, and they suddenly burst out laughing and held each other.

Still catching his breath, Nicholas said, 'So that is it, it will be just you and I together, as it should be!'

He turned to her and their heads touched as they looked at the sun setting across the reefs, small breaks colouring the sea, and they sat enjoying the closeness.

They held each other, feeling the warmth between them and listening to each other's breath. It was as though some unspoken restraint had formed between them since Nicholas's return, albeit not without difficulty as both of them were full of emotion and desire.

However, they each felt that they would wait for their marriage before allowing their emotions to rise out of control, as had happened previously.

Despite their self-control, they felt a bond strengthening between them. It was hard to explain, but a warmth from within rose between them, akin to feeling the satisfying heat when warming one's hands at a fire in winter.

No words were necessary as they slipped their arms around each other and enjoyed the feeling.

Their marriage was fast approaching and they both were feeling the rising tide of excitement.

Chapter 63

Tommy's Surprise

Nicholas lay on his bed in Tommy's house thinking about how relaxed he was, though quite melancholy if the truth be known.

He had dressed earlier, thinking he might visit John Roe this morning. But the main reason he was up early, apart from habit, was that he was mystified as to *why* he was so relaxed, a feeling quite foreign to him. Traditionally, he would wake and within seconds would be planning his day, barely stopping for even a coffee or tea, but lately he seemed to be of a different disposition.

He considered that finally, all of his dreams since he departed from lake Nyanza had now come to fruition and some part of him was at peace with his love for Victoria, the doubts had vanished.

He sighed and stretched and jumped when there was an urgent rapping on his door. 'Come!' he said.

Tommy burst in on Nicholas just as he swung his feet off the bed to pull on his boots.

'Nicholas, quick, quick now, dis is sumtin' ta see, ta be sure!' He frantically beckoned with his hands.

'What is it Tommy?' Nicholas asked looking at the excitement on his friend's face.

'Com'on Nicholas, ye'll see!'

They hurried out the back door and Tommy led him off to the right of the store shed and around the side of the men's quarters. Then putting his finger up to his lips for silence, Tommy took him by the arm and indicated he look around the corner.

Mnyama Ubaba stood, not thirty feet away, next to the corral fence, silhouetted against the rising sun. Tendrils of steam drifted from the beast's nostrils into the cool morning air, tinged orange in the morning Sun.

But that was not what Tommy had dragged Nicholas out to see.

Jack was seated on the black's back. Neither were moving, all was still.

Nicholas was shocked, and he saw there was no bit or bridle fitted to *Mnyama Ubaba's* head either. He looked at Tommy, who grinned and shrugged then leaned over and whispered in Nicholas's ear, 'Kinda magical ain't it Nicholas?'

Nicholas nodded as he took it all in. Tommy was right, it was a magical moment. The great dark horse silhouetted against the orange and pink dawn sky, and Big Jack melded onto his back, they looked as one, a faint orange tinge to their profile. Jack with his own huge frame did not look out of place at all.

Still they sat motionless, then Jack started to hum a song. Nicholas knew it was Zulu because of the extenuated "hmmm" Jack blended into it.

It really was a beautiful scene, he thought as Big Jack's soothing deep humming carried to them. He and Tommy retreated back to the kitchen.

'Dat, was sumthin' really special, Oi reckon Nicholas. Dat big fellow is workin' 'is way into the 'orses 'ead for sure an' certain,' Tommy said. 'Bloody marvelous!'

'Yes, I think you are right Tommy, and at least he is sitting on him!' Nicholas said, wishing Vicky could have seen it.

It was now only three days before the big day for Nicholas and Victoria and all seemed to be working well, people were coming to and fro Tommy's house, and Tommy himself was nervously waiting for his wagon train to arrive.

Nicholas and Victoria spent as much time as they could together – the wedding plans and preparation all now being handled by others – so they explored around the town at will.

That morning, one of the regimental privates from the 99th Battalion, rapped on the front door of Tommy's house, carrying an invitation to have morning tea with John Roe and William Burges at 10am.

Nicholas asked Jack to accompany them as well even though he was not invited. Nicholas wanted to test the water with regard to Jack being a free man having heard some rumours about William Burges's bias against Blacks – he had apparently said a few derogatory words about the abolition of slavery.

Jack could not stand under the low verandah and had to half crouch to get under the front lip. As he stooped down to enter the room, he came within a foot of Burges. Nicholas was amused at the momentary look of panic on Burges's face as the giant black man stood over him and stuck out his massive hand to shake the man's hand as Nicholas introduced him. Burges had no time to react otherwise and winced when Jack vigorously shook his hand. Nicholas flicked a glance at John Roe and was rewarded by a hint of a smile on the man's face. Smart man, thought Nicholas, realising Roe knew exactly what Nicholas was doing.

With the intent of excusing himself, Jack asked if he could look around the barracks. Permission given, he amused himself by wandering around the barracks, even climbing up to the flagstaff tower, where he sat taking in the sweeping view the small hill offered.

Victoria and Nicholas sat on the small verandah at the barracks chatting with John Roe and Will Burges.

John Roe, as was his nature, wanted to know everything that was planned for the wedding.

Victoria, her excitement bubbling over, told Roe that the ceremony was to be held at the rear of Tommy O'Farrell's house and the area was complete with a small dias and many chairs that had been made or brought in by Tommy for the event. Before long, and encouraged by Roe's prompting, Victoria was happily prattling away, her enthusiasm even engaging the magistrate.

They had a laugh when Nicholas told Roe that he didn't know who was more excited by the event, Victoria or Tommy.

John Roe then informed them that he was expecting the Anglican clergyman to arrive any day now, and as soon as he could arrange it he would like to have them meet Charles Clay and discuss the wedding ceremony. Victoria clapped her hands together exclaiming 'Wonderful Sir, how exciting!' She and Nicholas told him they looked forward to meeting the minister at his convenience.

Roe sat stroking his beard and was about to speak, when Burges suddenly stood, apologising, and informed them that he had some business to attend to. He explained that he and his family had taken up some 640 acres of land between Geraldton and Greenough, and he was expecting a large drove of sheep, which he believed would be close to arriving from the Avon Valley.

Some ten minutes later they saw him cantering out of the barracks.

John Roe said, 'Nicholas, in confidence, I can inform you that several new mining claims have been lodged by the Geraldine Mining Company, notably around the upper Murchison and also around the town of Northampton. They are primarily quite some distance from your claim and are for coal, lead, silver and copper. There are several other smaller claims lodged in the Northampton area by ticket-of-leavers and soldier pensioners. I caution that you keep your find as close to your chest as possible in the interim, or at least until you establish yourselves, yes?'

Nicholas considered this information carefully, before answering. 'I thank you Sir for your confidence and your information,' Nicholas said. 'Very few people know about the claim, but I guess as you said, it will not take people long to work things out, considering the amount of equipment we are shipping north. We will be extra vigilant and again thank you.'

Roe looked at Victoria and said, 'Sorry my dear, I did not bring you two here this morning to talk business and mining, you must be bored by all of this.'

Victoria replied, 'On the contrary Mr Roe Sir, I find it all very interesting and exciting!'

'Well, to change the subject, Peter Strudwich has asked for assistance to refloat the *Collette* this evening. Apparently he is expecting a king tide tonight and swears he will float the ship then. So, I am having the troops with some equipment and engineers go down to help if needed. Are you both going down to watch?'

Nicholas said, 'Yes, we will both be there to assist and watch Sir, perhaps we will enjoy your company? It happens that I have some excellent French cognac brought up for the wedding by O'Farrell, we can have a celebratory drink, yes?'

'We will look forward to that I assure you,' said Roe his small smile making a rare appearance.

The morning tea concluded, they stood to leave when Victoria exclaimed, pointing at the incoming trail from the south, 'Look Nicholas, that must be Tommy's express train from Perth City!'

They turned to watch as three of the long bed wagons trundled past the foot of the barracks. The three wagons were teamed up by oxen and accompanied by about a dozen men and were heading for O'Farrell's yard. Shouts of 'Ee-Yaa!' and the crack of whips carried to them from the team captains.

'I wonder what Tommy's surprise is. I could not pry out of him what it was, no matter how hard I tried,' said Nicholas.

They said their goodbyes to Roe and were joined by Jack as they mounted and headed toward the bay. 'Let's go to the beach and have a look at the progress on the ship,' said Nicholas and they headed off. Jack, as always, had strode well ahead, cutting across in a straight line to the bay.

Victoria said, 'Nicky, how can Peter get the ship back to the sea? I mean she has to be very heavy and is lying on her side?'

Nicholas looked at her and said, 'It will not be easy my dear, she is about twelve hundred tons. However, they have removed most of the cannon and ammunition and anything else that is of weight, so it *is* a bit lighter'. He continued, 'Peter has the support and help from the military now, and together I guess, they will jack up the low side somehow, the regimental engineer now assisting will be a big help.' 'Personally, I have never seen it done, most careening is done with the ship held vertical in slipways, so I am as curious as you are.'

Stopping on the small sandy rise looking down at the *Collette*, they dismounted, Nicholas slipping his arms about Victoria's waist.

Standing there on the sand, they could see and hear the hive of activity. Somewhere someone was peening steel with a large hammer, and the ring of steel on steel carried clearly to them. The "thock, thock" sound of several timber mattocks dominated as men swung the razor-sharp blades down onto the timber logs, and the jingle of harness and chain completed the cacophony of sounds.

Chapter 64

The Refloating of the Collette

Gazing down at the activity, they saw that the ship had already been turned about twenty degrees and the stern was now pointing out into the bay somewhat, although still at an angle. She had however, been jacked up some way to being upright. Her three main masts, at an angle of about sixty degrees, stabbed into the air, almost in defiance to the land side where her hull was shored up by several large box cribs of stout timber.

Sailors and other men were frantically digging out the sand on the sea side, no doubt getting ready for the king tide. They saw Jack snatching up a large shovel and splashing into the water and start digging with the sailors.

Nicholas could see that by having the ship at an angle to the water would expose more surface area to the incoming tide and therefore hopefully use less draft. He thought and marveled that turning the ship on her keel would have taken a mammoth effort and a lot of engineering nous.

Then he saw several large logs from the wharf stockpile had been dug in beneath the keel of the ship, which explained how the ship, despite her weight, had been skewed around. The logs were heavily greased and would now assist the haul to the sea when the tide was at its peak.

No substitute for experience, he thought, acknowledging Peter Strudwich as he did so.

Looking back across the bay, Nicholas pointed to a brigantine, the *Leander*, moored not too far from the corner where the *Collette* lay. 'Apparently, that ship has come from Fremantle, it arrived very early this morning. It has carried the first of several new families of the Pensioner Guards', that's retired soldiers, and there are a few single women,' he said to Victoria,

Nicholas stared at the scene before him. 'And oh look, there are two longboats from the *Leander* rowing over to the *Collette's* boats, they must be going to help!'

Victoria sighed. 'This so exciting, I never imagined such things could happen, and tonight she will float again! I love that ship, and Peter, it's as though it is a part of me now,' she said looking at Nicholas as he gazed out at the scene, nodding his head in agreement. 'Yes, she has played a big part in both of our lives when you think about it, bringing us together in fact!' He squeezed her. Victoria turned and kissed his hand, then snuggled into his arms.

They mounted their horses and made their way down to the ship. Nicholas called out to Jack, and the big man turned to him. Nicholas pointed to Victoria and himself and then pointed back to the house direction. Jack waved back and turned back to the work, which he seemed to be enjoying immensely.

Strudwich suddenly called out as he appeared around the bow splashing his way through the ankle-deep water. 'Hold up ye both!'

His eyes were sparkling with a mischievous twinkle and he said, 'The blessed tide will be up at about nine bells tonight and pray that we can slide my lovely back onto an even keel in the bay!'

Nicholas said, 'How much tide are you expecting Peter? More to the point, how much do you need?'

Strudwich looked back at the ship and said, 'Well, the moon will be bigger than it has been for at least three decades, so I am expecting about three and a half feet, maybe a bit more, so with the four boats pulling and those big wharf capstans the troopers and company engineers have rigged up to hold the timber skids,' – he pointed at the huge four-handle cast iron winches mounted on two box cribs about twelve feet square with heavy hawser and dual pulley snatches already attached – 'we should be able to do it.'

'Well done Peter, you are a clever man!' said Victoria and she went to him and kissed him on the cheek.

He said, 'Ahhh, look out, I am covered in dirt and sweat!' But both Nicholas and Victoria knew by his furtive glances back toward the *Collette* that he did not want to be seen showing any affection in front of his crew. Victoria giggled at his mock angry glare.

'We will see you tonight Peter, do you need anything?'

'Yes,' Peter replied, 'I need this to all go without a hitch! Now git ye two, I've a ton of work to do.' He grinned and walked back to his ship.

They chatted with many people as they walked the horses at leisure back to Tommy's house and paused at the Wu's house, but they were nowhere to be seen. Their neighbour simply pointed up toward Tommy's house.

As they walked back, they neither sensed nor saw Birch lurking in the shade of the alleyway next to the ale house and did not see the display of fury as Birch punched the side of the lime, gimlet and hessian wall, hate screwing up his face as though he was in pain, but Isaac saw it.

Birch went back into the ale house, got a good draught of rum and sat down at a table seething with hatred and made his plans for revenge.

As Nicholas and Victoria walked hand in hand leading their horses, and they approached the front gate, Nicholas suddenly stopped and cocking his head said, 'Can I hear music, a piano and…?'

Victoria said with excitement, 'Yes! It's coming from Tommy's!'

They hurried up to the rear of the house and stopped open mouthed at the scene before them.

An open sided tent had been set up beside the marriage dias complete with a wooden floor extending out to the patchy grass. On the floor and under the tent, two men were playing violins and a young girl with flaming red hair had a flute to her lips. But what was a bigger surprise, was Tommy.

He sat at a piano and was playing the beautiful lilting Irish tune.

Suddenly, Tommy stopped, stood and lifted the top of the piano.

'Gimme dat dere piana wrench!' he said to the man standing behind him, and added, 'Hit dat dere key until Oi' say stop!'

Grasping the 'T' shaped wrench, he reached into the harp and they heard the tone changing as he adjusted the strings and his assistant tapped on the piano key.

'Right, stop now, 'tis good! At any rate, she be pretty good fo' comin' all dis way from Perth on a wagon to be sure!' he said as he closed the lid again. 'Now let's start agin,' and went to sit down at the keys again.

Tommy looked up and spotted Nicholas and Victoria staring open mouthed at him.

'Well now, if it ain't me two favorite love birds,' he laughed, his eyes dancing and bright as buttons.

'Dis me lovelies, is me surprise Oi's been a waitin' fo', no weddin'at Tommy O'Farrell's was ever gonna take place wi't out some grand music, 't'wouldn't be right now Oi be tinkin.'

Victoria couldn't quite believe it and tears of gratitude welled up in her eyes. Nicholas put his arm around her and she said, 'Oh Tommy, you are so full of surprises,' and she ran over to him and embraced him, kissing him on the cheek.

Nicholas didn't know what to say, except, 'We did not know you could play a piano!'

Embarrassed now, (but also delighted) Tommy said, 'Well now, when Oi's a lad, Oi got taught by me Ma.' He sighed and added, 'Sorry, but we's got to get practicin',' and with that, sat back down at the piano.

He hesitated, then he said, 'Ya know, dere's dis new opera in London called "Lohengrin". 'Tis written by a fellow called Richard Wagner. Now, dey's got a song in it people are usin' fo' weddin's an' I's goin' to play it for ye ta start de weddin' as it 'tis called the "Bridal Chorus".' He turned back to the keyboard and tapping a beat with a small thin baton on top of the piano, they picked up the tune again.

Nicholas and Victoria sat on chairs and listened as the Irish group played some beautiful old ballads.

Victoria leant up and kissed Nicholas on his cheek and whispered in his ear, 'Oh Nicky, I am so happy, everything is like a dream!'

That night, almost the whole town gathered on the sand ridge to watch the *Collette* being refloated, there was even someone playing a fiddle somewhere amongst the crowd completing the carnival atmosphere.

It was a perfect night, the moon was just beginning to rise behind them, casting long pale golden fingers of light over the bay as it began its climb into the sky.

Four large wrought iron braziers had been strategically placed either side of the ship about fifty yards from each end and twenty-five yards apart near the shoreline. The blazing coal and timber fires cast orange dancing light across the water. There was nary a breath of air stirring, and Nicholas wondered if that were a good thing or not, but there was however, a gentle swell breaking on the shore.

Tommy, Whip, Robert and Bethany stood in a group with Nicholas and Victoria waiting for the start of the relaunch. Jack was down at the ship with Peter Strudwich as was young Adam, these days never far out of Peter's shadow, mused Robert.

They were soon joined by John Roe and Will Burges, Senior Constable Drummond and Augustus Gregory, who had just returned from the mine north of Northampton at the upper reaches of the Murchison River.

There was another gentleman with the party, and Roe said to Nicholas and Victoria, 'May I please introduce you to the Reverend Charles Clay. Sir, Nicholas and Victoria, the bride and groom to be!'

Clay was a thin looking man, with a sparse hairline. He was dressed in a dark grey suit and vest over a white shirt, open at the neck.

After the normal chats that one has when meeting people for the first time, he asked, 'Would it be possible to meet tomorrow, preferably at the place you are to be married?'

Nicholas replied, 'Certainly reverend, we can arrange for you to be picked up by buggy if that suits you?'

'I have my horse thank you. Shall we say ten o'clock tomorrow morning at the O'Farrell house, is it?' Nicholas and Victoria nodded agreement.

'Well then that's settled then. I apologise for not being able to stay tonight and watch this spectacle, but I have some other matters to attend, I look forward to discussing your wedding plans tomorrow!' He lifted Victoria's hand to his lips, and nodding to the men, turned and strode away.

Tommy produced a set of lead crystal glasses and a bottle of the French cognac and charged the glasses.

'To the *Collette*!' he said as they raised their glasses.

Peter Strudwich came striding up the beach to join them and before anyone could start a conversation, said to Robert and Bethany, 'Yonder is one very excited lad folks!' He pointed back to the small ship's skiff which was drawn up at the water line, young Adam holding the painter and looking up at them.

'I will row out to about fifty yards from the longboats between the 'awsers and snatch blocks, ye see?'

Robert looked at Bethany and she shrugged, not having a clue what he was talking about.

Peter said, 'I will signal which team of rowers needs to pull harder once we get 'er moving an' when the tide is at its peak. What I'm tellin' ye all this for is, Oi need someone to attend the small braziers in the skiff an' 'and me the brands so's Oi can signal the crews with 'em.

'So's, Oi'm askin' on the lad's behalf, can Oi take 'im out ta 'elp me?' He fixed Bethany with a fierce stare, that brooked no argument.

She met his gaze, with an equally fierce glare, then smiled and said, 'Watcher, be askin' me fo'? It's '*is* son!' she jerked her head at Robert, who almost collapsed in shock.

'All right then is it?' Peter looked at Robert with a huge grin on his face. All poor Robert could do was to nod his head and he greedily gulped at the cognac.

Peter said, still grinning, 'Right, that's settled then, where's *my* shot of that?' he pointed at the ornate cognac bottle.

Tommy poured him a glass, which he downed in one gulp, smacked his lips and said, 'By God that is beautiful! I hope you'se keep me a little after me lovely floats off that bloody sand!' With that he spun on his heel and quickly walked back to the skiff, calling out, 'Right then Adam, don't stand about like ye's bloody asleep, we's got work to do!'

Adam's voice almost squealed in delight as he shouted, 'Yes Sir,' and waved to his parents.

Nicholas felt a nudge in his ribs from Victoria, who indicated towards Bethany who had turned away but was unable to disguise that she was dabbing at her eyes.

Nicholas chuckled and said out loud, 'He a wonderful man that Peter Strudwich, not only master of the ship, but a master of manipulation as well!' They all murmured in agreement.

Nine bells on the note the tide reached its peak, the moon now bathing all in a golden glow.

The crowd fell quiet as they heard Strudwich yelling from his position in the bow of the ship's skiff.

'Take up!' he yelled, and the crews dipped their oars and took up the slack.

Adam handed Strudwich two flaming brands, which he held out. Peter was watching the slight swell as the waves slowly hissed ashore to run up against the ship's hull. As soon as the swell rose over the shoreline he yelled, 'Row! Row! Come on lads, Put ye backs into it!'

Strudwich dropped his right-hand brand down, but waving the port side brand, indicating the left-hand crew to row for all they were worth. 'Row lads, row,' his voice ringing out over the bay.

The soldiers strained against the capstan handles as the chained logs and snatch pullies tied to the logs under the ship tried to roll free.

'Second crew row!' he yelled and the longboat crew from the *Leander* took up the strain.

There was a muted screeching from the stern of the ship and a collective sigh from the shore crowd as the stern moved about six inches on the next swell.

Strudwich dropped his port side brand and raised the starboard side brand. 'Row,' he screamed, 'row.' Both crews now rowed with all they could muster. Again, a sigh from the shore crowd as the stern shifted a little more.

After an hour, the *Collette* had moved about two yards toward the sea from her first position, and the swell was now foaming about the hull, the stern still angled slightly ahead of the bow.

Peter judged it was time to concentrate pulling from the stern and had the starboard side longboat from the *Leander* tie up the stern, making it three boats pulling the stern. He knew that if they could get the stern to run on the greased logs, they could drag her off the beach, and the momentum would float the ship away from the shore.

It was another hour before they checked everything and were ready to start the pull again.

'Take up!' Strudwich yelled, both hands out now with the blazing brands. If she screws around just aft of the main mast she should start to run, thought Peter.

'Row, row, com'on lads get into it!' he yelled.

The ship moved about six inches and refused to move another inch. Strudwich held both torches together. 'Rest and water boys, take turns at keepin' the strain on, right now?' He could see the men's backs, shiny with sweat reflecting even from here.

Any man who has spent time at sea, or even on shorelines, can tell you about the cycle of waves. One can experience a normal pattern of waves, one after another with nary a difference, but every now and then a set or bracket of waves will appear, usually consisting of five or seven waves. Most times there would be a slight break in the normal wave cycle, then the 'freak' waves would come. There was usually a large wave after the first two or three and that wave can vary from about double the size to three times as big.

Later, Peter Strudwich, when asked how he knew a freak wave was coming, would just give his standard secretive tap on the nose and say, 'I can smell it man.' The truth was that he did not expect or even know that the bracket was going to occur when it did, in fact he would have bet that this would probably *not* occur, given the moon, king tide and the moderate weather. But occur it did.

The crowd was murmuring, and the not so subtle bookies moved through the people to take bets amending their original assessment, and there was now a great deal of chatter coming from the crowd.

John Roe and Nicholas stood a little away from the others, staring at Strudwich and the skiff, each holding a cognac.

Roe said, 'He has about forty-five minutes and the king tide will start to recede.'

'Yes,' said Nicholas, 'at least he has made some progress, but if he doesn't get this done now, they are in for a hell of a lot work and digging, shame, because it looks like they only need another three yards or so to get the float.'

They watched Peter Strudwich and were about to turn back, when Strudwich suddenly stood up straight in the skiff and turned his head to the sea, holding up his hand and roared out at the top of his lung's, 'HOLD, QUIET NOW!'

Silence slowly descended over the scene.

He did not move for several minutes, then screamed, 'Row lads, row for your lives, row!

There was a moment's hesitation, then the sailors bent to the task with vigor, the hawsers snaking straight then slapping back into the water as their oars, glistening in the moonlight, slid into the sea.

Strudwich was still screaming out his orders when it seemed as though he slowly rose higher then descended, only to rise again as the first waves of the freak bracket slid underneath them.

The first waves were about twelve inches higher than normal on that night, but the third was substantially bigger, and its sea span greater with it.

As the first wave slid under the *Collette's* hull, she skewed to the skiff's starboard side a little, then back as the first wave receded, followed by movement to the port side which gained about a yard, the three longboats lifting the hawsers in unison. 'Perfect,' grunted Strudwich as the crews maintained the tension. He held his breath as the second wave slid in. It slapped into the side of the ship with more strength than the first.

Victoria joined Nicholas slipping her hand into his and gripping it tightly as they watched the ship moving as though pivoting on an axle through the hull – first the starboard side slid down then the port. With more movement she was reluctantly but slowly moving to deeper water.

Nicholas was watching the masts for any movement toward vertical, but apart from some up and down movement as the waves hit and rocked the ship, they did not gain any height, 'Come on, go!' they all said, almost in unison.

John Roe normally taciturn, said with some degree of excitement, 'He is going to do it! The biggest wave is yet to come. His timing must be perfect or she will come back up the beach!'

They all held their breath as they heard Strudwich yelling, *'Wait for it lads, wait!.'* A moment's pause then, *'Row boys, row, one last time, row now!!'*

Again, the hawsers drew taught. A moment later the big freak wave moved rapidly beneath them, lifting the boats up high so that Peter and Adam were actually looking down somewhat from where they had been, Adam whimpered a little as he was frightened by the size of the wave and clutched at the side of the skiff. 'Easy lad, it's fine now,' Strudwich said calmly.

Strudwich could do nothing but watch as the big wave moved under the ship. The long sea span, slowly picked up the *Collette* and they all heard the timbers groan. Peter could see the main mast appearing over the starboard side of the ship as she gained clearance from the sand and logs as the keel started to descend.

The men on the longboats saw it too, and miraculously found some more strength, pulling on the oars as if their life depended on it.

Time seemed to stand still as the ship seemed to be suspended above the wave, then as the wave began to fade, she slowly began to slide out to sea. The keel, now free from the logs underneath, began its journey into the deepening sea, the ballast within the keel seeking the deeper water.

She gathered momentum, and the masts rose like defiant fingers into the stars and to the vertical.

Strudwich, still holding his breath, watched as the *Collette* slewed around on its shore tethers, its masts slowly waving back and forth.

There was a moment's silence, then an almighty roar erupted from the sailors and the crowd ashore.

Peter Strudwich stood beaming in the skiff, his beloved ship was afloat again.

The ship secure and her anchor deployed, the men rowed the long-boats ashore and amid many congratulations and back slapping, Peter Strudwich did not miss a man as he moved amongst the sailors and soldiers alike offering his thanks for the herculean efforts they had made. He stood helping the handouts of rum with De Freys until eventually he headed up to where Nicholas and Victoria were standing watching it all.

He said, 'There she be in all her glory a'gin! Now where's that foin cognac me hearties!' With an enormous grin on his face and pride almost bursting from within, he yelled with glass charged, 'To the *Collette*, an' may God bless all who sail in her!'

They all repeated, 'To the *Collette*!'

Peter turned and saw the sailors and soldiers mingling on the beach, celebrating with their free issues of rum. He looked out at the *Collette*, now bathed in golden moonlight as she rode proud at her anchor, and he longed to get back to sea.

Chapter 65

Edward Raymond Birch's Revenge

Nicholas and Victoria joined each other at the breakfast table the next morning along with Tommy, Seamus, Whip, Jack and Robert, while Peter and young Adam were now just returning from the ship, having gone down to inspect the *Collette* for any sign of leakage before the Sun had risen.

They burst in, Adam yelling, 'She's as tight as a drum!' imitating Strudwich to a word.

They all laughed at the boy's enthusiasm. Bethany had cooked up plates of eggs, bacon and rye bread, and as Peter and Adam joined them began to serve up.

'Well, what's next Captain Adam,' said Nicholas grinning and looking at the mountain of food the lad was now attacking.

His cheeks bulging, Adam talked around the food and gulping said, 'Well, we have to first get all of the extra halyards off the riggin' and masts, then we's gotta get all of tha' canvas back on board, then we's gotta get the cannon and gun cradles aboard, that'll not be easy, then all o' the ammunition, an' an' then…'

'Come on young man, eat ye breakfast now before it gets cold, an stop talking wit ye mouth full!' said Bethany gruffly and gave him a light cuff to the side of his head.

'Well Peter, you both have it all under control by the sound of it, well done!' Nicholas said laughing.

'Hmmm, yes it appears so,' replied Peter, a thoughtful look on his face. He was thinking about the boy's heartbreak and the time when he must sail, without the lad.

They were all sitting back relaxing after the breakfast and coffee had been served, when Bethany, out of the blue, suddenly addressed Nicholas. Fixing him with a steely eye she asked, 'So when are ye planning ta move out Nicholas?'

Caught completely off guard, Nicholas put down his coffee, and fixing her with his amber eyes, said, 'I beg your pardon Bethany?'

She shifted a little and almost back-pedalled under the intense gaze, obviously Nicholas was somewhat annoyed at the impertinence of the question. There was a shuffling amongst the group and silence descended around the table, apart from a slight cough from Robert. 'Er Be...'

One fierce glance from Bethany was enough to silence any protest he might have been going to offer, he shut his mouth.

'I means no disrespect sir, but ye can't be stayin' 'ere' no more now, at least not until ye's be married an all, now can ye? Shouldn't be 'ere now, Oi mean tain't be right even now tis' it?' She paused and went on, 'Folks be a talkin, an' best not ta be temptin' bad luck now as well?'

There, it be out, she thought. She had now regained her confidence and matched Nicholas's stare.

The silence palpable as Nicholas weighed up what she had said. Bethany cleared her throat and said, 'Oi mean…' Nicholas held up his hand, silencing her, and replied evenly, 'You are right Bethany, I was forgetting the correct protocol for weddings.' Suddenly he grinned and continued, 'My apologies Victoria, I am new at this wedding business,' she put her head down barely able to stop herself laughing.

'Where shall I stay Mrs Stokes, and how far away lest any improper thoughts travel to my intended?' he asked, his mischievous grin now back in place as the group twittered at his humour.

Bethany had it all worked out, with some slightly secretive help from Tommy, who was watching the scene unfold with humour and mischief creased on his face.

'Well sir, pardon me for bein' a bit presum…presump…shous,' she stumbled, 'but we's, Oi mean *I's* be thinkin with a little bit of 'elp ye could stay at the light 'ouse dwellin'.' Nicholas did not miss the "we's" word in her answer and flicked his eyes to Robert first…no, then to Tommy. Aha! thought so seeing the poorly disguised humour on his friend's face. Bloody hell! he thought.

He decided to let the lady off the hook, seeing as how she was the only one with enough gumption to broach the subject.

'That will be fine Bethany, I will move out straight after the reverend comes this morning for our chat, and I will be sure to make it obvious that, that is where I will be staying, all right?'

'Right then Nicholas, Oi'l get the lads ta 'elp, startin' right now! Dey'l make it all nice an' cosy fo' ye. Hee-hee!' Tommy cackled with some glee.

Nicholas tried to look stern, but failed, instead grinning back at his mischievous friend.

"An' tonight, we men are all goin' down ta tha' ale 'ouse to send ye off, if that'll be foin wit' everyone, yes?' They all agreed.

Isaac, appeared out of nowhere as he seemed adept at doing, and beckoned to Tommy. They stood at the back of the house, heads together. Nicholas looked over at them and saw Tommy's face creased in an angry frown, then he became slightly animated and was talking into Isaac's ear.

The tall man nodded his head and departed. I wonder what that was all about, thought Nicholas.

The Reverend Charles Clay arrived at the O'Farrell house promptly at 10am, and Nicholas, Victoria, Tommy and Peter Strudwich all sat down in the lounge room to discuss the wedding ceremony after formal introductions were made and coffee was served by Seamus.

Firstly, I must ask of which denomination are you both?

Victoria said, 'I am Presbyterian reverend and Nicholas is of the Anglican denomination. As you see we have both been christened in the name of God.'

Clay rubbed his hands together and said, 'Good, good, we therefore can marry under canon law, do we have any birth certificates Nicholas, Victoria?'

Victoria placed the two documents on the table before him. Clay scanned the documents and noting the registered and signed last page and where it had taken place, he carefully noted the dates of each.

He then opened a large book and after asking for a quill and ink pot, began to write furiously.

Nicholas produced the letter from Doctor Amendson and pushed it across to Clay, who looked at Nicholas.

'Permission to marry from Victoria's parents, Reverend Clay,' Nicholas said.

Clay quickly scanned the letter. 'Excellent, excellent. And in the absence of Victoria's father, who shall be giving away the bride?'

'That will be me reverend,' Peter Strudwich said.

Nodding, Clay said, 'Best man in assistance, maid of honour?'

Victoria broke in and said, 'Nicholas and I have decided we will not have either reverend, lest we hurt someone's feelings in choice. I will have just one assistant, Meili, does that present a problem Sir?'

Charles Clay looked at her kindly and said, 'No it does not, young lady, so long as you nominate who will witness the signing of the marriage certificate, apart from myself, and you will need two separate signatures.'

Nicholas said, 'We have asked John Roe to witness my signature and Tommy O'Farrell to witness Victoria's signature Sir.'

He said, 'I will need Mr O'Farrell's birth certificate Nicholas.'

Nicholas produced Tommy's certificate. 'Excellent! excellent!' said the reverend.

Clay wrote down the details, blotted the writings, blew on the ink, then snapped the book shut, at which he then reached for a smaller book. Opening it he said, 'Now let us discuss the format of the marriage vows and of the prayers we will use.'

Nicholas again passed over a sheet of paper, on which he had written some verse and words that he and Victoria had chosen to be inserted. He explained that they did not want to have a long drawn out ceremony, preferring to keep to a short format.

Clay picked up the paper and began to read, nodding as he read the inserts.

He looked up and switching his gaze between the two said, 'This is all fine. I myself am not one to drag things out so we will now look forward to the day!' he concluded smiling broadly at them.

'Until 4pm, Saturday afternoon then, and if you need any further counsel, I will be at the barracks.' He shook hands with Nicholas and gave a little bow to Victoria and left.

A crowd of well-wishers had already started to gather at the ale house, Tommy, Robert, Nicholas, Whip and Jack arriving a little later. They all came from the lighthouse where they had moved Nicholas's belongings, which wasn't much in essence, but what possessions Nicholas did have, were very important to him. He therefore did not want them left unattended, in particular his rifle whilst they had his send off. So, he had asked Tommy for two of his men to be stationed at the dwelling to ensure nothing was stolen.

They had already opened a bottle of rum and had sat out on the grassy knoll at the front and had consumed a half bottle between them, Jack even relenting and having a small glass.

Finishing off his glass, Nicholas said, 'Thank Christ we don't have to drink that Brady's rotgut you used to drink Bobby. Jesus, that stuff was potent!'

He told the rest of them about how Bethany used it to clean her pots and pans it was so strong, much to the amusement of all, Robert chiming in with his own version of the story about the black, after only consuming half a glass, outrunning an emu in Mullewa.

Eventually, with Sun now going, they all walked down to the ale house.

As they approached, Tommy suddenly excused himself and veered off to the west side of the ale house. Jack, walking somewhat behind the group and eyes searching everywhere was looking for Birch. Just before he entered he saw Tommy talking to someone in the shadows but it was now too dark so he couldn't see who it was. Within a couple of minutes Tommy, rubbing his hands together, returned to join the rest of them just as Peter Strudwich walked up to join them. 'Perfect timing Peter!' called Tommy as they all went inside.

The house was full of the *Collette's* sailors and quite a few of Tommy's men, all of course knowing Nicholas and wanting to wish him well, that is, all except one.

Birch, had heard of the gathering and had stationed himself in the corner of the ale house around 4pm. After several tankards and muttering to himself, he suddenly said out loud, 'Them fookers are gonna get what's comin' to 'em tonight, yes sir!' With that he banged his tankard on the bar.

The barkeep heard him and said, 'What be dat ye say man?'

'Nuttin. Oi just said I's be needin' another drink *now* an' not later tonight!' he said sarcastically at the man. "An' gimme a large pitcher of dat rum will ye!' Taking the pitcher and paying for his drinks, he left.

The Irish barkeep summoned up a young lad who was cleaning tankards and sent him scurrying off with a message.

Later, just on dark, Birch returned and sat outside at the rear of the building waiting for his opportunity to exact his revenge. He sat on a small wooden bench which was positioned between stacks of empty ale kegs lined up against the back wall, the pitcher of rum with him, which he diligently moved from the bench to his lips whilst he waited.

He had a muzzle loading .575 bore pistol, which was his own. The pistol was an old Joseph Wood muzzle loader, British built and a quality model but now outdated by the new Colt revolvers. He had brought along another similar well-worn pistol. Nonetheless they were powerful weapons, and at the range intended that night, did not need a great deal of accuracy. Both weapons were loaded and primed.

Periodically, he rose and peered back into the ale house through a two-inch wide gap in the hessian and plaster wall, which gave him a fair span of sight into the interior and enough space to aim the pistol through.

He wondered where Yuin, the big nigger and the others were.

Birch had decided that his prime targets would be Wilberforce and the big nigger, as far as he was concerned they were the start of all of his troubles.

He was wishing he had stolen one of the newer Colt revolvers that Strudwich had aboard the ship, then he would be able to kill maybe three of the bastards, in particular Yuin.

During the day, Birch had spoken to the first mate of the *Leander* and learnt that she was to depart for Fremantle on tomorrow's rising tide at three bells. He paid for a passage, reckoning, with luck and timing, he could get aboard after he had killed his targets and lie low until they were at sea, nobody would think to look on the ship.

A muted cheer went up inside and Birch got up and peered through the gap to see Nicholas and the others finally come into the room, followed by the nigger. There was a great deal of backslapping and hand shaking. Over the top of the crowd, tankards of ale were passed over to the new arrivals and the shindig got under way.

Almost three hours later, his insane hatred building by the minute, Birch still waited impatiently for his opportunity.

For the third time, he got up and traced out his escape route from the back of the ale house. He saw only the house grog cart in the rear lane and did not even notice or query why a horse was still harnessed to the cart at 10pm.

He had planned it well, he reckoned. After killing the nigger and Wilberforce, he would immediately cut to his left and would run up the rear laneway and away from the house about a hundred paces. Then there was a narrow lane which ran to the left again and down to the street. On the other side of the street, the lane continued, then ran straight down to the beach, where he had beached a little flat-bottomed dory he had borrowed.

Once he reached the street, he would casually walk across so as not to attract any attention. He would then calmly walk the one hundred yards to the dory on the beach and would quietly row out to the *Leander* and climb aboard on the open sea side so as not to be seen climbing aboard. Perfect, he grunted, reckoning if he kept it simple it would work out.

Two more hours passed. It was just on midnight and Birch looked again for a clear shot. So far, every time he thought he could shoot, some clown would step into his line of fire, the big nigger remained behind Yuin, watching everyone as he sat on his original drink, hardly touching the ale.

Finally, there was a challenge put down to arm wrestle, and after several men tried – and failed – there was one man left, Alby Newman. Birch knew this man and he was as strong as a bull, as yet unbeaten as far as arm wrestling went. Suddenly, the challenge was put to the object of celebration, Yuin.

After resisting the challenge for a while, Yuin finally sat down and placed his right arm onto the table across from Newman. The nigger immediately stepped up behind Yuin as the two clasped hands and waited for the call to start. Birch thought, brilliant! as he finally had a clear shot and knew he could not miss from here, his target no more than fifteen feet away.

Birch raised the pistol and lined up the rear 'V' notch with the silver bead. Jack's head swam in and out of his vision, his thumb reaching for the cocking piece. 'Damn, I shouldn't have had so much fookin' rum,' he cursed himself and lowered the pistol, taking great breaths of air to clear his head and rubbed his eyes.

Birch again lifted his right hand and the pistol, lining up the sights again, this time steadier and his vision a little sharper, his thumb now cocking the pistol.

He jolted a little when he focused on the nigger's head. Jack had stepped around between Yuin and himself and was a body-width closer, and through the blue smoky interior seemed to be staring straight at him with no small degree of concentration.

'Jesus! He knows!' Birch murmured. Slightly unnerved, he quickly refocused on the great head and began to squeeze the trigger.

Jack had entered the ale house on full alert as he fully expected Birch to be in there and would cause trouble. Jack swore that if he did, he would tear the bastard in half.

But Birch was nowhere to be seen. However, Jack could feel menace coming from somewhere, so he was never very far from Nicholas, who was blissfully unaware of Jack's angst. A few hours later, nothing had changed, apart from the amount of smoke and the noise. Jack had spotted the gap in the back wall several hours ago but dismissed it to a degree. Now, he stared intently at it. He sensed rather than saw movement beyond the gap and immediately stood at Nicholas's side, placing himself between Nicholas and the gap in the wall as he continued staring at the gap.

Birch was in a world of confusion – one second he was about to pull the trigger and squinted his eyes against the flash and then all he saw was a long, black leather-clad finger come down across his pistol between the flint hammer and frizzen. The hammer fell, but restrained, hit only the finger. Birch began to look up the arm that had caused his confusion but a loud bang erupted in his head and he collapsed to the ground. The last thing he remembered was the huge roar within his head as he slipped into unconsciousness.

Isaac stood over Birch, and lifting the hammer he flipped the safety lock on and lowered it gently down onto the frizzen. Then taking the pistol from Birch's hand, he turned and placed it on the bench beside the second pistol and slipped his blackjack back into his coat.

Suddenly, Isaac stiffened, his hand snaking under his coat in an almost fluid movement and he withdrew his razor sharp Rezin Bowie knife as he went into a fighting crouch.

Jack stood about ten feet from him, the moonlight reflecting on his shiny dome. He also was crouched, but he held his tomahawk in his right hand, already held back to throw it.

Time stood still as both men sized up the situation. Isaac slowly lowered his knife and swung it to his left, pointing at the crumpled body of Birch and then to the pistol.

Jack, once he realised it was Isaac standing before him, knew him not to be the sensed threat. He slid his eyes to his right, following the knife. The first thing he saw was the pistols on the bench and then he looked down at Birch. Not a twitch of emotion showed on his face, but the tomahawk vanished back into the pouch behind his neck, and he nodded and relaxed.

Isaac stepped back to Birch and made to lift the inert bundle, but a hand on his shoulder stopped him.

Jack leant down and with nary a grunt picked up the unconscious man and tossed him over his shoulder. Birch was no lightweight, at least not to the average man. Isaac was impressed and turning beckoned Jack to follow him. They reached the grog cart and Jack, none to gently, tossed the inert Birch into the back.

Isaac, beckoned to Jack and Jack bent his head to Isaac. The tall fellow, with his long-bent stovepipe hat whispered in a gravelly voice, 'I thank ye, but now ye must quickly get back in dere,' jerking his thumb back toward the ale house, then pointed at two constables standing in the lamp light just up the street. Jack nodded and strode back down to the alley and picking his time, entered the raucous crowd, heading straight to Nicholas, who was still locked in combat with Alby Newman.

Nicholas, straining with all his might, looked at Newman. Newman grinned and drove Nicholas's arm straight down onto the table with a bang.

The crowd erupted with a roar and someone started to sing as another began to play the fiddle. Nicholas sighed, massaging his arm, and looked up at Jack who still stood beside him. Jack just rolled his eyes and smiled.

It is going to be a long night, thought Nicholas.

Isaac drove the cart slowly along the road and turned into Tommy's yard, pulling up the cart at the open side of the store shed. He disappeared into the house, returning with a small bottle, some rum and a basket of bandages and went about mixing a strong draught of laudanum. Lifting Birch to a sitting position, he forced open his mouth and poured the mixture down Birch's throat. Birch coughed and spluttered but Isaac's hand was firmly across his mouth, forcing him to swallow.

As Birch slumped down even further, Isaac softly hummed an Irish tune, '*De ta de, de ta dee!*' as he went about his work.

A little while later Isaac pulled up beside the dory at the bay. Looking at his fob he saw it was 1:30am.

He lay the barrel rolling plank at the rear of the cart and slid Birch down the plank next to the dory and propped the stupefied man up against the side of the boat. Then getting onto the cart he disappeared up the laneway opposite, where he stopped in the dark shadow and waited.

Fifteen minutes later, in the moonlight, he saw a skiff pull away from the *Leander* and head for shore. As it slid onto the beach, two sailors jumped ashore and lifted Birch into the skiff and rowed back to the *Leander*. 'Yes sir, money talks,' Isaac whispered to himself. 'Piece of shite.' Isaac took one more look at the skiff, now almost halfway across to to the *Leander*, and grunted. He snapped the reigns and left for the house.

Birch was woken by the ship's bell ringing eight bells. He felt sick and his head softly jumped and pounded with each pulse of his heart. He lay, keeping still, and could not for the first few minutes work out where he was. Then he smelled the sea, the ship and the motion. He managed a smile, and said, 'By Christ, Oi've done it, Oi'm at sea!'

Elation rising through the drug and alcohol stupor, his eyes still blurred, he lifted his right hand up and went to grasp the side of the bunk to gain his feet. As he did so, incredible and all-consuming pain shot up his arm and he screamed at the top of his lungs. Flaying about, he banged his left hand on the deck beam only two feet above his head and screamed again as more unbelievable pain consumed him. Reduced to low sobbing, he tried to come to terms with what was happening. It was then he noticed the bloodied bandages on both hands.

Above him on deck, the captain looked at his first mate and said, 'Looks like our "guest" has awoken, best ye go and fetch that sawbones and 'ave a look at 'im. Don't forget tha basket o' dressin's 'e 'ad wit 'im.'

The first mate and the sawbones, who was a pretty rough sort of fellow and had come on the voyage north looking for a place in the settlement (some said he was more of a vet than a medical man), dropped into the bunk space under the steerage of the *Leander*.

They found Birch lying back on the bunk, his face screwed up and gasping in immense pain, but also swearing. 'Fook, fookin' 'ell, what's 'appened to me, where the fook am I?'

The first mate said, 'Ye's be at sea aboard the *Leander* matey, just like ye booked wit me.

'As fo' what 'appened ta youse, we dunno, 'tis 'ow we found ye when ye got ta us,' and shrugged. Birch just stared at him through the massive pain in disbelief.

'Well now, anyhows, I's got the sawbones 'ere to 'ave a look at ye wounds, or'right matey?'

The sawbones gently lifted Birch's right hand and began to tentatively unwrap the bandage.

He only got the top layer off when a piece of paper lifted off with the wrapping, ''Ang on a bit,' the first mate said. He picked up the paper and said, 'Dere's writin'on it!'

'Well what's it be sayin' man!' demanded Birch, grimacing in pain.

The first mate read it out loud:

Ye dabble in life, ye dabble in pain.
Three down and seventeen ta go
Don't ye ever be comin' back 'ere again.

'What's dat supposed ta mean?' scowled Birch.

The first mate shrugged, 'Bit of a poet, 'oo'ever 'e be. Continue,' he said to the sawbones.

Unwrapping the next layer, the man was puzzled by the lump on top of Birch's hand, and as he removed the wrapping he exposed three dark and discoloured severed fingers.

Birch, mouth open, stared at the digits, he sat for a moment trying to comprehend what he was looking at.

Suddenly he jumped, screaming as he cracked his head on the deck beam, sending the three fingers flying off his bandages. 'Ahhhhhh, fookin' 'ell, no, no, look at dis! Oo's done it, Oi'l kill 'em all!'

'No, no, no,' he sobbed, and lay back down again on the bunk.

The sawbones and the mate just stared open mouthed at the fingers now lying on the cabin deck.

'Jesus mate, a bit of advice, Oi wouldn't ever be goin' back dere ta thet place.' the first mate said and left the room shaking his head.

The doctor managed to give Birch another shot of opiate mix, although not as strong as what Isaac had given him.

'Not a bad job!' He muttered, examining the stumps as Birch glared at him. He dressed the right hand where the index and second finger had been amputated, and he lifted the left hand and did the same to the index stump.

'Oi'l bring ye some rum man, then ye best be considerin' them there words,' he said pointing at the note.

'That draught Oi gives ye will put ye ta sleep soon enough, try an' keep the 'and's up on ye chest, an' don't be getting' 'em wet at all, Oi'l check in on ye later.'

Chapter 66

The Wedding Prelude

*V*ictoria Lay in her bed, thinking about all manner of things. She could not sleep no matter how hard she tried. Every time she started to drift into a sleep mode, she would focus on something else.

Mostly she thought about Africa and her life at Herrgarden Grande. She suppressed a catch in her throat as she remembered her parents and the home and wished her mother and father could have been here for her wedding.

She thought of Baba Joe's tears when he learnt she had made up her mind to leave, and she pictured him wandering aimlessly around the stables and outside her bedroom window as he used to do, remembering how sad he looked when she left. With a heavy sigh and a supreme effort, she pushed the sad thoughts away.

She went through all of the arrangements and thought how only about three weeks ago she was in despair, wondering how it was all going to be done in time.

Everything had eventually come together for their wedding. Bethany had been a tower of help and she vowed she would never forget the big gruff woman's hard work and huge heart. Nonetheless, her families absence still weighed heavily on her, it was the only thing missing really.

But then she would think of Nicholas, and even though he had moved to the lighthouse keeper's house only that morning, she missed him already. She missed the echo of his voice around Tommy's house and his scent, but most of all his little touches; the kiss on her nose or slipping his arm around her waist to let her know he enjoyed being near her and was proud of her, or when he looked at her, love in his eyes.

She sighed and started to think of their tentative sexual encounters, and although yet to be fulfilled, they had been intense and transported them to another realm.

She could feel herself flushing as she remembered her tentative attempts at touching him, and his tender hands on her, and tomorrow night they would finally be alone. She tossed about in her bed as she imagined them together, her rush of feeling now almost unbearable. Abruptly, she sat up in the bed, her heart pounding with excitement. Stop it! she admonished herself. I must wait! But it was oh so difficult – she wondered if it was the same for Nicholas.

Perhaps not tonight as she of course knew he and all of his friends were at the ale house celebrating his remaining freedom, as was the tradition. She giggled a little, if only they knew. When it came down to it, her Nicholas never let *anything* stand in his way no matter what it was. It was a side of him that fascinated her, like treading the unknown.

She drew on her dressing gown and quietly walked out to the front of the house, noting it was almost 2am as she passed Tommy's beautiful grandfather clock, and she sat down on one of the verandah chairs and drifted, drowsy but still unable to sleep.

The settlement was quiet, except for the occasional muted cheer coming from the ale house and she rose to go back to bed, sure she would go to sleep now. A gentle breeze blew from the west as she turned and looked out into the bay. She could see the stern lights shining from the *Collette and* swiveling her eyes to the *Leander* saw her lights. She had her sails set, and Victoria could just make out the sailors calling out as the ship slowly got under way.

Victoria heard the clock chime 3am as the ship steadily gathered speed and sailed out to sea. She watched until all she could see was the pinprick of stern lights and a very faint smudge of sail in the soft moonlight, rapidly disappearing as the ship eventually turned west outside the reefs.

She went inside and laying down again was asleep within minutes.

Jack and Nicholas left the ale house not long after 3am and slowly made their way back to the lighthouse dwelling, where they dismissed the guards and sat outside, Nicholas drinking great gulps of water from a flagon.

He suddenly stood, swaying slightly and said to Jack, 'Look, there're lights at sea!' He fished his fob out and saw it was after 3am. 'It will be the *Leander* Jack, she was due to sail this morning!'

'I wonder what happened to Birch tonight, I was expecting him to join us and wish us well!' he laughed.

Jack looked at him with a deadpan face and said, 'Don you be worryin' 'bout Birch now Niclas, I be tellin' youse all about dis ta'morra, ho k?'

'What? Oh Jesus, my head is spinning. I'm going to bed Jack, okay? Goodnight.'

'Yaas, my friend, you 'ave 'ad too much ta drink, maybe more than 'tis good for you, hmmmm.' He started to laugh, 'You will not be able to start making the little *ingane!*' (baby).

Nicholas stared at him, not really comprehending what Jack had said, one hand on the door frame as Jack swam in and out of his vision. 'Okay, good night my friend,' and he staggered over to the bed and collapsed onto the down mattress.

The next morning, Nicholas woke to the cries of gulls and a pounding in his head. He sat up on the edge of the bed and immediately regretted it. 'Ah Jesus, what have I done!' he lamented, holding his pulsing head. Reaching for the jug of water, he drank about half of the water without stopping, then sat, hoping his massive headache would subside.

Nicholas reached for his fob watch and was shocked to see it was 7:30am – he was usually up at the crack of dawn.

He got up, and still fully clothed from when he went to bed, walked to the door.

The sunlight immediately hurt his eyes as he looked out to the sea. Jack stood, naked, thigh deep in the sea, his dark honey coloured skin glistening in the morning sun. Nicholas could see the crisscross of lash scars across his back.

Still holding his hand up shading his eyes, Nicholas walked out and stripped off, dropping his clothes beside Jack's on the grass and walked across the sand, diving straight into the sea. The cold hit him like a left hook and he rose beside his big friend gasping and spluttering.

'Good morning Niclas! 'Ow is de 'ead dis fine mornin'?' He grinned at Nicholas as his friend held his head trying to stop the pain.

He opened his eyes and grinned at Jack and glanced back at the shack. 'Oh Shit!' he exclaimed.

Standing open mouthed at the verandah were Meili and Bethany, wicker baskets on each of their arms.

Jack spun fully around at Nicholas's exclamation. There was nothing to do except relax and stand there buck naked. He put his hands on his hips and stared back at the women, raising one eyebrow in query.

Nicholas, on the other hand, immediately dived back into the sea, then sat down in the water, a strained and sheepish grin on his face.

Looking at the two men Bethany said softly, 'Oh my, my!' then switched her gaze to Jack.

Meili inwardly gawped at the magnificent physique, his dark skin glistening with water as though covered in diamonds and great slabs of perfectly formed muscle bunched on his frame. She was embarrassed but she could not have torn her eyes off him even if ordered. She found her heart a'flutter. Having never been so close to an unclothed man before, if ever, while the Chinese men she had partly seen were certainly not built anything like the huge black nude man in front of her.

This was the first fully naked man Meili had ever seen, and then to her shame she found herself dropping her gaze and staring at his groin, his genitals hanging free for all to see, and he just standing there looking at her and Bethany without any shame.

Apart from a slight flush on her face, no one watching could really tell if she had seen anything, as in typical Chinese fashion, her expression remained unmoved, but internally her body had responded, making her uncomfortable.

Bethany on the other hand, quickly noted the two fine specimens before her, took a mischievous step toward the two. 'No, no stay there Bethany, we are both, er.. unclad!' Nicholas shouted, feeling somewhat ridiculous at stating the obvious.

'Oi can see dat my man, Oi ain't blind. We's just brought ye breakfast an we'll gather ye linen as well.' With that she scooped up their clothes and spun around and went to walk back to the keeper's house.

'Hey wait, that's our clothes, leave them there please.' She ignored Nicholas's plea and stuffed the clothes into the larger of the two baskets, calling out over her shoulder, 'Ye's can come out when we've finished in 'ere.'

She turned to Meili and hesitated a second to see Meili's gaze still riveted on Big Jack, and she quickly looked back and forth between the two noting that their eyes were locked. 'Come on me girl, 'tis only a nekid man, come on,' she said guiding Meili into the house. Hmmm, she thought, noting the slight pink flush on the otherwise perfect white skin of the Chinese girl.

The two of them set the breakfast for the men, and Bethany purposely dawdled to keep the two in the sea. She hung their clothes on the pegs behind the door, and twittering with Meili, peaked out of the window to see the two deeply engaged in conversation. They slipped out of the door and snuck away without either of the men seeing them depart.

About fifteen minutes passed before Nicholas turned, and seeing no movement, called out, 'Hello is anyone there?'

Getting no response, they tentatively made their way back to the keeper's house. Nicholas went inside and saw the breakfast laid out, then noticed the clothes hanging behind the door.

'Cheeky buggers,' he said out loud. 'Come on Jack,' he said handing Jack his clothes, 'breakfast is served.'

After breakfast they sat in silence, each deep in their own thoughts. Nicholas was dreaming about his coming wedding, when Jack suddenly said, 'That girl, she be very beautiful Niclas.'

Nicholas looked up at his friend, a little taken aback by the big man's statement as he had never in the time he had known him, commented on any other woman other than Victoria and his memories of his betrothed.

Careful to keep his reply even, lest he make Jack feel embarrassed or seem disloyal, he said 'Meili? Yes Jack, I think you are right, she *is* very beautiful, such perfect hair and skin.'

Jack just nodded. There was some silence whilst Nicholas waited patiently.

Then Jack said, 'Very clean and beautiful! Hmmm.' After a moment he said, 'I wonder why dis girl no marry?'

Nicholas paused then said, 'Jack, Chinese culture is very different from ours. Victoria tells me Meili is twenty-three years old, within the right time for Chinese girls to marry. But moving out to Australia would have interrupted any plans she may have had because they are usually allowed to marry from age eighteen, I think, although I am not really sure, you understand Jack?'

Jack nodded slowly and said, 'Not like Zulu girls, by the time de girls have dere first moon an' have ma'be little titties, dey is ready an' marry! An', dey's bigger, especially 'ere,' he added, raising his hand up to indicate height. 'An ere!' he said laughing as he slapped his behind.

Nicholas replied, 'Yes, I know, it is different, Meili is in perfect proportion, just smaller, yes?' Jack looked at him and asked 'What is 'dis- *propor..?*'

'Ah, it means the shape is correct Jack, like this,' he stood and measured the height, then the width, and then made to shape the woman's figure, waving both hands down. Understand...*proportion!*'

'*Bukkayo, ilifomu?* Yes?' asked Jack in Zulu. 'Yes, that's very similar Jack,' Nicholas replied.

'But also, most Chinese men only have one bride, not like Zulu, who can have many wives, yes? 'The traditional Chinese people are a very old culture and place their sense of values first, especially family, before everything.

Jack said slowly, 'Hmmmm, Zulu 'ave values also first, an' sometimes only one woman, but mostly dey 'ave many more. Sometimes, death or thing's 'appen, an' de marriage fade away, dis I 'ave seen many times.'

There was silence again as Nicholas digested what the big fellow was getting at. Maybe he is thinking he might never see his betrothed and family again, Nicholas thought.

'Yaaas, she is very beautiful and clean, an' yet no marry? Hmmmmm,' he concluded shaking his great shining bald head.

He is attracted to her, Nicholas thought, though I can't blame him. Well, that would be interesting. He thought to josh his friend about it, then thought better of it. We will wait and see, he thought.

Jack suddenly said, 'Niclas, last night you wonder why dere be no Birch?'

'Yes,' Nicholas said nodding, 'I thought for sure he was going to cause trouble.'

Nodding Jack said, 'Ye don' 'av to worry 'bout Birch no more Niclas, de Isaac 'as got 'im!'

Nicholas stared at his friend, wondering what "Got 'im' meant.

Jack then told Nicholas all about what had happened and that Jack saw and believed Birch was trying to kill Nicholas.

'Niclas, de Isaac, 'e save your life, maybe de Jack too. Dis Isaac, 'e did good I think,' he nodded his head vigorously.

'Where is he now Jack, I mean Birch?'

'I's don' know Niclas, Isaac took 'im, never see 'im no more last night,' Jack said.

'Well that can only be good Jack, he is a nasty twisted man, best we never see him again!'

He wondered what that dark, frightening ghostly spirit of a man would have done with him, or what Tommy may have told him to do more to the point, remembering the animated discussion Tommy and Isaac had the previous day.

He rose and said, 'Well come on, best we get back and see if we can help Peter load his cannon.'

He suddenly laughed as he remembered Bethany taking their clothes. 'That cheeky Mrs Stokes!'

But all Jack could remember was a pair of beautiful, black almond shaped eyes looking straight into his own and onto something deeper.

Nicholas and Jack spent the day on the beach helping the *Collette's* crew winch the cannon aboard the barges, lashing them down so they could be towed out to the ship. It was hard work in the sun, and it wasn't very long before Nicholas – and most of the crew for that matter – had sweated out their hangovers.

Later that evening, Jack, Peter and Nicholas, sat chatting, sitting on some empty wine barrels Tommy's men had brought down from the ale house for them to sit on.

'Well it's been a hard day an' ta'morrow is yours and Victoria's big day, Nicholas, so now it be almost nine bells, an' I fo' one, be 'eadin' for me cot. Until tomorrow then,' Peter said and waved them goodbye.

Nicholas and Jack both decided to turn in for the night, Jack on the verandah and Nicholas in the room, a gentle and cool breeze blowing through the dwelling.

Victoria woke at dawn on the wedding day. She knew Nicholas would also be up and about and wondered if he was as disorientated and as nervous as she. She had a knot in her stomach and could not calm down.

Yesterday, Meili and her mother brought her wedding dress back to her, ready for the day and she looked at it for the hundredth time. It truly was beautiful. Meili had embroidered and hand sewn tiny delicate flowers onto the off-shoulder modifications.

She looked at her mother's wedding shoes, the low heel satin shoes shining even at this hour of the morning. She sighed and went out into the kitchen and got herself a cup of tea, then went onto the front verandah to watch the sky change colour as she and Nicholas both enjoyed.

She giggled to herself remembering Bethany telling her about she and Meili catching Nicholas and Jack naked in the sea. Bethany thought it hilarious how Nicholas was embarrassed and had dived back into the water to hide his privates, whilst Jack just stood there fully exposed and did not even bother put his hands in front of himself.

'E's got a tockley on 'im like thet great 'orse of 'is 'as got, my God, Oi's never seen such a thing, an' it was cold as well!' Bethany had said rolling her eyes. 'Meili couldn't get 'er eyes offern' 'im, could ye love. Oi think she be a bit keen on 'im!' she said winking at Victoria.

Poor Meili, not used to such indiscreet talk, went bright red in the face, and shamed, she ran from the room and ran down the street to her home. 'What'ed Oi say, what?' said Bethany looking at Victoria in surprise, who herself was somewhat embarrassed by Bethany's crude description.

Victoria said, 'I think you embarrassed her Bethany, she is Chinese and that sort of talk is off limits in their culture, at least as far as I know.'

'Well, she *was* starin' at 'im Victoria, an' e' was starin' right back. Oi's got a feelin' sumpin' is gonna 'appen between dose two, you mark my words. Humph, suppose Oi best be apologising to 'er, she's a loverly young thing. Can't say oi' be blamin 'im! She is a gorgeous young thing!'

'I will have a talk to her later this morning Bethany, I am sure it will be all right by the time you get around to apologising to her,' Victoria said, not letting Bethany totally off the hook.

Victoria walked down to the Wu's house. Isaac, still charged with her wellbeing, walking beside her. In fact, Isaac quite liked the duty, the lass talked to him completely freely, without any of the misgivings that made others abstain from talking to him. She prattled away in intelligent conversation, and even though he never acknowledged her, he guessed she had assumed it was not necessary for him to answer – she knew he was listening, and he did.

They arrived at Wu's shop and Victoria said to Isaac, 'I will be a little while Isaac, is that all right?' Isaac nodded imperceptibly and walked down between the buildings and started scouting the area, as was his cautionary habit.

Victoria sat with Meili and her mother Chen at a small table at the rear of the shop, one of the rare times Victoria had ever seen them not working. Tea was served. She loved the scented Chinese tea, hand rolled up into little balls with some flower petal. Initially they rinsed it with hot water and then poured more hot water over it before serving it from what was a very ancient eight-sided pot. It was a special moment, which she enjoyed very much.

Meili sat beside Victoria as they drank their tea in the morning sun and ate the small sweet cake that Mrs Wu had served.

'Today, is your ah, special day Miss Victoria!' Meili said, nodding at her, 'Hin how! And translated for her mother.

Victoria said, '*Oui*, today is the day at last! I wish to thank you for all of your help. You will be coming as my honoured guests, yes?'

Meili quickly translated for her Mother, who rose and clasping her hands together, bowed deeply and, hurried away. Meili said, 'She hurries to ah, tell father, we regard this as a great honour, thank you.' They drank their tea in silence, then Meili suddenly said to her, 'It is my mother and father's wish, ah, that I marry soon, they long for grandchildren to pass on their knowledge.'

Victoria, remembering the previous day said, 'Please forgive Bethany, she did not mean to upset you yesterday, she is not sensitive about other people's culture.'

Meili was silent for a little while and then blurted out, wringing her hands, 'She thinks I would be a good wife for Jack, but ah, this cannot happen, father would never allow it, I must marry a Chinese man and he will come this year to marry me.'

Victoria looked at the exquisite woman and saw some angst about the statement. She waited for Meili to continue, but then she noticed the hands had now stopped wringing and there was acceptance in Meili's eyes. Meili smiled and said, 'I must work hard and face the hardships to find the happiness!'

Victoria nodded that she understood, she must find a way to let Jack know, if indeed he was interested, that Meili was subject to an arrangement beyond any outsider's control.

Chapter 67

Est Conjunctio Animorum

Nicholas sat in the light keeper's house preparing his clothes. He looked at his fob again, as he had done all afternoon. Gone was his relaxed attitude. He was nervous and anxious, although he could not fathom why. He was about to marry the love of his life, happiness beckoned and it would fill the void he had carried around inside of him for years. He reasoned he should still be relaxed.

He fished out the fob watch again, it was 2:45, time he began dressing. Turning, went to the basin and shaved the stubble from his face, leaving only the moustache. He then plaited his black hair into a single braid and tied the end of it with a strip of black velvet.

Picking up his shirt, which was loose fitting and fashionable white, he shrugged into it.

He slipped on his beige trousers, which were held up with a shining dark brown two-inch-wide belt with a large polished brass buckle.

He drew on his calf-length dark brown boots, which he had polished to a near mirror finish, and stood. Next, he buttoned up the neck of his shirt and fitted his tie, which was a black, string style American adaptation.

A horse whickered outside and he strode to the door to find Stitch tied to the verandah. He had been immaculately groomed and shone in the sunlight. 'Hello old friend, today is the day at last!' said Nicholas to the horse, which nodded his head up and down and pawed at the grass, as if in agreeance. He looked around the corner and saw two of Tommy's lads doubled up on their horse and riding away.

Nicholas returned inside and put on a dark brown suede waist coat, which had six brass buttons sewn onto the front and buffed black leather shoulder patches on each shoulder.

He checked the inside pocket of the vest and felt the ring case there, taking it out, he again checked if the ring was still secure inside. Grunting, he placed it back inside.

'Complete!' he said out loud and went to the door and opened it. He swung up into the saddle, and patting Stitch on the neck, cantered away, waving to the two armed men still on duty.

'Good luck to ye's both now Mr Yuin, good wishes!' the pair called out.

Nicholas headed for the barracks to meet John Roe. He swung down at Roe's office and rapped on the door. 'Come,' Roe called out immediately and Nicholas entered to find Roe and William Burges ready and dressed, each with a tumbler of Scotch whisky. Roe picked up another tumbler and handed it to Nicholas.

'It is a beautiful day out there young man, perfect!' Roe said. 'To you both! May ye find happiness, good fortune and health Nicholas!'

'Aye said Burges, a fine couple ye both make, 'an I also wish ye both good health and happiness.

'Thank you sirs, thank you both,' Nicholas responded and extended his hand to both men.

'Well, we best get moving,' said Roe.

Downing their drinks, they mounted and cantered away to Tommy O'Farrell's house. As they slowed on their approach to the O'Farrell home, they were surprised to see that most of the settlement's folk were already at the house. Those not officially invited were nevertheless lined either side of the grassed area, which although still a little patchy in places, looked fresh and green.

Sailors and the locals were all dressed in their finest, with the *Collette's* crew turned out by and large in white uniform trousers, navy blue shirts and white seamen's caps.

Nicholas and his companions rode up past the crowd to light applause before alighting at the store shed and leaving their horses with the stable hands. Tommy came out to greet them, followed by Jack and Whip. They all shook hands.

'Welcome sirs, welcome!' he said to Roe and Burges. 'Could I be offerin' ye a drink now gents?' speaking half in his educated English and tinctured the rest in Irish brogue.

He turned to Nicholas handing him a drink and shaking his hand. Then, much to Nicholas's embarrassment, he stepped back and walked around him, issuing a low whistle. 'Ye don't scrub up too bad as a minin' dandy!'

Nicholas scowled at him. Tommy laughed and changed the conversation. 'Well now, here we be, de last moments of ye freedom as a single man, to be sure young man,' he said with a twinkle in his eyes. He hooked a finger around his fob chain and pulled out the piece. 'Yes sir, ye's got thirty-five minutes left my hearty!

'The women are all in de house now Nicholas, an' ye cannot be goin' anywhere down dere until Oi gets de signal from Seamus. Peter Strudwich is down there already, so 'ere, drink dis and calm down now, Oi'l be seeing ye down dere at de alter, so to speak. Oh, ho! dis be gettin' real excitin' now, ta be sure!' With that he spun on his heel and disappeared toward the back of the house.

Victoria sat in the lounge room in her bridal undergarments, with Meili and Bethany and a cup of tea in her hands, which were shaking a little as the nerves started to wind their way into her mind.

What's to be afraid of? she chastised herself. You will be marrying someone you have loved almost all of your life, he is devishly handsome, capable and is strong in mind and body, so what is the matter with me?' She worried and sipped at the tea. 'Bethany, can I have a little cognac or brandy in this please?'

Bethany went to the sideboard and got a bottle of brandy, pouring a little into Victoria's tea and another heavy nip into her own tea. She too was nervous for Victoria, and said to Meili, 'Meili?' raising an empty cup to the girl. Meili shook her head. Then taking Victoria's cup and bending down to her Bethany said, 'Calm down Vicky love, in about two hours, all is gonna be wonderful, an soon ye'll be 'appy with a foin and lovely gentle man. Youse two are made to be 'ere at dis moment, don't ye be worryin' none now!' And she kissed Victoria on the forehead.

Victoria gave her a wan smile and sipped her tea. 'Ugh,' she said screwing up her face, 'this is bloody well dreadful!' They all laughed.

They all jumped a little when a soft knock rapped on the door, and for a second she panicked thinking it may be Nicholas.

Victoria called out, '*Ah oui?*'

Then she heard Charles Clay call out. 'It is the Revered Charles Clay Miss Amendson, may I have a word please?' Victoria called out without thinking, '*Oui monsieur, enter!*'

'Jest a minute please reverend,' Bethany called out Bethany as Meili fetched Victoria's dressing gown.

Bethany called out, 'Come in reverend.'

Clay entered and said, 'If I may have a little word with you in private, it is almost time,' he said.

Bethany said to Meili, 'C'mon me beauty, let's go and check the catering and things, and they left closing the door behind them.

Clay looked at Victoria, noting the nervousness. 'I know you are a little frightened my dear, but this is normal, any step into the unknown is frightening, yes?' he began in a calming voice.

She nodded.

'But here we are, and soon you will complete one more step in your life's phase as most young people and in your case, couples do. I regard myself as a good judge of character and most times I am right. You have a good man and I can feel the love between you two. Now, you will marry and will become as one, before, and in, the eyes of our Lord. This is a wonderful time for you, so relax my dear and enjoy this moment as it comes to you.

'Let us pray.' With that they sat together and he intoned the prayer of blessing.

Victoria was not overly religious, but somehow the good reverend had calmed her spirit and she smiled at him as he excused himself and left, saying as he turned to close the door, 'I shall see you both at the altar!'

The door swung open and in marched Bethany and Meili. 'Right,' boomed the huge woman, 'let's get ye ready!' And the three of them went into Victoria's bedroom.

Victoria asked to be alone for the last moment to do the small things herself as she wanted to think about her mother and father. Bethany and Meili made to leave, but not before Bethany said, 'Ye's have thirty minutes me darling girl!'

Victoria looked at herself in the tall mirror. She wore a garland of the pink, yellow and white everlasting daisies with jasmine flowers from the plant at the rear of the house sown carefully onto a narrow white linen strip about a quarter of an inch wide by Chen. She now clipped it into her hair.

She had asked the Wu ladies to cut the gossamer thin and long veil her mother had worn on her wedding day. It was now pinned to the garland and hung only to the base of her neck and over her ears.

Her mother's very beautiful wedding dress – now her own with the sleeves and high buttoned neck removed so that the dress sat off both shoulders – looked simple and beautiful.

The dress had a figure hugging bodice down to the swell of the hip, where it came out to a full flair with three cascading layers of the finest French embroidered lace falling to just above the ground so that the low heeled satin shoes where just visible as she walked. The dress had a short detachable train of about four feet of similar material.

Around her neck, she wore a fine gold chain from which hung her sparkling engagement ring.

From her ear lobes, hung the pair of three-inch full circle earrings which had also once belonged to her mother.

Her hair had been softly curled and the lower half hung in golden tresses around her shoulders. The crown had been gathered up on the top and toward the back of her head, tied with a white satin ribbon, and came down in thick curls down her back.

She spun around slowly and turned around. Nodding at herself, she lifted the veil carefully, then went to the mirror and mixed and applied a pale pink, almost transparent, pomade to her lips and a faint application of crushed pearl powder to her eyelids. Finally, she applied a little kohl to her lashes. She lowered the veil and called out to Meili and Bethany to come and check if all was fine.

Meili had her hands to her mouth and Victoria saw she was smiling and nodding her head. She turned to Bethany, who stood silent and opened mouthed, moisture welling in her eyes threatening to roll down her face.

'Oh my!' Bethany crooned, 'ye look so beautiful ye's makin' me want ta cry me darling girl!'

'Now don't make *me* cry you two, all of this is made possible by you both, and Meili, my dress is perfect, you have made me so happy,' Victoria said.

'Bethany ducked her head out into the hallway, looking at the clock and exclaimed, 'Oh my goodness Meili we 'ave to get dressed!'

Victoria went into the lounge room and sat down to wait.

Meili was dressed in minutes wearing a traditional ankle-length Chinese dress, called a qipao, (cheongsam). This was a tight fitting, high-neck dress which split up to just above the knee. It was sleeveless and buttoned in a cross fold from one shoulder. The dress was of cream mulberry-worm silk and was exquisitely embroided in red, much prized in Chinese culture. Gold filigree adorned the edging of the dress and red embroided swirling dragon motifs and flower designs adorned the front and back.

On her feet she wore red and gold slippers. With her long black hair over one shoulder she looked a picture of Oriental elegance.

Bethany struggled to get into her heavy dark green and silver dress. Despite being invited as the second maid, she declined, gruffly saying, 'Thank ye Victoria but one, I ain't a maid anymore, two, I's too big, an' three, me dress is all the wrong colour, so no thank ye, I's just happy for you!' Meili and Victoria came to her rescue and helped her get dressed. The dress was her only dress, and she loved it. It was a neck-high buttoned dress, and getting a little tight as she commented, but they got her into it and Meili quickly and efficiently swirled her hair up and pinned it in place.

'Well, Oi think ye be very beautiful me darlin', an' now I's goin' out ta join me Bobby an' kiddies!'

She dabbed at her eyes and leant and kissed Victoria on the cheek and left.

Meili and Victoria retired to the lounge room to wait.

Peter Strudwich strode into the room, resplendent in his full captain's uniform. He wore cream trousers, black shiny calf-length boots and dark blue naval captain's jacket. He had chosen not to wear his hat, so his silver hair was swept back and tied with a bow at the nape of his neck.

He said, in awe, as he looked at Victoria and Meili, 'By God Nicholas is a lucky man on this day, you look such the beautiful picture my dear'. 'And you Meili, ye will be 'avin' every man in this colony wishin 'e was standing at the altar with ye!' Meili, not used to such gallant comments, blushed deeply and held her hands up to her face to hide her embarrassment.

He bowed to Victoria, and holding out his arm said, 'Shall we me girl?'

Victoria stood and took a deep breath as Meili fussed at the fall of the dress.

Victoria took Peter's arm and they stepped into the hall followed by Meili.

Tommy's 'quartet' were playing a traditional Irish ballad called "Mo Ghile Mear" as they stood at the closed door, waiting at the back entrance to the house.

Peter said, 'Here is Nicholas's ring my dear, 'twas his own father's wedding band.' Victoria took the heavy gold band and slipped into the tiny pocket secreted at her waist.

Twenty minutes earlier, Tommy had sent for Nicholas and his party and they were now seated in the front row, except for Nicholas who was standing to the right of the Reverend Charles Clay, who stood holding his Bible, speaking quietly to Nicholas.

Suddenly, Tommy stopped the quartet, and, seeing the signal, nodded to Seamus, who stood at the rear door, one hand on the handle.

Tommy began to play the "Bridal Chorus" as Seamus swung open the door.

Victoria and Peter waited a second for their eyes to adjust, then stepped through the door and onto the dark red and green hallway carpet which Tommy had taken outside for the occasion and which now lead to the pulpit.

There was a collective gasp and murmurs of approval as they came into full view and a further smaller sigh as Meili followed several paces behind. Most of the assembled crowd had never experienced such a wedding and dress, let alone seen a traditionally dressed beauty such as was on display to them all.

Nicholas turned and saw his bride coming toward him. She walked with her head held high, and to Nicholas she looked like an angel as she seemed to float toward him.

He felt his knees wobble as he stared. She was so beautiful he actually stopped breathing, his eyes seeking hers behind the delicate veil. Nicholas suddenly realised his mouth was open and he quickly closed it, trying to regain his composure.

Victoria looked only at Nicholas as she walked up the carpet, while he looked to her, like she was a goddess. He was immaculately dressed, and even though they had never discussed what he would be wearing, he was exactly as she had imagined he would look. Tall and so handsome, his dark hair on his crown shone in the sunlight and she saw the slight silver grey beginning at his temples as he turned to look at her. Locking eyes on him, she felt a little lightheaded, and Peter's right hand suddenly slipped under her elbow. 'Steady my lass, all is well,' he said.

Trance like, she came before him, and as she did so Peter stopped just before she drew level with Nicholas. Now Nicholas could see her eyes behind the veil, and his heart almost stopped. He leant toward her and whispered in her ear, 'My Vicky, I love you so and you look so beautiful it is beyond imagination.'

'Ahem,' said Reverend Clay seeking to break the stare between the two, 'let us begin!' Reluctantly, Nicholas and Victoria shifted their attention to the reverend.

They could hear Bethany sniffling on the seat behind them.

The reverend began, 'Friends and acquaintances, in the presence of God, the Father, Son and the Holy Spirit, we have come here on this day to witness the consecration of Nicholas Ryan Yuin and Victoria Lillian Amendson in marriage, may the grace of our Lord Jesus Christ, the love of God and the fellowship of the Holy Spirit be with you.

'Let us Pray.

God of wonder and of joy,
Grace comes from you and you alone are the source of life and love.
Without you, we cannot please you; Without your love, our deeds are
worth nothing.
Send your Holy Spirit and pour into our hearts that most excellent
gift of love,
That we may worship you now, with thankful hearts,
And serve you always with willing minds
Through Jesus Christ our Lord.
Amen.'

The gathering all, murmured Amen after him.

He went on extolling that the marriage was with God's blessing, and today was a celebration of Nicholas and Victoria's love for each other.

'For those who do not know of Nicholas's and Victoria's origins, and moreover their bond to one another, I will explain a little of this with their permission.'

Nicholas nodded.

The reverend told of their love for one another, which began in Tanzania and which had lain unrealised and unspoken through childhood. He then told of their journeys to eventually arrive at this point.

'Now, I must ask, is there anyone present who may give reason why this couple should not marry, speak now or forever ye remain in silence.'

There was not a murmur from the gathering.

Clay then turned to Nicholas and Victoria and said, 'The vows ye are about to take are made in the presence of God, who is judge of all and knows all the secrets of our hearts.

'Therefore, if either of ye knows a reason why ye may not lawfully marry, ye must declare it now. He waited for a moment.

'Who gives the hand of this woman for marriage?'

Peter Strudwich moved forward and lifted Victoria's hand to his breast and said, 'I Peter George Strudwich give the 'and of Victoria Lillian Amendson as proxy to 'er father in Africa, an' I do so with pride!"

'Thank you Captain Strudwich, you may step back,' Clay said.

The reverend opened his bible and read the passage as chosen.

He nodded to Tommy who began to play the ancient hymn, "All Creatures of our God and King".

The hymn finished and Clay turned to address the gathering and said, 'Nicholas please take Victoria's right hand in yours.'

Then placing his own right hand over theirs, the reverend said, 'Please repeat after me.'

He began with the nuptials, asking Nicholas to repeat them after him.

'Victoria, please take Nicholas's right hand in your own.' She lifted her hand from within Nicholas's and placed her own over his. And the reverend again covered their hands with his own.

He looked at her. Victoria and Nicholas were gazing at each other in obvious rapture. He sighed, cleared his throat and again said, 'Please repeat after me.'

Victoria repeated the vow.

'Nicholas?' said the reverend, waving his hand to them both, 'please.'

Nicholas began.

Animabus nostris fusio, our blending of souls, comes with equal and lasting friendship.'

Victoria answered as they had written and rehearsed. 'We share our common beliefs and thus make our trust and respect, this I freely give to you for always.'

'I hold this respect and trust as sacred and also give freely to you always,' replied Nicholas, smiling down at her.

Clay held a small purple satin pillow out and Nicholas had a small flash of panic as he momentarily could not find the ring in his vest pocket. With relief, he found it, and placed Victoria's wedding band on the pillow, the exquisite piece flashing in the sunlight. Victoria placed Nicholas's heavy gold band beside her ring.

Nicholas took Victoria's left hand and slipped the wedding band onto Victoria's ring finger and said, 'I thee Nicholas do bond my heart and soul to thee forever and always.'

Victoria took Nicholas's wedding band and placing it on his left hand, repeated his vow.

The reverend then said;

'In the presence of God and before this congregation,
Nicholas and Victoria have given their consent
And made their marriage vows to each other.
They have declared their marriage by the joining of hands
And by the giving and receiving of rings.
I therefore proclaim that they are husband and wife.'
Clay then took their right hands and said
'Those whom God has joined together, let no one put asunder!'
The Reverend Charles Clay, then said, 'Please kneel.'
They knelt on the small cushions in front of them.
'God *the Father,*
God the Son,
God the Holy Spirit,
Bless, preserve and keep you;
The Lord mercifully grant you the riches of his grace,

That you may please him both in body and soul,
And living together in faith and in love.
Arise! You may kiss the bride,' Reverend Charles Clay concluded.

They stood, eyes locked and smiling as Nicholas lifted the veil back over her head and bent, kissing his bride.

Cheers, whistles and loud clapping echoed around, and those seated came to their feet as Victoria and Nicholas turned smiling and faced their friends and well wishers.

Chapter 68

The Banquet, Speeches and Dancing

*B*ethany was openly weeping and even Robert had moisture in his eyes. Young Sarah, taking her cue from her mother, was also crying, although she did not really know why.

Nicholas saw Jack and Whip and waved to his friends. Whip was beaming in genuine warmth and clapping furiously. Big Jack stood head and shoulders over everyone, he was nodding his head, grinning and clapping.

'We must now sign the register you two, witnesses please?' he asked turning to John Roe and Tommy O'Farrell.

There was a little quiet from the guests and onlookers as they completed the signing.

Nicholas and Victoria shook hands with the reverend. 'A beautiful ceremony Reverend Clay, thank you!' Nicholas said.

John Roe shook Nicholas's hand vigorously and said, 'Congratulations Nicholas, I wish you both full happiness for always.'

'Thank you Sir,' Nicholas replied.

Roe then turned to Victoria and said, 'Look at that radiant smile now, congratulations, what a difference to the sad face I saw when we first met my dear, you absolutely look the perfect picture.' And he lifted her hand and kissed it. 'Beautiful,' he said shaking his head in admiration.

Tommy O'Farrell was almost beside himself with excitement and he shifted from one foot to the other. He put his arms around Nicholas and Victoria and kissed Victoria on the cheek and said, 'I be so happy for ye's, to be sure an' certain now, congratulations! From me an' all me lads!'

'Thank you Tommy, we are in your debt for this day,' Victoria said.

'Stop dis now, ye's be makin' me bawl now, stop it,' Tommy demanded. 'Ah, I's so 'appy for ye's, go on now and git and see all ye well wishers!'

They turned and stepped out amongst the people.

There were several wrought iron brazier stands with small buckets scattered amongst the invited guests, and in them Sarah, Robert and Adam had placed handfuls of the everlasting petals. The guests all showered Victoria and Nicholas with the dried petals. 'Oh wonderful!' said Victoria to Nicholas as they were covered in the pink, yellow and white petals.

Jack stood beside Meili, Chen and Lao Wu (his position not going unnoticed by either Victoria, Bethany or Nicholas) and was flanked by Whip and the Stokes family as Nicholas and Victoria turned to them and embraced their closest friends.

Meili came to her and smiling whispered, 'Turn around Mrs Yuin ah, I wish ah to take away your train for the dancing.' Victoria obliged and Meili quickly undid the clasps on the train, and folding it, disappeared into the house with it.

The bridal waltz commenced as Nicholas and Victoria swirled elegantly around the timber floor to music from Tommy and his companions. Soon they were joined by other couples, some from the onlookers, it really did not matter.

Whilst that was happening Seamus and a team of helpers were setting up the wedding banquet, bringing down trestle tables from the shed.

To one side was the bridal party table for the bride and groom, distinguished guests and those close to the newlyweds. The table was lavishly adorned with fine silverware, crystal goblets, white linen and elegant crockery.

On the trestles were two suckling pigs and many different plates piled high with vegetables, in particular a great dish of the inevitable Irish delicacy – potatoes. In addition, there was a great pile of the delicious crawfish from the bay. All of them had been cooked and shelled, save for some at the edges and centre for decoration. All sorts of cakes rounded out the feast.

After the bridal party had been seated, speeches were made by Peter Strudwich, who acted as the Master of Ceremonies, and John Roe, who gave his welcoming speech for the newlyweds.

Nicholas looked for his big friend and found him seated at the very end of the table, mainly because of his size, but noted again that he was seated right next to Meili. Catching Jack's eye, Nicholas smiled at him. He appraised Jacks attire. Tommy and Seamus had somehow managed to make a pair of trousers for Jack out of some light sail cloth Peter had given them, although a bit short at the ankle, the trousers looked reasonably presentable. He also had a dark navy blue sleeveless shirt, made up of two of the biggest shirts Strudwich could find, it did look a bit odd, but was better than nothing. He of course was barefoot.

Victoria felt she was in a dream, and everywhere was a sea of faces and well-wishers. Her cheeks were aching from smiling, though she worried she had forgotten to thank someone who had helped and looked around to check.

She too looked toward Jack and Meili to see that they were in conversation with Whip, but she noticed Big Jack's attention was almost completely taken by Meili.

As she looked, Isaac appeared, his face hidden by the ever-present stovepipe hat, he suddenly looked directly at her dipped his head almost imperceptibly and smiled briefly though warmly. She lifted her hand and gave a little wave. The smile vanished as quickly as it had arrived and he bent and spoke into Jack's ear. Jack nodded his great head and she could see him visibly relax, which was good, because she and Nicholas did notice he had been a little on edge during the day. They wrongly thought it was because of the Chinese girl.

Jack stood, excusing himself, and came up to Nicholas. She heard him say quietly in his deep voice, 'Niclas, de Birch, 'e was put on de *Leander* when she sail early this mornin'. 'E will nebber be a comin' back now, de Isaac, 'e jus tell me.'

Nicholas looked up at Jack's face to see a big smile on his friend's face. 'De Isaac, 'e be a good man!' said Jack, patting Nicholas on his back.

Nicholas grinned at him. 'Thank you Jack, that makes me feel very relieved.' Then he said, 'Jack?' 'Yas Niclas?'

'Best you get back to Meili, she will be missing you!' A cheeky smile tugged at Nicholas's mouth.

Jack just stood looking at Nicholas, his mouth open as if to say something, then closed, a confused look on his face as he looked up at Meili, who at that moment just happened to be looking straight at Jack.

'Nicholas, leave him alone, look now you have embarrassed him,' Victoria chided Nicholas.

After a few moments, Jack said, 'She be a very beautiful woman, Jack is *no* e'barrass.' He turned and walked back to his seat.

The bridal party were served their food at their table and the other guests filed past the other tables laden with food to return to the long trestle tables.

Speeches and toasts came and went, some droned on, others full of wit and good humour.

The night drew on, and after many dances with friends and acquaintances, Victoria was getting tired of it.

Suddenly, she noticed that Meili was not seated at the table, nor was she amongst the crowd. The Wu's were still seated at the table, as were Jack and Whip. She frowned and waited some ten minutes, then excusing herself, she went into the house looking for her friend.

Meili was nowhere to be seen and Victoria was starting to get really worried when she heard a very faint sniff coming from her room. 'Meili is that you,' she said opening the door.

Meili jumped when Victoria came in. Closing the door behind her, she saw that Meili was crying, her eyes red, and she sat on the bed, wringing her hands in angst.

Victoria came and sat beside her and put her arms around her. 'What is the matter Meili, please tell me?'

Meili shuddered and looked up at Victoria. 'I am confused ah, my, my heart it…it is no right, it…it is changing ah, what I do? Oh, oh, I good girl, obedient to father and mother wish, but…but I feel different!' She started to cry again and the wringing of hands began again.

Victoria guessed what was ailing her and said, 'Meili, after the wedding, maybe tomorrow or the day after, we will go for a walk in the evening and we will talk. Do not worry, I will tell no one about this, all right?'

Meili took a deep breath and nodded. 'I a good girl Victoria, I no…no want to upset parents ah,' she said.

'I think I understand what is the matter and we will find a way to make you feel better,' Victoria said and hugged and kissed Meili on the cheek. 'Now let us clean your face and we will go back outside.' Victoria went to the pitcher of water on her dressing table and dampening a face cloth, and gently wiped away Meili's tears, the cool water making her feel a little better. 'Come now.'

Victoria took her hand and she and Meili walked back to the bridal table, Victoria steering her to the opposite end with Nicholas and Peter Strudwich, seating Meili next to Peter.

A little later, she saw Meili smiling and in conversation with Peter Strudwich. Good, she thought, as Lao Wu and his wife Chen joined their daughter and Strudwich.

Nicholas stood and led his wife to the dance floor. It was a slow waltz and they moved around the floor as one. Victoria, her arms around her husband, whispered into Nicholas's ear, 'I want to go now my Nicky, and she moved, rubbing her elbow over his groin. To his horror, he felt himself stir immediately, and the tight trousers would hide nothing if he became further aroused. 'Very well my dear,' he croaked,' I will just get a drink.' She giggled, devilment in her eyes as he moved quickly away.

Jesus, he thought, I have no control! He sought out Peter and Tommy telling them they wished to depart.

Tommy's buggy was already in the drive way as the sailors from the *Collette* formed up two lines, each of them holding flaming brands on high.

They moved down between the lines amid more showering petals and shouts of congratulation. Nicholas lifted his bride up onto the seat, and walking around to the other side, leapt onto the seat. He spurred the horse and they drew away from the crowd and made their way to the light keeper's cottage.

Chapter 69

Sublime Intimacy

*A*rriving at the cottage, Nicholas and Victoria were congratulated by two of Tommy's armed guards, who left promptly in the buggy. Nicholas noticed Stitch and Victoria's mare pegged a little way from the house.

Nicholas then swept Victoria up in his arms and walked around to the front door, which was slightly ajar. He toed the door open and carried his bride across the threshold.

He gently put her down and latched the door.

Someone had placed her valise on the dressing table and an assortment of candles on the corner table. A large candle burned in the opposite corner by the bed, creating a warm and intimate atmosphere, throwing soft orange light across the bed.

Turning back, he gazed at her and felt the excitement surge through him as he watched the swell of her breasts rise and fall. Alone at last and nothing to hold back their emotions, he gently laid one hand to her cheek. She gave a tiny sigh and leant to his hand, no words necessary.

Victoria gazed back at him and found herself trembling at his touch and fell into his arms.

Nicholas leant down and kissed her with such tenderness she felt faint, and she allowed herself to be carried into a swirl of emotion which now enveloped them both.

Nicholas carefully and gently laid her down on the soft goose down cover of the bed. She gazed at him as he stared at her and she could see the outline of him rigid beneath his breaches. She reached out and lay her hand along the length of him and stroked him through the cloth.

He gasped at her touch and began to take off his vest. 'Wait,' she whispered, and then said softly, 'Unbutton me my love,' turning her back to him.

Nicholas first removed her garland and veil, carefully laying them on the small narrow table by the front door. Next he slowly gathered her hair, baring her neck, and laid it over her shoulder, he bent and ever so gently kissed her neck. She sighed and he felt her shiver and saw the goosebumps, golden in the candle light, swell on her shoulders, her hand reaching behind his head.

He searched for the embroidered buttons running down her back and began to unbutton the dress, continuing until he reached the last button just below her waist.

Nicholas peeled the dress away from her shoulders and it fell to the floor in a circle around her feet, leaving her standing in only in a pair of the palest of white and pink silk lace drawers, which finished just above mid-thigh.

He bent and gathered the dress, hanging it on the pegs on the door, and coming back to her, began again to gently kiss her neck. He nibbled at her ear and she felt his hot breath in her ear, her knees wobbled and she felt heat and moisture come to her.

Nicholas placed his hands on her narrow waist, her skin cool under his touch, and he marveled at her silky feeling and surreal softness. He turned her around slowly as she placed her hands around his neck and they kissed again, this time their tongues softly exploring each other.

Victoria's nipples were standing rigid and swollen as Nicholas, now trembling himself, placed his hands around her waist at her back, and gently bent her back, and leaning forward kissed one of her nipples, then drew it into his mouth.

Victoria gasped and was consumed by an almost painful but ecstatic feeling as he caressed her breasts with his tongue.

Nicholas lay her down on the bed and looked at her. Her golden hair was spread haphazardly behind her, and her breasts, the areola now swollen and topped by her rigid nipples, rapidly rose and fell as her excitement rose within her. He could see the love and longing in her eyes as she placed one hand on his bicep.

Still gazing at her, he stood and now removed his vest, tossing it on the floor, quickly followed by his shirt, he turned and sat on the bed, drawing off his boots and stockings, then, he bent and removed his trousers and turned to her naked.

Victoria stared at his face, his finely chiselled features and his neatly trimmed moustache and again felt herself stir, a fluttering in her stomach. She looked into his amber eyes, now warm and almost liquid. Lowering her gaze, she examined his broad chest covered in dark curls which tapered down to his groin.

She stared at him gently bouncing before her, and tentatively reached out to hold him. He gasped as her fingers encircled him. It was so hard and hot, such power, she marveled.

Nicholas reached down and undid the tie at her waist, then drew her drawers away and she lay back, opening her legs to receive him.

There was no pain, only a momentary burning as he gently and slowly entered her until they were fully joined. She whispered, 'Oh my Nicky,' as they lay still for a moment. She could feel his strength and heat as he pulsed within her. She moved her hips a little as she clutched at him. They began to move together, wave upon wave of surreal pleasure flowing over them.

So intense was the build-up of feeling that Victoria, her arms around Nicholas – his springy chest hair stimulating her nipples even more and feeling the muscle in his back rippling with every thrust, had lost any hope of control. She was being consumed by intense waves of pleasure and rising into a beautiful and intense plateau with no wish for it to ever stop. She had an instant of panic as the feeling peaked, then suddenly the pleasure crashed upon her like a wave and she was swamped by an orgasm that did not stop as Nicholas now moved rapidly within her.

She cried out and ran her hands down to his buttocks, reveling in the thrusts and the feeling of tensed muscle. She felt Nicholas suddenly increase his thrusting and then tense like a drawn bow as he shuddered, and an intense heat filled her.

Nicholas had felt his orgasm building but with great will power, he held himself in check, wanting Vicky to come to orgasm first. He was completely enveloped in his love's very being, she was so soft, almost impossible to feel! He felt he was in another world.

And then she began, first with rapid little sighs then pants, eventually crying out as she thrust to meet him, her hands now clutching him all over. Feeling Victoria's orgasm, Nicholas surrendered his self-control and increased his thrusting, and his own orgasm, more intense than he had ever experienced before, enveloped him as though his whole body was being squeezed by a giant hand and he too cried out as he too surrendered to their shared crescendo.

They lay breathless in the afterglow of their pleasure, Nicholas kissing away the little beads of perspiration on her upper lip, and gently kissing her eye lids, she running her hands over his back and arms. 'I love you my Nicholas,' she said.

'And I you forever and always my sweet,' he answered, bending, they kissed deeply, rekindling their passion.

Nicholas awoke a little later than usual. Opening his eyes slowly, he felt the warmth of his wife's body and captivated by her scent and softness, and he gazed at her shoulder and the top of her head as she lay cheek down on his chest. Victoria was breathing deeply and easily as she slept.

He placed his hand on her shoulder, instantly aware of the silky skin and warmth, and she uttered a small 'Mmmm'.

Nicholas thought he heard a noise outside the door, and thought to investigate, but did not want to move away from Victoria. He decided to stay put until she woke and he drifted off to sleep again.

Two hours later, he had to move to relieve himself and sought to slide out from under her. He did this with extreme caution so as to not wake his wife, and succeeding, swung his legs over, pulled on his trousers and quietly went and opened the door.

Rubbing his eyes against the sunlight he saw a tray of freshly cut fruit, some milk and slices of fresh bread at the door step. Suddenly ravenous, he bent to pick up the tray, but found that minute ants were also ravenous and they had invaded the tray.

Closing the door he began to blow away the little pests, and he placed the tray on the chair as he made for the sea and dived into the cool water.

Nicholas lay naked at the edge of the sandy beach, gentle waves washing over his lower half and the morning sun warming his face as his thoughts drifted back to yesterday and the wedding. He felt relaxed and happy as he doodled in the wet sand.

He heard slight noises coming from the house and got up, washed the sand from him, drew on his trousers and walked to the house. Picking up the tray, he made to enter when Victoria called out, 'No Nicholas, I am washing, wait please.' He chuckled to himself – a few hours ago all was happening and both were naked, and now he had to wait whilst she cleaned. Women are strange he thought, shaking his head.

He put down the tray again, flicked off some more of the little brown ants and looked around the corner toward the bay.

He could see the masts of the *Collette* over the sand dune and she had two topsails cracked. Jesus! he panicked. Surely he is not setting sail without saying goodbye! Then he saw the sail being rapidly furled and concluded that Peter or his new first mate De Freys were drilling the crew and practising up on the rigging to ensure nothing caught up when she sailed.

Nicholas was suddenly charged with energy as he realised the *Collette* was sailing today.

He walked around and started to saddle up the two horses, ready to canter down to the bay, when he suddenly stopped. Christ man what are you doing, you have just married, the *Collette* and Peter would have to wait!

He took the saddles off and walked around to the front of the cabin, just in time to see Victoria opening her valise which she had placed on the small round table drawing out a light cotton blouse and skirt. She looked at the fruit and said, 'We have a couple of visitors to share our breakfast my darling,' and she came into his arms, and reaching, nibbled his neck and licked at the beads of salt water scattered over his torso. 'Good morning my husband.'

'Good morning Mrs Yuin, and how are you this fine morning,' Nicholas replied, thinking she was like a little kitten as her pink tongue licked at his skin.

She drew his head down and kissed him in answer.

They dressed after nibbling at the fruit and eating some of the crusty bread, then walked arm in arm along the beach toward Champion Bay. There was reef exposed on the low tide, about one hundred feet from the cottage, and they carefully picked their way out onto it, barefoot, looking into the many small pools at the myriad small fish trapped.

Victoria looked up and pointed at the *Collette's* masts which again had some sail showing. 'Nicholas look, Peter would not be sailing *now* would he?'

Nicholas pointed at the exposed reef and said, 'No my Sweet, he will be waiting for the change in tide, sometime this afternoon I would think, or tomorrow morning, and any way I have dispatches for him to deliver to Sir Gregory Scott, which he knows he has to take with him.'

'Still, I am all excited now, perhaps we should go and see?' Victoria enthused. Tugging at his hand she pulled him off the reef and as they reached the shoreline, she snatched up her sandals and shoved him. Caught off-guard, he fell back on his rump as she raced away laughing before springing to his feet and chasing her back to the house.

They saddled the horses together and headed down to Champion Bay to find Peter Strudwich.

Reaching the point where a longboat was loading provisions for the voyage, they enquired as to Peters whereabouts, expecting him to be aboard ship. But the sailors pointed toward Tommy's and said he had gone back there to get his belongings.

Nicholas and Victoria cantered into the yard, and leaving the horses, went to the house, laughing and happy. They entered the lounge room to find most of their friends in a somewhat subdued mood, largely due to their overindulgence at the wedding party.

Peter Strudwich, Robert and Bethany were not amongst them, but they could hear Peter's voice at the front of the house.

Tommy sprang to his feet as they entered, immediately clutching at his head. 'Ah, ah,' he said quietly 'Ta be sure, Oi'm never ever gonna be drinkin' agin. Welcome Mr and Mrs Yuin, ye both be lookin' radiant!'

They all got up and congratulated them once again. 'Where are the rest of you?' Nicholas said, looking around.

Tommy answered for them all. 'Well now, Wilber's in dere,' he said pointing at Nicholas's room. "E's feedin' little Nimmy, Jack is up makin' love talk to 'is Ubaba,' he continued cackling at his own wit and clutching at his head, 'An' Peter, Robert an' Bet'ney are out on the verandah tryin' ta placate young Adam!'

Nicholas raised his eyebrow in query.

Tommy said quietly, 'Ah well now Nicholas, seems the young lad 'ad 'is 'heart set on sailin' wit Peter this afternoon, an' o' course 'is mother an' father, dey's aginst it, the boy is too young, but the lad is pleadin' like 'is little life is dependin' on it, an 'e is heartbroken.'

Nicholas and Victoria headed out onto the verandah, to find young Adam quietly crying, his mother's arm around him.

Victoria sat opposite them, she didn't know what to say, so elected to sit quietly.

Nicholas said, 'Well my friends, we'd best have a meeting shortly and I need to see you Peter about the dispatches.' Peter, glad to have the distraction as he had been trying to reason with the lad for over an hour now, said, 'Aye Nicholas, an' I 'ave ta be goin' up an seein' John Roe 'bout 'is dispatches fo' London as well.'

Nicholas said, purposely trying to distract the boy, 'Well now, we also need to discuss our getting back to our work at the Kalbarri Homestead and at your new business Robert and Bethany.'

He continued, stroking his chin. 'You know, Victoria, Whip, Jack and I are going to the homestead first to get things in order. But first we have to organize to drive our new cattle to the station, so Jack's huge bull, Kubi will have plenty of girlfriends. We really could do with an extra hand driving the cattle to the Murchison, after all Vicky's wagon needs a driver.' He was watching Adam for any sign of interest but all he saw was a shifting of feet, but, the lad had stopped sniffling.

So, he went on. 'The other thing is, I am told that the men do not have enough time to get fish for them to eat and dry at the homestead, so the skiff we have sadly is not being used.'

Strudwich catching on immediately said, 'Ye know, I gave thet skiff to ye's sayin' ye must look after it, since it came off'n the *Collette,* Oi'm not too 'appy thet it's no bein' looked after Nicholas.' He shook his head, "Tis a shame, seems it needs someone to be lookin' after it, a temporary captain for example.'

Nicholas gave an almost imperceptible wink to Robert and Bethany. The lad suddenly piped up, "As it got a mast and a sail?'

Got him! thought Nicholas. Victoria watched as Nicholas skillfully manipulated the lad.

'Well yes, of course Adam, but unfortunately I have no one to look after it, and none of the men there, apart from Wilber knows how to sail it anyway.

Silence descended as the boy sat thinking, his face changing as he sought to act surprised and blurted out, 'Could Whip be teachin' *me* 'ow ta sail it?'

Nicholas dragged his answer out, stroking his chin in mock thought. 'Yes, I suppose he could, but…you mean you would like that?'

Trying not to sound too eager, and in a somewhat gruff voice, which had the group almost burst out laughing, he replied, 'Yes sir, guess I would, but only if'n Oi be captain.'

Nicholas waited, again keeping the lad hanging. 'Excellent!' Nicholas finally exclaimed, 'the task is yours Captain Stokes.'

Adam looked up at his parents, his little heart almost bursting with pride and he had a grin to match.

'Understand this captain, your mother and father will also be needing you at the new store, so you will be just plain Adam Stokes when you are at home,' Nicholas said, 'and best you be minding your respect son and be askin' your ma and pa's permission first, yes?'

'Yes sir!'

Adam looked again at Bethany and Robert. 'Is it all okay Ma and Pa?' He was rewarded with smiles and nods of approval.

At two bells in the afternoon, they again gathered on the front verandah, Nicholas holding court.

'Right, Peter is setting sail at five bells, correct Peter?'

'Yes,' Strudwich replied, 'so I will say my goodbyes now, and until we be meetin' again,' and he made his way around the table. Turning to Victoria and Nicholas he said, 'I will see you down on the beach you two, at four-thirty, yes?' He saluted young Adam, who shot to his feet, saluting smartly back, but his lip was quivering. Strudwich stopped with one foot on the verandah steps. 'Ah me! Oi almost forgot!' he said as he came back up, and stooping to open his kitbag, he withdrew a fine British naval captain's bicorn hat, complete with gold braid, which he had intended to give Adam anyway, but now it was even more appropriate.

He had asked Meili to add some cloth stuffing behind the inner band so it would fit the boy's head a little better.

'From one captain to another, lad I want ye ta 'ave this gift from me, until I return then.' And with that he placed the bicorn on the boy's head. Adam was speechless, then suddenly stepped forward and wrapped his arms around Peter's legs. He shuddered, then Peter leant down and said quietly, 'Now, now, there'll be none o' thet now son, ye be a captain now, you hear!'

Adam stepped back and taking a deep breath, saluted Peter again.

Strudwich turned and walked down the steps to the buggy, tears in his own eyes.

Tommy sent a man to bring Jack down for the meeting, and when he arrived Nicholas began to organise what was to occur as they all prepared to head back up north.

Victoria loved the way her husband assumed control and organised things so thoroughly, it made her very proud and confident. She looked around the group and could see the respect on each and everyone's face as he gathered their attention.

'Right everyone, Robert and Bethany, I assume you will be wanting to depart for home as soon as possible…except for Captain Stokes here?' Nicholas asked, grinning and patting the lad on the back, the bicorn still perched on his head.

Bethany answered, 'We will be wantin' ta depart tommorra' mornin' at tha crack o' dawn Nicholas, we's all very excited 'bout what the men 'ave been doin' while we's bin away, an' also, Tommy's lads 'ave loaded up our wagons wit more goods fo' tha store!'

'That's fine, good, good,' Nicholas said.

'Now, we will be organising the drove of the cattle to the river the day after, or whenever we are ready. That means we will have Jack, Whip, Adam and two more of Tommy's artisans in the party, droving, and they will relieve Michael and Patrick at the homestead when we get there.

'Victoria and I will follow up the day after.'

Nicholas looked around. 'Any questions?'

There were none, so clapping his hands he said, 'Right! It's about a five-day trip so let's get things organised!'

That afternoon at 4:15, Nicholas and Victoria stood on the beach waiting for Peter to come ashore.

Victoria said, 'I will miss Peter very much she said, he is like father in many ways…' She stopped mid-sentence and Nicholas sensing her pain of separation, put his arm around her and gave her a squeeze.

Peter's skiff came around the stern of the *Collette* a few minutes later. The breeze was slowly picking up from the south-west and the *Collette* was straining at her anchor, they could see they had unfurled three quarters of the mizzen at the stern of the Blackwall to aid pointing her into the bay when ready to sail. Thus, she sat a little to the port side.

Peter jumped ashore, looking animated and happy as he was now about to get back to sea.

Victoria ran into his arms a soon as he got a little closer, hugging him and she said, 'I am going to miss you Peter.'

He said, 'Aye, and I you me daughter, ye be takin' care now, an' don't be takin' any lip from this 'ere young whippersnapper!'

'You take care of each other now, and I will see you soon.' He turned to Nicholas, 'Now Nicholas, ye 'ave your dispatches for me I be thinkin?'

Nicholas went to his horse and unstrapped a heavy wooden box about one and a half feet by one foot and eight inches deep, and carried it down to the skiff, the sailors taking it on board.

He then gave Peter a leather satchel. 'My dispatches, and the box to Sir Gregory,' he said.

'Right then,' said Peter gruffly and stuck out his hand. They shook and then embraced, and Victoria kissed him on the cheek, tears in her eyes.

Strudwich spun on his heel and strode down to the skiff, Nicholas following to help push off the boat.

As Peter was about to get in Nicholas said, 'One moment Peter, if you could deliver this for me I would appreciate it.' He withdrew an envelope from within his jacket.

Peter looked at the address and saw it was addressed to Ludwig and Lillian Amendson.

He looked at Nicholas and smiled, then jumped in the skiff. Nicholas heaved the prow and it slid out into the bay as the men pulled it round and headed back to the *Collette,* the wind behind them.

Victoria and Nicholas stood and watched as the skiff rounded the stern again. Fifteen minutes later, they heard shouted commands and the ship swung to port, just as the anchor swung clear of the sea.

As one, the mainsails came down and they heard them crack as the ship gathered momentum, dipping her bow into the sea.

Chapter 70

Afterglow – Friendship and Love

'Come on my wife,' he said grinning at her, 'shall we go back to Tommy's now and have dinner with them all?'

Victoria nodded but was not really feeling social after Peter Strudwich's departure, and everything seemed to be unravelling somewhat.

Nicholas suddenly said, 'Let's go see if Jack is still blowing sweet nothings into the Ubaba's ear,' he said laughing, seeking to cheer her up.

Jack was up by the horse paddock chatting to Tommy. Isaac stood leaning against the rear wall as they walked around to the fence.

'Ah me lovelies, welcome back. Peter has sailed away I see,' he said, patting the telescope he had in his hand.

'I was just tellin' Jack here dat I's havin' dat saddler, who come up wit the piana, 'e's makin' a mighty fine saddle for 'is horse but 'e needs ta go an' sit on some stuffin' or such for 'im to make the seat.'

Jack stood frowning, some part of him protesting about riding a horse still stirring within him.

'Maybe,' Jack rumbled.

Victoria went to him and put her arms around him and said, 'Jack, it will not hurt to get the saddle finished, you can still run whenever you like, yes?' She looked up at him as he swivelled his eyes down to look at her, still frowning. But she held his gaze with a beautiful smile and he broke, unable to resist his usisi. He gave a great sigh and said, 'Hokay, won't 'urt none I spose!'

He suddenly gave a low warbling whistle and within minutes they heard the drumming of Ubaba's hooves and the huge animal came galloping over the rise, to stand before Jack, dancing his head up and down. Jack reached into his overalls and gave him a large carrot. The connection now plain for all to see, Jack really loved his great horse.

Tommy, Nicholas and Victoria walked back to the house, Isaac as always, not far behind. Whip was near the wagons and Nicholas called, 'Whip, join us for a moment would you?'

Tommy said, 'Sweet Jesus girl, I 'ave been tryin' ta get the big git to get dat saddle fittin' for over an hour, an' you come an' bat your eyelashes at 'im an' 'e just rolls over an' agrees in two bloody minutes! 'E's as stubborn as a mule! Or maybe 'is 'orse!' Victoria just giggled.

'I need to talk to you Tommy, and the others,' Nicholas said. 'I have a business proposition for you.'

'Oh so?' Tommy said rubbing his hands together. 'Let's get a cup a tea or coffee and discuss it!'

They sat on the verandah and as soon as Seamus brought out the tea and coffee and some crunchy biscuits, Nicholas said to him, and having a dig at Whip, 'Seamus, do you think you could show Wilber how you make these before we go?'

Seamus looked at him with a smile, 'To be sure Nicholas, why be dis?'

'Well when Wilber makes biscuits for us they are so hard, we call them "denture breakers". We have to soak them in coffee to eat them, and even then if you're not quick they will cure the coffee solid!'

They all had a laugh, including Whip, then Nicholas said, 'Well, by tomorrow we will all head north again, except of course Tommy. So, I have had time to consider where we all stand with regards to the future, and also with what path we should look at with all of the things that we must face. So what I am about to propose is a plan with all of that firmly in mind.'

He took a deep breath and said, 'Right, let me get right to it! Tommy, firstly, you know I am going to be extremely busy getting the mine operating so will not have the time initially to organise anything else. Tommy nodded. 'In the future, if things are proven up and say in about six months' time, I am going to need a stamp battery, three head should do it or a four, so can you please see if you can source one, or at least where we can find one, preferably a "Californian" design. I will need a donkey engine and boilers to run it. If you agree, I will source payment from London, Sir Gregory Scott, he being my direct partner. What do you say?' he concluded looking at Tommy.

Tommy frowned, and stroking his stubble said, 'Dat'll be an awful lot of expense Nicholas, I means for one mine ta use now, an' what if da mine doesn't fulfil ye expectations? Oi don't means to put ye off, an' ta be sure I will find one for ye, but maybe ye might consider going 'alves in the battery wit me an' we could put it somewhere north of Northamton or even further up, den, we could charge a fee ta process the other prospects around,' he concluded.

Nicholas looked at him and after a few minutes of thinking said, 'Hmmm, that's really good thinking Tommy.' He thought for another minute, then said, 'Right, let's do it!' and he stuck out his hand and they shook on it. 'We will sort out the paperwork after.'

Jack walked out onto the verandah to join them and sat down, balancing on the rail.

'Now the next proposition I want to put to you is this!' Nicholas said. 'You know we have a magnificent Hereford bull at the homestead?' Tommy looked at him and his face creased in query. 'Aye, I have heard so, especially from Jack, his Kubi I tink 'e said 'e calls it, is that right Jack?' Tommy said.

The big fellow nodded.

'And, we have just brought thirty head of Hereford cows from you, so what I would like to propose is this!' he said. 'I wish to give my wife a wedding gift, other than me!' He laughed.

Victoria's head snapped up and she locked her eyes on him, one eyebrow arched in query.

'My love, I want to gift to you a forty per cent holding in the cattle business at the river!' Nicholas announced. She stared at him, gasping. 'Oh Nicky!' she said, lost for words as she absorbed what he had offered.

Before she could respond further, he turned to Jack.

'Jack for your hard work, loyalty, friendship and your love of cattle I want you to accept a five per cent holding in the cattle business at the river station.

'Niclas, I can't accept dis, dis is too much,' he said shaking his head, 'too much.'

Nicholas said, 'Well Jack, it's done, understand?'

Jack, looking down at the floor suddenly looked up and said, 'Does dis mean I be ownin' some of de cows?'

Nicholas said to him, 'Yes, you will own them with your *usisi*, no matter how many we can breed and carry. You will still work with me on the mine, of course, or do whatever is required.'

Jack was grinning and nodding his great head.

He then spoke directly to Tommy.

'Tommy, so… so also to acknowledge our friendship, what do you say about forming up a partnership. I have offered to buy out Sir Gregory Scotts holding in the Pastoral company, since the mine will now progress and the original expedition was all about mining anyway. I do not think Sir Gregory will object and I know he is not interested in raising livestock. Peter Strudwich has the offer with him. Assuming he agrees, I am offering you say… a twenty-five per cent holding? That would mean Victoria holding forty per cent, Jack five per cent, you twenty-five per cent and myself the remaining thirty per cent, what do you say?'

Tommy stared at him, open mouthed. It was a very generous offer and he couldn't quite believe it.

'I, er don't know what to say Nicholas,' he stammered, 'Er…I am a little taken aback by dis generous offer.'

'Well, Tommy, this settlement is to grow, I think we can all agree on that. What with the mining, the sheep industry and good farming land around here for grain – and now the government is building a land backed wharf, port and the new town– we will be in a prime position to supply beef to all, don't you think?'

'Aye, no question about that, as I be sayin', it's a very generous offer Nicholas and I accept of course.' He came and took Nicholas's hand, then swung around and took Victoria's hand raising it to his lips and said, 'Acceptable partner?'

Victoria, like Tommy, was stuck for words, and just nodded.

Jack said pointedly, 'What about de Whip Niclas?'

Nicholas, turning to Wilber, said, 'Ah, yes Jack, good point!'

'Well, my seaman first class, carpenter, gardener, boxer of note and also my loyal friend,' he grinned and walked over to Whip, who was now feeling decidedly uncomfortable, and put his hand on Whip's shoulder. 'We have been through some tough times to get to this point. You and Jack never questioned the "sentence" Peter Strudwich imposed upon you both, especially you Whip, after so many years at sea it cannot, in your heart, have been easy, this I know.

'Now before anyone asks, I have already spoken to Bethany and Robert about this and they are in total agreeance.'

He had their undivided attention now.

'I would like to offer you a full five per cent share of the new store, based of course, and to be dependent on, how much profit the store makes. The majority of your share of responsibility, your five per cent, will come from freighting. You will be in charge of the freight in and out of the mine and to and from Geraldton with the Stokes, working closely with Tommy's business of course. Robert agrees he will not be able to run the stock agency and the freight as well.'

Wilber's mouth was open as he digested what Nicholas had offered.

'I...I...' was all he could manage.

'Also, I want you to accept a two per cent holding in the mine, based on a yearly output in ounces per ton, or grams per ton mined. If you accept, know that there will be a cap applied to that yearly profit, but be assured it will be a fair outcome, this offer will be structured as a wage.'

He looked around at them all and said, 'We will have this all drawn up legally, so we all understand our commitment'. There was a lull as they were all lost in their own thoughts.

Then Nicholas said, 'All of this is because I believe in you all and value your friendship. What say you all?'

There was a moment's silence then Tommy said, 'I be tinkin' I be speakin' for all Nicholas, tank ye! Seamus, bring out dat fine Frenchy cognac an' some glasses!' he shouted.

Bethany came to Victoria and Nicholas and said quietly, 'I 'ope ye's don' mind, but Oi bin done an' asked Meili and 'er ma and pa to dinner tonight, ta say goodbye an' all.'

'Wonderful Bethany, wonderful!' Victoria said squeezing her arm.

Dinner that night was relaxed and intimate, a gathering of close friends and family, each with their own hopes and dreams, each now with their own sense of direction.

Tommy stood, tapping his fork on his glass for attention, and said, 'Attention please my friends, I've something ta say, if it please ye all!'

When they had hushed, he drew a deep breath and said in his 'English toff speech' as Bethany put it, 'Some people walk their whole lives, never able to take a chance, or maybe so lost that the chances pass them by without them noticing them, or perhaps no one will give them a chance either.

'But here tonight, we are blessed in our friendship and blessed also that we have a special bond. Let us toast to honesty, sharing and respect, an' of course, business!'

They all charged their glasses and raised them. 'Here, here!' they chorused.

Victoria looked around at them all and noticed that most of them were looking at her husband as they toasted.

Amidst the following chatter, Victoria turned to Meili and quietly said, 'We will be leaving the day after tomorrow or perhaps one day after that Meili, so perhaps we can go for a walk tomorrow afternoon, say about four-thirty, we can walk on the beach, just you and I, *oui?*'

Meili dipped her head and replied, 'Yes ah, the beach I like very much, very clean and cool. We can talk ah.' She smiled.

Nicholas and Victoria said their goodbyes to the Stokes family, thanking them. To say Bethany was excited about going home to see her home again was an understatement, shifting from foot to foot as lightly as a ballet dancer, despite her size, and chatting constantly.

Nicholas and Victoria led their horses and walked with the Wu's to their dwelling, said their goodnights and continued walking to the keeper's house.

They got undressed and lay on the bed in each other's arms, warm and comfortable.

'My husband made a lot of people very happy tonight, you are the most generous man in the world,' Victoria said sleepily.

Nicholas gave her a gentle hug, and said quietly, 'Man is nothing if he cannot share Vicky.'

She gave a huge sigh and he saw she was asleep in minutes, he lifted the quilt over her back. It had been a very hectic last few days he reflected, and then he too fell asleep.

The next morning they packed up their personal effects and rode back to Tommy's, electing to stay their last nights in Geraldton at their friend's house, it now being appropriate.

They had yet to decide exactly when they would leave and did not want to follow the drove to the river, mainly because of the dust, but also wanted some time alone.

Nicholas had business with John Roe and also with Tommy, contracts to sign and leasing ratification she knew. Tommy and Nicholas were in the great kitchen deep in discussion, so she dawdled around the house, finding it strange that Bethany was not there anymore. She found herself wandering out to the stockyards and looking for Jack.

Chapter 71

The Talisman

*J*ack was out in the back-holding yards amongst the cattle, walking it seemed, from cow to cow. She could see him talking to them as if they were his children. She watched as he soothingly ran his big hands over them and wondered what on earth he was saying to them. Either way, they were calm and placid.

He lifted his head and saw her, waved, and parting the beasts, came over to her.

'Hello my usisi, we be leavin' this afternoon, or ta'morra' mornin',' he announced.

'*Oui*, I know Jack.'

'Deys be fine cows, dese ones, better dan what we have at the river. My Kubi 'e be straight in love wit dese beauties an' make plenty more liddle ones!' he laughed.

Victoria laughed with him.

'Ubhuti, (brother) I must talk to you about Meili, do you mind Jack?'

'No, I don' mind, she is very beautiful, I's like her very much!'

'*Oui*, I know Jack, but it is complicated, understand?' He slowly nodded, listening to her.

'Meili's parents have arranged a Chinese man to come out from China for Meili to marry, and it was arranged she is betrothed, well before the

Wu's came out here. It is their custom, so she is still waiting for this man to come, do you understand?

Jack stared at her and said, 'Meili does not like Jack?'

'That is the problem ubhuti, she *does* like you! She is confused and caught in the middle of what her parents want and what her heart would like to do.'

She continued. 'She *does* have feelings for you Jack but listen to me now. She will *not* go against her parents' wishes. If she does they will cast her out of the family, understand? If that were to happen, it would destroy her spirit, *oui?*'

Jack stared at her while he thought about what she had told him.

'Hmmm,' he rumbled. 'I understand, dis arrangement. Often in my nation we 'av de parents and de king, dey make a marriage before it 'appens, when dey's liddle, an' in our custom if de man or woman break dis, dey be killed, an' maybe whole family! Like Nimit'je.' He nodded sadly.

Despite his new-found feelings for the Chinese girl, in truth Jack himself was in turmoil. In his uncluttered way of rational thinking, he had already made up his mind what course he should take to resolve things. He knew he had to do something or forever carry a burden within himself. That something was to discover what had become of his family.

'Yaaa's,' he said nodding. 'It 'as been many years, but Jack also be..teorotha. Sometime, Jack must go back to try an' find his maiden and maybe make de children, dis I must do first,' he said, placing his fist over his heart.

'After dat, if no find dem, I will be very sad, but den I will come back, an' *den,* I will seek Meili, if dis Chinee' man 'as no come to take her, hokay!'

He looked down at her and grinned.

Victoria looked at her ubhuti, realising that it could well be a couple of years before this could happen.

Jack, placing his hand on her shoulder said, 'Come,' and they walked back to the sleeping quarters at the rear of the shed.

She waited at the corner whilst he disappeared into the line of rooms.

He came out, and said, 'Open hand please.' She did as he asked.

He placed a stunningly beautiful talisman on a fine plaited silver wire and leather thong in her open hand. It was a perfectly clear pale green crystal about one inch long by roughly three eights of an inch wide and held in a fine silver cage. She examined it closer. The woven silver was so fine, it was like a spider's web.

From whichever angle she looked at it, it seemed to glow, almost with luminescence. The hair stood up on her neck and arms as she thought she could feel some kind of spirit coming from within it.

'My God Jack, this is so beautiful, where did you get it?' she said looking up at him.

'Dis belong to my mother an' before dat, 'er mother, an' 'er mother agin', many years old!' Jack said. 'Mebe from de far north!

'Usisi, you please give dis to Meili. In my nation, dis means she is beautiful, of de earth, colour and the beginning of life, you tell her I's 'er fren', she ever need Jack, she just hold it tight, he will be there, hokay!'

'Thank you ubhuti, I will give it to her,' she said, touched by his sincerity.

Later that day, Nicholas was preparing to ride up to meet John Roe and the magistrate William Burges.

Victoria came to him and opening her hand, told Nicholas about her conversation with Jack.

Nicholas gasped when he saw it, and fishing for his specking glass from under his collar, examined it.

'Vicky, this is very special! Extraordinary! Maybe thousands of years old!'

He looked at the talisman through the specking glass and said, 'My lord! It's an absolute perfect emerald crystal! I have never seen one, only read about it, wonderful! It looks like it may have come from ancient Egypt many years ago from the craftsmanship, certainly it is not made by the Zulu, although the thonging is not very old.'

Nodding, Victoria said, 'Yes it *is* a very intricate and fine work isn't it.'

Nicholas said to her, 'You know, historically, it is said that the Zulu came from the north of Africa originally, so I wonder. Jack must really feel strongly about Meili, no Zulu of his lineage would ever gift this to someone outside his people, she is very privileged!' Nicholas said.

Later that day Meili and Victoria walked hand in hand along the shoreline toward the light keeper's house. They eventually stopped at the cottage and sat at the table and chairs on the small verandah.

Victoria began to talk to Meili.

'Meili, I understand why you are so confused about your feelings and I want to relate some things to you that my mother told me when I was eighteen years old.'

She saw she had Meili's full attention, her dark eyes fixed on her.

'When I first knew Nicholas, we were very young and did not know that we were growing feelings between us, you understand?'

Meili nodded slowly and Victoria continued. 'I thought Nicholas was like a brother and I thought that way for many years, but in my heart there was a feeling that something was missing, that something was my deep love for him, and he also had the same feelings.'

Meili said, 'You mean, that you loved, but did not know ah?'

'*Oui*, exactly Meili. My mama told me that you can want to be loved so much that you do not see what is right before you. When this happens, one can close out all other thoughts, maybe even another opportunity for love.

'In her days when she was young, she told me of many girls she grew up with who were married to men who they did not love in their hearts but married anyway because the society of that time and parents demanded it. They never found happiness in their marriage, a little like what is expected of you at this moment, *oui*?'

Victoria looked at Meili, great tears rolled down her face as she sat quietly, unable to respond.

Victoria felt helpless and she had to fight back her own tears.

Meili, wiped at her eyes with her sleeve and took a great shuddering breath, then blurted out, 'I feel...feel, ah, that my heart is...ah, with Jack, but I don't know what to do!' She looked up at Victoria, wringing her hands, the tears starting afresh.

Victoria came and sat next to her on the bench seat and put her arms around her as Meili let it all out. 'I am confused, ah, I think what can be but I respect my parents' wants, oh, oh oh, what to do! She sobbed quietly.

Meili suddenly took a deep breath and dried her eyes. 'I must not be thinking only of myself!' She said and looked at Victoria. 'I must do the hard work, and must not put what I want first, so then I will get the reward ah.' The brave statement failed and the tears came again.

She cried softly into Victoria's shoulder and after a while said, 'I sense Jack feels for me ah, but it cannot be...oh, oh, what to do, what to do!'

Victoria waited until she calmed down, then she got up and shifting the small chair, sat in front of Meili and said, 'My sweet friend, listen to me now, Jack has feelings for you, *oui*, but he has something he must do first, before he can unlock his heart completely.'

She continued, Meili now looking at her with damp eyes. 'Many years ago, Jack was betrothed in Africa but he and his family were captured by slavers and taken across Africa. Jack and his betrothed were separated during a slavers' raid and he has not seen her or his family since, understand? He does not know if they are dead or alive, or where they are?'

Meili stared at her. 'Already bethrothed?'

'*Oui*, but just like you, as you are to marry a strange man, it is not so different, yes?'

The beautiful girl sat staring at her, but then slowly nodded. 'Yes, ah, it is opposite, but the same result ah,' she said sadly.

'He feels he must at least try to find his betrothed and family, and will, next year I think, go back to where they were separated to try to find them. Until he knows he will not allow himself to offer you what is now in his heart, understand Meili?

'He also does not want to interfere with your parents' wishes lest he hurts you, he knows that your family is very important to you. Meili, you do not know when this man will come to find you, or perhaps your parents may want to take you back to China so you can marry, *oui*?

'I mean, a lot can happen in our lives. My Pa pa always says, "we are not always in control of our destiny, and sometimes things are put in front of us for a good reason", you understand?'

Meili looked at her and nodding said, 'Yes ah, your father is a very wise man Victoria,' and she composed herself.

Victoria reached into her pocket and offered the talisman to Meili.

'Jack has asked me to give you this, it is a talisman from his nation, the Zulus. It is very old and has belonged to his family for many, many years. He said to tell you this, *"You are beautiful, of the Earth, colour and the beginning of life".* He said to tell you, you are his friend, and if you are ever in trouble, you are to hold it tight and he will come to you.'

'I cannot ah…' Victoria placed her hand over Meili's and the gem within it and said, 'Meili, it is done, you cannot undo his gift, it is yours!'

Meili looked at the beautiful gem in its spun silver cage. It seemed to pulse in her hand, and she said, 'What is this stone?'

'It is a very rare emerald crystal Meili,' Victoria replied.

Meili cried, 'Oh, oh, so beautiful ah! I do not deserve such a gift!' She tried hard to stop the tears once again but failed and she said, lifting the plaited thong over her head, 'Please tell him, I will keep it near my heart always ah.'

They headed back to Meili's her parents' house and on the way Victoria said, 'If your mother and father ask you who has given you the the talisman, you say I gave it to you, that is what happened anyway, it is the truth, *oui*?'

Meili looked at her and nodded, she reached inside her tunic and stared again at the pale green gem.

After dropping off Meili, Victoria walked up to Tommy's house and saw her husband still on horseback at the rear of the house and quite a lot activity happening at the rear of the shed.

Suddenly realising that the men had decided to leave this afternoon, she hurried, running up the side road. She found Jack, cinching the saddle and holding her horse by the reigns for her.

'Usisi, we go now, Nicholas say that you will ride the little way out with us, an' den, we will see you usisi when you get to the river,' Jack said. Then he looked back toward the Wu's house and asked, 'You give her the…' pointing at his chest.

Victoria nodded and told him, 'She said she will keep it by her heart always Jack.'

He said seriously, 'Very good, is good.'

Victoria said to him,'*Oui* my ubhuti, a time now for patience, don't you think?'

He looked at her, and grinning said, '*Yebo usisi, yebo!*'

Nicholas and Victoria trotted down to the gateway at the front of the house and waited for the cattle to come down the drive, Jack walking down with them.

As they waited, Nicholas saw Meili, standing by the roadway, some distance toward them from her parents' house. 'Victoria,' he said jerking his thumb back down the road. She turned and saw the girl, but also saw LaoWu and Chen standing out the front of their house watching. Jack did not miss Nicholas's gesture, and looked down the road to see Meili standing there. He went to move toward her when Victoria said sharply, 'No Jack! Her parents!' He caught himself mid-stride and stopped.

Before anything else could occur, the cows came down and Jack strode over to turn them north.

They were followed by Victoria's small wagon driven now by Adam, tied to the rear of which was *Mnyama Ubaba*. He clearly did not like being behind the wagon and skittered around dancing his great head up and down.

Jack came to his horse and walked with him and soothingly talked to him. The massive beast calmed a little and they headed up the small rise north.

On the crest Jack stopped, turned and looked back. Victoria saw him and also looked down the hill. Meili was still in the same place and Jack lifted his hand to his chest. She saw Meili lift her hand and wave. Victoria also noticed Tommy and some of his boys at the driveway, so she too waved, then they turned back and went over the crest of the hill and out of sight.

Just on sunset, Nicholas and Victoria cantered back to Tommy's. They were laughing and had raced each other back, Victoria winning easily as Stitch, although strong, was no fleet footed animal.

After dinner, they sat with Tommy chatting about all manner of things, but mostly about what lay in the future.

She and Nicholas had decided they would head north the next morning and take their time doing so.

Later in the evening, Nicholas and Victoria sat on the new wicker couch Tommy had procured and brought up from Fremantle with the piano.

Nicholas talked to Victoria about many of the things that had happened and what she could expect to see on their journey. She was listening with interest as she leant against him, then snuggled down against his chest, the cool evening breeze, chilling her just a little. She could hear the steady thump of his heart and soon began to fight to keep her eyes open, and before long drifted to sleep, secure and very much in love.

It was 6:30am and Nicholas and Victoria sat on the verandah. Both were dressed for the journey and had only to strap on their essentials to their horses to leave.

They were joined by Tommy, who was quiet. They knew he did not want them to leave, they had each grown very close, so it was a subdued trio who sat on the verandah.

Nicholas was lost in his own thoughts. He was thinking about all that had happened over the past three months – the discovery of gold, the trip to Geraldton, meeting John Roe and the bond that had formed with Tommy, and not the least, his and Victoria's coming together at last and their marriage.

He looked over at Tommy, who had his elbows on his knees staring at his coffee. He felt a pang in his heart and sighed, Tommy looked so sad. Tommy looked up and shrugged.

Nicholas, contemplating the most important things, and how he himself could now look to the future with some degree of certainty, was most pleased with how Jack and Whip's loyalty had evolved into a solid bond, like brothers.

He felt well pleased with events as they had unfolded, it being very satisfying to have direction and purpose. On the other hand, he knew they would need to step forward and be ready for anything, good or bad, and they had much to do.

Meili came up the driveway and climbed the verandah stairs. She had a calico bundle with her. 'I come to wish you a safe journey ah, and to say, do not stay away for too long.' she said and hugged Victoria, and turning to Nicholas, bowed low to him. Nicholas wanted to give the girl a hug and a kiss, but he knew she would pull away, it being part of Chinese protocol which forbade such open affection in public, even between couples, married or just in love.

She said, pointing to the parcel, 'Some *shuijiao* (dumplings) for your journey ah.'

She turned and quickly walked away, and Victoria watching her walk away and knowing what Meili was feeling, it made her a little sad. She vowed to make sure she kept in regular contact with Meili.

They strapped on their kit to their horses, then turned to Tommy. Victoria wrapped her arms around him, and hugging him, kissed him on his cheek. 'Thank you for everything Tommy, I love you!' she said.

All Tommy could do was nod.

Nicholas stood and took Tommy's hand shaking it firmly. 'Until we meet again my friend.' Again, all Tommy could manage was a nod, a brave front, but Nicholas saw the sadness in his eyes.

Suddenly Isaac appeared and came to Victoria. He handed her a small bunch of purple flowers, and dipping his head turned and walked away, leaving Tommy staring after him. His jaw open.

'I never!' he blurted.

They mounted their horses and, trotting out of the yard, they wheeled north and cantered over the rise. Nicholas and Victoria rode side by side, the cool morning breeze in their faces. Nicholas looked across at Victoria just as she did the same, and they smiled at each other.

After a while they slowed to a steady walk. It was not a long journey, approximately one hundred and twenty miles, and they chose to take the route via Northampton. Even then it would be around five days before they arrived.

Nicholas and Victoria took their time, enjoying little explorations on the way and their intimacy under the vast canopy of the Milky Way, with only the horses and campfire as companions.

Some write "The End", but I would prefer to say;
Dare autem somnia futurorum.
("Dare to dream of the future.")

Afterword

YUIN

Yuin, where did this name come from?

My grandmother, Gertrude Banks (nee Carlyon), often reminisced about her childhood growing up in the Murchison River area, in particular on or near Yuin Station.

My research has that the Yuin Goldfields were established in that era however found only a passing of information that Richard John Carlyon (my Great Grandfather) was the owner of Yuin Station and worked the 'Royal Standard Mine' nearby and on that property (He did have the lease of this mine). There appears no record of he ever owning Yuin Station that I can find and so no record of the rest of the Carlyon family in conjunction with Yuin Station or its history other than told to me by my Grandmother and my great Uncles, the research has, (other than the above) as yet failed to find any recorded mention of the Carlyon family in conjunction with Yuin Station or its history.

My Great Grandfather, was apparently a man of formidable intelligence and many talents, albeit he was of somewhat dubious character. I will reserve further information on that score for my next writing of the Yuin adventure-book 2- (factual insertions). Research has not produced any solid evidence on the naming of Yuin Station. It has been mentioned that it means "grass parrot" in Yamatje language, however this has since been debunked by people with knowledge of that language and of at that time.

There is a Yuin tribe that originated from the Sydney area of the period, its descendants are possibly still there today. I find no connection between the Murchison tribal peoples – or any other tribe in Western Australia – and the Yuin tribe in NSW.

Further research of the name finds ties with the ancient druid followings at Stonehenge in Britain and also strong ties with the Norse Vikings.

As I researched I also discovered another possible link in that mysterious name, that of an Indian religion, Shriva.

All have ties of what these religions or followings called the 'Bard' or branch of the walnut tree or the actual Walnut. Some of these links are a little vague but are there just the same.

What I have discovered however is another entity, that of the eagle, or as named in Norse and druidic culture, Yuin!

Using fictional license, I imagined someone with links to that or those religions named the station and area-Yuin, upon seeing our wedge-tailed eagles in abundance here in the Mid-West district of Western Australia.

Creating Nicholas Yuin's origins in England, and a unique name, I therefore formed the surname Yuin.

Geoffrey Robert Walker was born in 1948 and raised in the Eastern Goldfields' town of Kalgoorlie, Western Australia. He has three daughters: Rikki-Lee, Jessica and Jodie.

He is the youngest son of Harley and Jean Walker. Both parents have a long family history in Western Australia, as well as New Zealand and South Australia (his father's side) dating back to the early 1800s, and of which some of this first novel (Book One of a trilogy) is based.

Geoffrey was educated in Kalgoorlie, beginning primary school at Kalgoorlie Central Primary School and then progressing to Eastern Goldfields High School.

On graduating from EGHS, as it was known, he commenced an apprenticeship as an electrical fitter with the North Kalgurli Mines Ltd in 1965 and completed his apprenticeship in late 1969.

The '70s were new and exciting times for a young tradesman, with countless new mining processing plants being built across Western Australia. It was the real commencement of the iron ore mining industry, the start of a 'nickel boom' and many new gold deposit discoveries. Accompanying all of this activity was the development of new technogies and advances in the electrical field.

In this pursuit of new and exciting things, working 12 to 14-hour days, seven days a week for often twelve weeks without a break was not uncommon. For the young Geoffrey, it was the never-ending and fascinating challenge that presented itself every day that he hungered for.

As with every pursuit, there comes a cost. In his case it was relationships that suffered.

Then there was the other side of this work that he learned to appreciate and that was the never-ending stream of different people he met and worked with. He met men and women from many countries and walks of life – murderers, ex-soldiers, alcoholics, radicals and broken men from equally broken marriages. In particular, working with some exceptional tradesman to whom he owes much in his chosen field was a highlight. But above all he met and cemented solid relationships with good friends, some of whom he is still best friends with to this very day.

Geoff's first serious job on the Asian continent was in China, a job he enjoyed, and he literally fell in love with the country and its people. It was here that he was bitten by the overseas work bug.

Thereafter, construction work took him to the Pacific Islands, Africa, Asia and South America, where he saw another side of the world of the poverty, in particular the horrific gulf between the haves and have nots.

He has since partly retired and recommenced writing. This, his first work, is born out of human experience and a healthy respect for other cultures, people and their points of view.

Acknowledgements

I would like to offer thanks to the following:

Mr Raymond Cook. Thank you Ray, for your friendship, your absolute faith, assistance and encouragement and your sense of humour. Without you I may never have taken the first step in this work.

Mr Vic Yates. Special thanks to a true friend. I give these thanks for your unwavering belief in my ability, and your encouragement, without which it is possible I may never have completed this work. I consider myself very lucky to have a friend whose wisdom, even-handedness and sense of fair play has guided me over many years.

Mr John Keightley, who's belief and excellent knowledge of the English word has been a tremendous help during my final editing and corrections, many thanks John for your encouragement and knowledge.

The Pickawoowoo Group, thanks to Julie Anne and her group of professionals, what can I say- in a word, par excellence.

Of course, I must mention the encouragement of my daughters, Rikki-Lee, Jessica and Jodie who have steadfastly stood behind me during some difficult times during the many years of my writing this, my first novel.

No man could be prouder of his children than I.

Doubtless, there are many other people who have helped me in some way. If I have not mentioned you, please know that I have not forgotten you.

Yuin

The Dingo Mine

Book Two

GEOFFREY WALKER

www.ingramcontent.com/pod-product-compliance
Lightning Source LLC
Chambersburg PA
CBHW032029120726
47901CB00001BA/6